ICEFIRE TRILOGY

THE COMPLETE SERIES

PATTY JANSEN

CAPRICORNICA PUBLICATIONS

GET FREE EBOOKS

FIRE & ICE

BOOK 1 OF THE ICEFIRE TRILOGY

CHAPTER 1

SOMEWHERE NOT FAR from the edge of the plateau, where the goat track snaked up the rock-strewn slope, the rain had turned to snow.

Cocooned in his cloak, his view restricted to the swaying back of the camel, Tandor failed to notice until a gust of wind pelted icicles into his face.

He whipped off the hood and shook out his hair. The breeze, crackling with frost, smelled of his homeland. Oh, for a bath to wash off the clinging dust and the stink of the prairie lands, steam trains and the bane of his existence: this grumpy camel.

To his left, the escarpment descended into the land of Chevakia, its low hills and valleys bathed in murky twilight. To his right, the dying daylight touched the forbidding cliff face that formed the edge of the southern plateau, accessible only to those who knew the way.

Something flashed where the ragged rocks met the leaden sky. A tingle went up Tandor's golden claw, pinching the skin where the metal rods met the stump of his arm. Icefire.

Ruko?

He peered up, shielding his eyes against the snow. Golden threads of icefire betrayed the boy's presence, flooding Tandor with feelings of relief, urgency, panic.

Wait, wait, Ruko, not so fast. Tell me what's going on.

There was no answer, of course. Ruko conversed only in images, and Tandor needed to be close to the boy to catch those.

But Ruko's emotions had spoken clearly enough. By the skylights, something had happened while he was away. He flicked the reins to jolt the camel into a faster pace. The animal grumbled and tossed its head, but did as it was told.

Ruko waited at a rocky outcrop to the left of the path, seated cross-legged in the snow: an ethereal form, his skin blue-marbled, his brooding eyes black as a low-sun night. His chest shimmered where his heart should be. A lock of hair hung, dark and lanky, over his forehead; he shook it away in an impatient gesture.

Tandor slid off the camel's back.

He held out his two hands, one of flesh, the other a golden claw. *Come.*

Ruko rose, towering at least a head over Tandor.

By the skylights, did that boy ever stop growing? While Tandor had been away, he had discarded his soft childish look for planes and angles.

Ruko put his hand in Tandor's. The intense cold of it made Tandor gasp, but he steeled himself and sent a jolt of icefire into Ruko's arm.

The image of the two hands, the live one and the blue one, faded for a scene of chaos. Huge birds with tan wings, white heads and yellow beaks swooped down on the village, carrying Eagle Knights in their traditional red tunics and short-hair cloaks, the swords on their belts clearly visible. They landed their birds in front of the guest-house, jumped into the snow and ran to the houses, banging on doors, dragging out occupants. Adults, children.

"What, Ruko? What happened?" All those children Tandor had saved. He thought Bordertown was a safe haven, no longer frequented by merchants, no longer of interest to the Eagle Knights.

Images flowed through Tandor's mind. Snow crunched under his feet as Ruko ran from the village, while screams from women and shouts from men echoed. Trees flashed past. Crossbow bolts thunked into wood. And later, coming back to the main square, empty, except for deep tracks in the snow and a single child's mitten.

Ruko's shoulders slumped. There was a brief glimpse of the red-cheeked face of a girl, smiling, accompanied by shame and grief.

Tandor pushed Ruko's chin up. "No, Ruko, it's not your fault."

If anything, it was Tandor's. He had left the boy alone. But he couldn't have done otherwise; he had needed to travel to Chevakia, and Ruko couldn't leave the southern land. Across the border, where there was no icefire, Ruko would simply cease to exist.

"I'm sorry."

Ruko batted Tandor's hand away.

"Being angry with me doesn't help. What can I do about it?"

Ruko's fury burned inside him: his screams for his girl who was being dragged away by a Knight. His pounding on the Knight's back with insubstantial fists. Without the presence of the master, a servitor was little more than a ghost.

Ruko reached towards Tandor's belt for the dagger and the Chevakian powder gun.

"No—you're not to kill anyone. Stay here. I'm going into town to see how many children they took." There had better be some left, or his plan was in tatters.

Tandor swung himself back in the saddle. "Behave yourself." In case the order wasn't enough, he let icefire crackle from his clawed hand. Golden strands snaked around Ruko's legs and then into the snow.

Ruko glowered at him.

"Behave, and you will get your revenge, I promise."

He flicked the reins and the camel turned towards the town.

The southern plain spread before him, white, flat, the horizon bleeding into the grey sky. A gathering of low buildings lay in the snow like scattered bricks.

Smoke curled from the chimneys. Light radiated from the windows, golden rectangles that were the only spots of colour in the grey dusk, occasionally interrupted by the silhouette of a head: someone checking out this late visitor.

There was no sound except the squeak of the saddle and the croaking of the camel's footsteps in the freshly fallen snow. The soft blanket had long since erased the signs of the events Ruko had witnessed in the town streets. How long ago had that been? A few days, he guessed, no more.

If only I'd come back earlier. Stupid Chevakian trains, stupid Chevakian bureaucrats not allowing the camel on the train.

At a house with a deep front yard which held a shed, Tandor

tapped the camel's shoulder. The beast sank stiffly to its knees, uttering a protesting howl.

Tandor slid from the saddle and led the beast through a creaky gate, through the yard to the shed which stood slightly apart from the house. He pushed aside the bar across the doors, dislodging clumps of snow which rained over his glove and golden claw, and went inside.

The plainsman had kept his part of the bargain. The box in the corner contained straw and a bale of hay, albeit a very dusty one.

He tied up the camel and left it to attack the hay, and ploughed through knee-deep snow to the house, a sturdy construction of rough stone. The top floor was dark, but warm light peeped around the frayed edges of a curtain in a ground floor window.

He knocked. Locks rattled; the door creaked open. It was the plainsman Ontane himself who stood there, unshaven, dressed in a loose woollen robe. For a moment, he squinted into the dusk, but then he shrank back into the hall, pushing the door half-shut. "No, no. She be not here."

Tandor kept him from slamming the door with his golden arm, the points of his pincer-claw cutting gouges in the wood. "Where is your daughter?"

"Inside, but ye can't see—"

"I can't see her? Is that what you're saying? Three years ago, I brought you the child you'd always wanted, and now I can't see her?" Myra was one of the few children he'd rescued at that age; most he'd found abandoned on ice floes as infants.

"The man said—"

"The man? Most likely, he came from the City of Glass, didn't he? Most likely, he rode an eagle, didn't he? And most likely he told you to give up all your citizens with . . . defects." With each sentence, he thrust his golden claw closer to Ontane's chest. "Imperfects. Like me. Huh? Is that what he said?"

Ontane licked his lips and straightened his back. "He said we be punished if they found any such. They told us all to come out from our houses, and they ransacked any house where they thought we be hiding something. Then they lined up the children and took off with 'em."

"To the City of Glass?" *Please, let this not be true.*

Ontane shrugged. "How should I know?"

"All of them?" Tandor clenched his good hand into a fist.

"Yes, except . . ."

"Except what?" Tandor almost screamed.

Ontane tried to retreat further, but he already stood with his back against the wall. "No, no. I can't tell ye."

"Except the one who was born since the others left, is that what you were going to say? Except your daughter and her child?" All those children he had saved over the last fifteen years. All gone?

"Not born. Not yet. But they said they'd not take my daughter in the condition she be in."

"Let me see her."

"No!" Ontane planted his hands at his sides.

"Why not? Would I pay for your daughter's food if I wanted to harm her child?"

"Ye'll do to the child what ye done to that poor boy." He meant Ruko.

That poor boy lived with an abusive family from whom I saved him. *That poor boy* is only poor because you turned your backs on him."

Ontane muttered, "Not a surprise, that. He crackles with icefire, and the cold of him would freeze the kindest heart. Stupid as we be in your eyes, the villagers won't be letting such in their houses as they don't understand. Ye know ye can see through him? Here?" He put his hand on the position of his heart.

Of course you could. Ruko was a servitor. He had given his heart in exchange for his missing foot, and in exchange for never having to eat or be cold again. Tandor took a deep breath to calm himself.

"Have you spoken to him since?"

Ontane gave Tandor a what-do-you-take-me-for look.

"I have told you many times: he won't harm you."

"So ye say, so ye say. But many of us can't see him, even; and to the rest, he looks to be a spirit."

Unbelievable. The Imperfect children had lived here for as long as fifteen years; the villagers should be used to them. "I'll be taking Ruko. There is no point in leaving him here any longer. I want my sled to be ready tomorrow morning with a bear and supplies."

A look of business came to Ontane's eyes. "Usual fee, then?"

Tandor nodded. "The usual fee." He let a silence lapse and added, "Can I see your daughter?"

Ontane opened his mouth, but Tandor said, "No look, no business."

A silence, a few shifty eye movements, before Ontane said, "Only a look, then." Still eyeing Tandor suspiciously, he moved into the house. Tandor followed him through the hall, where a flapping candle cast long shadows over unpainted walls and a threadbare carpet.

They entered a dimly lit room with a blazing fire in the hearth.

In the chair against the far wall sat a girl, barely fifteen, propped up on pillows. Her face was pale and delicate, her hair dark but fine and straight. Her cheeks were red from the cold. A plain woollen dress stretched tightly over her distended belly.

Tandor breathed in deeply. The tingling of icefire snaked out from the child inside her: golden strands only he could see. Wild, untamed power. It called out to him, sang to him, like the voices of the mythical sirens said to be luring sailors on the iced sea.

He was sure: the child would be Imperfect. His life's work had finally brought success.

The girl's eyes widened. "Da, what's he doing here? Take him away!"

Her father pulled at Tandor's cloak. "Now leave, ye sorcerer. Ye've seen her."

With regret, Tandor let go of that tingling and retreated into the hall. He forced his breath to calm. "See? I mean her no harm."

Ontane said nothing; the suspicious look didn't vanish from his face.

Tandor forced a smile. "I'll let the child grow up with her, don't worry." After all, it was only in adulthood that the child would be of use to him.

Ontane snorted. "Let's say I believe that when it were seen."

He accompanied Tandor through the hall back to the door. When he opened it, an icy breeze blew in a flurry of snowflakes. Tandor stepped into the cold.

With his good hand, he dug in his pocket and flicked Ontane a silver gull. The coin caught the light as it spun through the air, before Ontane closed his fist around it.

The language of money convinces you easily enough. "My sled, with a strong bear. Provisions for six days."

Ontane nodded once and shut the door.

In total silence, Tandor strode through the village, trying to ignore heads vanishing behind curtains.

All you shallow greedyguts. Took my money while it was available, but cared nothing for the lives of the children who lived with you?

In all these fifteen years, nothing had changed. In fact, nothing had changed since his mother had fled the City of Glass. Well, things were going to have to change now.

The front desk of the inn was unmanned, but Tandor's ringing of the bell brought the matron hustling from a back room.

"Oh." She hesitated in the doorway, her eyes wide. For a moment, it looked like she was going to comment on Tandor's long absence, but she didn't. Clever woman. Had a nose for business. "Usual room?"

Tandor nodded.

He followed her up the stairs where she opened the door to a musty room and bustled in the fireplace to light the fire.

He asked her to fill the bath with hot water.

"My maids be gone home, but I'll see to it myself. I be always glad of giving the best to our best customer." She winked at Tandor.

Once, he might have responded, but the villagers' shallow bids to please him made him feel sick. The woman was about his age. Her face no longer held curves of beauty, but the lines of long, hard work. She cared nothing for him, or for the children. She only wanted his money.

"Ye be going after the children?" she asked when he failed to react.

"I'll do my best."

"Oh, it were such a disaster. My poor daughter lost her little boy as well. He be only four. Like a child, he were to her. Every day poor Poony be asking about her brother. What think ye they'll do with the children?" Her eyes glittered by the lamplight.

Tandor shrugged. He truly had no idea. Most Knights were from the Pirosian clan who couldn't even see icefire. They had been on a fifty-year mission to eradicate all remnants of the Thillei clan, but they wouldn't have bundled the children onto sleds if they wanted to kill them.

"And that mean bastard Ontane gets to be keeping his Myra. You know what I think? I think he paid the Knights so's he could keep her. He be willing enough to bargain with money. I think he—"

Tandor held up his hand.

"Yes, yes. The bath. I know. I be going."

Soaking in the tub not much later, Tandor transformed himself. First, he rubbed dirt from his skin. He washed dust from his hair until it was once again golden. Then he ran his golden claw through his locks until the colour leaked from it like honey, leaving his hair deep, glossy black.

Standing in front of the mirror, he blinked his eyes, let icefire crackle from his fingertips onto his face, and blinked a few more times. With each blink his eyes faded from brown, to grey, to green to a brilliant dark blue. The colour of his birth.

Then the hardest part. He called up a ball of icefire and shaped it into two symmetrical curls floating in the air. The curls descended towards Tandor's cheeks, one on each side. He closed his eyes and braced himself for the searing pain. The smell of burned flesh spread on the air. His mouth opened in a scream of pain, of punishment, of lust or satisfaction.

Panting, he opened his eyes, staring at his sweaty face in the mirror, where symmetrical curls of golden paint marked his cheeks, like the tattoos noble men in the City of Glass received when they became adults.

The Knights might have dealt him a blow, but he wasn't defeated. The children were in custody, but they were most likely in the palace, exactly where he wanted them.

He needed to know if he had enough Imperfects to freeze the guards for long enough to get into the palace.

By the light of the fire in the hearth, he dug a heavy book from his luggage and set it on his knees. Let's see, the guard level on the palace gates would be at a minimum because of the Newlight festival. He guessed there would be ten Knights. That meant he needed . . .

His pen scratched over the paper as he added up the numbers as he had learned from his grandfather's diary. He divided body weight by strength. He added up himself, Ruko, the boy in the city . . . that was not enough. He did have one other Imperfect: Ontane's daughter Myra. He crossed out the numbers and recalculated. Yes, that would give him enough power to take out ten guards, and once he was in the palace, he could draw on the fifty Imperfect children.

Yes, he could do it.

CHAPTER 2

ONTANE CROSSED his arms over his chest. He leaned back against the shed door, which he had just closed after dragging the sled out into the yard. "I tell ye, she be not for sale. Here in Bordertown we do the women's things different from how they do in the City of Glass."

"How much do you want then?" Tandor asked, while casually dumping his travel chest on the luggage rack of the sled. The white bear in the harness gave an annoyed snort. Ruko leaned forward over the driver's seat and patted the animal's furry rump while giving Tandor an impatient glance. Yes, Ruko wanted to get going. He had been waiting outside the inn at daybreak. That in itself was worrying enough. Ruko should not have been able to break those bonds Tandor had put on him yesterday.

"Ye never give up, do ye?" Ontane growled.

"No. A hundred silver gulls?"

"My daughter be not for sale!"

"I don't want to buy her. I want her to come with me to the City of Glass. I'll take her there, and I'll bring her back. Two hundred silver gulls?"

Ontane shrugged. He cast a shifty-eyed look at the shed doors, as if wondering if his wife or daughter were listening. "The Knights thought it too risky to take her a few days back, why should I think different now? She'll be needing another mother to be with her when she . . ." He spread his hands.

"My lady friend is one of the best midwives in the City of Glass. She has delivered hundreds of children and birthed nine of her own. Do you want a more experienced woman?" *Or would you rather I take your wife off your hands as well?* "Two hundred and fifty silver gulls?"

Ontane tightened his arms over his chest. "Bain't up to me to agree to something like this. Dara be sure to kill me if I do anything to the girl."

Tandor had only met the girl's mother once, a dumpy, unattractive woman with a permanent scowl on her face.

"Your wife will be glad you have the money to buy her a new carpet."

"There be nothing wrong with my carpet!" A blush rose to Ontane's cheeks. He snorted and looked down. "Although it be not exactly new . . ."

"Precisely. Women notice these things, take it from me."

"Hmph. What d'ye know about women?"

"Enough to know that I'm right."

Ontane sniffed and raked hair away from his face. "I mislike it. Why ye be wanting her anyway? I thought ye be hiding her here with us."

"I was, but your stupidity of bringing the Knights down on Bordertown has changed everything—"

"I tell ye again: it weren't *my* fault."

"Whoever's fault it was, I need to go into the City of Glass to get the children back. Including, I presume, your grandson's father. Don't tell me none of the other families in Bordertown question why you got to keep your daughter."

Ontane's face went red. "I told ye: the Knights didn't want to take her like . . ." He waved his hand toward the house. ". . . like that."

"I've not known the Knights to show such compassion. Maybe there was a bribe involved?"

"Hmph." Ontane scuffed his feet in the snow. "I want three hundred silver gulls."

"That's robbery!" But Tandor knew that, now Ontane had started negotiating, he'd won.

"It may be, but I'm the one that be happy with my daughter staying put."

"And with an old carpet on your floor. Two hundred and sixty."

"What do ye think I be? I want two-ninety."

"A man with a nose for business. I could just walk away from this deal and you'd get nothing. In fact, I'm in a hurry, so I best get going." Tandor picked up another of his packs and set it on top of the chest, then went about lashing both items to the luggage rack.

Ruko was jiggling his leg and fiddling with the reins.

"No, no. It bain't as easy as that, mister. Two-eighty."

"Da, what's going on?" The shed door had opened and the girl poked her head out.

"Go back inside, Myra," Ontane said.

"You're talking about me."

"We bain't."

"You can't fool me, Da. I heard you. What's it about?"

"The sorcerer wants that ye go with him."

The girl squeaked. "Go with him? Like this?"

She spread her arms. She was a thin, mousey thing with a fine-featured face, narrow shoulders and slender arms. One of her sleeves flapped empty below the wrist. While there might have been an element of beauty to her, Tandor's gaze was drawn to her swollen belly. It was hard to believe a female belly could stretch that much and still be part of her.

Tandor repressed feelings of discomfort. "My lady friend in the City of Glass is a very good midwife. She will look after you. Certainly a girl like yourself would like to see the marvels of the City of Glass again? You would like to buy some nice dresses from the city's best merchants, and go to the Newlight celebrations?"

The girl's eyes widened. "The Newlight celebrations? In the City of Glass? See the games? People competing from all over the land?"

"That's what I think I said, yes."

"Oh Da, it doesn't sound so bad. Can I go?"

Ontane snorted, and then shrugged. "I suppose your mother . . ." He shrugged again and met Tandor's eyes. "This, um, lady friend of yours . . ."

"Mistress Loriane, one of the city's midwives."

"And what if she . . . if it happens on the way, then? I be guessing *he* don't have any experience." Ontane nodded at Ruko.

Tandor repressed a shudder. "Look at it this way: the Knights will be back. If they find her here, you will never see her again. If she comes with us, there's a good chance that you'll see your grandchild. Anyway, my lady friend tells me that such . . . women's things have a habit of happening safely by themselves." He was groping for words. By the skylights, every word spoken delayed him further, with the chance that this dreaded thing would indeed happen before he got to Loriane's house. He'd heard a woman's birth screams once, while he stood, powerless, hidden between stuffy clothing in a dressing room. *Oh my love, if I'd known I'd do that to you.*

"It's all about your daughter's safety," he said, pushing away those memories.

"Hmph! Safety. It may be ye think it 'safe' to turn her blue and cold, like that ghost over there." Ontane pointed, his fingernail chipped and blackened from work.

Tandor met his piercing eyes. Ontane wasn't stupid. He knew that Tandor would have to turn Myra into a servitor if she was to be useful to him.

"She will be back here as you know her." Once he had control of the City of Glass, all the power of its Heart would be his, and he could return her in the original state. "Are we agreed then?"

Ontane fixed his gaze on his daughter, who smiled at him. "Please, Da?"

"Right then," Ontane muttered.

"Oh, thank you." She gave him an awkward hug.

Over his daughter's shoulder, Ontane mouthed, *two-seventy*.

Two-sixty, Tandor mouthed back.

Ontane's face twisted into a snarl, but he didn't protest. "Ye'll be the ruin of me." He hawked and spat in the snow to seal the deal. "Go get your things then, girl."

Tandor put his attention to securing his luggage to the sled.

Promises, promises. His life hung together with promises. Once he had established himself in the City of Glass, there would be no more promises. He raised his eyes to the sky. *Not even to you, Mother.*

CHAPTER 3

CARRO PICKED UP the cup from the merchant's table, feigning interest. A mother and a daughter had come to the stall and the mother had asked if the merchant had any good sets of tableware for sale, unwittingly saving Carro from doing what he dreaded for a few minutes.

While her mother spoke to the merchant, the daughter studied the items on the table, a dusty collection of bric-a-brac, the sort of things that remained after grandmother had died and all her relatives had scavenged her possessions.

The girl was nervously winding a thin strip of leather with a gull's tail feather attached around her fingers that marked her as one of the newly blooded virgins.

She let her eyes roam over Carro's short-hair Knight's cloak and the straps of his riding harness, which dangled from underneath. Her expression was one of fear or interest; he couldn't decide which. He knew her vaguely, like he knew most people here, or they knew him. His stomach churned. He did *not* want to do this, not in the safe haven of his childhood.

He glanced over his shoulder, between the crowded stalls with the garlands of yellow paper that hung from their canopies. A steady stream of patrons tottered out of the meltery, faces red from blood-wine. All those were signs that the Newlight festival was in full swing.

The Junior Knight Captain leaned against the wall, the map in his hands. He was looking straight at Carro.

"Can I assist the dear sir?" the merchant asked.

Carro started. The mother and daughter had left.

"Um . . ." He put down the cup he was still holding.

The merchant was a middle-aged man, his short-cropped hair and beard more grey than black. Age had lined his face, but his eyes were clear and blue. He wore black. Everyone in the Outer City knew what that meant.

"Oh, it's you." The man smiled. "I had been wondering how you were getting on with the Knights."

"Very well, thank you."

"You know that all of us in the Outer City are proud of you?"

Carro stands at the stall; the table has suddenly become a lot taller. The cover of the book feels rough under his fingers. He opens it, marvelling at the beautiful print on the pages of glossy paper. The book's scent floats on the breeze, releasing the smell of fifty years of hiding in a musty cupboard.

"I want this one," he says.

The merchant reaches across the table. He wears a short beard, black, the same colour as his clothes. It's the colour of the Brother-hood of the Light.

The merchant says, "I don't think your couple of foxes of pocket money would pay for that." He eases the book out of Carro's hands. "Besides, I don't think you want to be seen with this. Your father would whip you if he knew you had it."

Carro shivers. His father would, too. His father doesn't like the Brothers. It's illegal to possess anything that belonged to families who supported the old king. But he promised his friend Isandor. And the book is so *beautiful*.

Carro puts his hand in his pocket and closes his fingers on the gold eagle, the metal warm and heavy against his leg. It's not his money; well, some of it is, but most of it is his friend's. He takes it out and puts it on the table.

He says, "I want the book."

❄

"You'll be flying in the race today?"

Carro gasped. The words of the past were still on his lips. *I want the book*. He blinked at the merchant, who was waiting for a reply.

"Oh—um—the race. Yes, I will." His heart thudded. He hated how he had these spells where he drifted off into his memories.

"So you're here to visit your parents?"

Carro glanced over his shoulder again, where the Junior Knight Captain was still looking at him, drumming his fingers on the side of the sled. No way to get out of this. He closed his eyes and sighed.

"No. I'm afraid I'm on patrol. Do you have any illegal items?"

The merchant took in a sharp breath. His eyes widened. No, he hadn't expected that either, knowing of Carro's prior interest in old books.

Carro ploughed on, speaking rehearsed words with a tongue that felt like a tanned hide. "You can give illegal items to me now, and there will be no fuss. If I have to call my Captain . . ." He shivered. The merchant might tell the Captain that he had sold Carro some of those illegal items.

"No, no, you needn't do that." The man rummaged in the space under the bench and retrieved a box with a dusty assortment of bric-a-brac. There were some forks, silver, richly stamped with the crests of the old families of the Thilleian house. There were metal stands for lights—the silver globes gone of course—and a couple of sheets in neat print. Carro ran his finger over the paper, feeling the raised profile of the ink. It felt familiar. His books were like that. The old people used to have machines that melted ink onto the paper. Carro's books were still under his bed in his father's house, the books he hoped no one would find.

Carro took the box, meeting the merchant's eyes. He cringed with the anger in the man's expression. "I'm sorry, but I'm asking every merchant."

"Sure," the man said, his voice stiff. "You know this sort of stuff turns up every now and then."

"You should hand in any illegal material as soon as you get it." Carro hated his own words.

"I hadn't gotten around to doing that."

All lies. Carro wanted to hear no more, lest the merchant dig up uncomfortable truths from Carro's past. This was enough warning, for both of them.

Seated on a mound of snow, with his peg leg sticking out awkwardly into the narrow alley, Isandor opens the book on his knees. His skinny fingers trace the writing. He whispers, "Wow." A lock of glossy hair falls over his shoulders.

"A real diary from the time of the old king," Carro boasts. "The best he had. You should have seen his face when I showed him the money."

"You're a real hero, Carro."

Carro smiles. No one else calls him a hero.

"Who wrote this?" Isandor has a dreamy look on his face.

"The king's court historian." Carro bends forward and flicks the pages, trying to ignore his numb and cold fingers. Heroes are not bothered by cold.

"Wait." Isandor stops Carro's hand. There is a drawing on the page with many lines leading from one box to another. "Look at this. It's a map of the city with this thing they call the Heart."

"The Heart? There is no such thing." Carro feels uncomfortable. His father has spoken of this thing once and he'd seen it when he flicked through the book.

"It is the Heart," Isandor says. "It says so in the book. It's a machine under the palace. They say it's the source of icefire." Isandor raises his head. His eyes are distant. "You know this book sings?"

"Sings?" Carro shivers.

"Yes, can't you hear it?"

Carro shakes his head. "What song?"

"There isn't a song. It's like the band in the meltery. The music just plays on and on, but no one takes any notice of it until it stops. That's what it's like."

Carro shrugs. It's strange. Then again, Isandor has Thilleian blood, Carro is sure about that.

The old king only needed to reach into the air and icefire would spark from his fingers. He would kill people with it. Old people still tell the stories.

Carro carried the box across the marketplace to the sled, repressing memories unlocked by the musty smell. Other merchants, all people he knew, followed his every move with stone-hard looks on stone-hard faces. He wanted to scream that it wasn't his choice to do this job, that he'd been told to do it, that the Knights who had come with him were all older and hated him, that . . .

He dumped the box on the luggage tray of the sled. The Knight Captain strolled to the sled and rummaged through the contents in a bored fashion.

"Another load of old junk," he drawled. "You know, we've collected so many light stands over the past few days, one wonders where the lights are."

Carro didn't meet his gaze. The silver light globes were always gone by the time these items came to the market. Even if the lights had been complete when the merchant obtained the items, he would know better than take the globes to the market. They were worth a fortune, those bulbs that needed only icefire to glow.

The merchant hadn't given up everything he had, Carro was sure of that. But he'd hoped that by going to the Brother's stand first, he could spare the man a more thorough inspection.

No such luck.

The Captain flicked his fingers and pushed himself off the sled.

The other two Knights of the patrol moved towards the stall. One spoke, but they were too far away for Carro to hear what he said. The merchant shook his head. Then the second Knight grabbed the edge of the table and turned it upside down. Pots and plates flew every-where, shattering on the frozen ground.

As Carro had suspected, there were more boxes underneath—boxes holding far more damning material than the few stands and leaflets he had collected. He could see the spines of books and items of clothing in black and silver: the colours of the Thilleian house.

"You said you inspected that one?" The Knight Captain raised his eyebrows at Carro. "Are you Apprentice puppies capable of anything?"

Carro clenched his fists. The Brotherhood merchant was looking straight at him.

"I thought you would actually be of some use to us here," the Captain continued. "That's why I asked your Tutor if you could come. You *did* weasel your way into the knighthood from this slum, didn't you?"

Carro shrugged.

"Answer me when I ask you a question." The Captain slapped Carro in the face. "And look at me when I'm talking to you."

"Yes, Captain." Carro met the man's eyes.

"Then go and carry all that rubbish onto the sled."

"Yes, Captain."

Carro set off to the ravaged stand, past the yellow garlands that seemed to mock him. His cheek stung, but he resisted the urge to wipe it. Every merchant and many of the market's customers were looking at him. Carro, the pride boy of the Outer City. Carro, the son of a lowly merchant who had made it into the Eagle Knights. Carro, who had come back to betray his own people.

"I want that merchant watched," the Knight Captain said behind him to another member of the patrol. "See who visits him and what they bring, or buy."

CHAPTER 4

THE SLED SWISHED to a halt at a spot where a mound of snow broke the monotony of the plain. Tandor peered into the low sun, which trailed long shadows over the snow. Little diamond-like specks twinkled in the powdery surface untouched by man or beast. At the horizon, the sky faded from pink to the most delicate of blue. The tall buildings of the City of Glass were mere specks in the distance, glittering needles that reflected the sunlight in their glass façades. What tranquillity, what incredible beauty. This was home, this was what his heart had been denied all those years that his mother had forced him to live in the dust and noise of Chevakia.

"What are we doing here?" a whining girl's voice said. The bundle of fur that hid Myra from view stirred. Her head poked out.

"Enjoying the view," Tandor said. He'd grown weary of her complaints. Her back hurt, her head hurt, she was cold, she needed to piss. "You asked for us to stop somewhere you could piss behind a tree. Well, there aren't any trees on this plain as you might have noticed, so it will have to be a stack of ice instead. Here you go."

He jumped down from the sled, his footsteps creaking in the snow. The cool air that charged his lungs made steaming puffs of mist when he exhaled.

He unlashed a net from the back of the sled and took out an ice pick and a shovel.

"What're you doing with those?" Myra asked.

"Some big business."

She wrinkled her face, but pushed herself up awkwardly. With a bit of luck, she would go for a walk to the other side of the mound.

"You're welcome to watch."

"You're not just creepy, you're disgusting."

"At your service, lady."

She sniffed, let herself down from sled with a wince and waddled off. Good.

Tandor positioned himself so that the peak of the snow mound and the glittering buildings of the City of Glass aligned. His gaze tracked the barely perceptible line that marked the shore of the Frozen Sea, the flat plain of the iced-over bay to his left, and the soft, undulating, snow-covered hills on his right.

Yes, he was at the place the diary had described.

He glanced around, checking if Myra had gone. Ruko stood at the sled, glaring into the light. The bear fidgeted, shaking its shoulders and jiggling the harness. Steam blew from its nostrils. Ruko patted its back, to which it responded with an angry snort.

Tandor glanced at Ruko. *You deal with it.*

Ruko gave Tandor his usual fuck-you look and flicked his too-long hair out of his eyes. Tandor had tried to cut it, but the boy wouldn't let him near. With every step closer to the City of Glass, Ruko gained strength. He had heaved huge blocks of ice out of the sled's path with his bare hands. He had run after the bear when it got it into its mind to chase after a group of gulls and he had dragged the bear back by the scruff of its neck. Tandor had needed a lot of icefire to make Ruko let go of the bear.

Tandor swung his ice pick up above his shoulder and drove it hard into the mound. Ice chips flew in arcs of glittering diamonds. Two more hits and the point of the pick hit a hard object under the snow with a "ping".

Good. He was definitely at the right place. The secret had not been disturbed. There was hope yet.

A few scrapes with the shovel later, he had unearthed a door handle, a few more shovelfuls and the rest of the door had become visible, a plain metal surface, pitted and weathered over time. Tandor stuck the pick and shovel in the snow and yanked at the handle. It wouldn't turn.

He gathered strands of icefire from the air—much stronger this close to the city—and directed them at the door. Steam hissed. The metal vibrated and glowed. He yanked at the door again and this time it opened. Cold and stale air spilled out of the dark maw.

The bear gave a low growl, lifting one corner of its dark lips.

Tandor let his hand stray to the Chevakian powder gun he carried in his belt. Icefire oozed from the door, against which the gun was of course perfectly useless.

He felt a stab of anger at having shown such a basic Chevakian reaction. All his life he'd lived in the blasted foreign country. It had corrupted him.

He had even known that there was *supposed* to be a field of icefire here.

This was not the time to hesitate or make silly mistakes. He'd best hurry up before the nosy girl came back. If the past day was anything to go by, she'd be asking plenty of questions already.

He stepped inside and tripped over something. By the skylights, it was dark in here. According to the maps in the diary, there should be a light somewhere on the wall.

He stumbled to the side, hands outstretched, until his palms met slime-covered stone. A waft of cold air drifted in from outside.

Ah, there was the lever, the metal ice-cold under his fingers. He pushed it up. A light flicked on, cold and white and incredibly bright. It came from a round globe unlike the oil lamps used by the common folk in the city or the gas lamps in Chevakia.

The beauty, the wonder of it. How could the Pirosian Eagle Knights have denied the people of the City of Glass this technology? How could they have condemned the citizens to living in poverty as primitives while these wonders existed?

The room was dank and moist. Against the far wall, a staircase wound down into the earth, much like the dungeons in the palace, with which he had made unfortunate acquaintance, and just as slippery. Unlike the staircase in the palace, this was covered in slime from disuse, accumulated over all those years that water had seeped through the stone.

Tandor made his way down, groping along the wall for additional lights. A fear grew in him as to what he would find at the bottom of the stairs. What would remain of his plan if the machine was ruined by meltwater?

The stairs ended in a round chamber. A table stood in the middle, and on it, an array of jars and tubes and a large metal box with levels and buttons. He ran his finger along a glass tube. A tingle of icefire crept up his hand. What purposes had this strange equipment served? There might be some records of it, scattered in the antique shops of Chevakia and Arania, where refugees from the palace had taken their goods, but it was likely that no one would ever know. *That* was the crime the Eagle Knights had committed. All that knowledge lost. They had plunged the City of Glass into the worst period of back-wardness history had ever seen, and had condemned anyone who was not of Pirosian noble blood to poverty. Simply because they were afraid of icefire, and jealous of those who could see and use it.

At the far end of the room, a bank of tables lined the wall, their surface a maze of controls and dials, many of which were rusty and probably no longer worked. In the old days, this machine distributed the power for the city's heat and lights and for trains that flew along rails, much like Chevakia's steam trains, but without the smoke, the stink and the noise of the engine.

In those days, the machine they called the Heart of the City beat strongly in the catacombs of the palace. The more power was chan-nelled away, the more the Heart produced. Now, ignored and isolated, cocooned in its underground prison, its beat had faded to a feeble throb. Even after they'd seized power, the Knights hadn't been able to turn it off. Its fuel was contained within the machine, which dated from much further back.

Tandor sank into the chair that faced the panels and slowly extracted the key, which he had spent months travelling to find, from under his clothes. Discovering it, after a lifetime of searching, in a box of curiosities in a market in northern Chevakia, had been the culmina-tion of his work. If he could turn the distribution network back on, the Heart would again be powerful, and increased icefire would be available to all who could use it around the city. Then those people, the Thilleians, would make the southern land great again. Of course it wasn't quite so simple, even though his mother would like to think so; but it was a start.

The key was a strange thing, a thin strip of metal as long as his thumb, with two ridges on either side. He slipped the chain that held it in place from around his neck, feeling the stern eyes of his dead ancestors prick in the back of his head. They knew what he risked, and they knew of the glory of days past, and of the disasters. They also knew that he had no army to control the icefire the machine would produce.

They're in the City of Glass already; they will help me because they are destined to do so.

But he had to obtain their hearts for them to be unconditionally obedient to him. They had to be servitors, like Ruko. At the thought of Ruko, an unpleasant thought surfaced.

If I wait any longer, I won't be able to control him anymore. If I wait any longer, the Knights will kill the children, and then all my work will have been for nothing.

He stared at the controls and the dust-coated engravings in the metal surface. Levers stuck out of slots, their handles made from Chevakian wood inlaid with river pearl. There were little silica windows with silver embossing, now dark and lifeless. The work oozed beauty and craftsmanship.

I owe it to the souls of all the Imperfects who have been killed since the Knights took power.

There would not be a second chance. This was the best time of year, with the Eagle Knights distracted by the Newlight celebrations. Half of them would take part in the competitions and the other half would be drunk or in some woman's bed.

He didn't have another fifteen years to scout out another army. It was make do with these children, or not at all. He *did* have enough power to get into the palace.

I am no quitter, Mother, no matter how much you think I am.

He breathed in deeply and slotted the key into the panel. Strands of icefire bent to his hand. He pressed a button. A tiny light brightened, under a cover yellowed with age. Silver engraving reflected the glow. Underneath the ice on the plain between here and the City of Glass, in a pipe that contained threads that Chevakians called *wire*, a signal would travel to the underground power network to bring it to life. And under the palace, the Heart would respond.

Tandor went through the motions he had memorised from the diary. The network needed water to cool down. The underground passages needed to be opened up to let the heat escape. He slid up levers and turned dials. More lights blinked into life.

Everything seemed to be working the way it should. He had five days before the machine would come into its full power. This would be one sizzler of a Newlight celebration.

Cramped, shivering, Tandor rose from the seat.

He charged back up the stairs, across the slippery bunker and out into the brightness of the snow-covered ice. He heaved the door back into its place and used his pick to push snow over it.

Ruko waited in the driver's seat, the reins in his hands, an impatient scowl on his face.

Myra sat in the sled, rummaging through her luggage.

Tandor jumped onto the seat. "Ready to go? From here straight to the City of Glass. We'll be there today."

He expected a keen response from her. The prospects of visiting markets and shops had kept her happy for the past two days, but she wasn't looking at the horizon at all. Her underwear was bunched around her knees. His heart jumped. *Please, no.*

"Anything wrong?"

"I'm bleeding." She sniffed, wiping a tear from her cheek.

"What does that mean?" His heart thudded.

"I don't know!"

"Does it hurt?"

She shook her head. "It's only a tiny bit." But her voice sounded unsteady. Her face was very pale. He glanced at her underwear, spotting streaks of blood-tinged slime. Was that normal?

"Do you have any . . . pains?"

She shook her head again.

"You think you can hang on for a bit longer? We're almost there." *By the skylights, please.* He heard a woman's screams in his mind. Then the feeble cry of a baby, followed by the horrified voice of the midwife, *This one's deformed.*

"I think so," Myra whispered.

Tandor took a deep breath to calm his thudding heart. "Let's go then."

CHAPTER 5

THE EYRIE OF the eagle knights perched atop the second highest tower in the City of Glass, a place where windows had been removed and eagles and their riders could fly in and out freely.

Yellow feet outstretched, Carro's eagle glided into this dark maw that was its home. Air disturbed by its flapping wings propelled straw in little eddies to the corners of the landing area. At their tethering spots further into the building, other eagles squawked and ruffled feathers.

Carro unclipped his harness and slid off the back of his eagle. He swayed with the effects of too much bloodwine, but he forced his feet to move. Never mind the Newlight festival, there'd be trouble if he was caught drunk in the Eyrie.

Six birds stood tethered to the central bar. One of them was ripping at a mass of blood and fur that might once have been a Legless Lion cub. Two other birds were preening themselves, and one regarded Carro with a roving orange eye.

Carro tied the reins to the far end of the bar and threw his bird a hunk of meat. As if it knew that he was supposed to rub it down before leaving, the animal cocked its head and gave him a disdainful glare before it pierced the meat with its claw to claim it. Yet it didn't bend down to tear strips off the meat. It arched its neck. A series of spasms rippled through the animal's body. It opened its beak wide and spat a fur ball onto the floor.

A stable boy skittered past and shovelled it, still steaming, into a bucket. His eyes were wide. "Did you see that, how fast I got it?"

If he expected coin, Carro had spent his last money on drink. He shrugged, and continued to the door, bloodwine churning uncomfortably in his stomach.

That was not an honourable thing to do. But he had no coin left.

After the market raids, the men had gone to the meltery. The older Knights had been drinking hard and had challenged him to keep up. Which he had, just, including two trips to the alley at the back of the meltery to spew, standing over the pink-stained snow, hating himself for the waste of money. His father might be a merchant, but he was an Outer City merchant with nowhere near as much wealth as the city nobles whose sons usually went into the Knighthood.

He avoided the young stable boy's questioning gaze.

Later. He'd give double the going rate later. The thought only added to the misery he already felt.

He couldn't forget the merchant's shocked face, with the expression that said, *I trusted you*. Then there had been all those other merchants watching him. He'd *betrayed* his own people. What would they do when he came back to the Outer City two days from now, when he and Isandor flew in the race? Would they still cheer? What would the Knights do if they knew the full truth about him? There was no way, *no way*, he'd go back to his father.

He left the eyrie for the darkness of the corridor. Against the wall stood an eagle statue carved from opaque glass, with orange gems for eyes.

The Knight served his eagle; the eagle served the Knight.

It was said that the first eagles had been bred in the palace from the much smaller birds that lived in the mountains. Rumours went that icefire had gone into their blood and that this was the reason they were big enough to carry a fully grown man in leather armour.

The Tutors said that was nonsense spread by "certain elements", by which they meant the Brotherhood. But the Brothers said they spoke the truth about the eagles being giant forms of wild eagles, and many Knights believed it. This statue symbolised the first of those birds.

The Tutors and upper command didn't like it, but most Knights placed small offerings at the glass eagle's feet for luck. Carro stopped and stroked the cold glass neck, smoothed by the passage of many hands. He leaned his forehead against the glass, hoping it would clear his drunken head. *If you have any power at all, help me.*

Then again, why should it help him? He had never been brave enough to give an offering.

Carro's mother sits across the table, yelling at him.

"If I hear one more word about that nonsense . . ."

It isn't nonsense. Just because his mother fails to understand why the Brotherhood does things such as calculating the power of sunlight doesn't mean that it is *untrue*.

The things the Brotherhood teaches are true; he and Isandor did the experiment as it said in the book. They went out into the alley and let the light shine through the magnifying glass they bought at the markets. The intense spot of light caused the paper to burst into flames. The book told them this happened because of the shape of the glass and the direction of the sunlight. It also explained that you could do a similar thing with icefire.

They were laughing at their success when his mother found them.

Carro hangs his head. No use arguing.

"Go and help your father in the warehouse." She flaps her hand at the door, already bored.

"Yes, Mother."

Carro froze, his heart thudding, his cheek still against the glass beak of the eagle.

Voices echoed from lower levels of the eyrie, the meaning of the words inaudible. Carro heard his name in every shout, mockery in every bout of laughter. Even the wind whistling through the howling staircase shrieked his name. Carro, the betrayer. Carro, the gutless. Carro, who had to follow his cripple friend into the Knighthood.

"There you are, Apprentice Carro."

Carro gasped.

The Tutor stood behind him, hands on his hips. He was a man with a beak-like nose, much like an eagle.

Carro scrambled away from the statue, kicking a few coins across the stone floor. Blood rose in his cheeks. Had the Tutor seen how he'd embraced the glass eagle?

"Where were you? I expected you at training."

"With the Knight patrol. You gave me permission—"

"I did?"

"Yes, the patrol Captain—"

The Tutor slapped Carro's face, hard. "The Eagle Order has five pillars: Obedience, Honour, Honesty, Humility and Silence. You disregard all of them. May I remind you that your status is of no import amongst the Knights?"

Status? He had no status. His father was a lowly merchant. Oh, his status as the only Outer City Apprentice? His status as the Apprentices' pissing post?

His gaze on the toes of his boots—scuffed, unpolished—he said, "The Patrol Captain asked if I could come with them to the markets. You gave me permission to go." He'd done nothing wrong—except getting drunk.

The Tutor pushed Carro's head up and spat in his face.

"You disrespect me. And you're drunk. Go to your dormitory and sleep it off. Report for cleaning duty tomorrow."

The Tutor turned and made for the door. "And be glad I'm not giving you worse punishment."

Carro looked up defiantly, wiping saliva off his face with the sleeve of his tunic.

"And wash yourself. You're disgusting!" the Tutor yelled in the confined space of the corridor. The sound of his footsteps faded.

Carro went down the staircase which took him down to the Apprentices' dormitory, a long room with rows of mats against both walls. Blankets lay neatly rolled up at the head end of each.

A few older Learners huddled together on one mat, casting furtive glances at the door as Carro came in.

"And then," one boy was saying, "Then I could see her, right through her dress, you know, and man, does she have puppies."

The boys guffawed. One or two glanced at Carro.

"Heh, you look like you fell off your bird again," snorted Jono.

They always had to remind him of *that* moment, in his second-ever flying lesson, when his eagle had taken off so quickly that he hadn't secured himself in the harness.

Clamping his jaws, Carro crossed the room to the shelves at the far end and took a clean uniform from the shelf labelled with his name.

"Listen to me, then," another Apprentice said. "I seen her the day before yesterday. She were going into the baths. There were guards outside, and some went inside with her."

"Do you think they . . ."

More guffaws.

"Nah. She'll pick the real pretty ones. Like that one."

All boys turned to Carro. A grin spread across Jono's face.

"Hey, pretty boy."

One elbowed the speaker in the side. "Hush. He be selected, I think. I heard some Tutors talking about him."

"And they let him stay with us? Do they want him undamaged?"

Jono laughed aloud. For some reason, he'd been picking on Carro since the first day of their training. It started with comments on Carro's clothing, and his parents. Then there had been taunts about the Outer City, and about his clumsiness and his girl-like curls—which Carro had cut off at the earliest opportunity.

Carro kept his gaze to the floor. *Do not talk back, do not talk back.* With everything at the eyrie, that only made things worse.

"Hey, boy? You be a virgin?"

Carro stares across the room. The girl has hair like a bronze waterfall. It dances over her shoulders when she moves her head. She's come with the seamstress who is going to make some new dresses for his sister to wear to dinner parties to show off the material his father has imported from Arania. Then rich women will come from the city to buy the fabric.

Business. Fabric on the table and patterns spread out over the couch.

The pretty girl should be wearing the dresses, not his dumpy sister. The girl would look like a goddess. She should be outside, celebrating Newlight, but instead she's here with her boss on his mother's whim.

She smiles. Around her neck she wears a strip of leather with a gull's tail feather tied to it. She's freshly blooded and free to consort with whomever she wants. And she's watching him.

Carro's cheeks burn with heat. Distant thumps of festival music roar in his ears.

"Carro, I told you to get the account books. Why haven't you done it yet?"

Carro gasps. That's his father yelling at him. He'll be in for another punishment when the seamstress leaves.

He jumps up, but still looks at the girl, and doesn't see the table. He hits the corner with his knee. Cups go flying with loud clanks and clatters. Tea seeps into the tablecloth.

"You clumsy boy!" his mother yells.

The girl giggles.

Carro flees, blood throbbing in all sorts of uncomfortable places.

Carro sneaked into the bathroom as quietly as he could, trying not to catch the boys' attention.

His footsteps echoed in the room of tiles and stone. His breath made puffs of mist in the icy air. The fire from the drying room barely brought any warmth. A fat icicle trailed from the tiny window in the top of the opposite wall almost to the ground. The city buildings were so different from those in the Outer City. These buildings were open, square and cold. The houses in the Outer City were round, without windows, and had a central stove that kept the house warm all day.

Being a Knight wasn't meant to be comfortable.

He undressed himself, and rinsed the smell of bloodwine out of his clothes, shuddering at the memory of the Learner Knight from the patrol who kept buying him drinks when his stomach was already protesting. To get him punished no doubt. He poured several pitchers of ice-cold water over his head and then got to work on the bathroom floor. Cleaning duty: he'd done his fair share. He collected the broom and scrubbed the tiles.

When he went to hang his clothes to dry, he found the Apprentices who had been in the dormitory blocking the door to the drying room. Jono was in the middle of the group. He said lazily, "It think it's time the pet got a lesson, don't you?" He scratched the crotch of his trousers.

The girl's name is Kaila. She holds his arm and talks and giggles. Carro listens to her cheerful babble and wonders how he can guide her into the furniture-maker's warehouse. It's big and empty, and young people go there to lose their innocence during the Newlight celebrations. And now that he's managed to sneak her out of the house, he can think of nothing else. His whole body aches for it.

A couple of older boys block the street. Carro recognises some of them as his sister's friends. The pleasant feeling fades for an icy cold.

The leader of the group, a lanky boy whose name he doesn't know, pulls Carro's cloak off.

"Hey," Carro yells. His voice sounds high and boyish. Not the way he wants the girl to hear it. He wants to be manly; he wants her to think he knows all about having girls.

The boy holds the cloak out of his reach.

"You don't need that. You have enough blubber to keep you warm."

"Give that back to him," Kaila says. She lets go of Carro's arm—leaving a warm spot—and yanks the cloak out of the boy's hands.

"Hey, what have we here?" The boy grabs her arm. He reaches out and pulls the feather from under her cloak with a broad grin on his face. His mates are cheering.

"You keep your hands off her!" Carro shouts.

"Ah, she's yours, is she?"

Another boy laughs. "Do you guys reckon he knows where to put it?"

A volley of laughter cascades through the street.

"You know what," the leader says. "We will let you go."

Carro breathes out heavily, but doesn't understand. Let him go? They never let him go without humiliation.

Then the boy says, "And we'll come. We're going to watch."

One of the boys pushed Carro face-first into the wall. Others laughed. Hands yanked away the towel, which slipped past his thighs into a puddle on the floor. An icy breeze made his skin break out in goosebumps.

No. He would not think of what happened that day in the furniture-maker's warehouse, about the girl and her pale flesh and his own unwilling body, the laughter at his flaccid member, shrunken and shrivelled in the cold. The girl was crying; the boys were cheering, pushing him, jostling him. He could *not* do it.

And he would *not* go and relive it. He needed to toughen up; his father'd said it often enough and, as much as he hated his father, the man was probably right. He was *not* a pretty boy with too much fat and no muscle. He was *not* an artist with certain parts of his anatomy removed. He was *not* a boy lover.

Carro stands in his father's room. His father sits in his chair by the hearth, smiling.

Carro doesn't like the smile. When his father is angry, things are bad. When he smiles, things are worse.

But his father doesn't speak. He sits, saying nothing.

Carro grasps his hands behind his back and stands there, determined not to say anything.

But the silence lasts on.

Eventually he can't stand it anymore.

He asks, "You wanted to see me, Father?"

His father doesn't answer.

"Um—Father? I'd like to continue with my study."

His father says nothing. Doesn't even look at him.

What sort of silly game is this? Carro balls his fists, but knows getting angry will not do much good. Whatever he does, his father always wins.

So he stands there, and stares into the fire.

But his father still doesn't speak.

He gathers all his courage. "Father. I really need to study. Please tell me why I needed to come."

Another silence.

"Well, if you won't . . ."

His father raises an eyebrow, and goes back to staring into the fire.

"Father, I'm not going to stand here if you won't tell me what this is about. I have a lot of study to do. I won't let you keep me here and then punish me for not doing my work."

Carro turns on his heel and leaves the room.

In the hall he stops, panting, listening to his thudding heart, stilling his trembling limbs. He can't believe what he's just done.

Carro mustered his strength and pushed himself back, slamming his elbow hard into the nose of Jono, who was fumbling with his trousers.

Jono swore hard.

There were shouts, cursing, a jostle and few more boys pushed Carro back against the wall. The mixed taste of plaster and blood in his mouth was too familiar. Two boys on each side held Carro's arms.

"What did you think you were doing?" Jono stroked Carro's naked shoulders and let his hand slide down his back, between his buttocks. A cold hand closed around his balls.

"You thought you could beat me, pup?"

Carro dared not breathe. He whispered, "No."

The hand let go, and slid over the skin.

"You like that, huh?"

"Yes." No other reply was possible, not without making this worse than it already was.

Both hands now grabbed the sides of his thighs.

"I didn't hear that. Can you say it again?"

"Yes!"

"Beg me."

Carro pushed his eyes shut.

Jono hit him hard on the back of the head. "Beg, I said."

"Please!"

Jono came up from behind and rammed hard into Carro's arse. Carro couldn't restrain a moan. His whole backside was on fire.

"You like that, huh?" Jono's breath tickled in the back of his neck. Warm fluid trickled over his shoulder. Blood, from Jono's nose.

"Do I have a choice?" Carro snarled, with one cheek pressed against the wall.

Jono grunted and pushed deeper.

Goosebumps broke out on Carro's skin. The pain had subsided and now he was starting to go hard. It always happened. They'd fuck him, use him, and leave him, sore and aching for release. He hated how his body betrayed him. He hated everything.

Carro clamped his jaws. He would *not* scream or cry. Next time, he would hit harder and in a more delicate spot.

CHAPTER 6

"THE CITY of glass," Tandor said, gesturing at the horizon.

Since stopping at the cave early that morning, the sled had skirted the frozen bay, cutting across points and peninsulas. Now at last, the sled had crested the last hill on their path and they had an uninterrupted view of the point where the snow-swept white bay joined the southern ocean. To the right, fluffy clouds hung over the foothills to the mountains forming the border with Arania.

Straight ahead, where stacks of ice floes met the bay, the jagged peaks of the City of Glass reached towards the heavens, tall structures that reflected the light of the low sun. The palace tower protruded from the cluster like a broken stick. That was where Queen Jevaithi looked down upon them all from her rooms with the soft carpets, the ruffled curtains, the stuffed armchairs and the huge bed. Oh yes, the bed.

To Tandor's eyes, the City lay at the centre of a golden web of icefire that spread out over the plain, always moving and shimmering. By the skylights! He had never seen it as strong as this. In days to come, it would get stronger, and that was all his doing. It was the sign of power returning to the Thilleian clan.

Myra sat straight, wincing. She had stopped complaining but kept casting Tandor angry looks. Tandor alternated between finding it annoying and not even noticing. He had made it here without mishaps. Loriane would probably scold him for taking Myra, but now the women could worry about the women's things.

"You'll soon be warm in mistress Loriane's house."

"The cold isn't why I'm shivering. There's something creepy about this place."

She let her eyes wander to the jagged outlines of the city. Tandor wondered how much icefire she saw.

Ruko was pulling a hooded cloak from the luggage, the type worn by carriers of disease. Good boy.

Tandor nodded his appreciation; Ruko glared back and sent Tandor images of an infirmary ward.

No one will bother you, Tandor said by way of excuse.

Covering up avoided risky situations. If people saw a driverless sled moving by itself, there would be panic or, worse, arrests and questions.

A rush of images flashed through Tandor's mind: the same infirmary ward, but the patients bloody and injured in their beds. Red sheets. Some people decapitated, some with their bellies slit open and their intestines spilling out. A madman looking like Ruko, with a knife in his hand—

Tandor clamped down on the visions. He gathered icefire in his hand, and threw a loop of it around Ruko's legs.

The images faded, except for one: that of the girl Tandor had seen in Ruko's mind before.

Ruko's inaudible angry howl rang through Tandor's mind.

You love her? Tandor asked.

The girl smiled, and reached out.

If you do what I say, we will free her from the palace. If you disobey me I will turn you back into a mortal. . . . Tandor cast a glance at the chest strapped to the luggage rack. Ruko's heart was in there. Returning it to his body would not only return Ruko to a weakened, mortal state, it would make him Imperfect, and persecuted in the city.

Ruko pulled on the hooded cloak with jerky movements that oozed anger. While he stepped back up onto the driver's seat, his eyes met Tandor's. They both knew that Tandor's threat was useless. He needed Ruko to be a servitor for his plan to succeed.

Ruko flicked the reins. Even that simple gesture made Tandor's skin creep. With every step the bear took towards the city, the boy's power grew.

The bear started moving again.

The Outer City lay on a hillock to the right, a jumble of snow-covered humps, houses built by those exiled from the city after the Knights had taken power. Initially, it was nothing more than a camp, frequently razed by Knights to weed out the last remains of Thillei blood. These days, the settlement was a decent town in its own right, a gathering of buildings that had been thrown together without plans or foresight. It was the home of commerce and crime.

The traditional festival grounds were a temporary town made of colourful tents on the plain separating the Outer City from the City of Glass proper. It was busy; the breeze brought shards of music and clapping, and grumbles of bears from the sled parking area. A line of fences marked a course for racing Tusked Lions. They even had igloos for the animals. Tandor spotted the flapping wings of an eagle, and the grey and red uniform of a Knight. Yes, they would be out here in force, too.

Newlight meant free unlimited girls, most of whom were throwing themselves at the Knights, so most of those Knights wouldn't be looking too closely at what went on in the Outer City.

Ruko steered the sled along a track that was worn smooth by passing traffic, no doubt made by Lion-catchers returning to the city with the first of the animals to be slaughtered.

Soon, they had reached the ramshackle collection of houses, with Ruko negotiating the twisty streets. Getting lost was easy in the Outer City. No street was straight and the houses, structures locals called limpets, all looked the same from the outside: large conical shapes of ice. The ones that had just been resurfaced were pristine white, while the older ones had gone dirty and grey. At normal times, different colours of the doors distinguished the individual houses, but during the Newlight festival, most doors were yellow.

There were people everywhere: talking on street corners, watching artistes in colourful clothing juggling balls while standing on each other's shoulders, and lining up to get into their favourite eating houses.

The sled progressed at walking pace. The people would see a noble and a girl heavy with child and would see them as a man from the city's nobility with his breeder woman, nothing out of the ordinary.

A juggler performed an act with a set of burning coals and a huge butcher's knife. At his feet lay a stuffed pillow made from bear fur, symbolising the animal that would be ritually killed at the height of the celebrations. Newlight celebrated the end of the long, dark winter, when the sun first rose above the horizon after having been absent for months, and hunting trips were again possible. It was the start of a time of plenty, of new life, and of fertility.

The sled had gone past the juggler before the man got to the part of his act that involved stabbing the stuffed bear and ripping it apart. Usually, there was something inside for the children. Chevakian sweets, or bits of saltmeat. Tandor could taste it on his tongue.

By the skylights, the memories. His mother used to take him here for visits almost every year.

Myra looked wide-eyed at the scenery sliding past. For a short time at least, she seemed to have forgotten to complain.

They crossed the markets, with busy stalls and roaring fires, where people were eating hot food and warming themselves. Tandor felt the pull of icefire from the merchant who usually had his stall in the very corner. To the common people in the street, he sold crockery and bits and pieces he scavenged from old estates, but under his benches, he held forbidden items from the past. Little portraits of the King, a piece of cutlery with the Thillei emblem, scavenged from the palace storerooms. Today there was no opportunity for Tandor to see the man, but he'd come back later. First he must deposit this complaining child in mistress Loriane's hands.

Ruko halted the sled in front of a newly covered limpet with a blue door—just like Loriane to ignore the seasonal yellow-door decoration. The blue door was so familiar, down to the white snowflake patterns on the blue paint—Tandor had painted them—and the mark on the door which he had made trying to manoeuvre a chair inside. So many times had Tandor stepped through that door into Loriane's soft arms. He could taste her lips against his, he could feel the softness of her breasts under his hands. He could—

"Is this it?" Myra asked, frowning.

Tandor shook himself out of his memories. "Yes."

He jumped off the sled. A young couple came past and stared at him as he lifted the knocker and let it fall on the door. Why *would* a noble come to mistress Loriane's house? Good question.

Tandor ignored the gazes. He imagined the big round stove that was the centre of the limpet, where Loriane would make her heavenly soup. He could almost see her determined face, the cheeks red with cold, the slightly crooked mouth and the way one of her eyes always seemed to squint. No, Loriane wasn't pretty either. Her beauty was on the inside.

Why had no one opened the door yet?

"Well, your woman obviously isn't at home." Myra's voice sounded peevish.

Tandor wanted to snap at her. Yes, he was sore and tired, too—and how was he to know that Loriane would be out?—but he bit on his irritation.

"She might be at the festival," he said.

The remaining Imperfect boy would be fifteen. He might take part in some of the competitions. Loriane's brother was a butcher. He would have an important role in the festivities. Yes, that was it.

He climbed back into the sled.

Ruko's questioning mind touched his.

Tandor forced his thoughts back on the snow-covered field where the crowds and the tents had been. *And the eagles.* The place crawled with Knights, since a lot of them would be competing. Well, that was not to be helped.

Ruko steered the sled away from the house, and they went back through the same busy streets, drawing annoyed glances from pedestrians.

When they reached the festival grounds, the sled could go no further. The designated parking area was already full and the igloos occupied with bears. But never mind; they wouldn't stay long.

Tandor jumped out, after which Myra pulled up her legs and settled sideways on the bench. "You go and look for her. I'll stay here."

"No, you won't." He couldn't risk losing her now.

"I'm tired."

"No, you come. I promised your father I'd look after you." *And I didn't take you to play a stubborn adolescent either.*

Her face scrunched up briefly, but then she pressed her lips together and rose. "I don't know why you wanted me to come. So far, you've only been disgusting and nasty to me."

"You'll find out." He held out an arm. She took it, clambering awkwardly from the sled. A man walking past shot him a look that might have been disdain. Noble men of the City of Glass paid their breeder women to have their children but did not, ever, fall in love with them. He wanted to scream at those curious people, *the child isn't mine*.

A man walked past pulling a sled full of barrels. Bloodwine. That load was worth a lot of sore heads tomorrow morning.

To his right, at the bottom of the slope, stood several brightly coloured tents. Clouds of steam rose into the air from food stalls.

A bit further away over the plains, a group of eagles were coming in. This was the tail end of the long-distance race for Apprentice Knights, Tandor picked up from a shard of conversation.

A couple of youngsters were walking in the snow in bare feet, with bare legs protruding from blankets. Ah, the swimming. Didn't they make that race harder every year? Jump in the water, swim to the ice floe, climb on, get the token, jump back in and return to the start? By that time, most of the competitors were so cold that they needed rescuing, to loud jeers of the audience. Oh, the memories were coming back.

Soon, they were amongst the thick of the activity. Tandor wanted to run from tent to tent. Now that he was so close, he hungered for Loriane's touch, the twinkle in her eyes and the caress of her hands.

Loriane had once said she manned the drinks booth, so they looked at the food stalls. It was so busy that Tandor had to hold Myra close for fear of becoming separated in the throng. She shuddered under his touch.

The crowds at the swimming were so thick that even he, tall as he was, could only hear the splashes and the shouts. Further past the tents, nurses' sleds marked with green were doing a brisk trade shipping contestants off to the various Outer City healers.

Ah. As midwife, Loriane was a healer of sorts. Maybe she was on duty in the medical post.

A huge queue lined up there. Tandor pushed past the line. People glared, but said nothing at the sight of the golden curls on his cheeks. The advantages of being a noble.

In one tent, a couple of frazzled nurses were treating a young man with cuts all over his upper body. Tandor guessed he had fallen on the ice.

In another tent, a group of young men continued to brawl while Tandor tried to make himself heard. Where was Loriane? The young nurse thought maybe in the main post. Where was that? Her reply was interrupted by a loud burp. The next thing, one of the brawling youths projectile-vomited bloodwine all over his mates and collapsed face first onto the floor. Then everyone started yelling.

Tandor retreated. The smell of vomit made him feel sick.

"Have you seen anything that might look like a main medical post?" he asked Myra.

She didn't reply. Her face was pale; she seemed not to have heard anything.

A stab of irritation shot through him. "What's wrong with you?"

"What's wrong? Well, you're so good at being crude. In case you haven't noticed, having a child inside you puts a lot of pressure on your rear end. In case you don't understand that: my butt hurts and I feel like pissing myself with every step. I want to use the outroom." Her voice spilled over.

"But you did only just before we came here."

"Didn't you listen to what I said? I feel like that. All. The. Fucking. Time."

People were stepping back, leaving a small circle around them, keen expressions on their faces. At Newlight, fights were entertainment, no matter who was fighting.

He grabbed her arm. "Come. You're making a spectacle of yourself."

"No, I'm not coming anywhere. I've had enough."

She yanked her arm out of his grip and ran, shouldering people aside. Oh, by the skylights!

Tandor pushed between curious onlookers, but she had vanished. Great. That was just what he needed.

He stood there, gnashing his teeth when a shiver of icefire crawled over his arm. A brief golden thread snaked through the air. That had to be from Myra, but the thread had not come from the direction of the sled. Where was she going? Was she lost already?

Women.

He pushed through the crowd. The sensation grew stronger. Golden threads shivered and dissolved into sparks. At that point he realised that this icefire didn't come from Myra: the boy was here.

Stupid. He should have realised that. Myra had Thillei blood, but it wasn't half as strong as the boy's. Isandor had turned fifteen and would be out here looking for girls, maybe drinking if he had money, or taking part in a competition or two.

All Tandor needed to do was follow the tug of icefire and collect another of his children. Except the strand led him . . . to the eagles' pens.

Tandor spotted Myra before he found Isandor. She was at the fence, staring into the pen where at least thirty eagles were tied up on bars. She was even leaning her Imperfect arm on the fence. *By the skylights, get away before anyone sees you.* The place was crawling with Knights. There were at least ten of them in their distinctive red tunics with grey cloaks.

"Myra, come," he hissed at her. "I promise we'll go back to the sled now."

She didn't move, but stared ahead.

Tandor followed her gaze. In a group of a few young Knights stood a distinctive young man, lean and quite tall. His skin was milk-pale and his hair black as a low-sun night. Since Tandor had seen him last, his face had become more mature. He even sported a dark fuzz of hair on his chin. But his eyes were the clearest, darkest blue, the colour people called royal blue. It was Loriane's boy Isandor, and he was wearing an Eagle Knight uniform.

CHAPTER 7

ICE FLOES, belly slithers, what would they think of next?

Loriane pulled the thread and knotted it close to the young man's skin. She cut the needle free and covered the wound with a dab of paste to stop it going bad.

"That will become a nasty scar, I'm afraid," she said. On his forehead, too. Stupidity forever engraved on his face.

The man blinked, looking up at the canvas ceiling of the treatment tent. Light from the central fire flickered in his eyes. He was too drunk to respond, too drunk to feel pain. He also had been too drunk to swim, probably; otherwise he would not be sitting here.

"I've finished with him," she said to his friends who waited by the fire, hands outstretched to warm themselves. "Take him home and make sure he rests for a ten-night."

They mumbled agreement.

Loriane heaved herself to her feet and tossed her instruments—scalpel and needles—into the cooking pot that hung over the fire.

"Help me put his clothes back on."

One of the young men came forward and pulled his mate up from the chair while Loriane wrestled unwilling limbs back into armholes, sliding cloth over wounds she had bandaged earlier. The stench of bloodwine around the men made her gag.

The man's cloak, blood-splattered and dirty, went over his clothes. Then the two friends shuffled out with the patient.

Loriane sighed and sank down in the chair that still held the young man's lingering warmth. *Rest*. Like that would ever happen. More likely, she'd see him back here tomorrow with . . . let's see . . . alcohol poisoning, cuts from the ice, bruises from his fellow's fists or deep ugly scratches from trying to mount an eagle. Seriously, had she ever been that stupid at that age?

She so much preferred her usual patients: pregnant women who came to her for advice and who asked her to come to the palace birthing rooms to help deliver their children.

She should pack up and go home before someone brought the next victim. During the Newlight festival, there was always a next victim. She had been on her feet since this morning. They hurt. Her belly hurt.

As she picked up her cloak, the tent's outer flap whispered like it did when someone entered. A girl stood there, barely out of adolescence. Loriane knew her; she lived a few streets away, the daughter of a merchant.

"Mistress Loriane! Am I too late?"

Loriane sighed. "I was about to go home. Be quick."

"I'd like to get my ichina." The girl's eyes shone. "I got my first bleeding, just in time for Newlight."

All girls went through this trial, the ritual deflowering of their innocence. When they bled, they were allowed to consort with whomever they liked whenever they liked during the Newlight celebrations.

Loriane went to her medicine chests. She rummaged through her medicines for the jar of ichina, and measured out a small quantity of the red powder on her scales.

"You must take it on the first day you stop bleeding. You should mix it in a drink. It's most effective if you use it in the morning."

The girl nodded solemnly, but her eyes shone.

"Are you sure you want it now? Because you would have more chance next year. A girl's bleeding usually takes some time to settle before you can conceive." If that happened at all. Far too many women went barren.

"No, I want it now." The girl blushed.

All right—she fancied someone.

"Anyone important? If it is, you have to make sure you get a contract negotiated if you fall pregnant. Don't ask too much. They might use you again if they're happy with you."

The tent flap rustled again, letting in Aera, one of the Outer City's regular healers, an older woman with a severe bun on top of her head. She advanced silently into the tent, put down a bucket and peeled off her cloak. Underneath, she wore a sturdy dress. She rolled up the sleeves and started transferring chunks of ice from her bucket into a large pot of water that hung over the fire.

Loriane rattled off the other things in a businesslike manner. The girl left, happy and red-cheeked, clutching the treasure in her pocket.

"You go home," Aera said into the silence. "I'll take over. You look tired."

Loriane nodded. She *was* tired. Somehow, this child exhausted her more than the previous nine had.

"How long until you drop that child?"

"A ten-night, no more." Or tonight, she wished with all her mind, but so far none of the concoctions she gave her girls had worked on her.

"Urgh. Rather you than me. Whose is this one?"

"Yanko."

"Good catch. Hope he'll pay well for the suffering."

Loriane nodded non-committally. The world of breeders was far removed from this woman's life. Most of the bright-eyed girls who came to ask Loriane for ichina never came back again. Like so many of the city's women, they were barren. If they were lucky, they would snare a decent husband who would pay a breeder to have his children. If they found no husband, well, there was always the street, the pleasure parlours and the merchants who were always looking for workers in poorly heated warehouses.

Loriane donned her cloak, bid the healer good luck and left the tent.

She had feared there would be more people waiting outside for treatment, but the queues had gone and a sense of quiet had descended over the festival grounds in preparation for the night, when revellers moved to the Outer City's melteries.

Soon enough, the stream of patients would recommence, bringing unconscious drunks choking in their own vomit and men with gashes from fights.

With a shiver, she wondered what Isandor was doing. He'd been a boy this time last year, talking about the races with wide-eyed wonder. Now he was with the Knights and had a brooding handsomeness, which made her sure that by the end of Newlight he would no longer be a virgin. If a girl came to her door claiming to carry his child, would he have the money to deal with it? Could she cope with raising another one of those strange children that made her skin crawl? He was fifteen, not ready for any of this.

I was thirteen when I let myself be taken by the young noble Knight with the curly hair, and fourteen when I pushed out his son. After a day of pain, a beautiful baby with big bright eyes. She had fed the child and had never wanted to part with him. But the palace midwives had taken him away. The boy would be sixteen and living a world away in the towers of the City of Glass.

Oh, she had done well enough. With the Knight's money, she had been able to leave her embittered father. But no amount of money could take away the pain of losing her first child.

She wanted a different future for Isandor. She wanted to tell him not to touch any girls, but knew he wouldn't listen anyway.

"Loriane," a male voice called.

"I'm on my way home. Go to the help post at the festival." Then she realised she sounded snippy and added, "Unless it's an emergency."

"For you, there is always an emergency."

The next moment warm arms enclosed her from behind. The man's clothes smelled of exotic spices and oil.

"Tandor!" Could it be true? She leaned away from his male warmth.

Tandor indeed. By the skylights, where had he been? His blue eyes smiled at her. The street lamps glinted in the golden curls on his cheeks. He was wearing his noblemen's disguise again. He looked so good; he was here for her.

"What are you doing here?"

"Shh." He put a finger to her lips and pulled it away when his lips came closer. His kiss was hungry, and for a moment, she lost herself in desire.

His hands strayed to the taut skin of her belly. "Another one, eh?"

"It pays my food."

"Oh, Loriane, how many times do I have to tell you that you don't have to do this."

"And I'll tell you just as many times that I have no other option. I'm a fertile woman, and there'd be talk if I weren't carrying."

By the skylights, she was angry all of a sudden. Why hadn't he let her know he was coming?

"So, what *are* you doing here?"

"It's a long story. We need a safe place to stay, and I thought—"

"You thought Isandor's bed is empty so you can stay with me?" By the skylights, he was so transparent. "Tandor, you don't need to find silly excuses to stay with me, even though you always manage to think of some." Wait—he had said *we?*

She glanced over his shoulder. His familiar sled waited in the street, with the equally familiar cloaked and hooded driver. She had never seen the man's face, and had never heard him speak. Tandor had told her the young man had an accident and couldn't speak. His face had become terribly disfigured, he said. Would he have to sleep in her house, too? He never came inside.

Fur stirred on the back seat of the sled; a head lifted from what had looked like Tandor's luggage a moment ago.

"Can we go now?" asked a female voice.

Loriane stiffened. "Who's that?"

She pushed herself out of his embrace. Her heart thudded like crazy.

"This is Myra, from Bordertown."

His eyes met hers, intense, and she had no idea what that look meant.

Her lips felt stiff when she spoke her next words. "It'll cost to stay with me. This is the time of Newlight. There are no beds for hire anywhere in the city. If you stay in my house, I'll have to cancel a paying visitor I'd agreed to take."

"Loriane, Loriane, you know you're the worst liar in the world?"

Damn him. She shrugged and let a silence lapse. Then she let go of his arm, severing the last bit of physical contact between them. "Let's go."

He guided her to the sled, where he sat between her and the girl. She was a wisp of a thing, barely older than Isandor. It looked like she had travelled with him for quite some distance, with the amount of furs covering her and her wind-chapped, rough cheeks.

Tandor never said a word to the cloaked driver, but the man flicked the reins and the bear loped into action. Once they were out on the street, the going was slow. Groups of drunken youths came out of side streets, laughing and pushing each other, and generally not looking out for other people, let alone sleds.

"Busy," Tandor said into the uneasy silence. He kept his gloved hands ostensibly on his lap, as if uncomfortable with showing either her or his young lover affection.

Loriane turned her head away, seeing shops and groups of revellers pass through a blur of tears.

She thought he travelled to collect knowledge and to conduct his Chevakian stepfather's merchanting business. She thought he *belonged* to her; she thought that was why he visited the Outer City. She thought . . .

What did it matter?

The sled stopped in front of her limpet. Loriane stepped from the sled fighting her pricking eyes. She opened the door and stumbled into the short hallway. The air was cold and still in the space between the outer layer of ice blocks and the inner wall of the limpet structure. She had tossed a few bricks in the stove this morning, but they had burnt out a long time ago. Not even Isandor waited for her these days, not since he had moved to the eyrie in the City of Glass.

Loriane charged into the central room, not waiting to see if Tandor and his mistress followed. She opened the door in the side of the huge stove and flung in a few fire bricks—rubbishy ones. No point wasting her good bricks on someone who cheated on her. With a wick of fire, she then went around the circular room and lit the lanterns. Greasy curls of blubber oil rose past the sleeping shelves towards the ceiling. She indicated what had been Isandor's shelf, above her head.

"The bed up there will be yours, once I've—"

She turned. Tandor and the girl had come in after her. In the flapping light of the oil lamps, she saw how pale and tired the girl looked, and how young she was. And how incredibly pregnant.

Loriane froze, looking from Tandor to the girl.

Impossible. If Tandor had the necessary equipment, all her ten children would have been his. Or had he perhaps found a way. . . ? But then, why this girl? She'd been available for him all these years.

The girl gave her a desperate look. "Mistress Loriane, can I please, please use your outroom?"

Loriane played with the notion to refuse, but tucked it away just as quickly. She was a midwife first, always. "Sure, it's at the back over there."

The girl stumbled past the stove to the door Loriane had indicated, clutching her belly, leaving Tandor and Loriane facing each other in an uneasy silence. The fire bricks sputtered and hissed in the stove.

"Don't tell me that you took her all the way from Bordertown in that condition," Loriane said.

"She's in danger."

"From dropping the child on your lap, yes. What do you know about delivering a child, Tandor?"

His face hardened. Right, one didn't go there with him. "Must've been some pretty big danger for you to do something as stupid as that." She flung a pan onto the cookplate and reopened the door on the stove.

"Loriane—"

She grabbed the poker from its spot against the chimney and stabbed the dying coals under the bricks more vigorously than necessary. A volley of sparks flew into the chimney.

"—I will explain. There's a real danger to her—"

"No, just leave it. When you talk like this, everything that's real to you isn't to me." She hated how her voice sounded unsteady. Tandor was the only bit of colour in her dull life. She waited for his visits. She dreamed of travelling with him. *Why, Tandor, why?*

A small noise indicated that the girl had finished her business in the outroom, and remained standing by the door. Loriane couldn't help feeling sorry for her. Had she asked to carry his child, did he pay her, or—she cast Tandor a glance—had he played some sort of trick on her? How had he done it?

Loriane, jealousy is an ugly emotion.

"Come on, shut the door, come here and sit down. Let me have a look at you."

The girl sat down on Loriane's old couch and folded her hands in her lap. No, wait, one of her sleeves hung empty; she had only one hand. The other ended in a stump just above the wrist. Oh. That explained a lot. Tandor had said something about other Imperfects during his last visit. It was so long ago, she struggled to remember what it was.

Loriane kneeled on the carpet and pushed her hands under the girl's dress. The skin on her belly tensed into a hard ball. The girl took in a sharp breath.

"Does that hurt?"

"A bit."

Loriane prodded the skin, feeling bumps of the child's elbows and feet. "How long do you have to go?"

The girl shrugged.

"Do you know when you slept with a man?" She tried to see how Tandor responded to this question, but he had gone to the other side of the stove and studied the contents of her pantry, where she couldn't see his face.

"Many times," the girl whispered. "My father didn't like it, so we climbed into the hay loft. My father was furious when my belly started growing." Her face crumpled. "I wasn't the only one either, just the first one. Tandor says the Knights took the others to the City of Glass. Do you know where they are?"

Others? A chill went over Loriane's back.

Just what had Tandor been doing?

"The Knights discovered the sanctuary I set up for Imperfect children in Bordertown," Tandor said, still speaking at the wall.

Loriane could tell from the tenseness in his posture that this was important to him. So he had found himself a bunch of teenage lovers and was breeding an army of Imperfects?

He continued, "That's why I took her with me. The Knights didn't take her because of her condition, but they will be back."

"So you brought her to the one place in the land that's crawling with Knights. Some days you make so much sense to me, Tandor."

She pulled down the girl's dress, a coarsely knitted thing which barely fit over her stomach. Tears trickled down the girl's freckled cheeks.

Loriane hated herself for being so jealous, for admitting how much she had longed for him to come back. It had all been a waste of time.

She rose. "Come." And charged across the room.

When he was a small boy, Isandor, with his peg leg, had fallen down the ladder to his sleeping shelf a few times, so her brother had built him proper stairs. The girl followed Loriane up these steps to where Isandor's bed stood, untouched and musty. It was dark up here, and the air thick with rancid smoke from the lanterns. The light that reached from downstairs was feeble and orange.

"Take off your clothes and get in the bed."

Loriane snipped another lantern into life as the girl obeyed. First she took off her cloak, her jacket and her dress. In the pale light, she looked like a misshapen troll. Too skinny.

The girl hesitated. "Bottoms, too?"

She wore a coarsely woven pair of shorts, tied with a ribbon under her belly. Her bellybutton stood out like a weak spot on a waterskin.

"I'll give you some clean bottoms."

Myra undid the ribbon and let the garment fall to the floor, not looking at Loriane. She wore a piece of cloth between her legs, covered with blood-streaked slime.

By the skylights. "How long have you been bleeding?"

"Started yesterday." Her voice trembled. "I didn't know what else to do. I couldn't tell Tandor. . . . Does it mean . . . the child is harmed?"

Loriane picked up the cloth. The discharge was slimy, and brownish. "You've been having pains?"

She shook her head. "Is that bad?" New tears threatened in her eyes.

"I don't think so. It's just your body getting ready for the birth. It means that you will be having a child very, very soon."

"It hurts a lot, doesn't it?" Her voice was barely more than a whisper.

"If you panic and fight it. You should let the pains come over you and it will hurt a lot less." *But as skinny as you are, it will be a very hard job.*

The girl nodded but her face was pale. Oh, she was so young, and obviously no one had taught her anything about becoming or being a mother.

Shivering, Myra slipped between the covers of Isandor's bed.

Loriane draped the blankets and Isandor's bearskin spreads over her. Poor girl.

"I'll be back to bring you some soup. Eat it all. You will soon need your strength."

The girl nodded, but was already drifting off to sleep. Loriane guessed soup—and sleep for herself—would have to wait.

Before going downstairs, she pulled the string to open an air vent at the limpet's very top. For Myra's health, air laced with smoke and smells would never do. Too many people died from stale air inside their limpets.

Tandor paced around the stove.

The orange light made his golden tattoos glitter. His hair was smooth and glossy, tied back in a loose ponytail from his face, which was bronzed by the Chevakian sun. He was so handsome, so mysterious, it made her heart ache.

Tandor looked up where she had stopped on the stairs, white-knuckled hands gripping the railing. His face held a look of concern, a look that said she shouldn't be doing this in her state. As if she didn't know. Loriane raised her chin, daring him to say it, but he didn't.

"I'm angry with you," she said instead, still shivering. "You let that poor girl suffer. She's scared and in pain. She needs a mother to show her what to do and I have no time—"

"No, Loriane. I'm angry with *you*."

"Angry with me?" she whispered. "*You* are angry with *me*?"

"About Isandor. I saw him this afternoon. He's wearing a *Knight's* uniform. What's this, Loriane? How could you allow that?"

"Allow it?" She gave a hollow laugh while trying to keep her voice down so Myra wouldn't overhear. "You try and raise an adolescent boy alone and tell me how you can or cannot *allow* him to do anything. It was either the butcher's or the Eagle Knights. It was his idea to sign up. I'm happy for him. The uniform looks *good* on him."

Next thing she knew, Tandor had crossed the room and was looming over her. His mouth trembled.

"Looks good on him? By the skylights, *looks good on him?* Have you forgotten?" Spit flew into her face. "Have you forgotten who made me what I am, who killed my family and made me an outcast in my own country? Have you forgotten who is killing all the people of my clan?" He stopped to take a panting breath.

"No, I have not forgotten, but that's your life, not his."

"It's his life as much as it's mine. I saved him. I asked you to keep him safe, and where is he? With the *Knighthood* by the skylights. He's Imperfect, and the Knights will kill him. I don't understand why they haven't done so already."

"Times have changed, Tandor."

"They haven't. What do you know about it? How could you let him join?"

"Well, I never received instructions that he couldn't. And I couldn't have stopped him if I wanted anyway. He's a pretty wilful young man." *And much stronger than me, besides.* Frankly, Isandor was starting to scare her, with the wild look in his eyes. Those times, she wondered who his parents were, and wondered why Tandor had brought him, red and screaming, to her door with the end of the umbilical cord still attached.

"Just leave it, Tandor. It's his life. What is it to you anyway? I've looked after the boy and you've never shown any interest in him. And now you have your little family . . ."

Tandor's mouth fell open. Then he threw his head back and laughed, not a pleasant laugh. Loriane motioned for him to be quiet, gesturing upstairs to the sleeping shelf.

He snorted. "So that is what you think? You think the damage the Knights did to me can be restored like that? Yes, Loriane, this is about family, but much wider than your narrow understanding of it."

"I don't care about my *narrow* understanding of family! You intrude into my life, impose yourself on me, let me think you feel something for me, and then you think you can get away with this and I won't mind?" She turned away before she burst into tears and left the living room for the outroom, slamming the door behind her.

She stood there, panting in the dark. *Forget about him, forget him.*

She lit the wick and let its end sink into the oil reservoir of the light that hung next to the door. It was cold here in the washroom, and her breath steamed in the air. Tears were streaming down her face. She had been such a fool.

"Loriane."

She gasped. "Will you stop sneaking up on me like that? In my own outroom?"

"You're not using it." He glanced pointedly at the seat with the hole against the outer wall of the limpet's double layer. Natural sculptures of glistening icicles dripped down the inner cladding.

"I have used it." Loriane raised her chin and stalked past him back into the warmth of the central room.

Tandor spoke in a low voice. "Is that really what you think? That I have hidden all these young girls for my own fun and they're carrying my children?"

Loriane looked away. The accusation sounded silly when he spoke it aloud. She knew what the Knights had done to him, and if he'd been able to restore himself with icefire, he *would* have done so.

Tandor pulled out a stool from under the bench and sat down.

For a while no one said anything. The yelling and laughing of partygoers drifted in from outside.

Then Tandor said, "The father of Myra's child is a young man called Beido. He's fifteen, like her, and one of my oldest charges. When the Knights came to Bordertown, he was taken with the others to the palace dungeons. Myra is very upset about it."

Loriane saw nothing except the flapping light.

Oh, she had been such a fool. Such an incredible stupid, jealous fool. She turned away from him, straining to hold back tears. They came anyway.

His arms closed around her.

"Sorry, Tandor, I'm so sorry. I'm just a big emotional fool."

She leaned against his chest, listening to the heavenly sound of his heart beating. He stroked her hair. Everything was all right now. Things would be as they were before.

"Loriane, did you think I had abandoned you?"

"I shouldn't have, but I did. You were away so long."

"I know, but I'm here now. I'm not leaving you anymore."

She turned and faced him, meeting his royal blue eyes.

"I love you," she said.

"I know."

His lips tasted salty with her tears.

CHAPTER 8

AT THIS TIME of year, the land of the south knew no night. Day bled into dusk and slightly deeper dusk and then, slowly, the sun peeped above the horizon again.

Sick of watching Loriane sleep, Tandor had gone outside at the first hint of sunlight.

The drunken festival crowds had gone home, surrendering the streets to the humdrum of business: melteries replenishing their stocks of ice and distillates, cooks from the Outer City's eating houses haggling over the last vats of saltmeat, because certainly it would be the worst of shame to ask one's customers to eat only tubers and beans, with the only sniff of meat from the lard used to cook the pancakes.

No. Must not think of food. His stomach had felt queasy for two days in a row.

He yearned for freshly baked bread, and fruity muffins. *Chevakian* things. The food of his youth. He had become soft, corrupted.

In the chaos of the markets, no one paid attention to a noble roaming the stalls. Tandor pretended interest in the wares offered for sale, but he listened for anything that might be of use. From merchants, he learned there were no games today that Knights were likely to enter, which explained why the eagle pens remained empty.

Yet he had to find a way to talk to Isandor, because without Isandor, he would need one extra Imperfect for his plan to get into the palace. There was no way he could get his hands on the *other* girl.

He lingered at a stall where two men were discussing the swimming races to be held today while warming their hands in front of a grill sizzling with battered pieces of saltmeat. One man said that girls would win because they suffered less in the freezing water, to which the other man argued—

"Excuse me, do either of you know what's on tomorrow?" Tandor asked.

Both men turned to him, eyebrows raised.

"You're not from here?"

Tandor cringed. His accent always gave him away. *I'm a blasted Chevakian.* "I've been away."

"Good time to return," one man said.

"Tomorrow's going to be a big day," the other man added. "There's the long distance race for the Apprentice Knights, and the choosing of the Queen's Champion."

So— Isandor was likely to be back here tomorrow. He must find some way to talk to the boy and offer him something he could not refuse. But he had to be careful. He was not as young and strong as he used to be. As soon as he asked Ruko to help, Isandor would be suspicious. He was a trained Knight, and knew how to defend himself. On top of that, Isandor would be able to see Ruko very well and, with his interest in old books, Isandor might even know what Ruko was. Few books said good things about servitors, and fewer still fully understood the concept. He would have to change that, once he had his victory.

Meanwhile, securing Isandor's cooperation was going to be hard enough. Damn Loriane for allowing the boy to join the Knights. No, Tandor hadn't forbidden it, because the thought that Isandor would want to join the Knights had never even entered his mind. Why would a Thilleian do such a thing? Did he have so little regard for his heritage?

By the skylights, all his children were in prison, weakened, like Myra, or corrupted, like Isandor, and even Ruko.

What a mess.

Tandor arrived at the second-hand bric-a-brac stall that was run by a man who was an ordained member of the Brotherhood of the Light.

Last time he visited the stall, probably a few years ago, the man had sold him some interesting material from the old royal family, which had probably come out of the palace. He still remembered showing his mother the purchases. She had gone all misty-eyed over a small bronze statue and said, "I can still see it standing in his study." That statue now stood on her desk in Tiverius.

"Can I help the dear sir?" a man asked.

Tandor started and looked up into the bearded face. The stall owner had gone grey in those years, but this was indeed the Brother.

"I bought something interesting from you a while ago," Tandor said. "A bronze statue that belonged to the royal family."

The man obviously hadn't recognised him before, but he so did now. His lips formed the letter *O*, but his eyes showed an emotion not quite so indifferent. Surprise? Fear? It was hard to tell.

"Do you have anything new for me to look at?" Tandor kept his voice low.

"No, no. I don't have anything like that. It's illegal. The Knights took all I had. I should have handed it in before—"

"What sort of things?"

"All sorts. The usual knick-knackery, plates, cups, some napkins with the royal crest. All gone."

"Books?" Those were the most precious. Those books should *not* fall into the hands of Pirosians.

"Yes, there were books, but they're all gone."

"You have nothing left?"

"Nothing, nothing, nothing. It's a disgrace. I'm an honest business-man. What harm can a few cups and some forks do anyway? I mean— without the old royal family's stuff, what would we have to sell? Nothing good's been made since the Knights came to power. Nothing that people want to buy."

"Shhh." Tandor waved his hand. "I agree with you, but saying it aloud is dangerous."

"Not here at the markets it isn't. In most of the Outer City, it isn't. Many people are fed up. We're no longer happy to live in poverty while the Knights and nobles get everything. We'll no longer have any children taken away from their mothers' arms."

Tandor was surprised by the anger in the man's voice. He didn't know the resistance against the Knights had grown so much and was delighted with this turn of events. Maybe he didn't need to go as far as snatching Isandor away from the Eagle Knights' eyrie. There might be other Imperfects in hiding.

He clasped his live hand in his claw behind his back, feigning a relaxed pose.

"So," he said and licked his lips. "If I were to tell you that *someone* who's sympathetic to your cause might be looking for a person with a certain . . . imperfection, is there a chance I'd find such a person in the Outer City?"

A shrewd expression crossed the merchant's face. "There might be."

"Could you tell me?"

The merchant glanced aside. "The Knights have been rather keen to investigate us. I was searched recently, and things were taken. We fear . . . a raid, maybe. We might be . . . interested if someone were to offer this person shelter . . . if there is a certain . . . remuneration."

"An Imperfect?"

Another glance aside. "There's a boy. He's eleven years old. I've been expecting the Knights to get word of him soon. Rumour goes that you saved . . . others."

"This boy of yours, he's in the Outer City?"

"Yes."

"In your compound?"

The merchant gave a single nod.

Tandor considered his next response. At eleven, the boy was too young to be of much use, but it might be all he could get. He attempted some provisional calculations, but he couldn't concentrate under the merchant's hawkish gaze.

By the skylights, it had been so long since he had found an Imperfect, and if one sprang up just when he needed one so desperately, it could be a trap.

Tandor let the silence linger for a little longer before he put his hand in his pocket and drew out a golden eagle, which he deposited carelessly on the table amongst the second-hand jumble of cookware. Then he picked it back up. The merchant watched every move. Oh, he was keen to have the money all right.

"I'd be willing to pay, but I'm not sure if this boy is worth my money."

The man gave an indignant sniff. "I have not deceived you before, have I?"

"No, you haven't, but there is a first for everything." He grabbed some strands of icefire, which came so readily, and found and held the man's gaze until the merchant looked away.

"Don't stare at me like that. It gives me a headache. If you're going to stare me into revealing lies, you can stare all you want, because I don't have no lies. I won't lie about the money either. I'm broke."

Yes, Tandor was sure of it now: the man had felt icefire and had Thilleian blood. He took the coin out of his pocket again and put it on the market stall. "Tell me who this boy is and where to find him."

"You must promise you'll do him no harm."

Where did these people get the idea that he was out to kill everyone? "Would I harm one of my own kind?"

"Then come to the compound. But be careful, Brother, I can sense the Light in you. The Knights will sense it, too."

"Don't worry about me."

"May the Light guide you."

Tandor found it hard not to walk too fast from the markets, since it would only draw attention, but there was energy in his step that he hadn't possessed before. He pushed his way through the crowd that was waiting outside the door of the meltery. The shouting and bawdy music was audible even around the corner where Tandor stopped.

A cloaked and hooded figure came to his side, oozing out of the shadows between the limpets. Tandor tugged off his glove and parted the sides of his cloak. His hand of flesh and bone met Ruko's hand, blue and ice-cold.

Ruko, go and find me that boy.

There was no reaction, but he knew Ruko had understood. Moreover, Ruko was glad to have something to do. Without meeting Tandor's eyes, he pulled his hood further over his face and strode down the street.

Total obedience, that was how a servitor worked. It seemed Ruko's errant behaviour had been brought under control for now.

CHAPTER 9

JEVAITHI PICKED at her dinner, shoving bits of meat around the plate with a golden fork. They were perfectly cooked to her personal taste, but today even these morsels tasted bland. A feeling of pressure, an underlying thrum, coursed through her, a singing excitement that she didn't understand. She couldn't say when it had started, only that she had first noticed it yesterday. When she flexed the fingers of her left hand, sparks leapt off them all too easily. Those sparks her mother said no one must ever see.

Eyes unfocused, she stared out the window, where the glare of the light on the horizon silhouetted the buildings of the city. Directly before her, but lower down, was the Eagle Knight's eyrie. If she squinted, she thought she could see the great birds moving within. In past years, there had been days she had watched the Knights fly out and wished she could be one of them, but these days the sight of them just filled her with bitterness because she knew she never would.

She pushed her plate away.

"Not hungry, Your Highness?"

She glanced up at the dry sound of the male voice. Supreme Rider Cornatan stood a few paces from her, in the middle of her tower room. He was grey haired, stiff and reedy, and his short-haired Knight's cloak was held together with golden clasps in a never-ending display of status. Why did *he* always have to be here? Chaperoning her, watching over her as if she were his possession.

He was the *regent*, not her father.

"I have enough of children's meat." She put her fork down with a clunk to illustrate her point, then counted the heartbeats before he would say something about her childishness.

One . . . two . . . three . . . four—

"You are still a child, as I am sure I do not need to remind you."

Five. That was a poor score. He must be distracted. He deserved to work a bit harder for his presence here.

"It's almost my birthday."

"That's true, but until that day, you are a child and you will not eat any organ meat. We must consider your health. You know that, Your Highness, and you need not bring it up. Your birthday will come soon enough."

A chill crept over her back at his sideways glance and the change in tone of his voice: from harsh to something she couldn't fathom. One thing she knew: after her birthday, nothing would be the same.

For one thing, she didn't think Rider Cornatan was going to give up his power as regent so easily, the power he'd held since she was ten and her mother died. Rider Cornatan devoured power and twisted it. He sat at the table of the Knights' Council, his chair before the empty throne, and rebuked anyone who challenged him. He thought he ruled the world. Jevaithi wasn't even allowed to attend the meetings. Too young, he said.

Just look at the smug expression on his face. He thought she was dumb; he never made a secret of that. He thought she would let him continue as before.

"Rider Cornatan, I would like to discuss my attendance at the Newlight celebrations."

"Your attendance at the— No, Your Highness. I don't think it's appropriate for a girl of your age." Through clenched jaws. Good.

Now she put on her most innocent voice. "It is not appropriate that I want to show myself to the good people of the city who celebrate in my name?"

"Your Highness, there are far too many inappropriate things going on at the Newlight celebrations."

"All I ask is to take part in the traditions of my own people."

"Traditions?" His Adam's apple bobbed in his throat.

Jevaithi straightened her back; he knew perfectly well what she meant.

She was no longer a girl; she was a virgin, blooded three moons ago. He knew that. He had stood, straight-faced, as she came out of the bath chamber screaming, with blood on her hands. He had stood by the door as his own elderly mother explained to her what it was all about.

"You weren't seriously thinking . . ." His voice was indignant. "Your Highness . . . the men in the Outer City . . ."

"The men of the city who are celebrating are deemed unsuitable to take my blessed innocence as they do with every other newly blooded girl at the festival?"

"If you want to put it that way . . . Your Highness." His cheeks had gone red. "But I'd rather that you didn't—"

"Then, Supreme Rider Cornatan, tell me what the Knights have in mind for me, because surely the matter of my fertility—or not—must have come before the regent, and it is a matter that must be attended to as soon as possible. There must be an heir to the throne."

He nodded. "Yes, there must be." Dry-voiced and stiff-faced.

"If a young Learner Knight or an Apprentice isn't suitable for me, not even if he comes from the best family, then tell me, do I get a choice in this matter? Maybe we should discuss it?"

"Maybe." He sounded like he wanted anything but.

"Or maybe I should take it to the Knights' Council."

A shudder went over him. Oh, this was delicious. They *had* discussed it, she was sure. She was also sure that none of the Eagle Knights wanted to repeat the mess that surrounded her mother's succession. A virgin until twenty-nine, the Eagle Knights had squabbled over who from their midst would have the right to father her children, until they found that an unknown stranger had already done the job. But by that time Maraithe had been visibly pregnant, and in the face of the cheering citizens, all the Knights could do was smile with their teeth clenched.

"I don't think the Knight's Council should bother itself with such things," he said.

He turned to her, his expression now softer. "But maybe we could organise an excursion for you to the festival."

Oh glory, he was giving in already. The threat of the Knight's Council must give him panic attacks. She must remember that.

"However, I insist that you would need to be suitably attired."

"Is anything wrong with the way I look?" She held up her arms, letting air breeze through her dress.

"No, not at all. It's just that your dress . . ."

"Is a little revealing?"

He said nothing.

"Then I will order proper garments." She hated these flimsy garments the courtiers made her wear anyway. Layers of gauze so thin the wind breezed through them even when she walked around the room. They were designed to keep her indoors.

"You could do that." Rider Cornatan stopped pacing and stared out the window, hands clasped behind his back. A couple of gulls sat on the outside windowsill.

"I want a dress such as the maidens of the city wear. One that's warm enough for outside. I want to go into a real meltery and meet real men."

He stiffened. "Out of the question."

"Why? I will speak the words you tell me to speak. I will dance only with men you have chosen. Hire the meltery if you wish. Tell the owner to put guards at his door and let in only Knights. They don't have too much trouble drooling over my puppies when I'm merely walking past."

"Your Highness, where did you learn to speak so? If you were my daughter—"

"Which I am not. I am your Queen, and this is how my men speak about me. I listen to their voices, Rider Cornatan."

He let another silence lapse. She knew he would offer a compromise of some sort. A trip in the royal sled—she didn't care as long as she could leave this room. She didn't really fancy getting a close-up view of Knights drooling over her anyway. The junior Knights maybe, but the Senior Knights scared her.

"We could organise for you to witness a race and a walk over the festival grounds. Every year one of the Apprentice Knights is chosen to be the Queen's Champion. You could choose the winner yourself."

Yes, she could, but it was just another boring official function, not something she wanted to do. "Could I see the Legless Lions?"

His lips twitched into a smile. Was he glad she no longer mentioned men?

Hoping for a kiss and awkward fumbling in the dark with a young man of her age was futile anyway. The man who took her would be older, experienced, and in her bed for only one reason: to get his blood on the throne. She was probably facing that very man right now.

She had known it all her life.

There is no point fighting, Jevaithi, her mother used to say. The Knights do as the Knights want to do. She could still see her mother over there in the bed, pale and sickly. Devoid of the will to live.

"We can certainly arrange for you to see the Legless Lions, and the bears. Perhaps you would like to see the ritual killing?"

She shuddered at the thought of guts and blood on some beefy butcher's hands, but nodded. The longer she was out there, the more time she had to do *real* things and pretend she was a real girl. And real girls wouldn't mind seeing an animal killed. For them, it meant work and food. "Yes, I would like that."

Rider Cornatan bowed. "I will organise that for tomorrow, with your permission."

"You have my permission."

He bowed again and left.

Drained and still hungry, Jevaithi sank down on the bed. Her plate remained on the table, the sauce congealed into a jelly-like blob. A servant scurried to take it.

"You haven't eaten, Your Highness."

"No. Next time, I want you to bring me real food."

The man's eyes widened. "But Rider Cornatan says—"

"Never mind what he says. Bring me adult food. If he tries to mistreat you, come to me."

The man nodded and retreated.

She gazed out the window, where the people of the city moved about like little black specks.

She would try to charge into a meltery once she was out there. When they were surrounded by the people, Rider Cornatan wouldn't dare to lay a hand on her. The people loved *her,* not him.

Mother, maybe you gave up the fight, but I will be free.

CHAPTER 10

ISANDOR TOSSED a couple of coins onto the bar and wriggled sideways between sweating bodies to pick up the tray of drinks the barman had put there. A maid burst out the kitchen door, yelling at two younger girls who were collecting tottering piles of dirty glasses. In the din of the meltery room, Isandor couldn't hear what she said, but the gist of it was written on her face. Hurry up; work faster. The girls were rosy-cheeked, their hands red from alternately washing up in ice chips and tending the roaring fire, or stirring the giant vats of meltwater and mixing in spirits and berry distillate to make bloodwine.

Isandor lifted the tray with drinks carefully over the heads of a couple of fishermen and backed into marginally less-crowded territory. Here, patrons sat at tables, every chair occupied. Some talked, some were gambling, and here and there, a few couples were engaged in other activities. A layer of smoke hovered over the patrons. It wafted from the fire every time the door was opened, which happened a lot.

A heaving crowd on the dance floor made so much noise that it was hard to hear the musicians.

Carro and his cousin Daman sat alone at a table. Carro leaned his head in his hands and stared into the crowd, while Daman fiddled with the hem of his tunic.

"Hey, smile," Isandor said as he set the tray down. He regained his seat and distributed the drinks.

"That's easy for you to say," Carro muttered into his glass. His pale blue eyes had a haunted look to them.

Isandor laughed. "Yeah, we'll have this race in the bag, and then you'll just have the swimming and running races to win."

Carro clamped his large hands over his glass as if to retain the warmth of the wine. "The running and swimming are unfair competitions. I'm the only Knight Apprentice who can compete as Outer City citizen. It'd be embarrassing if I *didn't* win those races."

"Carro, have you noticed I'm from the Outer City, too, and I didn't even enter."

"It's different for you." He let the reference to Isandor's peg leg hang in the air. "Besides, the flying race tomorrow is important. Knights *live* for flying."

"And so we won our selection heat. Smile, Carro. We won. We're in the final."

"I almost fell off," Carro said. "Look, why don't you find another partner. You're so much better than me, you deserve someone who can actually control their bird."

"Carro, please . . ."

Why did he go into sulky moods like this? Isandor had thought it would get better when Carro was away from that horrible father of his, but if anything, being in the Knighthood had made it worse.

Carro shook his head and drank deeply from his bloodwine, staring ahead. Daman still fiddled with his tunic. His eyes were following one particular girl swept in the tide of dancers. Tall, with curved hips and tresses of honey-coloured hair, and completely out of his league.

"Hey, good evening boys!" A girl dropped into the empty chair. Her cheeks were red from dancing and bloodwine and her perfume mingled with a faint scent of sweat. Around her pale-skinned neck, she wore a simple strip of leather with on it, a gull's tail feather.

"Um, good evening, Korinne," Isandor said. "Still here? I thought you said your father wanted you home."

Stupid. That's sounds too hopeful. Bloodwine had addled his thoughts. He had to clamp his jaws to stop himself laughing, because laughing at the daughter of Rider Cornatan's closest advisor would never do.

"What's so funny?" she asked.

"Carro was just telling a joke," Isandor said.

"What?" Carro woke up from his moody thoughts.

Isandor gestured, *You deal with her*. All day, Carro had been staring at this girl like a hungry pup whenever she came near.

Carro began, "Oh yeah, I can tell you a good joke. Did you hear about the two Chevakians who went fishing . . ."

Isandor stifled a groan.

The girl continued to look at him, batting long eyelashes over her clear grey eyes. She fiddled with her feather. Yes, he knew she was available. He'd hardly had a chance to forget it.

"I guess you already heard the joke," Carro said, his voice flat.

"I just wanted to congratulate you on winning your race. It was amazing. I saw you come back so far ahead of everyone else. You flew really well." Then she glanced at Carro. "Both of you, of course."

Carro rose from his seat. He'd already finished half his glass and stood unsteady. "Can I invite you to dance, Korinne?"

"Knights can always ask me to dance." She giggled, and as Carro led her away, she gave Isandor an intense stare and added, "Whether I agree depends on who's asking." She winked.

By the skylights, that stupid girl just didn't give up. She had been following him around all night.

Isandor drank deeply from his cup, letting the bloodwine sting its way into his stomach.

"For someone who's had their first taste of booze only yesterday, you sure know how to put it away," Carro's cousin remarked.

Isandor had almost forgotten about him. "So," he said to Daman. "Do you know what happened when the two Chevakians went fishing?"

"I think we shouldn't joke about Chevakia. One day they'll invade us. You know, my father says . . ."

Isandor let his mind drift off. He didn't mind discussing politics, but not today and not with Carro's cousin.

Carro and Korinne came past on the dance floor. He was talking to her, his hand on her shoulder—too close to her neck—and his head bent towards her. He was too tall, and his steps too large. She held her body stiff, so she didn't touch him, and stared past him at Isandor.

Isandor averted his gaze. Between the dancers, his eyes met those of a much older man, a noble from the city proper, with golden swirls tattooed on his cheeks. He sat alone at a table. At more than twice the age of most patrons, he didn't belong here.

Isandor shivered. This was the man he'd seen after the race today, the man whose presence he'd *felt*.

"Heh, I think that one fancies you," Daman said, looking at Korinne whirling past.

"Does she really?"

"It's not fair," Daman went on, oblivious to Isandor's sarcasm. "The best girls are always taken by you Eagle Knights."

Isandor took another gulp from his drink, stifling the comment that Daman could have her if he wanted, and that if it was so unfair, maybe he should sign up for the Knighthood himself instead of whinging about it.

Before he could say anything stupid—and he was feeling rather drunk by now—Carro and Korinne came back to the table, both red-faced. Carro picked up his glass and took a large gulp from his drink.

"Oh, Isandor, you're not going to ask me?" Korinne said.

"Oh, come on, be a man to her," Daman said. "She's throwing herself at you."

Carro sank into his chair, his face hard, and didn't meet Isandor's eyes.

All right, so they had a disagreement. Let's see. It would have been about Carro treading on her toes or grabbing her too tightly? Next thing she would go back to her friends and gossip about it.

Oh, by the skylights. Isandor wanted to stay with his friend. No, he wanted to leave this stuffy place and walk with Carro back to the birds, or find some place quieter and away from pushy females, to have a drink and a good talk, but he couldn't refuse such a blatant offer by the daughter of Rider Cornatan's advisor. So he took the girl's hand and led her onto the dance floor, where it was so busy that bodies pressed into him from all sides. The musicians struck up a rowdy tune.

Soon, they were swept up in the tide of dancers, and Korinne attached herself to him, like a suffocating parasite. He had to concentrate hard to keep his gait even, to make sure that his empty boot didn't get stuck or pulled off his peg leg. The crowd heaved and surged. And he was attached to this girl, red-cheeked and bright-eyed with bloodwine, holding him more closely than necessary.

"You dance well," she said.

He just nodded. Never mind that he didn't think so, not when dancing had become a matter of life and death.

"I could dance with you all night," she said into the hollow under his chin. Her breasts pressed against his chest. When he looked down he could see into the deep crevasse between them.

Sweat rolled down his back. His hands felt like slippery fish. The scent of her perfume made it hard to breathe so he concentrated on his steps. One, two, three, four, one, two . . .

"It's so hot in here," she said.

This was the part where he should say *We can always go outside*. And then they'd go into the chill air, and he'd have to keep her warm with his kisses and no doubt she'd taken her ichina and was after a bit more than kisses, and that was all fine during Newlight, as long as the girl fell pregnant.

Part of him wanted to go, badly. No doubt she could feel that part in the space between his hips and hers. But he couldn't. It would mean taking his clothes off, and she would see his wooden leg. And although the Knights at the eyrie must have seen that he was Imperfect, no one seemed to have actually *noticed* it. He didn't understand why, and knew that someone would, one day. And while he was vulnerable, literally with his pants down, about to ride a girl, was not the time for that to happen. Especially when he was so drunk that he could barely see the opposite side of the room. He wasn't supposed to have lived. He knew no other Imperfects. According to the books, Imperfect babies were left to die on the ice floes, not to join the Knights, win races, or attempt to get any girls pregnant.

But it was so hot in here. He concentrated on his dancing. Korinne pouted. Isandor's heart was going like crazy. Would it hurt just to give her a kiss and see if he could do that? To see what it was like? But no, his body might betray him, like it did sometimes at night when he dreamed of the girl who came to the markets sometimes. She didn't know him, or how beautiful he thought she was. But for some reason in this dream she would come up to his sleeping shelf—he was always at home or some other place that was a weird combination of home and the eyrie, and he was always alone—and then she would take off her clothes, but as soon as she folded back the covers to get into his bed, he'd wake up and then he would be all wet. But he hadn't actually wet himself, since it didn't smell like piss, and it wasn't unpleasant at all, just embarrassing. Definitely too embarrassing to be thinking about now, since the thoughts only made his . . . problem worse. Korinne would be able to feel it now for sure.

Carro was sitting at the table with his cousin, who gabbled away, probably about some political thing, but Carro stared at Isandor with uncomfortable intensity, as if he knew what Isandor was thinking. His eyes said, *Get your hands off my girl.*

Sweat made Isandor's shirt stick to his back. Everyone was staring at him. He could see the question in their eyes. What was he waiting for?

Then, thankfully, the music ended. His face and ears glowing, he led Korinne back to the table, raising his eyebrows at Carro and hoping that Carro would get the hint and take her off somewhere to a dark warehouse. It might cheer him up. As for him, he felt like getting disgracefully drunk.

"Oh, do we stop dancing already?" Korinne said.

"I'm tired. I have to think of tomorrow's race and feed the birds. I think Carro would like one more dance with you."

A painful look passed over her face.

Carro was already getting up from the table, ready to take her hand, but she stepped back. "I promised my father I wouldn't stay out too long."

A feeble excuse. No girl promised their fathers anything during Newlight except that they'd do their very best to fall pregnant.

She extracted herself from Isandor's grip and ran out, her lips pressed together.

Isandor cringed. He hadn't meant to hurt her, and didn't know how he was meant to have rejected her without hurting her. What a mess.

"What, Carro? M . . . my sister laughed in your face, din' she?" The voice was haughty but the speech was slurred.

Oh no, Jono. He stood at the table, his usual smirk on sharp-nosed face. He had taken off his Knights' cloak, displaying the distinctive red tunic.

"Shut your stupid mouth." Carro took a step towards him.

"You in . . . ssssulted my sister," Jono said.

"She came here begging for a dance."

"Heh," Jono sneered. "Why sh . . . should my sss . . . sister ever want *you?*"

"Shut up!" Carro grabbed Jono by his shoulder.

A circle formed as other dancers stepped aside, faces keen and eyes wide.

"Oh, Carro, come, don't be silly," Isandor said in his friend's ear. "This isn't worth a fight."

Worst of all, the Tutor had warned that any Apprentices caught brawling would not be allowed to go out tomorrow.

Carro didn't move.

"Yeah, that'shhh right," Jono said, his arms over his chest. "Get y . . . your friend to sss . . . sort it out for you."

"Shut up!" Carro said again, this time louder.

"What? You're jjjjealous be . . . becaush your friend gets more girls than you?"

Carro lunged.

But he was drink-addled and Jono evaded him easily. Carro lost his balance and almost fell, but Jono grabbed him by his tunic. He drew Carro back to his feet. "So y . . . you want to fight? Let'sh fffight!"

"Carro, no," Isandor called.

"Don't, Jono!" Korinne said. "You'll be in so much trouble."

"Shut up, all of you!" Carro shouted.

He grabbed Jono's arms and tried to push him over. Jono stumbled backwards into the crowd, and fell. Carro was on top of him, and then Jono was on top of Carro, thumping his face.

Everyone was shouting and cheering.

Isandor grabbed the back of Jono's shirt, but he didn't have enough strength to lift Jono off. He was afraid his leg would slip away under him.

"Stop fighting, you two!" These stupid oafs would get them all into trouble. "Stop it, Carro, stop!" But they weren't listening, and any moment some older Knights would come and haul Carro off to the eyrie. He needed Carro in the race tomorrow. He—

Golden threads burst from his fingers. They crackled over Carro, as if he'd been caught in a living net of icefire. Carro and Jono froze.

And then the threads snapped into diamond-specks of light which scattered through the air and vanished.

Jono stumbled back as if stung.

Isandor's heart thudded in his chest so loudly that he thought the people around him must hear it. Had anyone seen that?

"That's right," Carro said while scrambling to his feet.

Isandor knew his friend couldn't see the golden glow, but Carro's eyes had gone hollow and distant again, as they did when he scared Isandor most.

Carro wiped blood from his brow. "I'm wasting my time here. I have better things to do than concern myself with the lot of you."

He pushed into the circle of onlookers and was gone in a few heartbeats.

"Carro!" Isandor shouted, but he had lost sight of his friend.

Isandor wrestled against the stream of revellers coming in through the meltery's doors. Young men pushed aside to let him through and young girls glanced at him with drunken longing. The bolder ones clapped him one the shoulder and told him good luck. He was *their* Isandor, from the Outer City, riding in the Champion Race tomorrow. Except he wouldn't be if Carro got into trouble.

Outside in the street, people lined up to get in. Some had their own drinks and were sharing flasks of wine around. An older Knight was kissing a girl in the light of a street lamp, his hands fumbling under her cloak.

Isandor stopped, both revolted and fascinated. Knights were supposed to hold up respectability. Much leering and inappropriate behaviour of course went on in the eyrie. Family visit passes being traded for the sake of going to the whorehouse. Money being used to bribe superiors to turn a blind eye. But it always went on *inside* the eyrie walls, never openly in the street.

Isandor stifled thoughts of Korinne's hips against his. He *could* have had her, snuck away somewhere in a warehouse. That was what *normal* boys did. *Normal* boys didn't run after their friends if they behaved like stupid oafs. *Normal* boys fought.

"Carro," he called into the emptiness of the street.

There was no reply.

He walked away from the meltery, breathing the cold fresh air. The streets became deserted. A single man leant against a wall, his eyes closed. Isandor stopped, intending to ask if he was all right and needed help, but realised that the man was so drunk that standing up was probably the most he could do. The front of his trousers was wet and had been frozen over. His mother would talk about something like that in gory detail for days. *You know frostbite leaves blisters on your* . . . He jammed his hands into the pockets of his cloak. Well, if this was Newlight, it wasn't much fun.

CHAPTER 11

ISANDOR WALKED ON in the grey-blue light of dusk. Above the roofs of houses, the skylights danced and shimmered in pretty displays of orange, pink and green. Far away, the sounds of partying continued, the crowd cheering the jugglers in the markets and the drummers at the festival grounds.

He had no idea where Carro had gone, but he didn't feel like going back into the meltery.

He might as well go back to the eyrie.

And then . . . golden strands snaked from the sky. Very briefly, they touched roofs and chimneys; they shimmered over the sloping sides of the limpets and crackled along the ground. A thread touched his hand and burst into a spray of diamonds. The display lasted a heartbeat before it winked out.

Icefire.

He stopped to look over his shoulder, his heart thudding. Icefire had never been this strong. Sometimes, when he stood looking over the city from the eyrie tower, the golden threads crackled over the city. They would bend to his hands, but they had never touched him, like they just had in the meltery. Icefire never ventured indoors.

"You felt that, didn't you, young Knight?" a soft male voice said in the darkness. The man had a lilting accent.

Isandor gasped. He'd thought he was alone. "Um—good evening."

The man was tall and lanky, with piercing eyes and a sharp face lined with age. There were golden curls tattooed on his prominent cheekbones. A city noble? With a foreign accent? Talking about icefire?

"Who are you?"

But he knew who this was: that man who had been staring at him in the meltery.

In answer, the man pushed back his sleeve and pulled off a leather glove. The white-skinned arm underneath shimmered and dissolved. The skylight gleamed on two golden rods extending from the man's elbow. At the end, they joined in a "wrist" of black stone, where he had a pair of crab-like pinchers.

Isandor stammered, "You are . . ." He reached for his wooden leg in an automatic gesture. In all his life, he had never come across another Imperfect person. When he had been little, his mother liked to remind him that children born Imperfect were left on the ice floes for the wild beasts to eat. Not even the riding eagles of the Knights would dine on such contaminated fare.

"My name is Tandor, and I'm a traveller. Come." He held out his good hand. A tiny crackle of icefire played along the skin.

"Why?" Isandor stepped back. Everything about this man radiated danger.

"We need to talk."

Need to? "I *need to* look after my eagle."

A flicker of distaste went over the man's face.

"You felt the icefire," he said again. "When you reach for it, the light bends to your will." It was a statement, not a question. "Do you know what that means?"

Isandor kept his silence. During the time of the old king, there were people who could *use* icefire, and who had done so to bring terror to the people of the City of Glass, by enslaving them as servitors.

"You're Imperfect," the man continued. "You helped your friend win the fight. I saw the icefire."

"There was nothing I could do about it!"

"No, there wasn't. I agree."

"Then why are you bothering me?"

"Others might have seen the threads, too. Maybe one day others will see the illusion you weave about your leg. Or they will notice how every person in the Knighthood you meet looks anywhere except at your leg. Or maybe—"

"Stop it! Who are you? What are you trying to do, destroy me?"

"To the contrary. I'm trying to help you."

"Some help."

"If you are aware that icefire weaves an illusion around your leg, you can make sure it never falters. That way, no one will ever notice." Then he added with a sarcastic tone, "Not even if you take off your trousers."

"Just go away, will you?"

"You don't want to learn how to hide your imperfections?"

Isandor wanted to shout that he had no interest, but that wasn't true. Being found out was his greatest worry. The Knights had never said anything about it, and every day, he feared that the subject would come up. "You can't hide it. You can make it look like there is a complete arm or leg, but they'll find out as soon as they touch it."

"Not if you learn how to control it."

"Control it? Isn't that the same as using it? Turning people into ghosts? Isn't that why, after the king was killed, all his people were sentenced to death?"

Tandor shook his head, an expression of pity on his face. "I see you're upset and confused. We should sit down somewhere and talk."

Every fibre of Isandor's being protested. This man was danger.

"Come," Tandor said again. "I'm buying. What I have to say is important. It will change your life."

His eyes met Isandor's in the light of a street lamp.

Isandor followed the stranger through the twisted streets of a quiet part of the Outer City. It looked like most people had gone to bed already or were hiding from the crowds inside the warmth of their limpets.

In an alley, away from the main streets, was an eating house, recognisable only by a small sign on the door of a limpet larger and with less steep sides than the surrounding ones. Tandor went in first.

Inside the circular room, most tables surrounding the stove were occupied by a selection of the best middle class citizens from the Outer City, men and women in middle age, dressed well and wearing jewellery—a far cry from the rowdy melteries. The cook was stirring a large pot and a kitchen hand was kneading dough.

Tandor went to one of the few empty tables. Isandor sat opposite him. Already, the warmth made him drowsy. It was even hotter than in the meltery. Couldn't they open a vent?

A waiter came to them.

"Bring some soup and bread for two," Tandor said.

"I'm not hungry," Isandor said. The bloodwine sat heavy in his stomach.

"I am," Tandor said. "And you should be, too. Adolescent boys are always hungry."

Isandor shrugged. *Not when they're drunk.* But he wasn't sure if he was still drunk.

The waiter left and they sat amongst the quiet murmur of the customers. Snatches of conversation drifted past, mostly about the Newlight festival and its various circus shows. Firelight gleamed in Tandor's tattoos. From this angle, he looked older than he had appeared at first. Isandor guessed him to be about fifty. His hair was glossy and black, his eyes . . . he couldn't look away from them.

They had that elusive hue citizens of the City of Glass called royal blue. He knew only one person with eyes like that; he looked at him from the mirror above the sink in the dormitory bathroom every morning.

"Are you my father?"

Tandor lunged across the table. The pincher-claw grabbed the collar of Isandor's shirt so tight that he could barely breathe. Isandor uttered a strangled, "Hey!"

Up close, the gold tattoos on Tandor's face looked frightening. Come to think of it, why did he have that sign of nobility? Certainly, nobles wouldn't pay for Imperfect children?

Tandor let a tense silence lapse, in which all Isandor heard was the roaring of blood in his ears. Diners on surrounding tables had stopped talking and stared at him.

"Let me go if you don't want the people to notice us," he whispered in a croaky voice.

Tandor blew out a breath. He relaxed and let go of Isandor's collar, his gaze still boring into Isandor's.

Isandor inhaled; the smoke-tinged air stroked his lungs. What, *just what*, was he getting himself involved in?

"All right, since you don't know me, I will tell you, once, and once only. Moreover, you will never speak of this."

Isandor nodded, nervously, tucking his tunic back into his waistband, too conscious of the glances at him. He was still in his uniform, by the skylights, and he should do something. This man could not attack a Knight without repercussion.

Tandor leaned on his elbows on the table. "My mother had the courage of a bear pup. When I was born Imperfect, rather than give me up, she ran away to the northern lands where she had heard people do not mind Imperfects. In time, she found a family, and married a travelling merchant and lived in comfort. The merchant collected old books, and as a boy, I became interested in them. I read that Imperfects are special people who have the power to shape icefire, and that they need to be in the vicinity of the City of Glass to use it. So I wanted to use that ability, didn't I? I was young, I was curious and I didn't get along with my stepfather, so I came to the white lands of the south."

He gave a hollow laugh. "Sounds simple, huh? What did I know about the southern laws and the Eagle Knights? I was a boy, just like you are now. I came to the City of Glass at the height of the tension over the raids on Chevakian border regions. I was both of southern stock and living in Chevakia and a prime suspect for being a spy. I was captured by the Queen's guards. They saw I was Imperfect, and judged me to be a king's supporter and too old to be abandoned on the ice floes—I might find my way back and come to haunt them—so the Queen ordered that I be changed so I could never father an Imperfect child."

It took Isandor a heartbeat to figure what Tandor meant, but then he realised. *Ouch.* He winced. "I'm sorry."

"If you don't want to attract my wrath, don't be. But no, I cannot be your father."

Isandor repressed the urge to shove his hand down his pants to check on his private parts, which felt larger-than-life and throbbing.

"And . . . are you? A king's supporter? A Thillei?" He had heard of such things whispered in the melteries, of people who said that the king should return. It was said that the Brotherhood of the Light organised meetings for these people.

A serving girl turned up with a tray containing two bowls of soup and a basket of fresh bread. Isandor found that Tandor had been right: he was enormously hungry.

He attacked the bread, dunking pieces in the bowl. The bread came away dripping with fat, which ran down his fingers as he stuffed the pieces in his mouth. Taste exploded on his tongue. Just like his mother used to make it.

Tandor put his spoon down and broke a piece off his bread. "There is one thing you need to understand. The Thillei are a clan much bigger than only the royal family. You cannot become one. You are one at birth. And you, boy . . . enough Thillei blood runs through your veins to make your eyes turn blue. There are few of us left. You, me and a handful of others. If it wasn't for me, there would have been none."

Isandor had suspected this, but hearing it spoken out loud made his skin crawl. He ripped a piece off a roll and mopped his bowl with it, disguising unease. Then another thought came to him.

"Then . . . when I was born . . . you paid for my mother to look after me?"

"Yes."

"Why, if you're not my father?"

Tandor gave him an intense look. "Don't you want to know who your real mother is?"

"Why should I? She wanted to kill me."

"How can you be so sure of that? Couldn't it be that someone else wanted to kill you, and she had no power to protect you, and gave you to me to bring to safety?"

Isandor scratched his head. He was beginning to feel sleepy from the bloodwine, and Tandor's stories were so confusing. Why should he care? Children in the City of Glass never grew up with the women who had given birth to them. They were breeders, like his mother.

"What do you want from me?"

Tandor shook his head, his expression sad.

"It is not about what I want or what anyone else wants. This is much bigger than the wants of individual people. It is about making the City of Glass great again, and about stopping the slaughter of children."

He hesitated. "I know this may not sound important to you, but I see in you myself when I was your age. I didn't know what to do with my gift. I was scared. I have found out how to deal with icefire the hard way. There is no need for you to do the same."

"You want me to be a sorcerer's apprentice?"

Tandor breathed out heavily through his nose. "Sorcery? I wouldn't use that despicable word, but that's obviously what the Knights have told you to think. Tell me this, though: do you think there is a good reason you should be punished if you were discovered?"

"I . . . can use icefire. I'm Imperfect. There are laws that forbid—"

"Is there anything that punishment could stop you doing, if you wanted?"

Isandor shrugged. "It's not as if I could *help* being Imperfect."

"Exactly. You can't help being what you are, but they will punish you anyway. Is that the way you want to live? I want to see you out of this slum. I want to see you soaring in the sky. You, and all other Imperfects. We need to save them, and I'm going to need your help for that. As . . . Knight, you would be perfectly placed to do that. Give me the word and I will teach you about icefire."

And then Isandor saw what Tandor wanted: to single-handedly change the Knights' view on Imperfects, to become a spy, or an agent. Did Tandor really think he was as stupid as all that? He respected the Knights, most of them at least. They were harsh but fair. He was determined not to let his wooden leg be a problem. No one needed to know. But on the other hand . . . if they found out, he would have to leave the Knights.

Damn this man. He was caught now. He couldn't refuse Tandor's offer or tell the Knights about him, or Tandor would tell the Knights.

He licked his lips. "What would you want me to do?"

A smile ghosted over Tandor's face. "A few days ago, the Knights discovered my safe sanctuary where I had hidden the Imperfects I rescued, mostly from the ice floes as babies, though some were older. Children who are now young people your age. The Knights broke into the sanctuary, flushed out all the Imperfects and took them away. As far as I know, they were taken to the palace bunkers, and we need to free them, if they're still alive."

"And you want me to do that. By myself." Isandor chuckled. "Do you know how many Knights there are at the eyrie? Do you know how many guards there are on the entrance to the prisons, if that's where those children are? How do you think I could even get into the prisons? I'm only an Apprentice—"

"I could provide you with a good illusion that would make you look like someone who *could* get into the dungeons. All you have to do is maintain it. That should be easy after I've trained you."

"Deliberately *use* icefire? Under the Senior Knights' noses?" Isandor found it hard not to laugh. This was getting ever more ridiculous.

"Then what are you doing with your leg? What were you doing back there in the meltery?"

"That was—"

"Icefire, strong and clear. You used it to scare that bully."

"I didn't mean to—"

"No, I know. That is where the problem lies, I've been trying to make it clear to you. You've been doing it and you have no control over it. One day, you will be found out. Or someone will betray you, like that halfwit friend of yours."

"Carro? He would never betray me." But a twinge of discomfort tugged at him. Carro had said such strange things recently.

"In the end, it comes down to a simple thing: children are killed and harmed because they were born with strong Thillei blood. You have the chance to help me save some of them. Will you do it?"

"If I help you, I will be cast from the Knights."

"You don't belong there anyway."

"Who are you to say where I do and don't belong?"

"You don't get the opportunity I'm offering, don't you? If you help me, I will give you *real* power." That last bit was almost a whisper.

Real power, like the old king, who had murdered thousands of people.

That was enough. Isandor strained his muscles to get up. "I'm going. I'm sorry, but I can't do what you want." He tried to sound angry, but he thought he sounded scared more than anything. "I'm an Eagle Knight and I will abide by their laws. The Knights serve the Queen with honour. They wouldn't do anything without her approval."

"Stop your naive daydreaming. Do you know how much power one fifteen-year-old girl has over an age-old institute of men?"

Isandor shivered uncomfortably, remembering the thin figure of a young girl standing alone before a coffin. So lonely, so small. Jevaithi.

"Do you see that I'm right?" Tandor said.

"I don't see anything except that you're telling me stories so I will come with you. I don't know what you want, but I don't like it. Find someone else to bother."

Isandor rose from the table, catching glances of fellow patrons.

"Good night, Tandor."

He turned and walked back to the door. He expected a shout, but none came. He opened the door and let himself into the cold night.

When he looked over his shoulder, Tandor was still sitting at the table.

CHAPTER 12

THE FOOTSTEPS of his hard-heeled riding boots echoing against stone walls, Carro strode through the corridor. His cloak flapped behind him. His riding harness creaked. Polished, clean, his hair slicked and bound by a leather thong, he'd done his best to make himself presentable, as if any amount of cleaning could chase away the ominous feeling that had become infinitely more ominous since his return to the eyrie.

When the Tutor had said the *high command wants to see you*, Carro had expected to deal with the Senior Knight who dealt with Apprentices.

Instead, the Knight at the entrance to the command centre had informed him that he was to see Supreme Rider Cornatan himself. Carro hadn't dared to ask why.

His face tingled with cold from the flight back to the eyrie and the air in the corridor did nothing to dispel it. Here, in the lower levels of the eyrie, warmth was as sparse as furniture.

Eagle Knights lived hard, simple lives. There was some aspect in that he liked. He had never felt comfortable with his father's opulence or his sister's obsession with clothes and hair ribbons.

Obedience, Honour, Honesty, Humility and Silence. He mumbled the Knights' mantra silently, as if to remind himself of the meaning of those words.

He had violated several of them in fighting with Jono. The Knights lived for punishing each other. There was a certain humility, obedience and silence in being fucked in the arse, but honour and honesty?

It hurt, that was all he knew, on more levels than one.

Yet, if he ever wanted to be someone in the eyrie, he'd have to endure it. This was what older Knights did to younger ones. Fit in, shut up and don't show your weaker side.

He failed on all three accounts.

Carro stands in his father's room. His father has the account books open on his desk. Long lines of figures stretch across two pages.

"Do you think I've calculated this right, Carro?"

Carro hesitates.

"Well? You tell me. You are so learned." There is mockery in his father's voice.

"I'd need to figure out the numbers. I need time."

"You need time. Ha, that's right. You have so many books, and you still need time to work out a calculation."

He laughs. He doesn't need to say that he thinks the books are a waste of Carro's time. Carro has heard it all before.

The books tell him that in the days of the old king, people had machines that could work out sums, but telling his father that would make him sound cocky. Some things are not worth the punishment.

Carro stopped, counting the doors he had passed since coming down the stairs.

Two, three, four, five. That's what the guard said: the fifth door. This one had to be it. Just a solid door, no different from the previous one, or the next one.

He knocked and waited, glancing left and right into the featureless corridor.

Strange, he'd have expected guards. The Tutor responsible for

Apprentice Knights had guards outside his quarters. So why didn't the Supreme Rider have any?

Before Carro could knock, the door clicked and opened. A dark room yawned beyond, polished stone bathed in emerald light.

No one met him in the door opening, and no one spoke, so Carro stepped inside, his footsteps echoing in the emptiness.

A stone chair stood in the middle of the room like a throne on a dais of black marble several steps high and with corners that looked sharp enough to slice skin. There was no other furniture.

A voice said, "Sit down."

Except there was nowhere to sit. The room was square, and entirely made out of black marble of the kind found in the mountains. The walls, too, were smooth, reflecting the soft green light.

The voice said again, "Sit down."

On the throne.

It seemed obvious. It was some kind of interrogation chair. Maybe the chair would get hot, like the chairs he heard they had in Chevakia. That would be his punishment. Pain and suffering. Rider Cornatan wouldn't even have to set eyes on him.

The tutor stands at the window, reduced to a silhouette against the low sun. The man's shadow falls over Carro's workbook, obscuring the print. He squints against the page, trying to read.

"What does it say?" The tutor's voice is harsh.

"It's a history of Tiverius."

The tutor drags a chair near the fire so that it stands on the middle of the carpet like a throne.

"Sit here. Read it."

Carro sits and takes the book on his knees.

"Sit up straight." The cane descends on the desk with a thwack.

Carro stares at the long Chevakian words.

"If you make one mistake, I'll hit you. I'll tell your father."

Carro wants to shout that he hates his father. Why does he have to learn Chevakian? His father hates the Chevakians. No Chevakians ever come to the City of Glass.

They would die if they did. He wants to die.

Gingerly, Carro climbed the dais, and sat down in the regal chair. The cold stone bit through his trousers, but he sat up straight as if he were royalty.

Just like Jevaithi would.

A tiny noise made Carro straighten his back even more. He would not be seen slumping in the seat. His heart thudded against his ribs. Punishment would not be far off.

But nothing happened, and his back became stiff and his buttocks very cold. What sort of punishment was this? The sort of unfathomable thing his father did.

Carro stands in the dining room. The dining table is so high that he can barely see what's on top of it.

His mother sits in the seat closest to the fire, his sister next to her. Neither says anything, but his mother looks at the floor.

Carro's boots leak melting snow onto the carpet, growing brown puddles seeping into the precious wool.

The door clangs behind him. His mother flaps her hand, and all of a sudden, Carro is lifted off the ground by the maid.

He kicks and screams while she carries him across the hall. The maid opens the front door and dumps Carro on the ground. Shuts the door. The lock clicks.

Carro bangs his fists on the door, but no one comes. Shivering, he sits down on the mat. It is wet and soaks freezing water into his pants. He draws his knees up to his chest, and waits. He doesn't have his coat. The wind cuts through his thin shirt. It is snowing.

A rumbling of stone on stone made Carro start. He turned, but the back of the chair blocked his view. There were footsteps, long and slow, hard heels on stone. Carro straightened, staring ahead, his hands on the armrests. *Don't show your fear.* There was a swish of a cloak, the creaking of leather and jingling of metal rings. It was said that although Supreme Rider Cornatan was too old to ride eagles, he wore his riding harness every day.

"Boy," said a voice that chilled Carro with its reminiscence of his father. "I'm glad you could come."

"Yes, sir." How was that for a sarcastic answer? The Supreme Rider was *glad* to see him punished?

There was a soft laugh, not unfriendly. "You have quite a lot of courage, for an Apprentice."

"Sir?"

"Quite a few discipline issues, too, I hear."

"I am sorry. I was not in my right mind. I'd been drinking." He didn't like this brand of humility. Jono had needled him on purpose.

"I accept your apology."

There was strange tone in the voice that puzzled Carro. Amusement, affection almost. Since when did the Supreme Rider concern himself with individual Apprentices?

"But that is not why I want to talk to you."

The Supreme Rider came from around the back of the chair.

Carro met the sky-blue eyes and then dropped his gaze, the wrinkled but powerful face etched in his memory. He pushed himself up from the chair. How had he ever thought *he* was meant to be sitting here?

"I'm sorry, I—"

"Stay seated."

"I'm sorry I got in a fight. I'm sorry I hit Jono."

"Forget Jono."

"Sir?"

"If Jono works hard and holds up the Knights' ethic like his father, he might get somewhere. For now, he's insignificant. Did you really think that's why I wanted to talk to you?"

"But I did start a fight. I'm not always very nice."

Rider Cornatan chuckled. "None of us are. If we were nice all the time, we would never get anywhere." He stopped in front of the dais, meeting Carro's eyes with his light blue ones. "The old king, for example, was a dreadfully mean person, but he was so powerful that even his family didn't dare disobey him. At the very end, he locked himself in the palace and sent his son and his daughter-in-law away. He said it was for their safety, but it was to distract the guards, so they were killed while he himself stayed in the palace."

Carro remembered the story, but he had thought the king had sent his family away and stayed in the palace as ruse, so that they could flee safely and that the unborn heir to the throne would survive. But he didn't dare disagree with Rider Cornatan's version. In fact he hardly dared breathe. Why did the Supreme Rider mention this?

"You know the story?"

"I do."

"Because you read the books."

"Yes." Carro looked at his knees. He wasn't sure if it was a reprimand. No one read those books in the City of Glass.

There were steps on the floor, and a hand touched his arm, weathered and wrinkled.

"Don't be shy. I'm impressed with you."

"Sir?" This visit was starting to puzzle him more and more. No one had told Carro he was impressed. No one. Ever.

Rider Cornatan smiled, and he looked more like a favourite uncle than a feared leader.

"I've brought you here, because I need you for a special mission."

Special mission? "Sir?" Doubt hovered in his mind again. He was only an Apprentice. What did he know that would make him eligible for a special mission?

"You haven't noticed I've already sent you on some unusual tasks?"

"You mean—when you . . . I went with the Junior Knights to the markets?"

Had Rider Cornatan selected him for that task? Carro felt sick. By the skylights, what was this going to be about? Who was he going to betray now?

"That was just a small job, that you handled well, I heard."

"Wasn't that because I am from the Outer City? That's what I thought."

"It was, but it was also because you are a very special young man, although I don't think anyone has mentioned it to you yet."

"Special?"

Rider Cornatan nodded.

Special as in good-special or bad-special?

"Come, boy, I'll show you something."

Carro rose from the cold stone chair, his head still reeling. Something very odd was going on here. There had to be a catch somewhere, there had to be.

CHAPTER 13

RIDER CORNATAN led Carro through a corridor made of dark stone into another room, also illuminated with the same eerie green light. The polished black marble on the floor contained the shapes of leaves and many-legged creatures such as Carro had never seen. The room was bare except for a table in the middle.

On a table lay a variety of things Carro surmised must be weapons. Long sticks of metal glinted in the emerald light that radiated from the walls. On the end of one of the sticks was a glass bulb with many carved facets.

Carro wanted to ask about it, but Rider Cornatan strode past the table and pressed a panel on the opposite wall. At his touch, an entire section of stone slid aside to reveal a hidden room.

There were four men in the room, two of them grey-haired Senior Knights in uniform. They stood near a stone chair similar to the one in the room where Carro had waited. On this chair sat a third man, in black, his hands and feet tied down by leather straps threaded through rings on the armrests and base of the chair.

The second-hand merchant who sold the books.

His eyes widened when they met Carro's, betraying an expression of utter panic. He was sweating, his face pale. The man showed no signs of torture, but there was a strange apparatus on a table behind the chair.

The last man wore a green protective suit with a helmet. The dark visor showed only his eyes. He was laying out snaking leads and sharp metal implements on the table with a heavily gloved hand.

Carro's knees felt weak. Oh, by the skylights. Was this all his fault because he'd betrayed the merchant? His dagger burned against his thigh. He felt like grabbing it and cutting the merchant free.

Rider Cornatan was talking to the Senior Knights.

One of them said, "Is that the boy?"

Rider Cornatan nodded, and his expression turned hard, as if he defied anyone to comment.

"You see, boy, what we're trying to do here is something very new. You will witness our first true application of knowledge we've acquired over the last few years. The Thillei have been saying it for a long time—"

"The Thillei? But I thought there weren't any left—"

"No visibly recognisable ones, no, but there are those who still practice the Thillei ways, and we might as well call them by their name."

Carro whispered, "The Brotherhood." He didn't dare look at the merchant.

"Very good." Rider Cornatan smiled first at Carro, then at his Senior Knights, as if he had proven a point. "Whatever can be said about the ways of the old king, the truth is that he had a vision for this land. When the Knights took over, they, naturally, abandoned his plans, but it has not been to the benefit of our land. Our people are poor. We no longer trade with our neighbouring nations. Instead, they laugh at us, and have erected barriers at their borders. They wish to ignore us and cut us out as if we were a festering sore."

He turned back to Carro, more intent than before. "It is said that because our land is frozen, we have nothing to offer, but that is a lie. We have much, and it has been right under our noses all the time. The power we call icefire can be used to drive machines that do incredible things: dig the ore out of the ground and make it into useful things, heat the caverns under the city and grow exquisite crops, then build fast trains to take produce to the borders. We have everything we need: we have water and we have unlimited energy. Why should we deny it exists?"

"But . . . but . . . that was what the old king did, and he became so powerful that he no longer needed his people, and he started turning them into mindless machines, the servitors."

Rider Cornatan chuckled. "Yes, that is the version commonly told at dinner tables, and it is also the very thing that has been holding us back. It's the belief that everything the king did was bad, the belief that we couldn't possibly use icefire differently and better. The power of icefire is ours. We have been blessed with it, and we should use it if we want to get ahead."

Carro realised why the sudden emphasis on confiscating illegal material: the Knights didn't want to burn it; they wanted to use it. That brought a whole new perspective to his own situation. He'd read about the old days—and *the Knights considered that a good thing*.

"Now of course restarting fifty-year-old plans is not easy, but we've made some breakthroughs, one of which I'm about to show you. I'm wondering, though, since you are doing so well: could you tell me the great weakness in our plan?"

All eyes were on Carro, as if this were some sort of test.

"Um . . ." He wanted to say *I don't know* but that would never do. "I . . . don't know much about icefire. I can't see it."

"Exactly!" Rider Cornatan smiled. "Most of us are unable to see or work with icefire. But there are those who can."

"Does that . . ." Carro swallowed. His gaze flicked to the merchant, who was sweating more than ever. "Does that mean you want the Thilleians back?"

"No. Their powers can be turned to true evil. Once infected with the sense of power, they tend to become corrupted. But we can learn from them."

"But the powerful ones were all killed." And at the same time, his mind squealed *Isandor*.

"Exactly. And that is where this man comes in. Go ahead." He motioned to the suited man, who pulled some metal frame from the table. It went over the chair to cover the merchant's head in a lock, with plates fitted to both sides of his head so he couldn't move it. The pale green light showed the man's face sheened in sweat. Another suited man had come into the room while Rider Cornatan was speaking. He stuck a very thin needle into the skin of the man's forearm. It had a soft balloon of fluid attached, which he hung on a stand.

The merchant struggled at first, but quickly gave up, and a stupid look came over his face, his tongue lolling out. A dribble of spit tracked down his chin. Carro's stomach lurched.

The suited man then dragged the table with the strange machines so that it stood in front of the chair. With click of a handle, he brought a light to life. There were two beams, which he adjusted so each shone into one of the merchant's eyes. His eyes were wide, the pupils dilated.

He started speaking.

At first, his voice was a barely audible mumble, made harder to follow by drool dripping from his flaccid bottom lip, but gradually words formed.

". . . no money . . . no money. Have to pay the landlord . . . Sorry, dear, but the Knights came and took all my stock. Now I can't sell it to the collectors. I have no more money, dear. Yes, I remember that man. He came to me before. He bought some books . . ."

Carro clamped his hands behind his back. The merchant was going to mention him as purchaser for illegal items, and that was why he was here.

"I have . . . no more books, but the stranger has lots of money. I tell him . . . I will tell him about the boy, the one who's Imperfect. He wants them, the Imperfects, you know. He pays lots. I can pay the landlord, dear. I'm sorry . . ."

The man blinked and then his eyes fell closed. The beams of light tracked over his cheeks, no longer focused on his eyes.

Carro's heart thudded against his ribcage. He was going to be punished for not letting the Knights know about Isandor, who had to be "the boy" the merchant referred to.

The suited man turned off the light and released the plates that pressed against the merchant's head. The merchant collapsed forward into the chair, gasping. He made a kind of *huuh-huuuh* sound while holding out a trembling hand as if trying to grab something he couldn't reach. The green-suited men were busy with their machine, and the Senior Knights spoke softly to each other, as if no one else were in the room.

But the man was still going *huuuh-huuuh-huuuh* and Carro wanted to do something about this whole awful business, but he didn't know what, and meanwhile the gasping and the *huuuh-huuuh* intensified, and the trembling hand looked like some sort of insect clawing at the chair's arm rest.

Carro couldn't stand it any longer. "Can you help him, please?" His voice sounded high and young.

"Take him away," one of the suited men said, muffled inside the suit.

Carro wasn't sure if he was the "him" referred to, or the merchant. The other suited man went to the chair and tried to untie the merchant's wrist straps, but he was leaning too hard into them, so he pushed the merchant back. As he did so, the man arched his back and with an explosive *huuuuh* projectile-vomited. It went all over the suited man's helmet and facemask. The suited man swore and dragged the merchant out of the chair, out of the room, leaving a foul-smelling trail on the floor.

Carro felt sick.

"Come." Rider Cornatan's voice sounded far off. "We'll leave the staff to clean this up."

He sounded so matter-of-fact, as if seeing people in this sort of distress was *normal* to him. He led Carro out of the room, gingerly stepping over the vomit trail, while Carro still heard the *huuuh-huuuuh* in his mind. He was used to brawls, and fights, and fellow Apprentices drinking themselves stupid until they spent all night puking their guts out in the bathroom. He had never heard anything so desperate as this man.

It was all his fault.

Meanwhile, Rider Cornatan kept speaking.

"As you are probably aware, since you helped inspect this man's wares, we had this merchant watched. He wears the black of the Brotherhood of the Light, but no longer lives in the compound. It seems he has taken a wife, and he is desperate to get someone to pay for the privilege of using his son. The child was born Imperfect, and his wife rejected it. The boy has lived with the Brotherhood ever since. The merchant passed the knowledge of this boy to another man, a visitor to the Outer City. He paid two gold eagles for the information, and vanished. At the moment, the boy is still in the Brotherhood compound. We are going to get him first. And that is where you come in."

Carro stiffened, alert now.

"You are familiar with the Outer City. No one will find it odd to see you wandering around the streets."

"So . . ." Carro swallowed. "You want me to get this boy, while some sort of stranger is also after him?"

Rider Cornatan chuckled. "Of course I'm not going to let you go without help. Let me show you something else." He walked to the table with the weapons in the other room.

Carro followed him, his head reeling.

It's cold in the lawkeeper's office. The room is bare with just a bench along the wall. A tiny window lets in a meagre beam of bluish light.

Carro sinks down on the bench. Cold and shame bites through his trousers. This is where *criminals* sit.

Carro's tears run across his cheeks like icicles.

Isandor says, "Don't worry."

It's easy for him to say. Isandor's mother comes to pick up her son. There is an officer with her.

"The merchant has put in a complaint," he says. "He wants compensation for goods broken."

Oh, why did they have to play with boomerangs so close to the market? Why did the boomerang have to hit the merchant's sled full of glasswork?

Isandor's mother puts an arm around her son's shoulder. Isandor looks up at her with his big blue eyes. "I'm sorry."

She says, "Don't worry. I know things sometimes break when you play." Her voice is warm. She smiles at the officer and the man smiles back. She's radiant, glowing and pregnant, one of the city's best breeders. "I'm sure we can come to an arrangement with the merchant."

They leave the room, their backs disappearing into the corridor.

Carro's parents won't be so kind.

No dinner, no oil for his lamp, and his books taken away from him; that is, if he escapes the whip.

He waits. It's cold in the room. The feeling inside him is even colder. No one is ever going to come for him. His parents are going to leave him here.

❋

Rider Cornatan had turned around, giving Carro a concerned look. "Are you feeling ill?"

Carro's heart jumped a beat. "No, no, I'm fine." He tried to push away lingering nausea from the smell of vomit and the hazy remains of the memory, and the realisation: the recurring memories were getting worse.

How long before he had an accident while his mind was off somewhere else? How long before someone discovered and declared him unsuitable for service? Declared him *insane*?

Rider Cornatan's expression wasn't convincing. "You looked out of sorts for a bit. Not an advocate of medical procedures?" He glanced back at the room with the chair, where the wall panel was just sliding shut again, and two Junior Knights were mopping the floor.

"No, no. I'm fine." A drop of sweat trickled down Carro's back.

"Good, then have a look at this." Rider Cornatan gestured at the strange contraptions on the table.

They were definitely weapons of some description. Eagle Knights used crossbows and poisoned arrows, or in close combat, swords or daggers. Carro reached out for the staff with the shining stone, but withdrew his hand, casting a glance at Rider Cornatan. Touching it wouldn't be very humble. Stupid that he had even thought he *could* touch these weapons.

Rider Cornatan laughed, his eyes gleaming with pleasure. "You like that, boy?"

"Yes." Carro hated how his voice sounded too innocent. His father always said *boy* and never used his name.

"Take it."

Carro picked up the staff. The metal felt warm, almost alive, in his hands.

"Try some blows."

Try blows? Where? Rider Cornatan didn't expect to be sparring with him? He was an old man.

"Stand over there."

Apprehensively, Carro went to stand where Rider Cornatan indicated, in the middle of the room. To his dismay, the Supreme Rider threw off his cloak and grabbed another staff off the table. While he strode across the room, the eerie light made his white hair almost green. He took up position opposite Carro, his legs apart, as if he were about to start a sword fight.

Rider Cornatan ran his hand over the metal rod of the staff. There was a noise like lightning.

Icefire! Rider Cornatan knew he couldn't see it.

"Yes, boy. That surprises you, doesn't it? Thought we had forgotten that the curse that taints our land can be *used* in more ways than one?"

He thrust out with the staff. A line of dust lifted from the floor.

Carro cried out, turned and tried to run. What sort of defence did he have against icefire?

"Use the staff!" Rider Cornatan's voice grated like stone on stone.

Carro grabbed the staff in both hands, but had no idea what to do with it. Dust now crackled all around him, making his nose itch. He swung the staff into thin air, like a blind man sword fighting.

"That's right. A good, honest Knight doesn't run like a coward. A good Knight stands his ground and fights with whatever weapon he has."

"But it's not fair . . ." Carro panted.

"Warfare is rarely fair, boy. Yes, the enemy will use icefire. So now, we will also. Come on, show me what you've learned." He swung the staff.

Sweat pouring down his stomach, Carro gripped the staff in both hands. He adopted a fighting stance, legs apart, swaying from side to side.

Rider Cornatan circled him. Slowly, watching with eagle eyes. The heels of his boots clacked on the stone floor. Carro's skin pricked. He turned on the spot, as he'd been taught in sword fighting, always watching.

Rider Cornatan chuckled.

"I see you've been taught well."

And then he thrust up. Lightning crackled around Carro.

Carro swung his staff. Too late. He didn't know what he was doing. However was he supposed to fight invisible icefire with nothing more than a stick? Rider Cornatan thrust again. The air was thick with the scent of singed clothing.

"Fight, fight," Rider Cornatan urged and punctuated each word with a thrust of the staff. He laughed. Maybe this was Carro's punishment.

He thrust faster and faster. Dust swirled in the room. Carro whirled, swung his staff whichever way seemed right, but Rider Cornatan always went faster.

Eventually, Carro could no longer keep it up. "This is ridiculous. I can't see what I'm fighting!" He stopped, panting, embarrassed about his outburst. "I'm sorry. You win."

He hung his shoulders. Humility. Lost to an old man.

Rider Cornatan laughed. "No. You win. Give me this." He took the staff from Carro's sweat-slicked hand. "Notice how the metal is cold?"

It was. Ice-cold in fact.

"You noticed how none of the rays hit you?"

Carro blinked. He couldn't see the rays, but hadn't felt anything either, so he supposed it was true. The floor certainly bore plenty of marks.

"That is because when you hold this weapon, it acts as a sink for icefire. When you're holding this staff, instead of hitting the intended target, icefire is all absorbed in this staff."

Carro's spirits deflated. "So . . . nothing would have happened to me even if I had not defended myself."

"Precisely." A smile curled the old lips. "You are special, because of what you are. Pure Pirosians are rare. Cherish it, keep it a secret and use it well."

Carro tried hard to feel misused or suspicious, but he only succeeded partially. He was *special*. He was more than Carro, useless boy from the Outer City, who was only here because the Knights wanted to spy on the Outer City residents.

"Apprentice Carro, we have a dire need of your talent. How would you like to be promoted?"

"Promoted?" Carro swallowed. This was getting stranger and stranger.

"The first Apprentice ever to skip straight to Learner? Your father would like that, wouldn't he?"

Carro flinched. What did Rider Cornatan know of his father? What did he know of what his father thought about him? Did his father have a hand in this? Was that the catch?

The carpet is dark red and has a pattern of squares within squares that Carro knows all too well. He stands just inside the door, his hands behind his back, his gaze on the ground.

His father gets up from the desk and walks across the office. Carro follows his father's movement from the corner of his eye. Don't go to the cupboard please, not the cupboard. He doesn't think he can stand any more work in the warehouse on the accounting books, but he will not cry, or the boys will tease him, all those boys who were already teasing him in the streets. It will just get worse.

His father opens the cupboard door. Takes a long time to select a big book. The stock-take records.

Carro closes his eyes and tries not to show his despair. He shivers with the intense cold in the warehouse.

He can feel the chill breeze as his father crosses to the rough table where he is sitting. The book lands on the table with a thud.

"I want this done by tomorrow morning."

Carro just nods, his mind numb. He fights back tears of despair.

His fingers will be blue and sore by the time the night is over. Then his reading tutor will hit him for not paying attention. Then his father will order the stove to be tempered, because the luxurious warmth is obviously putting his errant son to sleep.

And then . . .

Carro wobbled. Oh, by the skylights, why was he seeing these things?

Fortunately, Rider Cornatan hadn't noticed the spell. He was putting the staff back on the table. When Carro moved to do the same, his hands trembling, Rider Cornatan put his hand on the metal. "Keep it. I'm allocating you two elite soldiers. Get the boy and come back here. The soldiers are waiting for you."

"What—now?"

"Yes. Everyone is asleep or too drunk to notice. You should be able to take the boy on your bird. He's only a child. Bring him back here as soon as you can. Report to me directly. Don't tell anyone else."

Rider Cornatan turned to Carro and lifted up his chin with a single finger.

"Go on, make your family proud."

"My family hates me, especially my father."

Rider Cornatan's eyes met his, blue, intense. "I don't know about the rest of your family, but I can assure you, Carro, your father loves you very much."

CHAPTER 14

THERE WERE MANY questions Carro should have asked, but his brain was so numb that he was out the door before he remembered any of them. It felt like it had all been a dream, except he had the staff in his hands and his Learner's badge on his collar, and a fuzzy feeling in his head that told him that, yes, this was real, and if he wanted to come out of this alive, he had better obey orders. Someone was testing him, or teasing him, or using him as expendable bait, and all he could do was run along and hope he wasn't going to get caught in something sticky.

The two elite Knights waited at the end of the corridor that led to Rider Cornatan's quarters, both sharp-faced silent men at least ten years older than Carro. He had never seen them before. Their eyes were hard, their gazes neither approving nor disapproving, but Carro was all too aware of their muscled arms and lean physiques. Bodyguards or child-minders?

Their faces remained impassive.

They started moving through the dark corridor in the direction Carro recognised as leading towards the howling staircase. At night, there was no wind to make the jagged edges howl, and they climbed its many steps in uncomfortable silence. The sky was dark blue, too light to show any but the brightest of stars. Pink and green skylights shimmered above.

"You know where to find this Brotherhood compound?"

Carro had grown so used to silence that the man's voice startled him.

"I do." Carro explained the location on the far side of the Outer City. The men only listened. Evidently, they had been briefed on their mission.

They reached the eyrie, where dark shapes of birds shuffled and fidgeted as they came in. One of the Knights flicked the light lever up. The bulb sprang into life with its too-bright glow. The eagles stirred. Heads lifted from under wings, baleful eyes blinked. Both men had their birds untied before Carro had even done up his harness. His fingers trembled. He was fumbling with the staff Rider Cornatan had given him, not sure how to carry it. He settled on lashing his belt around the glass head. The stick banged against his leg, a feeling that was clumsy and awkward.

Carro untied his eagle. It hissed at him and flapped its wings, which made a few other eagles hiss and squawk.

Clumsy, clumsy.

At the opening, the two Knights mounted with fluid grace. Their birds stood ready, their eyes alert.

How had Rider Cornatan ever thought he could match men like these? Normally, the Apprentices mounted their birds from a platform, but it had been taken away for the night. Carro put his foot in the harness trying to imitate the Knights. He heaved himself up and almost overbalanced. The eagle flapped with his sudden shift of weight. Carro salvaged the situation by grabbing the handholds at the top of the saddle with both hands. The reins slipped from his hands, but at least he didn't fall.

One of the Knights gave a quick flick with his eyebrows before he launched the eagle out. Carro clicked his tongue and the eagle followed the other bird out, hurtling into the cold air that stung his face like the cuts of a thousand knives.

Carro was shivering, already struggling to hold onto the saddle.

Most of the buildings in the city were dark. Lights burned in the odd window here or there, but most decent nobles and proper folk of the City of Glass had gone to bed. The rest were partying in the Outer City, an island of light on the plain dark blue with eternal dusk.

Carro kneed his eagle into catching up with the others. The bird was unwilling and made no secret of its dislike at being woken up. The two Knights fell back and let him lead the way, over the festival grounds, mostly dark, over the market square, bathed in light and full of revellers, to the part of the Outer City furthest from the City of Glass. Here, Carro landed his eagle in a rough piece of land amongst warehouses. There used to be a warehouse at this plot of land, but it had burned down some years ago. He remembered the flames, which had been visible from his street. He and Isandor had climbed up the limpet roof to see the flames roaring into the sky. Now it was just an empty piece of land with mounds of snow and stone pillars which had once been the foundations of the building.

There was nowhere to tie up the eagles, and it would probably be unwise to leave them behind anyway, so he dismounted and led the bird by the reins into the street. Eagles were not fond of walking and the bird kept jerking its head up. Carro almost lost his grip on the reins twice before he noticed how the two Knights had the leather straps wrapped around their wrists. They also kept the reins very tight, so their birds didn't have the slack to get any force into the upward jerk. The Tutor didn't teach that. Interesting. It worked, too.

In silence, they progressed to the wall that was the back of the compound.

Carro hadn't expected guards at the gate, and indeed there were none. But now they couldn't take the eagles any further and there was still nowhere to tie them up. Instead, the two Knights tied their birds onto *each other*. Their reins were interesting as well. His tack was the standard length of leather, fastened onto the harness on one end with a metal ring and looped back onto the harness on the other end. Their reins were two separate pieces of leather, each lashed around the rider's wrist when in flight. They now tied one of these strips to each other, threading the knot through the reins of Carro's eagle.

Carro wanted to ask, *but what about if we need them?* He envisaged a tangle of feathers and wings as all three birds tried to take off at once and found they were attached to each other. But evidently, the Knights had considered this and had some sort of solution.

Carro felt so dumb. *I'm an Outer City pup, and they'll do their best to prove it with every step I take.*

The men took daggers from their belts. Carro untied the staff and unsheathed his dagger. He was unsure in which hand to hold which and his hands were too cold to do much with either weapon anyway.

They walked in through the open gates. On the other side was a small courtyard surrounded on three sides by a low building with a columned façade, very unlike the regular building style in the Outer City. Carro knew from earlier visits that the door was somewhere in the darkness between those columns, although he couldn't see it. This was the furthest he had ever gone into the compound, bringing a delivery from his father to the Brothers. Fabric for bed sheets, he seemed to remember.

Every time he'd come here, there had been children his own age playing in the snow. They had been rescued from abusive families, lived in the compound and received teaching from the Brothers. They had always seemed happy and harmonious. This was not a place of shouting and punishment; it was a place of learning.

Sometimes, in his darkest hours, Carro had considered seeking refuge here, but he had always thought it unfair to the children whose families actually *beat* them, the girls whose fathers came home drunk and raped them every night. Those children needed the Brothers, not him. Being ignored, ridiculed or scorned every moment he spent inside his parents' limpet didn't injure him or kill him.

He walked across the snow-covered yard and took the two steps up the porch. The two Knights followed him like silent shadows. From memory, the dining room was directly opposite the entrance, and the sleeping quarters were to the right. A glow lit up behind him. One of the Knights held a pebble no bigger than a fingernail, which gave off bright light. The first few windows they checked were store-rooms with lots of boxes, or classrooms with benches and tables. On a blackboard against the far wall, someone had drawn diagrams made of squares and triangles. Carro was unsure what it meant, but he had seen similar pictures in the books he and Isandor used to read, ones that spoke of calculations of icefire.

The next window looked into a living room of some kind, but a thick layer of ice made it hard to see. The second Knight gestured to a window further ahead.

Inside was a dormitory-style room with two rows of beds against the walls. In each of those beds was a child. The Knight tried the window, but it wouldn't open.

The other Knight gestured that there was an entry on the side of the building. They headed back into the courtyard and the Knight led through a passage between the building and the compound wall. There was an outroom at the back, and facing it, a wooden door. It was locked, but it took the Knights no longer than a few heartbeats to prise it open.

The quiet efficiency of these men chilled Carro. They had spoken no more than a handful of words since he had met them, and now he wondered if these men *ever* spoke. They certainly didn't seem the type to attend Newlight celebrations and start rowdy brawls in melteries, nor to get distracted by the presence of female flesh.

These were *real* Knights in the way he was not. Real Knights didn't party, didn't fight in melteries, didn't try to get into a girl's bed. Real Knights didn't even show off their status to their families and old friends. Real Knights didn't *have* old friends. They only had their jobs, and their superiors.

They went into the building, entering a straight corridor that stretched into darkness.

The fur-soled riding boots made not the slightest sound on the floor. The Knight indicated, *in here*. He pushed the door open, again without sound. The air inside was impossibly warm and laced with the smell of musty blankets.

The first Knight marched into the room, while the second shut the door, holding aloft the light. Meanwhile, the first Knight was yanking blankets off the beds, uncovering sleeping children who woke up to a hand pressed over their mouths. Carro clutched his staff and felt completely useless.

The Knight struck success with the fifth child. Carro felt a cold shiver in the staff before the Knight had pulled the blankets off the bed. He was going to say *that one* for the sake of being useful, but the boy already sat at the edge of his bed. The harsh light showed his foot, was missing toes. Imperfect. Two heartbeats later, the Knight had the boy wrapped in a blanket and was pushing him into the corridor. All silent.

The other Knight gestured, *Quick, let's get out of here.*

As Carro pulled the door to the dormitory shut behind him, the staff jerked in his hand, nearly causing him to drop it. He couldn't restrain a gasp.

Both Knights looked at him. One had slung the blanket with the boy over his shoulder.

"Someone's coming," Carro whispered. He wasn't sure if it was *someone*, but something was definitely happening. The metal of the staff was going alternately warm and cold in his hands.

The Knights had stopped. Neither spoke, but their sharp gazes roamed the corridor. Carro didn't even know their names.

They listened. All Carro could hear was the thudding of his own heart.

"Your imagination." The Knight closest to him gave him a disdainful glance and turned towards the door.

Carro shrugged, trying to be careless. Fine; these men thought he was an idiot, everyone did. He could do nothing but follow, even though the coldness in the staff increased.

They walked back along the path between the wall and the building, into the courtyard. Carro looked over his shoulder again. Saw nothing.

The staff chilled in his hands.

"There's something . . ." He didn't know how to continue. Speak of icefire in the presence of older Knights? Did they know what Rider Cornatan knew?

But the Knights broke into a trot.

Carro didn't question their motivation.

Quick, back to the eagles. Hurry up. The staff was jerking now. He took the lead in the courtyard, the two Knights close behind. Almost at the gate. There was a noise, a soft sigh as if someone expelled a breath.

Carro glanced over his shoulder.

Something moved at the dormitory window, a smudge of distorted air.

Quick.

Puffs of snow blew up in the courtyard, coming towards them.

Carro ran.

A loud crack reverberated between the wings of the building, followed by a thump. Carro skidded to a stop. One of the Knights lay face down in the snow. The second Knight, holding the boy over his shoulder, had his dagger in his hand, slashing uselessly in thin air.

Some artefact of icefire.

Carro gripped the staff even though its surface almost froze onto his hands. Something was in the courtyard with them, *something* he couldn't see. But he could see footsteps forming in the snow as the apparition walked. He waved the staff. The second Knight glanced around, his eyes wide, his dagger ready. His comrade hadn't stirred.

The second Knight's head jerked back. His face froze in a surprised expression. A loud *crack* echoed in the courtyard.

The man fell backwards as if in slow motion and landed on the icy ground with a dull thud, the blanket with the boy under him.

Carro wanted to run, but fear made his legs unwilling. He stared at the man's neck, bent at an impossible angle. The invisible thing *had broken the man's neck.*

Carro waved the staff like crazy. That *thing* was going to kill him next. "Begone, begone, whatever you are!"

A sudden gust of wind picked up, howling around the building. The air crackled. Snow sizzled, and blew into Carro's face. He stood stiff with fear. He wanted to scream, but could make no sound. It felt like his entire face was on fire.

And then quiet returned.

Carro stood there, holding the staff. His hands ached with cold. Snow had blown into heaps obliterating any footsteps the apparition might have left. Where was it now? All Carro could see were indistinct mounds of snow, two of which contained the Knights' lifeless bodies.

"Please, help." The voice was soft and muffled.

The Imperfect boy was pushing himself up from under the dead Knight, shaking snow out of his hair.

"Come to me," Carro called, still staring at the snow, expecting to see footsteps coming towards him.

He waved the staff. The metal was so cold it steamed. His hands hurt from holding it, but he was too scared to worry about frostbite. A deep keening filled the courtyard. Wind tore through the gate, throwing up a cloud of snow.

The boy had pushed the Knight off him. The man's head flopped back like it was attached to this body only by skin.

"Come now!" Carro shouted into the howling wind.

The boy ran, clutching his blanket.

Carro grabbed hold of him with his free arm, while hanging onto the staff with the other. The staff, and his hand, were rimed with frost.

He ran, whistled for the eagle, and then remembered the business with the tied-up reins.

But the eagles came, all three of them, flying low through the street, with their wing tips almost touching the houses on either side. The reins dangled loose—snapped? The two Knights' eagles kept flying, but his bird landed.

Carro heaved the boy on the saddle and clambered on behind him. One stroke of powerful wings and they were off into the night. Carro wrestled to gain control of the reins. His leather loop had broken, too; no, it had been cut.

The boy was shivering.

"S-s-so glad you came," he said. His voice was young and hadn't broken yet. "I thought . . . that blue thing were going to kill me like the others."

Blue thing? "What did you see?"

Carro shifted his weight to free his arm so he could lash the dangling reins around his wrist. He now saw how the tying-up trick worked. The knot still dangled in the reins of the eagle flying to the left of him. At his whistle, the birds had simply bitten through the leather. The Knights would replace the straps once they became too short.

"Didn't you see the blue man?"

"I didn't see anything." His teeth chattered.

"He were all shimmery and in places you could see right through him."

Just what was he talking about?

Carro had to concentrate on flying and the boy fell into silence. He didn't shiver so much anymore. Carro was too busy staying in the saddle to talk, and too busy worrying what Rider Cornatan would say about the death of two of his elite soldiers, men much more experienced than him.

Riding with the loose reins would have been tricky even during daytime, and the dead weight of the boy didn't help. The eagle laboured to stay in the air, but he made the eyrie.

Rider Cornatan was waiting at the back of the room, silhouetted by the light. Carro slid off his bird, the weight of the boy pressing him down.

It was only when he stood in the straw, and the boy slumped on the ground that he realised the boy had lost consciousness.

Rider Cornatan gave a sharp command. A Knight ran forward to lift the boy's prone body off the floor.

"Take him to the infirmary. Impress on the medicos that I want him to *live*."

Then the man was gone, and Carro faced Rider Cornatan. He couldn't bear looking up. He'd taken out two capable Knights and had come back alone. Rider Cornatan had given him the metal staff to protect the patrol, but he had run first.

"I can explain," he whispered, but the horror of that snap echoed in his mind. How strong was this invisible monstrosity that it could break a grown man's neck with such a loud crack?

There were footsteps on the floor, Rider Cornatan coming closer. Carro cringed. He would surely be beaten, punished for his failure.

Carro sits at the big table in the dining room. His sister is next to him, crying.

"Why did you do that, Carro?" his mother asks.

"Because she is ugly."

"That is such a horrid thing to say. I don't know how you let these things come into your head."

"But it's true."

His mother slaps him across the face. "You need to grow up. You want to be treated like a big boy, you act like one."

But a warm hand touched his shoulder.

"Look at me, Carro."

Carro raised his head, blinking hard to repress threatening tears. He couldn't help it—he always did or said stupid things that got himself and, most importantly, other people, into trouble.

Rider Cornatan's eyes met his. It was impossible to guess what went on behind that gaze.

"I know what it means to face the horrors of the Thillei legacy," Rider Cornatan said in a low voice. "There are certain things we simple human beings cannot fight. That is the true reason I sent you: because you alone have a chance. Had you not been there, the boy would have been in the hands of the enemy. You did as well as you could."

"Who . . ." Carro swallowed. Did this mean that the death of two capable men would be written off as inevitable? While it was *his* fault? "Who is this enemy?"

"That is what we need to find out. We might have thought that all Thilleians were dead, but it seems they are not."

Isandor. And then Carro had another chilling thought: did his friend have anything to do with this invisible monstrosity? It was Isandor's idea to read the books, but what if he had kept the most important of them secret?

"Now, I want you to clean up and rest. Go downstairs to my quarters and use the bathroom there." He winked. "I know it's Newlight. Don't stay too long, though. I believe you're racing tomorrow."

He passed an arm over Carro's shoulders and squeezed them briefly.

Carro's head was full of questions. What did he mean—don't stay too long? How could Rider Cornatan be so indifferent about the death of two men? What was he going to do with that boy? Why, if he wanted Imperfects, had he not noticed the one right in front of his nose in the eyrie, and what would Carro do if asked to betray Isandor?

But he left the room and trudged down the howling staircase to the Senior Knight quarters. When he came to the bathroom in question, he understood at least the first part of Rider Cornatan's remarks, because he could hear the sound of relaxed talk and laughter before he opened the door. It sounded like a party going on.

The room beyond was huge and impossibly warm. Steam drifted from the surface of a huge bath. At least twenty people sat in the water, on a bench around the perimeter of the bath.

"Hey, there's the hero!" one young man called out.

The others cheered, holding up glasses.

The group included some of the noble sons who had always been indifferent to him, men who should know about the deaths of two of their fellows. And, by the skylights, there was Korinne, seated in the water.

Their eyes met, and Carro looked away, acutely aware of his filthy clothes. No way to face a girl.

In a corner filled with benches and washbasins, Carro slipped out of his clothes and washed blood off his hands. It was warm in the room, and the laughter and cheerful voices made his ears ring, where he still heard that snap, that awful snap, of the Knight's neck breaking.

Footsteps in the snow.

Crack.

A servant came with a tray of hot bloodwine. Carro accepted a glass and drained it in one gulp. The liquid burned a way to his stomach. There. That was better. He slipped into the huge bath, not meeting anyone's eyes. The water stung his cold-numbed hands.

Carro leaned back against the side of the bath, letting the talk in the room wash over him. His head was becoming comfortably dizzy with the heat and the effect of the bloodwine.

"Hi, Carro."

Korinne had appeared on the underwater seat next to him. Her curls were flattened against her head and the bottom ends of her hair fanned out from her shoulders, partially covering her breasts.

"Um, hello," he said, and then he felt like he had to add something. "Have you been here long?"

Stupid question, really, seeing as what he'd been through.

"Not very long," she said. She took one of his hands and began rubbing it, examining blisters on his palms. "Flying out at night?" she asked.

He nodded, the simplest answer that didn't require him to lie.

"Didn't you wear gloves?"

Carro shrugged. He didn't want to talk about his mission. The flow of the water drew her hair away from her breasts, soft white orbs with dark nipples. He felt oddly detached.

"We were just getting ready for the party and were waiting for you." She ran her hands up his arm, meeting his eyes.

"For me?" Heat crept up his cheeks.

Was this the girl who had called him a clumsy idiot earlier that evening? By the skylights—was it only that evening? It seemed many days ago.

"Drink?" someone behind him asked.

Carro turned and took the bottle from the man next to him, a tall, dark-haired young man with olive skin. His shoulders were lean and corded with muscle.

The man met Carro's eyes; his were grey and uncomfortably intense. He had long eyelashes. His face was narrow, with a long, hook-like nose.

Foreign blood.

"Um . . ." Carro hated how he blushed. "I'm Carro."

The man chuckled. "We figured."

"And you are?"

"Farey."

His intense stare made Carro uneasy, but he felt he had to say something. He *wanted* to say something. Not to look like an idiot, for once.

"I haven't seen you at the eyrie before." It was an insanely stupid remark, he knew that as soon as it left his mouth. Apprentices never saw but a very small part of what went on in the eyrie.

Again that chuckle, breathy and nervous and very strange at the same time. "You wouldn't have seen me. It's my job to be seen only when I want to be." The grey gaze roamed Carro's naked shoulders, the pale skin of his belly.

Carro turned back to Korinne and made a show of unstoppering the bottle. His hands trembled. He drank a few swigs without tasting anything, and when he passed the bottle on, noticed how on the other side of the bath two noble sons faced each other. One was old enough to have the golden markings on his cheeks, the other was not much older than Carro. As he watched, the older Knight pulled the younger closer and kissed him full on the mouth. The light gilded the younger man's cheekbones, His eyes were closed; his hands slid down the older Knight's chest.

Blood roared in Carro's ears. He wanted to turn away, give his attention to Korinne, who was stroking his shoulders, but he couldn't. Men did these things to each other *by choice?*

Next to him, that strange Farey gave another one of his breathy chuckles. "You're not with kiddies anymore, boy." The tone of his voice made Carro shiver.

Carro didn't trust himself to meet the man's eyes. He forced his gaze back to Korinne, but saw sinewy, olive-skinned shoulders. "You . . ." He cleared his throat. "You have parties here often?"

"Not me." She laughed. "But Rider Cornatan invites his elite group here quite often, I hear. This is the first time I've been here. He asked me to come." Her eyes said *for you*.

She looped her arm around his neck. Her bare breasts pressed against his chest. Carro wondered what had made her change her mind about him. Nothing he had done, that was for sure.

But it was pleasant, and she was offering, and doing what she wanted, whatever the reason behind it, seemed easier than facing that strange Farey on his other side, and with all the uncomfortable feelings *that* brought.

He bent forward, pressing his lips on hers. She replied, eager and passionate.

The rest of the night passed in a drunken blur. When he stood in the deeper part of the bath, Korinne could loop her legs around him. It was easy to lift her in the water at the height he wanted her. She swallowed him, and he didn't object. His body obeyed his mind. For those few crazy moments, he ruled the world. He was Carro. He'd show his father how "useless" he was. Let his father beg him on his knees for forgiveness. Let his mother learn what it was to live in hardship.

If we are nice all the time, we'd never get anywhere.

He didn't suffer any flashbacks all night.

CHAPTER 15

JEVAITHI PULLED ON her thick furs and looked at herself in
the dressing room mirror. Lush, thick and pure white, the cloak had
been made in all haste for this visit. It suited her, she had to admit,
and brought out the lushness of her hair. She had the maid pin it up in
a loose bun today.

Underneath the cloak she wore a thick dress, tall boots, woollen
stockings and felt underwear over her usual silk finery. She twirled in
front of the mirror, admiring her new clothes, feeling like a little girl
again, like walking on her mother's hand. It was exciting, as if the
whole world was out there to be discovered.

She had even put some colour on her face. Lines of kohl and a fine
coating of silver paint accentuated her eyes.

Not too much or Rider Cornatan would object. She could almost
hear his voice: *You are still a child.*

No, she wasn't. She pulled up the leather strap she had insisted her
maid bring her, and let the feather dangle over her chest. It was a
crude thing, but one such as the new maidens of the city wore. It
made her feel grown up. It made her feel like she was in control of
part of her life, no matter how small that part was.

"Your escort is ready," a male voice said.

Jevaithi gasped and tucked the feather back under the white fur of
her cloak, her heart still thudding.

Rider Cornatan strode into the room. The dressing room! She should really talk to him about that. She was no longer a girl and he would have to start treating her like an adult, and an adult of the opposite sex at that.

He stopped a few paces inside the door and stared. Oh yes, she did not mistake the look in his eyes. She saw it in the Knights who attended her.

"Your Highness, you look . . . magnificent," he said. His blue gaze roamed her body as if seeking something to criticise, something that was too daring or too revealing for the citizens of the City of Glass to see, and, having found nothing, came to rest on her right arm, which she held in her pocket. Nothing untoward there either.

She stared back defiantly. *No, nobody will know.*

"Are we ready to go, then?" she asked.

"We are, Your Highness, unless . . ."

"Unless what?"

"Unless you would decide it's not safe enough."

Not safe enough? She frowned at him. "Is there a reason why I should change my mind about this trip? A reason that wasn't present when you agreed to take me? Which was . . . yesterday?"

His eyes met hers. He opened his mouth. Hesitated. "No, Your Highness, there isn't."

"Then let's go."

He was lying; she could feel that. Something was happening right here in the palace. And she bet it was something to do with those golden rays that wormed their way up from the ground to her tower room. Icefire, stronger than ever before. Whatever it was, he was worried, but would rather endanger her than talk about it.

Interesting.

She left the dressing room straight-backed, without looking at him. The fur lining of the cloak swished around her ankles. It was an unfamiliar sensation that left her feeling wonderfully warm and covered. For once, she wouldn't have to look at the world from a great height. For once, people would look at her face rather than her dress, or what they could see through the fabric.

The door opened, the Knights stepped to the side and then . . . oh, freedom. She walked onto the landing in front of her quarters. A breeze of frost-tinged air wafted up from the depths of the atrium, an immense triangular hall filled with bluish light, glass and mirrors. It was said that the hall had formed through the collapse of one building against another. When seen from here, the very top of the triangle, the theory made sense, and as far as she knew, the floors did slope in most of the unused other side of the palace.

Down below, far down, the palace workers moved like crawling insects, past the fountain, a triangular basin of water in the middle of the hall. Although blue with salts, dripping water had frozen in grotesque stalagmites at the foot of the burbling fountain. Miniature ice floes bobbed on the pond's surface, carved in the shapes of flowers and animals.

Lifts trundled up or down along rails set in the atrium's walls. There was the sound of ordinary people talking, laughing. It was intoxicating.

"Your Highness."

Rider Cornatan's voice broke her reverie.

A lift cubicle had come. Two guards stepped in, then Jevaithi and Rider Cornatan and then two more guards. The doors hissed closed. The cubicle jolted into action. Through the glass ceiling, Jevaithi spotted the jiggling chain that held the cubicle in place. The floors slid by. Sometimes they passed remnants of the destruction that had created the palace: twisted metal bent into elegant sculptures, haphazardly holding up sheets of grey stone. Molten glass carved into arches. Sometimes she wondered what weapon could twist stone and metal so.

Lights above the doors indicated that the lift had come to the ground floor. The doors opened and she saw more Knights, forming a guard of honour across the polished tiles of the atrium floor.

Through the glass wall of the main entrance Jevaithi spotted a sled in the street, surrounded by yet more guards. Were all these Knights going to come with her? There wouldn't be anyone left to guard the palace. Never mind her desire for an unobtrusive visit. She was going out, that was the important thing. Once she was amongst the people, she would try to stay there as long as possible.

As they were about to leave the atrium, a stiff grey-haired man came up to Rider Cornatan.

"You're going out?" he said in a low voice and his eyes flashed hidden meaning. He was a Senior Knight, with golden stripes for years of service on his collar. He had more stripes than Jevaithi had cele-brated her birthday.

Rider Cornatan nodded curtly. "Newlight festival."

"When are you back?"

"Why? Anything wrong?"

"Well—about the young lad you brought in last night . . ." Then he must have realised Jevaithi could hear what he said and he lowered his voice. They stopped walking. Jevaithi stopped, too, a few paces off.

The two men exchanged a few comments in voices too low for her to hear. Rider Cornatan's eyes widened briefly then he turned to Jevaithi.

"Continue on to the sled, Your Highness, I will be there soon."

Jevaithi didn't move.

Rider Cornatan raised his eyebrows in the way he did when he was annoyed. "I said I will be there soon."

"I am the Queen. I have a right to hear what is going on in my city, don't I? So I think I'd rather stay and hear about this problem."

"Your Highness, it's only a minor thing, not even important enough to discuss in the Knights' Council. It's certainly not important enough to delay our trip. You might miss the races." He turned to the Senior Knight. "We will discuss this later."

The man gave a stiff nod, but Jevaithi didn't miss the tightly pressed lips. *He* obviously didn't think it was a minor concern. She wondered if it had anything to do with the increase of the golden rays of icefire. If so, it wasn't unimportant to her either. Or maybe it had something to do with the more than fifty criminals the Knights had caught in Bordertown. One of her guards had let that information slip, but Rider Cornatan hadn't wanted to tell her how those people had been caught or what they had done.

"I think I should like to attend when the Knights' Council sits next," she said.

Rider Cornatan turned to her, his expression stiff. "We should start to think in that direction, yes, but I'm not sure you need to be introduced to the politics of running the land just yet."

Politics? There were the Knights and the Knights. What was so hard about that?

"I want to."

"We shall see."

He kept his face neutral, since he could hardly berate her with all these people present, but he would probably like to do so if the twitch of a muscle in his neck was anything to go by.

Her people were her protection. Once she was back in her prison, she would suffer. She thought of the gull's tail feather on the leather strap around her neck. The token suddenly felt heavy as stone. What if *Rider Cornatan* was to take her up on her advertisement tonight. . . ?

Quite a crowd had gathered to watch in the street. Held back by a couple of Knights, the people were all nobles of the City of Glass, dressed in their fine furs and gaudy headdresses. Women wore face paint and jewellery.

As soon as Jevaithi stepped out the door, a cheer went up.

She waved to the people as she had been taught. A Knight spread sand from a bucket so she didn't slip in the snow. Another held open the door to the carriage. She climbed up the steps and settled on the bench next to Rider Cornatan.

The sled was huge and white, drawn by four bears. Their white fur shone and was washed and groomed to perfection. They even had jewels on their collars and harnesses, which were made from red leather. One of the palace guards sat in the driver's seat. Two Knights stood on the front runners, and two behind, all prominently displaying weapons. So she was to have four minders, and Rider Cornatan, and the driver, who would stay with the sled. She could handle that.

With a flick of the reins the bears loped into action and started moving down the street. Jevaithi saw herself and the sled reflected in the glass façades of the buildings that lined the street. Pompous entrances were guarded by sculptures carved of molten glass. Behind the windows were racks of the finest clothing by the city's finest leather workers, or brightly lit benches with swathes of green plants. Customers stood in line for attendants to cut their fresh vegetables. No such things as mundane shops here. Through another window, customers sat drinking from bronze-coloured cups on dainty tables surrounding a giant glass sculpture of a dragon.

The going was slow in the streets. The Knights had to motion people aside, who then crowded along the street and in porches. They cheered. Jevaithi waved and smiled. A young man ran with the sled offering a tray of biscuits. They looked wonderful, but Rider

Cornatan's sharp glance stopped her from taking one. They could be poisoned, after all. Silly. She didn't care. If she died today, she would die having fun. Fifteen years old, and she didn't care if she never saw the sun rise on another day. If she died, she would have denied the Knight's Council the pleasure of using her body to further their aims. If she died, it would be without having a Senior Knight's handprints all over her and his child in her belly. If she died, it would be because she wanted to, not because anyone said so. Although, of course, there were better things than dying, and possibly other ways to escape her fate.

Escape. The taste of the word on her tongue was like that of a rare exotic fruit. Being out here amongst the people almost felt as good as escape.

They passed the city gates and the bears moved at full speed. The white plains spread out before her. Sunlight poured gold over the snow, casting long shadows and millions of glittering gem-like crystals.

An icy breeze bit into Jevaithi's cheeks. Her maids would probably complain about what it did to her skin, but she didn't care; she felt alive. Out here waited young men who didn't yet know the newly blooded virgin who would throw herself at their feet. She'd take herself off into one of the melteries, she'd dance, she'd flirt, and when the young man took the bait, she'd make sure it was out in the open, when none of the Senior Knights could make a scene.

Escape.

The jumble of low buildings that was the Outer City grew on the horizon at the same speed with which the excitement bloomed in her heart.

The buildings had been designed by locals and the people called them limpets. She had never been inside one—another task to add to her list of things to do after she ascended the throne on her birthday.

Before long, she could make out the colourful tents that had been set up on the plain and the fences for the animals. No Legless Lions yet, but one of her maids told her this morning that the festivities included a Legless Lion race. She would *have* to see that. Legless Lions were fun to watch when they ran on their flippers.

A number of eagles rose from the festival grounds. Knights in the saddles rode with quiet confidence. Low and gliding, they escorted the sled towards the tents. More guards. She'd escape them all.

Children ran out onto the plain, cheering and shouting when they met the sled. They ran along, stumbling through the snow to keep up with the bears. Their faces were red; their eyes shone with wonder. Jevaithi smiled at them and waved. The kids laughed and waved back, excitement in their eyes. She could hear their young voices: *Mother, I saw the Queen today*. What would it be like to be one of these kids, to live anonymously, to ride sleds down the hill, to build snow castles, to just walk around here without anyone watching?

The sled passed a fence and then they were amongst the festivities. The driver slowed the bears to a walking pace. The audience grew quickly. People ran through the pens, poked their heads out of tents, came with their families. Their faces were bright with happiness. The driver stood up on his seat and shouted, "Make way for Queen Jevaithi of the City of Glass!"

More and more people gathered along the sides, cheering and shouting. Someone started a chant, *Jevaithi, Jevaithi,* and before long everyone was shouting her name. Jevaithi waved until her arm ached. These people were her safety shield.

The sled came to a halt.

Rider Cornatan jumped off first and bowed, holding out his hand. "Your Highness."

If he was still angry about her insistence to attend the Knights' Council, he didn't show it.

Jevaithi stepped from the sled onto hard frozen ground where again a Knight was spreading sand. *They sweep the ground I walk on.* Rider Cornatan held out his arm to support her, but she waved it away. Her new boots were soft and warm. She wanted to walk in the snow, away from all these eyes. She wanted to run, be alone and free. She wanted to slip and fall, tumble in the snow. It looked soft.

But more Knights were coming up to her, all older men with lots of gold on their collars.

"How wonderful of you to grace us with a visit," a Knight said. She couldn't see his face because he bowed so deeply.

"Thank you for receiving me." She had to stay polite and formal, oh so boring.

"I have had the honour of being appointed as your guide, Your Highness. What would you like to see first?" He was still speaking to the snow at his feet.

"I should like to see the flying races," Jevaithi said.

"The eagle race pens are on the other side of the festival grounds," the Knight said.

"Then I shall walk there."

Rider Cornatan bent to her, whispering, "Your Highness, I don't think—"

"Walking is healthy."

He didn't dare protest.

"Lead the way, my good Knight," she said to the guide.

The guards cleared a path through the crowd. People crowded along the sides. Burly merchants, mothers with children, all chanting, *Jevaithi, Jevaithi.*

Jevaithi smiled and waved. She stopped to admire a young mother's baby, stroking the little head with hair soft as fur. A young man—the woman's older son?—stood, red-faced, slaving over a vat of steaming oil. Whatever he sold, the smell made her mouth water.

"Rider Cornatan, I'd like to have some of what he's cooking."

"It's saltmeat," he hissed at her shoulder. "You can't eat that, Your Highness."

"Why not?" She breathed the delicious scent that rose from the pot. The young man blushed furiously. He was perhaps only a few years older than her. Did he see her feather?

"Yes, I will have some," Jevaithi said in a clear voice.

The man scrambled to ladle a spoonful of steaming meat into a bag. Jevaithi reached forward, but a Knight had already taken the bag.

"With the compliments of my family, Your Highness."

"No, I won't have that. I'm a decent person. Pay him, Rider Cornatan."

He did. Unfortunately, Jevaithi couldn't see the look on his face.

The Knight held the bag for her while she slipped the glove off her left hand to pick up a piece of meat.

"Do you want some?" she asked him.

His face radiated distaste. "Your Highness, you may want to be careful what you eat. This is the Outer City, and it's not as clean as—"

She put the meat in her mouth. It was very salty and crispy, but hot and spicy. The taste exploded on her tongue. The taste of freedom.

"I shall be just fine." Anything that was this salty couldn't possibly be contaminated anyway.

By the time the group had made their way across the chaos of the festival grounds, the bag was empty. She had eaten half of it, and offered the other half to children along the way. Those children now followed the parade, along with hundreds of other people. Some came up offering her presents. A young merchant boy ran up to her and gave her a shawl made of thin silk. It was a beautiful thing, and he insisted that she keep it and that he didn't want to be paid for it. If his mother, who wove the silk, heard that the queen was wearing her work, the light might return to her eyes.

Jevaithi found it hard to keep her composure. These people loved her more than she had loved them. These were her people, not the Knights.

They arrived at the eagle pens.

Hemmed in by a frame of temporary metal fencing stood at least fifty eagles, magnificent creatures with gleaming white feathered heads, bright-yellow beaks and strong tawny wings. The beasts fidgeted and flapped, no doubt sensing the tension and activity around them. Each eagle was being attended by its young Knight. Most of them were Apprentices, boys of between fourteen and seventeen years of age. As old as she was. What would it be like, to fly on the back of an eagle? Did girls ever do that? They should have female Knights. Enough women in the city were infertile and lived as grumpy old maids. She should propose that, the first time she attended the Knight's Council. That would get those old men talking.

To the left of the pens was the official starting point, a square arena outlined by red paint in the snow.

Someone had made a viewing stand out of pieces of fencing. There were two benches, covered by bearskins and even a frame for a canopy, in case of snow.

This was where Rider Cornatan led her. Jevaithi felt embarrassed. Someone had made this just for her? She sat down, wrapping the furs around her legs. The Knights stood at attention. Rider Cornatan remained standing next to her.

A cheer went up around the pen. Eagles flapped and squawked, disturbed by the noise, which prompted their handlers to pull on their reins while ducking out of the way of flapping wings.

"What are the rules for the race?" she asked the Knight guide.

He bowed. "The contestants had a preliminary race the day before yesterday." She wished he would stand up straight and look at her. "The Knights you see here are the ones who came through that selection, the finest in the land. They fly in teams of two where they have to pass a message cylinder between them twelve times, and be the first team back here. If they drop the cylinder, they're out of the race. If they make an improper change, they're out as well. They're flying a distance of twenty miles. Part of it will be over ocean and dangerous terrain—"

A blast from a horn drowned out his words.

Something was happening in the pens. Each young Knight had untied his eagle and was leading his bird forward by the reins. Some birds walked stately, others found it necessary to snap and hiss at their neighbours. Silver coins glistened on the birds' harnesses. Bells tinkled on the reins. One Knight had painted gold spots on the bird's beak.

Jevaithi had been to the eyrie a few times, but she had never seen the birds so magnificently attired. Each Knight was dressed in a thick short-hair cloak and immaculate red tunic. They had keen eyes and proud faces, the sons of the city's nobles.

As they filed past, and lined up in the starting area, a young man amongst them drew Jevaithi's attention. He stood straight-backed and proud. His glossy black hair was tied in a plait. He wore no jewellery, unlike most other Apprentices—nothing that wasn't part of the uniform. His hands were red and rough from riding; his gaze was serious. He didn't wave at parents or wink at girls.

As she watched, a single strand of golden light snaked over his right leg.

She realised with a shock. *He's Imperfect.* How was that possible? All her life, she'd been told Imperfect children were killed after birth.

And there he was, looking at her, as if he knew . . . or felt . . . or saw what she hid, just like she saw what he was trying to hide.

The Knight next to her was still explaining the rules, but his words slid past her.

The Apprentice was about her age, teamed up with a boy taller and broader than him but much coarser in features, although this boy also stared at her, and at Rider Cornatan. Rider Cornatan even winked at him.

An older Knight blew a whistle. All the riders mounted their birds. Some put their foot in the stirrup and swung the other leg over. Some, like the Imperfect Apprentice, let their eagles crouch first. He definitely had only one leg, although it was cleverly concealed by a boot on the end of what she presumed was a wooden peg. Now that she was aware of it, she noticed the golden glow around his leg more clearly. Clever. Even his trouser leg stood up as if there was a proper lower limb inside. No one would notice. No one but her.

A second whistle sounded. Eagles poised, their wings spread. The crowd grew quiet. The Knights gripped their reins. The Imperfect rider glanced at her. Jevaithi couldn't contain a smile. He met her eyes squarely. He had heavy eyebrows, high cheekbones and full lips. His skin was pale with a tinge of red excitement. One corner of his mouth curled up, leaving a dimple in his cheek.

Jevaithi slid her hand up to her throat, pulling the feather out from under her cloak, but at that moment, there was another blast of the horn and the Knights were off with a flurry of flapping wings.

"It will be a while before they return," Rider Cornatan said, while Jevaithi looked after the eagle silhouettes which were fast getting smaller. "We could meet some of the Senior Knights."

"Let them come here," she said. "I'll wait."

She'd wait however long was necessary to see that young man return.

Rider Cornatan raised his eyebrows.

"If I am to choose a Queen's Champion as you said, I'd better watch the riders."

Rider Cornatan seemed happy with that response. She guessed it made protecting her easier for him. He sat down next to her, and said in a low voice, "On the subject of the Queen's Champion, Your Highness, I should point out to you which Apprentice has the highest points score."

"You already know that? Before the race has even finished? That's not how it should be done. I read the rules and it says the Queen or her representative can choose from all participants, as long as they completed the race and made all twelve changes. It is the tradition that the Champion is chosen from the first five, although my mother chose a different Apprentice on at least one occasion. The Queen's Champion is about fairness and skill."

He gave her a sharp glance, opened his mouth, but closed it again. "Yes, that it true, Your Highness. You read the books well."

"I thought I had better check the rules for what I'm supposed to be choosing." And it was not as if she had so much else to do.

She leaned back in her seat in mock-relaxed fashion. Her heart was hammering in her chest. She'd been openly defying and needling him since she left her tower room. Would he punish her when they returned?

A wry smile played over Rider Cornatan's mouth, also not a pleasant expression. "Pardon me for taking liberties, Your Highness. I should have said I can give you some good suggestions."

Oh, indeed. "Go ahead, and give me the suggestions, then. I don't know any of these Apprentices by name."

So she listened to a string of middle-ranked Knights extolling the virtues of the young Apprentices who had just gone out to race. The name of the Imperfect boy was Isandor, and he was a native of the Outer City. Even the name made her shiver. She very much wanted to ask about him, but she didn't, and the Knights volunteered little information. Her mother had always said, *If you want something that's not in your power to have, keep quiet about it until it is*. Several times, she found the question on her tongue, but one glance at Rider Cornatan stopped her.

She didn't want to bring the Apprentice in danger with her questioning, but she *had* to speak to him. No one, not even her mother, had mentioned that there were other Imperfects.

CHAPTER 16

ISANDOR HELD the reins tight and gazed at his destination over the bobbing head of the eagle. Even though he wore goggles and a facemask, his face was numb from the cold. There was no sun today, only a mass of dull white clouds. Darker clouds on the horizon promised more snow.

Isandor and Carro led a group of eagles which had detached from the main body of competitors about the halfway mark. One Apprentice had since dropped the cylinder in the frigid waters of the sea, disqualifying his team. Now they were on the home leg, the cylinder had passed from Isandor to Carro and back ten times. They still had two changes to make.

The other riders, led by Jono and Caman, were uncomfortably close. Carro wasn't flying well. He was using the reins too much to balance. He'd barely said anything since they got up this morning; he'd looked tired but wouldn't answer questions about what he'd done last night.

Carro's eagle was fidgety and snappy, probably tired, too. What had Carro been doing? Yesterday was meant to have been a rest day.

They had to win; they just *had* to. The winners would be presented to the Queen, and her gaze still burned in Isandor's mind. *Those* eyes were true royal blue. Her smile was more beautiful than he had ever seen.

The second last exchange of the cylinder was due. A Knight on a lazily circling eagle patrolled the change point. Isandor steered his eagle into a circle and swung the cylinder. It flew through the air, catching the light. Carro caught it neatly. He grinned, although his face was hard with fatigue.

"Now, come on!" Isandor yelled and pulled the eagle out of the spin. "We've almost done it."

Jono and Caman were now circling the change point, only a few wing beats behind, but Isandor could already see the festival grounds, and on the edge, the stands where the Queen was waiting.

Come on, come on, come on.

He saw her cheering—no not cheering, that was too undignified for a Queen—but clapping. He saw himself walking up to her to receive his medal as Queen's Champion.

No, he'd better keep his mind on the job. The Senior Knights always decided who would become Champion anyway, and they always chose a boy from the noble families.

Stop daydreaming. Do you know how much power one fifteen-year-old girl has over an age-old institute of men? Tandor's words came to haunt him.

The last change point. He brought his eagle into a tight spin so it circled Carro's.

Carro raised himself in the saddle. He was shivering, Isandor could see that even from his position. He lifted his arm and threw the cylinder. It flipped through the air, catching the light.

Short.

Isandor reached as far as he could, but his hand grasped thin air.

No.

For one horrible moment he stared at the twirling cylinder plummeting towards the gleaming ocean and the ice floes.

No.

Another moment and he had pulled the reins hard. The eagle screeched protest, but it pulled in its wings and dived. It went hurtling towards the ground. Isandor's stomach lurched. Freezing air cut into his face as the ground came up fast. His vision blurred from his watering eyes, but he focused on the tumbling cylinder.

Down, down, faster, faster.

He plummeted past the Knight who patrolled the change point. The man yelled out but Isandor couldn't make out the words.

He was not going to make it. *He was not going to make it.* The eagle couldn't dive fast enough.

Stop, stop, stop!

Golden light snaked out of the air. It wrapped around his hands, cocooned the eagle and caught the falling cylinder, freezing it in mid-air. Just a moment, and then Isandor had reached it and clasped his hand around the cold metal. A sharp pull of the reins brought the eagle soaring into the air again, its immense wings flapping. It gave a piercing cry.

Isandor stood in the saddle, balling his fist around the cylinder.

Yes, yes, yes!

"By the skylights, how did you do that, Isandor?" Carro shouted from his beast. His eyes were wide, pleading almost, scared. His lips were blue with cold and he shivered worse than ever. Isandor on the other hand, was hot and glowing from his victory.

Isandor smiled, but felt uneasy. Carro couldn't see icefire. But one day, Tandor said someone *would* see it.

"Never mind that, I've got it," he shouted at Carro, trying to sound careless. "Just don't fall off until we get there, all right?"

Carro returned a sharp look, and something flickered over his face. Worry?

Isandor didn't like to think about it. He had to concentrate, or he would fall off himself, as shivers overtook him.

The eagle flew lower, spread its wings and stretched out its yellow feet. It landed in the snow with a thump. People were cheering, but he barely heard it. The truth hit him hard. He had just used icefire to win the race, not just to bend it to hide his missing leg, but *use it* to his advantage. The old king used to do that, the old king, who had been the worst murderer the southern land had ever known.

In his mind, he heard Tandor's voice. *The Thillei blood is strong in you.*

No, he didn't want this. He wanted to be a good Knight.

The crowd had swelled since the start of the race. People were clapping and cheering. Isandor spotted his uncle in the crowd, waving wildly. He waved back, but felt sick. He had failed them all.

Isandor let himself slide from the saddle, clutching the cylinder against his chest. His heart was still going at a crazy rate. There was no escape. The bird handlers were hustling him and Carro out of the arena to the holding pens, where young boys threw steaming hunks of meat at the birds. He didn't dare look at his friend. Carro had the right to be angry. They'd lose all their points. Isandor didn't even want to contemplate what the Knights would do to him when he got back to the eyrie later today. Carro would never forgive him.

The crowd was yelling his name, and clapping and whistling and cheering. His eagle held its meat under a claw, but was hissing at the crowd, its wings spread. Isandor rubbed its head, burrowing his fingers in the feathers down to the hot skin. It was said that the animals were created through icefire and could feel its presence, and attached closely to those riders who could wield it. That's what he was: a dangerous freak.

"Apprentice Isandor?"

A Senior Knight was standing behind him.

"Sir." Isandor bowed, his heart thudding. This was it.

"Come with me," the man said.

Isandor followed him through the cheering crowd. He wished the people would shut up. There was nothing to cheer about. Hands were touching his arms, clapping his shoulder. Snatches of conversation drifted on the air.

". . . Did you see that?"

"What about the other one?"

". . . Queen is going to make him the Champion."

Oh yes, one of the boys would be the Queen's Champion, probably Jono, since he had the right family heritage. But first, his punishment, and the citizens of the Outer City loved that as much as they loved their blood sports.

They stopped at the base of the stand. The guards moved aside, giving Isandor a view of the Queen's legs, wrapped in thick bear furs. He bowed, unable to face pity in her eyes. "Your Highness."

The furs moved aside. The feet in dainty boots descended the steps. Soft boots and a cloak of fur white as snow. He bowed more deeply.

"Do not be shy," the Queen said. "Look me in the eye, Champion."

Champion? His heart missed a beat. He blurted out, "That can't be right."

Her laugh sounded like the tinkling of crystal. "Oh, you Knights are priceless. Don't be so humble. You won fairly. I have the honour of choosing the Queen's Champion, and I have chosen."

Next to her, the reedy man Isandor recognised as Supreme Rider Cornatan sniffed, his lips pressed together in a thin line. Oh no, *he* didn't think Isandor deserved to be Queen's Champion.

"I don't deserve the honour." *I cheated.* He let his head droop again.

A soft glove entered his vision and pushed his chin up. A strand of golden light seeped over her arm and into his face. He exploded in warmth.

Isandor looked into those dark blue eyes, and found himself drowning in her gaze. Her face was pale, her lips full and marked with just a touch of red paint. Long eyelashes were dusted with silver. She blinked.

Isandor had to look away. His gaze slid down her soft, white-skinned neck to the elaborately-worked fastening of her cloak. She wore a crude strip of leather around her neck. The shaft of a gull's tail feather poked just above the neckline of the cloak.

Somewhere at the edge of his hearing, over the roaring of blood in his ears, she said, "You do deserve it, Isandor. *I* wish to declare you my champion. It is *my* title, and *I* choose whom I see fit."

The barbs in that remark weren't intended for him.

Again he heard Tandor's words. *How much power do you think a fifteen-year-old girl has over an age-old institute of men?*

At this very moment, she had all the power in the world over him.

A junior Knight approached him with a box that contained the medal and Isandor was forced to step back from the stand to make room for the man. The Queen's hand fell back from his cheek, severing the warmth between them. The Knight hung the medal around Isandor's neck, but Isandor only had eyes for the Queen and how she kept her right hand in her pocket. He knew the signs. She didn't give him the medal herself, because she couldn't. She had only one hand.

Supreme Rider Cornatan came to stand next to her. "Your High-ness, there are some jugglers who would be honoured if you could watch their act."

"Certainly," she said, still looking at Isandor.

She took Rider Cornatan's proffered arm and let him lead her away, but even while she disappeared amongst the Knight guards, she kept looking at Isandor. Her eyes were intense, and pleading.

Isandor stood there, numbed, barely aware that the Junior Knight was speaking to him. "As winner of the race you will also get the honour of making the first kill of the hunting season. That ceremony will be held this afternoon in this arena. Be here on time so we can instruct you."

Isandor swallowed away that embarrassing, glowing feeling and met the man's eyes, registering what he had said. "Don't worry. I used to work in a butchery. I know how to kill a Legless Lion."

"Be there on time," the Knight repeated.

He turned away, leaving Isandor alone amongst the Senior Knights, some of whom congratulated him with stiff nods.

Someone said behind him, "Well, I guess you don't need to have a drink with me anymore, now you have all these new admirers."

It was Carro, with more bitterness on his face than Isandor had ever seen.

Should I warn him, should I not warn him, should I warn him?

Carro glared at Isandor who was receiving yet more congratulations from random patrons in the meltery. The man, someone Isandor must know from the butchery, clapped a meaty hand on his shoulder.

They had advanced barely a few steps into the main room. The door was still open, as more patrons followed, couldn't get in and then wondered what the hold-up was.

Carro jammed his hands in his pockets. He was tired.

Wan light slanted into the dimness, lighting up misty sections of heavy and smoke-tinged air.

The beefy man now left, towards the exit.

"Come on," Carro urged, pulling at Isandor's cloak. "You said we'd have a drink."

He dragged back a chair.

Seriously, if one more person was going to congratulate Isandor, he was going to scream. What about him? Had he not won the race together with Isandor?

But if it had been up to me, we'd have been disqualified.

Carro slumped into the chair, clenching his jaws.

Isandor paid for two glasses of bloodwine from a passing waitress and sank down opposite him, plonking the glasses down. He leaned both his elbows on the table and sighed. His medal dangled from his chest, glittering in the smoky light.

"Oh, yeah, life as a champion is so hard," Carro said and knew he sounded petulant.

Isandor looked up, meeting his eyes squarely. It wasn't anger Carro saw in that blue gaze, but something else Carro couldn't place. It chilled him.

"Carro, I didn't ask for any of this. You can have this medal if it makes you feel any better."

A moment of regret passed between them. Carro knew he was acting like a jealous toddler, but he could not, he just could not . . .

"Carro, we are friends, right?" Isandor said.

"Yes."

Friends, as long as Carro didn't tell Rider Cornatan what Isandor was, as long as no one found out. Friends, as long as it was appropriate for a Learner Knight to associate with an Apprentice, and an Imperfect one at that. Yet Carro had taken off his new badge, because he didn't want any talk in the dormitory about being favoured by the Senior Knights. He wanted to have *earned* his promotion.

"You are my friend. You can tell me what worries you," Isandor said.

"Nothing worries me."

Only that he had awoken late this morning, sweating and with his bedding tangled around his legs, plagued by a nightmare: Korinne and her father, Rider Cornatan's advisor, at his father's doorstep.

We need to talk business with you.

As the maid let them in, Korinne gave him a sly look from under her curled eyelashes, and placed her hand on her swollen stomach.

Payment. They wanted payment for his few moments of stupidity, and he wasn't rich, and his father wasn't rich, neither of them *wanted* a child, and as soon as Korinne and her father were out the door, his father was going to kill him.

What were you thinking, stupid oaf of a son of mine!

Carro wiped sweat from his upper lip. What was he thinking, indeed? It had been a setup from the beginning. She hadn't enjoyed it. He had, but he had known, even in his drunken stupor, that someone had ordered her to submit to him. Who was playing games with him?

And Isandor sat there looking at him with genuine worry in his eyes. Isandor, who had everything he wanted. His natural ability to fly well, his ability to make people listen, his innocence, and true innocent love. Oh no, Carro hadn't missed the look that passed between his friend and Jevaithi.

And that, he knew, was the root of it all.

You're jealous, Carro, simple as that.

Isandor slammed his glass down. He seemed to have taken to the drink just as badly as Carro had.

"You know," Carro said, swallowing discomfort. "You know I wish it was still last year?"

"Why?" Isandor asked, and then his face cleared. "Did she refuse you again?"

The truth was on Carro's tongue. *Get out before I can no longer hide you. It's the only way I can protect you.* He licked his lips.

The meltery door opened, letting in flash of wan light. People scrambled aside. Rider Cornatan had come in. The Supreme Rider looked around, spotted Carro and gestured.

Panic rising in him, Carro met his friend's eyes.

Rider Cornatan is after Imperfects. I don't know what he wants, but it scares me.

Someone is trying to buy me, and I don't know how long I can resist.

Treasure your virginity for as long as you can. Sex hurts and corrupts.

But he said none of those words. "Sorry, have to go."

"Me, too." Isandor rose from the table. His face looked drawn.

He faced Carro wordlessly, nodded stiffly as if greeting another Knight and left. By the skylights, was that what their friendship had become?

Carro drank the last of the hot liquid and set his empty cup on the table, clinging onto its lingering warmth. As he rose and crossed the meltery's room, his knees turned weak with fear. It occurred to him that, instead of his father, he now bowed to Rider Cornatan, who treated him far better, on the surface at least. But why? What did Rider Cornatan expect in return?

Carro met his leader in the middle of the meltery room.

"Good, boy." Rider Cornatan put his hand on Carro's shoulder and squeezed it briefly.

Together, they walked to the far end of the meltery's room, where there were private alcoves against the perimeter wall.

As they settled in an alcove, Carro hardly dared meet the Supreme Rider's eyes.

People on the main floor of the meltery pretended to ignore them, but Carro didn't miss the furtive looks out of corners of eyes. Jono had been sitting at a table somewhere, raising his eyebrows as Carro walked past in the company of Rider Cornatan resplendent in his full uniform and riding harness.

"The young boy you brought yesterday woke up this morning," Rider Cornatan said.

"Oh?" Carro didn't know what else to say, but obviously there would be something of great meaning following this statement, otherwise Rider Cornatan wouldn't have insisted on seeing him here in this very public meltery.

"He said that when you came out of the Brotherhood building a blue man attacked you and the other Knights."

"I can't tell. I didn't see anyone. I used the staff as you said I should, but I saw nothing. I just grabbed the boy as soon as I could."

"Yes, you did well. But, according to you, the two Knights were killed by something that snapped their necks. Something you didn't—or couldn't—see."

The voice quivered with meaning. Intense blue eyes met his.

"You mean a servitor?" His voice was barely more than a whisper.

A chill crept over his back. He should have realised it earlier.

"That's what I mean, indeed," Rider Cornatan said. "The Brothers have confirmed that they have the Knights' bodies, but they're hesitant to cooperate with our investigation. I think they know more than they're willing to say."

"But how can servitors exist?" His books had spoken of the slave-servants of the old king. They had no will, and did everything their master wanted. They could not be killed except when their master died.

"There is only one way: there has to be a Thilleian in the Outer City. One who is strong and has the capability to make servitors."

Isandor. Carro's heart jumped.

Isandor runs through the street, holding out a box. "For you, Carro. It's your birthday."

Carro stares. He doesn't have birthdays. His father made him work this morning. In the warehouse. No heating. No one said anything about a birthday at breakfast.

He takes the box. Opens it up and finds a book inside, a fat volume with a leather cover and thick, yellow pages. Doesn't know what to say. He's turning eleven today. "You shouldn't do that, Isandor."

"Why not? You're my friend."

Embarrassed, by someone who has so much less than he.

"But anyone . . ." Carro swallowed, hoping Rider Cornatan wouldn't notice his lapses in attention. ". . . any sorcerer who can make a servitor is very powerful." He didn't think Isandor could do that, but what did he know? Maybe he could.

"We must find this person." Rider Cornatan's eyes fixed his with uncomfortable intensity.

Carro looked down at his empty cup, bloodwine churning in his stomach. Once it came out that he had been friends with Isandor, what would that mean for him? Back to his father's warehouse? Death by accountancy?

Not that. Never that. He'd kill himself first.

"Did you enjoy last night?" Rider Cornatan's voice sounded far off.

Heat crept into Carro's cheeks. "Yes, I did."

"There were some elite young Knights invited, a special team of mine. Did you have a chance to have a word with Farey?"

The olive-skinned Knight who had been staring at him in a most embarrassing way.

"I did. We didn't say much—"

"Farey never says much. I've asked him to keep an eye on you. He leads a group of elite hunters. They scout out rogues that flee the city and spies to our lands. I was thinking that with your flying skills, you could possibly join them."

"Hunters?" They were special units of highly trained men. Jobs that attracted whispers and rumours.

Rider Cornatan drank. He seemed to be enjoying himself. "I think you could make a valuable contribution to our search teams. I wouldn't rule out rapid promotions. You, boy, are destined to do well."

Carro didn't think so.

"No, don't look like that. I think it's time you showed leadership. It's one thing to tag along with a group of others, but you need to learn how to give commands."

He? Give commands?

"I notice you're not wearing your Learner's badge."

"I . . ." Carro stammered. "Some of the Apprentices will tease me. They're already saying that I have no right to be here."

"Ha—and you let them say that to your face?"

Carro shrugged. What else could he do? "Apprentices are not allowed to fight. I've already been punished too much for that. Fighting will just make the mocking worse."

Rider Cornatan put a hand under his chin and forced him to look up. "Boy, take it from me: men never mock those they fear. I am giving you the means to hold power over your peers. You are a Learner. You outrank them. They should fear you."

"But . . ."

"If they don't fear you, punish them for their insolence, and punish them hard. I can assure you: if you do it well, you only need to do so once."

"I'm not sure I—"

"Yes, you could do it. Tell me, you don't think you *deserve* being bullied by these cowardly boys?"

Bullied? How about raped? "No, but—"

"There you go. You don't deserve it. Those boys are insulting you. You are worth more than ten of them. You know that, Carro. Promise me you will do the worst you can imagine to anyone who defies your orders."

Carro nodded, his cheeks glowing.

The man was the opposite of his father, giving him compliments where he deserved none.

"You're very quiet today, boy."

"I'm . . . a bit tired."

Rider Cornatan laughed. "You would be. By the way, Korinne was most insistent in asking if you were available to come again tonight."

Korinne, asking for him. Offering herself to him without being asked. Did she like him after all?

He nodded again. "I will be there."

"Very well, boy. That's the sort of thing I like to hear. Lift your chin and make sure *none* of your peers tell you what to do. You obey your superiors, and no one else. You understand that?"

"Yes, Sir."

Rider Cornatan hesitated, as if he wanted to say something else, but thought better of it.

CHAPTER 17

TANDOR KNELT in the snow in the shade of the alley, tugged off his glove with his pincer claw and put his hand flat on the hard, icy ground. In the feeble blue light of not-quite dawn, the area around his fingers glowed with a few specks of gold before winking out.

Yes, Ruko had come this way. The trail was half a day old at least, but Ruko had been here.

There were footsteps behind him, and voices of women. Tandor rose quickly and pressed himself to the wall on one side of the alley. The women walked past, casting Tandor strange looks that said, *What is he doing here at this time of day?*

Tandor waited until the women had disappeared from view and continued down the alley, kneeling and touching the snow. With each step he took, and each glance at the brightening sky, his despair grew.

Ruko was in trouble somewhere, or he would have returned long ago. It meant that someone out here could see Ruko and had a means of injuring him.

To add to that, picking up Ruko's trail became ever harder with the increasing strength of icefire.

Golden strands now frequently crackled through the air, escaped from the matrix that normally held its power.

The breeze carried the sounds of cheers, shouting and music. At the festival grounds, the common folk were watching the races. As yet they were blissfully ignorant of the increased level of icefire, but that wouldn't remain so. The Heart was coming into its full power soon, and he had recruited not a single servitor to help him channel that raw energy. There were limits to how much icefire the citizens of the City of Glass could stand without becoming ill.

Ruko!

A flutter of icefire responded, the tiniest of pulses.

Ruko?

The wind sighed through the alley, an exhaled breath of pain. The connection was weak. Ruko was injured and he was close.

The sound of children's voices drifted from the other side of a high wall at his back. Tandor couldn't make out the words, but the conversation held an edge of tenseness, the voices curious, more than just children at play.

He crept along the wall until he came to a gate, which judging by the amount of snow piled up on the ground, was always open. It led into a walled courtyard surrounded on three sides by a building with a columned façade. Made of mountain marble, the building was ancient, because it was a long time since any marble had been brought from the border with Arania. It was also a long time since anyone had used the inscriptions which graced the building's façade. Tandor remembered learning the formulae by heart. How to calculate the power of icefire at different points from its source. How to predict how many people could handle a certain amount of icefire, how to calculate how far the temperature would drop with increased power. How to convert icefire into heat and light. How he had hated those lessons with his mother.

A door opened in the rightmost wing of the building. A bearded man dressed in black came out, leading a group of children across the courtyard. Some were crying, some held the man's hand.

The Brotherhood of the Light was named not after the sun, but after the power of the Heart.

On the far side of the courtyard, two men came into view, heaving a large object between them that looked suspiciously like a body covered with cloth. There was another one already on the ground.

A little boy came out of a door onto the veranda, but was ordered back inside with a sharp command. Both brothers in black stood silent, balling their hands against their chests. One of the men went inside, but the other hesitated and glanced at a heap of snow against the courtyard's wall. Icefire leapt from the air, a single strand which forked like lightning. It shattered into golden diamonds, which rained down onto the snow mound.

The young man didn't react to the light spectacle, but Tandor had no illusion that he could see it in some form. The Brothers of the Light had been the old king's spiritual order. Further back in history, the order had served as a handy depository for idle noble sons, including princes with minor claims on the throne. As such, many of its current members would have traces of Thillei blood. This Brother's Thilleian blood had located Ruko.

Bless the boy. Weak and injured as he obviously was, he'd gone and buried himself under the snow. Now all Tandor needed to do was wait until the courtyard was empty.

Loriane shut the door to the inner chamber of the limpet behind her. She crossed to the table and set down her tray.

Myra sat cross-legged on the mat in front of the stove. The fierce glow from the fire gilded the folds of the girl's thin nightgown.

She didn't look up or open her eyes. Her hands on her knees, she sat there, counting and breathing slowly.

Loriane sat down and watched for a while. Maybe there was hope yet to prepare her for the birth. Her spot-bleeding had stopped overnight. Loriane might have a few days to teach the girl some relax-ation routines.

She felt guilty about not being able to help at the festival anymore, but if she was honest with herself, Loriane didn't mind losing out on treating drunken louts.

Myra opened her eyes. "Was that better?"

"Much better," Loriane said. "Now if you can take that off, I can examine you, before Tandor comes back."

"Did he say where he was going?"

"No." If she sounded snippy, she meant it. "Does he think I have nothing to do but pamper him?"

"Tandor doesn't pamper—"

"What do you know?" Again, too angry. Loriane looked away, ashamed to have let herself go.

"I'm worried about him," she said to the room in general. "He comes here, he does whatever he wants. He makes promises. He disappears."

"Does he keep his promises?" A lot of anxiety hung in the girl's question. What had Tandor promised her?

"Usually." Loriane heaved a sigh. "Come, lie down here. After that we better make sure the washing is dry and we have all those oils poured in jars."

"I didn't think being a midwife was so much work." Myra slipped off her nightgown and lay down on the couch as Loriane indicated.

"Oh, preparing the medicines is just a small part of the job. You don't even know about the times I get called out in the middle of the night and have to stay all of the next day as well."

She grabbed her basket of supplies and kneeled awkwardly. Her own belly was getting in the way of this job. She rummaged through and then realised the bottle of disinfecting oil was empty. By the skylights. She had more, but she had left it in the tent at the festival grounds.

"All right, this will have to wait."

The girl stared at the basket, her eyes wide. "What were you going to do?"

Clearly, no one had ever examined her. By the skylights, had anyone looked after this girl? Did the people in Bordertown just let women have their children—and die giving birth—like beasts?

She probed the girl's belly. The womb tensed up under her touch, hard as rock.

Myra gasped. "It hurts, it hurts."

"Yes," Loriane said and withdrew. "You know what I think? I think your pains have already started."

"I've . . . I've been having cramps all day."

"That will be it."

"Is that all?" She sounded too relieved.

"No, it's not." Loriane rose. She really needed that disinfectant so she could examine Myra inside.

Myra pushed herself up. She was trembling when she reached for her gown and hesitated putting it on. "Or do you want me to leave it off?"

"We're not getting to that stage so soon. That will be a while yet. You better do some more of those exercises I gave you."

Myra nodded and wriggled back onto the mat, crossed her legs and went on with the breathing exercises.

Loriane studied the girl's shape. The weight in her belly restricted movement of her spine, which she held at an uncomfortable curve. Her shoulders and hips were narrow, with not a scrap of meat on them. Loriane hoped, for all she was worth, that the father of the child was not too broad or big-boned. Myra was heavy for her thin frame, and a gentle start to the process like this often meant a protracted and painful birth, especially in young girls.

"Loriane, how many children have you had?"

"This is my tenth."

"Ten?" A stunned silence. "I don't know any woman at Bordertown who has had that many."

And lived to tell the tale, Loriane added in her mind.

"When is your child going to be born?"

"Soon." *Should have been a few days ago.*

Another short silence.

"I've heard that women in the City of Glass . . . sell their children."

"Noblemen pay fertile women to have children for them if their wives aren't fertile. Many of them are barren."

"Why?"

"They say it's to do with icefire. It may not kill us as it does with the Chevakians, but many of us can't have children."

"Yes, icefire is strong here. I've never seen it like this before."

Loriane studied the girl's face. She had forgotten that one of the attributes of being Imperfect was the ability to see icefire. Even when Isandor was still at home, he had avoided this very subject. She couldn't see icefire, not a single scrap of it.

"Someone paid for your child?" Myra asked.

Loriane nodded. She thought again of Yanko, and how much she doubted the child was his, and how she had no idea whose it could be. She hadn't been with a man except Tandor a ten-night earlier, but just last night she had seen again how he lacked the necessary equipment to do the job.

She glanced at Myra. Was there a way Tandor could have gotten both Myra and herself pregnant, even though he was no longer a man?

Yeah, that was wishful thinking. *Admit it, woman, this man has got you by the scruff of the neck.*

Loriane rose, rubbing her belly.

Now if Tandor would come back, she could send him out to get some disinfectant from the tent at the festival grounds.

Unless . . . She eyed his traveller's chest, which he had left open next to the bed. His thermals lay over the chest's contents. Whenever he visited, she usually gave him a few things from her practice, to use on his travels. He might still have some disinfectant.

She lifted the woollen underwear from the chest. There were clothes, neatly folded, and stacks of old books. A basket made of tough leaves unknown to the southern land contained an assortment of stoppered flasks, jars and boxes with foreign labels. She rummaged through the selection, recognising—she thought—ointment for cuts, syrup for upset stomachs and pills, but the latter were labelled in a language she didn't recognise. By the skylights, he even had face paint and perfumes. Did men use such things in the northern lands? With Myra watching, the sight of a large jar with a wooden stopper that she had seen many times before made her blush. Tandor brought this jar to her bed at night. It contained a gel which, when rubbed across certain sensitive parts, made those parts much more sensitive and made certain activities more pleasurable. She tucked that one away quickly.

But no disinfectant.

Tucked in a deep corner of the chest stood a jar made of clear glass with an elaborately-carved stopper. Clearly an item from an apothecary. The jar was heavy. The glass felt *warm* under her hands. Pink fluid inside suspended a fist-sized sac of soft flesh. A bundle of tube-like veins sprouted from the top, waving gently in the eerie bath.

The sac *pulsed* of its own accord.

Loriane stared at it, feeling sick. The pink sac was a human heart.

What had Tandor said again? That Ruko was restored in return for something he had traded? His heart? The old king used to do things like that.

Myra gave a soft gasp. "That *hurt.*"

Her words broke Loriane from her transfixed state. With trembling hands, she put the jar with its hideous contents down and dropped the woollen tunics back into the chest.

Myra had stopped her exercises. Her eyes were wide. "It hurts, Loriane."

"Yes, it probably does. Breathe as I've shown you. Nothing more I can do. It's all up to you."

Where was Tandor? What was he doing with that horrible thing in his luggage?

It took a long time for the courtyard to empty. When the last boys and the Brothers had finally gone, he ran across and fell to his knees at the snow mound. Faint golden strands of icefire showed the shape of a man underneath the snow. Tandor dug into the biting cold, scrabbling chunks of iced-up snow off Ruko's body. He lay curled up like an over-sized sleeping child, and didn't move when Tandor uncovered him. He was no longer blue, but a sickly grey.

Ruko, Ruko!

The response was weak, a mere tugging at the edge of his senses. Tandor breathed deeply, stifling panic that crept up from his gut.

What, *just what*, had happened to him? Ruko was supposed to be invincible. A servitor. You couldn't kill them unless you killed the maker. And *not dead* was just about the only thing that could be said in favour of Ruko's condition.

Tandor pushed the snow off Ruko's legs and tried to drag him to his feet. The boy was too heavy for Tandor to lift, so he picked him up under the arms and dragged him across the courtyard.

Tandor stopped at the gate. Where to now? He could hardly walk back to Loriane's house like this, dragging a body that most people couldn't even see.

There was a narrow passageway between two houses opposite the gate. Tandor waited for the alley to empty of women returning from the markets before he dragged Ruko across. The recently-fallen snow had been trampled into a hard cover, on which industrious citizens had spread layers of sand. As Tandor dragged Ruko across, the heels of Ruko's boots scratched into the sand cover, leaving tracks of pristine white.

There was no time to grab sand from the bucket that stood next to the door of a nearby house—someone was coming.

Tandor cursed, sending a burst of icefire to spread the sand and cursed again when icefire lifted all the sand and blew it against the outer wall of the compound instead. Icefire was so strong already, and he was no closer to getting into the palace.

He dragged Ruko further into the alley, sending another burst of icefire to obscure the alley's entrance from curious eyes. Passersby would see something that repulsed them, and made them look away. A drunk man, a dead animal, a pile of rubbish, two lovers engaged in an indecent act.

Tandor proceeded further into the alley, past a side entrance to a house, past steps and a rubbish bin to where the passage ended. He tipped the snow off the bin's lid and fashioned it into a wall, grabbing icefire from the air to melt the snow enough so it would stick together. The structure didn't reach very high, but it hid Ruko from view in case someone could see past the illusion at the alley's entrance.

By the skylights, what now?

He eyed the wall at his back. It was ages since he'd sneaked around the streets of Tiverius as a young boy getting away from his mother, scaling walls and climbing onto roofs. It wasn't just that he'd become unaccustomed to moving around in such a way—he was a prince, by the skylights—but the roofs of the City of Glass were too steep, ice-covered and utterly unfamiliar. *A man's survival instinct is honed and primed by his youthful scampering away from obnoxious adults,* his weapons tutor used to say. And Tandor's experience was all in Tiverius. In Chevakia.

He was a blasted Chevakian.

He sat on the cold ground, his back against the wall, sheltering behind the rubbish bin. There was no way he could move until Ruko recovered, but he didn't have the time. Someone was on the loose who not only knew he had a servitor, but who knew how to deal with servitors as well.

He loosened the clasp of Ruko's cloak and wriggled one of the boy's hands from underneath.

Tell me what you know.

Ruko's hand lay grey and pale in his live one. At first, Tandor didn't see anything, but when he grabbed strands of icefire and poured them into Ruko's prone form, images came to his mind.

The courtyard, the building of the Brotherhood shrouded in darkness. An unclear fuzz as Ruko walked through the wall. The boys' dormitory. There was someone walking around inside: three silhouettes escaping into the corridor. Beds against both walls, one of them empty but still warm. The three figures had taken the imperfect boy.

Blurry outlines as Ruko walked back through the wall, just as the three figures ran across the courtyard. One of them carried the Imperfect boy rolled in a blanket.

Two or three steps, and Ruko had grabbed the first Knight. Snapped his neck like an icicle, then the other one. But the third one, a slight man younger than the others, held a metal rod in his hands and waved it in the air indiscriminately. The rod pulled and tore at the very fabric of Ruko's being. Searing pain, blinding light. As the image faded, and Ruko slumped in the snow, the third Knight called out to the Imperfect boy, who scrambled from underneath the corpse of the Knight who had carried him.

Tandor ripped himself from Ruko's memories. The horrid image tore at him with the realisation of what the young man held. A *sink*. The third Knight, the inexperienced young man, was of pure Pirosian blood. No one could harm him, and while he held the sink, it attracted icefire. *Someone* had read the king's notes on the properties of icefire. And was using them against him.

What now. *What now?* The only servitor he had lay incapacitated at his feet. The Heart was beating and someone in the palace had started silly experiments with icefire.

He needed servitors. Isandor, the boy, Myra, or . . . did he dare hope that he could get the only other free Imperfect? Not without Ruko.

Ruko, I need you to recover.

He grabbed as many strands of icefire as he could and poured them into Ruko's prone form. The golden light resisted him. Making a servitor was easier than healing one. When the flesh was live and fresh, it would meld with icefire under the hands of a skilled worker. When he took Ruko's heart, it had fallen into his hands freely. As long as it beat, Ruko would live. But Ruko was his own entity, linked with the world through the heart in its jar in Tandor's travel chest. The flesh of his body had become old and scarred and resisted icefire from any other sources than itself.

Now that so much had been siphoned off by the sink, Ruko

needed to absorb more icefire to recover. And his very skin was resisting it.

There was only one way.

Tandor felt at his belt for his dagger.

Ruko barely flinched when Tandor drew a sharp cut across the skin of his lower arm. He stuck the dagger into the flesh and lifted up a flap of skin. The dark blue muscle tissue underneath rimed with frost. A trickle of blood oozed out of the wound and froze on his fingers, a light blue coating of crystals. He dug the tips of the dagger amongst tissue, hitting bone. Bits of nerve and gristle slid under his fingers. All blue and lifeless. Was there any hope?

He made another cut, this time in Ruko's neck. After peeling away the skin, he found the jugular vein, pulsing faintly, a dirty brown-orange in colour where it should be gold and fat with icefire.

Tandor reached out with his claw hand. Icefire crackled through the air and sprang from his arm to Ruko's vein. It glowed bright yellow before the colour seeped into Ruko's body. More, more. Icefire flowed down his arm. Ruko's battered body drank it in like a sponge. Tandor fed him as much as he could gather. Ruko stirred, a muscle twitched, but his eyes remained closed. Tandor let go of the icefire he was still holding. Its pull had become too strong for him.

Tandor breathed relief, tears pricking in the corners of his eyes. He couldn't restrain himself and bent over the boy in a hug. Intense cold crept through him. Frost rimed his cloak where Ruko touched it. Ruko's icefire still felt weak, but at least Tandor could feel it now.

So much of his plan hinged on Ruko.

Tandor sat with his back against the wall, holding Ruko's hand.

From his position in the alley, he could see a narrow strip of the street outside the Brotherhood compound.

A sled pulled by a bear came past. A Knight sat at the driver's bench, and a few more in the back, probably here to pick up the bodies.

Not much later three Knights walked back through the street. They were all young, with Apprentice badges on their collars. Tandor didn't move, counting on his disguises to keep him from sight. The fourth Knight was a Learner, and he looked straight down the alley in spite of the guards Tandor had put in place. Tandor didn't doubt for a moment: this Knight had seen him. This young man was a purest-blood Pirosian, and could not be fooled by icefire tricks. He would have been the one carrying the sink.

Tandor pressed himself hard against the wall, not daring to move. The young Knight was quite tall and broad for his age, with a determined face and a head full of soft black curls. He hesitated, but walked on.

Heart thudding, Tandor ran to the corner of the alley and looked into the street. The Apprentice Knights had stopped at the gate to the Brotherhood compound. The Learner was pointing into the yard. But Tandor didn't doubt that the young man would be back.

He needed to draw attention away from Ruko and the best way to do that was to give the Knights a more urgent problem to deal with.

Tandor opened the lid to the rubbish bin. Wrinkling his nose in disgust, he lifted up a slab of frozen fish bones and draped it half on top of Ruko. There. Now it looked like a snow fox had been at the bin.

The Knights still stood at the gates to the Brotherhood compound. One of the Brothers was with them, black amongst grey and red. They were in heavy discussion, gesturing and pointing.

Tandor turned into the street and walked away from the Knights. He disliked turning his back on them, and it cost him all the effort in the world not to run. But dignified citizens who had just come out of their house and were on the way to the markets did not run.

As he reached the corner, Tandor glanced over his shoulder.

The young Knight with the sink also looked up. Their eyes met. Tandor froze. A strand of icefire crackled from him to the shining staff on the Knight's belt, accompanied by a sharp jolt of pain in Tandor's chest.

Tandor gasped.

The man yelled, "There!"

Still clutching his chest, Tandor ran.

CARRO STOPPED, panting, in the street. The Apprentices of his patrol came to a halt behind him.

"Where did he go?" Inran asked.

They had halted at the intersection of two streets. Patrons spilled out of the meltery on the corner, talking and laughing in groups. To the left the street led to the markets, but more people obscured a clear view. Ahead a troupe of jugglers was performing an act. To the right was another meltery which was so popular that people queued up to get in.

Some Junior Knights were in the queue, raising eyebrows at Carro, like they wanted to ask why he was working while everyone ought to be enjoying themselves, or why he seemed to be leading this group of Apprentices when he was only a Learner, and a very young one at that.

Well, some of us have to do the work. And he thought of the Knights he had met last night, the ones who had died on duty, and the ones who held their parties in Rider Cornatan's bathroom. None of them mingled with the drunken crowds.

"Have you seen a man running past?" he asked the Knight.

"Well, if you mean seen a man run after the girls, I've seen plenty." The Knight laughed.

His breath smelled of bloodwine, and he wasn't pronouncing his words properly. "Hey, boys, forget the work and join us."

Carro turned away, not trusting himself to shut up. He wanted to berate the Knight, but he was an Initiate, higher in rank than a Learner, and he didn't want to obtain the label arrogant upstart because, ultimately, the punishment that would earn him would not be worth it. That's what Rider Cornatan had said: punish the ones of lower rank, obey the ones of higher rank. Even if they were drunk.

So he gave a half-hearted salute and led his group towards the markets, past the jugglers. Spectators blocked the way. Carro told Inran to clear the path. People glanced over their shoulders and frowned at them, at him, an Outer City boy so obviously obeying the other side. Yes, the Outer City loved the Knights, but only as long as they stayed out of Outer City affairs.

"We're not going to find him in this crowd," Jono complained at his side. "Why don't we go back to the festival grounds? The ritual killing must be about to start."

"Because that is not our job," Carro said. "We need to find this man." The staff at his side was only just warming up after that jolt of icefire that had gone into it, but he could still feel the cold, burning through his trouser leg.

"He's gone," Caman said, not meeting Carro's eyes.

"Then we will start a search of all the streets surrounding the markets." Carro clenched his teeth.

Jono scowled.

Punish them, Rider Cornatan said, and Carro had threatened extra duties, but both boys still challenged him. Both Jono and Caman were taller than Carro. His former bullies. Rider Cornatan must have known that when he selected these Apprentices for the job. Maybe because Carro had mentioned Jono.

Punish them hard and you only need to punish them once. And clearly, Carro failed at the punishing department.

"Move now. Markets first. Quick, get on with it."

Carro waited until the other boys had gone first. When he walked past, Jono's eyes flashed a challenge.

Isandor hurried through the streets, every step putting more distance between himself and the Senior Knights at the festival grounds and Rider Cornatan in the meltery.

Everything was wrong, even Carro seemed to sense that. Carro knew he'd used icefire to stop the cylinder falling, even though he hadn't seen it. His friend's voice still echoed in his mind. *How did you do that?*

He could still see the expression in Carro's eyes when the Queen had declared him Champion, a look that frightened him.

Carro frightened him.

A change had come over his friend since his inexplicable promotion. He was harsher, and to be frank Isandor didn't think the promotion was because of something Carro had done. Someone was advancing him for a reason. In his limited experience, those types of reasons were rarely good. Carro had been evasive at the meltery, as if he held some sort of secret, and what secret would that be other than that he knew Isandor had used icefire?

Maybe Carro was advanced under the condition that he spilled all he knew about the Outer City, and its inhabitants, about Isandor, about the Brotherhood and the old books they had.

There was only one option. Tandor was right about one thing: he had been born like this and couldn't undo abilities the Knights considered illegal. But rather than try to hide it better as Tandor suggested, he had to get out of here. Beyond the edges of the southern land there was a whole world he had never seen. Chevakia, Arania, a world without icefire, where no one would see what he could do, where no one even knew that using icefire was illegal, because there was no icefire.

He would run, before the senior Knights heard about his imperfection.

But he must bring food, and his own clothes. Beyond the border, a Knight's uniform would no longer be a disguise or a reason for respect.

He opened the door to his mother's house and stepped into the warmth of the hall between the outer and inner shell. The sound of voices floated through the door. His mother would be seeing some sort of customer, maybe that stupid Yanko, and he preferred to have as little to do with that business as possible. He was sick of defending his mother's reputation. No, she wasn't a whore, but while she carried Yanko's child, Yanko was entitled to see her as often as he liked. So she was a whore, of a kind. He didn't understand how she could easily give away children of her own blood. The whole business made him feel queasy.

The stand in the short entranceway held his cloak, but all his other clothing was next to his old bed on the sleeping shelf inside the main room. How to get up there without attracting too many questions? *Where are you going? What are you doing with that bag?* He could already hear his mother's voice.

There was a noise behind him.

A figure entered the limpet's front door and a burst of icefire hissed through the air.

Isandor didn't think. He dropped his cloak, raised his arm, sending a bolt to meet it. The strands clashed in mid-air, exploding into a rain of golden diamonds.

"So, you have *learned* something," a languid voice said.

Tandor.

"What are you doing here?" Isandor breathed quickly. Tandor had actually *attacked* him with icefire. "Are you crazy?"

"No," Tandor said. "But I'm getting impatient with your stupidity."

He stepped into the entrance hall, letting the door fall shut behind him. His complete hand moved to his waist and grasped the hilt of his dagger.

Isandor backed away, but there was nowhere to go. Tandor blocked the only way to the outside door. Worse, Isandor only wore the bare minimum of arms required for proper uniform rules. No crossbow, no sword.

"What do you want from me?"

"Same thing as before. Your help."

"And you'll get that from me when I'm dead?"

"Not dead. I wouldn't kill you. You know that. When you help me, I will give you unprecedented powers. You will not know pain, or death. You will never know hunger or cold. You will have two healthy legs."

The hand that held the dagger was covered in blue-tinged rime. Icefire crackled over the delicate crystals.

"I don't want any powers. Leave me alone."

"The Knights will find out what you are, and you know what they will do to you." Tandor's voice was low and mocking. "There is nowhere to run for you except to me."

"You're crazy."

"Not crazy, I'm right. I'm finally righting all that has gone wrong for our land. No Imperfect should be murdered for his ability. No children should be left on the ice floes. I intend to put things right. I don't care what you think of me. I need you. You will come." Tandor's bloodshot eyes stared like a madman's. "I'm out of patience and out of time."

A net of icefire flowed from the metal of his pincer hand.

Isandor threw up an instinctive defence. Strands of icefire clashed in mid-air. Shatters exploded through the hall.

Isandor groped for the door handle behind his back. Tandor's net hovered closer. Isandor strained to hold it off, but his golden stream was weakening.

Tandor laughed. "Out of ideas, boy?"

The door to the central room opened. "Oh, I thought I heard you, Tandor—"

Isandor stumbled back, into the heat of the room. The net of icefire melted away.

"Isandor?" she gasped. "When did you come in? Oh my boy, congratulations. The Queen's Champion."

Isandor hugged her, noticing over her shoulder how Tandor slipped the dagger back into his belt and smiled. Was he his mother's lover? By the skylights, no. She had to be more intelligent than that.

He was shocked how tired his mother looked, and how pregnant. He had never before realised she was quite so old and small and *fragile*.

"I . . . thought I'd come to see how you are." By the skylights, how could he get all his things and leave the city now?

She stroked his hair. "I'm sorry, but your bed is occupied."

"It doesn't matter. You know I can't stay. I have to get back to the Knights. I just needed to get . . ."

No, he couldn't say that, and he couldn't flee either. Tandor wasn't after him in particular, but was after Imperfects, and Isandor knew one other Imperfect. He must warn her. And he couldn't leave his mother to deal with this twisted madman alone either.

"I was . . . I was just going. I need to be at the hunt ritual." His courage sank. He had fully expected not to attend. He'd watched his uncle kill an animal often enough to know that he didn't want to do it.

"Oh yes, of course." She smiled. "I'm proud of you, my Champion."

Tandor still glared.

"Will I see you at the arena?" Isandor took another step towards the door, and then another one. Tandor watched him, but didn't move. *He didn't dare*. So Tandor cared about his mother.

"Maybe." His mother's gaze met Tandor's. "I was waiting for you to come back. You could give me a hand. I need someone to go to the tent in the festival grounds to get . . ."

Isandor ran.

CHAPTER 19

THE DOOR CLANGED and Isandor was gone, leaving behind a tense silence.

"Champion?" Tandor asked.

"Yes, Isandor was made the Queen's Champion. Didn't you hear that?"

"The Queen's Champion." Wasn't that one of those silly titles?

Her grey eyes searched his face. "You could at least pretend to be proud for me. He flew very well."

"He shouldn't be with the Knights at all."

"Tandor, we've had that argument already. You can't change the boy's choices. I don't understand why you're always so nasty about him. I'm sure he would have liked knowing that you wanted him to survive."

Tandor bit his tongue. Giving her answers she wanted would only lose him valuable time.

"Loriane—"

"No, listen, I need your help."

"Loriane," Tandor protested. With all his being, he wanted to go after Isandor, but with all these people in the streets, there was no way he could do what he wanted. He searched Loriane's face for signs of what she had understood of their confrontation. As Pirosian, he knew she didn't see icefire, but she had to suspect something. She had seen him facing Isandor. By the skylights, since when had the boy become so strong? He had never received training.

And why had Ruko not turned up yet? He should have recovered by now.

"I need you to run up to the tent at the festival ground and get a few things. It really can't wait, Tandor. Myra's pains have started."

Tandor started to protest, "I can't go out there. The Knights—"

"Then can you look after her while I'm gone?"

"What—me?" By the skylights, no.

"I don't see anyone behind you."

"But Loriane—"

"Just sit here with her and give her water if she wants. Rub her back if you feel like being useful." She yanked her cloak from the hook on the wall.

"But what if the child—"

"It won't," Loriane said, her eyes intense. "Trust me. This is going to take a very long time. I'll be back soon."

Soon? Tandor took in a sharp breath. The dagger at his waist burned against his leg, a freezing burn from where Isandor's icefire had hit it.

"Please, Tandor. All I want for you is to sit with her so she's not alone."

Panic welled up in him. Did she know about his past experience? Loriane's eyes were pleading. "Please, Tandor, be my hero. I don't know who else to ask."

Oh, my Queen. He bent forward and brushed her lips with his.

"How long?"

"Not long. I'll be back before the hunting season ritual starts. I take it you want to watch it?"

"Um—yes."

Lies, lies, all such horrible lies. If only he told her he wanted to make her his queen after he had defeated the Knights, if only he showed her his grandfather's ring, the Thillei royal seal, if he told her why he needed Isandor and Myra, if he told her why he needed the crossbreed child she carried . . .

Loriane would hate him, he was sure of that. And that was why he loved her.

She tied up the cloak's fastenings over the bulge of her belly. "Well, then, the sooner I go, the sooner I'll be back."

A few steps and she was at the door, which Isandor had so recently slammed behind him.

Loriane, be safe.

If there were reasons out there for her not to be safe, he had created every single one of them.

She blew a kiss to him and was gone.

Tandor grabbed the door handle to the inner room door, gathering courage. He listened, but heard no noise. Heard in his mind the screams of a young woman. Fifteen years it had been, and he had never forgotten.

His hand strayed to the dagger at his side. Myra was Imperfect. What if he. . . ?

Another deep breath.

He could just wait here, outside the room, until Loriane came back.

No, he couldn't. Myra was young and frightened. Ontane would hear about it if he left her alone.

He pushed open the door. Stale warm air wafted out of the room.

Myra sat on a low stool next to the stove, leaning forward. She breathed heavily and didn't look up when he came in.

Tandor stood there, frozen, until her breathing slowed. She looked up.

"Don't just stand there. Shut the door." Her voice was husky.

Tandor did, although he would rather have bolted out. He took a few uncertain steps towards the couch. The dagger bumped against his leg.

As if she felt his thoughts, Myra's light blue eyes fixed on it.

He gathered courage. "Do you want me to—"

"Don't touch me." Her voice was sharp and full of distrust.

That nightgown wasn't very thick, and showed the tight curve of her belly. She was skinny, just like . . .

"I won't," he said, swallowing nausea.

He settled himself on the couch. Her sharp gaze followed him, even when her breathing became harsh.

Then she bent forward, uttering a low moan.

Tandor folded his arms over his chest, pulling them tight to stop his trembling. The metal rods of his arm bit into the bottom of his other arm.

Myra's moan became a cry.

Tandor cringed, clenching his teeth.

Stop it, be quiet.

In his mind, he went back to that dressing room, the smell of furs around him. The shrill sound of a woman screaming. *Keep your hands off me! Get out!* A blood curdling scream.

Footsteps, the clanging of a door, voices, male and female.

Someone else runs into the room.

A female voice yells, *Push*.

Another bloodcurdling scream.

Tandor stands there, frozen, dizzy, while the woman screams and howls. There seems no end to it—

"Can I have drink?"

Myra's voice shook Tandor out of his nightmare.

"Yes, sure." He rose and almost fell from dizziness. He must forget what had happened and avenge what the Knights had done to her and his family. He must complete his life's struggle. His mother and other surviving Thilleians relied on him. She had not survived the massacre in order for her son to be such a coward.

Lies, lies, lies. He told everyone he was southern, but his mother had given birth in the merchant's house in Tiverius. He'd never even been to the City of Glass until his mother took him when he was about ten.

He was Chevakian, and a coward.

There was a carafe of water on the table. He took the glass out of Myra's sweaty and trembling hand and filled it up. His hand also trembled, and he spilled some water, which he mopped up with a towel.

By the time he had finished, she was moaning again, leaning forward with her elbows on her knees. The thin nightgown didn't do much to hide her pale skin. Her right arm ended in a withered stump just above the wrist

Tandor felt for the dagger at his side. If only he had the courage, he could solve all his problems now. He gripped the hilt, studied her back for where to cut. The dagger slid out of its sheath. He lifted it, gathering strands of icefire around his hand. And hesitated.

If he took her heart, what would it do to her? Would it freeze her in a permanent state of agony, making her useless for his purpose? What about the child? It could be killed. If he waited a bit longer, he could have two servitors.

He hesitated. Too long.

Myra pushed herself back up. Quickly, Tandor slipped the dagger back into its sheath.

"Can I have that water now?"

He handed the glass into her good hand. She gulped deeply and gave it back to him.

Yes, it would be better to wait.

The front door clanged.

Tandor flew up from his seat by the fire. Loriane came into the room, her cheeks red from the cold.

"And?" he asked. Behind him, Myra was still moaning.

She frowned at him. "And what?"

"Did you see where Isandor went?"

"No, I didn't ask. He went to the festival grounds, I imagine. He's got the hunting ritual to lead." Loriane looked past him, shrugging off her cloak. "Any progress?"

"I don't know. She told me to stay away from her."

"Tandor, I can't believe you." She dropped her basket and went to Myra, speaking soft words. The girl cried while Loriane rubbed her back. She gripped Loriane's hands.

"Don't go, please, don't go."

"No, I'm here now. Not going anywhere until you have that baby."

Loriane started unpacking items from her basket. Bottles, salves, bandages, all sorts of things. Tandor glared at her in the silence. Did she need all that? Couldn't she hurry things up a bit?

"There are a lot of Knights in the streets with a lot of gold on their collars," Loriane said without looking up. "I heard someone say that the Queen is there, and that it was she who declared Isandor champion."

"What—the queen? Jevaithi? In the Outer City?"

"I just told you."

Myra's gasps started again. Loriane was telling her to be quiet. Tandor waited for it to pass, scrunching up his hand behind his back.

When Myra had gone silent, Loriane wiped her face with something that smelled like mint.

"Thank you," Myra whispered. "You're doing so much for me. I'm sorry."

"Oh no, I wouldn't let another mother suffer."

Tandor clamped his teeth. Why didn't she hurry up with this dreadful business? "What is the Queen doing here?"

"I don't know. Watching the races, I guess." Loriane dipped the cloth in water. "I've heard rumours she wants to see the killing."

"Eeew." Myra said. "What's so great about that?" Her voice was husky. "I never watch. The tavern's much more fun to be around after Newlight."

"Well, there is that, too," Loriane said. "But I think she'll be heading back before that time. The Knights were tense and didn't look very happy to let her come here. Poor girl."

No, poor Tandor. His whole plan was falling apart. The children gone, Isandor with the Knights and the last two Imperfect children either out of reach or unwilling to help. The street was crawling with Knights, and Ruko had not yet returned.

Meanwhile, the Heart was beating at a faster rate than before, feeding more and more icefire into the air. If the children were in the palace, they might absorb some of it, but if he couldn't get to them soon enough, who knew what would happen?

He heard his own voice echoing in his mother's palatial living room. *But it's lunacy! I can't do all that alone.*

The spirits of our family will guide you.

By the skylights, Mother, what good were spirits?

He was stuck here with two pregnant women. He could run out, but there would be nowhere for him to go, except to be discovered by the Knights, and have them follow him back to his last Imperfect children. Jevaithi was here, but he couldn't use her; there were too many Knights. He might be able to use icefire, but he was not invincible, not alone; and what if that Pirosian with his sink was there?

He jumped when two hands grabbed his shoulders from behind.

"You are so tense, Tandor."

"Don't you have to look after. . . ?" He gestured at Myra.

"There's nothing much we can do except wait. She's not yet close to giving birth."

She massaged the muscles in his shoulders. Myra sat hunched over, breathing harshly through another pain.

Loriane continued in a low voice. "I'm worried about you, Tandor. It feels like something is going on. You bring this girl here, I don't know why. And what were you trying to do to Isandor? If I hadn't seen you come to my house with him as a baby, I might have thought you were trying to kill him back there. What has he done? I'd really like to know what this is about. Having you here is a risk for me, too. My clients are of the city nobility and I have taken enough of a gamble already looking after Isandor. You come here, barge into my house with a young girl about to give birth in the middle of the Newlight festival and I get no explanation. I'm busy, I'm pregnant, and I don't have time for your plans, even less so if you keep them secret."

"I told you life was too dangerous for Myra in Bordertown. I thought you understood that."

"Then why come here where there are even more Knights?" Myra asked

Tandor balled his fists behind his back. Why did sound carry so well in these damned limpets?

"She's right," Loriane said. "I believe she would have been much better off at home. She's only a young mother and it's not right to—"

"Don't talk to me about *not right!*" Tandor whirled.

A moan from Myra interrupted him. She clutched her belly, panting and crying.

"Calm down, calm down," Loriane said.

"It hurts, it hurts!" Myra screamed.

"Breathe like I told you."

Myra's screams faded into heavy panting.

Tandor turned away, looking at the door. All his hair stood on end. He could *not* stand this much longer.

When Myra's harsh breathing subsided, he continued. "I'll tell you what is *not right*. My family was murdered. My grandfather hacked to pieces as he tried to protect the wonders of the City of Glass and his throne. I was exiled. I have lived my *life* for this plan. I am not going to let it slip through my fingers."

"Tandor, what happened is a long time ago. It's not even something you personally remember." She let the shameful truth hang in the air: *You were born in Chevakia.* "Let it go."

"And let Imperfects suffer? Let Imperfect babies be killed?"

"I think Isandor is proof that things are changing."

"It is not. You know that. He would have been killed if it hadn't been for me, and he's only with the Knights because he shapes icefire around an illusion of the missing part of his leg, without ever having been taught how to do so, and because someone put it in his head that being with the Knights was a noble thing to do."

"Isandor is not stupid. He just doesn't care for your pointless quest for revenge." Loriane's eyes blazed with anger.

Not pointless. Tandor saw his mother's proud figure, exiled matriarch of his family. Isandor *would* return to the Thilleians, no matter what. Tandor *would* send the message that would end his mother's pain: *It is safe to return home.*

"Loriane, they *killed* my family. They're continuing to kill any children born with my family's blood. The Knights took the fifty children from Bordertown. I *saved* those children, every single one of them." His voice spilled over. The Knights would have left those children on the ice floes.

"For what aim, Tandor? That's all I'm asking. Because you saved Isandor, and then hardly cared about him until now. You never told me who this boy is. You never gave me any guidance. And now it seems I have done everything wrong by letting him do what he wanted."

Tandor stared at her, raising his clawed hand. "Oh, I give up."

"Give up? You never even started. You try and bring up a child. It's not some . . . possession you can dictate to. If you wanted him to see your ways, why haven't you been around more, and explained to him what he is and what you meant for him to become?"

"I have—"

Myra let out a wailing moan. She was rocking backwards and forwards on her stool. Loriane turned away from Tandor and massaged the girl's back, speaking soft words.

Tandor heaved a sigh of frustration and strode up the stairs to the sleeping shelves. He was trapped here, *trapped*, with two crazy women, while outside the Knights were looking for him.

Icefire streamed in from all sides. The Heart was producing more than ever before, and he had lost Ruko and Isandor, and he couldn't reach his one remaining Imperfect.

He lay down on the bed, even though the room was stuffy enough to make him dizzy. Loriane should open a vent.

He closed his eyes and cast his feelings out for Ruko.

But even the pillow over his head did not stifle Myra's screams from below.

Come on, woman, shut up and get on with it.

Then a cold breeze drifted over him. Not just cold, but freezing. Was that . . . Tandor pulled the pillow off his head and looked up. The wall next to the bed shimmered. First the rough planks that formed the inner wall of the limpet dissolved. An amorphous blob of blue rose from the middle. The blue become clearer and took the shape of a young man. Ruko stood next to him, blue and shimmery.

Ruko, his saviour.

He wasted no time in grabbing Ruko's hands. The boy was strong again. His anger burned, not just for the Knights who had come to Bordertown, but the ones who had injured him. Ruko wanted his girl back, and he was angry enough to kill everyone in his path. And he was Tandor's to command. The time for trying to solve this nicely was over.

So he ordered Ruko, *I want Isandor brought here. Alive. I don't care how you do it. Make sure that the Queen doesn't leave the Outer City. I don't care how you do that either.*

Ruko said nothing, but Tandor knew he would obey. Ah, blissful obedience and none of the women's silly protests.

CHAPTER 20

ISANDOR REARRANGED his cloak on his shoulders for what had to be the tenth time, ignoring the gazes of hundreds—no—thousands of people who were waiting for this ceremonial part of the festival to begin. The eagles in their pens at his back squawked and hissed, two of the Outer City's butchers talked to each other, their conversation accompanied by hand gestures towards the animal pens, and a young boy was sweeping the dull layer of sand off the snow-covered ground so it was again white.

Every time he put down his broom, golden sparks flew along the handle, but the boy gave no sign of having seen them.

To Isandor's eyes, the atmosphere in the arena thrummed with tension. Icefire sizzled and crackled through the air like he had never seen it before. Isandor couldn't believe he was the only one who noticed. Some in the audience would see it, too, but no one mentioned it, perhaps for fear of being labelled a sorcerer. Perhaps they hoped it would go away.

A large group of Knights gathered at the spectator stand to his left, where Jevaithi had come in moments earlier. Isandor had only spotted glimpses of her white fur cloak amongst the crowd of grey ones as she settled in the seating stand. The Knights carried daggers and swords, and Isandor even spotted a crossbow. The Knights might not be able to feel or see the icefire strands, but they knew something was going on, or they would not be as heavily armed.

He tried to catch Jevaithi's eye, but couldn't even see her head most of the time. He'd been silly to think that he would be allowed near her for the second time. And he'd even been so stupid as to think that he should warn her.

The citizens of the Outer City crowded around the perimeter fence, bright-eyed, to cheer on one of their own. Young girls with ribbons in their hair, older girls with their hair pinned up, wearing pretty earrings, with their leather necklaces and feathers prominently displayed. Younger boys with dreams in their eyes of becoming an Eagle Knight themselves.

In one corner of the arena, a couple of men were dragging a large wriggling shape in a net. The bark of the Legless Lion cut through the chatter of the crowd. The men would have caught the animal on this morning's hunting trip, the first of the annual harvest.

The men moved the net into the middle of the arena and drove stakes into the ice to pin the corners down before retreating to the perimeter. They were all wearing butchers' aprons. A nearly bald man —his uncle—winked at Isandor and smiled.

Oh yes, he would be happy. Isandor knew from past years that his uncle's back room would hold a number of other animals, waiting to be killed for the festivities, waiting for customers who would be flooding in after today to buy fresh meat.

From today for the next few moon cycles of high-sun, the butchery would be a place of activity, of large vats with salted meat and oil, stacks of uncured skins and racks of drying meat. During high-sun, the hunters harvested enough for the people to survive the dark low-sun days. Tonight, there would be a huge feast.

Jevaithi had settled on her bench, and the Knights stepped back to form a line around the stand.

"Are you ready, Apprentice Isandor?"

Isandor started, and nodded at the Knight who had come into the arena.

The three butchers came forward. One of them, Isandor's uncle, approached, handing Isandor a fearsome knife.

Isandor gripped his dagger's hilt, cold in his fingers, and drew it out of its sheath. The blade, sharpened by his uncle, gleamed in the sun.

The two other butchers were at the net, one of them undoing the knot that kept it closed. He glanced at Isandor.

"Ready?"

Isandor nodded. He took up a fighting stance, his legs wide.

His uncle yelled and the man pulled away the rope that held the net. All three of the men retreated.

As they did so, a strand of icefire crackled through the air like lightning, and struck the ground at the other end of the arena.

Some people gasped, but most looked around confused; they hadn't seen the icefire.

The Legless Lion writhed on the ground, trying to free itself from the loose net, splashing its flippers in puddles.

Isandor stalked closer, holding the dagger in a white-knuckled hand.

The animal's mouth opened, showing yellow teeth, emitting its fearful bark and a waft of fishy breath. The eyes, liquid brown, roved the arena. Did the animal see icefire? Did it see the citizens who had come to witness this spectacle? Did it see Queen Jevaithi, who had insisted watching her champion kill the beast?

Quickly.

Cut the heart, kill in one stroke, as it was done properly. Don't show his uncle his hesitation. He'd cut up carcases often enough in the butchery. There was nothing to it.

His uncle stood on the edge of the area, holding an axe at his waist. Ready for action.

The rope around the animal's flippers and neck dangled on the ground. Isandor grabbed it and with a sharp yank, he pulled the animal upside down, like he had helped his uncle do many times.

Before the animal could get up, he stabbed deep into the hairy chest. As the blade sank in, icefire crackled out of the ground. Strands exploded all around him. A golden glow burst, unbidden, from his fingers.

Oh, by the skylights!

The chest split open with a sickening snap, widening the cut he had made. The animal's heart jumped out. Isandor managed to catch it in his numb hands. Gold light poured from his fingers, filling the hole in the animal's chest. The lion barked and snapped at the rope around its neck, raising itself on clumsy flippers. Its fur had faded from mottled grey to an eerie blue, a faint glow. At the place where the heart should be, the chest shimmered.

Isandor stared from the throbbing heart in his hands to the animal. Severed arteries spilled no blood, but pure icefire. The golden threads snaked through the air, gathering to converge around the animal.

Around him, people in the stands stared. Some murmured in a tone of confusion. Someone said, the voice carrying across the pen, "Where is the Lion?"

A little boy pointed, but his mother clamped a hand over his eyes.

The Lion hobbled a few paces away from him, the net dragging through puddles, now half-frozen. It glanced at the end of the arena, where the plains beckoned.

"Oh no, you don't." Isandor lunged as fast as his wooden leg would allow, catching the Lion around the neck with one arm. Someone in the audience shouted. "Look, look!"

The animal's fur was rough and stank of fish, but Isandor cared not about the animal's snapping mouth.

But he was still holding the blood-covered heart, and the fur was greasy and slippery. The animal shrugged, and Isandor's arm lost its purchase.

He fell, painfully, on the ragged frozen ground. The heart rolled from his grip, still thudding, and came to rest against a block of ice. Sparks of icefire burst from it and leaked into the snow

On hands and knees in bloodstained-puddles, Isandor met the Legless Lion's deep blue eyes. Its fur rippled with tension. Whiskers twitched. The net lay free on the ground.

Isandor's ears roared, but through the sound, he heard the shouts from the crowd. *A servitor!* He scrabbled up, grabbed the netting, but before he could throw it over the animal's head, it waddled away, in the direction of the plain. A line of onlookers stood between the Legless Lion and freedom. People screamed and tried to run away from the animal, pushing into other people, some of whom looked confused, *because they couldn't see the Lion.*

The crowd cleared a small opening to the left, and the Lion took its chance.

Isandor shouted, "Hold it!" But it was no use.

A few heartbeats, and the animal was gone, a blue form fast disappearing amongst the tents. Isandor hobbled after it, but there was no way he could ever catch up.

Oh no, by the skylights!

People in the audience were screaming and pushing out of the arena. Others stood staring into the sky. Still others were talking to each other, confusion on their faces.

Isandor scrambled in the snow for the Lion's still-beating heart, scooped it up and slid it into his pocket, where it continued beating.

What now? Was there any chance of getting away unnoticed? Where to go in this confusion?

He looked up, straight into the Queen's eyes.

The Knights around her were shouting, but it was confusion, more than anger, that marked their words. Like Carro, most of them were Pirosians. They hadn't seen what had happened.

But Jevaithi just looked at him, unmoving, her eyes wide, her mouth open in an expression of shock. *She* had seen it.

In his mind, he was running past tents. People were screaming words he couldn't understand and running out of the way, tripping over their feet. He saw the shore where he belonged, where his females lazed on the ice floes. He couldn't get out of this maze; there was a fence in his way. A man ran after him, shouting unintelligible words.

No, no, he had to escape. He must get back to defend his females from the other bulls.

The image melded with the arena, the audience, Knights, his uncle staring with wide, bulging eyes.

All around him the Knights were stirring, and the first ones were already entering the arena.

He wanted to run, but his legs felt like they would buckle under him.

Carro stood with his patrol at the edge of the crowd at the arena. Being taller than many people had allowed him to see most of what had happened, but he didn't understand it. One moment, the Legless Lion was there in the net, the next moment, it was gone, and Isandor stood there, holding the animal's heart. And then Isandor ran, or tripped, and fell, and some people in the audience seemed to have seen something. Now, everyone was shouting and the whole festive atmosphere had turned into panic. Knights were forming a circle around the Queen.

"What happened?" he asked Inran next to him.

The young man was staring wide-eyed, at Isandor.

"I don't know what happened," another Knight answered. "One moment the Lion was there, and the next moment it was gone, become invisible."

A chill went over Carro's back. He had seen an invisible creature before: last night, when it snapped the necks of two Knights. A servitor, Rider Cornatan had confirmed. And he had just seen who had made a servitor by taking the animal's heart, just like it was described in the old books. Isandor had been behind the servitors all along. Isandor had wanted to read about the old king's practices because he wanted to *use* them. Isandor had deceived everyone, including him.

His heart thudding, he searched the crowd for Rider Cornatan. He would be with the Queen no doubt.

The Apprentices in his patrol were just as confused as everyone else. Jono was looking over the roof of the tent on the opposite side of the arena. Caman was observing a group of Knights trying to get into the arena, while Inran kept glancing over his shoulder. None of them knew where the real danger was.

"You. Stay here," he ordered.

Jono gave him a sneering look but said nothing.

Carro pushed through the crowd, filled with the uncomfortable feeling that he would have to discipline his patrol when they came back to the eyrie. They should be afraid of him, and they were not. But he'd deal with that later. The praise for what he was going to tell Rider Cornatan now would give him the courage to do what needed to be done. Hopefully.

Knights were pressing each other to see into the central area.

Carro pushed them aside. "Let me through, let me through."

His voice had become deeper, louder. They actually listened, and, after glancing at his Learner badge, moved aside.

Up to the viewing stand, where Rider Cornatan sat next to the Queen. All around, Knights were talking frantically, looking over their shoulders and left and right, frowns on faces.

Carro bowed before the viewing stand. Rider Cornatan acknowledged him, but the Queen just sat there, staring hollow-eyed at Isandor, her cheeks red, like she was deeply upset with his trickery.

Well, he should put an end to that.

The words burst from Carro's mouth. "The one you call a Champion shouldn't be here. He's a cripple. He turned the Lion into a servitor."

Rider Cornatan fixed him with his light blue eyes. "He's *what?*"

"A cripple. Ask him." There. That served him right. That horrid apparition last night had killed two good Knights.

"Imperfect?" Rider Cornatan lowered his voice and met Carro's eyes.

Carro nodded. The next question would surely be *Why haven't you told us before?* but he would have to handle that, too. *Because he has deceived us all.*

"Well, that would explain a lot." A smile crept over the wizened face.

Carro added, "There is another cripple in the Outer City, an older man. He was loitering around the area of the brotherhood compound. We followed him, but unfortunately lost track of him in the markets."

Rider Cornatan's face showed intense interest. He nodded, a satisfied smile on his face. "I see. You are proving your worth. Keep looking for this man. Let me know if you want more men." Then Rider Cornatan pushed himself up, his face set. "Now let's see about this young man. If what you say is true, you will have done the Queen a great service."

Rider Cornatan walked down the steps. A Senior Knight stepped in his way and held up a hand.

"The boy's dangerous," the man whispered.

"I know," Rider Cornatan said.

He pushed the man's hand away and continued into the arena.

Knights surrounded Isandor, but none had dared to touch him. In the confusion, no one seemed to have ordered them to do so. And yet Carro's friend wasn't arguing; he just stood there, with that gruesome heart in his pocket, still beating.

Carro could almost feel that someone was looking at him. He glanced over his shoulder into the Queen's eyes, which burned with pure hatred. She held her lips pursed and little white spots appeared at her upper lip and chin. Carro had to avert his gaze.

Isandor laughs. Gestures at the notice from the palace that Carro has brought. In curly letters, it says that Carro has been accepted into the Eagle Knights. Carro's father was against it, but he applied anyway. Isandor encouraged him. He wants to be a Knight, too, and his mother doesn't mind. He has already been accepted.

"Then we will join up together and we'll both be famous Knights." Carro laughs.

Then Isandor's expression changes to one of wonder. "Do you think we'll get to stand guard for the Queen?"

"Of course we will. All Knights do."

Isandor looks dreamy. There is something in those blue eyes Carro can't fathom. Something he doesn't want to fathom.

The Queen belongs to the Knights. She is *his*, with her honey-coloured hair and milk-white arms. Her eyes gaze into people's hearts. Carro has seen her twice, both from a distance. She is the most beautiful woman in the known world.

Yes, he will join the Knights, even though his father will hate him for it.

The Knights protect the Queen. He cannot trust a boy with a wooden leg to protect the Queen. The books say Imperfects are sorcerers. Carro is trying not to believe the books. They *are* only stories, after all.

"Apprentice Isandor?" Rider Cornatan's voice was hard and thin over the chatter of onlookers. He had pushed through the circle of Knights around Isandor and faced him directly.

Oh no, Rider Cornatan wasn't scared of sorcery. Real Knights weren't scared.

"Yes," Isandor said, his back straight and proud. His hair black and shiny, his eyes dark blue. Royal blue.

Carro's stomach squirmed. Oh, by the skylights, how he hated

Isandor. Even like this, he managed to look arrogant, like he owned the world, like he challenged Rider Cornatan to do something to him, even though he knew he could never escape.

And I am just a coward. Waited all this time to tell Rider Cornatan about Isandor. Can't even punish my own patrol.

Rider Cornatan looked Isandor up and down.

"Do you have any secrets, Apprentice Isandor?"

"Secrets, Sir?"

Rider Cornatan, lightning fast, kicked Isandor's legs from under him. He stumbled and tipped backwards into the fast-retreating Knights, and then fell in the snow. A blast of wind went over the arena, whipping at clothes and hair. Isandor's trouser leg had moved up, clearly displaying the boot stuck to his wooden leg. Everyone in the audience stopped talking.

Someone whispered, "A cripple."

"How is that possible? I thought they were all . . ."

"Watch out, he's going to blast us."

In the alley and under the cover of gathering darkness, Isandor lifts up his trouser leg.

"I do have a secret. I have a wooden leg, see? I can't run as fast as you can. People don't seem to like it. I don't know why."

Carro shrugs. "Why should people do that?" Isandor is just like him, someone people don't like very much. He also doesn't understand why.

Isandor bends closer, and whispers in Carro's ear, like *real* friends do. "They say that anyone who is born like this has magic. You know, icefire."

Carro shivers. Stares. "Do you?"

"Of course not. Do you see me making things disappear?"

"Um—no." But Carro doubts. His mother always told him icefire was real. She says she can see it. But his mother always lies.

"There you go. It's all nonsense. But we won't tell anyone that, will we?"

"Of course not." Certainly not his parents.

"It's a secret."

"A real secret, between friends?"

Isandor nods. "Friends forever."

Onlookers fled. People pushed away. Knights retreated to the edge of the arena. In the holding pens, eagle attendants shuffled back, pulling their eagles away, wide-eyed. Isandor lay there alone in the snow.

"What is this?" Rider Cornatan kicked Isandor's wooden leg.

Isandor raised himself, stumbling to get the leg under him. He still managed to act dignified, but the look in his eyes frightened Carro more than anger would have. It was not anger, not hurt, but a withering look of determination.

"Who said cripples could join the Knights?" Rider Cornatan asked.

"No one said they couldn't." Isandor's voice was cold as the southern wind.

A cold gust of wind blew eddies of snow in the corners of the arena.

"You should well know cripples can't even live in this city. You are an abomination. I don't understand why no one has seen it before."

"I've not hidden anything." Again, that confident tone.

That was true. Isandor had come up to the registration as he was, with his slight limp. Why had no one seen it? Yes, why? Everyone with half a brain could see that Isandor didn't walk normally. Yet no one had commented.

"How come you're even alive? Who hid you?"

"No one. I've lived with my mother in the Outer City all along."

Look at the cockiness of him. Look at him stand there.

"Well, whatever you did, you're finished now." Rider Cornatan stepped forward and tore the golden badge from Isandor's collar. "You will never darken the eyrie with your presence again. Thanks to my vigilant spies, I have saved the City of Glass from this evil. Take him away."

Knights closed in. Two grabbed Isandor under the armpits and yanked him up.

What were they going to do with him? Carro had flown over the jagged shapes of the ice floes earlier today. Anyone left there alone would be attacked by stray bears. Anyone put in the dungeons would die a slow death of hunger and disease. *Why did I say this? Isandor is my friend. He looked after me. He would never kill anyone. The fact that he made the Lion a servitor doesn't prove that he made the human one.*

Knights don't have Imperfect friends, the other voice in his mind said.

Isandor has been good to me. He's a good person.

But I've had enough of "good" people. I don't want pity. I want people to be honest. Right, they are honest, and don't like me. I want people to like me and be honest. No pity. I can't stand pity. I want to be accepted because of what I am, not because my father is a moderately successful merchant. I hate him anyway.

Oh, he was so confused.

CHAPTER 21

NO. ISANDOR!

Everyone was getting up, blocking Jevaithi's view of the arena. The citizens were filing out, most still trading gossip and uttering expressions of confusion. A whole group of Knights rushed into the arena and out again. Jevaithi presumed that they escorted the young Champion Knight away.

To the palace dungeons. She had to put a stop to it; she had to.

Rider Cornatan returned to her, his face red.

"With respect, Your Highness. We must take you to a safe place."

"What happened?" she asked, although she was sure she had seen it better than any of them. The animal had run off into the festival grounds in its blue state, leaving the Champion standing there holding the pulsing heart. The animal had become his servitor.

"It was inappropriate for your eyes. Rest assured, the Knight will be punished severely."

No. She saw an emaciated body, wounds from lashes, matted hair. She remembered. She had only been young when she saw the man who had been blamed for poisoning her mother. He'd spent ten years in the dungeons. "I would like to set eyes on him, who dares to perform these deeds before the Queen." She was trembling, fighting to keep control over her speech. That day, last year, she had presided over the poor wretch's execution. She didn't believe the man had poisoned her mother any more than she wanted him dead. He'd been

189

a palace servant. All the servants adored her mother. But the Knights had to have someone to punish.

"He'll be taken into custody." Rider Cornatan's voice sounded far off.

"Can I see him?" She ached to ask more, but anything she said could be dangerous. Rider Cornatan raised an eyebrow. He knew what she was, and probably had thoughts along the same lines as her fascination with the strange young Knight.

"I would think that inappropriate. Come, Your Highness, We must go now. It's getting late and this place is not safe at night."

Jevaithi stifled a sob. She must save that young Knight, the only other person of her kind. But how? The Knights controlled everything. They gave her the illusion of power as long as she did what she was told.

She took Rider Cornatan's arm and let him lead her away from the arena, which was completely abandoned now, save for a few remaining splatters of blood. To Jevaithi's eyes, they exuded a soft yellow glow.

People in the tents along the way cheered and waved at her, but she paid them no attention. In her mind, she saw those blue eyes, looking up at her with the boy's innocence. When she looked at him, declaring him her Champion, it was as if she had seen into his soul, as if their hearts beat in unison. If he was tortured, she would lie awake with the pain. If he was killed, part of her would die.

"We shall return to the palace as soon as possible," Rider Cornatan said.

For once, she couldn't find a reason to disagree with him. She longed for the warmth of her room, the comfort of her bed and the whisper of servants bringing her dinner.

She shuffled with her entourage, nervous Knights looking everywhere, Rider Cornatan holding her arm like an overprotective mother bear. They passed the food stalls, where it had become quiet. Stallholders were cleaning up for the night. Most of the revellers had gone into the Outer City to celebrate in the melteries. How stupid had she been to imagine she could ever dance with the local boys.

Stupid. Naïve.

Ahead, a woman screamed.

Rider Cornatan halted. The Knights at the front of the group had all stopped, a solid wall of cloaked backs. The woman's screams had turned into sobs. The Knights murmured. Hands went to swords, but most of the men just stood there.

"What's going on?" Rider Cornatan demanded.

"See for yourself, sir." The wall of Knights parted.

Jevaithi's royal sled stood abandoned on the plain. Splatters of blood marked the white paint and had seeped into the snow. The harness which had held the four magnificent bears lay empty on the ground. The bears themselves were bloodied humps of white fur in the snow.

Jevaithi took a gasp of stinging cold air and couldn't breathe out again. She clutched her throat, dizzy, blood pounding in her ears.

"No, no," she stuttered, fighting to repel blackness from the edge of her vision. Her beautiful bears, and the driver—where was he?

"Guard the Queen!" Rider Cornatan shouted, while he started running towards the sled with agility that belied his age.

Between the bodies of the Knights who closed in around her, Jevaithi saw how he jumped into the driver's seat and hauled up the body of the sled's driver. His head was bent back like a broken stick and his cloak dark with blood. His arms flopped by his side; his body hadn't been out here long enough to have frozen stiff.

"Don't look, Your Highness," one of the guards said.

"Who would do such a thing?" Jevaithi's voice sounded weak, even to her own ears. All of a sudden, she had trouble keeping her balance.

A soft warmth closed around her, the dense fur of a short-hair cloak, and a man's arms. It was one of the Senior Knights, a man normally calm and reserved. Jevaithi stifled her sobs in the man's shirt. She was shivering.

The Knights were shouting amongst themselves over her head.

"Who could have done this?"

"I'd say—*what* has done this? This wasn't done by a human."

"He's right. Look at the bears. No one can kill a bear that easily."

Jevaithi pressed herself deeper under the Knight's cloak, seeing images of a blue-tinged Legless Lion running from the arena. *No humans . . .*

"I want to go home," she said to no one in particular.

Why ever did she entertain such silly plans to go amongst the common people? There were murdering strangers out there. Poor, poor bears, poor driver. What had they done to deserve this?

"Shh, Your Highness. You are safe with us." The man's voice rumbled in his chest. He tightened an arm around her, while he continued to give orders to the guards.

Jevaithi felt warm, and protected. Was this the feeling kids had about their fathers?

She didn't know how long she stood there before Rider Cornatan returned. She heard his voice before he came into view.

"Where is the Queen?"

"Safe," the Knight said.

Jevaithi extracted her face from the warmth of his cloak.

Rider Cornatan came to a stop. Stared at her and then at the Senior Knight.

"I'll take care of her now," Rider Cornatan said.

A sharp look passed between the two men over Jevaithi's head. The Knight released her. Jevaithi reluctantly left the warmth of his cloak to take Rider Cornatan's arm. Even in times such as this, they jostled to be first in line to her bedroom.

The group started moving, away from the slaughter scene.

"What's happening now?" Jevaithi asked Rider Cornatan, doing her utmost best to sound composed.

"I've sent a messenger to the City. He'll bring back another sled. We'll wait for it to arrive."

"Couldn't I . . ." She licked her lips. "Couldn't I fly on an Eagle with a Knight? We would be back very quickly—"

The look he gave her stopped her talking. Obviously out of the question.

They crossed the festival grounds through the maze of tents and fences. Legless Lions barked in the distance. There were now so many Knights around her that it was impossible for her to see the cheering people. The Knights walked quickly, ushering the crowd aside. Jevaithi wasn't in the mood to be cheered.

They left the festival grounds, and clambered up the slope that led into the Outer City—through a wide street, where abandoned sleds stood in shop entrances, their terrified drivers holed up in alleyways by Knights. How many Knights *had* come from the city with her? How could someone still have killed the bears and the driver with all these Knights to guard her?

A person invisible to the Knights could do it.

They were now crossing the market place over trampled snow covered with sand. The Knights halted again in front of a cone-shaped building on the corner. The locals called these structures limpets. The writings had told her that there was a waterproof inner layer, made of ancient debris from the city before the Great War, a mantle of still air, and then an outer layer made from blocks of ice. This limpet was larger than most, and had three entrances. Someone had carved patterns in the icy outer cover.

A few of the Knights had gone inside. The glow of a fierce fire peeped through a crack between the doors.

There were shouts and bangs inside. The doors were flung open and lots of people streamed out, some speaking in angry voices.

Jevaithi shivered with the piercing breeze. She glanced over her shoulder towards the Knight who had offered her the warmth of his cloak.

The Knights moved forward, through the door and a short hall with racks for cloaks—all empty—into a room where the air was impossibly warm and laced with a tang of liquor and smoke. The inner walls, made from sheets of metal and other unidentified material, sloped slowly to a high ceiling. A balcony surrounded the wall, with stairs leading up to it. There were tables and chairs up there. Empty.

A huge metal stove stood in the middle of the room, a blazing fire within. Surrounding the stove were many small tables and chairs. A couple of red-faced girls were hastily removing glasses from the tables, many still containing dark red fluid. A young man was righting chairs that had fallen over.

"Your Highness, what a surprise and honour to receive you in my humble establishment."

The man who bowed before her was rotund and almost bald. Although his words had been polite, his tone gave away his extreme annoyance.

Oh, she could see why. He'd had a room full of drinking, paying patrons and the next thing the Knights barged in and tossed everyone out on the street. The voices of those paying patrons now drifted in from outside, shouts and jeers. A crash, the tinkle of glass. Angry voices.

"I would be happy if you let your customers back inside," Jevaithi said, making her voice as clear and regal as she could.

"For once, Your Highness, be quiet and stop your childish demands," Rider Cornatan hissed. She had never heard his voice as tight as this.

The flicker of hope that dashed across the meltery owner's face died instantly.

"Sit here by the fire, Your Highness." He indicated a soft, high-backed chair that had worn fabric but looked very comfortable indeed.

There was another crash of glass outside. A man shouted and something thudded against the door.

"I'm sure," she said, as peevishly as she could, while sitting down in the chair, "I'm *absolutely* sure that a street brawl is just what you need to calm things down, especially if your men are out there attempting to catch a Legless Lion most of them can't even see."

In two steps, Rider Cornatan stood next to her. He grabbed a strand of her hair as he bent to her ear and pulled hard. His whisper sounded like a hiss of air. "I'm warning you . . . you're behaving like a brat. You want to be grown-up? I'll show you grown-up. When we get back to the palace, I will take you to your rooms and teach you a lesson you won't forget in a hurry." He let her go and stepped back as if he had merely conveyed a private message.

Jevaithi shivered and leaned back in the chair. Her eyes met the meltery owner's. His were wide, shocked.

Yes, the common people loved her and that love was her protection, but tonight, that would not be enough.

CHAPTER 22

ISANDOR TRIED to run, but he never had a chance.

The Knights had blindfolded him and tied his arms behind his back before he could do anything. They pushed him out of the arena and through the crowd. As many people were cheering as shouting.

"Show them, show them!" a man yelled.

Show them what?

He struggled against the Knights' hands. "Stop pushing. I can walk. Where are you taking me?"

"To the only place sorcerers belong," the man holding him growled. "I hope you had a good look at the sky, because you won't see it again."

People around them were calling for the Queen, and then there were other voices from further away.

"Let the boy go, tyrants!"

"Down with the oppression!"

"Give us our houses back, and our businesses, and our money!"

"Death to Pirosian scum!"

There were more scuffles and screams. People bumped into him. Knights shouted in hoarse, out-of-control voices. Daggers came out of sheaths. The sound of people running. Something heavy landed near his feet with a dull thud.

Isandor tried to free his arm to pull the rag from his eyes, but the Knights held him too tightly. He wanted to see these people. There were still supporters of the old king in the Outer City? The revelation confused him. The deeds the king had done, according to the books about the fall of the royal family, horrified him.

But what if those books had been written by Knights?

He did remember that last book Carro had bought, the one that described all the wonders of icefire, not just the bad things. Deadly, but very useful and powerful.

Why had he never known that people still supported the old king?

He was running through the street. Even though he was blindfolded, he could see. People were in his way, running, pushing each other. Their unintelligible screams filled the air. Their words were garbled bursts of sound that meant nothing.

Some had sticks and tried to push him. He kept slipping, his flippers finding no purchase on the trampled ice.

I am much faster in the water.

The water, where the fish were fresh and wet and where the females waited for him.

He needed to get back there.

Isandor stumbled and gasped, realising how he'd been holding his breath and how lack of air had made him dizzy. By the skylights, what was wrong with him?

The Knights were dragging him along at a fast walking pace, having left the shouting crowd behind. Judging by the echoing footsteps, they were somewhere in the alleys of the Outer City. The ground was uneven, and every now and then, the Knight holding his arm kicked his wooden leg, and then laughed when he stumbled.

"Hey," he shouted. "Where are we going? Where are you taking me?"

His angry shouts echoed in the street, and were taken up by other voices.

"Where you be taking him? He did nothing," one man said in Outer City slang.

"You'll be taking him away like Merro," another man yelled.

"Where is Merro?" This voice was more educated.

The Knights sped up, tightening their grip on Isandor's arm. The sound of running footsteps followed them. Isandor was heartened by that. Certainly the Knights were less likely to harm him when there were witnesses. He had to face it. His time with the

Knighthood was over. He might as well make the transition into evil complete.

He reached out for icefire. The strands sizzled and crackled. He could feel them on his hands bound behind his back. His body drank in the power he had denied for so long.

"You go, boy. Show them," the man with the educated voice growled.

They want me to do this? Isandor felt the rush of icefire swirl around him. A *satisfying* rush.

Next moment, the rag flew from his eyes with a gust of ice-cold wind. The rope that held his wrists fell to the ground.

Isandor stopped, panting, still holding the strands of icefire.

The Knights had taken him to one of the darker alleys behind the markets. There were many other people here, but strangely no one took any notice of him. The Knights were shouting and swearing, their weapons drawn, their backs to him.

Isandor couldn't restrain a chuckle. They hadn't realised that *he* made the icefire whip up the wind? Amusing. He grabbed another strand. It crackled and sizzled when he whipped it over their backs. The men shielded their faces with arms and hands.

Isandor ran as fast as he his wooden leg allowed.

Behind him, a man yelled, "The prisoner! Stop the prisoner!"

Isandor skidded into a side alley only to find many people were already hiding there, all dressed in black.

A man at the front yelled, "Here he comes. Step aside, step aside everyone!"

People shuffled aside.

"This way!" a man shouted and opened a door for him at the back of the alley.

Isandor didn't think, didn't question; he ran through the open door, along a narrow passageway that zigzagged between limpets, their side doors, their outroom collection buckets, composting trays and broken furniture.

He ran and ran, charged by the power of icefire. His leg worked better than it ever had before. He felt like he was flying, *running like a normal man.*

All the time, he saw images of snow sliding under his belly, of partygoers in the streets running away and screaming their incomprehensible words. Where to go? Where was the ice plain with his females? Where was the ocean? This maze had trapped him. It was dizzying . . .

Breathe.

Isandor stopped, gasping.

He had to find that Legless Lion whose heart beat in his pocket. At times, he *became* the Lion, and Legless Lions could stay under water without breath for much longer than he could. If this went on, those images would kill him.

He made his way through the alleys, pulling his cloak tight around his neck so his red shirt wouldn't show. Shouts and cries rang in the night, sounds of fighting. The sky glowed orange ahead, and there were the telltale billowing clouds of a fire. Some of the limpets belonging to poorer families were made from light, foamy material that burned like fire bricks, and gave off thick smoke that made people who breathed it sick for days.

A group of youths tromped through the street, their faces hidden behind scarves, carrying sticks and shovels. He slipped in with the group, shaking his hair loose from the ponytail. No one protested the presence of one extra person.

". . . yeah, and they took Indo, too," one boy was saying.

"What? He wouldn't harm a puppy."

"Everyone who was there, they said. Did you see what happened to the Queen's bears?"

"Didn't see, but heard. And they think *we* did it?" This boy sounded angry.

The other boy shrugged. "We're Outer City folk. Can't be trusted."

"Always the same. We got to stop the Knights, you know. Stop them right here. We can't be ruled like this."

A few others grumbled consent.

The street opened out into the market square. Two lines of Knights stood on both sides of the meltery doors. Isandor recognised their uniforms: these were Jevaithi's personal guards.

Jevaithi.

What was she still doing here?

The group of youths marched on, but Isandor stopped, barely aware of their receding footsteps. Jevaithi, the only other Imperfect he knew who lived in the city. Jevaithi, whose eyes pleaded to him for help. And help he would.

Isandor stumbled across the square, deliberately unsteady, his eyes unfocused and his gaze directed at the ground.

"Hey, you!" one of the Knights said.

Isandor took the last few steps in a stumbling rush and leaned against the meltery's outer wall. His heart thudded in his throat. The Knights fell silent.

He swallowed a mouthful of air, and another one, and let it out in a mighty belch that made acid rise into the back of his throat.

"Hey, you. Move along," the Knight repeated.

"Be a moment," he said, slurring his words.

He dug under his cloak and undid the fastening of his trousers. He'd seen drunks often enough to know they always pissed every-where. Cold bit into delicate skin, and all of a sudden, he *needed* to piss. A yellow hole melted into the ice of the meltery's outer wall. The Knights laughed and continued talking. He was no longer a danger to them, just another drunk.

Finished.

He refastened his trousers and leaned against the icy wall.

The door clanged and two Knights came out of the meltery. Their voices carried over the square.

". . . should have been here long ago."

". . . is so embarrassing . . . what do you think she . . ."

"And all this on the whim of a spoilt brat."

Then he ran through the streets, his flippers slapping on the hard ground. Someone threw a stick at him, but it missed. He barked at the man; he tore the cloak off his shoulders. *The fur of my fellows.*

A deep gasp of breath. His face pressed against the ice wall. By the skylights, he had almost passed out. The Legless Lion heart beat against his leg, in unison with his heart.

One of the Knights called out, "Thank the skylights, there he is."

Isandor glanced over his shoulder, still panting. Another Knight was crossing the square at a trot.

"Got the sled," he shouted to his comrades.

"Good. Let's get out of here." One of the Knights went back inside the meltery.

"Hey, move along, you drunkard!" This shout was directed at Isandor.

"Jush . . . jush a moment . . ." Isandor stumbled a few steps, fell back against the meltery wall, swallowed air, and let out another burp.

"Disgusting," the Knight mumbled and went inside.

Isandor took as long as he dared to push himself off the wall, aware of the Knight guards' gazes on him. He moved away slowly, swaying on his feet. A faint breeze brought the sound of shouts and yells from elsewhere in the Outer City. The orange glow of fire had intensified. Once the surrounding ice had melted, those ancient building materials burned well. Isandor hoped the blaze was away from limpets of people he knew. He hoped someone was controlling the fire. He hoped his mother was all right.

The meltery doors opened, flooding the ice-covered ground with yellow light. A couple of Knights came out, long shadows over the empty square.

"We'll take you to the sled as quickly as we can, Your Highness."

Isandor couldn't believe his luck. She was going to walk right past him . . .

His vision faded. He ran on clumsy flippers. *I'm much faster in the water.* He shot out into the market square. Skidded to a halt. On the other side of the square was a building which glowed with yellow light such as humans had. There were a bunch of people gathered around it. What they couldn't see was that a blue man hid around the corner.

Isandor gasped. He recognised the blue form of the man, taller than him, broader and with expressionless black eyes. He carried a dagger in his blue-marbled hand, blood dripping from the blade.

This was a true servitor. Tandor's.

THE SKY HAD turned deep blue, and the meltery's owner had grown restless by the time the door opened, letting in a blast of cold air that made the fire in the stove flare up.

A group of Knights marched in and came to a halt before Rider Cornatan's chair. Saluted.

One stepped forward and bowed. "The sled has arrived."

"What took you so long?" Rider Cornatan's voice sounded annoyed. He broke his glare at Jevaithi, which he had managed to maintain for much of the time he'd sat opposite her. Undressing her with his eyes.

"There's a few houses on fire near the festival grounds, and the eagles had some trouble with the smoke, and when we got back, we had to come the long way. There are also too many people out to take the sled through the streets."

Rider Cornatan raised an annoyed eyebrow. "I hope you left an adequate guard with it."

"We did."

Rider Cornatan gave him a sharp look, but let the unspoken truth hung between them. No normal person could have inflicted the injuries that had killed the driver of the other sled. No normal human could have slaughtered those bears, and so there was no guarantee that this not-normal apparition wouldn't attack the new sled with guards.

He rose from his seat. "Let's go then. Are you ready, Your Highness?"

Jevaithi scrambled for her cloak, which a Knight held up for her. She met the meltery's owner's eyes across the bar, where he was putting away glasses.

"Rider Cornatan, can you make sure he is compensated for the earnings he didn't take while we were in here?"

Rider Cornatan grumbled something to a younger Knight, who went to the bar. A few of the men gave her strange glances, but the owner took the money and bent his head to her.

"Your Highness, you are always welcome here."

"Thank you."

She met the man's eyes and held his gaze while walking to the door, in a daze. *Please help me, if you can.* The citizens were her saviours, if she could still be saved after tonight.

The man didn't give any sign that he had understood what was going on. As citizen of the Outer City, there was probably nothing he *could* do.

Jevaithi followed Rider Cornatan outside, every step bringing her closer to the palace, to her bedroom.

A thin mist hung over the marketplace, a damper over the voices of revellers walking across. A powder-like drizzle of snow drifted from the sky. The air smelled of smoke.

The Knights started across the marketplace, with at least six close to Jevaithi. They were all taller and broader than she, and she didn't see much beyond cloaks and hands on swords.

She shivered. Something pricked at her senses. Icefire was thicker in the air than ever. It buzzed and shimmered, lining roofs and gutters. It danced on top of a lamppost. It didn't touch the Knights; it bent around them.

Maybe—she was getting ideas—maybe she could use it to defend herself, later, when she and Rider Cornatan were alone in her room.

A voice rang out from beyond her circle of guards, "Watch out, Your Highness!"

She turned around, and saw nothing but Knights' backs.

"Keep moving, Your Highness," the Knight behind her said. "There's nothing—"

"By the skylights!" another yelled.

There was a sickening snap. All around her, Knights were yelling and pulling swords.

Jevaithi shouted, "What's happening?"

Someone shouted, "Move, move!"

A man at the back of the group screamed, his voice descending into a beastly wail, which was followed by a hard snap, and silence. There was the sound of a sword being drawn, and another. Footsteps scuffling in the snow. Knights closed in around Jevaithi.

Silence, except for the Knights' breaths, which made puffs of mist in the air.

"Where is he?" a Knight asked.

"Um—just what exactly are we looking for?" another whispered. "Did you see what killed him?"

In the silence, Jevaithi shivered. She couldn't see anything with all these men in her way, but she felt it well enough: icefire burst from something a couple of steps in front.

The thing that killed the driver and the bears.

Another scream, short, loud and sharp. It broke off abruptly.

"By the skylights," one of the Knights whispered. There was horror in his voice.

Bodies pressed closer to Jevaithi. The short-hair cloaks smelled of oil and beast. Slowly, the Knights shuffled back towards the meltery. They nodded signals to each other, and Jevaithi found herself being lifted off the ground by a couple of strong arms. The Knights went faster, first at a trot, then a full run.

Men screamed behind them. A few Knights stumbled. A waft of cold air descended on Jevaithi. Through the gap between two of the Knights, she saw what they were fleeing.

A blue shadow, like the Legless Lion had been. This one was a man, taller than any of the Knights. His face was hard and white with a blue tinge. His eyes were dark holes without expression.

The protecting group around her fell apart as Knights drew swords.

"Go away, you spawn of sorcery!" someone yelled.

Jevaithi stumbled back, and would have fallen if it hadn't been for Rider Cornatan behind her.

"Careful, Your Highness." He put her back on her feet, and peered into the semidarkness.

He couldn't see the blue giant, nor could any of the Knights, some of whom were fighting a band of brawling youths who had come out of a street behind them. The Knights weren't even looking in the right direction. The blue giant grabbed one man by the collar of his cloak and smashed him into a lamppost. He didn't even scream, but sank in a boneless heap into the snow.

Jevaithi cried, "There!" and pointed at the fallen man. The blue giant was now coming towards her.

The Knights, including Rider Cornatan, jumped in front of her, even though she was sure they still couldn't see what they were fighting.

"There, there!" She pointed.

"Stay out of the way, Your Highness," Rider Cornatan snapped. "Or, you'll get in the way of our—"

The first of her guards fell.

Another group of youths burst into the square. One was running so fast he crashed into a Knight. The young man screamed garbled words. Following him was the blue Legless Lion, snarling, jumping around. The youth, who could obviously see the creature, was backing away, flailing his arms and shouting.

The Knights, who could not see the creature, mistook the young man for an attacker. One belted the young man on the head. His fellows attacked the Knight. Within moments, everyone was fighting each other, while the blue giant tossed bodies aside and smashed his way through the chaos.

He was coming for *her*, and the Knights couldn't see him.

"Stand aside!" a clear voice shouted.

A shadow sprang forward, putting itself between the blue man and the crowd. Yellow threads sparked from the cloaked silhouette, fanning out over the street. People yelled and ran in different directions. Most of them also couldn't see the golden strands. Icefire whipped up cloaks and crackled over the street in sizzling bolts like lightning that encased the blue giant in a shimmering net of icefire.

The Legless Lion jumped and snapped at the blue giant who was trying to push himself free of the golden threads.

"Come." The mysterious newcomer took hold of Jevaithi's hand. His voice sounded like that of a young man and his grip was warm.

"Before he kills everyone. I don't know how long this will hold him back. I'll take you to safety."

Jevaithi didn't question the order. She ran. The young man dragged her along. He turned sharply into a narrow alley where they had to squeeze past overflowing rubbish bins, out into another alley, around a corner into a narrower alley, past another group of brawling revellers, into another alley. *He knows the way.* Her companion was tall and lanky. He wore a Knight's cloak, but if there was an insignia of rank on his collar, she didn't see it.

He stopped at the door to some sort of warehouse, in a dead-end passageway. Their panting breaths sounded loud in the sudden silence. Puffs of steam floated in the blue air. He fumbled with something in his pocket.

"Just need to find the key." He gestured at the door. "We'll be safe in here."

His voice sounded so familiar that she reached out and pushed the hood of his cloak back.

The soft light showed the face of her rescuer. It was the flying champion, Isandor.

A strand of icefire snaked through the darkness, over her head. Jevaithi whirled just in time to see the ice wall behind her shimmering. A section of it went blue. Hardened, grey ice formed into a booted foot, a knee, a leg . . . Jevaithi stood as frozen. A blue-hued hand emerged from the wall.

"It's him," she whispered to Isandor, gripping his arm. "It's that blue monster."

Isandor retreated, pushing Jevaithi behind him. They couldn't run any more.

The alley ended here, in the door to the warehouse that belonged to Carro's father, and the blue giant blocked the only way out. Isandor reached for icefire, but he found only weak strands. He looked frantically for a weapon and found a snow shovel propped up against the wall.

The servitor detached from the wall, his face a mask of blue marble, expressionless, with black holes for eyes. He lunged.

Isandor hit out at the man. The shovel struck his arm with a bone-juddering clang like he had hit stone. The giant's aching cold shuddered through his bones.

Isandor fell back, dazed. How could that man have walked through a wall?

His view faded and he was jumping and barking. He snapped his jaws together, got a hold of the blue man's buttocks, but the blue giant just shook the Legless Lion off. He rolled in the snow, into a pile of crates.

Remember to breathe.

Isandor gulped air.

The Lion scrambled to its flippers, never ceasing its barking and snapping at the servitor.

Isandor picked up a snow shovel and flung it in the man's face, but he just batted it away.

The giant was too strong. He blocked the only way out of the alley. They were trapped.

"I'll make a bargain with you," Isandor tried.

The giant said nothing. He simply grabbed both his and Jevaithi's arms. The cold of the blue-skinned hand went through Isandor's clothes into his very bones.

"Keep me, but let her go," Isandor tried again.

Again, there was no reaction, not even to Jevaithi, who pummelled her fist into the man's arm. Silly, servitors only listened to their makers. This blue giant only listened to Tandor.

Isandor held his breath and looked at the Legless Lion. *Bite him!*

The animal surged forward, snapping and snarling, but the blue man pushed it aside as if it were a small child. An icy cold hand grabbed hold of Isandor's collar. Jevaithi was similarly constrained, and she was bashing the giant's arms, but he took no notice of her.

He dragged Isandor and Jevaithi out of the alley.

Jevaithi's eyes were wide with fear.

"I'm sorry," Isandor whispered. If he hadn't intervened, she might have made it back to the palace.

Maybe, maybe not.

"What's happening now?" she whispered. Her voice spilled over.

Isandor shrugged, too much of a coward to say, *Tandor is going to turn us into slaves*.

The blue man dragged them through other alleys, staying away from main streets, until they came to another warehouse. The Legless Lion, which had hobbled after them, sniffed the air and barked. From inside the building, barks responded.

A butchery.

The giant pulled a door open, pushed Isandor and Jevaithi inside, and slammed the door shut.

They were in a butchery backroom, much like his uncle's. A single icefire light burned in a bracket against the opposite wall. It gave off an eerie white glow, much brighter than the oil lamps used by most in the Outer City. White tiles covered the floor and walls. There were cages under the benches which lined the perimeter of the room. Inside, dark shapes moved about, snorting and sniffing.

Jevaithi stared, white-faced.

"I'm sorry," Isandor said again, and he looked away. It was his fault that she was in danger.

"Sorry about what? You've already helped me. The Knights were going to—"

"The Knights know you're Imperfect?"

She stared at him, wide-eyed. "You can see that?" Like this, she sounded like an ordinary girl, a very scared ordinary girl.

"I can see it in you just as well as you see it in me."

"It's the icefire that gives it away." She licked her lips. Her breath steamed.

Isandor said, "We must get out of here as soon as possible. The servitor is going to get Tandor, his master. I don't know exactly what he wants, but I think he wants to turn us into servitors, too."

"*Us?*" Her eyes widened. "What for?"

"We will be strong enough to break a man's neck. We can use icefire as he directs us. We can't disobey him."

"But what does he want with that power?"

"Kill the Knights? Rule the City of Glass? I don't know. I know that I don't like it and I want to get out of here before he comes back."

He inspected the door. It was bolted. There was a small window in the door, but even if it had been big enough for a person to climb through, which it wasn't, it had metal bars. There was another door at the back of the room, but it led into a storage room without doors or windows. The shelves were stacked with piles of frozen meat and folded parcels of skin. Nothing to use as a battering ram. There was no way out except that tiny window with metal bars. If he could turn himself into a long and skinny animal, he could get through. Even a snow fox could, he thought. The books had mentioned rumours of people so powerful they could change the physical shape of their bodies. That would be handy right now.

He shivered.

In his mind, he saw the blue man walking through the wall . . . He saw the blue Legless Lion hobble out of the arena; he felt the Lion's heart thud against his leg.

"Wait—I have an idea. It's probably stupid, but . . ." He hobbled over to one of the cages, and fumbled with the latch.

"What are you doing?"

"Help me. I'm going to open this. I want you to slam the door shut after one animal has come out."

"Why?"

"I'm going make a servitor. I have an idea. I could be stupid, but we don't know until we try."

She gave a small squeak, but nodded, her lips pressed together in a thin line. She took up position on the other side of the door.

All of a sudden it struck him how ridiculous this was, asking the Queen to do these things. Isandor hesitated.

"You know . . . for a noble girl having grown up in the palace, you're not afraid of anything."

"I am afraid," she said, and her voice trembled. "I'm just a lot more afraid of what will happen if I don't get out, or if the Knights catch me."

"The Knights? You're afraid of the Knights? I thought they protected you?"

That was what he'd always believed the Knights were about. That's what he had been *told* the Knights were about. They were the eyes and hands of the Queen, noble, honest—

She shook her head, her eyes blinking. "I live in a prison. I'm kept better than this animal here, but that is only while the Knights squabble over who out of their midst gets to rape me first. Tonight."

What?

"Don't look at me like that." Her voice spilled over. She covered her mouth with a white-gloved hand. Tears glittered in her eyes. "I don't want pity."

"Your Highness." Isandor reached out and touched her cheek. Such a vulnerable girl, too young to deal with this.

She looked up. "Don't call me that. I don't want it anymore. I want to be free. I want to go to the markets. I want to walk into the meltery and dance with the boys. I want . . ." Her voice spilled over in a sob. A tear ran down her cheek. She wiped it. "I'm sorry."

Isandor repressed an insane urge to kiss her, but he feared it would lead to all sorts of other things, and they didn't have the time for that.

"And so you will be free." He took the stick that stood against the wall and pushed the rope that dangled off the end through the eyelet so that it made a noose. He'd seen his uncle do this many times. "Stand there. Open the door. Slam it after the first animal has come out. I'll show you what I've been thinking." He sounded more confident than he felt.

She pressed her lips together, wiped her eyes and grasped the metal bars.

"Ready?"

Jevaithi nodded.

He opened the door to the cage.

A small female Legless Lion came out. Jevaithi slammed the metal grille on the nose of its mate, a young male. He yelped.

Isandor only had eyes for the animal, which hobbled about agitated. It wanted to go back to its mate, but Jevaithi stood in front of the cage, clamping a hand over her mouth. Yes, the animal stank of fish.

The Lion hobbled away but came to the opposite wall. It ran until it reached the corner and couldn't go any further. Isandor aimed with the stick. After three misses, he managed to slip the noose over the animal's head, yanking backwards. The Lion lost its grip on the slippery floor and slid over its belly. Isandor pulled the rope tight and wound it around the stick.

"Hold this."

Jevaithi's face was white, but she flipped both sides of her pristine white cloak over her shoulders and took the stick.

He took the animal by the back flippers and turned it onto its back. Then he pulled the dagger from his belt, just like he had done this afternoon, and lunged, while calling icefire from the air. The blade sank into the animal's chest. The ribs split open with a crack. Icefire lit the inside of the warehouse, flowing into the animal's chest. Isandor lifted out the heart, still pulsing, and stepped back.

"Let the rope go," he said.

Jevaithi looked on, wide-eyed. She relaxed her grip on the rope.

The animal wriggled itself out of the noose and rolled into a running position. Its fur had gone pale blue. It stopped and looked at him, waiting for him to tell it what to do. That's what servitors did.

Go, he told it. *You're free.*

With a jump of joy, the animal ran for the door, straight through it, and then it was gone. Yes!

Isandor turned to Jevaithi. "That's how we can get out."

"You're not suggesting that I . . ."

"It's the only way. You cut me, and I cut you. Then I walk through the wall, you pass both the hearts through the window up there, and then you walk through as well, and then we put the hearts back."

"But I've never—"

"Try it. You can do it. There is so much icefire about that it almost happens by itself, if you do it, as Imperfect. Practise. There's plenty of animals."

She looked sick, but nodded. "I'll try."

Isandor went to open the cage to let the second animal out. As it hobbled onto the tiled floor, the servitor female burst back through the wall. Isandor lunged for her neck and pushed the pulsing heart back into her chest. Icefire crackled through the room. The fur lost its blue tinge. The animal was whole again and frolicked through the room with her mate as if nothing had happened.

"I can't do that," Jevaithi stammered.

"Yes, you can. Try it." Isandor held out the dagger.

She took it, looking doubtfully at the animal which was shuffling sideways, playing with its mate.

"Kill it?"

"It won't be dead. It will be . . ." *your servitor, and its experience will torment you.* "It's only for a while. It's how we can escape. Please."

She gripped the knife in her sole hand. Isandor caught the animal with the noose and held it down for her.

She tightened her stance. Hesitated. Isandor held his breath.

Don't say you can't do it, because I might just agree. Who was he anyway, to think that this noble girl could kill an animal? He had to be crazy.

She pressed her lips together and stabbed. Golden icefire flowed from her single hand, even from her stump. The knife sank into the fur. Icefire crackled. The cut in the animal's chest flowered open.

The heart jumped out. Isandor caught it for her, warm and pulsing. She gave him a triumphant smile, and letting out a relieved breath at the same time. The Lion raised its head and tried to wriggle free from the noose. Its fur had gone blue and eerie.

"See? You can do it."

Her eyes were wide. She swallowed. "I'm . . . seeing things."

"That's because you see the world through the animal's eyes. Wait." He returned the heart to the shimmering spot in the animal's ribcage. The golden glow of icefire vanished, and the fur returned to its normal mottled grey. The Legless Lion barked. Isandor let the noose go.

Then he faced her again, peeling back his shirt to bare his chest.

"Do it to me. We can get out."

"No."

"You have to."

"No, I'd kill you." She shook her head, her face white as if she would throw up any moment.

He pulled her closer, the fur warm against his shivering body. The tip of the dagger dug into his skin, staining it with blood.

"If you kill me, I will die happy and free." His hand touched hers, and he had to stop himself caressing her skin. "If Tandor or the Knights get here before we get out, we'll be dead anyway. Do it, and we'll escape. Together."

"Are you sure?" She stared at him.

He nodded. "Please. Do it. Now."

She hefted the dagger, her hand trembling.

Isandor closed his eyes. They should have practised on the Legless Lions more. They should have . . . No time, no time.

He held his breath. "Do it, please." *Before I change my mind and I get scared.*

Impossible. He was *already* scared. Terrified. About to piss himself.

He felt, rather than saw, how her arm descended. The blade bit into his chest. A brief shot of intense pain. His scream died in his throat as ice cold invaded him. Silent wind whooshed out the hole in his chest. His life, seeping away from him. Death awaited him; he was—

Floating in the wind—

Everywhere and nowhere at all—

You are mine now. The voice was soft, but insistent. *I think I'm going to like it*.

He opened his eyes. The world had turned inside out. Shadows were white. The light against the wall was dark. Everything the opposite of what it should be.

There was only Jevaithi, holding his lifeblood in her hands. Her hair gleamed silver against her skin which was deep golden brown. Her eyes were rich magenta. She was so beautiful it hurt inside. He wanted to speak but couldn't. *I'll do everything for you*.

Here, take this. She passed him the dagger, while unbuttoning her dress. He stared at the dark skin, wanting to touch it, caress it—

Take my heart.

He didn't question the order; he was hers. He hefted the dagger and stabbed. Her face turned white even before he had the heart in his hands. It pulsed strongly, but it now looked dark in his eyes.

There was no time to contemplate the reason for the changed colours.

Here, hold this. He handed her the other heart. She cradled both in her single hand against her chest, his heart and hers, together. Oh, how he wanted to kiss her. Her eyes were dark and full of longing. Her voice echoed in his mind. *We'll kiss later*.

Yes, later, when they were safe.

He walked to the door and pushed his hands against it. Material bent around them. He pushed his arms further in, then a foot . . . He drew back, staring down at his two healthy legs. Two feet! In his mind, he was running over the snow plain, he was jumping over cracks in the ice, he—

No, he couldn't get distracted.

He pushed further through the door. Blurred shapes moved around him, and chilled him.

His leg came out into the clear air of the alley, followed by his hands. He pushed his head out. There was no one in the alley, so he pulled the rest of his body free of the door. Jevaithi moved in the darkness behind the little barred window.

Give me the hearts.

A white-blue hand passed through the window grille, holding an object that was too black for him to see. It fell heavy in his hands, ice-cold but pulsing. Safe. Then the other one.

The wall shimmered and Jevaithi walked through slowly, feeling her way with her hands. *Both* her hands. She stopped. Black eyes blinked at ten slender fingers, pale blue. The colour of her skin and eyes mattered nothing. She was so beautiful.

I'm free.

Her joy made him glow. He wasn't cold anymore. Tandor was right; he would never be cold anymore.

In two steps, he crossed the distance between them. He didn't stop to consider how he had never done what he intended to do; he bent and closed his mouth over hers. Her lips were soft and warm and willing. Her elation almost hurt.

I love you, I love you, I love you. Her inner voice sank deep into every fibre of his body.

He had to tear himself from her grip. *We must go.* They weren't safe yet.

Yes, I know that. Her gaze wandered to the hearts. *Will we put them back?*

He had intended to do that as soon as they got out, but he shook his head. Like this, they were strong. Like this, most Knights couldn't see them, and like this, Tandor couldn't make them his servitors. No, he had a much better idea, but that would have to wait until they were truly safe. He slid both hearts in his pocket.

Come.

They ran. The Legless Lion that was still outside hobbled along with them, even though the animal was now free. Or was it? Isandor felt in his pocket where he still had that animal's heart.

He ran, like a real person. His leg was whole and propelled him forward as if he flew. The joy, the elation, her warm hand in his—he was never going to let her go. He was going to rule the world, and put all the injustice right. He was—

Careful. Jevaithi's thought came like a shout.

She had stopped and yanked him back with tremendous strength. The Legless Lion couldn't stop quite so quickly and it slid into the street on its belly before finding grip with its flippers and hobbling back.

What is it?

Knights.

Isandor peeked around the corner and he could see them, too, a group of four.

They can't see us. He made to move into the street.

Wait.

What? He turned to her, to see worry crossing her face.

Don't you feel it?

Yes, he did. A pulling sensation that made him shiver.

Look. She pointed.

Black threads moved against the light blue sky, tendrils of mist streaming towards the Knights.

What is it? The pulling became stronger, as if threads were stuck to his skin and refused to let go.

Icefire.

Yes, in this state icefire looked black. *Leading to the Knights?*

The group of Knights had come closer. Their voices sounded far off, but the warmth in their bodies was close.

There were four Knights, and one, at the front of the group, held an object that attracted icefire, which wove over the Knights' heads.

Even through the tangle of black strands, Isandor recognised this Knight.

Carro. He was the one who held the object, a metal staff, poised as if it was a sword, with icefire streaming towards it.

"Which way?" one of the other Knights asked.

Carro waved the staff, his gloves covered in rime. "Something is very strong here." His voice sounded hollow.

He looked into the street where Isandor and Jevaithi stood, straight past them, and then moved the staff slowly so that it pointed at them.

No!

Jevaithi's shriek cut into Isandor's mind. She stood frozen like some grotesque ice statue. Dark strands of icefire flowed from her hands to the staff. The outlines of her right hand were already fading. Icefire flew from his body as well, dissolving skin into the air.

Oh, the pain. Like boiling water over his skin.

With all the force he could muster, Isandor shoved Jevaithi into a porch, out of the path of the black braid of icefire. Now it hit him at full force. Pain exploded in every part of his body. He wanted to, but couldn't, scream.

With immense effort, he picked up a lid from a composting bin and flung it at the Knights as hard as he could. It crashed into one of them, sending the young man toppling into the fellow next to him.

Carro yelled, "Watch out!"

The device had lost contact, and in that moment, Isandor covered the ground between them.

You betrayed me.

Carro couldn't hear him of course. He was wildly waving the staff, which made contact with Isandor again. White-hot pain flared.

He was dimly aware that a shadow leapt up between him and Carro. Something snarled. The next moment, the Legless Lion had thrown itself at the group. Carro stumbled and fell. The staff flew out of his hands, twirling and tumbling until it hit the ground.

Carro sat there, dazed, white-faced. His mates ran off down the street.

Isandor sat on hands and knees, panting.

The Legless Lion lay in the snow. It had jumped up to save him and had injured itself by touching the staff. Its body lay still, but when Isandor ran his hand through the rough fur, one flipper twitched.

Isandor flinched with the animal's pain. It lifted its head and blinked at him. He reached in his pocket and brought out the animal's heart.

Go, he told it as he slid it back into the hairy chest. *You have done enough.* The animal's fur shivered as it returned to its normal state.

The Lion let its head sink back onto the ground. *Sleep.*

Isandor rose. The animal would recover.

Jevaithi had come out of her hiding place and walked towards the staff which lay on the ground, absorbing lazy tendrils of icefire. Now that Carro wasn't holding it anymore, it had lost much of its power.

Don't touch it.

She bent over it, shuddering visibly.

Carro had retreated against the icy wall of a limpet, his eyes wide, trembling. He was looking at the Legless Lion, which had raised itself and slowly hobbled down the street.

Isandor grabbed the front of Carro's cloak, heaving him up until his feet came off the ground. His friend, taller than him, weighed no more than a sack of flour.

Carro's eyes bulged, still focused on a point behind Isandor. He gave a tiny squeak. "Where are you?"

Isandor hesitated. What would he do? He could easily slam Carro into the wall and kill him. He could break Carro's neck with a single snap. His hands ached to do just that. Carro had *betrayed* him. Carro had destroyed his life, his chance to be respected.

I would have been discovered anyway.

Isandor looked down into Carro's face. There were tears in his eyes. His lips were blue and shivering. One cheek was dirty from where the lid of the composting bin had hit him. A trail of blood ran over his face from a cut above his eyebrow.

He's just a coward. Carro did what people told him to do; he had always been like that.

Isandor got no pleasure out of killing cowards.

Prove yourself a real soldier, and we'll fight over this later.

He tightened his hold on Carro's cloak, swung his arm back and let Carro fly from his hands. His friend slid across the street like a rag doll, slammed into a heap of snow and remained there. For a moment, Isandor was afraid he'd used too much force, but then Carro raised his head.

Run, Jevaithi.

He took her hand, before he changed his mind, before he could no longer control his lust for blood. They ran through the streets, across the markets, where the merchants were guarding their stalls, eying a group of youths who stood outside the meltery. Isandor wondered if it was the same group he had joined briefly before rescuing Jevaithi.

The youths held sticks and shovels and stood together talking in low voices. Most of them had pulled their cloak collars over their faces. Acrid smoke billowed through the streets.

No one noticed Isandor and Jevaithi crossing the square. No one followed.

They went down the slope to the plain and the festival grounds, still bathed in the blue glow of eternal dawn. Aisles between tents were deserted, the previous day's activity only hinted at by the tram-pled snow.

Two Knights guarded the eagle pens, standing in silent reflection, hidden in the warmth of their cloaks. Neither stirred when Isandor led the way through the pens.

The guards might not have seen anything, but Isandor's eagle certainly did. It lifted its head and gave a series of clicking sounds that signified alertness.

Shhh. Isandor lifted the saddle off the fence and slung it on the bird's back, checking several times over his shoulder to see if anyone noticed. The Knights were chatting to each other, facing the other way where people were shouting and flames rose above the roofs. He fastened the clasps and stepped into his riding harness, belting it up across his chest

Ready?

Jevaithi nodded.

Isandor hefted her onto the eagle. *Hold on.* She grabbed the hand-holds on top of the saddle. He untied the eagle's reins and jumped up behind her, whistling at the bird. It spread its wings and with a whoosh of wind and flapping of wings, launched into the air.

There was a shout below them. A couple of Knights ran onto the snowfields, waving their arms. Too late.

All they would see was a riderless eagle flying over the moonlit landscape.

But down there, just entering the festival grounds was Tandor, running and shouting. He could see what Isandor had done, but there was no way Tandor could stop them.

Isandor laughed. He had fooled them all. He clutched Jevaithi to his chest, guiding the bird with his knees. He didn't need to hold on. He didn't need to breathe. The cold wind didn't bother either of them. They ruled the world.

CHAPTER 24

LORIANE GASPED and stirred, lifting her head off something hard that hurt her ear. She sat, to her surprise, on the floor of Isandor's sleeping shelf, leaning on the chair by his bed. One leg had gone numb and her ankle hurt where it pressed into the floor.

The fire in the stove downstairs had died to a pitiful glow that barely lit the furniture.

She must have fallen asleep, although she couldn't remember sitting down. Myra slept in Isandor's bed, her mouth open, her arm twitching by her side.

Loriane heaved herself to her feet. She did remember giving Myra the sleeping draught which had stopped her pains. The girl was too tired to continue, not having slept for two days, and all the hard work was still ahead.

A soft noise drifted up from downstairs, the sound of scrabbling on wood. If she was not mistaken, there was someone at the door, and now she guessed that the knocking had woken her up.

As quietly as she could, Loriane went down the stairs, across the main room, into the icy hall. On the way, she glanced at her own bed, but it was empty. Where was Tandor? He hadn't said anything about where he was going.

She opened the outside door a tiny crack. Against the faint light of the midnight glow above the horizon, she could just make out a dark figure.

"Mistress Loriane?" A male voice, young. She didn't recognise it. The man was much taller than her and wore a cloak. A Knight? She didn't know any Knights except Isandor.

"Who is it?"

"Please, I need help."

Loriane hesitated, registered that he hadn't answered her question. Illegal business? Something to do with Tandor? She wanted to say *He isn't here*, but that might betray Tandor.

"Please," the man said again, and she heard a wobble in his voice. "I'm injured. I don't know where else to go. The post at the festival grounds is closed, and you are the only healer I know. . . ."

No, Isandor wasn't the only Knight she knew. He had a friend who had gone to the Knights with him, a son of a fabric merchant, a pale and pasty boy. This might well be him.

Slowly, she undid the chain and opened the door.

He stepped into the hall, where the feeble light allowed her to see the young man better. She thought this was indeed Isandor's friend. He wore a short-hair Knight's cloak, wet and dirty. His face was covered in blood, which had plastered his hair against his forehead and run into his eyes.

"Thank you. Sorry for . . . waking you up. 'S too much fighting . . . in the street t' go . . . somewhere else. Don't want to go home." He needed to breathe through his mouth because dried blood blocked his nose.

She ushered him into the main room, motioning for him to be quiet, and gestured for him to sit down next to the stove. "I have a patient asleep upstairs," she said in a low voice.

She grabbed a clean cloth, wet it with water from the jar that sat on the stove, and passed it to him.

"Here, wipe yourself with this. Wait here. I'll be back."

She rushed up the stairs to get her bag. What a bit of luck that she had taken her kit from the medical tent in the festival grounds this afternoon.

The sound of her footsteps woke Myra. She jerked up and coughed.

"Myra?"

It was hot and stuffy up here with the simmering fire, but Myra was shivering. Her eyes were wide and distant and her breath came in shallow gasps.

"You're having pains again?"

Myra nodded and the next moment vomited all over her stomach. It was mostly water, since she hadn't eaten anything all day, but her nightgown was drenched.

"Oh!" Myra cried. She wrestled herself free of the blankets, rolled out of the bed onto hands and knees and sat there, alternately coughing and gasping and retching.

"Myra, Myra, calm down."

But the girl wasn't listening. Loriane wrestled the sodden nightgown off and stumbled to Isandor's cupboard to find spare clothes.

Where was Tandor? He could have helped her with the young Knight downstairs.

She yanked a nightgown out of the cupboard. Myra was crying. She was drenched in sweat, and, Loriane realised with a shock, pushing. Was she ready yet?

"Come, Myra, let me examine you first." She managed to get Myra off her knees but before she was back on the bed her waters broke, with fluid exploding all down her legs. Myra screamed. "Let me go. Don't touch me!"

She grabbed hold of the back of the bed with white-knuckled hands and pushed until she was red in the face, gasped for air and pushed again. More fluid dribbled down her legs and puddled at her bare feet.

Loriane's heart thudded. She had given the girl a lot of sedative; she couldn't have gone from sleep to this stage so quickly.

"Myra, just calm down. Breathe deeply. I only want to check you."

"I know about this checking of yours. It hurts. You keep away from me."

Loriane put a hand on the girl's shoulder. It was slick with sweat. "Myra—"

"Keep away, I said." Myra lashed out and hit Loriane. Her nails bit into the skin of her arm.

"Ouch!" Loriane stepped back. Red welts rose on her wrist.

The brat! She felt like hitting the girl in the face, but she knew that sometimes women in extreme pain reacted like that.

She schooled her voice to calmness. "Very well. I will leave you. I have another patient anyway." She started down the stairs.

"No! Don't go," Myra screamed. "I wasn't serious."

"But I was. I'll be downstairs."

And she strode off, feeling more welts on her face from where Myra had hit her. Oh, if Tandor came back . . . She balled her fists. Tandor, Tandor, all her trouble could be traced back to him. He came here, dumped this uneducated nutcase on her, and then spent all day gallivanting about town.

Oh, if he came back, she was going to tell him to pack up his girlfriend and take off with her, and to leave her alone.

The young man still sat next to the stove, holding the towel to his face. His eyes met hers and a twinge stirred in her. Just briefly, the way the light played over his cheekbone, she was reminded of a young Knight in the meltery, many years ago. He was strong and handsome, and as they danced by the firelight, he'd enclosed her gull feather in his fist and yanked it hard and sharp, so the leather strap broke. His intense eyes said, *you're mine*, and she had been delighted. With this Knight, a Learner like the young man sitting next to her kitchen stove, there was no fumbling in freezing warehouses. He'd rented a room in one of the Outer City's inns, a room with a large bed and a blazing fireplace. She had bled, just a bit, but he had been gentle, and he'd let her sleep next to him. In the morning, he'd given her a card with how to contact him, should that prove necessary. Which it did.

Never again had she carried a child for a Knight. Never again had she seen the young man, nor her baby boy with the face all squashed from birth. She very much doubted she would recognise either if she saw them again.

She set her things on the table next to the young Knight and proceeded to clean up his cheek, gentle around the edges of his cuts. She saw the handsome Knight's face, lit side-on by the fire. She felt his weight pressing on her, his warm skin against hers.

Once more, she was in the sled, her father driving it through the snowstorm. She sat in the back wrapped in furs, and every bump in the ice had cut through her belly like a hot knife. She'd been petrified of giving birth out there, on the snow-covered plains between the Outer City and the palace, but the child had taken a whole agonising day of pains to arrive.

Wails from Myra drifted from upstairs.

"What's with her?" the Knight asked, concern on his face.

"Well, you know I'm normally a midwife. . . ."

He raised his eyebrows, and then a look of understanding came over his face. "Oh. If I'm keeping you from your work . . ."

"Not at all." Loriane cringed and tried hard not to feel guilty for walking out on Myra. For once she was going to be tough like the midwives in the palace birthing rooms. Those women slapped misbehaving girls in the face, like that old hag had slapped her, not once, but three times. Myra would have to learn on the job what it meant to be a breeder. You only scream when it's bad.

She dabbed at the young man's face, dislodging clots of blood from his nose. Strangely enough, he didn't smell of bloodwine. "Well, someone certainly gave you a good beating."

A tiny shiver went through him. The shiver became a spasm. His muscles tensed up.

"Are you all right? Are you feeling sick—"

But he didn't react to her. His gaze was far off and his breath came in shallow gasps.

Loriane grabbed his wrist. His pulse raced like crazy.

Before she could do anything, he blinked and shook his head, meeting her eyes. Was there shame in them?

"What was that?" she asked.

He shrugged and looked away.

"Is there anything you're not telling me? Do you have a problem?"

His mouth twitched. He hesitated. "Well, I get these . . ." Then he stopped, shook his head again.

"These what?" she prompted.

But he would say no more and seemed reluctant to meet her eyes. She rinsed out the bloodied cloth, weighing up the risk of what she was about to say. She had seen little spells like this before, but he was a *Knight* after all, and Knights weren't *supposed* to be inflicted like this. But the condition could be quite dangerous.

"You know," she began. "Physical imperfection isn't the only type of defect caused by icefire. Some people have imperfect minds. They seem to find it hard to see the difference between a real experience and things that have happened in the past. They keep reliving memories, sometimes from long ago—"

"I'm *not* crazy." His voice was much too forceful.

"I'm not suggesting that at all."

"I'm fine."

"I'm sure you are."

A silence followed, broken only by Myra's moans. Loriane had washed all the blood off his cuts, which were deep and nasty. What by the skylights had he done to himself? The worst cut had collected half a bag's worth of sand. It looked like he'd been dragged along the street. But his injury was not what concerned her. This young man had serious mental trouble, and he was in denial about it.

She took a deep breath, gathering courage to speak again. "Just in case, I want you to know that ichina will help."

"Ichina?" He faced her now. "But that's for girls trying to . . ." His cheeks flushed.

"Ichina is a powerful medicine that will do much more than help girls conceive. It also helps a number of other conditions, although they're not common."

"So that's why we only hear about girls taking it?" He sounded relieved.

"Yes." She let a small silence lapse and then she asked him, "Do you want some?"

He hesitated. "If, say, a boy needed to take it for—um—other reasons, would that boy also have trouble getting a girl pregnant, you know, *before* he takes it?"

Loriane had to restrain a snort. Oh, these adolescents were so transparent sometimes. What had he been doing? Fooling around above his station, and now he was afraid his family would have to foot the bill?

"Quite likely." Although she didn't know this for sure. It wasn't important. The future would bring whatever it would bring.

He blew out a breath.

Loriane asked again. "Would you want some?"

He nodded, once.

At that moment the door clanged. Loriane turned.

"Tandor!"

His hair was wet, with frozen chunks of ice, and hung down the sides of his face in dirty strings. A dark stain marked his cloak and blood had dried up in a scratch across his cheekbone.

He wasn't looking at her, but staring at the young Knight.

"What are *you* doing here?" He spat the words out like broken teeth.

"Tandor," Loriane protested. "That's not how you treat—"

Tandor strode across the kitchen and grabbed young Knight by the collar of his cloak. "You let him escape!"

"I don't know what you're talking about, sorcerer!" The Knight's eyes bulged.

"Oh yes, you do, or you wouldn't be sitting here with your face bloodied up. You let them out of that warehouse, didn't you? And then you found that your friend wasn't your friend anymore?"

"I have no idea what you're talking about!" the Knight shouted.

"Hey, no fighting in my kitchen!" Loriane yelled, but the men paid her no attention.

The Knight scrabbled for his belt. He pulled out a long metal stick and jammed the point in Tandor's chest.

Tandor froze, eyeing the glittering crystal that pushed into his shirt.

The thing wasn't sharp at all, but Tandor let the young man go, his eyes wide. "It was you with the sink?"

"It was me." He let the staff sink ever so slightly.

Tandor's eyes roamed the young man's face. "Oh, I see."

"I don't see, Tandor," Loriane said. "I don't see anything at all apart from the fact that you're bothering my patient—"

"Loriane, he is—"

"I don't care who he is. The Healer's Guild made me pledge that I would help every sick or injured person who comes to my door. Get out or make yourself useful. Go upstairs and see if you can talk some sense into that girl of yours."

A brief smirk went over the young Knight's face.

Tandor pulled the Knight's collar tight with his golden pincer hand. "Don't even dare say it."

Loriane rolled her eyes. Why did men get so hung up about their dicks or lack thereof?

Tandor looked down. The Knight had the staff once more directed at his stomach. What was that thing?

"You think you're so smart with that toy, don't you?" Tandor snorted.

The Knight pressed his lips together. Blood was again running from the wound on his forehead.

"I'll get you, sorcerer."

"You wouldn't dare."

Tandor grabbed the young Knight's wrist in his pincer hand. Pushed the staff away and the Knight back into the one of the posts that supported the sleeping shelves. He lazily withdrew something from his pocket, a long metal barrel with a wooden handle. He pointed it at the Knight and poked the metal into the soft skin under his chin.

Loriane had only heard of the Chevakian powder guns, but she was sure this was such a thing.

The Knight's eyes widened.

"You should have known that you can't surprise me," Tandor said.

The boy swallowed hard. He clutched his staff.

Tandor laughed. "Ah, we *are* a coward, aren't we? Why don't you go and tell your Knights that the game is over? The game is over for everyone."

"Now stop this idiocy in my house!" Loriane yelled. "Tandor, leave him alone so I can treat him."

Tandor laughed, defying the Knight to make another comment. He didn't, and Tandor stepped back.

Loriane finished with the young man in silence, while Tandor leaned against the pillar. In a very demonstrative way, he took two bullets from his pocket, jackknifed open the barrel and slid the bullets into the magazine.

The young man gave him nervous glances. As soon as Loriane finished bandaging the wound, he jumped up.

Tandor clicked the barrel back into place and pointed the gun at the Knight's back while he ran to the door.

The door shut.

He had forgotten his ichina.

Tandor laughed. "If all else fails, a Chevakian powder gun will kill. Bang, bang."

Loriane whirled at him. "Tandor, are you crazy? What is this stupid behaviour about? That young man missed out on some important treatment because of you."

He smiled, but that only made her fury greater. The Knight was an angry young man, who might do silly things without treatment.

"He'll be fine."

"How do you know that? What do you know anyway? Why shouldn't he come back here with a bunch of Knights to question me? You haven't lived in the city for years. Things have been different ever since Maraithe died. She had the Knights in hand, but Jevaithi is much too young. They don't listen to her, and from what I've seen, they shelter her from the people. She hardly goes out, and the Knights just do whatever they want, so if they want to come back here and burn down my house, they will. I can tell you that. And it happens to people, I can tell you that, too. You know the merchant Merro—"

Tandor smiled. "Jevaithi is gone." Then he started laughing. "Jevaithi is gone with that boy of yours. I saw them fly off on his eagle. Towards the mountains. Bye, bye."

"Isandor?"

By the skylights, Tandor had gone mad.

"He was kicked out of the Knighthood for being Imperfect, to be imprisoned in the palace, but he escaped everyone, even me. He took Jevaithi from under their noses."

Tandor laughed, the sound a strange shriek.

Loriane had never heard him laugh, not like this. "Tandor, what's wrong with you?" He was telling lies, wasn't he? He was crazy; something had flipped in his mind.

"What's wrong, what's wrong?" Tears ran down his cheeks. "We're all going to die. That's what's wrong."

Loriane's heart thudded against her ribs, but she forced herself into calm.

"Of course we are going to die. Life is a terminal illness." *And you seem to suffer badly*.

"Loriane." He crossed the kitchen to her and scooped her in his arms. "Loriane, I love you." He bent forward and pushed his mouth on hers. His tongue met hers, hot and passionate. "There. I've said it. I love you, I love you."

Loriane pushed him away. "You're drunk." But she didn't smell any liquor on his breath. "Now you're either going to tell me what all this is about, or . . ."

"Or what?"

"It'll be morning soon enough and I'll have Knights on my doorstep, by which time you'll no doubt be long gone. I need something to tell them. What happened? What did you do? What am I going say?"

"Loriane, calm down."

"No, Tandor. I don't understand why you had to threaten him. I don't. You can't just come in here and create problems for me."

"Have I ever left you with a problem?"

"Are you kidding? My whole life is a problem of your making, starting with that baby you brought me. Who is Isandor, Tandor, why is he important to you and why have you never told me?"

"I mean a problem you can't handle?"

She snorted. "One day this whole game of yours is going to fall apart. Whatever game you're playing. And we're all going to suffer for it."

There was a scream from upstairs.

"By the skylights, Myra."

Loriane thudded up to the sleeping shelf. Tandor remained halfway up the stairs.

Myra was on her hands and knees on the floor, rocking from side to side. She glanced up between sweat-soaked strands of hair.

"I hate you." She spat out the words.

Loriane wasn't sure who she meant. Both of them, probably. Doubts about the father of the child resurfaced. Tandor hung around Myra too much not to be involved, and he still hadn't told her why he had brought the girl with him, rather than hidden her somewhere else. He'd lied to her. The child was his after all.

Why, Tandor, why? She looked at his handsome profile in the glare from the stove. She loved him; she hated him. It was time for her to break with him, to stop waiting for him to make sense to her.

"Tandor, stop whatever silly games you're playing and give me a hand. Hold her."

His eyes widened. "Hold her?"

"He's not . . . holding . . . any part . . . of me," Myra panted. Her voice was hoarse.

"Then sit still. I'm going to examine you, and if you hit me again, I'm going to belt you so hard your head is going to hurt worse than the rest of you. Understand?"

Myra nodded, but a pain took over. She rocked, and moaned and cried. Loraine washed her hands, cringing as her own belly tensed up. Stupid girl, by the time it came to the hard work, she would have no energy left.

"Girl, shut up. You're not going to get that child out by screaming. Now sit still." She crouched on the floor, awkward because of her own belly. Myra was crying.

She slid her hand inside the girl's softness. The womb tensed up. Myra screamed.

"It hurts, it hurts."

"Shut up. It's not that bad."

But then she probed with her fingers and felt that it was bad. By the skylights, she should have checked earlier.

"Tandor, do you have that sled and driver handy?"

He raised his eyebrows.

"The child is facing the wrong way. I need to take her to the palace."

Tandor's eyes widened. "The palace?"

In one hit, his face had lost its madness.

CHAPTER 25

FIRE LIT UP the sky. Flapping flames reached over the rooftops, spreading foul smoke in the air. People ran through the street, mere silhouettes in the dusky night. Some carried sticks as weapons, others had their faces covered.

Carro walked through the dark streets alone, cold air biting through his cloak. His face hurt, his muscles hurt, his head hurt. He'd fled Mistress Loriane's house without the medicine, but he could hardly go back.

He was sure that the man in Mistress Loriane's kitchen was the same he'd hunted earlier that day. Who was he, and what was he doing there? He might be dressed up as a noble, but he was no noble of the City of Glass. The man spoke with a Chevakian accent.

Carro knew he should seek Rider Cornatan urgently to tell him of this man, but on the other hand . . . Mistress Loriane had said that ichina would help stop the confusing memories. Surely there would be some ichina at the medical post in the festival grounds. The post was closed, but it was only a tent and he could easily get in. Taking medicine he needed wasn't stealing, was it? He'd rather no one else found out about it. It was a medicine for *women* and he had seen his sister prepare it many times. It never worked for her. But his sister was only his half-sister, wasn't she? Born from a different breeder. And what was wrong with him didn't have *anything* to do with a girl's ability to conceive, did it? Or rather—by the skylights, Korinne. *She* had probably taken it and was now waiting until she and her father could come to his door to claim their prize. He didn't want the care of a child. His Knight's stipend would never pay for a house and a wife, and *servants*. A Knight couldn't very well live in the Outer City either.

And he just didn't, *didn't*, want that sort of thing. Knights, especially Senior Knights, often paid families to look after their children, since most didn't marry. However, they were from noble families and had money, and they had lineages and inheritances to look after. He was only Carro, and no one cared about any brats of his.

Then you should have thought about it before you acted. He could almost hear his father's voice. His father was right, but his father was a jerk, and Carro would rather *die* than accept any help from the man.

Was that how he himself had come about? His father had been careless during the Newlight festival, but didn't care, didn't want him, got him anyway, and now Carro was about to do the same to a child of his? Rejecting a little boy whose only wish was to be liked?

A strange thought occurred to him: what if Isandor got *Jevaithi* pregnant? Isandor had no money at all; he didn't even have a family. Oh, that would be priceless, with all the Knights drooling over her and all the speculation of who would father Jevaithi's children. And then the Knights found she would have the child of a dirt-poor boy from the Outer City, an Imperfect at that. Hilarious.

Carro chuckled, then he started laughing. He laughed and laughed and couldn't stop laughing.

A man stopped and asked if he was all right, but Carro couldn't see him. The street, the people, the limpets, the orange sky above all blurred into streaks of light and dark. Tears of freezing water bit into his cheeks.

"Yes, yes, I'm all right," he said and the man left.

But he wasn't all right, wasn't he? He was crazy, damaged, sick. A common Outer City healer could see that.

He moved through the streets with the flow of the crowd, under cover of darkness. The air resonated with angry voices. People looked at him from the corners of their eyes. Young men in black formed little groups and spoke to each other in low voices. In a street nearby people were shouting. In an alley between two limpets, he caught a glimpse of a blazing fire and lithe silhouettes running away from a patrol of Knights.

Carro jammed his hands in his pockets and bent his head, hoping not to attract any attention.

Who were these people coming out in support of the Imperfects? Why were there so many of them? Did this mean the entire Brotherhood of the Light and all their pupils supported Thilleians? That they *were* Thilleians?

He had read of the time before the uprising against the king, when the common people stirred against those who held all power. There had been hordes of looters in the streets, demanding for the king to come out of the palace. The people had *lynched* the king's guards, hacked them to death and cut them up into pieces.

Something like that could easily happen again.

Carro slumps on the table. Rows and rows of numbers dance before his eyes. He could put his head on the book and sleep. All night, he's been sitting here. His fingers are cramped, his toes frozen.

One mistake in his additions, and he can start over. The figures never add up. Income and expenditure never balance. Records are missing or incomplete. One complaint to his father, and another book is added to the pile. No dinner until he's done.

He wishes that his father, like normal fathers, would hit him. Punishment by accountancy is cruel, slow, mind-numbing and, in the unheated warehouse, incredibly cold. His hands hurt. His feet hurt and he is beyond shivering.

"Hey, watch out where you're going!" a man shouted.

Someone bumped into Carro, a hard knock of a shoulder against his upper arm. Carro just stood there, gulping breath.

Carro mumbled an apology, rubbing his arm. One way or another, he must get the ichina to stop those spells.

If he left it too long, he was going to be expelled from the Knighthood, and he would have no other option than to go back to his family.

He felt himself sliding into another vision and had to steady himself against a lamppost. It was getting so bad recently. He was mad, not fit for duty. He was—

"Hey. Carro, isn't it?"

Carro looked up, into the grey eyes of one of Rider Cornatan's private hunters, Farey. He was out of uniform, wearing a cloak as dark and sleek as his hair. He raised his eyebrows at the bandage on Carro's face.

"I . . . I was looking for my patrol," Carro stammered, his tongue feeling like an overcooked piece of meat. He was still struggling to hold onto the present.

The eyebrows rose further.

Carro squirmed. This man had the ability to make you feel uneasy without saying anything. He added, "They fled."

"Real brave hearts, huh?"

Carro nodded, and looked aside. He knew what Farey would think of him: weak, unfit to command even a bunch of Apprentices. He had to *punish* the lot of them, and punish them hard.

"We . . . encountered some enemies . . . invisible ones." It seemed such a lame story, at least when facing this strange and very unnerving man.

"Ah."

It was too dark, but Carro thought a look of bemusement crossed Farey's face. His eyes glittered with mirth. Something in his smile made Carro shiver, not because he was cold, but because . . .

Both times when he had been to Rider Cornatan's bathroom, there had been more men than women, and both times, he felt the hunters considered Korinne a floozy who didn't belong there, and who was merely a plaything for a child.

Real Knights didn't play with girls; they played with other men.

Carro's heart thudded. What had Farey come to ask him?

"I'll . . . have to punish my patrol for running away."

"Yes."

"What about you?" He barely knew what he was saying. All he could see were Farey's grey eyes, intense and amused.

"My missions are always simple."

"Oh?"

"I was looking for you."

Carro's heart jumped. He saw Farey in Rider Cornatan's bathroom, his lean and muscled chest, his olive skin—

"I was asked to save your arse, and get you out of here before these riots blow up."

A nursemaid.

Farey had come as nursemaid. Rider Cornatan thought he needed a minder. He thought Carro was soft; Farey thought Carro was soft.

Carro paced in the empty hall, up, down, past the pathetic members of his patrol, whom he had dragged out of the dormitory.

He was still shaking from his encounter with Farey and the flight back through the freezing night air. He was shaking with anger, at himself, at his stupidity, at everyone for playing games with him.

"You stupid idiots," he yelled. "You left your commanding officer like a bunch of screaming girls."

The boys stood there, white-faced, dirty, eyes downcast, not looking at one another, especially not looking at him.

"What the fuck did you think you were doing?" Carro yelled, replaying in his mind how the Tutors yelled at him, and trying to copy. "We were to stay together at all times. Isn't that one of the things we learn?"

"We can't fight when it comes to icefire," Inran said, his eyes on the floor. "It's not a fair fight."

"No fight is fair!" Carro grabbed Inran's collar. Just as well he'd learned so much from watching the Tutor. "I can't remember fights being fair when I was at the receiving end of them. Did I run? No! Look at you lot. You decide to run off—by yourself. *Deserting.* Do you know what the punishment is for desertion?"

"There were two blue ghosts." Inran's lip was trembling.

"There were—what?" Spit flew from Carro's mouth.

Inran cowered back. "There were two blue ghosts. I was scared. I thought you'd seen them, too."

"Thought? You *thought?* Apprentices never *think* anything. You are not here to do any thinking. Your stupidity nearly got me killed. Is that what you wanted? Do you know who appointed me to this position?" Carro had to stop yelling to catch his breath.

Inran shook his head, blinking. He was one of the boys who used to egg on Jono and Caman when they teased Carro in the dormitory, but he didn't look so brave now.

Isandor looks up at him with those strong, blue eyes.

"All you need to do, Carro, is tell him you won't do it. You have been accepted into the Knights and you will have your own income. Your father can no longer demand that you do things for him if he's not paying for your upkeep."

"It's easy for you to say. You don't have a father." *That was a very nasty remark, Carro.*

Isandor fell into a moment of silence. Then: "Try it. Tell him you're busy. What can he do?"

"Give me a beating."

Isandor shakes his head, and Carro notices how fuzzy his friend's chin is becoming.

"Carro, you're sixteen. Your father won't beat you. He's an old man and you are stronger than he. He's afraid of you."

They should be afraid of me.

Carro let Inran go and paced back to the middle of the room, then whirled to face the boys. Inran stared at him with wide eyes. Jono and Caman were quiet enough, but looked absent-minded. They hadn't even listened to what he had said.

"What are you staring at? Get your rotten arses out of here."

The boys saluted and made for the door. Jono and Caman glanced at each other, and Jono smiled, a smile that said, *We haven't been punished.* Rider Cornatan would think had he been too soft. Not fit to command a patrol. These Apprentices should be so scared of him they wet their pants.

"Apprentice." Carro made the utmost attempt to let his voice sound harsh. How did Rider Cornatan achieve that?

The boys stopped in the doorway, Caman furthest into the corridor.

Carro had not forgotten Jono's taunts. The boys hated him all right; they had hated him from the moment he'd joined. They'd never hated Isandor, because Isandor wasn't special in the same way he was. Isandor was never any competition in the eyes of those pampered noble boys. That's why they hated him, because his presence threatened them. *Then you must hate them back.* Rider Cornatan's words.

Carro joined the two at the door and paced around them, slowly and deliberately.

"Do you need to be taught a lesson?"

Meet violence with violence. Payback time.

"You." He pulled Jono's uniform by the neck. Why had he never noticed that he had grown taller than the bully?

"Hey! You can't do that!" Jono squealed.

"Yes, I can. I'm your superior, like it or not, and you will respect me and obey my orders."

"I was obeying—"

"You were not."

Jono gasped a few words, trying to prise his fingers between his neck and the collar that cut into the skin. His eyes went wide.

A hand comes into Carro's field of vision, a hand filled with snow. The next moment, the snow hits his face, and the hand rubs it into his stinging cheeks.

Carro screams.

Someone is sitting on his back, knees painfully pressing into his spine.

"Stop it, stop it!"

His mouth fills up with snow. Carro spits.

Someone pulls his hair.

"Listen to me, you worthless runt," a boy hisses in his ear. "Any time we meet you again, we will repeat this. Understood?"

Carro nods. A cold lump of snow slides down his back between his clothes and his bare skin.

"Understood?" the boy says again, but louder.

Carro nods again.

The boy fumbles for the back of Carro's trousers, lifts the waist-band and shoves in the handful of snow.

The other boys are laughing.

※

Carro hated them, he hated Isandor, he hated everyone. No one ever respected him. No one. Even Isandor, a *cripple*, treated him like a weakling, like someone who needed help. He didn't need help. He could punish these boys just as well as everyone else had always punished him.

He tightened his grip on Jono's hair and slammed him face-first into the wall. Jono whimpered. His arm trembled under Carro's touch. Yes, yes, this was how it was done. They had to fear him, or they would run circles around him. They would laugh at him behind his back.

He ordered the other two, "Hold him."

They did as told and each grabbed an arm. Very quiet and obedient all of a sudden. Oh, they knew what was going to happen. They knew, and they didn't want it to happen to *them*.

Slowly and deliberately, Carro undid Jono's belt and let his pants whisper to the floor. His buttocks were scrawny and hairy, with a few angry red pimples. Goosebumps broke out all over his skin.

Carro squirmed and forced himself to think of Korinne—he repeated her name in his mind, saw her golden locks, her alluring eyes.

"Come on boy, what are you waiting for?"

She laughed, and her image faded. When he wanted the visions, he couldn't hold on to them. His cock was at best half-limp. Panic gripped cold fingers around his heart. Now he started this, he *had* to go through with it; this was how junior Knights were punished. He could of course use the belt to hit Jono, but that would be considered backing down. His . . . ability would be questioned. Carro the dud, he could just hear it. He had to do it, he had to, he had to. . . .

Inran and Caman watched him, their gazes hollow. They'd seen it before. They'd switched off in the same way they had when Carro was *receiving* this punishment.

They knew what was required.

Carro felt sick. Felt himself standing in the dormitory enduring the humiliation with clenched teeth. Oh, by the skylights! He had to do this properly. Rider Cornatan wanted it. *You must hate them back.* Hate, hate, hate . . .

Carro undid his own belt and clumsily pressed against Jono's backside. The skin was clammy with sweat. Carro remembered, felt the pain, his face pressed against the plaster of the wall. He ran his hands down Jono's sides in a mockery of a loving gesture, breathed hot on Jono's naked shoulder, and he grew hard. Jono squirmed away, but his fellows held him tight, white-knuckled fingers biting into purpling flesh, pushing him hard into the wall. Carro rammed in.

Jono screamed, his voice muffled into the wall.

"That hurts, doesn't it?" he whispered into Jono's neck. "You know what? It doesn't hurt for me. I never knew that."

He pushed harder. He was rock-hard now and should get this over with while it lasted, before he went limp and embarrassed himself.

"Ow! Stop. It hurts."

Carro grabbed Jono's hair from behind, arching his neck as far as it went. "Too right it fucking hurts. It's meant to hurt. You hurt me. Many times. The tables are turned."

Carro saw nothing, heard nothing. This was what he wanted to do to his father, his mother, to his sister, to the bullies in the streets. He was fighting, hitting them all back for pain they had caused him, slamming them into that wall. Carro won the fight, spilled himself with a triumphant roar. The feeling of ultimate power.

Carro withdrew, blood roaring in his ears. Jono was crying, and Carro tried to cut himself off from the sound. *By the skylights, be a man! Even I didn't behave like this when you did this to me.*

But there was blood in his crotch.

Carro ignored it, did up his belt and maintained a stiff and angry pose while the boys scampered from the room. When they were gone, he slumped against the wall.

The sound of Jono's cries would not leave him, and that feeling of power, and his unexpected lust. He kept seeing Korinne's face, and the image of Farey's eyes, the two Knights kissing in Rider Cornatan's bathroom . . .

His nails bit into the skin of his palms. Tears burned into his eyes. Who was he and what gave him the right to do things like this?

He didn't know how long he had been standing there when there were footsteps behind him. He whirled around to see Rider Cornatan coming into the room. The Supreme Rider said nothing, but approached Carro with quick steps.

"You're back." Carro heard a measure of relief in his voice.

Rider Cornatan's face looked relieved, too, more relieved than a leader should be over the fate of a single young man.

"I'm sorry," he said. He'd lost his quarry; then he'd found the invisible man but had fled from him. And the other Imperfect, the older man, was still at large. He hadn't achieved anything, except that he'd punished his patrol as Rider Cornatan wanted.

Rider Cornatan shook his head. "This is bigger than you. Bigger than all of us, I'm afraid."

"Is that what's going on? What those riots are about?"

"The whole of the Outer City is in uproar over the young Champion's dismissal. They see him as *their* champion. There are a lot of troublemakers on the streets out for a fight. They seem to have support from locals."

The black pit in Carro's stomach grew. "Just like when the uprising against the king started," he whispered.

Rider Cornatan stared in the distance. He nodded, once.

"We must stop this," Carro said.

"I don't know that we can."

Rider Cornatan met his eyes. Carro could guess what would happen next. As the only Knight from the Outer City, he would have to be involved in calming the people down. Except he could never do that. Didn't Rider Cornatan know that Carro wasn't exactly popular with many in the Outer City?

"I have an important mission for you."

See? There it was. Rider Cornatan was expecting far too much of him. And he was going to fail.

Carro sits at the desk in the warehouse. His father is pacing the floor.

"You, boy, when you're here, you're nothing but the lowest-ranking of my workers. You do not chat to the customers, or to other workers."

Carro nods and looks down to the columns in the book. For the last two pages, his handwriting has been atrocious, but his fingers are too cold to write properly. He wasn't chatting to anyone; he was only accepting a warm drink from the girl in the office, who had felt sorry for him.

"Are you all right, boy?"

Carro shook the memory out of his head. By the skylights, he still hadn't been able to get the ichina.

"I'm fine."

Rider Cornatan frowned.

"Really, I'm fine." Even to his own ears, he sounded nervous. "Tell me what you want me to do." He might as well face the disaster head-on.

"I'm going to send you out of the city."

"Sir?" That was the last thing Carro expected to hear.

Rider Cornatan looked away, almost as if he couldn't bear to meet Carro's eyes. The black feeling increased.

"The trouble started in the Outer City because we took the champion in custody for having lied about his condition. He used his evil power and escaped. At the same time, in a different part of the city, someone killed the Queen's driver and her bears and destroyed her sled. When a new one arrived, Jevaithi and her escort were caught up in a riot. In amongst the fighting, we lost her. We've found no trace of the champion or the Queen. But someone freed the champion's eagle. It took off for the mountains. We suspect that he released it himself, and that he's with the Queen."

Isandor with Jevaithi? Yet Carro had seen that look passing between them and he knew it to be true.

"I'm sending you with the hunters to go and find her. Understand that it's a vital mission. If we can't produce the Queen, the people of the City of Glass are going to turn against us." He lowered his voice. "Unless we can find the Queen, the Knights will be slaughtered. The Brotherhood has become too strong, and understand icefire much better than we do. We *must* have the Queen, Carro."

A vital mission all right, but why would Rider Cornatan send him with vastly more experienced hunters?

"Maybe you ask why I entrust you with such an important mission."

"Yes, I'm not experienced enough—"

Rider Cornatan drew something from his pocket and he gave it to Carro: a bundle of velvet, heavy in his hand. "It is because I trust you like no other."

"Sir, what. . . ?"

"Open it."

Carro folded the material back.

Inside lay a golden medallion with worked, scalloped edges and patterns stamped into the flat surface. A finely made gold chain hung from the eyelet at the top.

"Do you recognise this, boy?"

Carro ran his finger over the surface, depicting a Tusked Lion rearing on its hind flippers. He had seen this in his books. He swallowed. "Isn't this . . . the crest of the Pirosian House?"

A smile curled one corner of Rider Cornatan's mouth. "Very good. The crest of the Pirosian House indeed. You might have read, too, that there are only two of these medallions."

Rider Cornatan took the medallion from the velvet, unfastened the clip on the chain. He looped both sides around Carro's neck. He refastened the clip and arranged the medallion on Carro's chest, a satisfied look on his face. Carro held his breath, but still smelled the waft of musk and harness oil that hung in the Supreme Rider's clothing.

"Only two. One of these medallions belongs to the male heir of the Pirosians; the other, my son, belongs to his successor."

His heart thudding, Carro looked up into the wrinkled face. "You're . . . ." He hardly dared say it. "You're my father? My *real* father?"

The smile grew.

"But why . . . ." All that hostility, all those sniping remarks, the cryptic questions, the nastiness. The man he'd known as his father had been *paid* to look after him. Just like he knew Senior Knights would deal with their successors.

"Why have you grow up in the Outer City, with a man hardly worth his spit and a woman who would have been better off a whore?"

Carro flinched, felt a brief urge to defend the man and woman he'd known as his parents, but then a feeling of rightness descended on him. He had never fitted in. His father had always hated him. His mother, too. He'd looked too different from his sister to believe they were related. He'd just assumed that his father had used a different breeder for him and his sister, but now . . .

"I've not shared my rooms with a woman; that is not possible for me since Riders have sworn off such pleasures. But as Pirosian heir, I needed a successor. So I paid a young virgin of the purest Pirosian blood to give me one, for good money, and then hid you in a place I knew my enemies would not look and would not recognise you. The Thillei are more slippery than you think."

Yes, they were, Carro realised. The Thillei had tried to subvert him by letting Isandor befriend him. How could he have been so blind?

He clutched the medallion in a white-knuckled hand. He'd been stupid, stupid. "I won't let you down. I'll find our Queen."

Rider Cornatan's face hardened. "Listen, son. I'll tell you another secret. Jevaithi isn't *our* Queen. When the Thillei emperor was deposed, the people didn't want another dictator, so the Pirosian clan offered our female heir, since it was agreed that we should only have queens."

"Does that mean you are Jevaithi's father?" *I am royalty?*

"No, and that is where the problem lies. But we need to go further back than that. After the people had ousted the old king and instated the Pirosian queen, the Thilleians were desperate to recapture the throne. First, an agent infiltrated the palace and raped our queen. She fell pregnant, but the palace midwives managed to safely get rid of the child before it was born."

A visible shudder passed over Rider Cornatan. "That was probably just as well. The child was . . . not normal."

"What do you mean?"

"Have you heard of the legend of the crossbreed? The children of the purest Pirosians and the purest Thilleians?"

Carro did remember from the books. Old prints showed demon-like figures with claws and wings. He nodded. "But I thought those were all stories."

"Some of it no doubt is untrue, but when we have the time, I will show you a sample preserved in a jar in the palace birthing room. It's not just any sample, but this very child, as big as your hand, but already showing its animal nature. Old measuring equipment showed that the creature—I won't use the term baby to describe it—attracted an inordinate amount of icefire. It even used the evil power to change its appearance into shapes too horrible to contemplate, before it had left its mother's body."

"The child was alive?"

Rider Cornatan nodded, once, pressing his lips together. "When the healers took it from the poor queen's womb, yes. It took five people to kill it."

Carro felt sick.

"Anyway, after that disaster, the Queen was shaken, of course. We chose one of us to father the queen's child as soon as she recovered. It was done, and she gave birth to a healthy girl. However, we had never caught the Thilleian agent who was the father of the abomination. Soon after the birth of our princess, he, or someone else, came back and took the newborn baby, replacing her with another of the same age, who looked exactly like her, but grew up nothing like the Queen. You *do* know that Maraithe's mother killed herself?"

Carro nodded. Performers in the melteries still sang about the tragedy.

"That was because she couldn't live with the hatred she felt for her baby daughter, a baby that wasn't hers. You hear? *Maraithe* was a Thilleian impostor, but none of us realised. We thought we had eliminated all Thilleians."

But, Carro thought, that meant—

"Maraithe grew up normally, and never showed any sign of who she really was. We relaxed and, at that time, still suspected nothing. Things were good; the evil had been ousted. But then Maraithe reached maturity and we needed to find a father for her child. We thought to consider all possible candidates fairly. Some Senior Knights were engaged in battles of words and occasionally swords. Maraithe demanded a say in the matter as well."

Was that usual? Carro wondered, and then realized that there *was* no "usual". The system hadn't been in place long enough.

"Anyway, it was all a very lengthy process, and while we were debating a suitable father for Maraithe's children, time passed, and passed. Maraithe was twenty-nine, and all of a sudden, she was pregnant. She had said nothing, and one day she came into the Knights' Council in a tight dress that was stretching around her belly." He shuddered with the memory. "We put on a brave face, since it was much too late to ask the midwives to abort the child. The people had noticed her pregnancy, and you know how popular the queens are. For all we knew back then, it didn't really matter who the father was. But it did. Maraithe gave birth not two moon cycles later. Early, the midwife said, but she was carrying twins."

"Twins?"

"Yes. Jevaithi and a boy."

"What happened to the boy?"

"He was left on the ice floes."

"He was . . . Imperfect?"

"Yes. So is Jevaithi. That is the dreadful secret we keep. Jevaithi hasn't a drop of Pirosian blood in her veins."

Carro's head reeled. Queen Jevaithi Imperfect and no one had ever noticed? No wonder the queen hardly ever showed herself. Here was another betrayal. He'd sworn his allegiance. To protect her with his life. As many Knights did, he'd *dreamed* of her many a night, wanted her in his bed.

Rider Cornatan continued, "Now it appears that our enemies have taken Jevaithi back. I don't know what they plan to do with her, but with the potential of icefire, they could destroy everything and kill us. I don't think she'll have any hesitation in helping them. She hates us badly enough. That's why we must act now, before she has a chance to learn to use icefire. You must bring her back to calm the people. We must have her back here to control her. That's why I'm sending you. I trust no one else."

Carro wasn't trusting himself at that moment. *Jevaithi* was a Thilleian? A betrayer? A feeling of sickness welled up in his stomach.

"And the hunters?"

"My special team. You've met Farey."

"Yes." Carro fought to restrain a blush. Then he had another thought: every man in the Knighthood had known who he was all along? Now he understood the remarks the Tutor had made about his status.

"Find her and bring her back here, son, before it's too late and the evil spreads. Promise me."

Carro straightened his back. If he was highborn and Rider Cornatan said he was trustworthy, he must be. He'd sworn allegiance to the *throne* not to Jevaithi.

"I promise."

And what about Isandor? Capture him too? His friend?

If that's what it took to get his father's approval . . . Isandor was not his friend anymore; he shouldn't be.

Rider Cornatan looked into his eyes. "Can you say the word to me, just once?"

"I promise, *Father.*"

Rider Cornatan let go of his hands and closed his arms around Carro's shoulders.

"I love you, son. Never give up. The City of Glass belongs to the Pirosian House."

CHAPTER 26

THE EAGLE stretched out its feet, flapped huge brown and white wings and landed on the snow-covered hillside.

Isandor unlooped his arms to release Jevaithi. She slid from the saddle into the snow, stretching her arms and stamping life into her legs. He unclipped his harness and followed her down, drinking in the silence after the roar of wind in his ears for so long.

The surrounding landscape bathed in soft pastel tones: pale blues of pristine snow, the golden light of the sun low above the horizon, and pink and orange hues of the sky.

Isandor squinted into the sunlight. The mountains rose at his back, and long shadows cast the valleys between the foothills in blue shadow. The City of Glass was well out of sight, almost a day's flying distance away, but he felt its constant pull inside him. The City of Glass was his home; it was Jevaithi's home. She was the queen and all the people should listen to her. They should go back and get rid of the Knights. They should . . .

A soft sound yanked him from the uninvited thoughts.

Jevaithi ploughed through knee-deep snow to a wooden hut half-hidden by a stand of gnarled trees. She pushed open the door—it creaked, causing a big slab of snow to slide off the roof—and looked inside.

Anything? He was still feeling shaken, wanting to be rid of that need to return. He didn't *want* to return.

She shook her head. *There's cooking things, and a bed.*

We'll stay here tonight. Anything except go back there.

Why would people build this hut here?

It's a camp for high-sun herders. They brought their goats up here in the short period that the meadows weren't covered in snow. Isandor had seen the herders with their salted meats in the Outer City markets.

Jevaithi tracked back through the snow. Her blue-marbled form was not as substantial as it had been when they escaped. He could see *through* her. With the weakening icefire, their bodies would gradually disappear.

That was why the force of icefire pulled him back to the City of Glass. From here on, that feeling would become stronger, until it had grown into a physical pain in his ghostly body.

It was time to turn both of them back to normal.

He took the pouch from his pocket. To his eyes it was a solid black object that made him shiver. He closed his eyes and forced himself to put the bag into the palm of his hand. The hearts thudded, sucking in icefire with every beat. And with every beat, warmth in his hands grew.

Isandor had to fight the urge to fling the bag down the mountain-side, to be rid of the thing and live without hunger and pain forever.

But he couldn't let this feeling win. Hands shaking, he gathered a fold of his cloak into a basket and upended the bag into it.

Both hearts beat strongly, pumping hard to keep the icefire going, to keep the illusion alive. Jevaithi stood with her hands over her mouth.

Both hands; she would lose a hand if he put the heart back. She was perfect in her current state; she would never be any more perfect than this . . .

He would have to separate the hearts and they looked so perfect next to each other, beating in unison.

No.

Isandor closed a hand around his own heart, and lifted it to his chest, trying to absorb its warmth, but feeling repulsed by it. How could one be repulsed by life?

Here. He held it out to Jevaithi.

It lay, pulsing, in her hands. *Both* her hands.

Her eyes widened. *This is your heart.*

I know it's mine. I want you to have it. And he wanted it to be done quickly, before the urge to return to the city, or do something else stupid, became too strong.

You would forever be my servitor.

Isandor bent forward until the hand with which he still held Jevaithi's heart touched both their chests. He let his lips brush hers. She stiffened but did not withdraw. The tingle of frost made his blood stir. *And you would be mine. I want to be yours.*

I want you, too.

Her breath tickled over his skin. He sought her lips, teasing her with the most fleeting of kisses. She laughed and pulled him closer, pressing her mouth full on his.

A jolt of icefire bit through him.

Isandor withdrew. If he'd had a need to breathe, he would be panting. His need for her was so desperate, he would have ripped off her clothes and taken her in the snow, but that was not the sort of treatment she deserved.

He said, *If we take each other's hearts, we will be each other's servitors, but we will be whole at the same time. We can go beyond the influence of icefire, yet no one can ever make us servitors, because we already are.*

If I die, then you would die, too.

But you can't die unless I die. He smiled at her ethereal face. *Unless someone kills both of us at exactly the same time.*

A bright smile crossed her face. A glitter in her midnight-dark eyes, dimples in her cheeks. How he loved her.

She handed him back his heart. *Here. I want you to put it in.*

He took it and handed her heart back to her, his hands trembling. *You do it for me, too. Are you ready?*

To illustrate her readiness, she untied her cloak and unbuttoned the top of her dress, showing ethereal blue marbled skin, the fabric pulled back enough to show soft mounds of her breasts.

He pulled his tunic over his head. *Ready?*

She nodded, her mouth set. They each slid their heart into the other's chest. Icefire blossomed in the sharp burst, snaking out over the snow-covered landscape. Strands turned from black to golden.

Isandor's vision blurred. Pain tore through him like he'd been dipped in boiling water. He opened his mouth and screamed. The sound echoed in the mountains. His voice had returned. Then he stood there, panting. Jevaithi had fainted in his arms, but she was already opening her eyes, royal blue once more, and put her left hand on his bare chest, pink again, her right hand once again missing.

He kissed her, now warm and breathing. She gasped, clinging onto him, her breath warm over his cheek.

"Can you feel it?" She took his hand and placed it on her chest, between her breasts.

Their hearts beat in perfect unison. "I love you. I love you so much it hurts."

They stood motionless for a number of heartbeats. He let his hand slide under the cover of her dress. The skin on her breast was softer than he could imagine, but the nipple grew hard and erect under the touch of his fingers.

She giggled. "Your hands are freezing."

"Maybe we should go inside." He let a smile play around his lips.

She smiled back, nervously.

"Do you know how to make a fire?" he asked. "I need to look after the eagle."

"I'll try. I've seen people make fires."

"Up in your tower room?"

"Yes." And then she smiled again. "Imagine. I'm free. I can do whatever I want. I'm free!" Her voice echoed against the mountain. A bird screeched a reply.

Isandor gave her a last kiss on the lips before she ploughed through the snow back to the hut. Even the sight of her back, and her messy hair over her shoulders, made him feel giddy.

Jevaithi. He mouthed her name, like sweets on his tongue. *Jevaithi, Jevaithi.* And then, *She's mine.* Unbelievable.

He tied up the eagle, rubbed it down and gave it a chunk of meat from the saddlebag. The meat was frozen solid and the bird gave him a baleful stare. It didn't bother him. His wooden leg didn't bother him. His blood sang, his mind flew, deep breaths of freezing air made him feel dizzy. He was free.

When he went inside, a fire roared in the hearth. Warmth fell on him like a blanket; it made his cold-stiffened fingers tingle. Jevaithi came to the door to help him out of his cloak, her eyes bright.

"This hut is well-organised. I found some saltmeat and flour and—"

He stopped her words with his mouth. Her one hand strayed up his chest, fumbled with his tunic, while he peeled the dress from her shoulders with trembling hands. Dizziness threatened to overwhelm him; he felt like he wasn't here, wasn't doing this, like he was on fire.

She broke the kiss. "Should we go . . . over there?" She glanced at the wooden bed in the corner.

He picked her up and carried her to the bed which had straw poking out and a bearskin cover that released a cloud of dust under the weight of her body. She laughed. Isandor slid the silk finery off her until she was entirely naked except for the leather strip and the gull's feather. Her gaze still meeting his, she reached behind her neck and undid the knot. The leather strips fell over her breasts. She passed the trophy to him, her eyes twinkling. "Yours."

His. So beautiful. He sank down on the bed on his knees, awkwardly. He untied his wooden leg, put it on the floor, and then unbelted his trousers with trembling hands. The last of his clothing fell to the floor with a soft thud. She was watching him with wide eyes. Scared? Had she ever seen a naked man before?

"You're sure you want to do this?"

She nodded. A vein pulsed in her neck. Yes, she was scared.

He chuckled. "I don't know much either."

"What? You mean you've never . . ."

He shook his head.

"But I thought you Outer City boys all knew so much more than me." She laughed, but then her face grew serious. "Do *you* want to do it?" and when he laughed, she added, "What? It's a fair question."

He bent over her, supporting himself with a hand on each side of her shoulders and whispered in her neck, "By the skylights, I do."

"Well, that's settled then." She shifted her legs apart.

He could feel his heart going like crazy in her chest.

Isandor lowered himself, blood roaring in his ears. Naked skin whispered on naked skin. Oh boy, it was awkward. She had to wriggle her hand underneath to guide him to the right place. When he finally got the right position, she was so warm and so tight that the first time he pushed deep, he spilled himself in an uncontrollable shudder. Oh, by the skylights. He rested his head on her shoulder, still panting.

"I'm sorry. I didn't mean to do that."

"It doesn't matter." But in her voice he heard that it did. She was disappointed, had expected more.

"I'm sorry," he said again. "Did I hurt you?"

She shook her head, but he didn't miss the blood-streaked slime on the bedcover.

"It's all right," she said. "Girls bleed, the first time."

Isandor thought of his mother and the horrific stories she sometimes told about births gone wrong. "It's not fair. Girls get to take all the bad things."

He got up, filled the pot and set it to boil. In the future, he would have to do better than that. Look after her, love her better.

Jevaithi sat down on the bench while he stoked the fire. It was comfortably warm inside, and he was giddy with the feeling of love and independence. They could do this. He might be awkward, and she might not know much, but they would learn. They never needed to listen to anyone again.

He found some bowls and a pot and made hearty soup out of strips of saltmeat and herbs which he found on the shelf above the stove.

"Where are we going from here?" he asked. "Chevakia?"

"Chevakia! I don't care. We're free. No more Knights. No more Rider Cornatan to watch over me. Isn't it wonderful?"

He smiled, but deep inside suspected it wasn't quite so simple. That feeling of power he had as servitor still smouldered inside him. Jevaithi was the *queen*. People respected and adored her. He could wield that power to get rid of the Knights and give Jevaithi the throne that was rightfully hers. What would the people of the City of Glass do when they found out she was gone?

"Hey, dreamer." Jevaithi sat on his lap, pushing away the blanket slung over his shoulders. His naked body underneath responded pleasantly.

She gave him a sly look. "You want to try again?"

Sure, why not?

This time, things were much more satisfactory.

Afterwards, she fell asleep with her head on his shoulder. Isandor lay there, looking at her face by the glow of the fire, listening to the beating of both their hearts.

Yes, they would go back to the City of Glass one day, but not yet, not yet . . .

CHAPTER 27

RUKO WAITED by the sled outside Loriane's house. He had his back to the door and his arms crossed over his chest, and was staring into the street, not meeting Tandor's eyes. Anger rolled off him in waves. Tandor saw a young boy and the same girl he'd seen a few times, in a darkened corridor with metal-barred doors on both sides.

Great.

Tandor strode to the sled, flinging furs onto the seat for Loriane and Myra to sit on. Earlier, when he went out before, he'd already taken his chest out here, in anticipation of his move into the City of Glass, when Ruko had told him he'd captured Isandor and Jevaithi. *You could have been on your way to your girl already. I told you to go after Isandor. Why didn't you stop the boy running away?* Ruko should have been more than strong enough to restrain two adolescents.

Images of Isandor struggling against Ruko's grip came into his mind. Jevaithi, too. The butcher's warehouse. The door shut, enclosing the two teenagers inside. Then Ruko on his way to get Tandor.

All right, so Ruko *had* locked them up properly. That meant *someone* had to have unlocked that door. Tandor had seen the eagle fly over with Isandor and Jevaithi on its back, both in servitor forms and knew no one who could have turned them. Was there someone else who could make servitors? One of those pathetic Brothers?

Who saw you?

Ruko's arm muscles tightened.

All right, I didn't say it was your fault.

Tandor saw the rosy-cheeked face of a girl, one of the youngsters imprisoned in the palace.

Yes, I know it's taking a long time, but we can't go and rescue her until you help me to get enough Imperfects to get into the palace in the first place.

Ruko jumped up, blew a gust of frost-rimed air from his nostrils. He whirled at Tandor. Hesitated. Midnight-black eyes glared at Tandor from within the deep shadow of the hood of Ruko's cape.

No, you will not kill everyone. You will do as I say. I am the master.

Another snort of air, this one audible. Ruko whirled again and brought his fist down on the driver's seat with such force that the bench creaked. The bear let out a deep growl.

I am the master, Tandor repeated. He grasped for icefire and pulled it close around Ruko. The boy didn't move, yet Tandor could feel his anger strain against the icefire bonds. Did servitors ever break free of their masters? What happened if they did?

The door thudded shut behind him.

Draped in furs, Loriane and Myra shuffled into the street. Loriane had her arm around Myra's waist. The girl was crying, stopping every few paces.

Ruko settled into the driver's seat with a loud thump. He yanked the hood over his head and snatched up the reins so tightly that the bear grumbled.

Tandor pulled harder at the threads of icefire. *Careful.*

Loriane and Myra climbed onto the sled, very, very slowly. Tandor handed Loriane a few rugs, which she tucked around Myra. Tandor sat next to Loriane, on the far left of the bench, pressed against her because the sled only comfortably seated two people.

He released his hold on the icefire threads a fraction. Ruko snapped the reins. The bear loped into action, bouncing and kicking its hind legs in a way that was an indication that the animal was annoyed.

But now that they were underway, Ruko settled. He navigated the sled through the winding streets, avoiding busy thoroughfares. Through alleys and gaps between limpets, Tandor caught glimpses of fights, people running through streets with burning torches, buildings on fire, billowing smoke. The stench hung low over the Outer City.

Further, out over the plain, eagles circled, silvery shapes in the moonlight, Knights, no doubt looking for traces of the Queen. So many of them. Were there any Knights left to guard the city?

Tandor couldn't repress a smile.

While all the Knights were out looking for Jevaithi, he might not get a better chance to get into the palace, at least not any time soon. After a string of disasters things were finally looking up for him.

Ruko, to the City of Glass, as fast as you can.

Again, he saw the face of the girl.

Yes, we'll go and rescue her now.

Ruko flicked the reins. The bear increased its pace and soon, the sled left the twisted streets of the Outer City behind and came out into the open. Down the slope, past the festival grounds and onto the ice plain.

Myra was crying with every bump, and Loriane tried to comfort her. She cast Tandor poisonous looks. Did she have the faintest idea how pretty she was when she did that, her cheeks flushed, her lips slightly apart?

"Loriane, I love you." He gathered her in his arms and kissed her.

She pushed him away. "Spare your breath. You're up to something and I want to know what it is."

"I'll tell you." He kissed her again, tasting victory, in her, in the speed of the sled, in Ruko's anger. "After we come back."

"Now."

"No. After. Loriane, I love you. I wouldn't do anything to put you in danger."

"You swear you will tell me what this is about? I'm getting rather sick of your secrets."

"I swear it." *When I'm on the throne, you'll be the most powerful queen ever.*

"Deal." She gave him an intense glare that said *I'll believe that when I see it*. And she turned her attention back to Myra.

No one said much during the rest of the trip. Ruko urged the bear on as much as Tandor would allow it. Myra cried, but much less than before.

When the sled passed underneath a group of circling eagles, Tandor cast out a cocoon of icefire so they wouldn't see the sled. That was easy to do here, on the deserted plain, not so once he got into the city, where people with Thilleian blood might see it. The Knights didn't seem to be all that interested in who went into the city, though, because another sled ahead of them received no attention from the eagles either.

The tall buildings ahead grew and grew, dark and jagged silhouettes against a sky too dark for dawn and too light for midnight. Soon enough, the sled moved into the shadows of the buildings. Here, it was pitch dark and bitterly cold, with an icy wind gusting over the plain.

Ruko slowed down at the gates.

By the wan light of a single icefire globe, the three guards on duty were questioning a young nobleman who was trying to leave the city, and waved Tandor and Loriane through, without much of a glance at Ruko's cloaked form. Myra was again crying and a nobleman with a heavily pregnant woman in his sled could only be bound for the palace.

Once in the streets, the strong pull of icefire tugged at him. Golden strands of it snaked through the air, crawled up walls, slithered down windows, hugging all forms and structures that had once belonged to the ancient culture that had given rise to icefire. Tandor drank in the delicious feeling. By the skylights, he could do it. The children were here—he could feel them. Together they could tame the Heart. Tonight, the throne would be his.

The sled arrived at the back entrance to the palace.

A twisted iron and glass structure hung as an arch over the entry to the courtyard in front of the passageway that led to the palace birthing rooms. A few snow-dusted sleds stood in the open space, and a single bear dozed in the corner of the yard. Two guards stood at their post, one leaning against the doorpost, his eyes half-closed. The other guard had his back to the courtyard. As the sled swished through the open gate, he turned slowly, and as he did so, his eyes widened.

Tandor's heart jumped.

Stop as far from the door as possible, Ruko.

Had the man seen anything? Since when did Thilleians stand guard at the palace?

The bear halted with a snort and a grumble. Tandor rose and

pulled the hood of the cloak further over Ruko's head. Ruko batted his hand away, but Tandor grabbed the cloak's sleeve.

One of those men can see you.

Loriane helped Myra up, but when the girl stepped from the sled, she gave a cry and sank to her knees in the snow, clutching her belly.

Loriane glared over her shoulder. "This is ridiculous, Tandor, couldn't you have stopped a bit closer to the door?"

"No, I couldn't." He glanced at Ruko.

Myra struggled back up. Loriane put her arm around the girl's waist. When they shuffled away from the sled, she said over her shoulder. "You do remember your promise, don't you?"

"I do." *I will do more than that. I will put you on the throne, my queen.*

By the skylights, he loved her.

Tandor waited while Loriane and Myra shuffled across the courtyard to the entrance before stepping off the sled. Ruko stirred and rose from the driver's seat.

Wait here.

Tandor's heart was thudding. The man's attention had gone to Loriane and Myra, who were at the entrance to the palace. Myra had stopped walking and was having another crying fit, but the guard still glanced at the sled even as he spoke to Loriane.

Ruko snorted audibly and jumped into the snow.

No, you can't come inside. He's seen you. Stay here.

Ruko took two huge steps until his chest almost touched Tandor's. Cold radiated from his blue-skinned hands that could snap a man's neck.

Ruko was half a head taller, but Tandor didn't back down.

What's this?

A blue hand lashed out and grabbed Tandor by the collar with such force that he could barely breathe. The image of the girl again. Ruko's young lover.

Set me down.

Ruko's eyes met his, black and deep as the ocean.

Set me down. More forceful this time.

He couldn't use icefire in front of these guards, or he would have lashed Ruko without mercy. What was it with the insolence? Who was the master?

If you don't behave, I'll turn you back into a cripple boy.

Slowly, Ruko let go of Tandor's collar.

Tandor drew a grateful and welcome breath of fresh air into his lungs.

Loriane and Myra had gone inside and Tandor was acutely aware of the guard's gazes in his direction.

Don't you dare do that again. Stay here.

Icefire flared in a web of strands coming from Ruko's hands. Images of the girl burst into Tandor's mind. He thrust up his golden claw, slashing through the net. Ruko held on, but wasn't strong enough. The network of strands shattered into diamonds. Tandor ducked to avoid the projectiles and grabbed a handful of Ruko's cloak. Icefire crackled the length of his claw.

What's this, Ruko? I am your master. I command. You obey. I tell you it's not safe to come inside—

In his mind, Ruko ran across the courtyard, grabbed the two guards and snapped their necks.

No, you can't do that. There are many more guards inside, and we can't fight them.

More images of violence. Blood in the snow.

No, Ruko.

Dark forms of guards and Knights slumped in heaps, their limbs bent at impossible angles. Dismembered shapes barely recognisable as human. Blue hands slashing through flesh and blood. Bones snapping.

Ruko trembled.

No, Ruko.

The cloak was yanked from Tandor's grip with so much force that he stumbled backwards. Ruko walked away from the sled.

There were images of the front entrance of the palace, the steps dripping with blood. Severed limbs, heads torn from bodies, eyes staring lifelessly at the sky, Knights' badges defaced, their swords bent and molten, crossbow bolts between their eyes. Noble ladies in the snow with their clothes ripped off bloodied torsos. Nail and teeth marks in alabaster skin.

Tandor grabbed as many strands of icefire as he could muster and, never mind the guards, lashed them around Ruko's form.

You obey me!

The strands met resistance. They stretched and snapped, and hit the glass and metal arch over the courtyard entrance. The structure glowed and gave out a shower of sparks, while Ruko ran underneath, out the gate.

Tandor stumbled back a few steps and stood there in the middle of the courtyard, panting, to regain his balance, the horrific images fading from his mind.

"Um—sir?" one of the guards asked. "Are you all right?"

Are you all right? They had not asked that last time Tandor had encountered palace guards. Maraithe had to officially pardon him. He'd had to kneel before the throne, pushed down by a Knight, when getting to his knees with his recent wound was difficult. The pain, oh, the pain.

Maraithe had sat on the throne, with two rapist Knights next to her, her hands folded over knees. Her face looked drawn and pale. In his mind, he still heard her screams as she pushed out, unaided and denied medicine, the children he would never hold. It happened here, in the palace, a place stifled with haunting memories.

Tandor forced a smile. "I . . . tripped. I'm sorry. My son . . . he's at a difficult age . . ." A disaster. There was no way Tandor could get Ruko back under control alone. Servitors never disobeyed their masters. Never.

"Oh. I see." But the tone of the man's voice said that he didn't see at all, and worse, that he was expecting some kind of explanation, but there was no time for that now. Ruko was on the rampage and would kill anyone he encountered, and the only means of stopping him— Ruko's girl—was inside the palace dungeons.

He said, nodding at the door, "I'd like to wait inside, if I may. The lady . . ." He shrugged, feigning indifference, but his heart thudded. He *had* to get in, even if he was alone and helpless against the power of the Heart.

The guard eyed him. "Your breeder, sir?"

"Yes." Tandor kept his face impassive, no matter how much he hated these impersonal family arrangements.

The guard waved him through, but when Tandor looked over his shoulder, he noticed how both guards were leaning close to each other, and one was pointing into the courtyard.

The man had seen something: either Ruko or the icefire. Since when did the palace have Thilleian Knights?

And then he heard Loriane's voice, *That's your life, not mine. It happened fifty years ago, Tandor*. Could it really be that the citizens of the City of Glass were forgetting the clan feuds?

No, he decided. There were the Brothers, still teaching the Thilleian ways, and his mother, and all the people whose businesses had been destroyed by the Knights. They deserved revenge for what had been done to them.

Tandor would give them revenge, even if it was the last thing he did.

TANDOR STOPPED in the darkness of a niche and pulled a cloak of icefire around him. He cast out his rays of power, and compared the picture that the rays brought back to him with the map he had memorised.

Getting into the palace was one thing, finding the entrance to the underground passages quite another. He'd been lucky so far that no one had come out of the birthing room to question him on his presence. Most of the Knights were at the Newlight festival; he'd planned it that way. But he could never plan for what he found in the catacombs. Right now, what he needed most was luck.

The trail of icefire led him into the darkness of the corridor. Here, the walls were ancient and bleak grey, spotted with age and rust. The icefire trail oozed from an ink-black hole at the end of the passage. Tandor plunged into darkness. It seemed his mental probe had found the stairs to the underground chambers. His footsteps echoed in the staircase that seemed to have no end, zigzagging down and down. A metal railing disintegrated under his touch, caking the steps with flakes of rust.

With each step he descended into the bowels of the building, the tang of cold increased. The vapour of his breath froze in his hair and on the collar of his cloak. Icefire called beneath his feet. Down, down, down. His lungs laboured to take in the stale, breathless air, laced with an unpleasant smell.

On every corner and every turn, he stopped, listened for footsteps, voices, slitherings or pantings, jinglings or clinkings.

There were no sounds other than his own.

The stairs ended in a dungeon room where a single torch cast its flickering light over three walls of solid stone. The entrance to the stairs broke the fourth wall. There were no other doorways.

Tandor walked around the walls, inspecting the rough stone. From his time spent in the dungeons, he remembered the layout of the passages and cells.

Stupid, really, for Rider Cornatan to hold him prisoner in the dungeons all those years ago. Did the man know what icefire could do, of how he could scan and map the entire underground section of the palace, all its levels, its ramps and staircases, even down to the white lines painted on the floors by generations long past?

The flame on the torch flapped with a rancid breeze.

Tandor smiled. Of course.

That breath of air had to come from somewhere and had to be going somewhere. This was not a dead end at all. There was an illusion at work in this room.

For all he hated icefire, Rider Cornatan had no qualms using it, for the Knights of course would be unable to see the wall where Tandor saw it. With that knowledge, Tandor again walked the perimeter of the room, probing with icefire. This time, he found the passage, opposite the exit to the stairs. He pushed his clawed hand through the wall, then his other hand, his foot, and when it looked like his limbs were being eaten by stone, he walked through himself.

The familiar cold of icefire tingled his skin. A strong construction, this one, and he recognised in it the mark of his family. This ward might have been in place since his grandfather had left the palace, and he was the first of his family to walk through it since that time.

The Thillei are coming home.

He could see himself walking up the steps of his mother's house . . . no, she would come to him, here in the City of Glass, where he sat on the throne his grandfather had been killed defending. His mother would fall to her knees for him.

Your Majesty. Yes, he could get used to that, especially when coming from his mother's mouth. It was time that she learned who was doing all the work and who had the right to get the top spot.

He had entered another passage which slanted away from the bottom of the stairs at a weak angle. An orange glow of fire or torches flickered at the very end. There were no wall niches, nowhere to hide.

He had not encountered anyone, but if the Eagle Knights still used his grandfather's wards, they would also use the listening bugs, or might use his grandfather's famed live model of the palace, as his grandfather had described in the diary. If that was the case, they would know exactly where he was and where he was going.

There was no way of knowing how much the Knights had learned of using icefire, and what devices they were using. And this might all be a trap.

Yet the children were here. He could feel them close by, perhaps in the chamber ahead.

Fires burned in the hearth at the opposite wall of that room. People moved back and forth, silhouetted against the glow. Some carried heavy things. The figures looked strangely out of proportion, with thick arms and legs, and with large heads. When he came closer, he saw that they were wearing baggy suits. Hoods covered their heads, sealed by a plate of glass in front, through which the occupant of the suit could look out. The low light and the reflection in the glass made it impossible to see their faces. Chevakians needed to wear suits like that when they came to the City of Glass, not southerners . . . unless icefire was extraordinarily strong, like it would be around the Heart. *They're using it*. It was clear as it should have been before, when he encountered the sink. The Knights aimed to use this energy they couldn't see, or, for that matter, control. That's why they needed the children, as test subjects, as vessels and conduits for icefire. It was such lunacy. The children had no experience with using icefire, plus they weren't servitors. At crucial moments, they would never do as their masters wanted.

Oh, by the skylights! Did Rider Cornatan know what he was playing with?

He inched closer to the room, and the more he saw of its interior of tubes and machines, the more he knew he was right.

There was a commotion at the other end of the room. Two suited figures emerged from a doorway, dragging a third person between them. Thin, poorly dressed and not in a suit, the girl looked out of place, as if she'd been caught snooping. But the eyes drew Tandor's attention. Empty and hollow, they stared straight at him. She knew he was there. Icefire surged through him. He could barely clamp down on the crackling strand of golden light. Down here, he could no longer rely on the Pirosian inability to see icefire. Most of these workers would not be purebloods—Pirosians saved the best jobs for themselves; the part-Thilleian guard at the gate attested to that—and some would be able to see the strands, no matter how weakly.

Heart pounding, he leaned against the wall, listening to the girl's protesting screams. This was one of the Bordertown children. The others would be close by. If he could free just a few, he would have the situation in hand. He could turn them into servitors and take possession of the Heart. Once he was there . . . He clutched his dagger to his thigh. The throne would be his. The Thillei would return. The south would again be a force to reckon with.

The two suited figures stopped. They put the girl on a table and bound her hands to metal loops at the table's edge.

Another suited figure brought in a trolley on which lay an array of glittering instruments. The three gathered around the girl and covered her with a cloth.

The girl squirmed and bucked. The cloth slid off. The suited men yelled out. One pointed into the corridor.

Tandor released the icefire he had been holding. It crackled across the room in a jet of golden light. It hit the three suited men, knocking them to the ground, ricocheted off the wall, fractured and bounced back, until it formed a barrier across the room's entrances. Not much good against pure Pirosians, but he had to gamble that none of these people were purebloods. Tandor rushed into the room, drawing his knife from his belt. First, he yanked off the helmets of the suited men. If they had Pirosian blood, the bolt would merely have stunned them. He hit each of them hard on the head with the hilt of his dagger.

Then he went to the table.

The girl was thin, filthy, dressed only in a thin tunic. She looked at him, wide-eyed. "You are the man who came to Bordertown . . . the traveller . . ."

He put a finger to her lips and slashed the leather straps which held the girl bound to the table.

"Quiet," he whispered. "You thought I would leave you alone, did you?"

"They said you were dead." She met his eyes. Oh boy, could he feel the Thilleian blood stir in her.

He lifted the girl off the table.

She almost fell into his arms. Feeling her bony arms and the filth of her skin, a great anger surged through him. "Where are the others?"

Her eyes grew wide. "You can't get to them. You must get out. They'll capture you, too."

"I'll take that risk. Quick. Where are they? Show me. I'm here to free you all. There will be no second chances."

The girl hesitated, but pointed at an entrance, a dark maw of a passage leading further into the building.

"That way. There's a room . . ." She shuddered.

By the skylights, had they been treated that badly?

"Let's go then."

The girl stopped where the corridor ended in a t-intersection. Both ends of the new corridor vanished into darkness. Doors were set in the drab walls at regular intervals, all closed.

She pointed at one of the doors, unremarkable as the others. Tandor didn't need her directions; he could feel the presence of the children, enhanced by the strong glow of icefire beneath his feet. The Heart was close; and it was beating strongly.

"Stand back." He flung a burst of icefire at the door. It crackled over the smooth surface. The door vibrated and sprang open.

Tandor burst in through the opening before the display of icefire had died down. It was dark in the room, and the stink of human waste made him gag.

By the skylights! He stumbled back out into the corridor staring into that dark maw from which the stench now rolled into the corridor.

There was a tiny pinprick of light against the back wall. He sensed, rather than saw, the children inside the room; he felt overwhelming pain and misery. They were stirring, mumbling, weak, confused.

Tandor trembled with anger, because the children were not in any state to help him, or to run. Anyone to be turned into a servitor needed to be healthy and willing for the best effect. Tandor was prepared to compromise on the "willing" part, but these children simply weren't healthy enough.

"Any of you who can walk, get up and help the others." He would get the Eagle Knights for this, oh yes he would.

Sounds of movement—shuffling and scrabbling—came from inside the room. One by one, or in small groups, the children shuffled out. Rags, thin limbs, matted hair, many covered in their own filth. Many of them were wounded, sporting filthy bandages around arms and legs. They stood wide-eyed, blinking against the light. Tandor noticed a boy with a raw scar on his chest, and then another who had a filthy bandage in the same spot.

"What did they do with you?"

They didn't reply.

He examined the boy's scar. When he passed his hand over it, a chill went through him. "There's something underneath. What is it?"

The boy shook his head. He couldn't speak? Was he afraid to speak? He was not strongly Imperfect, just some of his toes were missing.

He turned to the girl who had brought him here. "What's been done to them?"

"The Knights put something under the skin. It makes you numb, like him. They were going to do it to me just now, when you came, but I'm one of the last."

"What is it?"

"I don't know. One boy opened the wound and took the thing out."

"What did he take out?" Tandor breathed fast.

The girl went back inside the room and came back with a filthy cloth. "We put it in here, so the men wouldn't see, but the boy died anyway."

Tandor folded back the filthy fabric. A clear diamond-shaped piece of glass slid out. As it rolled into his hand, strands of icefire bent and curled, stretching to its glittering surface, and simply disappeared there. The strands tugged at him, at the very power of his being. A low keening sound grew louder and louder.

Tandor snapped the fabric back over the stone. A sink.

All the icefire the children collected would be stored in that stone from where you could mine it but where it was useless to him, unless he could remove the sinks . . . He grabbed his dagger, but knew too well that his grandfather used to neuter Imperfects with sinks. Once the stone was inside the body, removing it always killed the subject. The Knights had outsmarted him.

While he stood there, wracking his brain for a solution, he realised that the children were shuffling in line, as if they knew where to go and were being told to go there.

The Heart.

It would come into full power today, and the sinks in their bodies meant that they were attracted to it.

Tandor ran around the corner. The line already stretched into the darkness, slowly shuffling.

He grabbed one of the children by the shoulders. "Stop, stop!"

The girl, a skinny thing no more than twelve years old with empty eyes staring into the distance, pushed him aside as if he were an annoying pup. Already, icefire had made her strong.

Someone had made half-servitors out of them without being properly in control of their minds. Now no one could communicate with them. They would run rampant. Like Ruko.

There was only one thing he could do.

Tandor closed his hand around the Chevakian powder gun in his pocket and pulled it out. The girl next to him gave him no attention. He raised the gun and pointed it at her head. She turned, showing her sweet young face. She had the fine curly hair that was common to the inhabitants of the border regions. Her skin was soft and pale with a few freckles, looking at him like a fox cub.

Fifteen years he had lived as travelling merchant to provide for these children. Many he had saved personally by grabbing the newborn infants from before the hungry mouths of wild bears. While taking them to Bordertown, he had fed them, cradled them, kept them warm. In his mind, he had already assigned them positions in his royal guard, repaying their service, and that of their foster families, many times over.

He loved "his" children. He left the gun sink; the girl shuffled on.

By the skylights, he was too soft, he *cared* too much, for a job like this. For all his boasting, he was no killer and not even the direst need was going to change that.

Mother, if you wanted this done, why didn't you do it yourself?

There had to be another way to stop the children.

Find the Heart. Without protection, he would probably die from exposure, but he had to try, or there would be devastation on a grand scale.

Tandor ran.

Ahead in the corridor, the children were going through a doorway from where the smell of must and disuse mingled with strands of icefire.

Tandor followed, into an eerie semi-darkness. In the dank room, the ceiling glowed with greenish light, casting harsh shadows on the walls. The floor sloped down in a spiral. Some time, a long time ago, someone had painted white stripes and arrows on the pale grey floor. There was a metal railing in the middle and flakes of coloured paint clung to some of the pillars that supported the roof. Other pillars had collapsed, or melted, causing the roof to collapse. In places, rust flakes piled up on the floor, mixed with bits of black that fell to dust when touched.

Tandor wondered what the old people would have used this construction for, and why this chamber had survived at all.

The call of icefire was stronger here than he had ever felt it in his life. His body sang with power.

He ran down the ramp. Two rounds of the spiral, three. Down, down, down. The light became ever brighter. All the children he passed glowed like beacons. His own skin also glowed, including the hand he never had, superimposed over the pincers of the golden claw. He resisted a look in his trousers to see if that part of him had been restored as well. Then again, he didn't need to check; he could feel it as he could feel his missing hand and rake his non-existent fingers through his hair.

Around the last bend and his target came into sight.

About the height of two men, and much longer than it was tall, the thing that was the Heart of the City glowed so intensely white that it was impossible to look at. The Heart's shape was vaguely rectangular, and plates of metal lay scattered around it—presumably the protection the Knights had installed and then removed. Some of the casing remained at the back, but all within was bright white. The air hummed so much that it vibrated in the light, creating an odd shimmering effect.

A single Knight guarded it, clad in a heavy suit, absurdly with a torch in his hand. What blindness that someone couldn't see this radiance!

Tandor let icefire rise to the tips of his fingers, but it wouldn't harm the man if he could stand here. He obviously had strong Pirosian blood.

This would call for valuable bullets. He felt in the pocket of his cloak, shielding his eyes from the glow of the square in front of him.

At that moment, a shape of light stepped past him. Through the blinding rays, Tandor saw the face of an adolescent man, strong-jawed. Dark hair flowed over his shoulders. The young man hit the knight on the side of the head. The Knight slumped, without having given an indication that he had seen the young man coming. His torch rolled over the ground and went out.

Tandor was puzzled. Who was this young man? Ruko was outside and few of the other children had been older than thirteen.

He turned.

Behind him, all the children coming down the ramp glowed, no longer skinny and filthy, no longer crippled, no longer small. Some had tossed aside walking sticks. The girl he had rescued from the table had grown to adult size. Her skin was no longer scabbed and dirty, but milky white. Under his eyes, she pulled the tunic over her head and stood there, naked, inviting. She tossed her hair over her shoulder and gave him a mischievous look, very much like Loriane would do, a look that challenged him to do what he could never do. Except now he could.

Loriane appeared in the air before him, naked, alluring. Tandor trembled, tossed by emotions he could by rights no longer feel. Once again he was a complete man, not a pale shade of his former self, damaged by the man he hated most in the world of the living and the dead. He closed the distance between himself and the illusion that wasn't Loriane, ran his hands along her shoulders. She felt real enough. Goosebumps trailed over her skin.

Oh by the skylights—what power!

Then he stepped back, forcing the image from his mind. This was an illusion, no matter that it was a very realistic one. Loriane was several floors above him in the birthing room. He was here in a desperate attempt to take control of this device, not to let it take control of him.

Several children sat on the ground, their bodies glowing, crying onto the shoulders of imaginary people they hugged.

Tandor understood. *This power shows us our deepest desires.* The young man who had just knocked out the Knight had been a boy whose wish it had been to become a strong soldier.

Wasn't it just disgusting that his deepest desire involved carnal pleasure? He should do better than that.

"Listen, everyone!" he called out. His voice barely rose above the humming of the device. None of the children paid him attention. He shook the shoulders of the nearest girl, who was so absorbed in her dream that she didn't react, not even when he slapped her in the face.

The young muscular man who wanted to be a soldier just stood there, staring at the brightness, eyes wide open.

They still have their hearts, Tandor reminded himself.

It was unlikely that he could still turn them into servitors, but he had to try. He fumbled for the dagger.

The girl had grown taller than him. Tandor grabbed her hand. She glowed and her touch burned even in the hand he was not supposed to have. With his real hand, he wielded the dagger and stabbed.

As soon as the knife made contact with her luminous skin, a surge of icefire went through him. It burned through his senses. He held up his hands to catch the heart, but too late, realised the icefire was flowing *out* of him *into* the girl. The scar on her chest glowed white.

Tandor struggled, but couldn't let go.

A young man took hold of the girl's shoulders. Another jolt shuddered through Tandor's body. A third child joined. That figure, glowing too much in Tandor's pain-stricken eyes to determine gender, grabbed the next person. Tandor braced for the jolt, and still screamed when it came. He was still panting and sweating when there was another jolt, stronger still.

The rectangular shape of the Heart had lost some of its brightness. Still, the glowing figures were joining up, linking hands. Strands of icefire now flowed from the rectangular device into the children.

They were sinks. The device was voiding itself, its power flowing into the children's bodies.

The next jolt was so strong it turned Tandor's muscles to jelly. Shivering, crying, he fought to stand upright and found he couldn't. The two figures on either side of him had grown so much that his legs hung off the floor. His hand burned with intense cold. His trousers were wet from where he had lost control of his bladder. And still the rectangular shape became more visible, less strongly glowing, but more silver, like a giant metal box, with leads, pipes and other protuberances on the outside. Some ancient device the function of which he could only guess. A weapon.

Jolts of icefire made him scream, his voice raw. The pain made him sick, but his insides were empty.

Then the jolts stopped.

The circle of hands around the Heart was complete.

The children, or the grotesque, glowing shapes that had been the children, held its power now. The thing itself was no more than an ugly dented metal container.

No one moved.

The surface of the machine trembled, and shivered as if someone had kicked it. Seams split apart. Shafts of light shone through, and expanded, etching into the ceiling. There was something *inside* it. The ground rumbled. The ceiling split open, hissing smoke. Debris rained from the stone and lit up where it intersected the beams. The children let Tandor drop to the ground.

Tandor sat there, dazed, while a firework of icefire raged over his head. The children, now constructs of light, breathed icefire. Their mouths spewed it when they spoke. Strands snaked away from their circle of hands, pulverising stone. Pipes burst, spewing forth water that glowed with icefire, ice-cold water too contaminated to freeze.

Tandor screamed. "Listen to me!"

But his voice didn't rise above the crackling and the rumbling. He gathered strands of icefire in his hands, tried to wind them around the legs of the grotesque figures. The strands fell away or snapped when the figures moved, as if they were simple threads.

No control, no control over this monstrous creation.

Too much exposure. The Knights shouldn't have removed the protective casing. They shouldn't have played with things they didn't understand and couldn't see.

He shouldn't have come here not knowing what the Knights had implanted in the children. He should have realised the danger. He should have shot the children.

It was too late. The power was out of control and he was no match for it.

Tandor ran.

Up the ramp, as fast as he could. His legs ached, his lungs burned, but he didn't stop. He ran and ran.

At the door that led out of the twisting ramp, he almost crashed into a group of Knights.

"Get out, get out!" His voice was hoarse.

They just stared at him, their faces already peeling from exposure.

Tandor ran through the experiment room, back to the stairs that led up to the entrance of the birthing room.

Loriane! He had to get her out of here. He ran up the stairs.

Blood pumped in his veins. His face was burnt; he could feel the sting of cold air on raw skin. The numbness of the injury was wearing off.

Up, up. Black spots danced before his eyes. He missed a step and stumbled against the wall, bracing himself with his hand. By the skylights, the skin on his arm was peeling in big slabs, leaving raw and oozing flesh. The sight made him feel sick.

While he stared at it, the ground rumbled deep below his feet. Tandor listened, holding his breath. The floor vibrated with a low keening. The sound increased in pitch, and increased until the metal-and-stone construction of the building sang. Tandor ran. He almost blacked out, but he ran. Up, up, up, into the corridor. Into the room at the end.

"Loriane, *Loriane!*"

The room was empty, beds abandoned, a trolley of medicines upended in an aisle.

Tandor ran towards the exit.

"Loriane!"

The guard post was deserted. Shouts drifted in from outside.

"Loriane!"

The roar of an explosion overtook him.

MYRA SAT stark naked, legs spread on the birthing chair. Sweat-soaked hair clung to her head.

The elderly palace midwife knelt on the cushion facing the girl, and placed a basket with soft towels under the chair. She nodded at Myra. "You're almost ready."

Myra's expression was distant. Her lips trembled, and then she muttered, "Help me, help me, help me." With each *help*, her voice became louder. Her breath sped up, her legs trembled, her one hand dug into the flesh of her thighs. She howled.

The midwife cursed. "Oh, come on, girl. It's not going to happen with screaming. If you want to be a breeder, you've got to do better than this. Push, by the skylights. Push, push."

Myra wailed and panted. Tears ran over her face. "I can't. Please help me, Mistress Loriane."

"She's right," Loriane said. "*You* have to do this. We can't help you any further if you don't want to be helped."

While Myra wasn't looking, the midwife reached between the girl's legs, trying to examine the baby's progress.

Myra screamed and kicked. "You're not touching me!"

"Right. That's *it*." The midwife wiped her hands on her apron and rose. "I've had enough. I'll be back when you decide to behave." She walked off between empty beds where women who shouldn't be walking had vacated their beds to get away from Myra's screaming.

Myra, her eyes wide, stared after the woman's broad back. "She can't just leave me!"

"Yes, she can," Loriane said. "You're behaving like an idiot."

"But I'm going to die."

"Yes."

Myra's eyes widened. She clearly hadn't expected that answer. Her lip trembled. "Mistress Loriane? You're kidding me?"

"No, I'm not. You *will* die if you don't do what we say."

"I don't want to die."

"Then for all you're worth *shut up*."

The girl was shivering with another building pain. "I'm scared. I'm so scared, Mistress Loriane, please help me, please . . ." She threw her head back.

Loriane covered the girl's mouth with her hand. "Shut up, shut up."

She kneeled at the pillow the midwife had just vacated, put her hands on the girl's sweaty and blood-slicked thighs, fixing her with a hard stare. "Or I'll tell Tandor that you behaved like an idiot."

Myra clamped her lips, her eyes blazing with anger. "I'm not an idiot."

"Good. Now shut your mouth and push."

Myra pushed. Her face went red until she gasped for breath. Then she pushed again. Loriane patted her knee, knowing that girls didn't like being touched at this stage.

She whispered, "Very good, keep going, keep going. You're almost there."

Myra pushed and pushed. Drops of fluid dribbled on the towel in the basket under her.

The silence was heavenly.

Two of the women who had left came back, peeking around the corner of the door. Their eyebrows rose. They had probably expected Myra to be dead.

Loriane glanced at the door. Tandor needed to come back quickly. If this was over, she could maybe ask the midwife for an examination, but after that, she could stay here no longer, neither could she go to the sled with a driver no one could see, or wait in the sled for a man who wasn't supposed to be in the palace.

Another contraction. Myra was really getting into it now. She pushed and panted, and pushed. The midwife came back and joined Loriane with set of instruments that included forceps and needles and gut thread. This was not going to be easy.

Loriane rose, sore and stiff from sitting in the uncomfortable position. The child inside her was kicking her in the ribs. It wouldn't be long before she had to come back here herself.

Myra pushed and howled and pushed. The midwife was easing out the baby's feet, and then the abdomen. Her calming words were wasted on Myra, who was hysterical. "It hurts, it hurts!"

"Keep going, keep going."

The head of the baby shot out, followed by a gush of fluid. Myra screamed. The child fell into the midwife's hands, wet and slippery and covered in bloodstained slime.

Loriane's stomach cramped. She turned away from the group, scanning the room for a bowl to throw up.

A healthy cry drowned all the women's talk.

"That's a big boy," one of the women said.

But then someone gasped.

"By the skylights," the midwife said in the silence that followed. "He's Imperfect."

"I know, I know," Myra cried, her voice hoarse. "Give him to me."

"I can't. He . . ." The midwife licked her lips. She was still holding the squealing infant.

Loriane swallowed bile, and swallowed again, quelling her stomach.

In her haste to get Myra to help, she had forgotten the rule about Imperfect babies. She hadn't even considered it, since Imperfects were hardly ever born these days.

"Give her the child," she said, shouldering her way into the group.

The midwife gave her a strange look.

"The girl is from Bordertown, and will be going back there." She eased the squealing boy out of the midwife's hands and proceeded to cut the cord. She wrapped him in towels to still his cries. Everyone in the room had gone very silent.

Myra looked from one face to the other. She was leaning back in the chair, still bleeding from a good tear, sheened with sweat, white-faced and totally spent. She had suffered for three days. It was probably a wonder she was alive at all. *If this had happened in Bordertown, she might not have been.*

"You had best fix her up," she said to the midwife.

Carefully, she lowered the child to Myra's swollen breast. The girl gasped when he latched onto the nipple and then started laughing, and crying.

Loraine's eyes misted up. How could she have forgotten her first time? That incredible relief after all the pain. The healthy baby at her breast. That boy would be sixteen now. Unlike her, Myra would keep her little boy.

"I'm still going to have to report this to the Knights," the midwife said. "They have been very strict on Imperfect births recently."

"The Knights are at the festival. The guard is really light. If I take her out tonight—"

"Back to your house? Like this? She needs to be under observation. We need to notify the father's family—"

"She's from Bordertown, and there *is* no breeder's contract." Please, she really didn't want to argue about it now. Even the thought that Myra *might* lose her baby made her chest constrict. She still saw the nurse walk away with *her* beautiful boy.

"No contract? How can that be?"

"Because . . ." Loriane spread her hands. Tears pricked in her eyes. *Because she loves this boy.*

The midwife raised her eyebrows.

"Please, just let me take her home."

"I didn't think you would—"

The floor trembled.

"What, by the skylights. . . ?" the midwife said.

The other women stopped chatting and glanced at each other. The door creaked open letting in a waft of freezing air, and a guard. He looked around the room wordlessly and disappeared, leaving the door open. The frosty chill settled in Loriane's stomach. Tandor had gone down there. He was doing something stupid. He was always over-confident, that was how he'd become maimed in the first place.

She heaved herself to her feet and waddled towards the door. When she was halfway across the room, the floor rumbled again, more violently this time. Dust and plaster rained from the ceiling. A chunk of stone came down behind her, scattering bits over beds and couches. And something, *something* she couldn't see or describe made the air hum with tension.

Tandor, for sure. Tandor never came for just a social visit, and Tandor had *wanted* to get into the palace, that's why he was here.

Loriane turned, her heart thudding. "Myra, come, now."

All around, women scrambled for their bedding and warm clothes. Myra just sat there, clutching the child. She probably couldn't walk unassisted. Loriane ran back into the room and pulled Myra up. "Come on, Myra. We *have* to get out."

The girl's eyes were wide. "What's happening?"

"I don't know, but there are fifty floors above us, and I think I'd rather be in the street if this building is going to collapse."

The floor rumbled again.

A group of knights burst from the corridor into the courtyard, into the snow . . . which was melting into sludge. Steam rose from the ground. Bears bucked and pulled in their harnesses.

Loriane walked as fast as she could, dragging Myra with her. The girl's steps were insecure; she was probably close to fainting. The boy had started crying, muffled in the towel. Myra stumbled. Her face was deathly white. *Yes, yes, I know this is a cruel thing to do to you.* "Come, run, run."

Myra couldn't walk fast, let alone run, but Loriane pulled her along.

When they arrived in the courtyard, the floor heaved again.

Loriane pushed Myra into the sled and stumbled in herself. No Tandor. No driver.

"Go, go," she screamed at the bear and yanked the reins.

At that moment, there was a roar behind them. The ground trembled and bucked. Metal creaked. Glass crashed behind her.

The bear reared, pulling the front of the sled up with its harness. The animal sprang forward, and bounded out the gate.

Too fast, too dangerous.

The back entrance of the palace was in a narrow street, half-blocked with rubble. People were running out of every entrance; people lay in remains of collapsed façades. One woman hung on for her life to the crumbling construction that had been an apartment floor. A breeze stirred up her nightgown, giving Loriane a view of her pallid body. An instant, and then the sled whooshed past. People ran out of entrances on both sides of the street, screaming and pointing. The bear plunged into the fleeing crowd. Loriane yanked the reins, but couldn't stop the animal. In the mayhem, people fell, causing others to trip over them. People in flimsy clothes, people with bleeding wounds. Glass was everywhere.

The ground bucked and rumbled. Debris fell down from the towering buildings that lined the street. More glass. Pieces of stone. People screamed over the deafening noise. The bear was growling and snapping at bystanders that blocked its way.

Then there was a thundering rumble behind them, and a huge whoosh. A cloud of smoke and dust filled the street. Every bit of glass that was still intact shattered. A rain of razor-sharp fragments pelted down. Loriane threw her and Myra's cloaks over both of them, and when the pelting stopped, she peeked out.

Silence, except for the creaking and groaning of metal.

Loriane climbed from the sled.

The street behind her was blocked by a heap of rubble. In the dusty air all she could see was the structure of the palace gates, no longer attached to anything. The buildings were all gone.

The only people here were ones who no longer needed help, burnt and bloodied corpses, their skin blistered, limbs ripped.

Someone whistled; she recognised the sound.

"Tandor?" Her voice sounded like that of a lost child.

The way back through the street was blocked with the ruins of collapsed buildings. She shoved aimlessly at pieces of rubble. There was far too much of it, and she had no chance of finding him, certainly not without help.

The stupid idiot.

"Someone please help me."

No one replied. Everyone here was dead. The ground was freezing up in a hard layer of ice. Soon, the pieces of rubble would have frozen onto each other.

"Tandor, I love you," she screamed at the silence. She had never said those words aloud, but they were true, true as she stood here, carrying someone else's child, and wishing it was his, wishing for his arms around her, wishing for his voice to tell her everything would be fine.

On top of the rubble appeared a tall, bear-like figure, stepping from block to block without hesitation. At first, it seemed like the figure floated in the air. It looked like some kind of demon, with strange protuberances sprouting from its upper body. Then it came closer and Loriane saw that the figure carried someone, but still did not appear to have legs. The arms and head, too, seemed only half there. Tandor was real enough, but was he alive?

All his hair was gone, the skin on his face horribly burnt, peeling in places, black with soot and blood. Parts of his shirt were missing and the skin underneath burnt. Blood dribbled from a deep gash in his good arm.

"Tandor!" She wanted to touch him, but the thing that carried him turned its head. It was human, of a fashion, but consisted merely of a thin skin of dust, transparent in many places, ethereally grey in others.

As it walked towards the sled, Loriane realised that it was Ruko, the invisible sled driver, covered in dust.

He put Tandor down on the furs in the back seat. His skin glistened with weeping burns. His eyes were closed, his mouth slightly open. He breathed shallowly. Loriane took his arm and felt his pulse. It was regular but weak, although that could be because her hands trembled so much. Loriane and Myra wrapped him up and sat down on either side of him so he wouldn't fall over.

The driver flicked the reins and the bear started off through the street.

They passed many other injured, some beyond help. People with limbs blown off. People so badly burned that their faces were a mess. Some walked, but many did not, bleeding their life's blood into the dirt-smeared snow. There were guards and Eagle Knights, all horribly burnt, trying to help each other, or too busy simply trying to stay alive as exposed skin grew blisters. The air hummed with tension.

You can't see icefire, Tandor had once said. *That doesn't mean it's not there and it can't harm you. It just harms you less quickly than it harms others.*

The buildings on both sides of the street were badly damaged. Glass blown out, floors collapsed, people's furniture sucked into the street.

The number of people increased as they went. Streets flowed with a sorry tide of humanity. Previously well-dressed nobles clutching jagged scraps of clothing and carrying their loved ones, some of whom beyond help. Old people fell and didn't get up. Sometimes, someone would haul the fallen back to their feet, but no one stayed around to make sure they remained that way.

The ground still rumbled; buildings shuddered with some unseen force. People shielded their eyes to light Loriane didn't see. Exposed skin reddened with the blisters of icefire burns.

They reached the markets where a great number of people were crowded in the corner, with more people spilling into the square from the streets that led into it. Something Loriane couldn't see seemed to block the other side of the square.

Myra gasped.

"What is it?" Loriane asked.

Myra pointed. "Over there! Can't you see it? It's a huge . . . person. Like—made out of light. And there's another one, and . . . ohhh! It's Beido!"

Loriane stared where Myra pointed, and saw . . . nothing. No, that wasn't entirely true.

It had started snowing, and steam rose off the place where the girl pointed. Then Loriane saw them, too: huge shapes, at least thirty of them, maybe even more, outlines made of steam.

They formed a circle, towering over the city. The figure facing the people in the square held out its steam-wreathed hands.

"Beido! Beido!" Myra's voice barely rose over the screams of onlookers, but it seemed the figure heard her. A long tendril of steam curled towards the sled. Ruko tied the bears' reins to the sled.

"Look, this is your son." Myra uncovered the baby's head.

Ruko rose from the driver's seat, his hands planted at his sides, facing the steam figure.

Loriane said in a low voice, "Sit down, Myra."

"But that is Beido!"

"Myra, please—"

Loriane couldn't see the flash of icefire, but she could feel how it took her breath away. People around her fell . . . and died. Blistered faces froze in screams of agony. Eyes wide open stared at the sky.

Myra screamed, "Beido, no, don't, Beido!" Then she grabbed Loriane's arm. "He isn't listening. Make him listen!"

"I can't do anything. I can't even see him. Sit down." Loriane yanked Myra back into the seat.

But Myra continued to scream. "Beido, Beido! What are you doing? I'm here. Beido!"

A patch of steam grew in the sky directly overhead. Mist flowed out of the steam figures to join it and form a kind of dome, which was extending downwards.

Loriane reached for the driver's shoulder. The dust was ice-cold. "Please, get us out of here."

The sled remained where it was. People in the square were falling over, clutching burned faces, skin peeling from flesh, glassy eyes staring at the sky. The screams made Loriane shiver. This was hundred times worse than Myra's screaming.

"Come on, Ruko, if you want us to live."

Myra was crying. "I don't know what they're doing. It's like . . . evil. Something has bewitched them. Get us out of here, Mistress Loriane."

"I'm trying, but I think he only listens to Tandor—"

Ruko yanked the reins. The bear roared and raised itself on its hind legs, pulling the front of the sled off the ground. It charged forward, towards the steam figure, towards the crowd and the edge of the bowl-shaped steam shape that was growing fast in the direction of the ground.

Loriane shouted, "No, no not that way!"

Her shout was futile; neither of them could have stopped the animal.

The patch of steam in the sky had grown into a half-complete dome, blocking the view of the sky, but ahead, a path was still clear.

The bear growled. The sled jostled and bumped over the bodies, which flopped under the sled's runners like rag dolls. *They're all dead.* Loriane closed her eyes. It was so awful and they were not going to make it. The rim of mist was sliding towards the ground . . . *They were not going to make it.* They were . . .

The sled cut into the mist. Myra screamed. A gush of intense cold took Loriane's breath away. She clutched the seat, squeezing her eyes tightly shut.

They were going to die, they were going to die, they were . . .

And then there was only the sled, the padding of the bear's feet and the swishing of the runners in the snow.

Myra cried, "Oh, Beido. What happened to him? Do you think he let us go because of our son?"

Loriane looked over her shoulder to see the ring of steam shapes close the dome of icefire. For the life of her, she couldn't recognise a face in the steam shapes. Her heart was still thudding like crazy.

"Maybe," she said, but she had no idea what had happened. She stared, too numb to cry, at the destruction around them, at the people still running, many covered in blisters.

Ruko was urging the bear into a run. Much of the dust had blown off him, making him once again almost invisible.

No one spoke for a long time. Myra cried softly. The whole city was covered in the hideous mist, which was expanding outward, eating up shapes of buildings. The sound of shattering glass drifted on the wind. Loriane could barely breathe for the acrid smoke.

When the bear charged out the city gates, the Outer City came into view—a mass of fire, billowing smoke and flames.

Loriane felt sick. She muttered, "My house."

Eagles swooped low over the festival grounds, and a crowd of people were throwing projectiles at them. But even some of them had become aware of the destruction in the city itself, and the outwardly expanding deathly cloud.

"My house," Loriane said again. Her practice, her friends, her patients. Isandor. "What am I going to do?"

Myra touched her shoulder. "Bordertown should still be safe."

Loriane bit on her lip to stifle tears. "That's where he's taking us, isn't it?" She nodded at the invisible driver.

"It's our home," Myra said.

The bear veered to the right, where the horizon merged with the sky.

Eagles whirled overhead, as powerless as she.

Getting to Bordertown would take at least three days. They had no food and no shelter. Their clothing was not good enough for such a voyage. Tandor and Myra needed care. She was exhausted and her belly felt hard as a rock. Every bump in the ice hurt.

But the bear knew the way. It ran and ran and ran.

A Word of Thanks

THANK YOU very much for reading *Fire & Ice*.

As author of this book, I would appreciate it very much if you could return to the place where you purchased this book and leave a review. Reviews are important to me, because they help readers decide if the book is for them.

In book 2 of the Icefire Trilogy, Dust & Rain, we follow Loriane, Isandor and the other refugees into Chevakia, a country actively fighting against icefire and the people who can wield it.

Also be sure to put your name on my mailing list, which I use to notify subscribers of news and new fiction. For everything else, please visit my website at pattyjansen.com.

DUST & RAIN

BOOK 2 OF THE ICEFIRE TRILOGY

CHAPTER 1

SADORIUS HAN CHEVONIAN dropped the pile of barygraph read-outs on his desk. Pages and pages of plotted squiggly lines slid over the wooden surface.

On top was a different sheet with a hand-drawn graph, a red line which jumped up sharply towards the right hand side of the page. He picked up that sheet, shook his head and frowned at the young man who had brought him these data.

"Up by this much?"

His new student, Vikius han Marossi, nodded. Silver embroidery glittered on the young man's white tunic, showing the insignia of the Chevakian doga, the government assembly.

The young man had left the door open and sounds of voices drifted in from the hall, mixed with the slapping of sandals on stone. A breeze that carried the tang of summer ruffled the curtains and nudged at the lingering chill in the room, a hint of the fury of hot weather to come. As chief meteorologist, Sady knew all about the weather; he could feel summer in his bones. And yet . . .

He looked at the graph, as if staring at it would change that ominous red line, and shook his head again.

"What happened? When I checked a few days ago, sonorics levels were at three motes per cube, but now they've at twelve?" Three was normal for this time of the year; twelve was slightly above the highest average level in the middle of winter. He wiped sweat from his upper lip, rechecking figures in the table on the second page, in the idle hope that the attendant of the met station who had plotted the graph had misread. He hadn't.

"It looks like we're in for an interesting summer." Sonorics, the deadly rays that came from the southern land, an ice-covered plateau so mysterious that it didn't have a name, dictated the weather patterns across Chevakia.

"I'm not sure I would call it interesting. I find it frightening." Viki's tone was timid. He held his hands clasped behind his back and stared intently at the desk.

"Viki, straighten your back and look up."

The young man did as Sady told him, a startled expression on his face. Mercy, since when did the Scriptorium send him jackrabbits for students?

"Imagine you're making an important announcement to the doga. They're not going to listen to you if you mumble, and they won't take you seriously if you slouch."

"Um—I'm sorry, Senator."

"Viki, if ever you're going to be chief meteorologist, you will need to show more confidence. How else are you going to tell selfish senators that, no, their district isn't going to get an allocation of maize production, because the air current predictions are wrong and the harvest will certainly fail?"

"Um . . ." Viki went red in the face and went back to staring at the desk.

"Stand up! Look me in the eye. Tell me what you'd say to them if you were in this situation."

The young man straightened again, his eyes wide. "Um—I'd say that they were wrong asking for the allocation, Senator. I'd tell them about our high sonorics measurements and that they predict unseasonably cold weather in the south which means much less rain in the north. I'd show them the maps and show them how I calculated—"

"No, no, Viki."

The student gave Sady a startled look. "But I have to—"

"You should always keep it simple. Don't explain to them how you calculated the prediction. That not only bores them to tears, but it shows that you feel the need to justify yourself because you're not sure of your calculations."

"But—"

"Confidence, Viki. You'll need confidence in your work or the farmers and the districts will howl you down, especially those in the North. They seem to think that the sheer act of predicting is going to make it happen."

"But you can only predict rain when the circumstances indicate that there will be rain."

"Exactly, but do you think they care? Rain is money to them. If I predict rain, the doga gives them money to plant crops, simple as that. Then of course, there is no rain, the harvest fails and the meteorologist gets the blame."

"But that's . . ." Viki's eyes were wide.

"That's how things go if you're not careful." Sady sighed and shuffled the papers on his desk. He felt no patience with his student today. Those data were really too worrisome to ignore. "Have you looked at any other border stations?"

Viki pushed another bundle of papers across the table; his hands trembled.

Sady leafed through the graphs. Same results. Automated devices were all recording low pressure, and the manual measurements taken by faithful meteorology staff in the stations reported high humidity, low temperatures and out-of-season increases in sonorics. Not just one station, but Ensar, Fairlight, Mekta, all of them reporting levels of twelve, thirteen, even fourteen motes per cube.

Mercy, what was going on?

"Senator, begging your permission . . . I made this." Viki put a roll of paper on the desk. Sady frowned and unrolled it: a map, showing isobars across the country.

It was a neat piece of work, impressively detailed. He gave Viki an appreciative look. "Now that is what I call initiative. That's what I'd like to see more of."

The young man blushed.

Sady moved some papers aside and spread the map out over the table. Wavy lines ran parallel to the escarpment that formed the border with the southern plateau, a pattern that sometimes occurred in midwinter, but even then the pressure lines were usually less crowded. There was a huge low-pressure system building up.

Sady met the student's eyes.

"Any idea what it means?"

"Um . . ." The young man's cheeks went red.

Sady sighed. "Viki, this is not a trick question. I don't know either. Nothing like this has happened before. This is not a seasonal pattern. At this time of the year, we'd expect the low pressure systems to retreat to the far south and the air flow to swing around to the north."

The young man looked up, his lips forming the letter *o*. "Well, in that case, I was thinking . . . I mean . . . low pressure is usually associated with a rise in sonorics, because sonorics tends to increase the air humidity."

"Yes, but why?"

Viki hesitated. "What if . . . if the people in the City of Glass were releasing sonorics deliberately. . . ? Could they, if they wanted to?"

Sady shrugged, uncomfortable. They knew so little of the workings of the southern land and the source of those deadly rays that influenced far too much of Chevakia's weather. Some sort of machine, the classic works said, somewhere under the City of Glass. No one knew if this supposed machine was a physical thing or a myth. Sady wasn't sure the southerners themselves knew what it was. Then, fifteen years ago, after the border wars, the barriers went up and no one travelled to the south anymore. Right now, he certainly didn't want to worry about whether southerners could manipulate it, although the thought chilled him. Sonorics were deadly to Chevakians.

"Viki, please give the Most Learned Alius the message that I wish to see him." Sady didn't really expect much help from an academic who did not share his practical experience, but his old tutor had made an extensive study of sonorics and was without a doubt Chevakia's most knowledgeable expert on the subject.

"Certainly, Senator." Viki bowed and left the room at a trot.

Sady grimaced. *Really? Am I that frightening? I must be getting old.*

He shook his head. No need to worry too much over this student. After his traineeship, Viki would probably choose to move on to a career in academia—or so Sady hoped, because the youngster really hadn't the aptitude for a life as doga meteorologist.

Sady rose and went to the window.

Laid out before him in perfect geometric patterns, the splendour of Tiverius spread towards the horizon. Rows of terracotta roofs basked in the sun along perfectly straight streets, interspersed by stone buildings with columns. Trees bloomed along the roadsides, even numbers on both sides. Down in the courtyard, a man with a water truck was watering the flowers in the planter boxes.

A warm breeze stirred the curtains. A few moon cycles, and it would be midsummer, not at all the time high sonorics levels usually happened.

Sonorics levels wouldn't need to rise that much before they caused trouble. At twenty motes, it would taint the harvest, at thirty, set off the first alarms and affect exports to Arania. Chevakia couldn't afford not to harvest in the southern border provinces. The northern region was too dry to produce much more than camels and the occasional crop of maize.

He didn't want to start panic, but . . . why now? Why at the start of summer, when the annual cycle should be approaching its lowest level.

Back at his desk, he pulled out a writing pad. He scrawled on the top page, *Authorise dispensaries to start stocking salt tablets for general public use. Authorise protective suits to be taken out of storage and sent to border regions.*

This he took to his secretary in the next room, who took the note, looked at it and met Sady's eyes in a wide-eyed look.

The expression of worry cut Sady deeply. He only vaguely remembered the time of uncertainty before the barriers went up, but he had heard the tales told by older folk. The young man would have seen the barygraph readouts this morning. He would have heard the tales, too.

"Just to make sure," Sady said, hoping he exuded a confidence he didn't feel. A confidence that, following such a rapid rise, the levels wouldn't hit twenty motes per cube and trigger the lowest-level warning.

The man nodded, but similarly didn't look convinced.

Not good. Not good at all.

CHAPTER 2

Oh, morninglight, oh evenlight,

How you wake me through the night.

Oh morningstar, oh evenstar,

How do you guide me from afar?

JEVAITHI'S CLEAR VOICE faded amongst the trees, in the rustle of the wind through the pine boughs, and the singing of the birds.

She breathed the scent of grass and pine resin, letting the taste of it flow through her lungs. It was beautiful. It was strange; it was new. All her life, she had only seen the whiteness of the plains around the City of Glass, whenever her minders had deigned to take her, which wasn't often.

For the first time in all her life, Jevaithi was free. There were no courtiers telling her to behave, no ladies-in-waiting telling her to wear hideous clothes; there was no Rider Cornatan watching over her. She could dance, she could sing, she could roll in the grass.

The dress was filthy, but it didn't matter. The grass was soft and the wind was warm, although today it had been quite chilled, but she and Isandor had their furs, even if they were full of sticks and seeds and smelled of each other.

There was plenty of food and it was so easy to catch that even she, with little experience in hunting, had made two kills. Fat birds with webbed feet and funny, broad beaks. She'd learned to pluck and clean them, and cut them up for roasting. The Chevakians must keep these for eggs, because they found many of those.

There were even milking goats, although they were tricky to catch and even trickier to milk.

But it was fun. Goat's milk was tangy and smelly, but it filled her stomach.

They had seen no people.

The large house down the hill seemed empty. Once it must have been a magnificent residence, but now the paint had faded, moss covered the roof and the garden was an overgrown mess. In the fields surrounding it, the farm machines moved backwards and forwards by themselves, chug-chugging and belching steam. There was no one in those machines; Isandor had checked. How did they move?

And why was there such a large house with all these empty rooms? Why did no one look after the machines? Why were there big barns with grain just sitting there? Where were all the people to eat it? Chevakia was such a strange place, such a rich place to let all these buildings stand empty and let harvested crops uneaten.

There was the swishing of footsteps through grass.

Isandor stood at the edge of the golden wheat field, holding his hand above his eyes and squinting into the distance.

His face was so serious that Jevaithi wanted to go and hug him, but he'd been very distant ever since they had let the eagle go. He had told her that he'd wanted to be an Eagle Knight, not a leering one like the Knights who had guarded her, but an honest Knight. Of those men it was said they loved their birds more than their women. The bird that had carried them here all the way from the City of Glass had been his, briefly. As he had taken the harness off, it had flown away in the direction of the border. Isandor had watched her fly off until she became a little speck that disappeared over the horizon.

Jevaithi had asked, "Where will she go?"

Isandor had said, "Probably back to the Aranian mountains, to the mountaintops where her kin roost." And the roosts of the giant birds were said to be holy in the eyes of the Knights. Of course the eagle would go back where she could be free.

But Isandor was not free. He stood staring at the sky, with that expression of sadness over his face. The glare from the sun carved sharp angles in his face. Jevaithi didn't dare ask if he was looking for the bird to come back. Her heart—his heart inside her chest—ached with his sadness and at the same time felt warm with love. He didn't deserve sadness.

Isandor was handsome, he had the perfect royal blue eyes, black glossy hair that she loved to stroke and comb, and a few funny hairs that poked out of his chin. He tried to cut them off with the dagger and she said she liked him better with the hairs.

He didn't need to be ashamed about being a man.

She approached him through the grass and was just about to touch him when he turned around abruptly, seemed to see her for the first time, grabbed her hand and pushed her face first against the trunk of a tree.

Jevaithi barely had time to protest. "Isandor, what—"

"Shhh!" He flung his cloak over her and pressed himself against her. Under the cloak, it smelled of sweat, wet fur and pine resin. She could feel her heart beating like crazy in Isandor's chest. His arm tightened around her. All around in the forest, the birds were making alarmed noises.

"What is it?" she whispered in the darkness under the cloak, but at that moment there was a faraway cry she recognised: the plaintive, high-pitched trill that took her back to her tower room prison in the City of Glass, where she would stand with her nose pressed against the window watching the Knights soar past on their birds.

And she could almost feel Rider Cornatan's presence, always watching her. She could feel his gaze burn through her thin dress.

The eagle was surely going to see her; eagles could spot a snow fox on an ice floe from heights where you couldn't even see the rider on the bird's back. Soon, the bird would come down, and bring its mates. There was no way they could fight a couple of trained Knights. She should run, while she still could.

But Isandor's arm enclosed her like a vice, keeping her pressed to the trunk of the tree.

"Keep as still as you can," he whispered. "Eagles can only see you if you move."

Every nerve in her body was telling her that he was wrong, but it made sense. He had been an Apprentice after all. He knew eagles better than she did. She kept still, controlled her shivering muscles which were aching to run, and hardly dared breathe.

Those moments under the cloak felt like eternity, but eventually, Isandor relaxed. He retreated, leaving a cold and sweaty spot where their bodies had touched.

Jevaithi pushed the cloak off her head and squinted at the bits of blue sky peeking between the trees.

"Is it gone?" she asked.

Isandor was squinting at the sky, too. "I think so."

"It wasn't your bird, wasn't it?"

He shook his head, looking serious. "Lucky we let the eagle go. She would have given us away."

"Please do your best to hide us from them. I don't want to go back. I want to stay with you always." She hadn't thought that the Knights would find their position so quickly.

"It's not going back that worries me," Isandor said. "If the Knights catch us, why would they take you back to the City of Glass? It suits them if the Queen has had a terrible accident and won't ever come back. That way, with no Queen and no heir, they can do exactly what they want, and Rider Cornatan won't ever need to give up his power as regent. He can just call himself king. He's probably already done that."

He was right. These Knights weren't here to capture her; they were here to kill her. She had thought there was nothing worse than having Rider Cornatan in her bed, and of course she'd been stupid. There were worse things. Much worse.

"Please, Isandor, help me."

The worried expression on his face hurt her. He held her close, but another chilled wind blew through the forest, which suddenly seemed very harsh and foreign. And there was a tang in the air. If she hadn't known any better, if she hadn't been in Chevakia, she would have thought it was a flare of icefire. That couldn't be. There were barriers. She had seen them herself, felt their eerie influence, endless walls cutting through the landscape, made from metal plates set at an angle. She didn't know how they stopped icefire, but just watching them from the back of an eagle they gave her the shudders. There *was* no icefire here.

"I'm cold."

He didn't meet her eyes. Would he feel it, too, the tang in the air?

Huddling together, they studied the alien intense blue sky. The sun was much further above the horizon than it would ever be in the City of Glass, and cast harsh shadows over the grass and Isandor's pale skin.

He said, "We should probably get under cover. The door to the shed down there is open. I tested it, and there's no one in there. It will be safer, and warmer. I've found some hay that will make a nice bed . . ." He gave a wolfish grin. "Come."

He took her hand.

They gathered up whatever little things they had brought and carried the filthy bundles through the field. The grain came up to her knees and when the ears hit her legs, they tickled. She no longer laughed at the feeling. The sight of the bird wheeling in the sky had awakened a deep fear in her. Running away might work well for Isandor, but could she ever feel safe?

The shed looked rather forbidding, a structure without windows, made from a material that was grey and had countless longitudinal waves. If she hadn't known any better, she would have thought it had come from ancient times. But this was most certainly Chevakian-produced.

Isandor opened the shed door; it creaked.

Jevaithi followed him into semidarkness and a musty smell of dry grass. There was a big dark shape inside, like a big crouching animal. Jevaithi hesitated; she felt so small and nervous. "What's that?"

"It's one of their machines. I know it looks scary, but it doesn't do anything. Come over here."

Jevaithi walked past the machine, running her hand over the smooth metal and breathing its strange scent. The machine was almost as tall as a house, and was one block of metal bigger than she had ever seen before. It had a large wire cylinder on one end and stood on a set of tractor wheels. At the top was a long arm. She wondered what it was for.

Isandor had collected a couple of the strange rectangular cubes of hay as they had found stacked up in another shed. One as a table, two as chairs. A plank held treasures they had collected so far: a rusty fork, a broken pot and a couple of flat rocks for the fire. There was also the clumsy basket she had woven from straw, with three eggs, and a couple of pieces of fruit they had collected.

Isandor spread his hands. "Behold, our first home!"

She forced her worries from her mind and threw herself in his arms. He stroked her hair, but didn't say anything. He was worried, too. She could feel that in the way his heart beat in her chest.

"I think we can't keep running," she said. "We should hide instead. We should become farmers. We can keep goats and keep these funny birds."

"They're called ducks."

"Never mind. We'll look like Chevakians, and no one will recognise us."

"We don't know how to be farmers."

"That doesn't matter. The machines know how to be farmers. We can just let the machines do the work for us."

But her words had a hollow ring to it, and even Isandor would feel that they were fake. They would never be farmers. They didn't even eat anything that had come from a plant. Plants were treasures that took up important decorative positions in rich nobles' houses in the City of Glass. While her body frolicked in the grass, her mind was back in the palace.

She wondered how Rider Cornatan would use his power now that she was gone. Abuse it, rather, because she no longer watched him. And she wished she could stop thinking about the City of Glass, about how the people might suffer in her absence, because the thoughts made her feel guilty.

She had always thought that she had no power, but she did stop the Knights taking power completely, because the people wanted to see and hear *her*, not the Knights, and the Knights served *her*. But there was no point in having these thoughts, and it was not fair for those feelings to creep up on her.

"I think we will go back, one day," Isandor said softly. "It's not right, being free while the people we care about aren't."

No, it wasn't. Her room servants, those people closest to her, might be punished. They might be turned out into the street without a way to support themselves. Was that the way she wanted to reward them?

The people of the City of Glass loved her. They stood along the roads and cheered, and while she held herself proud and waved and envied them for their freedom, their love for her was very real. She challenged the Knights where she could get away with it. Even through her horrific illness and dark moods, her mother Queen Maraithe had raised her with pride. *You must always honour the people. If it weren't for the people, you wouldn't be what you are.* No she wouldn't. Without the people, the Knights would have raped and murdered her long ago.

The people in the City of Glass would miss her. They might revolt; they might be repressed by the Knights. They might accuse the Knights of making her disappear, and the Knights wouldn't take kindly to such accusations. Rider Cornatan would make sure that all those dissenters would be punished, and that would make the people only angrier, and would play into the hands of the Brotherhood of the Light and the sorcerer Tandor, whose motives she didn't understand, but who would be sure to stir up unrest. A shiver crawled over her back. Her escape might lead to the deaths of many people. She'd acted selfishly.

"Then what do you think we should do?" she asked, and she hated how discomfort laced her voice. And she hated how his words cut through the dream of being free.

"I think we'll need to hide for a while until the Knights stop looking for us," Isandor said. Which wasn't really an answer. "Then we can find somewhere to live."

She nodded, but knew it wasn't so simple. As long as she, or a child of hers, was alive, the Knights would hunt her.

His worried face broke into a smile. "Hey, don't look like that. We'll survive. I'll always be with you."

She smiled, too. "I love you."

His lips sealed on hers.

They rolled in the hay, clothes discarded along the way until they lay naked and panting, in the afterglow of lovemaking.

He whispered, "I love you so much it hurts me here." He held his hand to his chest.

She put her ear on the bare skin next to her hand. Their hearts beat in unison; she could never get enough of hearing it.

She would never leave him, never, never leave him out of sight, wherever they went.

"Love me again," she said. "Love me again and again."

He did.

But love did not solve her deeper worries.

CHAPTER 3

"THEY WEREN'T even listening!" Viki protested, spreading his hands in a gesture of frustration. His eyes, wide and brown, met Sady's, while he swerved to avoid a uniformed guard coming the other way in the corridor. They were walking back to the office from the morning's doga session where Sady had cringed through Viki's presentation on climate patterns.

"I told you that showing calculations and tables would bore them," Sady said.

"There was only one sheet of calculations and one table. You said to show the maps, so I showed mostly maps. I did what you said, honestly."

Viki was right: he had eliminated most of the calculations and dry data tables; he had made the maps bold and pretty. It was just that . . . the senators had been more interested in discussions about train lines to the north. Sady felt a deep shame about that. What a way to introduce a young man to the world of politics. *We only listen when there is something in it for us.*

"I know you did. I'm sorry, Viki. I'm not sure what I would have done differently." Would they have listened had he given the talk himself? The data was serious enough.

They went around the corner and up the stairs. Their footsteps echoed in the open staircase. Marble columns and rich wall hangings.

Carved wooden doors and leadlight windows. Splendour was everywhere.

They passed a group of senators who gave him glances that bordered on pity. Poor Sady, who listens to him? Poor Sady, who cares about meteorology? Some people said it was fast becoming an irrelevant discipline, that everyone already knew what there was to know, that one only needed enter a date and weather data in one of those new calculators that were being developed by the Scriptorium, and be presented with best dates for planting crops.

At the top of the stairs, Sady turned left and charged down the corridor. Viki had to run to keep up.

Someone behind him called, "Senator Sadorius, can I have a word?"

Sady stopped and turned around to see Proctor Destran mir Parkeshian behind him. Oh, mercy, that was just what he needed.

Viki said in a low voice, "Do you want me to continue to the office?"

"Stay here," Sady said. Destran would most likely want to talk about Viki's presentation.

Viki stayed, clasping his hands behind his back and tensing his shoulders. His face resembled that of a hunted rabbit.

Destran caught up and gave a customary bow. "Senator."

Sady returned the greeting. "Proctor."

From close up, Destran resembled a scarecrow. Lanky and taller than most people, he always walked hunched over, as if life were a great burden. His heavy, hooded eyelids increased that impression. His hands were like veined spiders; his neck had as many wrinkles as the neck of a very, very old turtle. Exposure to sunlight in his childhood had made his skin blotchy and age had brought the breaking out of many small, polyp-like warts over his face and neck.

The man's narrowed eyes met Sady's. "I heard you authorised the distribution of pills and suits."

"I did, for the border regions only."

"I understand you didn't ask doga permission?"

"No, I didn't. Within limits, I don't need approval." Destran would know that.

"Don't you think you overreacted?" Destran's gaze was intense.

Sady stared back. "No, I don't. Some border stations were recording sonorics levels of fourteen motes per cube."

"The warning limit is twenty."

"Yes."

There was a moment of silence. Destran continued staring and Sady continued meeting his gaze. A cold draft made the curtains behind Destran stir, and matched the icy atmosphere between them.

"I cannot see a reason for this," Destran said. "There is no evidence that we are under any kind of sonorics threat beyond what we can cope with."

"The rise is rapid and completely out-of-season."

"And the twenty motes per cube is a failsafe, arbitrary, nothing-could-possibly-happen-at-this-level kind of limit."

"My greatest worry is not the level, but the timing of it. We've never been able to test the precise effects, because, as you can understand, we are reluctant to send our people into the south. So yes, the upper limit is somewhat arbitrary, but the safety of Chevakians should be the first priority for the doga."

"Within reasonable assumptions."

"And you, Proctor, are suggesting that nothing of what you've heard today is reasonable? That the measurements my student reported are all fake? Are you suggesting that the measurements taken by our own met stations lie?"

Destran spread his hands. "No, I do not."

"Then what?"

"I think your reaction is completely out of proportion and unwarranted."

"This has the potential to become an emergency."

"So you seem to think, but tell me: who is going to pay for this extravagance?"

Ah, now they got to the real problem. Sady hated poor budgeting masquerading as policy, and Destran seemed to excel at the activity.

"Safety is more important than budgets."

"Up to a point." Destran continued, "But, to please you, I've asked for independent advice about this issue, and that's what I wanted to talk to you about."

"Independent advice?" It came out as a sarcastic remark. There was no one in the country who knew more about weather patterns than him. That's why he was Chief Meteorologist.

Then Sady noticed another man who had stayed back with Destran's aides, but now came forward.

Tall, grey-haired, straight-backed, the Most Learned Alius cut an impressive figure. As head of the Scriptorium, he oversaw academia and the tutoring of students of the arts and sciences. Sady hadn't seen the man for some time, and his dark clothing and age made him sterner than Sady remembered him. And what was with the beard?

Alius bowed and Sady returned the greeting, wondering if beards were the latest fashion in the Scriptorium. Then again, he had not known academics to take much notice of fashion. "Well met, Most Learned. You know your student, of course." Sady nodded at Viki, who stood a bit back, staring at his formal tutor.

"Oh yes, I know him." Alius smiled, and the corners of his eyes crinkled. "That was an entertaining talk, young man."

"Um . . . um . . . thank you, Most Learned." Viki's stammer was back in full force.

"I am being sarcastic."

"Ummm . . . excuse me, Most Learned. I do not understa—"

Alius shook his head. "My dear student, I turn my back on you for five seconds, and you've already become the politicians' mouthpiece."

"Um . . ." Viki opened and closed his mouth a few times, like a fish gasping in the air.

"How much time have you spent analysing these data?"

"Um . . ."

"Did you just throw them into a graph and present the results without any background research?"

"I did background research." Viki's voice spilled over into a squeak. "I'm aware of all the protocols in the Meteorological Manual—"

"That's just a silly book of rules. What do you know about sonorics? I mean—really know about it?"

"I know that sonorics are rays akin to a magnetic field, and that the source is somewhere in the south. Exposure to the rays distorts the soft tissue of the human body by collapsing the cell membranes. Sonorics increases the humidity in the air which is how we can detect it . . . um . . ." Viki swallowed and shrank back further under Alius' continued death stare.

Sady couldn't stand this verbal caning anymore. It was one thing for two senators to swear at each other, another entirely for a senior academic to tear into an inexperienced student, and one who hadn't even made a clear transgression at that.

"I think your student did everything right," Sady said.

"*You* think so?" Alius' eyes were intense. "What do *you* know about sonorics? Have you studied the precise properties of it?"

"Not sonorics." Sady had to concede the point. It had been Alius who had conducted those studies, who had helped construct the barrier that protected Chevakia. "Is there anything new to report about sonorics that we should know?"

"At this stage, there is no need to cause panic in the public. There is no proof that there will be any damage to the barriers below at least fifty motes per cube and no proof that levels such as measured in the border regions will cause harm whatsoever."

Destran nodded. "There appears no reason for your unilateral action. I must assume that it was taken for political purposes."

"You would disagree that this rapid rise is highly unusual? That we need to caution people in the border regions?"

"No, I don't disagree," Destran said. "We have issued travel warnings for the south."

Sady didn't make a habit of swearing, but for fuck's sake, *travel warnings?* What good would that do? He stomped into the office after Viki, and shut the door with a thud.

"Mercy, Viki, the day Destran defeated Milleus was a sad one. I bet my annual stipend that Milleus wouldn't be so hesitant to take action. What's up with him, Viki? No money, money, always the same excuse. Well, he has all our taxes, what does he *do* with the money? Pay off his northern supporters who keep him in position?"

They were all rhetorical questions, of course. Viki scuttled to his temporary desk in the corner, took his maps and looked busy. He was way too young to remember the great Milleus han Chevonian, Sady's brother, who had been voted out ten years ago.

Milleus wouldn't have allowed Viki to have been drowned out by catcalls. Milleus wouldn't have let issues of budget stand in the way of Chevakia's safety. Admittedly, that hadn't always gone in his favour, but Chevakia had been a safe place. It had been Milleus who'd had the foresight to let Alius build the barrier that had protected the country for the last fifteen years.

Sady heaved a sigh and dropped in his big seat behind his desk. The feel of the smooth leather gave him no comfort today.

He swivelled the chair to face Viki. "Anyway, what was going on there between you and Alius?"

Viki gave him his usual startled look. "Nothing."

"Well, that looked like an odd kind of *nothing* to me. I don't recall ever being so petrified of my tutor. Why was he abusing you? *Politician's mouthpiece*. We're all mouthpieces of politics. Chevakia *is* politics."

Viki had no answer to that. He kept looking ahead of him. Avoiding Sady's eyes?

Sady sighed again. "Listen Viki, it's fine to tell me, because I can help: is there anyone at the Scriptorium who threatens you or makes you feel unsafe in any other way? Do you ever feel that you are not allowed to speak your opinion because it doesn't conform to certain opinions held by the senior academics?"

"No," Viki said, much too quickly. "No, not at all. Why are you asking?"

"Because I don't believe you. As long as I can remember, I've never heard anyone from the Scriptorium utter political comments. What is going on over there? What has gotten into Alius? What's with the beard?"

Viki looked at him, and blinked. "He's allowed to have a beard, isn't he?"

"Well, yes, but it seems strange to me. Not just the beard, but his entire behaviour. He wasn't like this when I studied—"

"Like what?"

"Like . . ." Sady shrugged, looked for words to describe his feeling, and couldn't find any that satisfied him. Aggressive, defensive, evasive, anything an academic was usually not. "Like . . . Alius always used to be more open about everything, willing to discuss. It's like he's made up his mind about this and he doesn't like being challenged."

"Well, he did build the barriers. Maybe he feels the need to defend his work to people who suggest it's not up to the job."

That was actually a really good point. And one that worried him. The academics were supposed to be impartial and non-political. And now, for some reason, Alius had decided to support Destran and consider people who opposed him an enemy.

CHAPTER 4

THE BEAR RAN across the snow-covered plain, up hills, down the other side. From the passenger seat, squashed between Tandor and Myra, Loriane could only see its bobbing back, and the reins dangling from the invisible driver's hands.

Wherever she looked in the white landscape, she could see no other people, and there hadn't been any for at least a day.

At first, when the mangled ruins of the City of Glass were still visible on the horizon, there were other refugee sleds following, families fleeing in the clothes they had worn when disaster struck, woefully inadequate for the cold. A lot of nobles, because they had sleds and could get away quickly.

But one by one, the other sleds had fallen behind until no one was left. Those sleds had to stop for the night while Tandor's bear kept going, up, down, up, down over the undulating landscape. This was no ordinary sled and no ordinary bear.

Occasionally, an eagle wheeled overhead. Loriane would cover Tandor up for fear of being recognised, but those eagles seemed to be searching only for other birds and their riders. Yesterday, she had seen a small group of them join up and make their way over the horizon in the direction of the Aranian mountains. If even the Eagle Knights abandoned the city, then what hope was there for the rest of them?

Loriane thought of the ruins, the fire and the broken bodies. The explosion she couldn't see, and the human-like shapes made of steam, one of which Myra had recognised as the father of her child. She thought of the thousands of people who didn't have sleds, and who would have been overtaken by the horror of the invisible icefire, and would have died through its burning as all those had died in the city itself.

The bear ran, the runners of the sled swished in the snow. The driver didn't pull the reins once. It seemed the animal knew the way.

Tandor's weight lay heavy against her side. Bits of his face and hands were exposed between the furs, showing peeling skin and weeping blisters. His eyes were shut. The eyelids fluttered every now and then, but Loriane's prodding didn't wake him up.

Myra was still recovering and slept a lot. Sometimes Loriane managed to wake her up to feed the baby, at other times, when the child cried, she took it to her own swollen breasts. The suckling made her stomach tense up badly, and she stopped doing it for fear of bringing on the birth out here in the snow. The baby cried a lot.

She had found out that the driver could hear her voice and that he would obey her, as long as she used Tandor's name in the requests.

They had little food. Loriane had scoured everything on the luggage rack, but she hated going through Tandor's things, fearing she'd find another horrid item like the beating heart which sat in its jar in the chest that she dare not touch.

She had only found a small box containing dried and salted meat— frozen solid—frozen fruit and cubes of a dark type of bread Loriane had never seen before. Its unfamiliar taste made acid burn in her throat. She nibbled dried meat and stayed away from eating too much snow because already she had to ask Ruko to stop the sled more often than she thought his patience allowed. Whenever she asked for a stop, he would get off the driver's seat and kick snow about, and would goad the bear until it slashed its claws at the air, and growled. The first time that happened, Loriane told him to be more careful, and Ruko threw snow in her face. She was afraid to anger him any more.

It was not to be helped; Loriane had to change Myra's bandages.

After her horrific breech birth, the girl was still bleeding quite heavily and Loriane hoped they would get wherever they were going before her supply of clean cloths ran out. The bandages needed to be rinsed, bleached and boiled, or Myra would still get sick and die of fever.

After that was done and Myra was peacefully feeding the child, Loriane would stumble off into the snow, her own baby's head threatening to burst her full bladder. There was nowhere to squat, no place to hide and after the business was done, she left an embarrassing patch of yellow in the snow, something she was sure eagles would spot. So she covered it with snow, kneeling awkwardly, but still she was sure the eagles would notice. She couldn't help it. She was tired, weary and sore, and more than anything, she wanted the roiling in her belly to stop. She wanted Tandor to wake up so that he could hear her abuse about how stupid and selfish he'd been. And then he was going to tell her what he did, and he was going to fix it before she killed him —which she should have done ages ago. He was trouble, and she'd known it all along, but somehow she thought that dangerous streak made him romantic. Stupid, stupid, stupid.

Most of all, she wanted a dry and warm place where she could rest and from where she wouldn't move until this cursed child had been born. Then she would kill that child, too, because it was part of Tandor's machinations. Fancy that—out of all the ten children she had grown inside her, she couldn't get rid of the child she least wanted.

When night came on the third day, the bear loped into a scattering of houses spread in the snow as if someone had thrown a bunch of firebricks. They were odd, blocky things spaced widely, so unlike the limpets from the Outer City which sat close together like Legless Lions conserving warmth. But houses meant people, and help, and food. Welcoming tendrils of smoke curled from chimneys; warm light radiated from windows.

Myra sat up straight, looking with wide eyes, the word *home* spelled on her face. This then, was Bordertown, the edge of the southern plateau, and as far as they could go without running into Chevakia.

Loriane was too sore and weary to be disappointed with the town's small size. Her feet were cold and she had long since given up trying to pick icicles from her hair. Her backside felt like one solid bruise, and she needed to piss again.

The bear seemed to know where it was headed.

They turned into the yard of a house as unassuming as the rest, a two-storey affair with a shed out the front. Tattered curtains covered the windows. There was light on the ground floor. As the sled came to

a halt, the front door was thrown open and a woman stood silhouetted by the warm light of an oil lamp in the hall.

"Myra, be that you?"

"Ma!" Myra cried out.

Myra threw aside the furs, scooped the baby in her arms, jumped
off the sled and waded through the snow.

The woman came out of the house and met her daughter in the
yard, enclosing her in a hug. Myra was crying, her sobs interspersed
with, "It was so awful . . . the whole city is destroyed . . . everyone is
dead . . ."

The boy started crying, muffled between the two women. Myra
unwrapped the furs that covered his face.

The woman gasped. "What a big boy."

"That's what the midwives said, too."

"What be his name?"

"I haven't named him yet, Ma. I wanted you and Da to be there."

The woman lifted the child from his sling, while he continued to
protest loudly. Her brow was unusually heavy for a female, her nose
coarse and her mouth wide. She had skin red and rough from working
in the cold, and big, widely-spaced front teeth. The word *ugly* came to
Loriane's mind.

A man had come to the doorway, leaning against the doorframe.

Myra's mother held the baby out to him. "Look at him, Da. Your
grandson."

But the man, black-haired and unshaven, was staring past his wife
and Myra to the sled, his suspicious piggy eyes narrowing when they
met Loriane's.

"Where be the sorcerer?" His mouth twitched. "That be my sled
and my bear."

Loriane said, "Tandor is injured. Can we please—"

"Who be you?" Eyes narrowed at Loriane. "You be the city
whore?"

"Da!" Myra hissed. "Mistress Loriane has helped me. I was in pain
for *three days,* not one day as you said, Ma. The baby was facing the
wrong way and I did so much screaming I couldn't talk for two days.
Without Mistress Loriane, I would have been dead."

The man studied Loriane's face. His suspicious look didn't vanish.
"That be so?"

"Please," Loriane said. "Could you offer us a meal and a bed?"

"It'll cost," Myra's father said. He crossed his arms over his chest.

"I can pay."

"Two silver gulls?"

Loriane swallowed hard. She had no money. Never in her life had she begged for anything. "Yes." Her voice sounded unsteady. She had never lied either.

"You can't do that, Da."

"Myra, we bain't rich people. If we don't ask money from visitors, they'd ruin us."

"I didn't pay anything for her help. It's only fair that she gets to stay for free."

"Myra, get inside," her mother said.

"Why? I'm not a child anymore."

Her father said, "Ye be fifteen. Ye know nothing about money."

"But I know about what's fair. And this isn't—"

"Go inside."

"Da, you can't do this—"

"Please!" Loriane called out.

They were all silent, staring at her.

"I'm happy to sleep in the shed, but can I *please* use your outroom?" Loriane's voice cracked. A few days ago, a thin and very pregnant girl had asked the same question while standing in the warm and comfortable room of her limpet. At the time, Loriane had been angry with Tandor and had thought of refusing.

"Of course you can," Myra said. "Come, I'll show you."

Loriane pushed Tandor aside and rose slowly from the sled's seat, wincing at a stab across her belly. Neither of Myra's parents spoke although Myra's mother's eyes widened and fixed on Loriane's belly.

Myra crunched back through the snow and took Loriane's arm to help her down from the sled.

"Mother, Father, this is Loriane. She and Tandor will be staying in the upstairs bedroom. Loriane, this is my father Ontane, and my mother Dara. She has a bit of healing knowledge. I am sure that between the three of us, we can help your child into the world safely. Come."

"Leave it, Myra." Her father eyed his wife, and she shot back an angry look at her husband. "Mistress, go with my wife. She'll show ye the way."

The woman stomped off without a further word. Loriane followed her into the house, through a dark corridor with a threadbare carpet, into a damp kitchen, where a pan bubbled on the stove. Whatever was in the pan smelled strongly of game meat, and Loriane wasn't sure if the smell made her feel hungry or sick.

The woman flung open the door at the back of the kitchen. An icy wind came in. "The outroom."

In the gathering dusk, Loriane stumbled into the freezing shack. There was a wooden plank with a hole, where she sat to do her business a few measly drops at a time. It burned. The child's head inside her pressed on her bladder and relieving herself made little difference to her discomfort.

The sound of angry voices came from the kitchen.

Loriane wriggled off the seat.

There was no jug of water to wash herself, only a stack of cloths she dare not use. The baby kicked in her ribs, hard.

Both Myra and her mother were waiting for her in the kitchen. Myra still held the child in the sling and leaned against the wall. Her mother was stirring a pan. Neither looked at the other.

"Come," Myra said into the icy silence and started up the stairs, so narrow and steep that Loriane had to support herself by running her hands along both walls.

The upstairs bedroom was tiny and freezing cold, with a hearth in the corner—empty—and just enough space around the not-quite-double bed to walk.

Loriane stood there, fighting back tears. She just wanted to go home, and not be dependent on these people who clearly didn't want her. It had not been much of a life but it had been hers: her modest limpet, the income she earned, her patients.

Isandor. She had always claimed that he was a burden to her, but at the same time, she loved him too. He was a good boy with a good heart. She hoped he was far away from the City of Glass, in a place where being Imperfect didn't matter. If it was true that he had fled with the Queen, she hoped that they were happy.

"I've got to . . . I've got to get Tandor," she said, to find the entire family standing in the doorway.

Behind them stood Ruko, carrying Tandor. Well, she couldn't see Ruko of course, but Tandor floated in the air as if carried by invisible arms.

Ontane turned to Myra. "Letting the mistress here use the room be one thing, but I don't want *him* in my house."

Loriane wasn't sure if he meant Tandor or Ruko.

Myra gave an annoyed snort. "Why do you keep going back on your promises all the time? Can't you see he's injured?"

"Ye keep out of it, girl."

Myra turned to her mother. "Ma, you heard him, didn't you? Da agreed, didn't he?"

"My agreement didn't include sorcerers and ghosts," her father said.

Her mother said, giving Loriane a prim look, "Myra, dear, ye have to understand. Our safety comes first. We still don't know what the sorcerer—"

"Stop it! Just stop it!" Loriane shouted.

Silence.

"Take him back down, Ruko—"

"No!" Myra yelled. "You call yourselves my parents? I'm ashamed of you. If you make them sleep in the shed, then I'll go there, too."

"Don't ye be stupid," her father said.

"Then he stays here. I brought them here. They're my guests. Now get out and give them some rest." Myra ushered her parents out the room and shut the door. "Put him on the bed." This to Ruko.

Tandor floated through the room onto the bed. He groaned, his eyes half open.

"You stay here and make yourself comfortable, Loriane. I'll go and get some water to wash, some firewood and make sure to bring you some food," Myra said and left the room.

Loriane dropped on the edge of the bed and sat there, staring in front of her. In a thin strip between the tattered curtains, a thick layer of ice covered the window. It was bitterly cold and her breath steamed. On a table in the corner of the room, a fur blanket moved and spread over Tandor, as if it flew by itself.

Ruko sat down on the other corner of the bed; she saw that by the way the mattress was pressed down.

"Look, Ruko," she said. "I think you better go somewhere else.

These people are nervous about you." Never mind the other people, *she* was nervous about him.

By the skylights, he could kill her and she wouldn't notice before it was too late. The old king's servitors did that, according to the rumours.

She said into the silence, "You've done enough for Tandor. We can manage now. Can you wait with the sled?"

He didn't move, and she didn't know how to make him move. His cold and silent presence in the room made her shiver.

The door opened and Myra came back into the room, carrying a tray with two steaming bowls of soup and a roll of bread, still warm.

Loriane spooned up the soup. The first couple of mouthfuls were unsettling, and she wasn't sure if her stomach would tolerate the food, but then she grew comfortably warm, and wolfed down the rest, as well as the roll.

"Thank you," she said to Myra, who was busying herself lighting the fire. "You're not eating?"

Myra shook her head. "I eat with my family."

She threw a few chunks of wood—real wood—into the hearth, and started them burning. Flames licked the rough surface. Loriane had hardly ever seen wood used for furniture, let alone the wastage of it being burned.

Loriane glanced at the corner of the bed. Ruko hadn't moved. She had never seen him eat, but Myra ignored him completely, so maybe he didn't need to.

She took the other bowl of soup from the tray and set it on the bedside table. "Help me get him up."

But Myra had settled in the chair by the hearth feeding her baby, and it was Ruko who got up from his corner of the bed. His invisible hands lifted Tandor by the shoulders and propped him up against the pillows. The same invisible hands draped the cover over Tandor.

"You don't want to eat anything, Ruko?" she asked him.

"He can't eat," Myra said. "That's why he asked to be changed."

"Wait—he asked for this?"

Myra nodded. "He is one of the Imperfect children Tandor rescued from the City of Glass. There were about fifty of us living in Bordertown. He placed us with foster families."

She nodded at the bed where Ruko sat. "Ruko was unlucky to be placed with a family who only cared about the money Tandor paid them. They treated him badly. I don't exactly know what happened, but the man, a woodcutter who used Ruko as a labourer to haul his sleds, was said to be fond of young boys—"

There was a crash in the corner of the room and one of the soup bowls lay in pieces, remnants of soup oozing down the wall.

Myra shifted forward as if to get up. "Hey, don't do that. My parents are already stretching their tolerance by allowing you in here. Breaking things does not help your cause. You want to help your master? You behave!"

The corner of the bed pressed down again.

"Can you see him?" Loriane asked.

"Yes. He's sulking. He was always an angry little boy."

Loriane could stare all she wanted, but saw nothing.

"Yes, I said *little boy* and I'll say it again as long as you behave like one."

She gave a sniff.

"Anyway, then he started to grow too strong for the woodcutter to abuse, and the man stopped feeding him, and locked him in the shed and would come out at night to whip him—"

The corner of the bed moved.

Myra turned her head. "Yes, I know the whole village could hear you scream and we did nothing. I was thirteen, all right?" She glared and let a silence lapse. Then she sighed. "So because he was constantly hurting with hunger and cold, Ruko asked Tandor to take his heart so he would become a servitor."

"His heart?" Loriane thought of the beating heart in the jar in Tandor's travel trunk. She'd heard about the servitors, but had always dismissed the stories as myths.

"Yes. If you take the heart from someone with icefire in his blood, someone with Thillei blood, this person becomes trapped between life and death. He's still alive, but can't speak. He doesn't have a real body, and can walk through walls. But if he wants, he can pick up things and destroy things. You can't kill a servitor. He only dies if the master dies."

She glanced aside at Ruko, a questioning, curious glance.

Myra continued in a low voice, "We could all feel Ruko's pain on the night that Tandor did it, but afterwards he calmed and we lived peacefully—most of us with our families, but Ruko out in the snow. He doesn't feel cold. He doesn't get hungry. He's happy, as far as a person like him can ever be happy— All right, you're not happy, fine."

A cold feeling crept over Loriane's back. She didn't like this invisible angry adolescent. She'd found Isandor and his brooding moods hard enough, and he'd at least been visible to her.

"And what does Tandor want? What is his grand scheme? Do you know anything about that?"

Myra shook her head. "I don't think anyone knows. But he wanted to take the other Imperfects back from the Knights. Because the Knights came here and took all the Imperfect children into the palace, except me. So when he came to the City of Glass, he wanted to get into the palace. What he did once he was in there, I have no idea."

Eyes half open, Tandor slurped soup from the spoon Loriane held out to him.

Loriane said, "He sure did something. I mean—look at him. What's going on, why can't he talk? He must have been doing something really, really stupid." She poked Tandor's chest. "Something happened while he was down in the dungeons. The explosion was his fault, I'm sure of it."

"When he visited, he sometimes spoke of the Heart of the City and that he wanted to find it."

Loriane had heard rumours of this thing. "Do you know what it is?"

"One day, a long time back, he showed us some pictures. It's a kind of machine from way back before memory. Apparently, the people who built the glass towers played with it and it blew up on them, killing everyone who knew how the machine worked. Then the old King tried to regain the knowledge, but he only abused the power."

Loriane said, "In the City of Glass they say there was a war back in the old times, and all the people who built the city got killed—"

"And then the royal family discovered it and used its lingering rays to power the lights, the trains and the glasshouses—"

"And to make servitors to suppress the people who couldn't do anything with icefire."

"Tandor told us that the Pirosians were jealous."

Loriane felt herself get inexplicably angry. "If the King hadn't used the power badly there would have been no need for jealousy. So the Pirosians banded together and formed the knighthood—"

"Using the eagles which only grew to that size under the influence of icefire."

"That's ridiculous. Did Tandor tell you that eagles are really the souls of the dead, too?"

Myra and Loriane glared at each other.

Then Loriane shrugged. "No one knows what's true."

"And who, exactly, discouraged people to learn to read?"

"And who, exactly, has been trying to bring the servitors back?" Loriane gestured at Tandor. "He doesn't care about you. He didn't care about any of us, only about his crazy scheme, whatever it was."

Myra shuddered and clamped her hands around herself and went on in a more gentle tone, "I think he wanted to breed us Imperfects. He would come in occasionally and bring all of his children together in the guesthouse. The last time he did that, it was very different. He no longer had toys for all of us, but he'd give the older boys things like necklaces and told them to give them to girls they liked. And then he gave us drinks . . . you know, the kind parents wouldn't allow us to have. And then it turned out he had rented the entire top floor of the guesthouse and said we could all stay the night, and . . . you know . . ." She glanced at the baby. "That's how he happened."

"It's all Tandor's machinations. He wanted you to have that baby. He wanted me to have my baby."

Myra frowned at her. "When is your baby due?"

"The baby *was* due days ago. I don't think this is a normal child."

Tandor stirred and mumbled but his words were inaudible.

Myra stared at Loriane, her eyes wide. "Are you sure?"

"I'm not sure about anything until this child is born. Listen, I want you to do something for me. In my bag you'll find a pot of salve. I want you to put it in." Lucky she'd had her healing and midwifery bag with her when the city exploded.

"Put it . . . in? Inside you?"

"You wanted to be a midwife? You can start with me."

CHAPTER 5

PAIN.

Pain was all around.

Tandor heard women's voices, but the meaning of their babble floated outside his range of hearing. He couldn't see who the women were, but one of them had to be Loriane. Lovely, down-to-earth, *Pirosian* Loriane. The other was probably Myra.

He couldn't see where they had taken him, but after days in the cold on the sled, they were now inside. Myra's house, probably.

Ruko was there, too, a glowering presence on the edge of Tandor's vision. His figure was a mere silhouette, a dark form soaking up all icefire.

Tandor tried to move, but he couldn't. Cords of icefire bound his hands to some ethereal substrate that he couldn't feel.

"Get these off me."

Ruko came to stand next to him, looking down, his hands behind his back. The recalcitrant lock of hair obscured one of his eyes. One corner of his mouth curved up.

"Who put these bonds on me?"

"I don't know why I believed that you could control all that power unleashed from the Heart. I thought you were a sorcerer, but you're just a simple weakling."

"You're not answering my question." Why not? Ruko was a *servitor*. He should obey his master's command. On that subject, why was he speaking? Unless Tandor had also entered that space between life and death occupied by servitors and other magical beings.

"I can see no point in answering stupid questions. Whoever put the bonds on you was a smart person."

"How dare you talk to me like that?"

"I will talk to you however I like. You broke your promise. You told me that we would free Peonie."

So it was all about a girl? "I can't do anything about that until you untie me."

"No." Ruko trailed an ice-cold hand over Tandor's neck. "It's too late to change your mind. I think I'll have great pleasure killing you." He closed the hand around the base of Tandor's throat. His black eyes burned with anger.

Ruko's touch felt like burning fire, but Tandor laughed. He didn't know how he still could laugh, but he did.

"I'll remind you: you're a servitor. If you kill me, you die as well."

"Then I will have died a worthy death."

"Oh, just stop it with the rubbish. Untie me, and we'll go and find this girl of yours."

"No. I don't believe you anymore. I'm going to kill you, and all the people you care about, in the same way you took Peonie away from me."

"And how do you think the girl will love you when you're dead?"

"I'll be dead, anyway. She was the only one who cared for me, ever. You turned her into a murdering monster."

"It was nothing to do with me. It was the Knights who put sinks in the Imperfects' bodies. They caused this disaster to happen."

"You lie, you lie!"

"I don't, and if you take these bonds away, I can show you. There are ways in which I can turn her back to normal."

"You lie. I have believed you far too long."

"But you want her to join you?"

Ruko hesitated. His dark eyes looked suspicious.

"Anyway, supposing you would kill me, and you'd survive, do *you* have a plan how to rescue her?"

Ruko's lips twitched.

"See? You have no idea. You can't do it. If you take away these bonds—"

"Shut up!"

"—I can show you—"

"Shut up! I don't believe you anymore."

"Cut these bonds."

"No!"

"Cut them, I said. You're my servitor. Obey me."

Ruko folded his arms across his chest.

Tandor yanked, but his arms would not come free. He tried to call icefire, but it would not come.

He could see his own shape on the bed. He could see two vague figures of the women, but they couldn't hear him. His bond to Ruko was a bright blue strand of light, and Ruko sat, clear as life, on the corner of the bed. He wanted to sever the stream, but he couldn't. He wanted to scream at the women for help, but he couldn't.

And he couldn't show Ruko how scared he was.

"What are you going to do with me?" he asked.

Ruko smiled, not a pleasant smile. "That's better. From now on, *I* am the master."

Tandor snorted. "Most people can't even see you."

"No, but that can be fixed."

By the skylights. His travel chest contained the jar with Ruko's heart. He could, if he knew how, or had access to someone who could bend icefire, turn himself back into an independent person.

CHAPTER 6

WITHIN A FEW very long days, Sady went from being a senator too academic to warrant much discussion to being one of the most-discussed senators in the city of Tiverius. Everyone knew about his distribution of salt pills. Everyone had their opinion, too, mostly unfavourable. Budget problems were bad enough already, they said. He should have asked for permission, they said. Maybe he should have, but it had been within his spending limit without having to ask permission.

Destran then halted the distribution of those pills, at which border regions which hadn't yet received supplies sent a veritable avalanche of telegrams asking why they didn't get the pills while the neighbouring district had received them.

With his distribution program cut short and half the southern districts angry at him, Sady asked for funding to visit those southern regions to measure and map the changes in sonorics himself, and to quell the anger. Because he wasn't every senator's golden boy right then, the application was refused.

Every time certain senators passed him in the corridors of the building, they felt it necessary to make sneering comments. That he wanted to draw attention to the Meteorology office; that he talked up the sonorics crisis just so that he could have more staff and money. An anonymous person sent him a table of data showing effects of various levels of sonorics on humans.

Sady read the report, feeling increasingly sick. The experiment had submitted people with no natural tolerance to as much as three hundred motes per cube. The work was littered with comments like, "Subject showed severe nausea, disorientation and bleeding from nose and gums," or "Subject died after three months." Yes, it also showed that maybe Chevakian sonorics safety standards were a little on the cautious side, but mercy, this table meant that someone had actually done this work on human subjects. On Chevakians. He thought of all those girls who had been abducted from the border villages, none of whom had ever returned.

He was unable to trace the origin of the report, although he strongly suspected that it was a translation from a southern document, and that it must have come from some dark corner of the Scriptorium library.

Meanwhile, Viki's reports of the levels at border stations inched very slowly in the direction of the twenty motes, but not convincingly so, and each time he presented the figures to the doga, Destran asked for a second opinion from the Scriptorium, which either failed to arrive or spoke in very vague terms, and offered Destran an excuse for not spending money or resources on the problem.

The more time passed, the clearer it became to Sady that he couldn't afford to be caught in whatever political reason Destran and Alius had for not acting. Something needed to be done, and needed to be done urgently, while Chevakia still had the opportunity to act.

So one morning, he sent out Orsan, the faithful leader of his personal guard, with a message to a lady he hadn't seen for many years.

When Orsan returned, he was informed that the Lady Armaine wasn't interested in seeing anyone. The note she sent him was quite rude, but it made him smile. Lady Armaine might be old, but she certainly hadn't lost any of her bite. There was a fair chance that the old hag secretly relished the attention.

Everyone in Tiverius, or at least everyone in the inner city, knew the house of the merchant family whose oldest son had married the haughty southern beauty. Her dark-haired children, now well into middle age, were features of the district. Girls both, they had inherited every bit of their mother's pride, and married into well-off merchant families themselves.

Sady had been only a small toddler at the time the woman had arrived in Tiverius, but he remembered the gossip, especially since she had come into the city alone and pregnant, had given birth while staying in the merchant's house, and had subsequently married her host, a man more than twenty years her senior.

Sady remembered her son, an arrogant, sleek, black-haired youth with the bluest eyes he had ever seen. He came to Sady's school when Sady was in the highest grade, and caused a lot of fights by being an incredibly rude and outspoken little creep of a kid. Sady was never quite clear what became of the boy after he left school, save that his mother had taken him on an extended trip to the south when he was about sixteen or seventeen. By that time, Tiverius was in a full-scale diplomatic conflict with the City of Glass over the Knights' kidnapping of women from the towns on the border. The surly teenager had taken over some unidentified part of his stepfather's business and had been one of the few people who regularly travelled between Tiverius and the City of Glass. Not needing protective suits was no doubt a great advantage for him. He would be able to blend in perfectly in the City of Glass.

He used to be on the doga's books as a spy, but as far as Sady had been able to trace, hadn't delivered reports for many years. How the family lived was anyone's guess, because their merchanting business didn't appear to be bringing in a lot of money. They had no physical office, no shops, no warehouses, and yet they were still considered one of the wealthiest families in Chevakia.

The merchant had long since died of old age. Sady hardly ever saw the son anymore, but the woman's two daughters, the ones resulting from the marriage to the merchant, and their mother, still lived in the family house and Sady decided to pay them a visit in person.

Like most merchant houses, the residence was a huge sprawling affair, comprising several buildings, courtyards, pools and other such extravagances in Tiverius' dry climate.

The merchant had built it back from the street on a hill. A solid wall surrounded the land, with a forbidding fence attended by a doorman in family colours.

Sady introduced himself. "Senator Sadorius han Chevonian from the doga. I'd like to see the lady of house."

The guard's eyebrows rose. "The Lady Rosane?"

"Armaine." Such southern names, too. For the life of him, he couldn't remember the son's name, the arrogant little creep.

The guard's eyebrows rose further. "You're sure you mean to see the mistress' mother? She is very old and hasn't left the house for months."

"Yes, it is her I wish to see."

The man gave him a weird glance. "We have a standing instruction not to let anyone talk to her."

"I wrote to her and she should be expecting me." He held out the letter.

The man raised his eyebrows. "Doesn't it say here that she doesn't want to be disturbed?"

"Has the lady ever welcomed anyone? Yet doesn't she complain when people don't consult her? I'm about twice your age; I am familiar with her tricks."

"Fair enough. Come along, then. But don't blame me if she starts swearing at you. She's got a temper and is not exactly accommodating these days."

"I'm willing to give it a try."

The man led Sady through a magnificent garden where water burbled in ponds with fat yellow fish, and shrubs were neatly clipped into miniature shapes depicting birds and bears, similar to the plants he had seen in the houses of the rich in the City of Glass. The garden beds in between the bushes were paved with pure white stones, so it looked like snow on the ground.

He became overwhelmed with memories of his two trips to the City of Glass, the pristine whiteness and the scents of cooking meat —almost the only thing southerners ate. The absolute bitter cold that no one in Chevakia would have experienced before. The claustrophobia of being stuck inside a suit for days on end. The smell of the inside of the suit. The feeling that everyone in the City of Glass was on edge and you could get arrested for the simplest transgression.

They went up the stone steps into a wide and airy hall with mosaic floors, large double doors and stained glass windows.

The guard knocked at one such door and stuck his head in. "A senator from the doga is here to speak to you, mistress."

Sady couldn't hear the reply, but it sounded sharp. He was

expecting to be refused, but the man stepped back and opened the door fully. "You're in luck. She's in a good mood today."

Sady entered a magnificent high-ceilinged drawing room with a mosaic floor and plaster friezes on the walls. An elegant row of pillars supported the roof. The doors into another garden were open and let in the breeze, which billowed up the curtains. The cold edge to the breeze didn't seem to bother the woman who sat at a solid wooden desk in the middle of the room.

Sady hadn't seen her for years, and she looked much older, her face lined with deep wrinkles. Her hair was now snowy white, and tied in a loose bun at the top of her head. Over her thin shoulders she wore a heavy embroidered robe, too hot for Tiverius, but something that would not have looked out-of-place indoors in the City of Glass.

She was writing something in a thick book, her hand gnarled with age and corded with veins. Sady glanced at the curly script, wondering how many people in the south could read and write. Not many, he thought. During his visits, he had never spotted any scripts.

She looked up from her work. The eyes that met his over the rim of her glasses were cloudy with age, but still dark blue.

"Forgive me, lady, for interrupting you," Sady said. "The matter at hand is quite urgent."

"You have already interrupted me. We might as well get it over with." Her voice was educated, with the slightest of accents. Sady had almost forgotten what a southern accent sounded like.

"I'm here as a representative of the Chevakian doga," Sady began. "My name is Sadorius han Chevonian."

"Oh yes, I remember you." She cocked her head. "Weren't you one of those pesky kids who used to tease my son? What was it you used to call him? Mudhead?"

Mercy, did she really have to dig that up? To be honest, the kid's behaviour was asking for it; even the teachers said so. At some stage, Sady must have participated. Not something he was proud of.

"So, you've become a politician, like your useless brother." She chuckled. "Yes, yes, I think this talk will be interesting. Sit down there, young man. I cannot stand having to look up at people."

Sady sat, meeting her blue eyes. "Just to clear up any misconceptions, I'm not here for any political purpose."

She laughed. "That's what they all say. I am sure, senator, that once we get to the real reason you've come here, we can get the discussion to political subjects in no time. But do tell me, because I'm interested now, what makes you so insistent on seeing me?"

Sady bit his tongue. He had secretly hoped she might have mellowed with age. "My question is simple, Lady. Are you aware of anything that is happening in the City of Glass?"

Another cock of her head. "Why do you ask me? You know I am not in contact with the City of Glass on a daily basis. I was a refugee, as you are certainly old enough to remember. They killed my family."

No, she certainly had lost none of her bite. "I understand, but at the moment, we have no one else to turn to. I am the doga's chief meteorologist. We have recently measured a recent sharp rise in the level of sonorics. Under the influence of the cold air streams, there is a huge supercell developing over the southern continent, a storm the likes of which we haven't seen for many years. You see, low pressure systems can be induced by a rise in sonorics and we are afraid that—"

"Yes, yes, you don't need to spell out all the details for me. I know. I wasn't born yesterday, you know?" She laughed at her own joke.

Sady met her eyes, wondering how much she knew about this subject. There were rumours that some people in the south had formulae to calculate the energy carried by sonorics motes, and that they did so in order to predict how many people they could kill and how many buildings they could destroy with it. And that brought his thoughts back to that uncomfortable piece of research circulated by unknown sources in the doga. *Subject died after three months.* Imagine the pain and suffering encapsulated in that simple line.

He asked, "Do you know then why this is happening?"

She laughed. "Don't your machines give you the answers you need?"

"Our sonorics metres and barygraphs tell us the patterns, but we need to understand what causes them, and what we can do about it."

"What you can do?" She laughed. "Once the Heart roars, watch and see glory return to our land. The process has been set in motion; there is nothing you can do, except buy our marvels, when they become available."

"Wait—this increase is the result of something people have done?"

"What do you think? That we are as helpless as you?"

"But the power cannot be controlled. When I visited the City of Glass, the Eagle Knights told me—"

"Knights!" She laughed. "They wouldn't know anything. They pretend the whole thing doesn't exist. It is they who spread these rumours—rumours which you Chevakians have been oh so quick to believe—that this power is magic and uncontrollable. Did you think anyone could derive real power out of a myth? That you could run heating and trains from something that's magic? The Knights have been trying to stifle it, for the only reason that *they* cannot see it, or do anything with it. Out of sheer jealousy, they condemned our land to poverty. But when the Knights couldn't stop the Heart working, they dragged it down under the ground as far as they could. You thought your barriers worked so well? Ha, no, that's because the Heart has been sheltered by layers and layers of stone for many years."

Sady knew that to be a lie. The Most Learned Alius had done a lot of work on the barriers, and they were effective; measurements proved that. But the suggestion that this machine could be made to emit more of the deadly rays worried him deeply. If it was true, it would be a disaster.

"Then what has changed now? Did they uncover the machine?" He didn't believe any of this, but it was always easier to get what you wanted out of people if you agreed with them. One of the despicable sides of diplomacy.

"No, not them. The Knights thought that only when they eliminated all the elements that supported the royal family could they seize complete control over the south, but they forgot that people have memories, people have books, even in the City of Glass. Some people travel to all the corners of Chevakia and Arania to find these illegal books that were smuggled from the City of Glass at the fall of the king."

Sady glanced at the book on her desk, and remembered stalls of dusty old books in the marketplace, and the great libraries: the multi-storey treasure of the Scriptorium, and his brother's extensive library. And some dark place that housed the book with the horrible experiments. He regretted that he'd never had much patience for study out of dusty books.

She continued, "Books have become quite valuable in certain southern circles recently, initially as curiosity. Those old, forbidden books show a City of Glass none of the current population recognises. In those books, they will see the trains. They will see the comfortable houses, heated glasshouses with lush plants, and they will ask: why can't we live like that anymore, if it means no more hunger and cold? And then they find out that some people have been using the remaining power of the Heart, and have been practicing the knowledge of the old royal family and want to rid the land of the ignorance perpetrated by the Knights—see we're already into politics." Her eyes twinkled.

"I didn't ask about politics. I want to know about what is causing this rise in sonorics."

"I told you: the touch of the royal heir has woken the Heart of the City again. A time of justice and glory is coming."

"You call that glory? My whole country is under threat of this thing!" He spread his hands in a gesture of frustration.

"Tut, tut, tut." She gave him a sharp look. "Do you think we would not consider you, our valued neighbours?"

Sady hadn't meant to shout in an esteemed lady's presence. This was not a doga session. He let his hands fall back to his sides. "Sorry." Then he sighed. "I care a lot about Chevakia. I'm sure you understand why this doesn't make me happy."

"I see no reason for you to be unhappy. Once the Eagle Knights are gone from the City of Glass, Chevakia will gain a very wealthy trading partner. Relationships between the City of Glass and Chevakia are already much better than those we have with Arania. It would be wise to capitalise on that, once the City of Glass starts exporting—"

"But sonorics are dangerous to us!" How many times did he have to say this?

She cocked her head. "At high levels, yes, but no one is suggesting that any Chevakians move to the City of Glass, although, with medication being developed now, I would not rule that out in the future."

"Medication?" There was nothing other than salt pills, and they were not particularly effective; they merely helped restore any damage from low-level exposure. They did nothing about long-term effects.

"Yes, you should ask your academics about it."

Alius. A piece of the puzzle fell into place. That was why the Most

Learned cared so little about sonorics. But why keep such an important discovery secret?

He started to wish he'd come here much earlier.

Also, how long had these revolution plans in the City of Glass been going on? Who was involved? Obviously the old royal family and the Eagle Knights, but what side did the citizens support?

"Who is currently the ruler of the City of Glass?"

"The Queen, as normal."

"This is not Maraithe, but her daughter?" He remembered being made to kneel for the fragile wisp of a woman, wearing gauze-thin garments and seated on a throne made of carved glass. He remembered how hot it was in the room—and inside his suit. He remembered that she barely spoke a word, but that a Knight did all the talking.

"Mar-ay-the," she corrected him. "The daughter's name is Jevaithi."

It was the first time that Sady had heard the name. "She is—how old?" He remembered a toddler girl with golden hair being snatched away from him by her minders. He had only been told that she was the crown princess much later.

"Sixteen."

"You cannot be serious about a girl that age having any influence."

"No, she doesn't have any influence at all. The regent is an Eagle Knight by the name of Rider Cornatan. Jevaithi is a puppet queen, a prisoner of the Knights. Her birthday has passed, and she should by rights have ascended the throne, but the Knights are holding on to power. To the people of the City of Glass, the royal family is sacred, even the old king, twisted a man as he was. They will not be happy to see the Knights continue to rule the country. And now, thanks to the books, they understand how the Knights are denying them prosperity. The citizens are angrier and angrier. They are getting ready to fight and take back what is theirs."

The last southern king was said to have been a figure of unspeakable evil, and the Chevakian government at the time had been glad to see him gone. Sady remembered his parents talking about it at dinner. They saw the royal family of the City of Glass as a *threat*.

"This development worries me." He could already see the reaction of panic in the doga. "If the doga hears about this, the senators will ask for all army units to be mobilised, in case the conflict spills over into Chevakia. If history is anything to go by, that is highly likely."

"It won't happen this time. Unlike the old kings or the Aranians, we're not interested in war, or expansion of territory."

"And when . . . do we get to know about this change in regime?"

"The revolution is being taken care of as we speak. With as little violence as possible. My son will have more information once he returns."

"All right. I'll speak to your son." Mercy, that would be an exercise in cringing. "Meanwhile, and until we have this medicine, do you have anything I could tell the Chevakians about the situation? 'The south has increased sonorics so they can have a civil war' doesn't quite do it."

She gave him a sharp glance. "You don't believe a word I say, and are making fun out of me."

"I reserve the right not to believe anything until I can verify it."

Another hard stare. "All right." She pulled a little book across the desk and picked up a pen.

Sady watched her veined, paper-skinned hands as she scribbled something on a page that looked like . . .

She ripped the page out of the book and handed it to him. "Here, maybe that will convince you of my sincerity."

Yes, a bank draft indeed.

Sady put it back on the desk. "I couldn't possibly accept this."

"So, you don't want to visit the southern regions to measure sonorics and map weather systems and to reassure the people?"

How did she know about his request? "It would be seen as a political bribe."

"From whom to whom? I'm an old woman, and I can spend my inheritance any way I like. See it as a gift to those who worry about the effects of struggles in my country."

"But . . ." She was right; senators often received donations from rich patrons for projects that the doga wouldn't fund.

"I know the rules. We will ask nothing in return. There are no secret deals. It's simply a sign of goodwill."

Sady opened his mouth to protest, but she continued. "While you're there, in the south, of course . . . I agree that this current Proctor is an indecisive incompetent ignoramus. So, with our blessing, visit whom you intended to visit and if you find him amenable, return to Tiverius with someone who is not too scared to make the hard decisions. It is my guess that it was already your plan to visit such a person."

She gave him a long stare over the rim of her glasses. Those blue eyes penetrated into the depth of his soul. Mercy, how could she guess that he had been thinking about asking Milleus to come back?

"One other thing, senator. Let's do away with this nameless southern land thing. The Knights banned the land's true name, and no one could ever think of a suitable alternative. My country will no longer be The Country That Shall Not Be Named. Its true name is Peria."

Seated behind his desk opposite Sady, the most Learned Alius raised his bristly grey eyebrows and folded his hands while regarding Sady with a calculated expression. "She told you that?"

"Yes. Is it true? Are you working on such a medicine?"

He sighed. "I would really have preferred her to have kept quiet about this."

"But such a medicine would be a great breakthrough." Sady recalled Alius saying, many years ago when he had been a student himself, that such a medicine would be impossible.

"Yes," Alius said, and he folded his hands on the table.

Sady glanced at the table against the far wall, filled with equipment and trays of glass cylinders each exactly one cube in volume, that would be sealed with a glass lid on one side and a gel-covered paper on the other. When placed in a heat chamber, the gel absorbed any sonorics-charged motes, which showed up as brightly lit spots in a strong beam of light. "Then why not tell the doga about this medicine? Why involve southerners, and no Chevakians?"

"There are Chevakians involved, from a range of backgrounds. Also southerners, for obvious reasons. Every participant was asked to keep it quiet."

"But why?" Sady was almost screaming with frustration.

"Academics do not work well in the public eye. The ideas behind the project are . . . pretty controversial. The financial backers of the project didn't want to cause a storm unless we were certain that it would work."

"And does it? Work, I mean?" He had an uncomfortable thought about that report on sonorics studies on people.

"Yes."

"Then why not make it public?"

"We're not ready yet. There are tests still to be done."

"How long? We could really use this medicine right now."

"I understand completely. We will do our best to get it ready as soon as possible."

Sady rose to leave. He had not specifically asked Alius about the Lady Armaine's implication that he had received southern money, but it seemed that it had been used to fund good work, and Alius obviously had no problems accepting it.

Still, the bank draft burned in Sady's pocket.

On the way out, he wandered through the Scriptorium library, but the books about the south were in a special section which he could easily access as senator, save that his visit would be recorded and he wasn't sure what signal that would send. Foreign relations were not his responsibility; the senator who was responsible for them might object to his invasion of his turf and Sady already felt the pressure of general opinion on him.

"What do you mean, 'What's wrong?' " Sady asked.

"You've been really grumpy the last few days," Lana said.

Sady faced the other across the wooden table in the kitchen, in the manner they ate their meals every night—Sady in his work shirt and Lana still wearing her apron.

"Have I?" Sady asked, rubbing his hand over his face.

"Yes. It wasn't Serran's fault that the neighbour's ducks got into the garden."

"He is the *guard*." Mercy, he hated to see the mess the birds had made in his pretty private space where he often sat to read and enjoy the sunshine. And he was more annoyed that no one had noticed the birds before the kitchen staff.

"Guarding the gate. For *people*. The ducks flew over the wall."

"He's the guard and should have noticed. And if he's too busy at the gate, he should have organised someone else to do it."

"Still, he's upset that you got angry at him." Lana got up from the table carrying both their empty plates. "You want more soup?"

"No, thank you."

"See, there you go. You're grumpy. You never refuse my soup, and I've made soup for you since your father gave me this job."

"Oh, don't you go like that on me. You're starting to sound like my mother." But she was right. Lana was always right when it came to judging people.

Sady sighed and let a silence lapse. "Suppose I *am* grumpy. I just don't know what to do about this sonorics situation. It isn't bad enough for an emergency, but I want the doga to prepare. Instead, it's like no one wants to make any decisions. I don't have anything to back up decisions I'd *want* them to make."

"No additional data?"

"No. Sonorics have been stable."

"But that is a good thing."

"It would be, if I didn't suspect it's only temporary, and if the level weren't so high. After I spoke to Lady Armaine, I don't think anything about the south is random anymore. We're getting a reprieve, but no one can take advantage of it. And I can't tell anyone that I got my information from her." They'd laugh in his face. "Seriously, Lana, there is only so much I can make of this low depression and building storm. I can make it sound as bad as I can, but in the end, it's only weather, never mind that it usually goes hand in hand with high sonorics."

He sighed again and stared at the table. "No one takes meteorologists seriously. They'll only hear the predictions they like to hear. I can predict disasters, but all they want to know about is their crops and whether the neighbouring district gets a higher cropping allocation."

"Poor, poor Sady." She ruffled his hair.

He smiled at her. She'd been his housekeeper for as long as he could remember, but she was more like his friend. She knew everything about him.

Destran pushed approval for another road-building scheme through.

Viki fumbled through another presentation which showed no significant increase or decrease in sonorics levels. People started to get angry with Sady for ordering resources be put into distributing the tablets and suits. If stored in suboptimal conditions, the tablets had to be replaced yearly at great cost to the doga.

No one made any moves towards appointing southern informants. Lady Armaine's son did not return.

A strange kind of tension built in the doga. Sady wasn't sure what caused it. Maybe Viki's rather emotionless reports of relentless higher-than-usual sonorics started to grate on people, the levels just short of twenty motes per cube. Whenever any issue remotely related to the border regions or the south or cropping was raised, senators expected Sady to speak up, but when he didn't and said that he couldn't, because he had no reliable data or the particular subject wasn't his field of expertise, one or two suggested he go on a trip to the border regions. Most notable was that one of those was a northern senator, who was also the first to mention the big V-word: vote of confidence. In Destran, that was. Destran, who kept sidestepping the issue of sonorics by saying there was no problem, which there wasn't—yet. Destran, who continued to claim lack of money.

By the end of the fifth day of these antics, with no sign of the low pressure cell evaporating or sonorics going down, Sady went to see the northern faction leaders. He really wanted that southern trip, so that he could assess how feasible it would be to strengthen the barriers and, failing that—because there was no way such a major undertaking could be done quickly—how quickly they could evacuate the region in the case that might prove necessary. And he was determined not to use the Lady Armaine's money to fund the trip. That meant he needed northern money.

He disliked doing regional deals for favours, and knew this had the potential to blow up in his face, but without their support, the doga would kill itself debating roads and train lines and the fairness of allocations for education, and whether northern children should get special allowance when coming to Tiverius to study. . . . Vote of no confidence indeed.

❄

"We are sick of Destran's paralysis," the northern senator Shara said in the comfort of her top floor office. Firelight played tricks with the folds of her northern region dress and on the gloss of her skin, black as obsidian. She fiddled with her glass, not meeting Sady's eyes while she went on a rant about all that was ill in politics, which included things Sady agreed with, and things he did not.

Here, under the roof of the building, they should feel the heat radiated through the roof, a sign of the fury of summer to come, but the weather had turned unseasonably cold.

"If we are to challenge Destran, now seems a good time to do it."

"Who is we? Who do you propose in his place?" Sady asked, feeling slightly uncomfortable. He didn't like using this regional voting to his advantage. It was exactly what he had always agitated against. That way, the meteorologist position was not bound to any region, and the positions of power were usually held by central region delegates. Like himself, like— "Milleus?"

She shook her head. "We want you to stand."

"Me?" They had to be kidding. "I don't have any support. I don't want the job."

"I don't think anyone ever wanted that job, Sady. It's not much of a job, but someone has to do it."

What she said was certainly true. Most Proctors had the job thrust upon them through circumstances. But most of them had been flamboyant, outspoken, strong characters. Everything he was not. He shook his head. "I wouldn't be any good at it."

"I think you will be."

Mercy, no. "I'm not standing and that is definite. It will be Milleus or no one."

Shara met Sady's eyes, intense. The northern senators knew they didn't have the numbers to field a candidate of their own. They were too divided for that.

"I don't know, Sady," she said.

Sady said, "We both know the doga can't go on like this. We're paralysed with indecision. Not just about this issue, but every time someone has a good plan, the group of doubters scuttle it with committees and requirements to draw up plans and have them approved. The only thing that happens is that the stacks of paper grow ever higher, but nothing is ever decided. And if something by chance does make it through, there is never any money to implement it."

"But by asking Milleus to return, you are also asking the senators to vote against every step forward the doga has made in the last ten years."

"Like what? All the doga has achieved in the last ten years is a division between the northern and southern provinces. So the provinces have more autonomy. What has that achieved except more political bickering over roads and trains? More indecision and building projects caught up in endless streams of bureaucracy. We need the unity more than ever." That was not quite true. Destran had put Milleus' rampantly negative budgets back into line, but he seemed to have taken that a bit too seriously recently.

"But . . . bring back Milleus? Are you serious? He's an old man."

"He is decisive. He steered us through the Aranian war." *And he will steer us through a southern war, if one happens.*

Sady saw his brother at the head of the victory procession through the streets of Tiverius. How had the people cheered him. Arania had attacked, but they had been well and truly defeated.

"Times are different now," Shara said.

"Not as different as you'd think."

"Have you asked Milleus if he even wants to come back?"

"I know my brother. He'll say no, but if we present him with a majority vote in the doga, he will." *Or at least he had better*. Sady set his glass down and leaned back in his chair. "Chevakia will need his experience. Whatever happens with the weather, we're facing a crisis, because we've already delayed putting in some crops too long. There will be shortages. The current senators know nothing about how to run the country in a crisis, especially one generated by a country we know so little about. Remember the fear the Eagle Knights struck into the hearts of the border regions? Remember all the young girls who were lost? Milleus was a senator then."

Shara sipped, and gave a little shudder. Most of the girls would have died from sonorics sickness soon after arriving in the City of Glass if they hadn't died at the hands of raping barbarians before that. And then some sick mind had gone to write a report about it, as if taking the girls to the City of Glass was an experiment.

"That was all before my time," Shara said.

"It's before almost everybody's time, including mine." Milleus was fifteen years his senior. "We need the experience."

For a while, he stared into the leaping flames.

Shara continued, "Sure, not everybody is happy with Destran's achievements. With the right campaign, I think someone else could have the numbers to topple him."

Sady nodded. "Destran's support is not as strong as it was when . . ."

Another uncomfortable memory. Shouting in the benches of the amphitheatre in the doga assembly hall. Senators fighting like street urchins. And his brother standing silent and defeated at the dais. Moments later, he had thrown off his cloak, and walked out, never to return. When Sady came to the Proctor's house later that day, his brother had already been packing.

"I know when I'm not wanted and this is it, Sady. A man can only take so much. I've worked my entire damn life for this. I've. . . ."

The slam of a lid on a box had been accompanied by the shattering of porcelain.

Milleus stared at shards of pottery on the floor. "Suri loved that vase."

Suri. Ever since her death, Milleus had not been the same. Yet, he had never noticed how lonely she was. Poor Suri. For years, Sady had watched her become unhappy, knowing that she might have been better off with him than with his brother.

He should have done something. He should have told her how much he loved her.

Tears stung in his eyes.

"So what do you suggest?" Shara's voice shattered the painful memories.

Sady made a decision. "I'm travelling to Ensar in the morning."

"What? I thought you were still trying to get funding for that approved?"

"I've found some alternative money." He thought of Lady Armaine's bank draft on the corner of his desk. "I'll travel through some towns on the way. I think I can garner support for Milleus in the south of the country."

She nodded. "That is reasonable. Dangerous, though. Destran will know you're doing it. It'll only take him a short time to find out where you've gone."

"It's the only thing I can do. He's going in for the battle. He knows he's flailing and that something is up. Right now, he's probably at a meeting of his supporters."

"Probably," she agreed.

"So, let's get to business. What are the feelings amongst your northern colleagues?"

"Without calling a meeting, I would guess that Destran probably still has the numbers amongst them, but people are smarting because the northern irrigation project has been delayed for so long. If . . . someone came in and promised some set dates on it . . ."

Typical regional politicking. There wasn't enough water for all districts to get as much as they thought they needed. Yet, he couldn't say the obvious truth; he needed the North's support. Never mind that it would come to haunt him, because this was going to be a bad year for the north.

"I'm sure Milleus would hear your concerns." *Or he had better*.

"We don't want an audience; we want a decision about projects we've applied for. My constituents are sick of coming off second best."

"There is a more immediate threat to Chevakia."

"Only to the south, don't forget that. The northern regions are sick of propping up the south. The people haven't forgotten that when we had the great sand storms, which were a threat to the north, we had to beg for assistance and even then it was slow in coming."

"That was Destran's doing. You might point that out to your faction."

She nodded, slowly, but still didn't look entirely convinced.

"Sady, I still wish you would put forward a different candidate. You might as well know. Milleus was not well loved amongst my regional colleagues. He was a selfish, discriminatory pig, and what happened in his personal life was plain unacceptable to many of us."

"What happened in his personal life is none of the doga's business."

Shara fixed his gaze, her mouth twitching. "It was unacceptable nevertheless."

"So you would vote against?"

She shook her head, slowly. "I don't think we have an option. Our faction doesn't have a candidate with enough support across all regions. No faction does. If you would only stand—"

"No."

"But we would demand some sort of apology from him—at least the female delegates."

Sady nodded. Suri. He'd hate to broach that painful subject with Milleus, but it had to be done. There were just too many rumours about what had happened. Not even he knew the full extent of the story except that Suri had killed herself—there was no doubt about that—but no one knew why.

She went on, "Out of the two—Destran or Milleus—Milleus would have more clout. Yes, he has the experience, and I'm sure you'd get a much higher support for him if he has clear plans. If you're asking for Intention to Vote, then I would give it, providing he clears up the air on his personal business."

"I am asking." And there was no time for committees to be looking into Milleus' private life. It still would have to be addressed after the crisis.

She went to the desk in the corner, pulled out paper and a pen. For a while, the only sound in the room was the popping of the fire and the scratching of the pen on the paper. Then she passed him the note. *Intention to Vote.*

"Thank you. I appreciate it." He folded it in his pocket.

Not much later, he was on his way home, but having visited the leaders of all regional factions. In his pocket, he held the Intentions of five of the factions, about fifty votes in all.

The house was dark when he came home, and he spent some time rustling about with pots until Lana stuck her head around the door.

"Sady, what in the heavens' name are you doing?"

"Cooking. I'm hungry."

She sighed. "Sady, Sady, didn't I ever tell you that you can always wake me up? That's what I'm here for."

"But . . ." he started to protest, and then she smiled at him, and the tension faded.

"Sit down." She went into the cold cellar and retrieved some soup, which she heated up with a fat slice of bread. "Now tell me, how come your work is more important than having a proper dinner?"

"I'm travelling to Ensar in the morning."

She sucked in a breath of air. "I thought there was no money."

"I . . . found some."

He wished she wouldn't look at him like that. Questioning, one eyebrow raised. "It's all right. It's political money. I'm going to see Milleus." Mercy, Milleus had better be worth the trouble. He did *not* like lying to Lana.

"You're not going to ask him to return?" Her eyes were wide.

"Well, actually . . . I am."

"I never thought I'd see the day. That is good news." Her eyes twinkled. She had never made a secret of her fondness for Milleus.

The vote would be tight, and he hadn't been able to sway everyone he'd hoped to convince, but Sady was sure that if he could get Milleus to come out of retirement and back to the capital, more people would follow. People had not forgotten how his quick decisions had won the war against Arania, and how well he had taken up the command of the Chevakian army, how he had used Chevakia's balloons not just to repel the Aranian invasion, but to follow the fleeing army home and take their capital. In the doga building hung a banner with the crest of the Aranian king, taken from the palace by the victorious soldiers. Tables had turned. The attacker had become the attacked. Thanks to Milleus, the people of Chevakia slept well at night.

They would not have forgotten.

Thanks to Milleus, they would again sleep well. As for Sady, he never slept too well, and the next day, he was up annoying the household staff before dawn, packing his travel bags and his instruments, leaving Viki to mind his office in Tiverius, all fingers and toes crossed that the next few days would be boring and routine on the meteorology front and that whatever bugged Viki about Alius wouldn't come to a head.

CHAPTER 7

THE ENGINE PUFFED and chugged and thumped. Goats bleated, jostled each other and nosed around in the feed trough.

Hoses vibrated. The pipe spewed sloshes of milk into the vat; first a gush, and then a steady stream, which slowed to a mere trickle.

There. The next lot done.

Milleus pulled the release. A hiss of steam escaped the vent on top of the compressor. Suction pads disengaged from udders and flung back to their positions under the arm of the milking machine. As one, the goats lifted their heads from the feeding trough and bolted for the gate of the milking pen.

"Mercy! Be calm, the lot of you. Just *what* is wrong?" Milleus straightened, squinting against the glare of sunlight and the shimmering air. He scanned the edge of the wood up the hill, across the golden field of grain.

Only a few days ago one of his prize kids had disappeared, a female, too, born from one of his best milkers, which would have fetched a nice price at market. Milleus had taken his carbine, and scoured the woods, but had found no trace of it, not even a half-eaten carcass. The goats had been nervous ever since.

A *shadow* fell over him. Huge, dark, blotting out the sunlight. Just a heartbeat, and then it moved uphill, over the golden grain field.

Mercy!

A bird, no, a *bird* circled above him, a stark silhouette against the blue sky, with powerful wings of such size as Milleus had never seen. As fast as his old bones allowed, Milleus scrambled to the gate, pushing through the mass of jostling goats.

Over the gate, into the hot darkness of the shed, past the flickering lights of the milking machine. Up there, on the shelf. His hand closed on metal.

Thank goodness for the gun.

Hands trembling, he found the magazine of bullets and clipped it into the holder. Outside the shed, a mass of goats assailed him, having somehow found their way over, or through, the gate.

The bird soared over the forest, wings perfectly still.

The shadow passed over once more, way out of range of the gun. Milleus tracked the dark shape with the barrel, his heart thudding. The eagle wheeled, gaining height. A few lazy wingbeats and then it was gone over the crest of the hill. Milleus stood there, watching. The eagle didn't return. The sky was deep blue, without a single cloud.

Well, that was one explanation for the disappearance of the goat. Fancy that, a southern eagle. They were native to the mountain range between Arania and the south, but the largest ones, the really large ones, big enough to carry a man, lived only in the Eagle Knights' eyrie in the City of Glass. Such beasts were said not to be natural, and this was a beast like that. Riderless.

Someone lifted the latch on the gate.

Milleus whirled, aiming his gun, cursing himself.

At the gate stood an olive-skinned man with salt-and-pepper hair, in a long red robe dusty from travel.

Milleus lowered the gun. "Sady?"

"It's me all right. Milleus, you old billygoat." Sady let the gate fall shut and rushed across the milking pen, his arms spread.

Milleus set the gun next to the milking machine.

They met each other amongst the goats. Milleus revelled in his brother's hug and returned pats on the shoulder. It was so long since he had seen Sady, all the way in Tiverius where he'd sworn never to return.

"What's with the gun?" Sady asked.

"Tell you the truth, brother, I just got the biggest fright. There was a southern eagle scaring the goats. Did you see it?"

Sady shook his head. "I just came from the station. An old guy gave me a lift to the gate."

That would have been Andreus, the old nosey always ready for a chat. "Look at you, Sady. Not a day older. What in all the heavens are you doing here? The meteorology stations playing up?"

The laughing crinkles faded from around Sady's eyes. Grey-flecked brows lowered. "Don't tell me you haven't heard."

Haven't heard what?

"Sonorics levels have risen all along the border stations."

"How much?" By rights, Milleus *should* have heard, but he hadn't, because he hadn't been into town, because he'd been avoiding talk, and finger-pointing, and gibbering women.

"Much more than usual for this time of the year. We're sitting at an average of seventeen to eighteen motes per cube."

"Hang on, Sady. This time of the year sonorics levels usually go *down*."

Sady nodded and stared over the field in a moment of reflection. There was more to the story, much more. Something serious was happening.

"Come to the house," Milleus said.

Not much later when they sat over tea and biscuits in the kitchen, Sady told his story, about sharply rising sonorics, about the rising measurements from all border stations, about the increased sonorics levels Sady had measured in this region.

"And also, there are rumours of an uprising against the Eagle Knights in the City of Glass."

"Really? Who told you that? Didn't think Destran kept any of our southern spies on the doga's books."

"No, but that doesn't mean there are none to be found."

Milleus eyed him and Sady met his gaze squarely.

"Don't tell me you've asked *her*."

Sady expression closed.

"All right, so you *have* asked her. You know who is she is, right?"

"The old king's daughter-in-law."

"Too right. Anything she says will be coloured through a thick layer of revenge."

"I'm not trusting her." Sady sounded defensive.

"No, and make sure that you do not *ever* trust her."

"It's just that we have no one else to give us information. At least she won't feed us southern propaganda. She hates the Eagle Knights' regime as much as we do."

"Yes, but that's propaganda, too. We hate the Knights for the border raids, which they may well have recognised as a grave mistake by now. From memory, no one was too friendly with the old royal family either. It's been a relief to most Chevakians that they haven't had to tell their children scary stories about *magic* since he was disposed."

He met Sady's eyes squarely. Sady wouldn't remember any of that fear, but Milleus did. The time of Chevakian ignorance about sonorics, the time before Alius and his barrier. "Do not trust her, Sady. Do not, under any circumstance, accept any of her favours. Do not believe what she says. Find another informant. It's not as if there are no southerners at all in Tiverius."

Sady folded his hands around his teacup and stared at the table. Milleus read the signs.

"You've already gone in too deep with her?"

"I needed the money for this trip. The doga wouldn't sign for permission."

"Pay her back immediately."

Sady gave him a *what with?* look.

"Mercy, Sady, Destran gets his taxes. The situation can't be as bad as all that?"

Sady spread his hands. "That's the way it seems to be."

"Who of us is going to say 'I told you so'? Destran is a dithering fool trying to please everyone and pleasing no one in the process."

Mercy, he was angry. Milleus did *not* want to hear about Destran. The doga had voted him in. He was *their* problem. He met Sady's eyes, more irritated than he should be. He was done with politics.

"Let's talk about something else, Sady. I'm sick of this subject. How are you?"

Sady shook his head. "I'm here to talk about this. It's serious." Sady's eyes were pleading. "Something needs to be done."

"Good. Tell Destran that. What would the doga propose to do? What is causing this rise? Hasn't anyone investigated that? What does the Scriptorium have to say about it?"

"Not much, and that's the odd thing. Alius is acting strangely—"

"He's always been strange—" Academics, Milleus had no patience for them.

"Not like this. He's evasive." He hesitated, as if he deliberated on saying something and decided against it. "And ever since I've raised the issue, Destran is stalling on giving me extra funds for sonorics testing and safety measures. I've sent out some scouts, and some balloons, but no one has yet come back with an answer. I need more funds for better equipment and more people."

"My guess is Destran probably doesn't have any funds. All spent on his roads projects and other things to appease the districts. Doesn't keep a free reserve for emergencies. He can't withdraw any of his money streams for the fear of losing votes. Districts have been voting through their wallets the last few years. Sady, you don't have to tell me all this. Is there anything I don't already know that's not going to make me fume with anger?"

"Yes. This." Sady placed something on the red- and white-checkered tablecloth. A folded envelope. "Although I hope you deserve it."

Milleus took it, frowning. He knew what it was before he opened the envelope, but he opened it anyway, his hands trembling. It was indeed as he had feared: a petition from more than fifty members of the doga—for Milleus han Chevonian to come back to the capital and once more stand for the position of Proctor.

Oh mercy.

His life flashed before him: his quick ascendancy as popular senator. His appointment as senator responsible for the army. The Aranian invasion and the crushing defeat of the Chevakian troops which were but poorly organised, poorly equipped and poorly motivated. His lobbying with the Scriptorium and the young student who had developed an air ship. His speech in the doga. *We are going to build these things. We are going to win.* How had they all cheered. How had they lined up to volunteer for service. How had they hammered, sewn, trained. The magnificent sight of seeing the air ship fleet take off. And then the victory of that first battle. Milleus had gone on the airships to show his commitment.

Meanwhile, the south had assumed that since Chevakia was busy, they wouldn't miss a few girls from their border regions. The balloons had gone after the eagles, and young and brilliant Alius had designed the barrier, and no Eagle Knights had ever come back.

After the war, when concerns turned from freedom to taxes, that's when things started falling apart. When governing the country became a series of monotonous, mindless tasks to do with stupid trivialities. So the doga wanted a younger leader, someone who liked that sort of stuff.

"I can't." Milleus let the paper fall.

Sady watched him, his face unreadable.

Fifty signatures. Mercy.

"You have to, Milleus. Destran might be a good administrator, but he's hopeless in a crisis. If Destran carries on like this, it will be too late to do anything when we need to. You're the best hope we have. The south is up to something. Arania is nervous. There could be war. The *army* wants you."

"They don't vote in the doga."

"I know, but they want you anyway."

Milleus didn't know what to say. Couldn't say anything. Silence fell between them and stretched on for uncomfortable moments. Sady expected a "yes", that was clear. Milleus picked up a spoon and scraped the bottom of his empty cup to gain time for thinking. Found some strands of reason. There were many capable men in Tiverius both younger and more loved than he. He would be held to glorified incidents that hadn't been so glorious even at the time they happened. War was dirty business. Properly preparing a country for one meant discounting a lot of people's voices, running straight over their very valid objections like some sort of army general.

"I have the farm now. I'm happy here."

Sady spread his hands, and rolled his eyes at the kitchen. Pots and pans teetered on shelves. Most of Milleus' pantry was on the kitchen bench, as were the plates he used regularly. Dirty clothes spilled from a basket in the corner. "Happy? You call this dust bowl happy? This outpost? You, who always were in the thick of it all? I ache to see you so, brother. You have no one even to talk to. Ever since you've come back here to live, you've been alone. This place is run-down, a pale shade on what it used to be like as the Proctor's country estate. It needs painting, the garden needs weeding, the roof needs cleaning. This was once a lovely house, back then."

Milleus glared at his brother. One word about Suri's death, and about how he should visit his sons more, and he'd bash his brother's face in. His jaw moved stiffly when he spoke. "After a life in the doga, I happen to like being alone, so I don't have to listen to all these nattering voices around me."

Sady harrumphed. "Take a look at yourself, brother, covered in mud and shit. I'm used to seeing a proud man, not a lowly farmer. And when I look at you, brother, I still see a highborn man, not a farmer. I see a highborn man hiding from the world, just because once, and I mean *once*, forces conspired against you."

"What? Are you calling me a quitter? I have worked this land with my own hands and turned it from a dust bowl into a profitable farm."

He glared at Sady and his brother glared back.

Milleus blew out a sigh and leaned back in his chair. "Honestly, I've done my bit for the country. I'm too old."

"The doga needs you."

"Trust me, Sady, the doga does *not* need me. I'm nothing but an old man who's run out of ideas." He put a dirt-stained hand on his brother's shoulder. "Do me the favour and stay the night before you head back, but talk to me as my brother Sady, and not as Sadorius han Chevonian, politician and mouthpiece of the doga. You are welcome at my table, brother, but understand one thing: however much you talk, and whatever has happened, I will not come back to Tiverius with you. I'm done with politics, and that is my final word."

CHAPTER 8

LORIANE WOKE UP in a soft grey light.

Her first thought was that she was not in her own bed at home. The second realisation was that a warm body lay nestled against her, which a glance confirmed to be Tandor, still on his back. But his arm had shifted and now lay over his chest. His breathing was regular. He was definitely getting better.

The third realisation was that some ruckus seemed to be going on outside the window, with people shouting. The fourth realisation, as she heaved thick furs aside, was that she'd been asleep for a long time and that, despite the salve Myra had put on, her pains hadn't started. The bandage had shifted and the salve, slimy and warm, was leaking onto her left inner thigh.

By the skylights, was this child ever going to budge?

Loriane stumbled to the window and shifted the sides of the curtain apart.

By the feeble light from the not-quite dawn, she could make out people in the yard, outside the shed where Tandor's sled still stood. There were men and women, standing around a sled talking. The sled's bear lay in the snow, its head resting on its paws.

Loriane didn't understand who those people were and what they were doing here, so she dropped the curtain and turned back to the room. She was so weary.

The thought of another day of having to cope with Myra's bickering parents and being away from her comfortable home made her eyes prick.

Where was she going to live now that she couldn't return home? Not here, that was certain. What was she going to do with this child she didn't want?

Tandor gave a startled snore, as if he had heard her.

"Tandor?"

His lips moved, but no sound came out.

"Tandor, can you hear me?"

A bottle hovered through the air—Ruko was still in the room—and was pressed to Tandor's lips. He drank the water in big gulps, spilling some over his cheek.

"Tandor, I know you can hear me. Can you stop this nonsense and talk to me?" She wanted to shake his shoulders, but something grabbed hold of her hand, a hard, ice-cold grip that closed around her wrist like a vice. Ruko.

She tried to wrench herself loose. "Oh, by the skylights, let me go. I'm not going to harm him." Or at least not until he told her what he'd done and how to fix it.

The grip loosened.

She grabbed her clothes off the chair in front of the hearth, which had almost died and only gave off the merest glow of heat.

Harsh voices sounded outside, a group of men arguing. She went to the window again, but the group was behind the barn and she could only see their sleds and bears, steam rising from their backs by the light of the street lamps.

Loriane slipped on her clothes and winter cloak and left the room. Everything in the house was still dark. As quietly as she could, she crept down the stairs, through the quiet corridor, the dark kitchen, and out the back door. First, the outroom.

While she sat there on the cold slab of wood, the shouting between the houses intensified: men's voices, the words just out of hearing; the swish of sled runners in the snow; the growl of a bear.

She hoisted her clothes back up and went outside.

Fresh snow had fallen overnight, covering the yard with a pristine layer of white. The sky was never completely dark at this time of the year, but it was dark enough for a couple of stars. There was a single lantern in front of a house opposite the road, and by its light, she could see silhouettes of people walking past. People with sleds, people carrying packs. Many more people than lived in this small town. Bears snorted clouds of steam into the air.

There was a group of men camped in front of the shed doors. One was shouting at another group of people in the street. She feared going up to them—what would they do when they discovered that she had food and had slept in a warm bed?—but maybe she could hear what they were talking about from inside the shed. When would it be safe to go back to the City of Glass? How many people had died? Whatever news she could snatch.

The shed door was open. The air inside smelled of straw and animals. It was pitch dark and Loriane inched ahead foot by foot. On a bench she found a lamp and a lighter, and a bit of fumbling later, the tiny flickering flame lit the hay shed.

A sound such as Loriane had never heard before issued from somewhere in the dark corners. A growl—not quite aggressive. More like a call made by mating Legless Lions.

In the corner, in a box surrounded by wooden planks and filled with straw, stood a most unusual animal. Much, much taller than a bear, on knobbly, spindly legs, with a long neck curved upwards, a body strangely out of proportion, bearing a flabby hump on its back. The fur was shorter than the bear's, brown, shaggy and moulting in clumps. The animal had an elongate head, with large, mournful eyes and long eyelashes like a pleasure-house girl. Its nose was soft, with slits for nostrils. The animal lifted one side of its soft lips, showing huge yellow teeth, and stretched its neck up in a curious way.

She had often heard Tandor speak of a camel. Was this such a beast? She heard people rode on them. This one didn't look very friendly.

The straw behind her rustled.

Loriane whirled around, but could see nothing.

"Ruko?"

There was no reply; it must be him. By the skylights, he creeped her out. Myra had said he could walk through walls. He could just pick up a knife and kill her and no one would be any the wiser, and no one would ever catch him. The time of the old King must have been frightening for his enemies, and she was fortunate indeed that she didn't live in his time, never mind the trains and other marvels. Icefire was evil, and she wanted nothing to do with it.

A strip of flickering light came in between the shed doors. The shouting had stopped, but there were still a lot of voices.

Loriane pressed her face against a crack between the doors and peered outside onto an area where at least six sleds had stopped, sheltered from the wind by the shed walls. There were families with children, elderly people, a man with nobility tattoos on his face caring for someone injured, an elderly woman, she thought. They had made a fire in Ontane's yard, and built a rough igloo out of snow. Three bears were tied to the lamp post in front of the house, which was a laughable sight, because the animals could easily rip the post out of the ground if they wanted, but they were resting, shaggy heads on their paws. The poor things were probably exhausted.

Loriane listened, but whenever the people said something, they spoke of boring things, like, *Can you fill this with clean snow?* Or, *Has your brother come out of bed yet?* That sort of thing.

She was getting cold when over the general noise of the camp, someone shouted,

"This be my house. I want all of ye gone by morning. There be plenty of room at the inn and they cook for ye, too."

Loriane cringed. Ontane.

Some men laughed.

A woman closer to the shed said, ". . . annoying old bear. Easy to talk for him in his big house and nice fire." She spoke in a city accent. "Come, help me, it's getting light now. Let's see if we can open this door, so gramma and the little ones can be out of the wind."

Loriane just stepped back in time when someone pushed hard against the doors of the shed, but the bar that locked it was heavy and the wood new, so it didn't give. Until they came back with something heavier, or found an axe. Desperate people did desperate things.

Meanwhile, more sleds arrived, swishes in the snow. Shouts of women, crying children. Reunions of families with their loved ones. Loriane caught snatches of conversation.

". . . just a wall of steam. It came over the house and it exploded, just like that . . ."

". . . and when we left, there was this incredible, horrible sight. Do you know that the entire Outer City is on fire?"

"... No ... I haven't seen anyone who looks like that. A man and two little girls?"

"Twins. My husband."

"My husband says the icefire is coming this way."

"Yes, her husband is one of the Brothers of the Light." This voice was sneering.

"Well, say what you want, but I'd rather travel with her husband than with people who have no idea what they're fleeing. Tell me—what did your husband say?"

"He's a minion for the old royal family, that's what, and it's them that caused this trouble."

"Oh, do us a favour and shut up. Don't listen to her. Tell me what your husband knows."

Loraine stood there, staring into the darkness.

This was just too frightening. Tandor had sometimes spoken of the Brotherhood of the Light. He'd said they were poor, ignorant idiots with good intentions. All she knew was that they ran schools and orphanages. And did mysterious calculations. The orphans they raised often became successful merchants, because they were good with numbers. Some of them also disappeared. Malicious rumours said that the Brothers sacrificed these children, but a more likely rumour had it that they left the country.

She wanted to go out and ask why these people blamed the Brotherhood for whatever had happened, but she had no idea how many people were outside the shed and was too frightened to open the door, lest the shed be overrun by refugees.

And if the people found out Tandor was in the house, they would lynch the man who had caused their misery. Once she had asked Tandor about his relationship with the Brothers and he had said there was none, and she had asked him about rumours that some members of the old royal family were still alive and he said that if she meant Thillei, yes, they definitely were, else why would there still be Imperfects, and they'd gone into a long discussion about what to do about icefire: use it or ignore it, and it wasn't until later that she realised how deftly he had avoided answering her question. And she also realised how much she didn't care about a conflict that happened more than fifty years ago. And how much she should have.

There were heavy thunks outside, like an axe hitting wood, and then a shout, "Hey, ye city folk, keep yer hands off my fence." Ontane again.

A man replied; Loriane couldn't hear the words, because the thunking continued unabated.

Ontane swore, and there was a hard bang, and then the sound of footsteps coming into the back door of the shed.

Loriane stiffened, but it was Ontane, his face red from the cold, snowflakes in his hair and the fur collar of his cloak. He stopped a few paces inside the door, held his storm light up, and looked around. In his furs, he looked like a malformed bear waddling on its back legs.

"Mistress, what d'ye be doing here?"

"I heard the noise. I wanted to know what was happening."

"Ye tell me; they all come from the City of Glass. Ye know what be going on there better than I, why they all need to come out here like they own the place."

"I suspect they have nowhere else to go," she said, her voice soft. "There is nothing left of the City of Glass. They're tired, cold, hungry and scared."

She met his eyes and he looked away. He *had* taken her in, even though Myra had a lot to do with that, but she suspected that underneath that blusterous attitude, he did have a heart.

His shoulders slumped. "Let's go inside. It be warm there. Dara will have some breakfast. Ye look like ye could use some."

But when he pushed open the back door it was to find a big group of people at the door of the house and Dara, bewildered, in the doorway.

"Anything you have," a woman shouted. "We'll pay. I have two young children to feed."

"We need blankets!" another woman shouted.

"My father broke his leg. Do you have a medic in town?"

Dara just stood there, while people at the back of the crowd were jostling each other for space.

"Oh, the blighting freeloaders," Ontane muttered. He shut the shed's side door, produced a key from under his clothes and locked it. "Come, mistress." He ploughed through knee-deep snow towards the crowd. "Ye lot, stop harassing my wife!"

Everyone in that crowd turned to Ontane and started shouting at him.

Ontane yelled over their voices, "Dara, get inside and shut the door. Ye lot, it be the end of winter and we have no food to share. Go out there in the forest and hunt your own. There be rabbits and moose—"

There was a shout across the street, at a neighbour's house. A woman had come outside with a crate of bread.

As one, all the refugees ran across the street, pushing to get through Ontane's gate. Young men vaulted the fence. At least a hundred people crammed into the neighbour's yard, and soon fights broke out.

Loriane followed Ontane to his house, through the trampled snow.

She was angry. "You could have shared some of your food. Those people are hungry and desperate."

"Precisely. They be desperate and we don't have enough to feed all of them, not even the ones who have money—" He stopped in the doorway and stared. "Quick, inside. There be a lot more coming."

He shut the door and shoved two bolts shut. They stood there, staring at each other.

"What can we do?" Dara said. Her plain face was wide-eyed. "They'll swamp the town. They'll ruin everything, like the Knights did."

"We go elsewhere," Ontane said. "Let's hide at Zany Peak."

"But they'll wreck the house if we bain't here."

"We'll lock it up. In any case, it be better than let the mob kill us." He looked at Loriane. "Sorcerer awake yet?"

"Not when I last looked."

"How be he?"

"Not so good, I'm afraid. He's alive, but barely conscious."

"Let's go see him." He started up the stairs.

In the upstairs bedroom, Tandor was still asleep. Loriane folded back the bloodstained cover. The low light showed up the burned blisters like ugly sores. Weeping skin glistened. A muscle in his neck twitched.

Ontane's throat worked. "He be able to ride?"

"Like this? He can't even sit up. And I don't think I could take any more fleeing."

"Ye have to, mistress. See that?" He flicked aside the curtain.

Loriane looked.

By the feeble blue light, she saw hundreds of black specks on the snow plain, thousands even. "Are they all. . . ?"

"They all be refugees wanting to eat. By midday, there be hundreds of 'em outside, and some of them been talking . . . I dunno. A wall of steam coming after them. I don't like the sounds of this, mistress. Ne'er liked the Queen's magic much, and him over there . . ." he nodded at Tandor ". . . he knows more about this magic than he let on, doesn't he? He went out there looking for the magic and it looks like magic found him instead, didn't it?"

Loriane had nothing to say to that. She was out of ideas, and too sore and tired to care.

"If we . . . go, how long will that be for?" She shivered at the thought of having to give birth somewhere in the snow, or some cramped hut, with Ontane watching.

"Not long. The wife will be with us, and we have food. You be comfortable, mistress."

Loriane shrugged. She was far from convinced, but it seemed like they didn't have a choice. She took Tandor's hand and stroked the feverish skin. Tears blurred her vision. She was so tired.

CHAPTER 9

SADY SPREAD the map out over the camp table.

The automated barygraphs hadn't lied. He had half-hoped that the devices, such as the one that stood at the base of the telegraph pole in the forest clearing, had malfunctioned, and that the massive dip in air pressure some instruments had recorded yesterday was the result of a mere error. But the protective glass was intact, and so was the tiny bellows that contracted and expanded with the air pressure, which was inversely driven by sonorics, and the thin needle, precision-mounted on a rod of crystal, which didn't expand much with heat. The crystal acted like a seesaw; the bellows pushed or pulled one end of the needle, and the other, longer, end went up or down, touching thin copper wires set at intervals. Each time the needle passed such a wire, it would send a signal down the line. Most of the barygraphs Sady had visited in these few days had the needle stuck well below the lowest sonorics reading. With all the will in the world, he couldn't call this an error.

If nothing else, the sky confirmed the low-pressure reading, with scudding clouds which looked, for all he could think, like it was going to snow any minute.

Mercy, snow in summer. There was a massive low-pressure cell building up over the southern plateau. Thankfully, sonorics had remained stable. Too high, but still stable.

"Senator, are you ready to go?" a soldier behind him said.

Sady turned around, both annoyed and appreciative of the men who had offered to help him in Ensar, after he'd come back from his private and useless trip to see Milleus and found the train delayed. Typical, the local official said, and he'd gone into a diatribe about how the doga needed to give the district more money for trains.

Money, money, everything was about the lack of money.

"The balloon's almost ready," the soldier said. "Waiting for your directions."

He was holding these men up, and they had better things to do than hang around waiting for him. "Have you been able to contact the Tiverius office?"

"Yes, briefly, although the line has a lot of static."

"Any important news?"

Sady had wanted news from Milleus, that he had changed his mind; but so far, the old bear had been completely silent.

"Vikius han Marossi sent a couple of missives for you. He says they're urgent."

Sady took the paper from the soldier. In irregular block letters, the man had written out Viki's message, *Senator Sadorius han Chevonian, please confirm meteorology handbook rule 23 and confirm that I can apply it.*

Sady shook his head. Had Viki truly never sent a telegraph and didn't he know that every character added cost?

Rule 23 regarded the collection of rooftop rainwater for human consumption. The quota system that allowed residents to keep a certain amount for their gardens wasn't easy to explain in a few words. If more water had been collected than necessary in a citizen's tank, then that house could use the excess water for ornamental gardens.

The next sheet said, *Senator Timmonian won't give me access to the city's water storage.*

Oh, mercy, what had happened in Tiverius while he'd been away?

Sady groaned. *Viki, Viki, what have you done?*

He had hoped to hang around here a few days so that he could still pick up Milleus if he changed his mind at the last moment, as Milleus was wont to do.

But now . . .

No, he couldn't stay. His duty lay in Tiverius. Viki's clumsiness was causing an avalanche of disasters. Milleus could find his own way there, although by now, Sady felt it would be unlikely he would. What then? Nominate himself to stand against Destran? Was there another option?

He let his gaze roam over the campsite. The soldiers had packed their tents into the balloon's basket and spent most of the past hour inflating the massive air bubble which now towered over the trees. Squally winds tugged at the gasbag. The balloon was weighed down with bags of pebbles, each bearing a stencilled image of the two crossed guns over a gear blade, the sign of the Chevakian army. Little boys would scour the woods looking for these ballast bags and return them to the nearest authorities for a small payment.

Sady sighed and rolled up the maps. He wished he had more time to take measurements, but his current understanding of the situation would have to do.

The soldiers folded the camp table as soon as Sady had removed the maps.

Sady clambered into the gondola and sat down at his usual spot at the back, out of the way of the crew, who were now throwing off ropes, rolling them up and stowing them.

"Where to next, Senator?"

"We head straight back to Tiverius."

Sady considered that balloons were pretty handy and, given the grim situation, he felt almost guilty for enjoying his balloon ride.

One day, when all this trouble blew over, he would have to wrest designs from the army and start a civilian balloon transport service. Much nicer than the smelly train he'd taken out here.

Thanks to the soldiers who had taken pity on him, poorly dressed as he was in an unexpected snap of cold, and waylaid by a train malfunction, he was now back in Tiverius two days early, and had been able to take sonorics measurements at height as a bonus.

Now, though, as the buildings of the city tracked under him, and the soldiers who manned the burners were letting air out to make the balloon sink to the ground, his feet itched to get back to the doga and deal with all the disasters he would find there. And the inevitable confrontation with Destran.

And before that, his impending admission of failure to his

supporters. He could not tell the fifty senators who had signed intent to vote that his mission to bring back Milleus had been unsuccessful. If he did, *he* was a failure and they would never trust him again. Yet he did not want to stand for Proctor. He did not, he did not. He was not the right kind of person, not flamboyant enough. They would compare him with his brother; they would sneer about the fact that he had never married, that his brother's poor ways with women had rubbed off on him. They would say that he was his brother's mouthpiece. No Chief Meteorologist had ever challenged. He didn't even represent a district. It was a recipe for disaster. But was there an alternative?

A northern candidate would never get enough votes. There were no suitable southern candidates. Destran's cronies were out of the question.

His thoughts were going around and around in circles.

Sady caught the train from the army barracks. The city, which would normally be basking under a blue sky at this time of the year, was shrouded in heavy cloud. The citizens on the train were talking about it, and one man shared Sady's feeling that those looked like snow clouds.

He alighted from the train at Tiverius' central station and, from there, walked across the city's central square, perfectly paved, with trees planted at equal intervals. The columned, marble doga building basked in a flash of brilliant sunlight that peeped between the clouds. A gust of wind tore through the young leaves, sending a flurry of flower petals over the pavement.

Sady held both sides of his cloak together with one hand and ran up the steps. He felt lonely, abandoned and insignificant.

The wind was not as strong in the courtyard, but here his footsteps echoed eerily. Where was everyone? Sady went into the tall columned main entrance of the building and up the steps to the second floor corridor where his office was.

He was about halfway up the steps when he heard the agitated voices. A man was shouting. Someone else replied.

He turned the corner and found himself at the back of a crowd in the corridor.

Oh, mercy, they weren't standing in front of *his* office, were they?

"You can't do this!" a man shouted. "We need to be notified of any change in cropping schedule in advance."

Heart beating fast, Sady shooed people aside. "Excuse me, excuse me, can I get through?"

Some people in the crowd turned.

"Senator Sadorius!" someone shouted. More people turned.

"Senator, what's this about the change in cropping schedules?" someone else asked.

"Do you authorise the change?"

Someone else yelled, "He says we can't use water collected from our roofs anymore. So what are we supposed to do?"

Someone at the back of the crowd added, "Yeah, whose stupid idea is this?"

Change in cropping schedules? "Wait, wait, wait!" Sady advanced into the group. "Can someone tell me please what is going on?"

"He did it!" a man shouted, and pointed at the door of Sady's office, where Viki stood, red-faced, clutching a bundle of notes.

To his credit, Viki straightened and answered with a clear voice, "I did nothing unauthorised. I'm following the doga's protocol and the meteorology handbook."

"It's irrational!" a man shouted and others agreed.

Sady raised his voice. "Quiet, calm down!"

They did, glancing at each other from the corners of their eyes.

Sady looked around the group. There were men he recognised as regional representatives, and even merchants. Mercy, he'd hoped Viki wouldn't create some sort of disaster in his absence, and it looked like the young man had done just that. On top of everything else that had happened.

"Viki, would you care to explain?"

"Well, I—" He glanced nervously at all the people demanding his attention.

Sady jerked his head at the office door. "Inside."

When the onlookers grumbled, Sady added. "I'll be back shortly."

Viki disappeared into the room, and Sady followed, shutting the door behind him.

He took a step towards his desk, and stopped.

Every flat surface in the office had been covered with curling snakes of data read-outs, maps and papers. Some had spilled onto the floor.

"What in the heavens has happened here?" Sady grabbed one, glancing at the data, but needed time to fully make sense of it.

"I haven't done anything," Viki said. "I was just following—"

"Please start at the beginning."

By now, Sady had an ominous feeling about where this was going. The unseasonable cold wind was not as innocent as it seemed. The massive low pressure spikes he had measured had made it even to the capital.

Viki swallowed. "Well, after levelling off, sonorics levels suddenly went up after you left, and they crossed the twenty motes level in the border regions. First in the Fairlight district, so I used the doga's protocol to stop exports from there—"

"Viki, you can't just do that one-sided . . ."

Viki turned around and handed Sady a readout. "I can't? Look at this. I followed protocol, from the handbook!" His voice spilled over with emotion and his eyes glittered.

Sady looked at the graph Viki held up. The plotting machine had skipped up to a larger scale so that the red line hadn't risen off the page. Twenty motes, twenty-seven, thirty-six. Fifty-nine. And still, the direction of the plotted graph was up. Mercy. Blood rose to his cheeks and ears while he looked at the graph. He licked his lips. "This is a verified measurement?" The readings were nothing short of horrific.

"Look at the others. They're all close. One measurement I could discount as a transmission error, but all the measurements are like this."

Mercy. Out went his prepared words for scolding Viki. It seemed Sady himself would have acted every bit as the young student had—perhaps with more authority, but still. While he'd been away, the Fairlight district had been bombarded with sonorics. "Have you heard if the barrier is still holding with this strain?"

"It is, according to the latest news."

Sady's heart was thudding against his ribs. The town of Fairlight was very close to the border. There were thousands of people in the district, a fertile agricultural area. "Do we still have a telegraph line to Fairlight?"

"Fairlight is hard to get on the line at the moment. Too much static. But the line hasn't gone completely. We can try. Any message you want me to send?"

"Yes." Then he hesitated, knowing that what he did wish to say, *get your backsides out of there*, would cause a flood of panic and outrage. "I'll deal with it in person."

But by the time Sady had dealt with the chaos outside his office, and he had made his way to the telegraph offices, the link had been severed.

Worry rising in him, he went to the Scriptorium to ask Alius about that new medicine, because he had a feeling it would be needed soon. However, Alius wasn't in, and he had to contend with leaving a note. He made the text as urgent as he could, but figured there was a good chance he'd have to chase it up, given Alius' recent record of replying to his messages. Damn, if only he could understand why the man had decided to hate him so much.

After a brief bite to eat in the building's canteen, where he was besieged by senators wondering where Milleus was and other senators still smarting over Viki's dealing with the situation, he prepared for that afternoon's doga session. A quick glance at the agenda had him shaking his head with frustration. Funding for bridges and a new Scriptorium in regional towns was all very well, but there was no mention of the crisis, except in the section *Questions raised by members*, and he noted, with a sense of satisfaction, that it had been Viki who had entered the question *How will we deal with rising sonorics levels at our borders?*

Mercy, maybe the young student had more courage than he had given him credit for.

He gulped his food and too-hot tea while outside the window, over the administrative wing of the building, snow clouds gathered.

The signs were bad, and the doga was wracked with indecision and paralysed by a body of senators who didn't like to hear bad news and were all too happy with Alius' strange *don't worry* message. If there was a new medicine, Alius had better turn up with it soon, or he was going to evacuate. In fact, he scribbled a note which he asked Orsan to take to the stationmaster, to send any free trains to Fairlight for evacuation, his lack of funds be damned.

Folding the note, Sady rose, and as he pushed his chair back under the table, he made a decision. He owed Viki and Shara. He owed his long-dead parents; he owed Milleus. He owed Suri and her sons, and the love he had never been able to give her. He owed this city. For years, his family, friends and colleagues had taken the burden of looking after the country. It was his turn. It might destroy or kill him, but he was going to challenge.

CHAPTER 10

MILLEUS SHIFTED the van into "brake" and it rolled to a stop just before it hit the fence. A cloud of steam burst from the pressure vent in an angry hiss. He flung the door open, dropped out of the van and slammed the door after him, as if it was to blame for his mood.

Mercy, mercy on his brother if ever he got his hands on the blabbermouth.

In his mind, he could still see the town shopkeeper's smiling face, hear his voice, "So it is true, then, you will be standing as Proctor?"

He had wanted to wring the man's neck, wanted to shout, *Who in the blazing wastelands has told you such nonsense?*

But two of the man's customers had been standing in the corner of the shop, wide-eyed. Next thing the whole town would be talking about him returning to the doga, no matter that he had told the shopkeeper there was not a shred of truth in the rumour.

If a politician says he won't stand for an election, it probably means he's about to win it. He'd said this himself so many times.

Well, not him. Return to the doga—pfa! They'd voted him out well enough. What had gotten into the brain of Sadorius han Chevonian to suggest they'd wanted him back?

Fifty signatures, that's what. That's almost half the doga, almost a majority.

He blinked, staring over the golden fields of grain, fruit of years of dogged labour, but saw instead the chamber of the doga, the men and women who debated Chevakia's future seated in rows of benches.

Facing him. Listening to him. They each had their copies of plans spread out before them. Not the precise details, oh no, never that, but enough to see what the army had in store for the unsuspecting Aranian attackers. Balloons. Air attacks.

The senators were loving it. From the moment he brought out those plans, he had ridden on a wave of support all the way into the Aranian capital.

Pfa, enough of this. His time in politics was over. Leave an old man to his retirement.

Peace. Quiet. Harvest time.

Milleus stomped into the control shed. Flung the door open. Lights flashed on panels on the wall. The harvester . . . He pressed a few buttons and returned to the shed's entrance to look up the hillside. Over there, beyond a copse of trees was a shed that housed the machinery. In a moment, the door would open and the harvester would come out in a cloud of steam, followed by the bin truck, ready to cut and collect the grain and bring it to the storage bins next to the house. The bin truck would chop up the straw and bundle it into bales which would keep the goats comfortable in winter. A marvel of modern technology.

He *loved* being here, being one with the farm, the fields, the goats. Anything that threatened the farm . . .

Rising sonorics levels. Sady was right. As Proctor, he *would* have done something, and Destran should act. He should be organising emergency supplies. He should be writing a letter to the southern Queen demanding an explanation. He should be sending delegations, and spies.

Milleus sighed. It wasn't *his* problem. Destran had wanted the leadership; Destran had called him incompetent. Well, let Destran find out the new meaning of incompetent.

The field was still empty.

Where was the harvester?

He went back to the panel and found all lights flashing orange. A malfunction. He pressed the reset button, and tried again. Immediately, the lights flashed orange again.

Mercy, what a day.

Well, there was nothing for it, he had to go look and hope it wouldn't require a mechanic, because he hadn't the time for waiting for parts to turn up; and with this unseasonable cold spell, it might rain and the grain would get too moist.

He jumped into the van and revved it up the hill, leaving behind a cloud of hot steam.

The door of the harvester shed was closed. Possibly jammed. Well, that wasn't hard to fix. He jumped out of the van and entered the shed through the side door . . . into the point of a knife.

"Mercy!"

Holding the knife was a wide-eyed, longhaired youth, about fifteen or so, with intense blue eyes and unruly dark hair. He wore an odd garment made from—of all things—empty seed bags.

He was not alone. Milleus caught a flash of someone else in the shed, movement under a heap of fur.

In one practiced swoop, he hit the knife from the youth's hand. *See, don't play with an old man. I'm tougher than you think.*

The boy went sprawling. Fell hard on his backside. A wooden leg shot out from under him.

Oh mercy, I've just hit an invalid.

A defensive invalid, though. The boy scrabbled in the straw, dirty hands searching.

Milleus kicked the knife aside and put his foot on the blade. Slowly, keeping his eye on the youth, he picked it up. "I'm sorry, but what are you doing in my barn?"

The youth said nothing, but stared at Milleus with those intense blue eyes.

He was too thin. Not a fighter, too young to be a trained soldier.

He had set up quite a neat camp here, with a box for a table, bales of straw for a bed—so that's where the bales from the hay loft had gone—and furs for sitting. Right in the harvester's path. And that was why it wouldn't come out.

The furs stirred. A pale face peeped out between them, then vanished again. A girl, Milleus thought.

"Don't be afraid. I won't harm you. I just need to get my harvester out." He gestured, wondering if the youths understood his words. With their furs and pale skin, they looked awfully foreign. They looked *southern.*

The girl had now lowered the furs. She was about the same age as the boy, had honey-coloured hair, grey eyes, and only one hand.

Her face, pale as moonlight, wore a scared expression. She spoke a few words to the boy, equally scared, to which he replied in a soft voice.

Oh mercy—they were just runaways. Milleus stepped further into the shed, holding out his hands. "My name is Milleus." He didn't know if they understood, so he bowed his head to show he didn't intend harm.

The girl threw the furs aside and rose, arms by her side. A skinny thing, she was, with arms thin as sticks and legs with bony knees. Her skin was deathly pale.

"We thank you, farmer." Her voice sounded awfully formal. "We apologise that we have not asked permission to lodge in your shed."

Milleus would have laughed if there hadn't been that chilling tone to her voice, that self-assured toss of the head.

"Who are you?"

At this, the boy stepped between her and Milleus, holding a protective arm around her.

"We will go if we can't stay." His accent was much stronger and rougher.

Go, where? Into the forest? "No, no. I'm not telling you to go. I just want to know who you are, and how you got here, and what you're doing in my barn."

Did they have family in Chevakia he could notify? Were they planning on going anywhere?

"I am Isandor," the boy said, taking another step closer to Milleus. He was a hand's width taller than Milleus.

"And what about your friend?"

"Does not matter." His voice was abrupt.

"Just her first name. Seeing where you've come from, I'm not going to contact the authorities in the City of Glass, am I?"

A hostile look. Then a flick of the eyebrows. "Nila."

"What?"

"Her name is Nila. No more."

"All right."

Well, maybe they *were* involved in some shady thing in the City of Glass. Maybe the girl's rich parents wanted her back. Mercy, what was he to do with them?

"And what did you intend to do here? Do you have any family?"

"Can work," the boy said, showing a white-skinned arm corded with muscles.

Well, that could be a temporary solution. Milleus did have a large pile of firewood to be chopped, and his back did happen to have developed an aversion to wood chopping. Not to mention gardening.

Besides, the guest wing to the house had been empty since he had last entertained the collected ambassadors here . . . he couldn't remember how long ago. He carried the keys in his pocket. Everything would probably still be there.

"All right. You can stay here until I find another place for you. One thing, though, I will promise you: if you are in any way involved in a crime against a person or property either here or in your home country, you are asking the wrong person to help you. I will find out, and I will pass you onto the authorities. So you better be honest and swear you haven't killed anyone or stolen anything."

"We would never do such a thing, farmer," the girl said.

Farmer. What did she think he was?

"My name is Milleus han Chevonian," he grumbled. "Milleus for short." *Retired Proctor of Chevakia, so you better watch it.*

Then again, his name didn't mean anything to her, or if it did, she didn't show it.

"Nice to meet you, Milleus. We are grateful for your help."

Milleus turned away. He was too old to take this formal talk from someone barely a quarter his age.

You're just a grumpy old man, Milleus, who has stopped caring. "Now if you will take your stuff out of the way, I can get the harvester to work."

The youngsters shifted their possessions which included straw-covered furs, eggs, the old pot which he used to feed the ducks—so that's where it had gone—and some women's underwear. He chuckled at that and wondered what Andreus' wife would have made of her bloomers disappearing.

He pressed the manual button to open the large shed door. The boy gave a frightened squeak when the mechanism hummed into action.

The girl said something to him, and he relaxed, but still watched the door until it stopped moving.

"Come. I'll take you to my house."

For once, Milleus let the harvester do its work by itself. He took all of the youngsters' possessions—their furs and some clothes almost too dirty to touch—and put them in the van. It took a lot of coaxing to get the boy anywhere near it. He pointed vehemently that he wanted to walk, and continued to do so after Milleus had turned off the engine, but Milleus told the girl in no uncertain terms that he would not have *her* walk all the way to the farm; that was not the way Chevakians treated their women, and she spoke to the boy in their strange language, and eventually his stance softened.

Milleus wanted to help the girl into the van, but the boy had evidently decided he was not going to let her out of his sight. An arm around her side, he helped her to the van, speaking in a strange language, and then he squished himself in the front seat next to her, his long limbs at odd angles.

"There's a seat in the back, it's much more comfortable," Milleus said, while climbing in the driver's seat.

"I sit here," Isandor said in his intense way. He held onto the girl's shoulders and hand.

Oh mercy, have it your way.

Milleus started the van and drove back to the homestead, accompanied only but the puff of the engine. The boy held a white-knuckled hand over the girl's fingers. The girl stared at the various gauges, the pressure-metres, the water level metres, the temperature of the engine. At times, Milleus thought her lips moved, as if she wanted to ask a question, but she didn't. She puzzled him, much more composed than her flighty companion.

They arrived at the house and he pulled up at the front door. The youngsters got out, staring wide-eyed. Yes, Milleus knew the doors needed painting and the straw roof supported a veritable botanic garden of native succulents. Some were even flowering, pink daisies that moved their little heads with the sun.

Milleus opened the back door to get the filthy bundles of cloth from the back, and when he shut the van, the boy had closed his arms around the girl, nuzzling the skin in her neck. She spoke a few soft words; he smiled, his eyes all dreamy.

Milleus remembered a day too long ago, when the most beautiful woman he had ever seen waited in the garden surrounded by both their families. Music played and people laughed, but he only had eyes for her. Suri, *his* Suri in her beautiful dress, flowers in her hair.

"Come." He stomped into the cool hall, not sure why he was so angry, and wishing he weren't. He dumped the dirty clothes in the laundry and returned to the youngsters in the hall. They still held each other, hands intertwined.

"You live here alone?" the boy asked.

"Yes." *Do you have a problem with that?* "Come. I'll show you the rooms."

He pulled his key ring from his pocket and found the age-blackened key to the guest quarters. The door creaked when it opened and a waft of stale air spilled out. He half-expected some ghost of the past to come flitting down the corridor, Dena or Horus or any of the other long-gone servants. But his footsteps sounded hollow as he went into the linen room. The sun slanted through dirt-streaked windows.

"You'll want some sheets."

He had to yank the door to the cupboard hard, but the sheets inside were still neatly folded, although the bunch of herbs Dena used to put on them had fallen to dust with age.

Two sheets each, a pillowcase. Blankets were on the beds as far as he remembered. He hoped nothing had eaten them. He put everything in a pile and led down the corridor.

The first room . . .

Mercy, the Aranian ambassador used to stay here. Ghosts of the past flew by. The scent of tobacco, the chesty laugh, the rough voice. *Milleus, surely you will join me for a drink?*

The room was musty and empty, but a folded blanket lay on the bed, an empty pitcher stood on the table by the window—mercy, the cobwebs! Milleus cleared his throat.

"Isandor, you can sleep here." He dumped two sheets and a pillowcase on the bed. "And you . . ." He left the room again.

Suri's mother's room had an elegant couch, a table, a marble fireplace, a large four-poster bed with frilly curtains that were—or used to be—pink. Sunlight had faded the fabric, as well as a patch on the carpet, which used to be dark red, and was now dirty yellow. Mercy, the dust.

But the girl stood in the doorway taking it all in, letting her strange grey eyes roam. Her expression showed neither approval nor disapproval.

"This will be your room," Milleus said into the uncomfortable silence. "There is a bathroom at the end of the corridor if you want to get freshened up. You'll find some clothes in the cupboard. I hope there's something that fits you." Mercy, some of those were Suri's clothes. "I'll be in the kitchen. I'm afraid the fare on the farm is pretty simple—"

"Thank you so much."

Milleus nodded, and left.

In the kitchen, he busied himself with the fire in the stove, and then unpacked the seldom-touched items from his pantry onto the table, after clearing this morning's plates. Mercy, mercy. What did he have to feed two hungry children? He could not really use that stock powder anymore. It looked suspiciously mouldy.

Soup? Some bread? Well, that wouldn't last more than a day. He'd have to go into town to buy more. And he must buy some vegetables, too. At least he had plenty of meat and milk and cheese.

He set a large pot to boil with bones and herbs. Fresh soup would be good, never mind the powder.

There was a small noise. Milleus looked up to see the youngsters at the door, still holding hands. In Sady's hunting gear, Isandor had gained about ten years in age. Yes, Milleus was not mistaken—he did have dark fuzz on his chin.

But the girl . . . Nila, although he didn't for once believe that was her name . . .

No. You can't wear that dress.

Suri whirled around so that the pretty frills formed a full circle around her thin waistline. *Oh Milleus, thank you. It's so pretty!*

He laughed and scooped her up in his arms, stroking the soft belly that did not yet show the child within.

A pretty house needs a pretty woman.

The girl—Nila—had just such a thin waistline. Her hair, done up in a delicate bun, was straight and very southern, but the dress fitted her. *No, not that dress.* Milleus turned, cleared his throat and put the soup on the table.

"There's no fancy tableware, I'm afraid." Yes, there was, in the cupboard in the dining room, equally unused and probably dusty beyond redemption.

"It doesn't matter," the girl said. "Thank you."

Milleus scooped soup into bowls and distributed big chunks of bread. Isandor gulped the soup, holding his spoon in his clenched fist like a farm worker, and ate like someone would run off with his plate.

Nila sat up straight like the highborn girl Milleus was sure she was. She held the spoon in her dainty hand, and ate slowly, pulling little pieces off the bread before putting them in her mouth.

Milleus took his own plate and sat down. Isandor had taken Milleus' usual spot and he had to sit at the head of the table.

"Now, about you two. You came from the City of Glass?"

"From the south," Isandor said.

All right. He wasn't answering the question. "How did you get here?" The City of Glass was a long way away. The mountains across the border were pretty high and as far as he knew no one lived there.

"We had . . . we had a bird."

Oh. Milleus saw. The bird he'd seen a few days ago. But then again . . . "You let it go?"

"The bird is free."

"Is anyone after you?"

Isandor glanced at Nila. "Maybe."

"Maybe or surely?"

"Maybe. Don't know."

"And those people who are after you, who are they?"

"You ask many questions for a farmer," Nila said.

"I am giving you lodging. I think I have a right to know such things. Especially if they could lead to trouble."

"No one will harm you. It is us they want."

"And you didn't commit a crime?"

"No. I swear by my heart." She picked up a knife and held it, point to her chest.

"Oh, no, no." Milleus eased it from her hand. "We don't do that sort of thing here. We just promise."

"I promise."

Milleus normally lived and ate in the kitchen, but there was only one comfortable seat, so he told the youngsters to go to the adjacent room while he cleared the dishes.

When he entered the room, Nila sat in one of the chairs, half-asleep, her cheeks flushed, but Isandor stood at one of the many bookshelves.

"You have . . . many books."

"Yes. They're all big volumes about boring things."

A boy this age would hardly have interest in politics, philosophy and statecraft. Even he hadn't touched most volumes for many years. Who knew why he even kept all this stuff. Isandor's blue eyes roamed the titles. Big leather-bound volumes covered in dust.

He pulled one book off the shelf.

Military strategy in the Aranian war.

Mercy, how had he and the Aranian ambassador discussed this tome—until they were both red in the face and so drunk they fell asleep on these couches. Anything better than to disturb Suri's sleep and provoke her wrath.

"You read this?" Isandor asked.

"Long ago." Hah! He helped *write* it.

Isandor flicked through pages of diagrams and tables. "You use balloons in war." It was not a question, and something about the way he said it made Milleus stop cold.

"Yes, the Chevakian army uses balloons."

"Balloons better than eagles. Eagles carry one rider. Bows, arrows, maybe gun. Nothing heavy."

"But an eagle is fast and you can use a knife or the bird's claws to cut a balloon."

"You use nets. Riders can't cut. Not many have guns. I say if you have balloons you win the war." Again, it was not a question. He shut the book and put it away.

Mercy, the boy had *military* training.

A Knight? A deserter? A spy?

But his smile was too disarming. If he was a real spy, he wouldn't mention this so freely. And he would be much older. Yet Milleus made sure he locked the door to his sleeping quarters that night.

CHAPTER 11

FLAMES LEAPED in the night, against the backdrop of forest, unfamiliar dark shapes that were *trees*, where creatures hid and rustled and hooted. The sky above was dark and full of stars like the sky in the City of Glass at low-sun.

As someone new to lands devoid of snow, Carro found his senses were all askew. The smells, the sounds, the feel of the ground under his feet, everything was different. And even the nights were so incredibly *warm*.

A shiver crawling over his arms, Carro finished rubbing his eagle and put the brush back in his kit bag. So neat and tidy it was compared to those of the hunters. They had non-standard bags, and non-standard saddles. Jeito wore a harness, but the other two didn't. They'd laughed when he asked about their uniforms.

Farey knelt by the fire, using a fearfully sharp knife to slowly pull the skin off the animal Nolan had shot. Carro had seen him do it. A single shot from a Chevakian gun, from the back of a plummeting eagle, not wearing a harness.

And Rider Cornatan wanted him to *control* these hunters? That had to be his idea of a joke.

It brought up memories of the abuse at the hands of his fellow apprentices, and the eyrie he was glad to have left. It made him think of the promise he'd made to his father. *Bring them back, dead or alive, but preferably dead. Avenge the Pirosian house.* The medal that hung on a chain under his clothes burned against his chest. He was no heroic soldier.

"Hey, Carro." Farey jerked his head at the pile of wood Nolan had collected. His hands shone with grease and blood.

Carro needed no more instructions. Tend to the fire. It wasn't an order so much as a task. Everyone else was busy, too. They were all pieces of the puzzle that formed the achievements of a well-oiled team. Trying to command would be useless at best, at worst would earn him disrespect. You did not order these men.

He knelt inside the pool of warm orange light and poked the burning logs into a pile.

Farey's knife worked at the carcass. His muscles cording in his arms, he was hacking the head off the animal. Bones cracked.

Nolan just returned from the creek with a bladder of water, some of which he poured into a pot. Teeth flashing, Farey grinned and threw the head of the animal across. Splash, in the pan.

"Oy!" Nolan shouted. "You wanna get me shirt all messed-up?"

Farey snorted and rose. With his long face and yellowish skin, he looked part-Aranian. Long black hair hung on either side of his face. He looked nothing like he had in the palace, yet this image was the real Farey. Had Carro met him in another life in the streets of the Outer City, he would have walked around the block.

Farey oozed danger, in his smile, in his intense look and in the way he went to stand behind Carro and breathed over his shoulder so close Carro could feel the warmth of his body, and he didn't dare breathe for fear of being stripped of his pants and raped. That's what happened to junior apprentices, after all.

Farey laughed. "The pup is scared, huh?"

"No," Carro said, but it came out as a strangled sound.

"Oh, quit that, Farey," Nolan said. "He's been a good replacement for that idiot we lost."

"Yeah, he's not half-bad," Farey said, tracing Carro's shoulder with a hand glistening with grease and blood. Carro's heart thudded in his chest. "You fancy him, huh?"

"Quit that, I said."

"Yeah, you fancy him." Farey let his hand drop. "All right. You can have him." But before he turned away, he pulled Carro against him. Carro could feel his cock through two layers of clothes.

"Hey, come and help me," Nolan said.

Carro stumbled to the fire, his heart still thudding and blood roaring in his ears, and, embarrassingly, in other places.

"Thanks," he mumbled to Nolan.

"Look after the fire for me," Nolan said, his eyes meeting Carro's in an intense look.

He transferred the pot to the fire, hanging it up on a wire frame. "Don't make them flames too high, or you can scrub the soot off."

Carro nodded, and pushed the logs a bit further apart.

Farey had pushed a stick through the carcass and hung it above the fire. He sank down with a sigh of satisfaction, wiped his hands on his trousers and pulled a bottle from his pocket.

"Want some?" He held it out to Carro, who took it from his bloodied hands.

The spirits were strong and burned in Carro's throat. He wiped the mouth of the bottle and passed it to Jeito, who was studying a map. His long hair hung forward over his shoulder. Jeito's fingers traced lines on the map. Long fingers with rings. Sometimes, when Jeito raked hair behind his ear, Carro thought he looked feminine. He was certainly not tall and lanky like Farey, or strong-jawed and stubble-chinned like Nolan.

But he'd seen Jeito with a knife, and he'd felt the strength in the grip of those fine-boned hands, and he'd seen how Jeito set fire to a farmhouse with an entire family locked inside. More than anyone, more even than Farey, Jeito scared him.

"Where are we, then?" In the group tasks were strictly divided, and it seemed talking was Nolan's task. He was perhaps the youngest of the three, and with his soft honey-coloured curls and hazel eyes, he must have a lot of Chevakian blood.

Jeito grunted. "We've searched this area." He circled a spot on the map. "Tomorrow, we're going here." He pointed at the map. His shirt hung open at the front, showing soft, hairless skin. "They're around here somewhere." Jeito's finger circled the district on the map. There was a small farming village, and a larger town called Ensar.

Yesterday, they had spotted a riderless eagle, circling high. They tried to follow the animal, only to find that it was heading back over the mountains and that it had neither a harness nor listened to whistles. A wild bird? It might have been a coincidence, but they expected the Queen to be around here somewhere. Any further north and it would have been too hot for the eagle.

Carro nodded. "I think they've hidden somewhere in these hills." He tried to sound authoritative. "I wouldn't be surprised if they let the bird go, since it will give away their position. I think we—"

"Don't think too much," Farey said. His teeth flashed a warning.

"I know Isandor better than all of you. We grew up together." That was why Rider Cornatan had sent him on this mission, wasn't it?

"What you know would fit in a brain the size of the nail on my little finger," Farey said.

"Whoa, calm down," Nolan said. "What Farey means is that obeying orders is not the way we do things here, with us. We're hunters, you know, and we don't like being bossed around like you . . . would be used to."

"Shut your trap, blabbermouth. I don't need you to explain what I said. The pup's got ears. We'll have him along, if he doesn't fuck up, but I don't want him to get any illusions about commanding us."

"You're as blunt as the sword smith's hammer."

"And your mouth's gonna kill you one day."

But Farey gave Nolan an affectionate smile as Nolan handed back the bottle, and a cracking slap on the shoulder. Nolan threw himself on Farey and the two rolled back in the grass. Carro jumped up, ready to discipline his team, but they were laughing, pushing away each other's hands until Farey lay on his back and Nolan on top of him, having pushed Farey's arms flat on the ground.

Nolan grinned. "Who's the pup now?"

In a flash, Farey got his legs under him and bucked up, sending Nolan flying in the grass. He jumped up and ran into the darkness.

"Cut it, idiots, will ya?" Jeito snapped. Then his shifty glance met Carro's. "Oh, sit down, academy boy. They're just stirring each other up."

Branches cracked and Nolan came back out of the forest.

"Stop teasing the pup," he said to Jeito, picking grass out of his hair. "I was like him just two years ago."

"That long already, feels like two moons." Sarcasm dripped from Farey's voice. "Hey. You think there is any hope for this one?"

"You gotta be fair. He can't help who his family is."

Jeito raised his eyebrows.

An uncomfortable silence fell. Nolan blushed.

Eventually, Jeito said, "Family?"

Nolan shrugged and met Carro's eyes. He mouthed *sorry*. "You don't have to tell everyone if you don't want to. Me and my big mouth."

"You can say that again," Farey growled. "If you shut your trap more often, we'd be in a lot less shit."

Carro looked down in an uncomfortable silence. *You don't have to tell anyone if you don't want to.* With these young men, nothing but the total truth would do. He spoke, still looking at the grass.

"I found out . . . before I came on this mission . . . that the people who raised me, an Outer City merchant and his family, were paid to do so. My real family . . ." He licked his lips, didn't know what else to say, or how to say it, and pulled the medallion of the Pirosian house from under his tunic.

Three pairs of eyes fixed on it. One grey, one blue, one brown.

"Oh frolicking skylights," Jeito said. "You're Rider Cornatan's son?"

Carro nodded.

Farey whistled between his teeth. "That's some name to live up to. What'd you do?"

"What do you mean—what did I do?"

Nolan explained. "Well, the Knights normally send us poor boys when they misbehave in the Knight's training. You know—to toughen them up."

Oh.

"They usually don't stick around for long," Jeito said. "Can't hack it."

"Hey, but you're not too bad," Nolan said, meeting Carro's eyes. "But tell us—what did you do?"

Carro shrugged. He didn't do anything, as far as he was aware. Maybe that was the problem, or maybe even his father thought he was worthless and wanted to stick him away, somewhere he couldn't do any more damage than he'd already done. The shame of the Pirosian house, a blot on his family.

"He speaks Chevakian, that's what he did," Farey said.

"Oh." Nolan looked disappointed. Then he shrugged, took the

bottle again and drank deeply. "Want some?" The skin around his eyes crinkled. Something about that look unsettled Carro.

Farey used the sleeve of his tunic to pick up the stick and turn the meat. Fat dripped into the fire, hissing into the flames. Jeito sat next to Farey, and whispered in his ear. Farey smiled. Jeito slapped Farey's chest in a playful gesture.

The next thing they were kissing, a deep, passionate kiss that made Carro all hot and uncomfortable in certain places.

Farey's hands moved down Jeito's shoulders. Jeito sank slowly onto his back into the grass until all Carro could see was Farey's back, and Jeito's long-fingered hands.

Carro took the bottle, meeting Nolan's eyes. "Don't mind them," Nolan said. "They're always clowning."

Carro shrugged. He couldn't take his eyes off that scene. Firelight flickered over Farey's back, and the rings on Jeito's hands, their bodies rubbing against each other, totally absorbed.

He swallowed and asked, "So . . . why are you here?"

"Isn't that obvious? I speak Chevakian, too."

"Your mother is Chevakian?"

Nolan nodded. "Yes. Before you ask me, I'm one of the slave children, born from a kidnapped woman. Never fitted into the City of Glass, so . . . I became a hunter, a spy."

You don't need to be half-Chevakian not to fit in.

"You've been doing this two years?"

"Sure have."

"Is it good?"

"You kidding? Best job I ever had. Better 'n playing cook in the Knights' mess, I'd say. No, the worst job I had was washing up and cleaning the kitchens. What about you?"

Carro shuddered.

"Doing my . . . my stepfather's accounts . . . all through the night. I was so cold. And when I complained . . . he would bring me more work." He stopped because his voice choked up. He stared into the fire, but Nolan said nothing, and he continued. "All night, I would sit there. He wouldn't feed me until I finished, and if I fell asleep, he would bring me more work. I was cold, and it was scary in the warehouse in the dark . . ."

"Hey," Nolan said. There was warm sympathy in his voice. He

reached out, and when Carro didn't react, put his hand on Carro's shoulder.

"They treat you bad, huh?"

The fire swam in Carro's eyes. He blinked and blinked, afraid to cry. If the Knights at the Eyrie heard that he, Carro, had cried . . . if his father heard it . . .

"You know, we all been hurt," Nolan continued. "That's really why they put us here. None of us fit in. Farey's half Aranian, Jeito . . ." He shrugged. "Well, he speaks for himself. They hurt us and poke us, and hope that we grow into tough men. And you know? We don't. Because we're too hurt, too cut up inside. But us, we look out for each other."

Carro nodded. He wiped furiously at his eyes, aware that Farey and Jeito looked at him, haunted looks on their faces. Not one of them laughed.

Jeito lifted the bottle to his lips and drank deeply. "Nolan blabbers too much, but he speaks right. It was no place for any of us, the City of Glass."

They all fell silent.

Somehow, Carro didn't care as much as he should. The City of Glass was far away and the warm wind in his hair was far too enjoyable. And what was more, ever since they had crossed the border, he had suffered no more debilitating flashbacks.

He lay back in the grass, staring at the star-dotted sky. The cooking meat made hissing and sizzling noises and spread the most delicious smell. The drink glowed comfortably in his belly. *We look out for each other*. No one had ever looked out for him. No one perhaps except . . . Isandor. But Isandor was the other side, now. He understood; Isandor was Thillei, a sorcerer, kidnapper of the Queen, to be exterminated. He could never be a friend.

"You all right?" Nolan said.

"Yeah."

Nolan's hand found Carro's shoulder, caressing the skin through his clothes. Carro lay still, his heart thudding.

"Hey, relax," Nolan said. His hand wandered down Carro's chest, to his belt.

Carro jerked away.

Nolan withdrew his hand, and raised himself on one elbow, meeting Carro's eyes.

"It's all right," he whispered. "We never hurt each other."

But . . .

The firelight played on Nolan's face. His eyes were sincere. He'd taken off his shirt. There was a bulge in his pants.

Carro stared through the haze of confusion. Were they all male lovers? Was he one? Whenever the Knights had violated him, he'd always become aroused. He'd had Korinne, but he hadn't really *loved* her, had he?

Long moments passed. Nolan reached out again, took Carro's hand and placed it on his bare chest. "Feel it."

Nolan's heart thudded under his fingers, through the warm and sweaty skin. He bent closer, his breath tickling in Carro's neck. Carro wanted to give in, wanted Nolan to fuck him. But that was what the Knights did to apprentices for punishment. It hurt. Nolan nibbled the skin under his ear, and ran a hand over Carro's shoulder. His lips moved up Carro's jaw line.

Men don't kiss.

Carro jerked back.

"Does it scare you?" Nolan asked.

Carro nodded. He disengaged from Nolan's touch and rolled on his back.

"It's all right," Nolan said softly. "I can wait."

Carro nodded again. But he was rock hard and wanted to go somewhere private to relieve himself. No, he wanted someone else to do it. He lay there, looking up at the stars, his heart thudding.

"Look," Nolan said.

A short burst of light tracked through the sky.

"Quick, make a wish."

They were silent for a bit.

Then Nolan asked, "What did you wish?"

"I'm not saying. It's supposed to stay a secret, otherwise it isn't a wish." But Carro didn't know what to wish. He would have wished for himself to do well so his father would love him. He might have wished for his hallucinations to stop, but they seemed to have stopped of their own volition since crossing the border. Now, he just wanted to be free of the guilt he felt about his hot, naked desire.

"Well, I wish I had loads of money and a big palace with swimming pools and all that stuff they have in Chevakia." Nolan pushed himself up. "Better go and check the food."

Before he could stop himself, Carro raised his hand, as if he wanted to say, *wait*.

Nolan hesitated, and sat back down, and leant over Carro. "So you do want it?"

Carro panicked. He wanted to scream, *No!* But he was so hard it hurt.

Nolan whispered, "About your wish." The skin around his eyes crinkled with his smile. "You didn't happen to be thinking of me? You've been ogling me for days."

Nolan reached up and felt for Carro's hand. Warm flesh met warm flesh. Something connected. Nolan shifted closer and as if it was the most natural thing, folded Carro into his arms. His curls smelled like saddle oil and unwashed hair, but very male. Nolan lifted his face, and the next moment his lips met Carro's. Moist, hot and eager.

Carro had never been kissed like this. He'd forced himself on a girl, he'd been forced to kiss when he didn't want to, and had other boys force themselves on him, and there was that incident, in the Eyrie where he had felt compelled to punish his patrol, that he didn't even want to think about.

None of those times were anything like this.

Nolan's hands were tender and questing. His callus-hardened hands warm under Carro's shirt. His breath was heavy in the gathering darkness. Nolan took off his shirt, but Carro shied away when Nolan reached for the fastening on his pants.

"What?" Nolan whispered. His lips glistened with moisture.

Carro shook his head.

"Why not? I want to fuck you."

Carro shook his head again.

"There's no need to be scared. Although . . . I was scared, too, the first time. Everyone tells you it's wrong."

Carro said nothing. He was breathing deep, panting breaths. His heart was thudding against his ribs like crazy, but his cock was hard as rock and dribbling slime into his pants. "I'm not—"

"A male lover? No, we're not. Those words are for men who are too scared to do what their heart tells them. We call ourselves wolves. We move in a pack and if ever we need to be with the wolverines, we fuck them fast so they can get on with the breeding and they don't bother us anymore."

Carro grinned. Wolves. He liked that. Moving in a pack, no obligations to nagging women, and their parents wanting payment for offspring. No need to let himself become trapped in a marriage for the sake of appearance. He'd be independent, like his real father, and not a limp dishrag like the merchant.

"All right," he whispered, his voice hoarse. "Show me."

Nolan did.

They were beyond the reach of the glow of their fire and found each other purely by touch. There was nothing Carro hadn't seen or done before, but Nolan was gentle, and Carro forgot his doubts. He even forgot what those doubts had been.

Some time later, when the sky had gone black as midwinter night in the City of Glass, he lay in Nolan's arms in the grass staring up at the flicker of firelight on the tree trunks. The branches made ghostly shadows which jumped about like a bunch of those other horrid things Chevakia had and the City of Glass did not: bugs.

Farey called out into the night, "Hey, you two, stop clowning. Look at this!"

Nolan let go and raised himself, pulling up his trousers. Carro pushed himself up and scoured for his pants and shirt on the forest floor. He shook leaves off and jumped about on one foot while getting into his pants. He stumbled into the clearing a bit after Nolan did.

Jeito pointed at the horizon.

"What is it?" asked Nolan, staring where Jeito pointed.

"There's . . ." Jeito's eyes were wide.

They all stared at the horizon, which, as far as Carro could see, looked just as it had before. But a cold chill went over him with a breath of icy wind. He heard faint echoes of voices in his mind. If he couldn't see it, but he could hear the nagging voice of his stepfather, then it could only be . . .

Nolan whispered, "Icefire."

Icefire here in Chevakia?

CHAPTER 12

SADY SPENT most of the next few days talking to fellow senators, mostly in factions, because there wasn't the time to do it individually. Four trains had left for Fairlight, and he needed a decision before they could return. So he was going to challenge at the next session, because the authority to send trains wasn't his to make unless he won.

Over the years, the doga senators had developed a ritual for these canvassing meetings. It meant he announced his visit to the owner of the office some time in advance. The faction leader or senior senator would call in all the faction members, and the potential challenger would sit at the senator's desk while everyone else stood around the perimeter of the room. Sometimes, there would be food.

Over all his years in the doga, Sady had attended several of those canvassing sessions. They happened with disturbing regularity. He had always been in the audience, always somewhere at the back, closest to the door. He had always disliked the backstabbing and had often wondered why the backstabbers couldn't just get on with their work and leave the leadership to do theirs.

He saw that attitude in quite a number of his listeners, those who leaned against the wall, arms crossed over their chest. They were probably happy enough with Destran's performance and saw no reason for a challenge, or they didn't care. They thought a challenge was a waste of time and resources. He knew; he'd thought the same so often.

But this time was different. This time, the country was at stake.

Then again, he wondered if those challengers hadn't thought exactly the same thing every time they challenged. With all the abuse for not much of a stipend, certainly senators did this for the love of the country, and they challenged because they believed the current Proctor's hold on the situation was broken.

Some challenges had been successful, some not, but all challengers had believed they were doing the right thing. And for all of them, life had never been the same. There was no way he could go back to being a quiet senator after this.

So he watched the preliminary votes, or intention-to-votes, in a detached numbness. Destran still had many supporters. Too many, if he had to be honest.

He spent a long time before the meeting staring at his account balance, as if the action of staring at it would somehow increase it to a level high enough to pay for the sending of the trains if he failed to gain office.

"So what happens after the meeting?" Viki asked, in a low voice, when walking through the corridors to the doga session where he had planned to make his move.

Everyone knew it was coming, and senators scrambled out of his way, or gave him pitying looks.

"I win or I lose. Either way, you will be the Chief Meteorologist." Sady felt tight as a wound spring. If he won, funding for his projects would be a battle, but if he lost, he'd have to cut Viki's stipend to pay for the trains before resigning in disgrace.

Viki nodded, his face determined.

Sady hurt inside. He could be cutting short the young man's career as meteorologist, just now when Viki had become a lot more confident at handling requests and no longer fell apart when a senior senator asked a tricky question.

"You'll surely win," Viki said in that disarming way of his.

"I don't think so. I don't feel confident at all."

"But if you lose, what will you do?"

"I can't go back to being a quiet senator. There would be constant distrust surrounding me." At least he had never taken up the offer to live in doga-owned accommodation, but still, his stipend would be gone, and he'd need another way to pay for himself, never mind the staff. He could teach meteorology at the Scriptorium, or maybe in Arania . . . "I might join my brother on the farm."

He'd said it as a joke, and he tried to convince himself by laughing, but it came out wrong. Mercy, he was tense. It wasn't just his situation that worried him. He worried about the consequences to the country if he lost.

They arrived at the hall, Sady in front and Viki walking behind him, clutching his notes with more worrying meteorological data. No one had been able to raise Fairlight on the wire. Communication with Mekta was patchy at best. There was too much crackle on the lines so that not even the automated barygraph readings could be trusted. Because of the line outages there had been no reports of sonorics measurements, which had to be taken in person by the local meteorology officer. Sonorics in the border might well have spiked, but there was no way of knowing.

The senators at the hall's entrance stepped back to let Sady and Viki through into the richly wood-panelled hall. There was a broad stairway leading down into the hall, with the senator's benches on both sides. Men and women who had been talking to each other on the stairs stopped and watched Sady and Viki walk past. Others, already seated, stopped talking, too, and by the time Sady sat down in his usual bench, almost every senator was looking at him, including Destran, who sat on a chair behind the dais, nervously shuffling through his notes.

Sady pretended to ignore the attention. He made a show of studying the meeting's agenda, in an outwardly calm way. Inside, his nerves raged. He had never imagined what Milleus had felt when he took over, although he remembered that day well. It was in the middle of the Aranian war, when senator Milleus had taken up his former position as army lieutenant, and he and his balloon squads had taken the first victory against the western invaders.

Proctors were rarely elected at term. The Chevakian people usually re-elected whoever was in charge until that person's colleagues staged a coup. The challenges were the subject of much gossip and street theatre. Tomorrow, his name was going to be all over the gossip circuit. He'd heard some rumours already. *Who did you say was going to challenge? You have to be kidding.* Tiverians were said to be staid and calm, but they loved their political bloodlettings.

Everyone in the hall took their places.

Destran rose from his seat and opened the meeting. He listed the agreed agenda points and asked for emergency items to be added. This was a formulaic requirement normally read without much enthusiasm. It was also an invitation for a challenge.

At this point, everyone fell quiet and looked at Sady, and Sady rose, as if in a dream, a very bad dream.

"I have a point to add."

Destran glared at him. Standing here in the spot of light coming in from the ceiling, he looked very old and tired.

"I want a vote of no confidence."

The entire hall broke out in cheers and shouts.

Destran hammered the dais and eventually a semblance of silence returned. He continued glaring at Sady. "And why do you think that the doga will vote against me?"

Destran had been challenged a few times before, and had always won comfortably. If nothing else, he was surprisingly tough to unseat. Because he divided his opposition.

Sady ploughed on. "A good number of senators have become distrustful of your handling of the sonorics crisis. By pretending it doesn't exist, you—"

"And Alius continuously confirms that there isn't half as much a crisis as you say there is," a senator yelled at the back of the hall. "You're all making this up for your own advantage."

"Alius is not coming forward with any kind of solution about this, even though I've asked him, even though he promises that we will have medicine. But that aside. Alius is not a meteorologist. He does not see the large patterns and the looming food shortages. We cannot wait any longer. We don't like this situation any more than anyone else here does. Ignoring the facts does not make them go away. I want this country to survive. I want every person in Chevakia to be safe."

He looked all around the hall. "Destran continues to play down the danger. The truth is, the earlier reprieve we had from rising sonorics has been brief. The truth is that levels are rising rapidly. The last-measured level of sonorics at Fairlight was seventy-three motes per cube. Last measured. We have lost contact with Fairlight. These levels may well pour so much energy into the barrier plates that they will shatter. The truth is that a massive low-pressure cell is building over the southern plateau. There will be a snowstorm like none of us have seen in our lifetimes. I have taken it upon myself to send four trains for the evacuation of Fairlight. The drivers have risked their own lives to volunteer for this job. I have risked my life to visit the border regions. There are as yet unconfirmed sighting of eagles in the region. My sources report civil unrest in the City of Glass. That is what we're facing, and this situation will not go away by ignoring it. Are you willing to go on with a Proctor who stands by and does nothing?"

The hall descended into shouting and yelling, until Destran hammered on the dais, and by the time a measure of silence returned, a group of senators at the back of the hall were chanting, "Vote, vote, vote."

They were mostly Sady's supporters, and he noted with unease that a lot of other senators didn't yell support.

"Senator Sadorius han Chevonian, are you challenging?"

"I am." Never had two words meant more for Sady, not when Milleus said them, not when Destran said them. A trickle of sweat ran down his back. "I am challenging for the sake of Chevakia, because I want our land to survive and defend itself."

A lot of senators cheered.

"So, we vote." Destran's voice had gone flat and emotionless. "All those in favour of the challenger, Sadorius han Chevonian."

Hands went up. Not as many as Sady had hoped. He noted several of the senators who kept their hands down had stood at the back of the room during canvassing meetings. Destran's support was still strong.

People started moving around to lobby others to change their vote, both ways. The arbiters shouted for people to stay seated, but still, there was so much chaos in the hall that counters had to recount three times before the result was announced.

"Sixty-three in favour."

This was followed by shouts from the audience.

Any vote for Proctor needed a two-thirds majority, which he clearly didn't have. Which Destran didn't have either.

Senators already lined up to negotiate with him. More money for alternative industry to reduce the central region's dependency on mining. Sady could agree to that. There would have to be the revival of a lot of military industry, which would benefit the central region, because of the mines.

More money for education in the south. That was harder to promise, because no one knew what the immediate future would bring for the south. He sent Viki to the telegraph office for the latest news. The response was erratic, with reports that would take a lot more time to appreciate, and still no news from Fairlight. The wildly fluctuating sonorics levels prompted some to say that the barygraphs were broken.

While this was going on, factions were convening on the floor, and changing their votes to stand in blocs. Message boys delivered their requests to the rival candidates.

The north demanded its railways if they were to vote in favour—Sady cursed at that. But he desperately needed the north's support, so he made some sort of half-hearted promise on the damned train lines.

Mercy, he hated these kinds of votes-for-money deals, and they didn't stop with the demands from the north. The east wanted better telegraph lines. The west wanted export regulations to Arania to be relaxed. Mercy, mercy. Even if he agreed to some, there were always other demands, and other senators claiming unfairness because senator so-and-so got their wish. They were all like little children around the honey pot. And he was the bee stupid enough to have been caught in the frenzy.

The more the process wore on, the more he wished he could follow the one senator who walked out in disgust.

At the end of the afternoon, there was another vote which delivered a grand majority of two . . . in favour of senator Sadorius han Chevonian. So in the still-noisy hall, he walked down the stairs and took the ceremonial cloak and hammer from Destran, whose face twisted in a sneer. Whose face reminded Sady of Milleus' when that same fate befell his brother. He wanted to say sorry, except he was not, really. He didn't dislike Destran as a person, and his likes and dislikes had nothing to do with politics anyway. Besides, Destran looked furious.

He hissed through clenched teeth, "You and your family are all the same. Enjoy it while you can. It won't last." He turned abruptly and stormed out, leaving Sady to stare at his retreating back, feeling the literal and figurative weight of the Proctor's cloak on his shoulders.

Mercy.

What had he done?

CHAPTER 13

DARA AND MYRA spent a long time packing, far too long for Loriane's liking. She had nothing to pack and, with more and more people streaming into the town, wanted to be gone as soon as possible.

She carried her meagre possessions into the shed, where the bear was snorting nervously and the camel stood chewing peacefully and Ruko sat atop Tandor's chest. Well, she couldn't see him of course, but something threw a ball of twine into the air and caught it again and again.

"We can use Tandor's sled," Loriane said when Ontane stumbled into the shed after her, carrying a heavy travel chest.

He put his load down. "Where we be going we can't use a sled. Snow stops quickly down the side of the platform."

"Then how are we going to get to this hunting shack?" By the skylights, she hated the idea of another trek.

"We walk, and take the camel and a cart."

He pulled a rough cloth off a strange contraption in a corner of the shed. It was completely made out of wood—it had to be worth a fortune—and moved smoothly on the ground on two round things on either side.

"What, ye never seen wheels, mistress?"

Loriane shook her head. Like the sled, it had a tray and two beams on which to tie the animal.

"Cart." She repeated the strange Chevakian word.

He slapped his hand on the tray. "We'll put all our things here and your man on the saddle."

Loriane was going to say that he wasn't *her* man but couldn't muster the energy. She went up the stairs, ignored the piercing stare from Dara in the kitchen, and tried to get Tandor to sit up. He mumbled some incoherent words, but wouldn't open his eyes more than a sliver. His face looked horrible, half-covered in caked blood. Most of his long hair was gone. But for all she could see, his injuries were superficial.

"Come on, Tandor, stop behaving like this and help me." She shook his shoulders. His eyelids flickered, but he did not otherwise react to her. "Tandor, come on. I can't move you by myself. I've had enough of this. I know you can hear us, so help me, by the skylights."

But her words made no difference.

Slowly, she dressed him in his filthy overclothes. She had scrubbed some of the caked and dried blood and mud out of his cloak, but the furs smelled terrible.

His eyelids flickered and his eyes seemed to gain focus.

"Come on, Tandor, talk to me."

He opened his mouth, but at that moment there was a rushing sound and she was roughly pushed aside so that she fell into the chair that stood before the hearth.

"Hey, watch out!" she yelled at Ruko, who was now lifting Tandor off the bed. "Tandor, tell him that he's rude."

But Tandor had gone back to being non-responsive.

Ruko carried him down the stairs, and Loriane followed, glad for his assistance, because she wouldn't have gotten him down. In the shed, Ontane had put a saddle on the camel and was lashing a pack to the cart.

Dara strode into the shed carrying another pack, which she added to the pile already waiting to be put onto the cart. Ontane heaved the pack his wife had given him onto the cart.

"There be something you wish to take, mistress?" Ontane asked.

Loriane glanced at Tandor's chest on the sled. It was much too big to fit onto the cart with all the packs Dara had brought. Yet she couldn't leave it here. They might not come back. The refugees might destroy it. Tandor never travelled without it.

"I . . ." She walked to the chest, fingering the lid.

"It be clear that we can't take that entire thing," Dara said, before she turned away and left the shed, no doubt to get more packs from the kitchen.

Yes, Loriane could understand that, but why did this woman have to be so rude about it?

If she left Tandor's things here, vital information could be lost. She should at least take something. The books, at least.

Yet she shuddered at the idea of going through Tandor's things and finding goodness-knew-what. Like that horrid beating heart in the jar. She couldn't even blame rude and simple-minded Dara for not wanting to take that. What would she do with it?

She braced herself and pushed the lid—

—*No*, Tandor screamed in his mind, *don't take it.*

Ruko laughed. "They won't hear you. They're stupid, meaningless people."

"They saved me."

"They prevented you being saved. They are stupid."

"Why are you talking like this? You are meant to listen to me. What are you doing here? I thought I told you to guard this town."

"I'm not going to listen to a weakling like you. There's no point staying here. You don't command me, and the others don't command me. I'm going with them to Chevakia."

"You can't. You'll vanish as soon as you cross the border."

"Then I'll just have to return to my normal form, won't I?"

—the lid opened.

Dara walked past again with another look at Loriane. "Take some of his clothes, but we'll have to leave the rest of that thing here."

"I'd like to take all of it."

Dara's eyes widened. "Don't you see there be no room? We need food and blankets and the tent. We have no room for silly things like books."

"I have hardly anything to take. This can take the space for both of us."

"But we can't—"

"Look!" Ontane said.

Tandor had stiffened. His eyes were wide.

Loriane said, "See? He knows we're talking about him. He doesn't want his things to be left behind. There is important information in Tandor's books."

"And I'm saying that everything on that cart is for all of us. Food, blankets, tent—"

"I have to take it, or I'll never find his family—"

Ontane stepped between them. "Ladies, ladies, stop the fight—"

—"I forbid you to return to your normal form!" Tandor called in that place between life and death.

Ruko laughed. "You forbid? You have no say over me anymore. Never had any, coward. I've had enough of hanging around in this stupid village."

"And you'll have to hang around here some more. I want you to see what happens with all these refugees here—"

"I'm coming. Watch me." He went to Tandor's travel chest.

—Myra screamed, "Look, Da!" and pointed.

The clothes that lay atop the contents of the chest moved by themselves. Then the invisible hands rummaged through the contents underneath, pushing aside underclothes and books, and unearthed the glass jar with its grisly contents.

Lifted it. The jar stopped in mid-air.

Ontane stood watching, his eyes wide.

Myra came up behind him. The baby in a fur sling across her chest gave out muffled cries.

Ruko, for it must be he holding the jar, turned to her and held it out to her. The contents of the jar pulsed with blue glow. Myra's eyes widened.

"Da? Mistress Loriane? What's happening?"

"I think he wants you to take it," Loriane said.

"What is that thing? It's . . . disgusting." She shrank back.

When Myra made no attempt to take the jar, Ruko retreated. The jar went up, and before anyone could do anything, Ruko had smashed it on the ground. Myra screamed. Even Tandor uttered a cry.

Shattered glass lay in a heap in the straw, and amongst it, the pulsing heart.

Ontane muttered, "By the skylights, it be alive."

But Myra was still staring at the spot where Loriane suspected Ruko to be, in the middle of the barn.

"What?" she whispered. "What do you want me to . . ."

She knelt on the ground.

Her mother shouted, "Myra, don't touch it—"

—Tandor jumped forward, but his virtual body was insubstantial and his real body still refused to obey his will.

He grabbed hold of Ruko's arm, but his hand went straight through it. Ruko laughed.

"You have to learn how to be a ghost."

"What are you going to do in Chevakia?"

"I'm going to offer my services to this mistress of yours, because she seems to have more backbone than you."

"She's my *mother*, by the skylights, and she's a horrible old woman. She cares only about revenge, no matter who gets hurt."

By the skylights, he did not want his mother to get her hands on Ruko—

—But Myra had already picked up the pulsing heart in her hands. She rose, holding it out. The fluid from the jar dripped off her hands and spread a pungent odour through the shed.

The heart vanished, as if eaten up by the air.

—Tandor lunged.

He fell straight through Ruko's body and landed hard on the floor, next to his body. He scrambled up, called strands of icefire and lashed them around Ruko's upper body, even while the heart vanished into his chest.

Ruko twisted and snapped the strands, but as his body oozed icefire and faded from the in-between world, one strand hit him in the back of his head and looped around his neck. The strand stretched and grew thinner and thinner—

—There was a flash of light. Myra screamed. Loriane clapped her hands over her face.

When Loriane uncovered her eyes, a young man stood in the middle of the barn. He was longhaired and filthy, dressed in a ripped shirt and trousers held up only by a piece of string, clothes far too small for him. He was skinny and his arms were covered in bruises and scratches.

Dara was staring at him. She whispered, "Ruko? Is that you?"

He said nothing, just stood there. Like Isandor, he had only one foot, bare and red from the cold, the other leg ending in a wooden stump. His eyes were black and hollow.

"Ye always said he be gone, here's yer proof that he didn't," Ontane said. "I always seen him, every time the sorcerer brung him in here. Believe me now, woman?"

Dara snorted. "I don't know that he be real. He don't look too real to me. Hey—you, say something." She stepped up to stare into the boy's face.

"Hey, can you hear me?"

—Tandor laughed. "You thought you could get away from me?"

Ruko's voice was distant, his form in that in-between world little more than insubstantial mist. "Fuck you. I'll get you. Your control over me is only weak."

—He said nothing. His face was impassive and menacing, Loriane thought.

"Hey!" Dara poked him in the chest. "An adult asks you a question."

He merely stepped back.

Dara snorted. "See? He be nothing but a ghost. Body be here, but the brain be somewhere else. I always said the sorcerer be up to no good."

All of a sudden, Ruko jumped into action. He flung all of Tandor's possessions inside the trunk and snapped the lid shut hard. Then he heaved it on top of the cart with a thunk.

Ontane protested, "Hey, that be the space for our things."

Ruko didn't react. Without a word, he turned to Tandor—

"Come, old man, the situation has changed. I am real and you are not. I think I'm going to have some fun."

"Ruko, I forbid you—"

"—you're my servitor now." He laughed.

✳

—and heaved him into the saddle of the camel as if he were no more than a small child.

Dara was elbowing her husband in the side. "Go on, stop him. That be the place where we need to put our things."

"Stop it, woman. What do ye think I can do? Have ye seen how strong he be?"

"Oh, ye men be useless!" She stomped to the cart and tried to heave off Tandor's trunk, but she couldn't lift it. "Hey, you! Take this thing off, or we'll have nothing to eat!"

Ruko had been tying Tandor's legs to the saddle straps, but now he wheeled around.

Ontane yelled, "Watch it, woman!"

Ruko pushed Dara aside. She fell bottom first in the straw.

"Ma!" Myra yelled.

Dara screamed, "Did ye see that? He hit me! Do something about that creep, useless lump!"

"There be no time for fights. There be room for our packs to go on top." He picked up a couple of bags, but Ruko had taken the camel by the lead and was leading it towards the door of the shed.

"Hey! Wait!" Ontane yelled, hobbled after the cart and flung the bags on top of Tandor's trunk.

"We still need to get some things from the kitchen," Dara protested.

"No time. You already spent so much time packing. We best move our sorry backsides afore everyone out there wakes up to where we be going and wants to come with us. There be only so much space in the hunting shack."

Ontane lifted the latch and pushed the shed doors.

They would only open halfway, because the refugees had built an igloo outside. Ruko let go of the reins and gave the doors a huge shove, simply pushing aside snow heaped up behind them.

Loriane expected to be swamped with requests for food and shelter, but all refugees were further down the street, staring in the direction of the plain.

Behind her, Myra gasped. "By the skylights."

"What's going on?" Loriane asked.

"The whole sky is crackling with icefire." She gave Loriane a strange look. "You can't see it?"

Loriane shook her head.

"This is like the wall we saw in the City of Glass. The dome of icefire, expanding outwards."

"Can you see . . . anyone?" Loriane asked. Myra had told her that she'd seen her boyfriend, the father of her baby, as a giant figure of burning icefire.

Myra shook her head. Her eyes glittered.

"Is it going to stop when it reaches the edge of the plateau?" she asked.

Ontane shrugged. "It'll stop at the border. Chevakians have barriers."

Ruko turned the camel into the street.

They crossed the village, where refugees hung around their igloos, camped in the lee side of buildings. There were even some Knights of junior rank, trying to organise people into some sort of order. Loriane caught shards of yelling. ". . . and then, once we've registered all your names, you will be given passes for food . . ."

"Hmph. Wonder where he be planning to get food from," Dara muttered.

A man asked where Ontane and his group were going, and Ontane mentioned relatives in some place that meant nothing to Loriane.

"You should tell them about what's coming," Loriane said.

"They'll find out soon enough. We'll have a head start."

As awful as it was, he was right, and she hadn't the energy to protest.

The crowds grew thinner and they left the last of the houses of the village behind. From here, the path sloped constantly down, and soon they reached the edge of the southern plateau where the steep cliffs fell. Far below them spread the rolling hills of Chevakia, looking furred and black in the morning light.

It was the first time in her life that Loriane saw land that was not covered in snow. She understood that what looked like black fur from here were *trees,* even though she had only seen pictures of those strange things.

The terrain plunged off the cliff-side into a tangle of rocks. Ruko led the camel deftly through places where Loriane couldn't see a path. Ontane had been right in that the sled wouldn't have gone down here. At first, there was still a meagre cover of snow, but it was wet and sometimes frozen over. Later, it was just wet.

The cart had enough trouble getting through with all the rocks and the steep slope. Ruko walked at the front leading the protesting, camel, and Ontane at the back pushed the cart when the terrain was too uneven for it to roll across. Sometimes he and Dara both needed to hang on to stop the cart rolling down. Sometimes they needed to lift the cart over rocks. It was slow going, it was wet, and as the day progressed, Loriane grew ever more weary. She was top-heavy, out-of-balance and half the time couldn't see where she put her feet.

Some time in the morning, she stepped on a particularly slippery patch of mud and fell hard on her side.

"Loriane!" Myra called.

Loriane sat there, wetness seeping into her clothes. It had started drizzling and thick clouds of mist billowed up the cliff side, obscuring the land below from view.

That mist now revealed the stumpy form of Dara, rushing back. "Mistress Loriane, are you all right?"

"Think so."

Dara grabbed her under the arms and heaved her back onto her feet. "By the skylights, ye be even bigger than Sinna was with the twins. You must be exhausted."

"I'm all right," Loriane said, but she felt tears pricking in her eyes. "Is it far to where we're going?"

"Oh, if we'd be going where we planned to go, ye'd already be there, but since we can't—"

"What do you mean—can't?" She hated how her voice spilled over. Yes, she had noticed how Dara and Ontane had been fighting, but she had been too busy not falling to hear what they said. "Why didn't you say anything before? Where are we going?"

"Truth be told, mistress, I wish I knew that meself." Ontane came stomping up the path. "But with that spectacle of icefire coming, we'd not have been safe. The hunting shack be only uphill from town."

"Then where to? All the way to Chevakia?" Loriane stared into the mist.

"If that's what it takes, yes."

"I can't walk that far."

"You'll have to, mistress, nothing be helped."

Myra gave her father a furious look. "Can't you at least help her?"

"Child, what do you think we're doing here? It be hard enough getting the cart down this rotten path without you women bellyaching. I wish, too, that we could put our feet up in the shack, but that bain't going to happen, and whether you complain or not, it can't be helped. I'll say it again: it can't be helped."

"No need to be rude about it," Myra said. When her light blue eyes met Loriane's, her expression softened.

"Take my arm," she said.

She held out her left arm. The sleeve of her right arm hung limply below the shoulder.

For some reason, Loriane remembered taking the little bundle of fur from Tandor's arms containing Isandor. A premature baby, his eyes unfocused, his arms and back covered in sparse but unusually long black hair. The stump of a leg withered below the knee. In the first days, she had worried about the frostbite to his single foot, and she had worried about looking after an imperfect child.

Isandor, where was he now? Would she ever see him again?

They kept going.

At first the path was steep, slippery and snow covered. Soon the mist overtook them and turned the world dreary and grey. Ruko led the camel, the beast picking its way between the rocks as if it knew the way. On occasion, it would stop and then everyone would have to lift the cart over some rock or another, but those times became fewer and further in between.

They encountered no other people, although sometimes Loriane thought she could hear voices amongst the rocks behind them, but even when the view cleared occasionally, she could not discern any movement further up the cliff.

When the path allowed, Myra came to walk next to her.

"Have you named the babe yet?"

"His name is Beido," Myra said, and her eyes glistened. Beido was the father of the child, one of those Tandor had gone to rescue, and failed.

"Was his father . . . like Ruko?" She glanced at Ruko's back, at the head of the column, leading the camel.

"No, not like that." Her eyes went distant.

"What happened to him back there in the shed with Ruko? One moment I couldn't see him, and the next, I could."

"When his heart was in the jar, he was Tandor's servitor, his utter slave. But servitors can't exist where there is little or no icefire, so he needed to have his heart back, or otherwise he couldn't flee with us."

"But he's still a ghost."

"I don't know why that happened either. It almost looks like the conversion back was incomplete. Maybe it needs someone with more skill than I . . ." She shuddered.

"I didn't know that conversion back was possible." Loriane had always heard that the king's servitors had died when the Knights killed the king, and that this was the only way to kill a servitor: by killing its master. "I think this icefire is evil. I don't know why Tandor is playing with it."

"There are good things—"

"When you can use it to enslave someone, I don't want to know about good things. Why can't we forget about the whole dreadful business? In the City of Glass, we all lived together, and then Tandor comes in with his talk about Pirosians and Thillei as if there were only two types of people. Things don't work like that in the City of Glass, not at least in the Outer City. The Knights don't have just Pirosians; they have Thillei, too, and all kinds of people in between, other clans, whose names you won't even know. All those clans have intermarried, and all the breeders will have been from different clans." But, she thought with a chill, those with a high percentage of pure blood tended to be more fertile, especially within the Pirosians. And there were legends about the strange occurrences of offspring of two pure members from different clans. She'd seen some crude drawings in the books kept by midwives in the palace. Most of them were very old, and current midwives dismissed the reports of malformed children with six limbs or with *wings* as fantasies. Those children were, they said, badly malformed Imperfects drawn to look more dramatic to justify their sacrifice to the wild bears. If those things existed, the midwives would have preserved the foetuses in jars.

Looking after Isandor, Loriane had changed her views on Imperfects. The Knights liked to picture them as evil demons, but they were just people with limbs missing. She suspected that over time a lot of the palace midwives had come to think the same, so trying to hide their deeds behind demonic depictions of the Imperfect children seemed only a logical step.

Just like the making of servitors was evil, so was the insistence of the Knights on killing all Imperfects.

As they descended the path, Loriane cursed herself, and Tandor, and the camel and the glutinous, slippery substance Myra called *mud*.

Never having seen a ground uncovered by snow, Loriane wasn't impressed by it. It rained—and rain was like snow, only wet—and progress down the rocky slope was slow. Myra helped her, the babe asleep in a sling on her back.

Loriane wished many times that she carried hers outside of her body instead of within it. She was sure that by now the babe had gone well over its expected date. Her legs ached and pressure of the babe's head made her need to seek privacy behind rocks many times. She would re-emerge, just as aching and sore, and having earned another scornful look from Dara. Yes, she slowed down their progress. Yes, they heard voices up there and the horde up there was probably catching up, but she couldn't help it.

By the time they reached the furry mass that Myra called the forest, Loriane was bone-weary.

An odd thing it was, too, this forest. In the City of Glass, little grew outside, even in the high-sun season. On occasions when she had been in nobles' houses, she had seen the "greenhouses" they kept, in which they grew plants. Little waist-high things they called trees that their keepers clipped and kept tidy. Those things were nothing like this. These trees were huge, with straight trunks and feathery branches which flapped in the wind. They made so much *noise*.

And she really didn't like making camp amongst the pillared trunks, where a fire cast flapping shadows into a mass of tangled wood. Anything could be hiding out there, and they would have no means to see it.

At least Tandor had recovered a little. Still strapped to the harness on the camel's back, colour had returned in his skin.

In this forest, they stopped for the night.

What Ontane had called a tent turned out to be little more than a canvas roof. Loriane lay down next to Myra and her babe, under the cover of furs and blankets. But she couldn't get comfortable and couldn't sleep. Her back ached, her belly ached and her legs ached. The babe wriggled inside her, kicking her ribs.

After staring into the darkness for what felt like an eternity, she rose, and picked her way into the forest. In the pitch dark, she crouched for another agonising piss. This time, she sat down on a fallen tree trunk and rubbed her fingers across her wetness. Imagined the pain, the stretching, the sheer hard work of pushing out a child. Nine times, she had done it. Nine times, she had felt the slimy head emerge from her body. Right now, she'd welcome the pain with open arms. She'd do it silently, because no one of the family needed to know what was going on. In any case, there was no need to scream. Screaming was for first-timers. She squatted, her back against the tree trunk, gulping deep breaths as she would do when pains became intense. She waited for tightening aches across her belly, but felt nothing of the sort. She dug her icy hands under her layers of clothing, took her swollen breast in her hands and rolled the nipple between her fingers until it hurt. Previous times she had done this, it had brought on the birth pains. This time, all it did was make her sore. She cried silently up at the stars.

Please, please.

CHAPTER 14

MILLEUS SIPPED his tea, leaning his elbows on the kitchen table. Firelight flickered through the kitchen, making Isandor's hair glisten. He had dropped his spoon by his empty bowl and leaned his head in his hands. For a moment he sagged, then he jerked up and looked into Milleus' eyes, a guilty expression over his young face.

"Oh. Excuse me." He rubbed his face.

"You're tired." Milleus said. It was not a question.

Both youngsters had worked hard all day. Isandor had chopped the entire pile of firewood and had helped Milleus straighten the collapsed fence.

Nila stared into the fire, her look distant. She was also tired, her cheeks red from being outside. She had spent all day in the garden, doing an admirable job for someone who had never seen a plant that didn't grow in a pot.

Milleus asked what they ate in the City of Glass, and Isandor said there were no vegetables, but that everyone drank milk or ate meat, dried, salted or frozen. Nila said people grew some things in greenhouses under the city.

To which Isandor said, "No, not much."

"Yes, people grow things, and eat them."

"Not us. I never had any." He switched to his own language, and they exchanged a few words.

"Not everyone eats vegetables," Nila said, and Isandor nodded, as if it was a consensus summary.

It became ever more clear that the two came from different backgrounds, and this was probably the reason why they had run away.

Milleus said, "Look, why don't you two go to sleep. I'll clean up."

"No, you have been so kind to us," Nila said. "We must help."

"No way. You've done enough."

She had even cleaned up his living room and kitchen with a dedication and precision of someone who did very little of that kind of work. He was almost ashamed of the mess in his cupboards. Mercy, the beetles! Some of the crockery hadn't been touched for years and a thin layer of mould and dust covered the white porcelain. But this morning, she had taken it all out, wiped the plates and put them back.

"Please," he said. "Go to sleep. There will be plenty of work tomorrow. I can take care of these three bowls."

That seemed to sway her.

"Good night." She rose, came to him and gave him a peck on the forehead, just like his daughter-in-law used to do. She smelled of sunshine.

Isandor got up, too, and they both left the kitchen.

Instead of cleaning up, Milleus leaned back staring into the fire. He hadn't seen either of his sons and his grandchildren since he'd come to live on the farm, now a few years ago. He couldn't get his son's angry look out of his mind, that day at Suri's funeral, as if he said, *you killed her*.

Never.

Never would Milleus have thought that Suri would take her own life. She seemed happy, even though they had slept in separate rooms for years. They had come to a silent agreement to make the marriage functional. He brought in the money—she took care of the family things.

That day when he had come home and found her on the couch, white and not breathing, felt like an absurd nightmare. At times, when he thought of Tiverius, he would think that he'd come back to his usual home, the Proctor's residence, and that Suri would be there waiting for him.

Why had she done it? Why?

Because he didn't care about her, the gossip went, because he ignored her.

It was untrue. He did care for Suri; he cared a lot. It was just that she didn't find she could return his care in the way he desired back then: by coming to his bed. She had always been afraid of intimacy, her mother had revealed. At the time, he'd been talking about retiring to a pleasant place in the country. He had sometimes wondered if that prospect frightened her too much. Sometimes she would shut herself in her room and wouldn't come out for a whole day, not even for dinner. She grew thin and gaunt.

These days, there was no use stewing over it. He'd gone over all these things so many times, he couldn't possibly add anything new to it. It happened, and it shouldn't have. He could possibly have helped, but he hadn't seen it coming. In any case, it could never be changed.

He heaved himself to his feet, bones creaking. Mercy, he was too old for all this hard work. Never mind the bowls. He'd wash them in the morning.

He banked the fire and shuffled out of the room. When he walked past the guest wing corridor, he heard a squeaking noise, like a door opening.

Oh, those youngsters weren't . . .

He went back into the kitchen, opened the door as quietly as he could and stalked into the garden. Mercy, it was cold tonight. Most unseasonable.

There's something going on in the south. Sady's words. He wished he'd questioned his brother more.

It was dark in the garden, with the newly weeded beds deep with dark soil that spilled over the top of his boots when he accidentally stepped in it.

Soft light radiated from the window of Suri's mother's room, gilding the tangle of bushes in the courtyard between the main house and the guest wing. Milleus clambered through the overgrown mess and glimpsed inside, feeling dreadful and sure that the kids would be looking back at him, jeering *ha, ha, gotcha!*

But both of them were much too . . . involved with each other to have taken note of any noise Milleus made. Firelight glowed over the pale skin of Isandor's back, half-covered by the sheet. Nila lay under him, legs apart, rocking her hips with each languid thrust, her eyes closed and mouth open in total bliss.

And images from the past rushed up at him.

"A whore?" Suri's eyes had burned with anger. "You went to see a whore?"

The word hurt.

"There were six of us, and she was a dancer. It's the custom in Arania. It's how men entertain important guests. Nothing happened." Entertaining, that was all he seemed to do since entering the doga.

"Milleus, how could you?"

"Suri, I swear, it was nothing. Not important." Not counting the urgency-filled moments he'd spent in the bed in the upstairs bedroom. Sorry, but sometimes he liked to be with a woman who enjoyed his touch, or had the grace to pretend.

He reached out and snaked an arm around Suri's waist.

"You will always be my princess."

A kiss, full on the lips. "Want to be my princess right now?"

She squirmed away. "Milleus, you're drunk."

"Yes, deliciously so."

He guided her down on the bed. She spread her legs willingly enough, and that was an improvement on last year, after she had just lost the baby, but she cried when he entered her.

He bit down a curse. "I won't do it anymore if it hurts you so much."

She said nothing—he knew how desperate she was for a child— but held her breath through much of the action when she lay under him, frozen, while he tried to do the job as quickly as possible.

There was nothing enjoyable about it. He had imagined things so differently.

So different from Isandor's relaxed movements. As if he had all night, and indeed he did. No wonder they had still been asleep this morning when he found them in Suri's mother's large bed, curled up against each other. They could do as they wanted. They were young, they were free and they were very much in love.

Milleus turned away from the window. Nothing he could do about it. If there was any damage, no doubt it had already been done. Who was he to say what the youngsters couldn't do? Were they going to listen to an old bitter man blathering on about marriage before intimacy? What was marriage worth anyway? The girl's parents had probably wanted to marry her off to some dirty old man with money, and she had chosen her lover without money instead.

Isandor worked hard. Nila had cleaned his entire kitchen and sitting room. They were honest, good kids. He'd feed them just as well in the morning, and if they were still here at the start of winter, he'd be standing by to help the girl give birth same as he did with his goats. There was no scandal in bringing into the world the next generation. Heavens knew this house could do with a pair of little feet.

Love was beautiful. There was far too little of it in the world. There had been far too little of it in his family.

He walked back through the garden, cold and alone, wiping a wet trail off his cheek.

If love is so beautiful, Milleus, why did you ignore all those who loved you?

Sady had been kind enough to think of him as someone worthy of support. Fifty signatures. And what had he done?

There was a soft noise, somewhere in the garden. Footsteps, heels on the paving of the garden path.

Someone stood at the front door, a dark shadow.

There was a hard knock on the door, one of those that made the door rattle in its frame.

"Who is there?" Milleus called out, his heart thudding in his chest.

A gasp. The figure turned. "Is that you, Milleus?" A familiar voice: his neighbour Andreus.

"Yes."

Milleus half-ran to the front door, trying to draw attention away from the light in the room across the courtyard, and the activity within. He might not mind it, but this was the country, and people in these parts were old-fashioned.

"I . . . I had to check on the goats," he said. "Wait. Come in."

Next thing he'd be accused of running a shameful house for fallen youngsters. People in the district talked enough about him already.

Into the kitchen. Milleus turned the wick on the oil lamp up. His hands trembled.

"Now what brings you here at this time of the day?"

His neighbour stood on the doorstep, eyes blazing. "Don't hide it any longer, Milleus. You've got them, don't you?" His gaze rested pointedly on the table and the three bowls from dinner.

"Got what?"

"Who, not what, and you know very well what I'm talking about. Those two people that creep on the bird was looking for."

"Mercy, man, what are you talking about?"

For a moment, the man faced him wordlessly, then he said, in a low voice. "This man on a giant bird came to my house. He didn't wear the uniform, but everything else about him said Eagle Knight. Frightened the wife and children. He said he was looking for some people in the district and said I was going to help him find them. I said I wasn't going to do nothing of the sort and that I knew nothing about no strangers in the district, and then he did this to me." He held out an arm, the skin blistered.

"A burn?" Milleus' skin crawled. He'd seen the bird, but it hadn't landed, and now he knew that had been because the rider had seen Sady approach.

Something going on in the south.

The man's eyes flashed. "A burn all right! He had no weapons, Milleus. Fire came from his hand like lightning. But that's not all. I went to the physic emergency practice to have it attended, but I wasn't allowed in the surgery because I set off the sonorics alarm. When the physic held the sonorics meter to me, it went right up into the red. I had to scrub naked and take decontamination tablets. This creep of a man uses sonorics rays, Milleus." He dropped his voice and held his hand to his mouth, and added, in a whisper, "As in the war. It's filthy foreign magic. And here you are: sheltering the people he's looking for. Why don't you just hand them over and let them get out of here? Let them sort their own filthy problems in the south."

"Why should I give refuge to criminals—"

"Milleus, for the sake of the district you proclaim to love, shut up. I know you're sheltering these people, because I don't, and my neigh-bours don't, and there isn't anyone else to hide them except you."

"They could hide in the forest for all I know."

"And you're feeding the forest three lots of dinner."

Point made.

Milleus sighed. "Can you tell me why you have suddenly become so keen to help a man who has crossed our borders illegally? He *says* the people he's looking for are criminal, but how do you know if that's true?"

The neighbour's eyes flashed. "You're a windbag, Milleus. You can say all these great noble words, but you know nothing of the struggle of the common people. You say these words, but who suffers for them? I don't care what the creep's squabble with those two people is. If we hold out, this man will bring friends and work his magic to harm us. Do you want that? Do you think this foreigner cares who you are? Some has-been member of the doga. He'll be long gone before anyone from Tiverius knows he's here. Give them up. Let him take his trouble home."

Milleus shook his head, while panic filled his chest. He had to protect Isandor and Nila and their young love. Find out who they were, sure enough, but criminals, they weren't. "They're innocent. They're only children."

"Give them up!"

"No."

"And I'm telling you you'll be sorry soon enough, and all of us will suffer for it."

"If that is a threat, you had better reconsider."

"Reconsider what? As far as I know, you're no longer Proctor and you have no power to threaten anyone. I thought, this morning when I heard the rumours that go around the district about you, that you had some guts, but now I see. Get with it, Milleus. You're an old man and no one listens to you."

Red anger flashed before Milleus' eyes.

"Go home, man, before I act on my lack of power to issue threats."

The man glared at him, then turned on his heel and stomped away to his waiting van.

Milleus stood in the doorway, breathing hard.

In his pocket, he clutched the letter. *Fifty signatures . . .*

Who was a powerless old man?

CHAPTER 15

NOLAN LANDED his bird next to Carro's on the dusty farm road. The eagle shook itself and folded its wings. Nolan slid off and gave Carro the knotted rope he used as reins. Carro took it from Nolan's hand. His skin briefly touched Carro's palm. Nolan looked up and met Carro's eyes.

Neither said anything. They knew the drill.

Nolan pushed open the creaky farm gate and crossed a vegetable yard to the door of the house. Such strange houses they had here, too. Walls made from stone blocks and straw roofs.

Burns well, Farey had said yesterday, and had proceeded to demonstrate with an old cranky farmer who wouldn't tell Farey if he'd seen the two fugitives. The farmer's family was hiding behind one of the windows in the house, and when Farey had taken off, he'd flown over the roof and dropped a burning torch.

Woof. The straw burned almost better than the ancient material that formed the roofs of many houses in the Outer City.

Farey laughed.

The old farmer and his family ran for shelter.

They'd frightened a few more families, and with each further house they came to, Carro was more afraid they'd find Isandor and Jevaithi. They had seen the riderless eagle. The beast had been too far away to recognise for certain, but it *could* have been Isandor's. The more he thought about it, the more sure he was that it *had* been Isandor's, because there were only a few wild eagles left, and the books said that in the mountains they didn't grow large enough to carry a man. That only happened under influence of icefire in the City of Glass.

So yes, they would likely find Isandor soon.

Isandor would recognise him, and would plead forgiveness or some such, and Carro didn't think he'd be able to look his former friend in the eye while Farey ran a knife through his heart. There were so many times that Isandor had helped him, or saved him . . .

Nolan knocked hard on the farmhouse door.

After the shoving back of bolts and creaking of hinges, a man opened, holding a sword.

In one movement, Nolan had his staff out and yanked the sword from the old man's hand. It flew through the air and clattered to the ground at Carro's feet.

Carro slid from the eagle, which looked at him as if it wanted to say *Is that all you can get me to eat?* Holding both sets of reins, he knelt and retrieved the sword. The weapon was old and blunt, of the type sometimes sold in the antique markets in the Outer City as having belonged to Chevakian soldiers during the Aranian war. The man was a veteran, clearly.

Meanwhile, the man was whimpering and Nolan shouting in Chevakian. The man was crying, shaking his head. A woman was crying, too.

By the skylights, shut up! Carro wanted to clamp his hands over his ears.

A gust of wind brought a chill.

And Carro's vision faded. He heard, not the cries of the peasants in the farmhouse, but those of fighting youths in the City of Glass. The streets were dark with gloomy pinpricks of light from the odd street lamp. He saw brief glimpses of burning houses and groups of people running through the snow. It had been the night Isandor and Jevaithi escaped.

He tried to banish the memory from his mind.

By the skylights, he thought he'd been cured of the damned affliction.

"Hey, Carro! Carro!" Nolan shouted.

Carro jolted back into full consciousness.

Nolan was running through the yard, pursued by a younger man carrying a powder gun. The peasant stopped, aimed, and there was a loud bang. Something whistled through the air. The eagles pulled on their reins, flapping huge wings over Carro's head. He was almost dragged up into the air.

Nolan flung himself over the fence, scrabbled up, swung himself on the eagle's back and kicked the bird into motion. Carro followed, heading into the icy breeze. Thick smoke billowed up behind him. He tried not to think of the farming family, and what Nolan did to them. Once, when he was young, he had seen his father mistreat his mother—

She was crying and yelling at him, while Carro, about six at the time, hid behind the door.

Carro sits on hands and knees on his sleeping shelf, looking down into the central room of the limpet.

His mother yells, "If you do this again, I will tell my family!"

To which his father responds, "And what do you think they are going do? Admit that their daughter is a selfish sea cow and take her back so she can continue to be a selfish sea cow?"

Carro sniggers, then covers his mouth with his hand, so they won't realise he's listening. It's so entertaining to hear his father yell at someone other than him.

His sister sits next to Carro; she's crying. Carro grins at her.

His mother yells, "My parents will demand to have back their loan. Don't you dare forget what makes you a successful merchant, whose money it is."

"I don't need your damn money, woman."

"No, you just need a sex slave."

Carro clung onto the reins, his hands sweaty.

He had been way too confident lately, had thought that because the visions were gone, he had been cured of them, but not so. Worse, the only thing that could help him, the ichina herb, was not available to him here and the hunters would cast him out if they found out he had an illness. They would tell his father. And his father would disown him, like everyone in his life had disowned him.

So he hung onto the saddle, and peered down to the forest, sweating and feeling sick. He must not give in to these visions. He must banish them.

The hunters' temporary camp was a clearing in the forest big enough for the eagles to land. In the morning, they had piled their camping gear at the base of a tree and put branches on top and covered the fire with dirt and sticks.

It still lay as they had left it; Farey and Jeito were still out.

They went to prepare the camp silently.

Nolan strode to a tree, unhooked a bag from a tree and tossed his bird half a sabre-wolf carcass with the same careless gesture as he had hunted, killed and cut up the animal yesterday. The eagle claimed its prey with a yellow claw. Carro's eagle got the other half of the beast, which Nolan threw with such force that it bounced over the ground and the eagle had to hop after it, only to find that its tether was too short. It gave an annoyed cry. Carro ran to shift the carcass before the bird decided to try chew through the tether. He glanced at Nolan while he did this, but Nolan looked the other way.

While Carro and Nolan relit the fire and uncovered the gear, the birds were ripping up their prey, snapping bones and crunching them in their beaks.

It was so silent that Carro could hear the wind rustle through the trees. Nolan was still not looking at Carro.

Finally, Carro couldn't stand it any longer. He said, "I did something wrong, didn't I?"

Nolan looked up. Oh, his eyes were furious.

"That guy almost killed me. I thought you were there on the look-out! Why didn't you warn me he had a gun?"

Carro had been dreaming, on the verge of getting another spell, but he couldn't say so. He had no medicine for it.

Carro shrugged. "Sorry. I was . . . looking the other way. Thought I saw something."

Nolan's hard stare met his. "I thought you'd look out for me. I thought you cared."

Carro shrugged. "Sorry," he said again.

Sorry was hardly appropriate, and he knew it. You could not say *sorry* so easily to someone who was in love with you. And Nolan was in love. He had said so many times while making love, but Carro hadn't worked out what he thought. Every time Nolan touched him in intimate places, he thought back to the abuse at the eyrie, and he felt the stone under his hands as he clawed at the wall to get away from the tormentors with their cock up his arse. Nolan didn't hurt him as much as the abusers had, and for a while, in the middle of it, he could enjoy the pure sensation. But later, he always wanted to wash the filth off. It was when he crouched near the creek, trying to clean the sticky stuff out of his hair down there, that he felt a seed of hatred grow deep inside him for the way men and women used sex to manipulate others.

He raised the water bladder to his mouth and drank deeply. Nolan was still looking at him, but Carro didn't return his gaze. By the skylights, wasn't it possible for any adult to have *friends* while keeping your clothes on? He finished the water and went to refill the bladder at the spring.

Here, away from the pile of saddlebags, their makeshift shelters and the firewood, the wind soughed through the pine trees. It was a lot colder than it had been yesterday, and the sky was white, rather than blue. Carro shivered. It seemed the cold had quietened the birds.

The grass rustled.

"No, you're not getting away from me that quickly."

He gasped. Nolan blocked his path.

"Looking the other way. That's rubbish and you know it. You haven't been the same all day. Is it because of something I said?"

Carro shrugged. "Back there, at the house . . . I wasn't thinking. We've done so many of these farm calls that I didn't expect the fellow to charge at you. I am sorry." He looked at the ground and felt all the thoughts he had inside seething at him. They were saying *come on, coward, do something.* "I'm probably not very good at saying it."

They were standing on the bank of a creek, and the grass here was green and kept short by animals that came in to graze at night. Farey would set his traps and catch the weirdest creatures. Things he called "hares" with soft fur and long ears and strong back legs with lots of muscle that was good to eat.

"Hey." Nolan reached out and touched Carro's arm.

Carro flinched.

"It's all right. The fellow gave me a fright, but I survived. You were dreaming. Come on, confess, what were you thinking about back there?" His eyes were playful.

"Er—nothing."

"You're sure?" Nolan's hand found its way under Carro's shirt. His fingers caressed the soft skin.

There was just no getting away from it.

When they returned to the camp in semidarkness, Jeito had returned. A fire blazed in the clearing and a cooking pot stood in the flames.

"Smells good," Nolan said.

Jeito raised one eyebrow. The light from the flames lit Farey's face; he stood near the eagles, grooming his bird, listening to every word they said.

Carro didn't know where to look. These men could see straight through him. Even though he had washed in the creek, he could still smell Nolan on his skin. He had no doubt Jeito would know what he and Nolan did at the creek.

Jeito was holding a map and scanning the campground they'd covered so far. Jeito's hair, tied back in a ponytail, flapped with a gust of wind that nearly tore the map out of his hands.

"Oh, fuck!"

Jeito knelt in the grass and spread the map out there, using stones to keep it in place. Not for the first time, Carro noticed Jeito's fine, long-fingered hands. In view of Nolan's clear Chevakian background and Farey's Aranian heritage, Jeito was an enigma. Small of build and southern in appearance, with a fine face, but ruthless with his dagger. Yet, Farey seemed protective of him. Carro got that they were lovers, and had been for a long time, but neither seemed to mind if the other strayed.

"You still think they're in the region?" Nolan said, all business, coming to stand behind Jeito.

When Jeito didn't reply, he continued, "One farmer said he'd been missing things from his garden. That one there . . . The farm with the goats and the big old house. There's tracks in the grain."

"An old man lives there," Farey said from under the trees. "He had a visitor last night. I think it was one of the neighbours, one of the ones we roughed up."

"They're warning each other, huh?" Nolan said.

"Not used to being spied on from the air."

The accuracy of these men was disturbing. Things they picked up he never would have. If Isandor and Jevaithi were in the area, they would surely be found. There were only a few farmhouses left that were yet unmarked by fire. What would Isandor say if he found his friend had been sent to hunt and kill him and the young Queen?

"I've spotted some soldiers on the road, over there." Carro pointed at the map, away from the unmarked farms.

Jeito looked over his shoulder, a hint of irritation flitting over his face. Did he sense the deliberate change of subject?

"I saw them, too," Nolan said. "There were four."

"Four is not an army." Jeito's voice had a *What do you know?* tone about it.

Nolan shook his head. "It's a spying unit. Or a special mission squad."

Jeito raised his eyebrows. "What would they be doing here?"

"Same thing we are?" Nolan said. "They were doing something strange. They had a long section of cloth which they spread on the forest floor. Then they took a crate of silver cylinders from their vehicle. There was a frame attached to it, and they attached the cloth to it. Then there was a burst of air and a flame, and a section of the cloth bulged. And a bit later, it had grown bigger."

"By the skylights, what was it?"

"I think . . ." Carro hesitated, remembering his books; he hadn't seen the thing, but he'd been too busy staying on the eagle. "I think that thing is going to fly. I think it was a balloon."

Nolan laughed. "That a balloon? It was huge and lumbering, and *slow*. Our eagles are much faster."

"They are, but they don't carry heavy weapons." He'd learned about balloons in his books, even though he had never seen one. "You know that Chevakia defeated Arania with an army of balloons?"

"They did not. You're just making things up. Chevakians would be too dumb to think of using things that fly."

"Actually, he's right," Farey said.

Silence was instant. Farey didn't speak much but when he did, everyone listened.

"The Chevakians had hundreds of balloons. In each balloon there were up to ten soldiers. The carried heavy weapons and vats of powder which they dropped on the ground. There were explosions every-where, and fires, and people burnt to cinders. My father lost many of his cousins that way. The balloons are a great evil. Many people in Arania are still angry about it, and curse at the King who has gone weak and panders to Chevakia."

"But what are they doing here with that thing?"

A moment of silence followed. Wind whistled through the trees. The Chevakians might have had word that the Queen was gone. The Chevakians had all kinds of strange magical equipment to carry their messages.

"We need to warn the Knights."

"You don't think they already know?"

Jeito shrugged. "Question is: do we care if the Chevakians do our job for us?"

"Course we do." Nolan's voice sounded indignant. "No bodies, no payment. Leastways, not for me. Yeah, yeah, I know." He held up his hands. "I still care about getting myself some silver gulls so I can buy things in the City of Glass. I happen to like going back home every now and then."

Jeito scowled.

Carro felt sick. So that was the deal. He knew that the patrol was meant to return the bodies, and he had some idle hope to prevent the killing. They could always say that the remains were too badly burnt to return. But no, it seemed that wasn't going to please the Knights.

"Right, so let's keep an eye on these Chevakian scouts. They know the country better than we do."

He and Farey exchanged worried looks.

"Do you think it had anything to do with the flare we saw last night?" Nolan asked.

Jeito shrugged, but looked worried.

Farey said, with a glance at Carro, "It worries me that we haven't heard from the Supreme Rider, especially since you are with us. I'd have thought he'd be sending us gulls every day."

"How often does he normally contact you?" Carro asked.

"Once every few days," Farey said.

"Why don't we release a messenger gull?" Nolan asked.

"We haven't heard back from the first one yet. We only have one left, and none have come to replace it."

They all looked at the small cage hanging in a tree, holding a white bird with orange legs and a fierce beak.

Jeito shook his head and there was another silence.

"That never happens," Nolan explained to Carro. "Whatever Rider Cornatan thinks of us, he's normally good with his replies. He always sends gulls if we're out. He gives lots of instructions."

"Too many," Farey said, and then glanced uneasily at Carro. "Tends to meddle a lot, telling us how to do our jobs and all that. He says he used to be part of the raiding parties in Chevakia. He'd find the best women, claim them there and then, and take them to the City of Glass, letting the silly noble soft guys think they'd actually sired the children the women bore."

"Quit talking about that, will you?" Jeito said.

An uncomfortable silence fell. Like Nolan, it seemed Jeito had been one of those children. Did that mean Jeito was his half-brother?

"That's right. We were talking about sending out gulls," Nolan said.

Jeito said, "Not much good talking. I think we should send this one. Not much good sitting here yabbering about what might have happened when we have a chance of finding out."

Farey nodded. "Can't argue with that logic."

Jeito had taken a leather folder out of his saddlebag. When he folded it open, it revealed thin sheets of leather and a pen. He went to write a note with a cramped, childish hand. Carro spotted spelling mistakes, but he didn't dare point them out.

Meanwhile, Farey had retrieved the cage with a messenger gull. The bird hissed and pecked at Farey's hand when he inserted it in the cage, but he took it out without the loss of one feather. Jeito gave him the message, rolled up in a tiny cylinder. Farey tied it to the bird's foot and threw the bird up into the air. It gave a single undignified squawk and flew off into the dusk, leaving the hunters in silence.

The flames of the fire hissed. A chill wind made Carro shiver. Shadows trailed through his mind, of the merchant, and a dark cavernous warehouse, but he managed to hold the visions at bay. Not a sound came out of the forest, as if the world waited for a disaster to come.

They sat down and ate, all in silence.

If something had happened in the City of Glass . . . Was this war? Were they now marooned in hostile territory? Or was this just another of his father's silly tests?

CHAPTER 16

LORIANE AND THE family got up early the next morning, all of them miserable and with not much inclination to talk. A dense mist had settled over the mountainside, dulling any sounds. Loriane kept looking up, expecting to see Eagle Knights searching, or expecting to see hordes of refugees bearing down the mountain, but seeing nothing in that dreadful forest. And she didn't know what was worse: fearing the refugees might come, or fearing they wouldn't come, meaning that everyone up there had been killed.

There were sounds she could not identify. Something was up there, just behind them. She knew they were being followed and sooner rather than later this thing, or these people, would catch up. And it scared her, not being able to see any further than those infernal *trees* all around them.

At first light, Ontane had stoked the fire, and now Dara had put on a blackened pot of water in which she had tossed a couple of handfuls of dried meat.

Branches cracked and Ruko came from the forest with a bloodied animal of sorts. He sat down at the fireside and effortlessly tore a hind leg off the creature and ripped the skin off with his teeth. Blood ran down his chin.

Myra whimpered, looking up from feeding the baby. "That's disgusting."

"He's likely lived like an animal the last few years," Ontane said. "He don't know any better."

"He could be considerate and do it somewhere else," Dara said, giving Ruko a harsh glare.

Ruko ignored her. Loriane wasn't sure if he heard anything at all. Sometimes she thought he did, and sometimes she thought she didn't. If his transformation meant that he was now free, he seemed to be more protective of Tandor.

Dara kept urging, "Ontane, ye must do something about him."

"What do ye want me to do, woman? Ye know he hears us. Ye know he doesn't listen except when it suits him. Ye know I didn't invite him along, and ye know that if he hadn't come, we'd never got the cart down here, over those rocks."

"I wanted no sorcerers with us."

"Jus' shut yer complaining for a change."

Dara rolled her eyes at her husband. She ladled out jelly, a thick, gloppy substance congealed from the extract of the salted meat. It had a stale, rancid smell that made Loriane's stomach churn.

Myra pulled a face at her bowl. "This is like cement."

Dara snapped at her. "Ye be the cook next time, and if it still be too thick, ye can go piss in it."

Loriane was so weary of this family's bickering. She wanted to be alone.

For all the jelly's stickiness, it allowed Loriane to pick up little clumps of grain and shove them between Tandor's cracked and scabbed lips, under Ruko's suspicious glare. Earlier on, he'd tried to feed Tandor pieces of the raw meat, torn off with his teeth, but Tandor refused to eat them.

He seemed a little better; at least, he swallowed the tiny mouthfuls. At times he opened his eyes a sliver. He mumbled a bit, but even when Loriane held her ear to his mouth, she couldn't make out what he said. She didn't think his physical injuries still stopped him speaking. His wounds had scabbed over and, although ugly, they were not life-threatening. His breath still smelled sweet with icefire.

By the skylights, Tandor, wake up and stop this charade.

She met Ruko's eyes, deep black and hollow. His pale face never showed any emotion, but just the look of it made her shiver. Whenever someone came close to Tandor, he would watch. Sometimes she wondered: did Tandor control him or did he control Tandor?

Loriane ate some jelly, too, but spewed it back out moments later. Myra saw her, and looked concerned. Yes, Loriane knew. She was weakening. If this went on for long, she wouldn't have the strength for the birth. With every moment that passed, the child grew bigger; eventually the head would be too large to fit through her birth canal, and when she couldn't pass it, she would have to ask Myra to use Tandor's knife and cut the child up inside her and bring it out in pieces. She had done that a number of times over the years, and only three of those women had survived. And that was when the thing was done by her with all her experience, in the clean surroundings of the palace, and not by a young girl on a dirty forest floor.

They went on. Packed up, tied their belongings to the cart pulled by the camel and descended further down the hill.

Ruko went first, leading the camel, limping on his wooden leg. He stayed with Tandor, attending every step, and wouldn't let anyone near.

Ontane and Dara came next, with Ontane walking next to the cart, and Myra and Loriane made up the rear.

Ontane and Dara's voices carried in the still forest.

"Ye be wrong, woman! I'm not sure what I heard last night, but there be people higher up the mountain. All those poor buggers camping in town be following us."

"That's why we must leave the road. If we go into the forest now, there be a path that goes up from here to the shack—"

"Dang it, woman, don't ye *feel* it? There be icefire all around us. I don't know what happened, but something happened and I'm not going to hang around here to find out."

"We hide and the people will pass."

"And where do ye think *they* be going? They be fleeing the icefire. Nah, I won't stop until we be safe on the other side of the border. I feel it in my bones."

"You remember what happened last time we went into Chevakia?"

"That be twenty years ago. It be different now."

"It bain't. They be the same people. The old folk will remember the raid by the Eagle Knights. They still hate us."

"I say things be different now. Shut up, woman."

"No, because ye be wrong. We go to the hunting lodge, wait until they pass and go back home. There be nothing in Chevakia for us. I don't want to go there."

On and on they went. Loriane closed herself off from their voices, but caught Myra rolling her eyes.

"Are they always like this?"

"Yes, pretty much. Da likes bossing people about, and Ma doesn't like to be bossed about, so whatever he says, she never agrees. He just likes arguing. Are you . . . you're not married, aren't you?"

"As a breeder?" Loriane gave a hollow chuckle. "I have far too many men wanting to use my services."

"Doesn't it ever hurt . . . you know . . . giving away the child that you suffered for? Don't you ever wonder where all those children are? I couldn't imagine giving him up . . ." Her voice cracked and she patted little Beido on the back.

Loriane saw the baby boy in her arms. She saw him suckling at her breast. Felt the despair when a nurse in the palace birthing room had torn him from her arms to give him to some merchant. Since the boy had been born to an Eagle Knight, he would not even have had the joy of living with his natural father. Isandor was . . . not a replacement, but his presence and needs as a child had comforted her. After that first time, it had become easier.

She shrugged. "That's the way it's done in the City of Glass." But she hated how her voice sounded unsteady.

"Whose child is this?"

The path widened and Myra could now walk next to Loriane. The rest of the group was quite a way ahead.

Loriane hesitated. It would be so easy to say *Yanko* but ultimately it wasn't true, and she wanted answers. The time for lies was past. Yanko was probably dead, and her contract with him would never go ahead.

She said, in a low voice, "I don't know."

Myra frowned. "What do you mean? How can you not know? This man is paying for it, isn't he?"

"Well . . ." Loriane hesitated again. "Yes, he's paying." She blew out a breath. "But he's not the father of the child."

Myra's frown deepened. "You were with another man—"

"No, it's nothing like that, because otherwise, if I'd cheated, I'd keep that a secret. I'm not like that. I wouldn't give a man a child that's not his. The truth is, I wasn't with a man for some time before I made the contract, but I was already expecting when I signed it. The only man who came to my house in that time was Tandor. Yes, Tandor sleeps in my bed, and he gives me pleasure. But you know how he is. Damaged."

Myra nodded.

"There is no way Tandor can father a child. Yet, there is no other man I've touched."

"What about any of your patients?"

Loriane shook her head. They were all female anyway.

"Or the apprentice Knight you cared for?"

Isandor? "I would never do such a thing. He's my—" No, Isandor wasn't her son; he wasn't even closely related in blood. Isandor was purest Thillei, and she . . . Tandor had often told her that he was attracted to her because of her pure Pirosian heritage. "I raised him. He's as close to a son as I'll have."

And then she felt chilled. She had never considered Isandor. He hadn't touched her; just the thought revolted her; he was her son, even if only in mind. But such thoughts, of course, did not worry Tandor, and it might well be . . . after all, you did not need to sleep with a man to become pregnant; you only needed his seed, and Tandor always liked to rub her with salves and concoctions which he said he'd bought on his travels.

Slowly, the group made its way down the wet and muddy mountainside.

Fortunately, it had stopped raining and the path was less slippery. It was warmer here, too.

The ground became less steep, and the path wider and less rocky. But the walls of green forest unsettled Loriane, though they offered her handy spots for a pee. The trees made unfamiliar noises in the wind, and there were animals, too, moving in the foliage. She didn't like the idea of animals moving, out of sight.

Myra walked next to her, but since the path was less steep, she needed no assistance. Walking wasn't any less of a struggle, though. She was one big hurt. Her back hurt, her legs hurt.

Myra said little and patted the infant. Like all children born with a lot of weight on them, he was a good baby, asleep most of the time with the rocking of his mother's body, and drinking greedily from her breast at stops. Loriane found it hard to watch the bond between Myra and her son. Out of her children, she had only fed two or three and then only once, after birth. Isandor was the only child she had cradled against her stomach, watching him fall asleep with the nipple in his mouth.

There, she was thinking about Isandor again. *I hope the boy made it out alive.* Her stomach stabbed at the thought.

At about midday, they came out of the forest into a field of green. Sunlight peeked out from between the clouds, and Loraine couldn't get over the amount of colour in the landscape. The grass was so green it almost hurt her eyes. Flowers, which were a delicate rarity in the City of Glass, grew by the side of the road. Animals, not ones she recognised, buried their noses in the greenery, chomping on bits of grass. Their coats were outrageously orange-brown with large blotches of white. They had big wet, pink noses and sometimes one would curl its tongue in to one of the nostrils.

Loriane couldn't have imagined a place like this. Her world, her memories and imagination were white. They passed through forest, and then a few more fields. Some with animals, some with waving vegetation. Grain crops, Myra said. Sheep. Goats. So many new things she couldn't name. For a while, Loriane almost forgot her discomfort. She looked around and marvelled at this strange, intensely coloured world.

Then she became aware that Myra hadn't said anything for a while, and no longer answered her questions. An eerie dense silence had settled over the land. The birds were quiet; the breeze had stopped.

"Myra?"

The girl walked next to Loriane, her eyes hollow.

"Myra, what's going on?"

"Don't you hear it?" Myra's voice sounded haunted.

Loriane listened. If she was very quiet, she could just make out a low hum.

"You mean that noise? What is it?"

"It's horrible," Myra whispered. "It's crying."

Loriane felt chilled. "Is that the thing following us?" She thought people were following them, somewhere higher up the hillside. Refugees.

"Make it stop," Myra cried, clapping her hands over her ears. "Please, make it stop."

"Where is it coming from?"

"I don't know, just make it stop."

Loriane cast a panicked glance ahead, but Myra's parents were out of hearing, although Ruko and the camel had stopped as well.

"Come." She dragged Myra ahead until she came to where Ontane and Dara stood.

"What's going on?"

The sound was much stronger here, not just a low hum but a high-pitched keening.

Ontane pointed. "He be frozen to the ground."

Ruko stood stiff like he'd turned into stone. His eyes wide, muscles straining, staring ahead.

Loriane looked.

Up ahead loomed a thing like she had never seen before. Across the road stretched a row made of huge sheets of metal, each larger than a house. Their mirror-like sides reminded Loriane of the windows in the buildings in the City of Glass. These metal sheets didn't touch each other, but each had been placed upright on a pedestal and set at an angle like shading lamellae. There were hundreds of these things placed in an overlapping pattern, cutting through the forest as far on either side as Loriane could see. The metal plates were taller than trees, and seen from a distance, the air around them shimmered.

"What is that thing?" Loriane whispered.

"That thing be the reason my husband turns to jelly each time he comes here. He be a coward. You feel anything?" It was a challenge, not a simple question, the way Dara turned everything into a black-or-white statement.

"If it's something to do with icefire, people *do* feel it differently." It did have something to do with icefire, because otherwise Ruko wouldn't react to it. Out of all of them, he was probably the most sensitive.

"Pfa," Dara snorted.

"The barrier is singing," Ontane said. His voice had an ominous tone.

Myra's face was hollow. She clamped her arms round herself and shivered visibly. She had stopped in the middle of the road. Her baby cried, but she paid it no attention.

"Myra?" Loriane shook her. Her skin was hot, like she was running a fever.

"It's bad," the girl whispered, staring at the metal wall.

"Bad? How can a—" A dreadful howl interrupted her.

Tandor's face was drawn in a snarl, mad and wide-eyed. Ruko had a hard job trying to keep him restrained.

"Tandor!" She ran to the camel. "Stop it. Tandor, listen to me."

He was having some sort of fit, his eyes rolling. He screamed unintelligible words, kicked out, almost hitting her in the face.

"Stay away." Myra pulled her aside. "He can't hear you. He'll only hurt you."

"What is this horrid thing?"

"The barrier is singing. It hurts."

"But it's just . . . a wall of metal." Thick metal sheets, she could see that now they were closer.

"We have to pass," Ontane whispered, looking over his shoulder. "I know this thing can't hurt us, but—"

Ruko let go of the camel and bashed full-speed into Ontane. They both fell to the ground. Ruko was screaming unintelligible sounds, the first sounds Loriane had heard him make, and Ontane was yelling at him to stop.

"Help! Get him off me, woman!"

Dara took the cooking ladle from the crate at the top of the cart and hit Ruko over the head with it. Ruko crumpled.

"There," she said, her voice full of satisfaction. "That suits him."

Ontane scrambled up. He picked up Ruko, bundled him into the cart and lashed Tandor more securely in the saddle. Dara's face was set like cement. Myra stared ahead, as if she had to do her best to concentrate.

Ontane asked, "Mistress Loriane, do you feel the pain?"

"Not me, but then I can't see icefire even in the City of Glass."

"Good. Lead the camel. Whatever any of us tell you from now on, ignore it, no matter how we scream. Here . . ." He held out a cloth strap. "Tie me to the cart. Myra too."

Loriane did as he asked. Dara refused to be tied and looked at Loriane with suspicious eyes. Her face looked white, though, and when the caravan set in motion, she clutched her husband's arm.

Slowly, they inched towards the sheets of metal. The camel was snorting and tossing its head. It almost yanked the rope out of Loriane's hand.

"Hold it!" someone shouted, and recognised that voice.

"Tandor!"

His eyes had lost the dreamy look and met hers squarely. But pearls of sweat beaded on his forehead.

"Loriane, don't cross this thing. Don't run. Don't—"

His voice spilled over into a scream, hoarse and haunted. Loriane didn't understand a word of what he was saying. Rumours went that in their subconscious, when they were sick or losing their mind, people always returned to the language they grew up speaking. Tandor had grown up in Tiverius. Loriane tried to close herself off from his screams. Tandor was the most fiercely southern man she knew. He hated Chevakia. She didn't want to know that in his nightmares he spoke Chevakian.

Keep going, keep going.

Tandor kicked and screamed. Ontane starting mumbling, his eyes closed. Myra was pulling at the strap that tied her to the cart.

"Let me go. Let me go." Her voice sounded like a shriek.

Loriane kept walking, hoping that the camel would continue to follow. If the beast decided to bolt, she couldn't stop it.

The keening sound grew so loud it hurt her ears. The barrier loomed up ever closer, the sheets of metal towering over her.

"Hurry up, you stupid bitch!" Dara shouted. "They're all going crazy, don't you see?"

By the skylights, even Dara was affected.

What if they all decided to bolt at the same time, or attack her, or whatever it was this dreadful noise made them do.

Stop it, stop it, stop it. She repeated the words with each step, drowning out the shouting.

The sun came out and large shadows of the wall's segments fell over the road. They passed into such a shadow, and then between the metal shields.

On the other side, the sound level dropped quickly, and soon the air became calm. Dara stopped shouting, and then Ontane and Myra, until only Tandor still mumbled. When even he had stopped, Loriane halted and untied Ontane and Myra's hands. They both looked pale like ghosts and neither said anything. Tandor had slid sideways in the saddle. Ruko on the cart was still out cold.

Ontane sank in the grass, his face sheened with sweat

Loriane slipped off her cloak and wiped her forehead. Phew. How could a couple of plates of metal have such an effect on people?

She breathed deeply, sucking her lungs full of sweet air, and then became aware that Myra was staring at her.

"Myra?"

"There is no icefire here. None at all."

CHAPTER 17

IN THE YELLOW-ORANGE light inside the tent, General Finnisius put the map on the table. Sady pushed himself to the edge of the chair so that he could see. The map showed the border regions, from the gentle hills of Ensar, east, to the rough country of Mekta and the rich agricultural region of Fairlight, with the southern platform at the bottom of the paper. The barrier was drawn as a thick black line interrupted only in the most mountainous terrain at the back of the little pocket of civilisation that was Solmeni. It also showed the telegraph line, of which Sady understood some poles had been uprooted by bad weather and that was why Fairlight wouldn't come on the line. Fixing the problem was taking a little longer than he had hoped.

General Finnisius pulled the map so it faced Sady. "If there is going to be a southern attack, we are likely to see birds here, and here." He jabbed his finger at the main railway at Fairlight, and the gently sloping road at Ensar. "As you can see, these are all strategic points where roads and railways provide access to the southern platform to quickly move an army on foot. We have already seen an increase in the number of scout birds reported in the Ensar region."

Sady nodded. Milleus had even mentioned seeing a bird. He should have asked about it when he was there, even though Milleus had said that the bird was without a rider.

"We are as prepared as we can be, without going into full preparation for war. We have balloons ready to counter their eagles. We have nets to protect the balloons from claws and beaks. We have light-weight armour and shields to protect the balloon crew against their crossbows. But one thing I can tell you, Proctor: a skilled Eagle Knight is a deadly weapon. They're quick, frightfully accurate and some of those birds are big enough to wear armour."

Sady nodded while stifling a yawn. Not that he was bored, but he was so incredibly tired. It was cold in the army command tent, and he felt fearfully underprepared for a discussion about military strategy. Milleus knew all about military, having served himself. But Sady . . . he had spent two days going through the doga's financial mess to find money to pay creditors, a mess that was worse than he had expected. Much worse.

"Are we prepared for any weapons they might use?"

"They use crossbows. They also use poison darts, but their range is very much smaller than that of our powder guns. On the ground, they use crossbows and daggers. Those are the weapons we know about."

"Do we need to worry about the ones we don't?"

The general hesitated. "I don't know how much I should mention about this, certainly not to the troops. The southerners are rumoured to have sonorics weapons. They would gather sonorics and somehow shape or bend it into a single destructive beam. But I cannot find anyone who could verify the existence of this kind of weapon. I don't know if the current rise in sonorics has anything to do with it."

The most recent measurement they had was fifty-nine motes per cube at Ensar, but Ensar was further from the border than Fairlight, and Sady feared what he would hear when the line to Fairlight had been restored.

"Do you think . . ." Sady swallowed. "Do you think they're increasing sonorics *in order* to use in attack? Maybe they are trying to break the barrier?"

"I'd like to think not. They've always wanted either food or women, and they're not going to get either of those if they kill us. Besides . . . apart from the border raids, which weren't particularly well-planned strategically, they have never shown any sign of aggression."

"Are there signs that they've established a base in Chevakia?" Sady had received some terse notes from the Lady Armaine to come and see him about unknown southerners in the city, claims which he had been unable to verify, and hadn't had time to chase up.

General Finnisius shook his head. He took a deep breath as if preparing to dive.

"Just between you and me, Proctor, I'm having some difficulty with this situation. A threat may or may not come, but we don't know what shape it will take. My men can prepare for battle, and we're doing our best, but I don't know how we can prepare for an enemy we cannot see. I'm afraid you may need to call in the assistance of people with different skills than mine. Pure military manoeuvring isn't going to solve this."

Sady nodded. "I'm in contact with Alius. We will start distributing his new medicines soon."

Or, more accurately, Alius had better turn up with his wonder medicines. He hadn't had time to chase that up either.

The general stared at the map, chewing his lip for a bit and then he said, "To be honest with you, Proctor, some of the men are scared and there is a fair amount of unrest in the ranks. I cannot, with a clear conscience, send my troops to be the front line of this emergency when I don't know how to prepare them. The men have accepted that to sign up involves risk, but if I ask them to deal with something that looks like *magic,* I'm afraid that there may well be problems."

He met Sady's eyes squarely when he said that, and Sady felt a chill. *Magic.* For years, the Scriptorium had tried to stamp out that word. There was no such thing, they said; everything could be explained, measured and calculated. They thought they understood everything. Their calculations had worked. The barriers had protected the country. But that said, the common people of Chevakia never really *understood* sonorics, and there were those who still called it magic. Those who couldn't afford education and sent their sons to serve in the army.

The warning look in Finnisius' eyes said, *Give me something to tell my men or we'll risk mutiny.*

"I have no reason whatsoever to ask any of our soldiers to enter southern lands," Sady said.

Finnisius nodded.

"I will not ask soldiers to do anything except defend Chevakia."

Finnisius nodded again. "And this medicine? The men have heard the rumours about it."

"The army will get first priority when it becomes available. I will get that distributed to the troops as soon as possible."

Finnisius nodded again. He still seemed to be waiting for more. What else would he want to hear? "Any other problems?"

"Well—I hate to raise this with you at a difficult time, but some of my men have not received their monthly stipend."

Mercy. What was going on? "I will look into it as soon as I get back. The men who defend the country are our utmost priority."

Finnisius breathed out audibly. Were those the words he'd wanted to hear?

What a mess. He hoped that Alius was getting close to providing those magic pills, or there would be real trouble.

He stared at the map and the regions where soldiers might soon have to fight. Declare war. That was his power. Get the people out first. He was glad he'd sent those trains to Fairlight.

"All right, General. I will leave you to your work."

The general bowed and Sady left the tent in company of Orsan and two of the Proctor's guard.

Outside, a cold wind whipped his hair to one side. Sady pulled the sides of his cloak closer around him, and walked back through the camp, past the balloons flapping at their tethers, gusts of wind howling through ropes and loud bursts of fire spewing from burners.

Soldiers greeted him, full of cheer, but he felt uneasy. He hated being unable to give these good men the assurance that they would not be fighting "magic". He had no idea what was happening, other than that, whatever it was, Chevakia was ill-prepared for it, and he was ill-prepared to be their leader.

The camp lay on one of the hills that surrounded the capital, and from here, he could see across the valley. Low grey clouds scudded across the sky, brushing the tops of the ranges on the northern side of the city. In the valley, a grey kind of dust called ghostcloud shrouded the buildings in a soft light. Ghostcloud happened during dry spells in winter, when strong pressure gradients drew winds from the north, and dust from northern deserts fouled the air.

The difference was that it was summer, and that the wind was from the south. There should not be this much haze.

＊

People waited at the entrance to the doga building to see him. Accountants carrying thick books—

He'd have to get to the bottom of the financial problem as soon as possible. It was clear that this budget crisis had been going on for quite some time. No wonder he hadn't been able to get money to travel to the Ensar region; the doga survived by shuffling debt from one account to another; there *was* no spare money.

But first, he went to see Viki, in his old office. It was disturbing how quickly places didn't feel like they were his anymore. Viki had dragged the desk closer to the window so that he could put a large drafting table in the room, and both this table and the desk were full of barygraph readouts and maps, strewn about in disorderly fashion. Some were even on the floor, with indication that they had been there for a while, judging by the dusty footsteps on them.

Viki sat at the drafting table, crunching up his face in concentration while drawing a map. Rolls of paper lay around him and spilled over the edges of the table. Mercy, what a mess.

"Have you seen the increase in ghostcloud?"

Viki looked up briefly before returning to his work. "What do you think I'm doing here?"

Seriously, did everyone have to snap at him these days?

Sady walked to the table and looked over Viki's shoulder. He was drawing an air pressure map, which displayed a large low-pressure cell with closely spaced pressure lines on its eastern side.

"Is that Fairlight?" Sady pointed at the end of a solid straight line, very close to the high-gradient area.

Viki nodded and kept drawing.

So that was where the telegraph poles had blown over.

The winds at the weather front would be southeast, bringing air from the slopes that led up to the platform. Agricultural areas and forest.

"Why the ghostcloud?"

"It's not ghostcloud," Viki said. "There are fires on the slopes to the southern platform. It's smoke."

"*That* many fires that the smoke travels all the way over here?"

Viki spread his hands and met Sady's eyes with an expression of exasperation. "Why does everyone expect me to have the answers?"

Because you're the meteorologist. Having answers is your job, even if you don't. "What about sonorics?"

"Sixty in Ensar, forty-six in Solmeni, nineteen in Twin Bridges."

"Twin Bridges?" That was halfway between the capital and Fairlight.

"That's what I said." He kept drawing.

Filled with worry, Sady went to his office, where he had to wrestle past a long line of people queuing up to see him.

All Chevakian citizens had the right to request an audience with the Proctor, and the queue was more or less a permanent fixture, so that there was even a food vendor allowed to come into the building to sell his wares to those waiting.

In the past, Sady had never taken much notice of those people and what their reasons and demands for speaking with the Proctor were. Back then, he'd known that it wasn't his business and that someone would deal with it. Now that someone was him.

As soon as the people saw him coming, they started yelling.

"Please see me first. I've been waiting for a long time and have small children at home."

"I was here first! The farmers of the city ring need your intervention."

"Proctor, please—"

"But I've come all the way from Solmeni to ask for help with my children's strange illness. Please, I don't know where else to go."

What? Solmeni was in a dead-end pocket of land to the east of Fairlight. Surrounded by the southern cliffs and forest. A railway track went into the town, but the line stopped there.

Sady turned around and looked at the woman. She was thin, wore the long-sleeved garment and colourful head scarf of the type often worn by farming women, adorned with beads made from seeds. Her skin was tanned and wrinkled from having spent much time outside.

Everyone in the queue took the fact that he had stopped as a sign to start yelling more loudly.

"Please, Proctor, see me first."

"No, me. I was here first."

"I have nowhere to sleep. The landlord has kicked me out."

Sady turned to the last speaker, a middle-aged man. "In that case, you'll be better off going to see the housing office." He gestured to the peasant woman. "If you could come with me, please."

"But I was here first! Proctor . . ."

Sady strode into his office, avoiding the protester's gaze, feeling awful and guilty.

A week ago, he would have promised to see all these people, and he would have questioned why Destran didn't do so. Now he knew there wasn't enough time in the day, and that the queue never stopped, no matter how many of them he saw. And that there would always be more people to go back home disappointed.

He shut the door after the woman had entered his office.

"Sit down." He cringed at the mess: the financial books in big tottering piles. Pencils and pencil shavings everywhere.

The woman took the big leather seat opposite his, folding her hands between her knees. Eyes wide, she looked around the office.

"So you've come all the way from Solmeni."

She nodded. "I got a lift with a travelling merchant to Twin Bridges and then got the train from there."

"How long did that take you?"

"Three days."

"Do you know anything about what's going on in Fairlight?"

"Not Fairlight. That's a long way from us."

Not that far, when seen from here, but never mind. "So tell me about your children?"

"Not just mine, but a lot in the school as well. They have been sick to the stomach, sir. Especially the little ones, and all red around the eyes. I took a bundle of them to the clinic in Twin Bridges—that's why I rode with the merchant—but the medic wouldn't see them and won't come back with me. So I got angry and said as physic he has to see them, right?"

Sady nodded. That was part of the physic's pledge, to see every person in need.

"I said they were the town's children. Our future, you know. And he still wouldn't see them. I asked him why and he used a lot of big words—like I never learned. We teach things the kids can *use* at school, not filling their heads with big words, and I asked him to explain, but the physic couldn't make any sense. So I said I'd go and complain. And he said feel free, but I don't think he really believed I would do that. But I did and here I am."

"I am glad that you did."

She smiled a brown-toothed smile.

"Are there any other people in the area with the same illness? Adults?" Why hadn't he heard about this before?

"Not that I've heard, Proctor, but then again, most are in the farms away from the town. Like ours. My man said he liked the hill so he built the house there. You should see the view—"

"Could any adults be sick at home?"

"Could be, why are you asking? All I want is the physic seeing the little ones."

"And he will." Sady slid a sheet of official paper across the desk and wrote a note reminding the clinic of their obligation. As he signed his name, he figured that over there in Solmeni, many people wouldn't even know that the leadership had changed.

He rolled the paper up and handed it to the woman. "I'm going to send someone back with you."

She stared at him. "But that's not necessary, Proctor, much as I appreciate it. Just signing an order for the physic to treat the little ones will be enough. I thank you for that. I know that you and your people are busy and all that—"

Sady rang a bell, and a moment later Orsan came in. In a few quick words, Sady explained that he wanted a small team to return with the woman.

"I want them to take sonorics measurements—and suits," he whispered. "If there's any spare carriages, make sure they get hooked up to the train."

Orsan's eyes widened; he understood. He nodded and, with a quick salute, was out the door.

Mercy. Solmeni was well within the borders. First Fairlight and now this.

What if this evil came to Tiverius? What if the barriers failed? What were they facing?

CHAPTER 18

MILLEUS SLID the truck into neutral and let it coast until the tyres hit the kerb in front of the Town Hall. He glared at the building's facade with its pompous columns. The gentle rolling hills of the town stretched out behind it, with their sprawling timber houses, but the main street was a neat row of solid stone buildings in a mockery of a streetscape in Tiverius. Somehow, it looked even less like anything in the capital. These monstrosities, built from funds squandered by Destran, were all fake.

Mercy, he always grew cranky if he had to go shopping.

But with the youngsters on the farm, he needed decent food, and this morning his second pair of work trousers had come apart and he didn't know how to fix them. He'd grown tired of asking Andreus' grumpy wife and didn't want to ask her after having rebuffed her husband the previous night—she didn't do that good a job anyway. And he didn't want to ask Nila—she was doing so much already and he wasn't sure if she had sewing skills—so he was going to ask the tailor in town. He was, after all, not a pauper.

And that meant shopping.

Despite the pompous façade of the Town Hall, council positions didn't occupy office bearers full-time, so the tailor doubled as the town's mayor, and a visit to have trousers fixed had a second purpose, as everything does in politics. Milleus wanted to know if the southerner the neighbour had mentioned had been elsewhere in town and what the local authorities were doing about it. There was a small army unit stationed at Ensar, and he'd like to know if they had been called or had asked for reinforcements.

Southern Eagle Knights on the loose in Chevakia. If that was true, it was a clear violation of the border agreement. Why wasn't the district swarming with army units? Oh yeah, they were probably still waiting for their supplies.

Mercy, he had sworn never to look into politics again, leave the whole lot to stew in their own mess, but what if the doga just didn't *know*, through collective bureaucracy and incompetence, that there were southern spies foraging around? In his day, they would call in the ambassador, but apparently no one had thought to reappoint an ambassador after the anger over the kidnappings of girls by the Eagle Knights had abated.

Yet he knew there were several southerners in the city. They called themselves merchants, but everyone knew they were spies. If nothing else, he remembered that the lady Armaine had been a gathering point for southerners and their sympathisers in the city. They would certainly know what was going on in the City of Glass. Why didn't the doga—

Pfa, he should stop worrying.

He opened the van's door—it creaked—and slid out of the cabin. His trousers, a sorry bundle of cloth, lay on the bench next to him. He tucked them under his arm, shut the door and crossed the street to the tailor's shop, opened the door, stepped inside . . .

A siren wailed. A high-pitched scream that made him want to clamp his hands over his ears. He stopped, frozen, on the doormat, while the door blew shut after him.

The shop's sonorics alarm.

Milleus just stood there, his heart thudding, like a little boy caught snooping in the pantry.

The alarm quietened. There were yells and shouts inside the shop. Shufflings and clangings. A few moments later, someone burst into the shop through a back door, wearing a full protective suit. Stopped.

"Milleus?"

The voice was that of the tailor, muffled inside the suit.

"Yes, I wanted to have a pair of trousers fixed, but . . ." Milleus stared at his own reflection in the suit's helmet visor.

The tailor walked around Milleus, passing the sonorics meter over his farm clothes. The needle jumped on the dial. Not very high, but it definitely moved.

"Where have you been?" the tailor asked inside the suit.

"Just the farm." Milleus' heart was still thudding.

Andreus had said that something like this had happened to him, but he'd been visited by the mysterious Knights, and attacked. Wait—he had shown Milleus a burn. And where would a burn come from other than some sort of sonorics-based weapon? That wasn't supposed to work this side of the barrier.

He asked, "When have you last checked the sonorics readouts?"

Every day, the meteorology officer drove up to the shack not far from the back of Milleus' farm to read the sonorics levels, which he then telegraphed to Tiverius, and Sady.

Milleus couldn't see the tailor's reaction in the suit, but the man opened a drawer behind the shop counter and drew out a set of hand-written measurements. There was also a sheet of graph paper. He'd seen Sady's work often enough to know how to read it. The highest level of sonorics was sixty-nine motes per cube. Twenty was considered dangerous; fifty was the lowest all-clear level for the barrier. No one knew at what level it would break, but it would do so explosively.

"Look at this." Milleus pointed at the end of the graph, where the squiggly line rose towards the top margin of the paper. The needle on the sonorics meter which lay on the bench jumped when his hand passed it. So much else made sense. The unseasonably cold wind, for one.

"You reported this?"

"All sent to Tiverius," the tailor said.

"Has there been a reaction?" Mercy, why hadn't there been any advice from the capital? "Why are there no warnings up in the street? Why is no one doing anything? Has the army post been notified? Where are the emergency suits?"

The man took a step back. "What do you mean? We were following our normal procedures . . ."

"Even with figures like this?" Milleus gestured at the paper. The needle on the dial jumped as his arm passed. "Someone needs to go and check the barrier. I don't understand why that hasn't already happened. Hasn't the doga's chief meteorologist been here to tell you that sonorics were rising without explanation? And you didn't think to warn anyone to limit time spent outside? You should have rung the bell."

"We discussed it in the council. Tiverius said not to worry, so we didn't. We didn't want panic—"

"No, instead you'll have panic now. You could have started an evacuation before panic hit. Oh—wait—you haven't enough passenger trains available, and the suits are still in storage in Ensar, waiting for authorities to approve their transfer. And half the local army unit is on leave to attend the northern ballooning competition."

The man took a further step back. "Now, wait, Milleus, you can't go accusing—"

"It's true, though, isn't it? You haven't done anything, because the district hasn't the resources and because the politicians are sitting on their comfortable arses pushing documents from one side of their desks to another. They're passing the problem off to someone else, and meanwhile nothing happens. You value your political career over the safety of the people."

"But Milleus, tell me what we could have—"

"What you could have done, with no money? Watch me."

Milleus turned on his heel and strode back out the shop. The alarm started wailing again.

The tailor ran after him.

"Milleus, stop! You have to come inside and—"

Milleus wheeled at him. He felt oddly alive, perhaps more alive than he'd felt in years. "Have to scrub and decontaminate? Never mind that. If I'm contaminated, everyone in town is. I'm an old man, so whatever sonorics is going to do to me, I'll take it. I'll protect the young ones, though."

Mercy, a whole crowd of people had gathered outside the shop, hurling questions at him as soon as he came into the street.

"What's going on?"

"Milleus, I heard you are going back to Tiverius."

"What is the doga doing about those southern spies?"

Milleus held up his hands. "Listen, everyone, listen." And when relative calm returned, he continued, "Everyone please back away a few paces. It seems my farm is contaminated. I have just set off the sonorics alarm."

People stumbled away from him, mothers dragging children. Whispers went around. Milleus picked up his name a few times. The feeling of satisfaction it raised in him was surprising. In his voice, he heard echoes of the past, of a hall full of senators, one by one raising their hands in favour of a general mobilisation of all Chevakian men. That had been one month prior to the Aranian offensive. It had been the most important reason Chevakia had won the conflict. Preparation. His hand went to the pocket of his trousers holding the letter with the fifty signatures. He still meant to burn it. He didn't know, in fact, why he hadn't already done so.

"The sonorics level has risen dramatically near the barrier. Before anyone asks—the barrier is holding for now—but I don't think anyone can guarantee anything in the future. As a way of precaution, I want everyone here to go back home, warn your neighbours, collect your family and most important possessions, including any protective gear you may have, as well as provisions, tents, if you have them, take your trucks, carts and animals and go to Ensar. Make yourselves known to the local garrison and await instructions. By leaving now, rather than waiting for authorities to notify you, you will ensure that nobody needs to panic. But do make sure you tell any family and friends you may be in contact with. Make sure you look after people who are sick or the elderly. Don't leave anyone behind."

A wide-eyed woman at the front asked, "What if you don't have protective clothes?"

Mercy, did they have nothing? The older farmers would have suits to deal with the occasional flare-up, but all these young families would have settled after the barriers were installed. "The suits are made of resin-coated fabric. Substitute anything that is thick, and finely-woven. Winter jackets, truck canopy covers, tents, that sort of material. If you have any, it helps to dip the fabric in paint or wax." Of course they wouldn't have the special resin used for the official suits. It contained metal-dust, which made the suits so heavy and hot.

"Will rain jackets do?" asked a man.

"Better than nothing. The important part is not to expose any part of your body unnecessarily."

There were a few more questions, all asked in orderly fashion, and then, somewhat to his surprise, the first people started moving off. Mercy, people were actually doing what he said.

He watched the crowd disperse.

"Now you'll have panic." The tailor had come onto the footpath behind him, still in his suit. A few women also waited. To buy thick fabric inside the shop, Milleus guessed.

"Panic at this stage is better than the alternative. Any preparation for what may come is better than none. Every step people can put between themselves and the barrier will be beneficial, if the barrier doesn't hold."

Milleus let the threat hang between them. If the unspeakable happened and the barrier shattered, everyone in town would be dead within days, no matter how far they walked.

"Anyway, I'll go back to the farm to get my goats. You better go and serve your customers."

"I can't let you leave like this, Milleus, you really have to come inside with me now."

"And be scrubbed? No thank you."

"You'll endanger the people you live with."

"And just exactly who is that?" They glared at each other for a moment. "I'm old, and if a little bit of exposure to sonorics will kill me in twenty years' time, I'll be dead anyway. So just back off, and let me do my work."

He crossed the street to his van.

The man stared after him through the visor of the helmet, but Milleus felt uncomfortable. *Back off and let me do my work.* Those exact words he had used many times as proctor. They were the words that had led to praise but eventually to his downfall. Too much, too brash, too fast. Not enough communication and consultation with his workers. He liked to boss people around.

Well, sometimes the situation didn't lend itself to endless talks. And anyway, he was no longer in politics, and right now he'd best go back to the farm to start packing.

The youngsters would have no trouble with sonorics, but he wasn't so lucky, and he wasn't sure about the goats. Anyway there was no way he was going to leave them.

He reached the van, opened the furnace door and flung a couple of shovelfuls of coal inside, pumped the bellows a few times and checked the water level in the tank. Steam hissed from the escape valve.

Then he climbed in and drove off. Already some vans were on the road, travelling in the other direction.

People still listen to me. It surprised him every time. It warmed him. It made him think of the old times, when he used to come to the district with his guests, and go hunting, and have good times.

His hand strayed to his pocket.

Oh, curse Sady and his signatures. He was *not* going back to the doga. They didn't want him; they voted him out.

But they're incompetent.

Never mind. Let them stew in their own problems.

There are lives at risk. I should do something.

Milleus' white-knuckled hands tightened on the steering wheel. Curse Sady, curse him all the way to Tiverius.

When he crested the next hill, he noticed a column of dark smoke at the edge of the forested hills. High above it, a few shadows darkened the sky: huge birds circling.

His heart missed a beat. Mercy, the farm, the youngsters, the Knights who had come to the neighbour's house and still had to be somewhere in the area. The neighbour might be a cranky old bastard, but Milleus didn't think the man had lied about those things.

Mercy, mercy.

He slammed the boiler escape vent shut. Pressure in the boiler increased. The pistons of the engine thunked and thudded. The truck's speed increased, windows rattling, the wheels jumping over bone-jarring bumps. This old farm truck was not made for speed. Down the valley. Up the hill. The air became hazy with smoke. The scent of burning wood grew stronger and he was pretty sure that the labouring engine was not the only source. Now he could see clouds billowing from over the hill. Milleus groped on the back seat for the gun. It had to be his house. There *were* no farms other than his.

Mercy, mercy.

The van crested the hill and his house came into view.

Orange flames licked at the roof of the guest quarters. Most of the house was still unaffected, but once that straw roof burned, it wouldn't stop by itself.

He pulled out gears and then let the weight of the van carry it down the hill, honking the horn. Into the driveway, between the paddocks where the goats stood bleating at the fence. He crunched into the pebbled yard, braked hard, spraying pebbles everywhere, opened the door, jumped out, pulling the collar of his shirt over his nose. Smoke drifted into his face. He coughed.

I'm too old for this.

"Milleus!"

The front door of the main section of the house had opened, and Isandor and Nila stood there, white-faced and dirty. Isandor carried Milleus' meat cleaver from the kitchen. Thank the heavens they were safe.

"Come here! To the van!" Milleus called.

Isandor took Nila's arm and they ran across the yard. At that moment an enormous bird flapped up from the other side of the house. As it rose into the sky, Milleus noticed that there was someone in the harness.

Milleus gasped. "Quick! Come!"

But there was no time for them to hide; they were in the open. Surely the rider would see them and come back, and then Milleus would have to fight sonorics weapons he had no idea how to fight. He pointed the gun, keeping it aimed at the bird, not even sure if the measly hunting bullets would bother something that big.

The eagle flapped lazily over the roof of the house. Milleus could see the rider on its back, black curly hair flapping in the wind, his face turned towards the scene in the yard. Surely any moment now . . .

Milleus raised the gun, keeping the point aimed at the eagle. Just a bit closer . . .

But the bird kept rising. The man on its back looked down, but did nothing.

Isandor and Nila reached the cabin and clambered in. They squeezed into the front seat, panting, faces smudged with soot, smelling of fire.

Milleus stared after the bird, now even further out of range, and lowered the gun. It had reached the treeline at the top of the wheat paddock and showed no sign of turning back. Surely the rider had seen the two come out of the house?

"Your house," Isandor gasped. "We have to put out the fire—"

Milleus grabbed his arm. "Nothing we can do. Don't endanger yourself." A gust of wind carried burning straw to the kitchen roof. In the guest wing, the fire had spread to ground level. All his furniture, his memories, all beyond rescue.

Mercy, his library.

"How did this happen?" he asked.

"The men came to the house and banged on the doors," Nila said. Her eyes were wide. "We didn't open for them. Then they broke the windows and climbed in. We hid in the pantry. They didn't see us. They got angry and smashed things. And then they set fire to the house."

"Who were they? Eagle Knights?"

"They were not in uniform," Isandor said.

"Hunters," Nila said, her eyes wide, and whatever hunters were, they had to be something really bad.

"But now they've seen you. Are they likely to send a ground party?"

"The Eagle Knights do not violate the border without the Queen's consent."

Milleus was surprised at the anger in Nila's voice. Her determined, soot-streaked face had an expression that chilled him, and reminded him how much she *wasn't* like Suri.

He turned the van's engine off and let himself slide from the seat. A breeze blew clouds of smoke across the yard.

Over the sound of snapping and burning wood, he became aware of an eerie sound: a mournful keening, something he had hoped never to hear: the singing of the barrier under the pressure of sonorics it was absorbing.

"Come, help me pack whatever we can salvage from the shed. We must go."

He had some stores in the shed . . . and the goats. He was *not* leaving his goats.

CHAPTER 19

NOT LONG AFTER Loriane and Ontane's family passed the barrier, the road grew wider and rutted with tracks. Pools of muddy water covered the road in places, making passage difficult and messy.

Tandor sat unmoving and rigid, atop his camel, and Ruko lay, still unconscious, over the luggage in the cart. Neither had shown any sign of waking up, although Tandor's face twisted in awful grimaces at times, as if he was trying to say something. Loriane hated seeing it, but after a few times, she ignored the horrible faces; they were probably just caused by muscle spasms.

Ontane led the camel. Dara and Myra walked behind, with Loriane following.

The going was slow.

The camel could not be shooed to go any faster. Loriane suspected that the animal was tired. On top of that, the tracks were deep and broad, much further apart than the wheels on their cart, which meant that the cart moved on an angle a lot of the time. Loriane wondered what sort of vehicles the Chevakians used that churned the road up so much.

They passed the occasional house, and a few times Loriane saw vehicles. They were nothing like Ontane's cart. Much bigger, most with four instead of two wheels. Some had harnesses like they were meant to be drawn by animals, but some carts were huge and bulky, with barrels of dark metal, with chimney-like protuberances on top.

There would be a covered cabin for people to sit, with chairs covered in fabric. Ontane said that those carts moved by themselves, through fire in their metal bellies and steam.

Tandor had often spoken of the Chevakian engines, but somehow she had never taken him seriously. Back then, his talk hadn't mattered to her. Chevakia was far away and not a place she'd ever visit.

At one house they passed, a woman stood on the doorstep staring after the group. She held a broom and wore a neat and crisp dress, and a clean apron. She had dark hair, and didn't look as Chevakian as Loriane had expected—didn't they have sandy-coloured hair?—but this was clearly a woman from a much more civilised family than anyone except nobles in the city of glass could ever hope to be.

Loriane imagined what they must look like to her: a bedraggled group of travellers, their filthy clothes and their shaggy camel. The camels in the fields were much leaner. Their fur was short and neatly brushed. Most wore colourful harnesses with bells that tinkled as they walked.

Loriane had never felt ashamed of herself, not even in the Outer City, but now she did. Her clothes were dirty and she hadn't washed in days. The machines frightened her, as did the strange animals, and the smells and the colours. There was so much *light* here. More than that, she felt so *backward* and stupid, and the people's expressions only confirmed that.

"People here don't like us much," Myra said when Loriane mentioned it to her. "The Knights used to come and raid this area. They'd kidnap the older girls and take them to the City of Glass to serve as breeders."

Loriane knew. There'd been that year, shortly after she started work as healer, that the birth rate at the palace almost doubled. Many of the Chevakian girls brought in by their masters were closer to death than living. Many had died in childbirth. Others had birthed malformed children before dying soon afterwards. And those were just the ones who had made it to the end of their pregnancy and hadn't died horribly before that time. Chevakians didn't survive long in the City of Glass. Even those who did developed horrible skin sores which eventually crept into their bones. The kidnappings had been nothing but a sad waste of young lives. Not even the surviving half-Chevakian children were entirely comfortable. Many, now Isandor's age, had left, and lived, if not in Chevakia or Arania, on the edges of the southern plateau.

They came among more closely set houses, blocky and painted white. Yards had high walls, and in each grew at least one spreading tree. Children came out of gates to stare, bare-footed in the sand. It was so much warmer here that Loriane sweated under her dress and cloak. She hated the smell of herself. In the City of Glass, there were no smells, but here the earth breathed filth with every breeze. Everything stank, even the flowers on trailing vines by the side of the road.

The road was no longer a dirt track, but paved with smooth stones. Flowers grew in planter boxes, a riot of colour that hurt Loriane's eyes.

Ontane and Dara, ahead, argued as usual.

Dara was suggesting that they set up camp in the field before going into town to get food.

"That's just disgraceful," muttered Myra, glaring at her mother. "You can't expect mistress Loriane to sleep in a tent when there are guesthouses. Even Tandor never wanted me to sleep in a tent once we arrived in the City of Glass. You should say something, mistress Loriane."

Loriane shook her head. "Soon, I'll be taking Ruko and Tandor off your hands and let your parents be."

"What? You're not going to travel like this?" Myra's eyes were wide.

"I don't see what else I can do. I'll sell something from Tandor's chest to buy another camel. Ruko knows how to look after it. Tandor has family in Chevakia."

"But they live in Tiverius."

"Yes."

"But . . . mistress Loriane, do you know how big Chevakia is? We're only in the very southern province. This is the border town of Fairlight. Tiverius is days away from here. Days and days."

Loriane shrugged. "It really can't be helped. I have to go, and your parents have their own concerns. They don't want to come with me."

"Then I will." Myra's face was set. The baby in the sling was starting to stir and make noises, and she patted it. "I'm not going to leave you alone."

Loriane didn't know what to say. It was a nice gesture, but she really preferred to be alone, and people referring to her state as if it were a great illness made her angry. She had given birth alone, twice before. Once in a night with weather so foul she couldn't possibly travel to the palace. Once in her practice rooms when she'd left going to the birthing rooms much too late. Once, too, she had to instruct the sled driver to assist her when the child refused to wait until they were at the palace. She wasn't afraid. Her body was used to it.

They were still bickering by the time they entered the village and had come to what looked like a central town square. Under a collection of trees some sort of market was in progress, a handful of stalls where vendors sold fruit and brown things in baskets. Another sold fabrics. There was also a woman stirring a large pot over a fire. To the right, a makeshift pen held a handful of young camels. The scents of dung, cooking and *people* made Loriane's stomach churn.

The people noticed the group of travellers. Merchants stopped doing whatever they were doing and watched. Children came around and asked questions. Loriane didn't understand them. Tandor sat high on the camel in the bright sunlight. His head lolled to one side and he was drooling over the front of his cloak. Ruko lay like a deadweight on his stomach on top of the bags. Ontane had him lashed down so he wouldn't fall off. The skin on his hands looked blue.

Villagers blocked their path until they were surrounded.

"Get out of the way, ye lot," Ontane called. "We'll not be doing ye any harm."

The people chattered in Chevakian.

Ontane pushed Myra forward. "Ye talk to them."

"What do I ask?"

"Ask them where we can find an inn—"

Dara interrupted. "I said we shouldn't stay in this town. These bain't our friends. If we go in an inn, they'll rob us."

"Please, Ma, stop it. It's not as if we have anything worth stealing."

"Myra! Don't you dare be rude to your mother."

Myra faced her father, eyes blazing. "I'm a mother, too. I need rest. We all need rest."

"We do," Dara said. "And if I'm to cook a meal, I'll need time to buy some things, and I need hands to help me carry things."

"Then what do ye want me to do, woman? Why are ye always bossing me around? I be doing the best I can and you—"

"Stop it, I said! Both of you! I'm sick to death of having such stupid, selfish, bickering parents."

Loriane touched Myra's arm. "Please, Myra, it's all right." She just wanted to be gone.

"No, it's not all right. You need rest."

They continued walking, because arguing was not going to bring a solution.

Their progress across the markets was slow. There were too many curious onlookers.

A couple of women were feeling the fur on Myra's worn cloak. Ontane was shouting at the villagers to leave his daughter alone. Dara glared at them, her arms crossed over her chest. Loriane suspected that her defensive stance didn't help the locals' mood, but at least the villagers left him and the camel with Tandor alone.

Then a couple of men in brown uniforms pushed themselves through the crowd and came in their direction.

By the skylights.

"Tandor!" Loriane clutched his leg, hoping for him to wake up. He spoke fluent Chevakian and would know his way around.

But he didn't wake. Everyone was arguing and yelling around them. Loriane understood none of it, and panic rose in her. It was a bad idea to come here. They were going to be locked up. They would be punished for something they didn't understand they'd done—a sharp pain lanced through her belly.

She gasped.

Oh, little one, not now.

But the pain built, and burned. She had to stop walking. The yelling voices of people around her faded into meaningless noise.

"Loriane!" Myra put an arm around her shoulder, and then there were women all around her, touching her. She panted, chest heaving with deep breaths. Oh, this *hurt*.

One of the brown-uniformed men called out. The crowd parted at his words. Two other men formed a chair linking their hands and heaved Loriane off the ground. In the throng and smell of bodies, she fought not to scream. It was like someone was trying to poke through the skin from the *inside*. She put her hand on the spot and felt a sharp bump. By the skylights, what was that?

"Put me down! Stop!"

The men kept walking, jostling her and yelling at the people ahead, presumably for them to get out of the way. A woman came to walk next to her, holding her shoulders and gibbering words which she took as soothing.

"Stop! Where are you taking me—aaahhh!" Another stab of white-hot pain. Loriane grabbed instinctively for the spot. By the skylights, what was this? The bump had moved to the side.

"Loriane!" Myra came running from behind.

"Tell . . . them . . . to . . . put . . . me down." A surge of bile burned in the back of her throat.

In between fighting to get the words out and struggling not to throw up, Loriane realised she'd screamed, something she'd sworn was for first-timers.

Myra spoke in halting Chevakian; the men put Loriane on her feet, and scrambled out of the way as she threw up her lumpy jelly, and a second time more jelly, bile and blood.

By the skylights.

Cold with sweat, shivering and very afraid, Loriane stared at puddle of vomit. Blood. This babe was eating her from the inside.

"I told you that you needed to see a healer," Myra said, behind her.

"I don't know what a healer can do. I've tried all the things a healer can to make this child move, but it's bewitched. This is going to kill me."

Myra went white in the face.

Loriane swallowed a further surge of bile. "Myra, we need some place away from people. Not a guesthouse, a barn or some such. I'm going to have to ask you to do something very unpleasant."

She retched and coughed. By the skylights, the vomit went up her nose. She coughed, but that only made it worse. Her stomach cramped.

Myra nodded, her face white. It seemed she understood.

Loriane bent over and retched. More blood. Retched again, and again, until it felt her head would explode. She grew dizzy and fell to her knees.

Oh, by the skylights! She leaned over, panting. For a moment her vision went white.

It was a number of heartbeats before she realised the world had stopped.

No one moved to pick her up.

No one moved at all.

No one spoke.

Everyone stood still, eyes wide, staring at the sky.

There was only one sound: the same mournful keening she had heard when they passed the barrier, and it was increasing in volume. A woman screamed.

One of the brown-uniformed men shouted something and all around people started running, hurling themselves at doors.

The volume of the keening increased.

People screamed, crowding before doorways, pushing each other in, scrambling over the fallen, punching others out of the way.

Loriane scrambled up, clamping her hands over her ears, looking at Myra for a clue what to do, but Myra's face was just as bewildered.

Windows shattered, showering glass into the street.

Then there was bright flash of light, a moment of intense silence, a gust of wind and an enormous bang that shook the ground. Roof tiles flew into the street. The entire facade of a house collapsed. A cold wind tore through the street, ripping washing off lines, overturning market stalls and rubbish bins.

And there was silence.

CHAPTER 20

IN THE PLACE between life and death, Tandor shook awake when Ruko laughed. He sat up, a lingering chill of a cold blast still clinging to him.

"What was that?"

"Didn't I tell you we'd win?" Ruko said. "The stupid Chevakians put up their silly walls, but we're much stronger than that."

Tandor tried to look outside that place, and recognised none of the twisted shapes that he could make out. He didn't even see his own body, nor that of Ruko. All he could see was some sort of valley with hills made out of rubble on both sides.

Where were they, and how long had he been asleep?

Had he even been asleep?

He now remembered the pain that made him pass out. They'd passed the barrier, which meant that they were now in Chevakia and the fact that he was conscious in this place meant that icefire had penetrated . . . that the barrier had shattered.

Now he realised what he saw: those were not hills, they were the remains of houses reduced to rubble. Those were not boulders in a streambed, they were dead bodies in the street.

"No." He tried to push himself up, but he was still tied to the chair. "Loriane!"

There was no movement.

"Loriane!"

The child. He needed her child. The hybrid would be the only way he'd be able to control the onslaught of icefire.

If Loriane had been killed, all was lost.

"She can't hear you," Ruko sneered.

"Shut up."

Ruko laughed.

Tandor twisted on the chair, and all of a sudden a rush of icefire found its way into the place between life and death, and ripped the bonds. He was free.

He jumped off the chair and landed in the real world.

The smell of rubble. An overwhelming smell of fire. Moans from people caught under the rubble.

People with burned skin peeling off exposed limbs.

"Loriane!"

Something grabbed him from behind.

"Loriane!"

It was Ruko, pulling him back into that prison. The real world faded. Tandor swung around, and hit Ruko with his clawed arm. The metal went straight through him.

"Let me go!" He had to find Loriane. He had to rescue her and the child. He had to stop her going to Tiverius.

"You will do as I say," Ruko snarled. He tied Tandor back to the chair.

CHAPTER 21

LORIANE UNCURLED herself, sucking lungs full of air with an familiar tang. She was lying on a pavement of a street with tall houses on both sides.

She would have sworn she heard someone call her name. A voice that sounded like Tandor.

A haze of dust hung in the air. The ground was covered in glass and debris and, underneath that, dusty bodies, unmoving. Close to her, a couple of burly men in uniform, eyes open and glassy. Further away, a whole heap of people in front of a door. There was no blood, but no one moved, and the coating of dust made it look like they had turned to stone.

Loriane scrabbled up, awkward and top-heavy, but no longer in pain. Then a fleeting thought: does this child inside me feel icefire? She patted her stomach, but couldn't find the sharp bump anymore.

The breeze that went through the street was icy cold.

Where were the others?

Several houses had lost windows or parts of walls. Straw roofs had been blown off, and the entire town had gone eerily silent.

"Loriane!" That sounded like Myra.

Loriane turned around and almost tripped over a body behind her, half-buried under a piece of wood that had fallen off a shop awning. Every bit of exposed skin on the villager's face and hands was red and covered in blisters. He stirred and moaned, his eyes half open and showing only white. She had seen that before, after the explosion in the City of Glass.

Icefire.

That was the familiar feeling in the air.

"Myra, girl, you be all right?" Ontane emerged from the dust of a collapsed façade of a house, with the camel in tow. Tandor still sat on it, dazed, his hair rimed in dust, but otherwise unharmed.

Myra ran to embrace her father. The baby in the sling made muffled cries in the tight space between them.

What remained of Tandor's hair had turned white with a fine riming of white dust. His eyes were open, and Loriane noticed that the skin on his face had started to peel.

"Tandor? Did you just call me?"

He didn't answer, but when she took his hand, he moved his and squeezed her fingers. His blue eyes stared into the distance.

"Tandor, can you hear me?"

He squeezed her hand again.

"Please, talk to me. Tell us how to find your family."

But he didn't respond to that. His face contorted into frightening expressions. She swore she could hear someone laughing.

On the cart, Ruko sat up. A piece of debris had struck the side of the cart, and the wheels were out of alignment. Ruko glared at her over his shoulder. Somehow, his expression seemed less detached than before.

"Ruko? Do you know where Tandor's family lives?"

But he still wasn't speaking. He was looking at Tandor, though, and she wondered if they had a means of communication.

"We need to get out of here," Ontane said. "Before the Chevakian army turns up and accuses us of destroying this town."

"Where to? That was their accursed barrier that just exploded, dear husband," Dara said. "Haven't you noticed that we live on the other side? We might as well go home now."

"And what do ye think we'll find up there, huh? If the icefire down here be strong enough to kill everyone, it will be strong enough to kill us up there."

She didn't reply, but her face was set, her arms crossed over her chest.

"Be there anything we can do without you arguing about it,

woman? I tell ye now, ye be free to go back home, but I bain't coming."

Dara snorted, but didn't leave either.

Ontane held out his hand to Loriane, not noticing that he stepped in the puddle of blood-stained vomit, and helped her clamber over the debris of a collapsed shop awning. There were several *people* underneath.

With Ontane leading, they picked their way through the street, which had turned into an unrecognisable mess. Stalls had been ripped apart. Houses collapsed. Bodies were everywhere, covered in blisters, some still alive, most of them dead. In fact, apart from Loriane and the family, not one person was walking. A sickening scent of dust mingled with that of burnt meat hung in the air.

"What do we do now?" Myra asked.

Ontane shrugged. His face was haggard. "See if we can find another camel and cart for mistress Loriane, and keep going. Don't ask me where."

Well, damn it, there went her chance to leave this bickering family behind.

Dara still had her arms crossed sullenly over her chest.

Loriane was just so tired. "Please, I want to find a quiet place, away from the town."

"I agree," Dara said. "We wait until it be safe to go back."

"I don't mean that. This child is killing me. It's not normal. I want someone to cut it out."

"Mistress Loriane!" Ontane's face turned white.

"Be that . . . be that really necessary?" Dara didn't look so happy herself.

"It's not coming out by itself, and it won't, because it's too big. I can tell Myra what to do. I've done it a couple of times." More often than she cared to remember. There was a *reason* girls were made to wait until sixteen before being allowed to take part in the Newlight Festival.

"I'm not letting my—"

"Ye can't ask Myra to—"

Ontane and Dara started speaking at the same time, then stopped and looked at each other.

"Congratulations. The first time you two agree on anything is when it's something that has to be done."

"Myra, I don't want ye to do such a horrid thing," Ontane said. "I'll do it."

Dara said, "What do ye know about women's things? I'll do it."

They glared at each other.

Myra stepped between them. "Right then, if we can all agree, let's go and find a safe place."

With great difficulty, they made their way back to the market square. They saw no survivors.

They stopped to consider which way to go and of course Ontane and Dara argued over it.

Ontane said, "I think we keep going that way. The other way's the road we came—look!" His eyes widened.

Loriane turned. Over the rubble of collapsed houses, she could see the hillside that led up to the plateau. She didn't see anything—wait, she did. Higher up the slope clouds of white whirled, covering the green trees. Snow.

There were also clouds of steam, or smoke rising from between the trees.

"Is there a fire?"

"A fire? Can't you see it, Mistress Loriane? The trees be alive with blue flames. It be following us."

Loriane stared up the slope but could not see any blue flames.

"Icefire," Myra said.

"Great, and what now?" Dara said. "So much for all your wonderful ideas."

"You, woman! Ye be full of talk about what to do, but when ye actually have to make a decision—"

"Yes, it be always my fault, of course. It bain't like *you* ever make any mistakes, mister know-it-all! I still think we would have been just fine at the hunting shack, but no, you—"

"Stop fighting!" Myra screamed.

Silence.

Dara and Ontane stood facing each other, both glancing sideways at Myra.

"Hadn't we agreed to help mistress Loriane first?"

Ontane grumbled an unintelligible response. Dara looked the other way.

Loriane just wished they'd stop acting like little children. Honestly, if this was what having a family meant, then she was glad she had never married.

"Look," she said. "I appreciate your help in getting down here, but don't feel like you have to stay with me. I'll ask Ruko to help me." Her child was important to Tandor, and no doubt Ruko would protect it.

"Well," Ontane grumbled, "it looks like there be no time for that nasty business. I vote we be getting out of here as soon as possible."

At that moment, there was a harsh whistle somewhere in the distance, and a sound like Loriane had never heard before.

Myra's eyes widened. "A train! Let's go to the station."

The building Myra called the station was on the other side of the markets. Once it might have been painted white, but half of the entrance had collapsed, showing exposed bricks and timber. Getting there was a struggle. The camel was jittery. Loriane guessed it could feel icefire. The cart was too broken to be pulled with ease; the ground was covered in rubble.

In front of the building, they halted and Ontane untied their packs from the cart. The moment he touched Tandor's trunk, Ruko pushed him aside.

"Hey, you," Ontane yelled out. "Behave yourself, for all ye've been a parasite on us the last few days."

"Let him," Loriane said. What Ontane said wasn't true. Ruko had come along to protect Tandor, and had never eaten from the family's supplies. She added more quietly, "Ruko, we're going on the train here. We'll have to leave the camel, but we need to get Tandor up into that building."

Ruko said nothing, but turned back to the cart and took care of Tandor's enormous trunk

Ontane slipped the headgear off the camel's neck. "We'll turn the beast free. It may find its own way home, if it knows where home be."

Loriane followed the family up the rubble-strewn stairs into the station. She'd be prepared to walk all the way, or ride in the cart. She thought setting the camel loose was a bad idea, and didn't like the sound of the word "train".

After clambering underneath a half-collapsed arch, they came onto a paved area, from where two very straight strips of metal led towards the horizon. Rails, Myra said. For the train, although the train itself was nowhere to be seen. Taking in water, Myra said.

So there was no train at the moment, but there were unharmed seats under the awning of the roof and Loraine sank down gratefully, ignoring Dara and Ontane's bickering over the absence of a train, and whether it would or would not leave. Ruko sat next to her, guiding Tandor. It was the first time he had come close.

She glanced at him and wondered what went through that head of his. He was staring ahead, the light from the field on the other side of the tracks reflected in his eyes. There had to be some secret to speaking with him.

"Ruko, have you ever been to Tandor's family?" Loriane asked.

As usual, Ruko said nothing, but a big tear tracked down his cheek. He reminded her of Isandor and she wondered where her son was. Ruko was just another boy, broken and turned wild by living in the wilderness for years.

Loriane took his hand. It was warm. They sat silently, while Ontane and Dara bickered and Myra rolled her eyes while feeding the baby. Loriane's other hand was on her stomach, feeling the movements of the baby's feet through her belly. The child was facing the right way, and everything felt normal again. One ride in this train, and she would be safe. Maybe everything would be fine after all.

Voices echoed in the entrance of the building, and a group of five young men arrived. Strong and healthy all, with dark hair and wearing fur cloaks. Southern men without a doubt.

They nodded at the family, but didn't approach to talk. Deserters from the lower ranks of the Knights, Loriane thought, and knew that other refugees would have no love for them. They sat in the far corner of what Myra called the platform.

Soon others came in, all southerners. Families, silent children, women with haggard faces, and then the physically wounded. Burns mostly, but also broken limbs and frostbite from those who had fled in the clothes they were wearing.

They talked to whoever wanted to listen.

Their stories were all equally haunting. Some had come from the City of Glass, others from Bordertown. The ones from the City of Glass were mostly nobles or those who had been in possession of sleds. They spoke of a wall of icefire following them and burning everyone who was too slow.

Many had been fleeing constantly without sleep, and had festering sores that needed urgent attention. Loriane did what she could, but without materials, that wasn't much.

The platform filled up more and more. No one seemed to know where they were going, except out of here. Wherever the train went when it came, wherever there was work, wherever someone had some distant relatives or some acquaintance who had long forgotten about them. Most of them had no knowledge of Chevakia, and knew no one, no matter how vaguely, who lived there. It didn't matter, they all waited for the train that still hadn't entered the station. Word came that a second train had entered the town.

Scuffles broke out as some people were trying to leave again, arguing all of Chevakia was dead and there wasn't going to be a train, but the platform was too full and no one knew where to go.

Still the people came. The old and the very young, in a sad, stinking heap of humanity that soon spilled out the station onto the adjacent square.

Ruko had to fight for the bench they had secured for Tandor. He was well enough to stand up, but couldn't do so, or they would lose their seat.

Dara surprised Loriane by bartering some of their saltmeat for a blanket from a group of young men who seemed to be travelling together. When she spread the blanket over Tandor, the Knighthood crest in the corner was clearly visible.

Myra helped where she could. She caught a baby as it slid from the distressed mother's body, while next to her the boy's father succumbed to his injuries. Six more people died before she could attend to them.

There was nowhere to leave the dead. No space, no platforms for laying them out as was the custom in the City of Glass. There were no wild animals to come for their meat.

Fights broke out over the meagre supplies some people had with them.

Then there was a loud whistle in the distance and such hissing as Loriane had never heard before. A few children near the edge of the platform pointed and screamed. One of the children's mothers looked and screamed as well, and a young man yelled, "A train, a train!" Using the Chevakian word.

An older man yelled at him, "Use the right language. We once had trains, too."

A few people gave him suspicious glances, since he was clearly a supporter of the old king.

With much hissing, the huge thing rumbled into the station like some monster.

Mothers drew their little children out of the way, screaming at the older ones to stand back. Children cried and everyone stared at this huge, dark, gleaming and hissing thing.

Loriane felt awed. If this was the technology Chevakia had, then why didn't the Southern Land have this kind of magic? Tandor had even spoken about it. He said he had old books that showed the trains in the City of Glass. He even told her where to look for the remains of the tracks. She had never cared. Why not?

She searched the crowd for the man who had made the remark about trains, and found him surrounded by a couple of others engaged in serious discussion, pointing at parts of the train.

The train came to a complete halt. Despite the refugees' fear of its hissing steam, the boldest ones soon opened the doors and clambered into the carriages where there were rows of seats. Bewildered attendants aboard were pushed aside in the tide of humanity; they were helpless. Healthy and sick, strong and frail scrambled aboard.

Anything to get out of here.

Ontane managed to clamber into a wide door and held out his hand to Myra. In the stream of jostling people, they pushed Tandor up, followed by their luggage, which included Tandor's chest, under close guard of Ruko. Ontane then heaved Loriane aboard and Dara followed.

There were no seats in this part of the train, just a large carriage, with straw covering the floor. Loraine guessed this was how camels travelled. The air even smelled of the beasts.

While others clambered in the door, they secured themselves a seat in the corner of the carriage, and draped Tandor on a heap of straw. He was shivering and mumbling. Loriane covered him with their new blanket, meeting Dara's eyes. A thought crossed her mind that, away from her whingeing husband, Dara might be a successful healer, or merchant.

Still, people were trying to push in, but there was no more room in the carriage, and plenty of people still on the platform. Someone blew a whistle. Steam hissed past the open door. People screamed; a few young men pushed themselves in, stepping and stumbling over the knees and legs.

Men yelled out the door that there would be another train, that they could see it.

The train chugged into motion, and the crowd of people crammed on the platform slid from sight. The screaming and crying for loved ones who had become separated lingered a bit longer.

Silence descended. The only sound was that of the machine that pulled the train and the rumbling on the rails. Loriane had expected to be afraid, but it was much like being in a sled.

Wind blew in through the open doors.

Soon people started asking questions. Where was the train going?

No one knew.

Tiverius, someone said. Others said they had family there, but didn't seem too certain when asked where their family lived.

How long would that take?

Again, no one knew.

The man in black who had known about the trains was with a group of similar fellows in the same carriage. They were explaining to children and anyone who would listen how the trains worked.

"You know anything about this thing of icefire that's following us?" Dara asked them.

"It's power that has escaped from the Heart," a man said. His black clothing looked more clean and unruffled than that of the others, and his white-flecked beard was neatly clipped. "The Knights tried to stifle it, because they wanted to make sure that the people were poor and never understood the riches of icefire. Only because they, themselves cannot see it and cannot feel it or do anything with it. But the Heart doesn't like to be locked up. Its power built and built until it exploded from the earth."

"And before, this power was used for trains?" a young girl asked.

"Yes, that, and much more. The Knights denied us the riches. The Knights wanted the power gone. But you cannot stifle the Heart . . ."

Ontane was making frantic hand movements.

Dara mouthed, *What?*

He whispered, "They be rebels, and we don't want anything to do with them."

"And ye liked the Knights so much?"

"Please—these rebels be dangerous."

"Ye remember how the Knights used to come into Bordertown and rape the women?"

"Shhh."

"I haven't forgotten, husband. I haven't forgotten that the people who called themselves our parents let it happen—"

"Dara!"

She glared. "That be the first time in years ye haven't called me 'woman'."

"Just shut up. We mind our business, and get into nobody's way."

Dara turned away, her face tense. Loriane guessed that had Ontane not been there, she would very much like to join the black-clad men. However did she put up with such a selfish prick as husband? However did he put up with such a prune as wife? How come Myra had grown up as kind and open-minded as she was with parents like them? That had to be the greatest miracle of all. Of course, she'd only lived with them a few years, since Tandor had brought her, but she knew the girl loved them and they loved her, despite all their bickering.

Loriane stroked Tandor's hot forehead. She lifted the bandages. The wound didn't look too bad, but she worried about him. He should have woken up by now. His wounds were healing faster than she had thought possible, and there didn't seem to be a reason for him to remain half-conscious. Unless . . . unless icefire kept him asleep.

Either way, she was uncomfortable sitting cross-legged on the floor next to him. Her back ached. She was sore all the time.

And the train rumbled on.

Some people munched on whatever food they had been able to bring. Men stepped over sleeping bodies to piss out the open door. Women could do no such thing.

Soon, Loriane found herself crouching in the corner, the darkest place she could find, dribbling piss on the straw. Her bowels twisted and churned, ejecting jets of brown, bloodstained fluid, and she wasn't the only one. Many of the weaker people didn't even bother getting up but let it run into the straw where they sat. A young boy close to her was sick. The sound of retching made her cringe. The smell followed soon after.

With that, and the stinking wounds, the vomit and sun baking on the roof of the wagon, the smell became unbearable. Only those close to the door got enough fresh air, but as the train continued, the air became hot, and those close to the door had red skin from the wind and became thirsty. The young men in black organised a rotating scheme so that everyone got a turn at sitting near the door.

Somewhere on the far side of the carriage, a woman wailed when her child stopped breathing. The little boy, covered in blisters and ugly sores, couldn't have been more than a year old. There was nothing to cover him. Nowhere to put him aside so the mother took off his shirt and draped it over his head.

When an old woman died, the young men pushed some straw in the corner and stacked the bodies on top. They were soon joined by the body of the woman who had given birth on the platform. Fever, Loriane knew. The woman's adolescent son clutched the child, but Loriane knew that without its mother, it would soon die. She would offer to feed it, but she hadn't eaten for two days and was desperately thirsty and didn't think she'd have much milk to share.

Myra sat against the wall where they had secured a place, and clutched her baby. No one had any water, and Myra didn't have enough milk either.

The train rumbled on. Steam trailed past the windows.

Forest replaced fields, and then came wide expanses of grass. Groups of camels roamed the countryside. It grew warmer, even as the sunlight turned golden.

Then came night.

Several of the wounded did not stir the next morning. The young men again stacked the bodies in the corner.

A man, who must have done some nursing work, started arguing that they should remove the dead from the carriage.

"What do you mean—remove?" yelled the mother of the young boy, her face stained with tears.

"Well . . ." He looked at the door, over the jumble of dirty and stinking bodies.

"How dare you suggest that!"

"It's in the interest of all of us. If the bodies stay here much longer, they will go bad, and all of us will get sick."

"I will not put my son to rest without a proper ceremony."

Several parents agreed with that.

The man retreated, mumbling about having been to Chevakia before and knowing how quickly things went bad here.

Loriane's belly cramped from sickness and hunger, and the foul smell that grew worse as the sun rose. At night, she suffered another bout of stabbing pains. Same thing as before: strange sharp bumps moving under her skin. She put her hands on the spots, pushed back, and felt the bumps moving, too sharp to be knees, too strong to be hands. She sat like that for a long time, sweat rolling off her back. In her mind, she kept seeing those drawings of malformed children.

There was another pregnant woman in the carriage, and occasionally, they threw each other anxious glances, hoping and knowing that the babes would be better off being born once they got off this train. Loriane was scared. By now, she had to be almost a moon overdue. Not long, and the birth would become impossible.

Tandor, what did you do?

But Tandor had no answers. He sat in his crazy stupor, moving where they told him to go, but not communicating with anyone. Ruko sat next to him, protecting him from people who came too close, and making sure he wasn't hurt. Loriane was glad for that, but the two of them seemed lost to everyone else, and she didn't know what she could to bring them out of their stupor, so that either could tell them where Tandor's family lived. Worse, Ruko had locked Tandor's chest and wouldn't let anyone near it.

The train rumbled on.

How long was this going to last?

CHAPTER 22

IT WAS A GLOOMY circle of faces that gathered around the fire when the sky began to darken. A cold breeze whistled through the pine trees, blowing any heat from the fitful fire away.

It was amazing how quickly Carro had become used to the mildness of the Chevakian climate. He liked it.

"I found this," Jeito said, holding up a wet and bedraggled bird. It had the orange legs and white feathers of a southern gull, and the red paint on the beak to show that it was a bird belonging to the Eagle Knights. A baleful light blue eye blinked, but that was the only sign of life it displayed. "Found it flapping about in a puddle of mud next to the creek."

Carro recognised it as the bird they had released to fly to the City of Glass with messages for Rider Cornatan, and requests for instructions. They had been away for more than ten days now, and not one bird had reached them with further orders or updates on how the Knights coped with the Queen's absence.

Jeito untied the note it had tied to its leg. It was the same note he had attached to the bird a few days ago, except now it was dirty and wet. He crumpled it in a white-knuckled hand, and let it fall in the grass.

"What has happened?" Farey asked, his face in expression of shock. "We've never had any birds fail to reach their destination."

It was the first time Carro had seen Farey worried.

"Maybe the bird was blown off-course," Carro said.

Jeito and Farey gave him dirty looks.

"A few options," Jeito said, his voice low. "Either the bird fell ill, it got lost, or it somehow couldn't reach the City of Glass. Apart from being wet, the bird looks healthy enough, so that leaves the other two."

"I'm not liking either of those," Farey said.

Carro struggled to make sense of it. The birds used icefire to navigate. They were much more sensitive to it than humans, and could detect it even in Chevakia. They always knew their way back to the City of Glass. It was where nature told them to go in summer, after having spent the winter on the Aranian shores.

"What could have happened?" Jeito asked.

Farey shrugged. "Bad weather?"

"Maybe," Jeito said, but they all knew the underlying truth: bad weather of the type that disturbed animals' navigation involved the release of icefire. Not only that, they *had* seen a flare.

"What do we do now?" Nolan asked.

"Stick to our orders," said Farey. "Find the highest in command."

"Go back to the City of Glass?" Carro asked. He didn't want to go back to the City of Glass. He didn't want to face his father, or any of the Knights, or, for that matter, Korinne.

Farey nodded, slowly.

The hunters packed up the camp at first light.

Carro was nervous, looking about him for an excuse so that they could stay. A night of fitful sleep hadn't changed his mind. The obligatory sex with Nolan hadn't changed his mind, nor had the promise of being able to stay in luxury in his father's apartments in the palace. The pool where the hunters held their orgies, the empty-headed girls like Korinne who came only so that they had a chance of securing a good payment for carrying a senior Knight's child. All those thoughts made him sick.

Carro did *not* want to go back to the City of Glass. He did *not* want to face his father. He did *not* want to go back to having visions and having to hide them. And he especially did not want to have to take a girl's medicine to help alleviate them.

But the others were ready to go, supplies packed on their eagles.

"Come on, Carro," Nolan said, and smiled in that leering way of his.

Jeito snorted, already on the back of his bird.

Farey was even less talkative than normal. He was by far the oldest of the group, and his silence unnerved Carro more than anything that had happened so far.

He untied his eagle from the tree and jumped into the saddle. He left his harness dangling. The saddle's leather showed the shine of frequent use. At least none of the Knights would ever tease him again for being clumsy.

Then they were off with a flapping of wings. The countryside glided under him, with its neat fields and forests and burnt-out shells of farmhouses. At least no one would ever question him on the two people he had seen running towards a Chevakian truck from the last farmhouse they burned, one with long black hair and an awkward gait, one with honey-coloured hair, whose Chevakian farm clothes didn't hide her fine figure. Carro had avoided his worst fear of having to witness Isandor's death.

They came to a road which was unusually busy. The vehicles were all travelling in the same direction.

"The Chevakians are fleeing," Nolan said and he laughed. "That's how scared they are of us. This land will all be ours. We don't even have to fight for it."

Carro felt sick, remembering the flames and Farey's murdering of people whose only crime was not to reply to questions.

Ahead lay the area the Chevakians called the wastelands, forested hills that slowly climbed to the southern plateau. From up here the hills didn't seem so tall, and in the distance the cliffs of the plateau were already visible. It was strange, Carro contemplated. He had never thought about it, but the plateau was as if a giant had cut out a section of land, and pushed it up from the earth. He wondered if in history before human memory icefire had anything to do with this strange layout of the land. After all, the City of Glass was said to have been built by an ancient civilisation and destroyed in an evil war. The machine sometimes referred to as the Heart was said to be a construct of that civilisation. Living with his stepfather, Carro had learned not to believe everything—his stepfather distrusted everyone—but surely there was a reason for those rumours to exist? Even if they were spread by old Thilleian books. It couldn't be coincidence that his father had approved of him reading those books.

"By the skylights, look at that cloud," Nolan said, pointing at the horizon.

Carro looked.

At the horizon, sitting atop the plateau was a huge black roiling mass of cloud. Lightning arced across the top.

"Some bad weather, that is," said Farey.

"Do we have to go through?" Carro asked. There was an uncomfortable chill in his bones and he felt a strange disconnect between what his eyes saw and what he experienced, as if the world wasn't real.

"We may have to shelter until it blows over."

Nolan had his hand above his eyes to shelter them from the biting wind. He squinted at the cloud. "I've never seen anything like this."

"Agree it's not normal for this time of year." Farey's voice sounded far off.

Carro shook his head to banish that disconnected feeling, as if he was about to get a vision, but the cloud morphed into vaguely human shapes, and one had the face of his stepfather.

By the skylights, already those damn visions were returning. He glanced aside at Nolan, who looked at him. "You all right?"

Carro nodded, his face stiff like a death mask. He noticed his dangling harness and knew he should clip it on before a full-scale vision struck, but Nolan was watching and would think him a weakling, having learned how to ride without a harness just recently. A tough hunter didn't use a harness, storm or no storm.

But as they came closer, it turned out that the blackness wasn't just a cloud. Along a long storm front, the trees were on fire. Entire trees exploded, spraying embers everywhere.

The embers whirled and formed human-like figures made solely of fire threaded with lightning.

Carro shook his head. He was surely imagining things.

"Stay together!" Farey yelled somewhere in the distance.

Next to Carro, Nolan struggled to keep control of his bird. It flapped and bucked, threatening to throw its rider off.

Farey steered his eagle into the cloud and disappeared from sight. Jeito followed, but Nolan's eagle refused to obey its rider's command.

Carro went in after Jeito. The moment his bird plunged into the roiling mass, something hit him that made his entire body tingle. All around him, human-like figures roiled.

"Stop," he yelled, fighting to keep visions at bay.

But he couldn't see Farey or Jeito, and he couldn't see Nolan behind him.

He yanked at the eagle's reins. But the bird was plummeting down.

Carro knocks on the door and walks into the room.

Standing by the window, Rider Cornatan turns. "Do you bring me the fugitives, son?"

"Yes," Carro says, and somehow he's come in carrying a stretcher, and on it is a hunk of bloodied meat. It barely looks human except dangling from it is a ponytail of black hair.

"How do I know that this is him?"

It is Isandor, because of the hair clip.

Isandor. He and Jevaithi had been staying with the old farmer. He hoped they were safe. The south would gain nothing from their deaths.

Smoke trailed past him. Still, the eagle was going down.

"Up, up!" Carro pulled the reins, but the bird took no notice.

Carro knocks on the door and walks into the room.

Standing by the window, Rider Cornatan turns. His face twists into a sneer. "Do you bring me the fugitives, son?"

"They escaped," Carro says. "I think we know where they are."

Within a heartbeat, Rider Cornatan's face twists into a snarl. "You *know*? What good is knowing alone? If you know, what are you doing here and why don't you bring me their bodies? I thought you would do me proud, but you're as useless as the rest of those weaklings."

His hand flicks out and slaps Carro hard in the face.

Ow.

Carro ran his hand over his cheek. It burned like fire. He looked down his tunic to see a trail of black. He must have been hit by an ember.

The eagle was still descending in slow circles. The mist had become acrid smoke from the flames below. A strong breeze carried the sound of exploding trees.

"Carro!" someone shouted in the distance. "Carro, what the hell are you doing?"

Carro gave up trying to control the eagle. Some strange voice in his head told him that the bird knew the way and that whatever fate awaited both of them, it was inevitable.

He squinted through the shards of smoke and when a breeze cleared the air, he could see the burning forest. Amongst the exploding trees walked a huge, human-like figure made entirely of fire.

The moment Carro saw it, the figure turned its head up. It pointed a flaming hand and a bolt of lightning shot into the sky. It missed Carro and his eagle. The bird swooped, leaving Carro to clench its labouring body hard to stay in the saddle.

He laughed and punched the air.

"You can't get me!"

The figure on the ground ripped a tree out of the ground and swung it in a great arc while fire spread over the crown. Then it let go of the tree, which flew into the air, but rose far short of Carro's eagle. Again, the bird swooped.

But as Carro hung onto the saddle, he noticed two more flaming figures plundering their way through the forest. One was smaller than the first one, the second one much bigger. His laugh fell flat.

He yanked the eagle's reins again. "Up, you stupid bird!"

Too late. The large figure pointed, lightning gathering around its outstretched hand.

Carro dug his heels into the eagle's sides. "Up, up!"

Carro's vision went white. The reins slipped from his hands.

Carro knocks on the door and walks into the room.

Standing by the window, Rider Cornatan turns. His face is triumphant and his smile chills Carro. "Are the fugitives dead, son?"

"Yes," Carro says, and somehow he's come in carrying a stretcher, and on it is a hunk of bloodied meat. It barely looks human except dangling from it is a ponytail of black hair. The carcass is a Chevakian goat's and the hair is Carro's own.

Rider Cornatan walks around the stretcher. "How do I know that this is him?"

"Look at the hair clip," Carro says, clutching the dagger behind his back.

Rider Cornatan bends over and at that moment, Carro jumps, plunging the dagger deep into his father's back, so that the point comes out the other side.

Rider Cornatan staggers, a surprised look on his face. He tries to speak, but blood oozes from his mouth. His eyes unfocused, he slumps forward over the goat carcass.

He whispers, "Why, son, why?"

Carro was flying, flying, like an eagle. He spread his arms and legs and the wind flapped past him, roaring in his ears.

The thought crossed his mind *I'm falling, and I'm going to die,* but he didn't care. He'd done his duty and rid the world of a great evil.

He was a hero.

Historians would sing his name.

He was dead.

"What the *fuck* were you doing?"

That voice sounded far too real and it sounded far too much like Nolan.

Not dead, then.

Carro opened his eyes with a great effort.

He was on the ground in a forest clearing where dark pine trees rose around him. Directly above him was a face, the features blurred, but clearly Nolan's.

Carro tried to speak, but he couldn't. Everything hurt, even breathing.

"You would kill us all trying to rescue you from that fire?"

Carro shook his head. He didn't honestly remember what he had done. He only remembered his father's eyes as he stabbed the dagger into his heart. He remembered his father's rasping voice. Why indeed?

"That was the stupidest thing I've ever seen anyone do in my life," Farey said. He poked into the fire, sending sparks flying.

"Where . . . where are we?" Carro's throat hurt.

"Well back into Chevakia. We can't get home that way."

"At least now we know why the gull came back," Nolan said.

Farey glared at him.

"Did you see those fire devils?" Jeito asked. He had his arms clamped around himself.

"Yeah, what are they?" Nolan said.

"Fire devils are constructs of icefire."

"But those things looked human."

"They *are* human."

"You're kidding me."

Jeito shook his head. "I've read about the old king's creatures. He had servitors, but he had ones that were way worse than that. There were beings that could change their shapes at will." He stared into the fire. "They could fly. Some people said that eagles were descended from these creatures."

For a while the silence lingered. Carro wasn't sure what to say. A few months ago, he would have laughed at such tales. The fact that they were in the old books meant nothing. Books were full of stories; but now he had seen the working of icefire, shown to him by his father, and he had seen human figures made out of fire. There might be some truth in those old tales. There were other things in those books: shape shifters, crossbreeds, living ice. Who was to say what was real and what a myth?

"Well, since it's clear we can't go to the City of Glass, what do we do now?" Nolan said.

Jeito gave him an irritated glance. "Is that all you worry about—what do we do now, what do we do now? Can't you think for yourself?"

There was a haunted expression in his eyes. Worried about family, Carro guessed.

Farey reached out to his lover and squeezed his shoulder. "We'll find a road of some kind," he said. "There are a lot of people travelling. I'm not sure where they're going, but they'll be going somewhere. Meanwhile, stick to our orders: try to find the fugitives and kill them. Also, follow where everyone is going and find any of the senior command. We'll confiscate one of these vehicles and send the eagles to roam. They'll attract too much attention. If we travel by road, we can remain hidden. One of us goes with the eagles each day."

CHAPTER 23

THE LIGHT HAD turned orange, and the pine forest cast long shadows over the road. The haze amongst the trees shrouded the straight trunks in a veil of purple.

Milleus drew a hand over his eyes while steering the van with the other. Up ahead, the van they'd been following since the last village crested the hill and became a silhouette sharp against the yellow sky. The van that had followed them had already stopped for the night, and they'd passed a few camps along the way, where people were making fires and children huddled in blankets against the biting southern wind.

"I'm tired," Milleus said to no one in particular. He cast a glance over his shoulder, where Nila lay across the back seat, half asleep, a slice of bread still on her lap. She had been hungry; he had given her the bread, and she hadn't eaten it. He didn't know what to think about that, which only intensified the feelings of unease in his own stomach. He had been contaminated with sonorics. With less severe contamination, it always took a few days for the effects to show. Was he feeling nauseous because of that, or from the worry about his health? Rumours of the barrier having shattered were coming in too frequently for them to be untrue. The same was true for the many reports of huge birds circling the sky.

He had tried to contact Tiverius in a few of the villages they had passed through, but the lines were either busy or out. Or there were huge queues at the few stations that did work; he was too impatient to wait his turn. Meanwhile, he looked for signs that people were falling ill from sonorics poisoning and found no evidence.

The only one who seemed off colour was Nila.

On the seat next to Milleus, Isandor unrolled the map and traced his finger across the line that represented the road. "There's a village a bit further down the road. We can stop there."

Amazing, how quickly he learned. Milleus would have sworn that the boy had attended some form of tuition in Chevakian. "No, we stop here. There's a glade on the other side of the hill. There's a spring nearby and plenty of firewood." He knew the place from his hunting days.

Isandor threw him a sharp glance. "Why you always stay away from people?"

"I'm not staying away from people. We need grass for the goats."

But the boy was right, and by the looks of things, he knew it. Two days they'd been on the road, travelling in a loose convoy of trucks. Normally, it only took a day to get to Ensar, but they had to stop frequently to let the animals graze. Isandor would collect handfuls of grass and heap them on the floor of the trailer. The goats had to be milked by hand. It took a lot of time, more than he wanted, and people passed them on the road.

Nila would set up a roadside stall to sell milk to other travellers. Milleus would stay with the goats, avoiding the looks people gave him.

They *recognised* him. Closer to Tiverius, that happened more often. Old men came up to question him about politics.

"Are you going to fix things in the capital?"

"The doga should send the army across the border."

"Why isn't anyone doing anything?"

Milleus made non-committal responses, going over excuses in his mind. He was too old to become involved. The rumour that he was returning to the city, however, travelled faster than he did, and he felt like he was caught up in an unstoppable wave that was outside his control. It seemed people expected him to return, whether they wanted him to or not. He still hadn't burned the letter in his pocket. Damn Sady. Return to Tiverius.

Well, he'd do no such thing. They were merely on their way to Ensar to get out of immediate range of the border. When they got to

Ensar . . . what then? He knew no one there. His only family was Sady —in Tiverius. Well, the only family still talking to him, that was.

The van reached the top of the hill and the turnoff to the glade, where he had camped so often in his younger days, with Sady and some senators, or with foreign ambassadors. He could still hear the laughter and the baying of the dogs. He could smell roasting meat over the fire, he could hear the Aranian ambassador telling his tall tales. Memories.

Milleus killed the engine and leaned on the steering wheel. Rest. Food. Sleep.

Isandor pushed himself out of the van. The grass was knee-deep and lush green and Isandor left a track when he limped out of sight to the trailer.

The goats must have seen him coming. They were bleating and jostling each other, making the van rock.

Isandor opened the tailgate with clangs of metal and then the whole herd rumbled out, with much bleating and jingling of the chains that held them together. Isandor whistled and they quietened.

Mercy, the boy was good with animals.

Milleus pushed himself out of the driver's seat. He'd best make a fire for cooking while Isandor set up the tent. In his hunting days, they always left a pile of firewood under the trees. He wondered if it was still there.

Nila emerged from the van, rosy-cheeked and with mussed hair.

"Sleep well?"

She looked better now.

"Yes. I'm hungry. Do you want me to get water?"

Milleus pointed her in the direction of the spring and, for a while, everyone went their way, Milleus making the fire, unpacking the cooking pot and peeling vegetables, Isandor milking the goats. He had learned this trick yesterday and seemed to enjoy it; his young hands were certainly much better suited to it than Milleus'.

Nila was just coming back from the creek for the second time, with bottles to fill the goats' water trough, when the putter of an engine disturbed the peace.

The last rays of the sun glittered in the window of another van entering the glade.

Oh mercy. Milleus didn't want company.

The van stopped on the other side of the glade. A young man came out, followed by a toddler and a woman. The man greeted Milleus briefly, but then went about his business of setting up a tent.

Well, that was fine then. They were nice young people, looking for quiet.

But while he was lighting a fire, another van came down the road. This one with four passengers, youths all. They stopped on the far side of the glade, almost amongst the trees. They had no tent, but unrolled bedding on the forest floor. Three of the youngsters had glossy black hair and one curls which glowed golden in the light of the fire.

Foreigners. That was fine with Milleus, too. No one who would pester him about his plans to return to Tiverius. He didn't point the group out to Isandor. At least two of those youths looked awfully southern, and one Aranian. But Isandor must have seen them, too, and made no move to talk to them. In turn, the foreigners kept to themselves and mostly sat behind their van where they made a fire out of sight of the glade.

Mercy, I'm a coward. Yes, he knew. In a way, he was afraid to find out what the youngsters' crime was. He liked them. He didn't want anything to happen to them. If he found that they'd stolen things or harmed people, he would feel betrayed. Yet, something in him told him that he really *should* find out why they were important enough to warrant search parties.

Pfa—Nila was probably just a rich man's daughter. And children were valuable enough in the City of Glass.

But, the little voice argued, the rich nobles of the City of Glass don't control the Eagle Knights. Each were a class of their own; he knew that much about their strange society.

The Lady Armaine used to wrangle invitations to doga functions; she used to shadow him at dinners, holing him up in dark corners while pressing her ample cleavage under his nose. Yeah, no goddess, that one. A power-hungry snake, more like. No doubt she revelled in all this renewed attention on the south. He could almost hear her voice. *I am a southerner. I know what is going on in my country.* No, she didn't. She'd left over fifty years ago, and hadn't travelled there since her son ended up spending some time in a southern dungeon as teenager.

He only shivered at the thought of what she would do to Destran, the spineless gasbag. What was she telling him now? *Oh, it's only a temporary flare. No need to do anything. Knights in the border provinces? Don't worry, they're just looking for some dangerous criminals. No harm will be done to anyone.*

Why wasn't this district crawling with Chevakian soldiers?

Mercy. He should go into the towns and do something, instead of hiding here with the refugees and the outcasts.

They'd been travelling all day and had seen not a single official or soldier. The people could be forgiven to think that Tiverius didn't care.

In fact, Milleus was sure the doga didn't care. From what Sady had told him, they were far too busy fighting for their political survival. The people of the district would be disgruntled and support him, ride all the way to the capital with him and march into the doga . . .

Pfa, what nonsense. You're an old man, Milleus han Chevonian.

They ate and Nila announced she was going to sleep. She looked tired, too. Milleus still couldn't shake the feeling that she wasn't well.

Isandor got up to accompany her to the tent, his arm around her shoulders. She leaned into him and let him caress her. Milleus guessed Isandor would probably not come back to the fire either. Last night, Milleus had gone to sleep in the van trying to block the soft noises from the tent.

But soon after the youngsters had gone into the tent, the flap moved and Isandor came back out. The flickering glow from the fire danced over his face. Was it a trick of the light, or had the ungainly black hairs on his chin increased? Maybe he should lend the boy his barber's razor.

Milleus held out an empty cup, for tea, but Isandor shook his head. "You watch when we sleep. I get up in the night and watch you."

Milleus frowned.

Isandor cast a quick glance at the van with the southerners.

"It's all right," he said. "I think they're just refugees. None of them look like full-blood southerners."

"The Eagle Knights use elite teams called hunters. They're mostly half bloods and other outcasts from the City of Glass. They are the most dangerous soldiers the south has."

The intensity in his eyes made something click for Milleus. All of a sudden, he understood what Isandor had done. "You're a deserter."

Isandor squinted and let the silence linger for a few long seconds. Then he said, "Of a kind, yes."

Milleus thought he knew the kind. He was well-familiar with armed forces and what superiors sometimes did to men they didn't like. With his wooden leg, Isandor would fit the bill of someone these tyrants loved to pick on. He fought to repress a shudder.

"Is that why they're after you?"

"They want to kill us," Isandor said.

"These foreigners don't look dangerous."

"No." Isandor's eyes were intense; they said *I think they could be.*

"All right. I'll watch them."

Isandor nodded in that intense way of his and went back into the tent.

Milleus sipped from his tea and stared into the fire. One piece of the puzzle put into place. Isandor had been an Eagle Knight apprentice, or whatever they were called. That's why he knew so much about military strategy.

The thought again crossed his mind, *What if he's a spy?* But he discarded it just as quickly as he had before. Certainly a spy would never flaunt that type of knowledge. Nor could he see any government, not even the dictatorial south, appointing mere teenagers as spies.

That left the enigma of the girl. Because Nila wasn't her name. What did she have to hide?

Their voices and rustling of blankets were soft in the tent. They really were very considerate. And anyway, how much did you need to hide that you were in love?

He sighed. Saw Suri at the dining table a few days before she took her own life. One bright look, a smile. Not at him, but Sady. What was going on between them? He'd asked her.

So it's fine for you to see prostitutes and it's not fine for me to have a friend?

It was not the same, and she wouldn't see that. If she wanted a playboy, whom she paid, that was fine, but his own unmarried brother . . . she refused to say whether or not she ever slept with Sady. "That is just such a ridiculous question, Milleus. You don't understand how ridiculous." His best guess was that her refusal to answer the question meant that she had.

And Milleus had . . .

Jealousy was an ugly emotion. There was no excuse for what he had done, for what he would have to forget. The marriage had been bad from the start. He should have known the moment she became reluctant to be touched. He should have let her go, but he'd never wanted to push her. He should have . . .

He'd expected her to run out on him, find another man, but *kill* herself?

"Mind if we join you?"

Milleus started at the sound of the young male voice.

The young father stood there, holding a lute. The young woman, the toddler's mother waited just behind him.

Milleus shrugged. "Sure. Sit down. Want some tea?"

The young couple sat down and introduced themselves. They were from one of the towns they had passed through and underway to Tiverius, because the man had family there.

"It's much safer to go there than stay in Ensar," the young father said. "If anything happens, do you think the doga would let it happen to the capital?"

His eyes met Milleus' and Milleus felt uncomfortable, but there was no suspicion on the man's face. He was possibly too young to have remembered the glory days of Proctor Milleus han Chevonian.

Milleus shrugged. "Politics don't interest me much." *Liar.*

The subject changed to travel experiences, and then goats. The young man played his lute, and the music drew three of the foreign youths to the fire. There was a lanky young man with olive skin who had to be Aranian, an adolescent youth with curly golden hair but hazel eyes who had to be a Chevakian half-breed. The third person turned out to be a young woman with silky black hair and intense blue eyes. Under a too-wide shirt of thin material, her figure was thin, androgynous. She moved with the grace and stealth of a sabre-cat. Milleus didn't doubt the strength of those corded muscles. But her eyes were wide and held a kind of innocence that only came with youth. She was gorgeous in every way.

The young father sang and the foreigners shared bottles of a heavy, sweet liquor. Milleus felt drawn back to the pleasant memories he had of camping in this glade. In those days, there had never been any women, but the southern woman seemed to fit in perfectly. She laughed with the boys, she swore enough to colour the ears of a soldier, she drank like them—straight from the mouth of the bottle— and her deep sensual voice carried a promise of living fast and dangerously, like a man, like a soldier. The golden-haired youth had a huge store of bawdy jokes, and in between passing the bottle they laughed themselves silly.

The more he drank, the more Milleus looked at the sleek-haired beauty. She returned his glances, secretly, over the shoulder of her hawkish Aranian friend. Milleus wasn't used to drinking so much anymore, and somewhere in the back of his mind a voice told him to get out before there was trouble and go to sleep. The voice sounded like Suri, who used to be angry with him when he was drunk. Mercy, when he was drunk he used to do stupid things. Like force her into his bed. It was a wonder those two useless sons of his weren't born with alcohol in their veins.

He rose, so unsteady on his feet.

"Look, I better go to bed. 'S a long day t'morrow." He couldn't even talk properly anymore.

He stumbled to the van. Remembered vaguely that we was supposed to stay awake to guard the tent. What for? These half- southern youngsters were just louts.

They haven't told you who they were and where they're from, the little voice in his head said.

"Ow, mercy, sh . . . shuddup." He put his hand on the door of the truck's cabin. All right, he'd guard the truck. He'd just sit in the cabin and—

—the pale-skinned woman slipped next to him, bottle in hand.

"Don't go yet." Her voice was deep and sultry, unlike any woman's he had heard before. She leaned against the truck and tipped the bottle to her mouth. A rivulet of moisture ran from the corner of her mouth down her chin, over her neck.

The firelight gilded her thin blouse and the merest of curves underneath. A nipple, hard and erect, pushed the fabric.

Something stirred in him.

Milleus tried to shake himself out of his stupor. *You're seventy-one years old and you're drunk.*

"Why don't you come with me?" She flicked a glance in the direction of the forest.

Beyond the glow of the fire, tree trunks stood as dark sentinels.

A few moments of unattached passion. He had plenty of money, and she needed it. Come to think of it, that was probably how the four of them survived. She'd been scouting him out all night. Since the young father made an unlikely customer, she had set her eyes on him.

Mercy.

He should go to bed if he knew what was good for him. Go to bed and listen to Isandor and Nila's lovemaking for much of the night.

He shook his head. "I'm an old man, twice the age of your usual customer, I bet."

She gave a crooked laugh. Her blue eyes were intense.

"You'd be surprised," she said. She trailed her fine-boned but wiry hand over his arm. He shivered, feeling the blood stir inside him.

"I think you had better go and bother a younger man."

"Really?" She raised her eyebrows.

"Don't fl . . . flatter me." His voice was unsteady from the drink, but his crotch glowed pleasantly.

"I like older men. I think you could show me a thing or two."

Oh woman, where do you think I've been the last ten years?

On the farm with the goats, that was where. He hadn't been near a woman for a long time, had no idea if his body was still up to the task; but it might be, it just might.

Who would care, really, if he spent his own time and own money on a bit of pleasure? The goats wouldn't eat any less, and Isandor and Nila wouldn't know. He was meant to watch the southerners, and he was just watching them very closely. Even if the youngsters did find out, they might realise that not just young people had fun.

"Come." She pulled his hand. Milleus stumbled a few paces, swaying, and then regained his balance. Mercy, it had been a long time since he'd been this drunk. She draped her body cat-like against his. Warm and smelling of female perfume. It wouldn't take long, oh no, it wouldn't, he could feel it, he still had some fire in him.

"Ow, let's go, then."

She gave him a mischievous smile.

He hooked his arm in his, and drank another good swig from the bottle. She offered it to him; he took it and gulped the burning fluid. Oh, his whole body was throbbing *most* pleasantly now.

But somehow, in his drunkenness he registered that she was pulling him towards their van, and he vaguely remembered that he vowed to keep an eye on Isandor and Nila.

"No, no, Lady. I have a nice van. There's a lot of . . . room inside . . ."

"I have all my oils in the wagon. I'll give you a good rub."

But Milleus wasn't interested in a rub. He wanted to . . . hell, he wanted to fuck her hard, not care about decency, and wake up the youngsters with the noises they had plagued him with.

"Let's just go in the forest." From there, he could keep an eye on the tent; he'd promised Isandor.

"All right." She gathered up her shoes.

Holding her hand, he led her between the trees. He stopped a few paces in, pushed her against a tree trunk.

"No," she whispered. "Not here. I don't want my friends to see. They can't know what I am."

Oh, rubbish. Everyone knows what you are. "Your friends are drunk as anything. Just stay still. I won't take long."

In one movement, she pulled her shirt over her head. "Catch me."

She jumped a few steps and he chased after her, and managed to get hold of her arm.

He pulled her into a close embrace in the shadow of the tree trunk. She panted, arching her back, undoing the fastening of her trousers. He slid his hands over her skin, breathing the scent of her hair. The muscles on her belly were firm, her breasts soft. Blood roared in his ears. It had been so long . . .

A branch cracked behind him.

Milleus gasped, suddenly wide awake.

Hang on.

Somehow, her *catch me* game had taken him far enough in the forest that he could no longer see the tent, where his two southern fugitives lay asleep.

"Wait."

"What?" she said. She was stark naked, and the firelight gilded small breasts. "Come on, I'm waiting for you." She pulled his arm.

"Gotta check something." He shouldn't have left the fire.

He yanked himself free, and ran, half-stumbling through the forest.

The tent was silhouetted against the firelight. He couldn't see anyone near it, but a shadow stood beside the foreigner's van—the fourth member of the southern group, the young man who hadn't come to the fire.

Milleus ran, all effects of alcohol banished from his mind.

"Isandor, Isandor!"

He reached the tent, at almost the same time as a dark figure rushed out. The man crashed into Milleus and swore, or so Milleus presumed, because he didn't speak Chevakian. Milleus thought it was the Aranian youth.

Then there was Isandor's voice, also not in Chevakian. A knife flashed. Someone screamed and a second figure ran from the tent, his head wrapped in a headscarf. An engine started up.

Nila came to the tent entrance holding a flapping candle. "Milleus? Who was that?"

Isandor scrambled out after her. He opened his clutched fist in the pool of light cast by the candle. There was a handful of fur in bloodied his palm. "Knights."

Nila clasped her hand over her mouth. "They cut you."

"It's nothing." Isandor wiped the fur on his trousers. His gaze was on the edge of the forest where the foreign van no longer stood. "They were not here to capture us. They were here to kill us. I woke up because there was a noise. I saw the knife."

"Who were they? How did they get in?"

Isandor met Milleus' eyes.

Milleus felt heat rise to his cheeks. Yes, he was supposed to have been watching. And just as well one of the foreigners stepped on a branch. "I was in the forest—" And then he felt like he needed to explain. "Taking a piss."

Isandor frowned. "With a woman?"

Milleus looked over his shoulder. The foreign woman was gone, of course, but Isandor would have seen her.

Isandor's blue eyes met his. Then he gave a wolfish smile. "Oh."

Oh indeed. Milleus didn't know whether to feel stupid or victorious. Had he been near the fire as he ought to have been, nothing would have happened.

"It's not safe here," he grumbled. "I'll sleep in the tent with you."

He went to get his mat and lay down, after stopping for a good spew behind a tree. Mercy, he'd feel like a wet dishrag tomorrow morning.

Somewhere in the dark beyond his vision Isandor and Nila kissed and whispered to each other. Milleus pulled his bedding over his head, irritated that the itch inside him had not been stilled.

He lay staring into the dark until silence returned and still couldn't sleep. His mind churned.

He'd been stupid. Not just about a silly pair of pretty eyes, but about everything he cared about, and everyone who cared about him.

And he had grieved over his sour marriage and Suri's death far too long. He might well have another twenty years of fire left in him. Seventy-one was old, but he wasn't dead yet. If he was still up to misbehaving himself, he could be useful to someone. He would have to go and fix the mess Destran had made, find out what foreign spies were doing here, and why there had been two attempts on the youngsters' lives. When all that was sorted, he would go to a matchmaker to find himself a woman. Not too young, mind because he didn't want any more children.

Tiverius then, it was.

Damn you, Sady.

CHAPTER 24

CARRO STARED at the hunk of meat in his hand. The yellow light from the fire glistened in fat dripping down the bone over his hand and down his arm.

He had taken a few bites of the leg from the animal Nolan had shot, but was no longer hungry. This life sickened him. The way Jeito and Nolan had held up a family of refugees and confiscated their van and their food, and shot the father when he protested too much, the way Nolan enjoyed stealing from others on the road.

Why couldn't they even leave refugees in peace?

The whisper of voices in the back of his mind had almost become constant, an itch he couldn't scratch. It had whispered at him while they ran back to the van after having been disturbed, and during the mad ride through the forest, and the lonely drive on the dark and deserted road and the hours no one had said anything in the cabin. Farey drove like an idiot, and now that the sky was turning blue in the east, they had finally stopped.

Jeito and Farey sat on the other side of the fire, casting him occasional glances. If they hadn't known about the fire in the house and how Carro had ignored the two people fleeing from it, they knew now. Nolan had settled between them and Carro, as if he couldn't make up his mind who to support.

No one told any jokes now.

"So . . . straight to Tiverius from here?" Nolan asked into the silence that had lasted too long.

"No point hanging around here now they're all on alert," Jeito said, with a sharp glance at Carro. "Remembering that both of them can use icefire, and if the barrier has really broken, they'll burn us to ashes if we try again."

"We almost did it," Farey said, staring into the fire.

Again, Jeito glanced at Carro. Carro shivered in a breeze of cool air. So that had been the secret. Jeito was a woman, or could be, if he wanted to. Or maybe he was one of those confusing people who were born both.

"Clumsy pup," Farey snarled. "Stepping on a piece of wood. Why did we ever agree to take you?"

"It's not fair," Nolan said. "Carro has never been here before. He doesn't know how there are branches on the ground that can break and how much noise it makes when they do—"

"Oh, just shut up," Farey said. "We had our chance. We've blown it, thanks to him, deliberate or not."

The haunted grey eyes met Carro's. Carro looked away.

And the strange thing was: he didn't feel sorry. He hadn't planned to do it, but Carro could still see it before him, a dead piece of gnarled wood. He could feel himself lifting his foot, and stomping down on the twig.

Crack. Deliberately, as far as he had ever done anything deliberate. Which, admittedly, wasn't often.

Why?

To make up for the fact that he had betrayed Isandor? Because he still called Jevaithi his queen no matter what Rider Cornatan—his father—said? Because the merchant, his foster father, had despised her and therefore Carro must adore her?

Because Isandor was my friend.

Isandor and Jevaithi weren't doing anyone harm. They were fleeing with the old man, fleeing something that they, with their southern blood, didn't need to flee. They could have taken the old man's farm, and they didn't. They were helping him and his flock of noisy animals. And the old man, a Chevakian if there ever was one, seemed to care about them.

Care. That was the key word. Had he ever cared about anyone?

Not his stepfather, certainly not his stepmother or his stepsister. Not Korinne. Not the Knight Apprentices, not even the man who had claimed to be his real father. And here, Farey scared him shitless, Jeito scared him more if that was possible, and Nolan was just an innocent bumbling idiot who happened to be good with a blowpipe and dagger. Carro found his proclaimed love increasingly wearying.

Could he care for anyone or had this horrid abnormality of his mind robbed him of that, too?

He'd watched Isandor and the old man from a distance, talking to each other, laughing, smiling. A pat on the shoulder, a hand getting out of the truck. Caring for each other, even though they were not related, total strangers as little as a moon ago.

By the skylights, Carro, you're jealous.

Carro threw the bone and remaining meat in the fire and rose to go into the forest for a piss. To clear his mind and consider what to do now.

"Yeah, that's right, walk away when things get hard, that's how you live, isn't it?" Jeito shouted.

Carro froze, met Jeito's eyes and felt cold at the naked fury in them.

"You're a coward. You need some balls. Come on, tell me. Why did you do it?"

"I did nothing," Carro said.

"Too right you didn't. You've been nothing but a burden to us ever since we let you come along." When angry, Jeito looked more female.

"I had to stay behind. We all agreed on that. They would have recognised me."

"So instead, you betrayed us." Jeito rose. The firelight glinted on the boning knife in her hand. Yes, her arms were thinner than his, but corded with muscle.

"Whoa, Jeito." Nolan stepped between them. "Calm down. It was an accident."

"You know nothing about accidents. Get out of the way, oaf. I'll kill him!" Jeito pushed Nolan aside with far too much ease, grabbed Carro by the collar of his shirt and drew him up. Muscles quivered. The firelight shone through Jeito's thin blouse. She had breasts. But muscles, and a face with angles and planes like a man.

Carro tried to pull his shirt loose, but Jeito's grip tightened; he could barely breathe.

"You just fucked up my chance at getting back to the City of Glass with the Knights. I've been waiting for this for years, and you come along, you little creep. . . and you fuck it all up. You hear that? You fuck it up!" She screamed in his face and shook his collar. "Fuck, fuck, fuck! That's what you are, a little fuck! I'm going to kill you."

"Stop it!" called Farey.

Jeito froze. Licked her lips and gave him a sideways glace. Farey was the only one who had any kind of influence over her, even if only because he was much taller. Maybe he fucked her, but Carro had no doubt that was only because Jeito let him.

"Calm down," Farey said. "There's no point in fighting over what has already happened. The damage is done, and we won't get a second chance. It's not our task to deal with Carro's stupidity. If we do, we'll only be punished. Remember who he is. Let his father take care of it."

He looked at Carro, his dark eyes full of hatred.

A chill made Carro shiver. His father. His father who wanted him to kill the only friend he'd ever had.

Maybe he should just . . . vanish, become a foreign spy in another country, like Farey. Run away.

That's how you live your life, isn't it?

"Yeah, you're right." Jeito chuckled and let Carro's collar go. "I think I like that. Let his father take care of it."

"All right, so if we've decided that, let's quit fooling around with this stupid van, take the eagles and go to Tiverius," Farey said.

Nolan raised his eyebrows. "You know something we don't?"

"There was a bird. We've been ordered to join up with the other Knights either in the west or Tiverius. Tiverius is closer."

"Why didn't you say so?"

Carro was glad Nolan had turned his anger on Farey.

Farey flicked his eyebrows. "Why should I tell you anything that you might let slip out while you're fucking the traitor?"

Nolan's eyes grew wide with indignation. "Hey, have I ever betrayed you in all the time I've been with you?"

Neither Farey nor Jeito spoke.

"Come on, really?"

Farey rose, leaving Nolan standing there, still without an answer.

Carro didn't know where to look. Because of him, people got into trouble. Because of him, people died. Maybe he would be better off dead, too.

Farey let out a long whistle.

Jeito walked to the fire. While whooshing wingbeats of the approaching eagles disturbed the predawn silence, she pulled out a log that burned on one end. Carro realised what she was going to do just before she threw it, trailed by a stream of embers, into the truck. The canopy burst into flames almost immediately.

"There," she said, rubbing her hands. "Never liked that Chevakian devilry anyway." She wiped her hands on her trousers—a very female gesture now Carro knew the secret—and scratched her eagle's neck. The bird bent down and rubbed itself against her shoulder, to which she responded by ruffling its feathers. The bird stretched out its head at a weird angle, presenting more of its white-feathered neck to her.

"Oh, you stupid bird," she muttered, and scratched, sending a cloud of down into the air.

Even Jeito—murderous, evil, two-faced Jeito—cared about something.

One jump, and she sat on the bird's back, face aglow with the light from the burning truck.

"Come up, pups, hurry up. I'm not waiting for the Chevakian army to turn up to investigate the fire."

Carro lifted the harness over his bird's head. It snapped at the straps and hissed while he attached his bedroll.

Yes, I know you hate me, too.

Then they were off into the predawn. Farey knew of an abandoned shed where they'd sleep until dark, and from there on, it was straight to Tiverius.

Even Nolan was giving him looks that said, *Don't you dare trying to sneak off.* And where would he go anyway?

He had no home.

Tiverius was bigger than the biggest city Carro had ever seen. Even in the dark, and from a distance, the spread of lights dazzled him. There were no tall buildings, like in the City of Glass, but there were so many of them. Street after street with neatly planted trees and regular streetlights. He'd read of Chevakia, of course, but had not appreciated just how many people would live there, and how impressive and peaceful it would look.

Farey had made the hunters wait until dark before approaching the city, so no one would see them. He even knew where to go. Farey had probably been here before. He had not shown the note he was said to have received to anyone, but somehow, neither Jeito or Nolan questioned the order. When Carro asked Nolan about it, he said something about Farey having skill with tampering with the Chevakian *telegraph* whatever that might mean. It seemed the hunters *did* have a post deep in Chevakia, and had a base in Tiverius. Maybe they'd always had it, but none of the hunters was answering Carro's questions anymore.

After skirting the city's outer edges, they flew over hilly terrain where the ground was dark with trees and dotted with lights from the occasional farm.

It was in such a farm that the eagles landed, a low arch-shaped building of the type he had also seen near the border. The open end of the arch was blocked with a number of open sheds. The courtyard was bare and it was here that the eagles landed.

A young stable boy came out of the nearest shed to take the eagle's reins. Now Carro saw that there were more eagles under the canopy, at least ten birds, none of them familiar.

Under the balustrade that surrounded the courtyard, a senior Knight waited, also someone Carro hadn't seen before. He greeted Farey with a single nod of his head, and a hand sign that Carro didn't recognise. Farey mumbled something.

"The eastern road, he told me," the senior Knight said.

"What, now?" Farey spoke in a low voice.

"Immediately."

"Tell him to go fuck himself," Farey snarled. "They won't arrive until daytime. I haven't slept for days. These soft Chevakians don't do anything at night."

"Then send one of your sissy-boys—aaah!"

Jeito stood very close to the senior Knight. Carro couldn't see much by the soft dawn light, but if he wasn't mistaken, Jeito had the man by the balls.

"See what these sissy-boys can do?" she said, her voice menacing.

The man's face glistened with sweat. "Go. Do whatever. But don't come to me when he gets angry."

"The fuck he won't. Come, let's find a bed," Farey said and stomped off. Jeito followed—the senior Knight took a step back—and then Nolan, but when Carro walked past, the senior Knight held him back. "No, not you."

What? Carro stared after the hunters' retreating backs, his heart thudding.

"Your father wants to see you."

Oh, by the skylights. "He's here?"

"Not right now, but I've been ordered to give you some work that you're said to be good at. Something he needs done urgently."

Carro wanted to say, *It's all a lie, I'm not good at anything,* but he only nodded, so the Knight preceded him into the building.

Carro sees his mittened hands atop a wall. Isandor stands behind him in the alley.

"Can you see anything yet?"

Carro peers between the limpets ahead, pointed roofs half-hidden in thick roiling smoke. The breeze blows some of it his way. He coughs and shakes his head.

"Must be a warehouse on fire."

He hopes it's his father's. He hopes his father is inside the building and that the door is locked—

The house was a dark affair with high stone halls in which all noise echoed relentlessly. A few Knights sat to eat in a room with long tables. Carro didn't recognise anyone in this room. Several Knights sported injuries, especially faces and hands.

"What exactly happened in the City of Glass?" he asked.

"What, you don't know? Where have you been?"

Carro opened his mouth and then remembered that hunters never spoke of their missions.

"Just came in from regular patrols in the countryside."

The senior Knight chuckled. "Those hunters are quite fearsome, aren't they?"

Carro almost reminded the man that the fact that he still had his balls had nothing to do with his senior Knight rank, but he didn't. "Wherever I was, it wasn't in the City of Glass."

The Knight let a pause lapse. Then he said, "No one knows what caused it, but there was a huge explosion under the palace. The entire city has been destroyed. Many died. The people were talking about huge ghosts made out of steam."

Another senior Knight walking behind them broke in, "I reckon the sorcerers did it. Those evil ones in black."

"There have always been Brothers of the Light in the Outer City," Carro said. "They're idiots, with all their formulae and calculations."

That earned him a lot of harsh glances.

Carro was going to say that the Brothers never hurt anyone, and that no one would have as much knowledge of the old King without the Brothers having preserved some of the books, but he didn't think these men would appreciate that. So he just kept walking.

Visions niggled at the edges of his mind. Snow-covered plains and sleds made from pieces of rubble they found in the back alleys of the Outer City.

A man, shouting at him, probably for coming into his yard to filch bits of rope or pieces of dried fish.

The constant fear of running foul of his foster-father. Knowing that whatever he did and whatever time he came home and whatever the state of his clothing, the merchant would be angry anyway. Seeing Isandor being led away by his mother, her arm on his skinny shoulders.

. . . and all of a sudden, they arrived in a large room where old furniture had been shifted to the side to make place for a couple of dining tables of varying height, shoved together and surrounded by a mismatched lot of chairs. An ornate, high-backed chair stood at the head of the table. Heavy curtains covered the windows, faded and frayed, and the room was lit only by smoking oil lamps on the walls.

For some reason, Carro thought of that black stone room in the palace where he had first met Rider Cornatan.

Another, less-senior Knight came from somewhere at the back of the room, frowning at Carro.

"I'm supposed to do some work for Rider Cornatan," Carro said.

"Your name?"

"Carro."

Eyebrows shot up. Another glance up and down his dirty uniform.

Carro was sweating under his shirt. Any moment now and he was going to be challenged about the veracity of his name, about his mission, about the state of his clothes—

"So, you're the famous boy, eh?"

Carro cringed.

"Your father's not in, but he left you some work to do. Sit here."

Carro sat. He clutched the medallion through his clothes. Maybe he should just give the damn thing back. Surely Rider Cornatan had other sons.

"Here you go." The man had returned with a pile of books.

Books? "What am I supposed to do with them?"

"Check them. The Supreme Rider tells me you're really good at that."

Carro took the top book off the pile and opened it.

It was a ledger.

What? They were kidding, right?

"You might wonder why we worry about finances while there's a war going on?"

"Um—yeah." His mouth had gone dry. He fought the visions clawing at his awareness. Of his father carrying a big pile of books. Of his hands aching with cold. Of his father dousing the flames in the hearth, *Heat is for soft boys*. Of lines and lines of numbers dancing before his eyes.

"Well, money in Chevakia is important, and we need money to buy things so that we can survive here. The caretaker of this house has run off, leaving the books in a mess."

CHAPTER 25

TO SADY, the afternoon session of the doga—the important debate to discuss the vital tightening and redistribution of the budget—felt like stepping in tar. As soon as you thought you'd crossed it safely, it turned out there was some sticky residue on the sole of your shoe that kept leaving its mark all over the floor.

Sady seemed to have stepped in a patch of northern railways and had so far been unable to wipe the contamination from the afternoon's debate.

Yes, the north would support spending on distributing suits to the southern regions, if the promised expansion of the northern railway remained unaffected by the budget cuts. Yes, they would sign for the injection of non-existent funds into the balloon industry, if the old trains got new carriages. Yes, they would vote with the central regions in favour of Sady's proposals, providing that—you guessed it.

An eastern senator summed up Sady's feeling. "And I would like my honourable colleague to elaborate on how we are going to finance this railway."

Unlike the other senators, Sady couldn't yell and shout; and he wanted to, because with every hour that passed, he discovered more financial mess. The latest disaster he had uncovered was that someone appeared to have taken a number of the doga's finance record books from the treasury office, and not only didn't anyone know where they were, but no one had missed them.

The doga was wasting valuable time with this kind of nonsense, time they should have spent discussing what to do about the unfolding crisis in the south.

And Destran, at the back of the hall, looked like he was enjoying himself. The debate about railways went around in circles, and Sady kept glancing at the door, wondering what held up General Finnisius, who was meant to address the doga on the progress made by the army on the balloons, and was running late. The general had always been very punctual in previous meetings.

The thought clawed at the edges of his mind, *something has happened*. It was about the time that the trains from Fairlight would be expected back, and he hoped that the majority of Fairlight's citizens had taken the warning to get on.

And then this stupid meeting . . . Sady leafed through his documents, which detailed the agenda for the meeting that wasn't happening in any orderly fashion, but which he couldn't steer because the proctor was not allowed to interfere in the debate; the speaker was meant to be doing that, except the speaker was a central senator who had voted for Destran, and was obviously still sore about that. Every time someone mentioned an important point, he ever-so-subtly allowed senators to derail it with trivialities, like the stupid northern railway.

Sady had the documents with measurements from his trip to the border towns all done up, but there had already been some rumbles about who funded his trip, because he'd had to declare Lady Armaine's sponsorship, and this was causing all sorts of political spot fires about southern spies, about her loyalty and about whether or not she could possibly be called Chevakian. And that was just amongst his own office staff.

Never, ever, trust this woman.

Sady hadn't seen her since his trip and now wished he'd had nothing to do with her. Nothing of what she'd said about the south had been verified through other channels.

The scout he had sent with the peasant woman to Solmeni sent an alarming report from Twin Bridges this morning. The town's lines to the south were all out. The town was shrouded in smoke from forest fires, but it was unseasonably cold.

A vicious storm, Viki said, and showed him the crowded isobar lines having made their way into southern Chevakia.

Sady had asked Viki to contact the border stations on the telegraph, but he had received no new data. He wasn't sure Viki knew how to get the most out of the automated barygraph network, and wished he could do it himself, but writing new code for the machine took time, which he no longer had, having to discuss railways to the north instead.

And he hoped Viki would have the sense to keep trying. If his awful premonition was true and the barrier had shattered, sonorics in the city wouldn't increase for a number of days. Those days were crucial, since they could find out how far the menace would travel and how strong it would be. The city did have some defences. There were guidelines, a plan to keep people indoors, and, if necessary, an evacuation.

But he needed data to justify taking those measures.

No one knew what had happened. Not a word from the City of Glass, although Sady had made sure that messengers had finally been despatched. His trip to Milleus to seek out his wartime experience had been in vain, and none of the data he had gathered could convince the doga of the urgency of the threat. His support margin was too small to allow him to push through hard decisions. He was a leader without a real mandate.

Milleus, old goat, you let us down when we needed you.

Someone tapped Sady on the shoulder.

"Proctor?"

He turned to see his office boy behind him.

He mouthed, "What?" The office staff didn't usually come into the doga hall. His heart skipped with the nervousness that had never left him these last few days.

"There's a soldier in the office, Proctor. He insists that you come with him."

"We're in the middle of a session. Can it wait?"

The boy shook his head. "He said it's urgent."

"Is the message from General Finnisius?"

"He says the general has a problem. Please, Proctor, he was most insistent."

Sady heaved himself out of his chair. Senators fell quiet even before he hit the dais with the hammer. "You are going to have to excuse me. I have to adjourn the session. Something has come up."

There was some unhappy grumbling in the hall, mainly from northern senators.

At the back of the hall, Destran said, loud enough for him to hear, "Adjourning the session won't save your arse."

Some senators laughed.

Sady gathered up his documents and left, feeling chilled. His term would be a short one, he feared, having achieved nothing, and leaving the doga in more upheaval than it had been when he came to power—was that only a week ago?

In his office, he found that "the soldier" was the Proctor's personal guard Deri, who was normally stationed in the guard's post on the building's ground floor, but performed other tasks while the Proctor was in the building.

"What's this about?" Sady asked.

"Major Orsan asked me to come and get you. It's an emergency. The escort's down the corridor. Orsan says to bring your monitoring gear."

"But General Finnisius—"

"Is already there, Proctor. Please."

"What is going on?"

Deri didn't know any more, except that it was an emergency. Orsan was not someone prone to theatrics and neither was Finnisius, so Sady collected his cloak and his field box of sonorics measuring gear and followed him into the corridor.

A breeze came in through the open window, biting and cold.

In the courtyard of the doga building, two lines of soldiers faced each other in a changing-of-the-guard ceremony. The tassels on their epaulettes flapped in the wind. Soft green leaves that had grown on the trees with the beginning of spring now lay on the ground.

A young member of the city guard waited at the top of the stairs, his face anxious. He fell into step, taking up position on Sady's other side.

"Any report on what's happening?" Sady asked him.

"About midmorning, a train with what appeared to be refugees turned up at the station."

Mercy, the people from Fairlight. Finally.

"Stationmaster needs your advice urgently on what he should do. Thinks that you should make a decision because they're contaminated. Major Orsan is there, trying to keep them under control. It's not easy, Proctor. These people are in a bad way, and they're angry. They're not in the mood for being friendly, and we're still trying to find someone to communicate with them."

"Communicate?" Rebelling refugees? Certainly not the citizens of Fairlight.

"Yes. They're all southerners, sir, and we haven't found anyone who speaks Chevakian."

Sady turned to the man, his heart thudding. "Southerners?"

"Yes, I thought you understood that."

"Surely there must be some of the citizens of Fairlight on the train."

He shrugged. "If there are, we haven't found them yet."

"How many people are there?"

"Oh, I don't know. The train was packed. Many of them. Many are injured. They look like they've been burnt. There's dead people, too."

"Have you measured them for sonorics?" Sady felt his grasp on the situation slip from under him.

"Off the scale, sir. Station's been sealed off pending your advice."

Burn injuries meant extreme exposure to sonorics. Southern people, too, who were supposed to be resistant. The scale of this disaster made him feel numb. Was this what the Lady Armaine called rebellion?

He forced himself to focus on immediate needs. He could not have these people loose in Tiverius contaminating everyone else. "How many injured?"

The man shrugged, but he read the answer in his eyes. A lot.

"Well, let's see what we can do." He certainly sounded a lot more confident than he felt.

While they walked, he found some strands of reason. There was a field on the south-eastern outskirts of the city that was used sometimes by travelling troupes of artistes or cheapskate merchants. He would ask the army to set up tents there. The only trouble was, he would have to close the main road to Ensar because it went through the field, but they would have to set up diversions.

The marketplace bustled with the normal kinds of activity, which seemed surreal after his recent experiences. A young man and his wife or sister pulled a heavy cart full of fresh glistening fish. The man interrupted his work for a cheerful, "Good afternoon, Proctor," and other merchants echoed the greeting.

Sady had the feeling that soon, all normality would be blasted out of everyone's lives, that something was brewing the likes of which Chevakia had never seen.

The station was on the other side of the marketplace. There were soldiers at the station entrance, blocking the way in. A few confused passengers carrying bags of shopping waited and argued with them.

"But how can I get home?"

"I paid for the ticket."

Beyond the blockade, the steps into the building were empty.

The soldiers would not let Sady through until a man in a protective suit came down the stairs. He pushed up his hood. Orsan. His face glistened with sweat.

"Sady, I'm glad that you're here."

"How many people are in there?"

"Hundreds. The train was crammed."

Sady glanced into the dark maw of the station building, where he saw no one, but heard the murmur of many voices. A breeze carried a stink such as Sady had never smelled in his life. He gasped. "What's that awful smell?"

"Sorry, sir," said a man in station attendant uniform. "There was nothing we could do. We had to let them out of the trains. They're all on the platform at the moment, but many of them were dead, and the wagons . . . The line master says there's another three trains coming —" His eyes were haunted.

They were the trains he'd sent all right.

"Any citizens of Fairlight on the trains?"

"Not that I've seen," Orsan said. His eyes went distant.

Sady shivered in a cool breeze. He had never seen Orsan dishevelled like this. "What happened to them?"

"Your guess is as good as mine, sir, and at the moment I'm not sure I'll like your guess any better than mine."

Dead. The barrier shattered.

"Where is the stationmaster?"

"In his office, sir, with the driver." The station attendant continued, "What do you want us to do with these people, sir? They're anxious and nervous and I don't know how long we can keep them here. We need more guards."

"Already notified and on their way," Orsan said.

"Let me talk to the people," Sady said.

"No, sir. No one should go between them. These people are desperate. There's hundreds of them. They're hungry and sick. They'd rip you to pieces. They crackle with sonorics, all of them, and I don't know that any speak Chevakian."

Sady breathed in deeply as a waft carried fresh air across the marketplace. He scoured in his pocket. Found a handkerchief and pressed it over his nose. "Then find me a suit. I'm going to talk to the stationmaster."

What else could he do? He had to get this mob out of here somehow, in a way that didn't make them angrier than they already were, and after a three-day train ride from Fairlight in that stench, he guessed that would be pretty angry. "Where is General Finnisius?"

"Gone to mobilise the troops, sir."

Good. At least someone was getting a measure of what the situation required.

Someone handed him a suit. Sady pulled it on over his clothes. He hadn't worn a suit for a while, and the musty smell reminded him of his trips to the City of Glass. But even while the weather was unusually cold, Tiverius was much warmer than the City of Glass, and he was sweating inside the suit as soon as he'd done up the helmet.

"Come," he said, keen to get out of the suit again as soon as possible, because a proctor who'd fainted from heat stress was no good to anyone.

A heavily armed guard of four accompanied Sady up the stairs.

People crammed on the platform behind a barrier of armed guards in protective suits.

They were clearly southern people, with a dominance of dark hair, pale skin and blue eyes, and the latter were rare in Chevakia. Many carried packs and blankets of dirty fur. The people were dirty, too, sweaty, greasy-haired, red-faced.

Even through the suit, the stench was incredible. Sweat, dirt, vomit, excrement and overriding all that, the all-pervasive smell of decaying flesh.

A woman screamed and tried to run past the guards. The crowd surged and pushed. Soldiers struggled to keep them on the platform, guns levelled at the people. Civilians, all. Frightened out of their senses. Hungry, desperate. Contaminated. They had despair in their eyes, weeping sores on exposed skin. Horrific injuries.

Three more trains. Mercy, what were they going to do with them all? There were at least . . . he let his eyes roam the heaving crowd . . . at least a thousand people here, if not more. Yes, probably far more than that. Three more trains?

Sady swallowed nausea.

Then, in the middle of the seething crowd and between the suited bodies of two guards, his eyes met those of a woman sitting quietly serene. She wasn't exactly young—early middle age—but she was hideously pregnant. She wore a plain brown dress and had a mass of black curly hair tied at the nape of her neck. Her face was pale, her cheeks red and incredibly alive. She saw him, and her gaze held his. Her expression didn't radiate despair; it radiated hot anger. A woman having fled for her life, crowded onto a train, a woman proud and dignified even after all this hardship. A woman who didn't deserve this.

Just a moment, and then he'd lost sight of her.

The guards led him up the stairs to the stationmaster's office, which overlooked the platform.

The stationmaster stood at the receiver behind his desk, talking to the mayor. Both wore suits but no helmets. Sady entered the room, shut the door and lifted the helmet off his head. After exchanging greetings, he asked, "Someone told me the train driver was here?"

"Gone," the stationmaster sighed out. "Sat here not two counts and spewed all over the floor."

Yes, there was a wet patch, recently cleaned.

"Sonorics illness?"

The stationmaster shrugged, then handed Sady a printout from the station's sonorics reader. A wriggly line tracked over the paper, rising slowly, until it jumped off the edge of the paper. One hundred and fifty motes per cube. Mercy.

The stationmaster pointed. "That was when the train came in." The figures were clear enough. "Driver said the refugees were on the platform when he pulled into Fairlight, and there was nothing anyone could do about them boarding. The Fairlight station was completely overrun. None of them paid for their tickets. None of the train attendants could stop them coming in. The attendants are all amongst the dead, with their clothes soaked with shit and vomit, and blood running out of their eyes." He didn't need to say *sonorics illness*. "Story's the same for the other trains."

"Where are those trains?"

"We managed to stop them at Curly Loop. Waiting for your orders as to what to do with them, sir."

What to do? What *could* they do? Send the army and shoot all the passengers?

"Are there any citizens of Fairlight amongst them?"

He shrugged again. "Driver said he didn't see any, but he said that there was a lot of smoke in the area, and shortly before he entered Fairlight, there was a bang loud enough to shake the ground."

That bang would have been the shattering of the barrier, and the locals couldn't flee—because they were dead. If they had somehow survived and made it onto the train, they would have died on the way. How many people lived in the Fairlight region? He hardly dared add up the numbers. Thousands dead. Tens of thousands. All people Chevakia needed for food production.

Then another horrible thought: Milleus. Some of those towns down Ensar way hadn't responded recently either. He wiped sweat off his forehead. When he had a moment, he must make more of an effort to get in touch with Milleus, brotherly grudges be damned.

"I want to speak to General Finnisius. I also want a team in there to take out the dead and select the most desperately ill and their families."

"We tried to collect the bodies, sir," one of the guards said. "But they won't let any of their relatives out of their sight, even if they're dead. Some people say . . ." He swallowed. "Some guards say that these southern strangers eat their dead."

"Oh, nonsense. You don't believe that, do you?"

The man looked away. "None of them appears to speak Chevakian, sir."

"Then get an interpreter."

The man's eyes widened. "But where do I find—"

"Go and get Lady Armaine or one of her daughters. Don't pretend to me you don't know where she lives."

"Yes . . . yes, sir." The man bowed, put his helmet back on and trotted out of the office.

Never, ever, trust this woman.

Sady heaved a sigh and turned to Orsan, and noticed with satisfaction that General Finnisius had come in. "The army is at your service, proctor."

"Thanks, Finnisius. We need to establish a contact, a leader, and we need tents to house them. I want the army to set up a camp on the field on the Ensar road. We need vehicles to take them there and we need men to put up the tents. I want the route to be fenced off for citizens."

"What about the people who want to use the Ensar road?"

"Put up signs that they should use the Mekta road instead."

"Yes, sir."

"I want drivers and anyone working with the refugees to wear suits. I want all army personnel out of the camps before the refugees move in. We need to process the refugees first by decontaminating them. No one is to deal unsuited with anyone before decontamination. We need a temporary hospital. We need food."

"We can deal with the tents and decontamination," Finnisius said.

"All right, arrange it."

Finnisius left.

He turned to the mayor. "Could you ask the hospital to send a team, and for food for these people? Report to Orsan."

"I can do that, proctor." The mayor met his gaze squarely. He was a tall man, with short-cropped curly hair, quite handsome in his late middle age. "What account do I use to pay the merchants for that food?"

It was a valid question, and probably made out of innocence, because Sady didn't think the mayor of the city had much of a reason to be aware of the financial woes of the doga, but it chilled him to the core. What account to use to save thousands of *foreign* lives?

"Use general expenditure."

"But—"

"I'll make sure there will be extra funds to cover this event." He hoped he sounded confident, because he didn't feel it. He really needed to find those missing books and get someone to get to the bottom of this financial mystery.

"And wait."

The mayor stopped with his hand on the door.

Sady undid the chain he wore around his neck. On it dangled a small key that would unlock a cabinet in the town hall. He gave it to the mayor, whose eyes were wide.

"Do you want me to ring the bell, sir?"

"Yes. Once only, at this stage."

"Yes, sir." He bowed and left, leaving behind silence and the murmur of the crowd downstairs, the residual hissing of the train's engine, the shouts of soldiers, all muffled by the presence of a floor between them and the platform.

"Ringing the bell? Is that really necessary?" asked Orsan.

"Precaution." Or so he hoped, but if whatever the City of Glass had unleashed made its own citizens flee, then what hope did Chevakia have?

Then he turned to the stationmaster. "Do bring the other trains in here as soon as you clear the platform. We'll process the refugees at the station. Also, cancel any inbound trains. Keep Westside open, and the Curly Loop as well. Close the main line."

"But the people going to work—"

"When the mayor rings that bell, no one will be going to work. I want this part of the city sealed off, together with a corridor we will use to take the southerners out of here."

The stationmaster nodded, feebly.

"We'll need some help from the refugees themselves, but I want to wait until we have some interpreters who can talk to them—"

"Two young men have just come in to offer their services as interpreters, proctor."

"Excellent. Take them to the platform and let them explain what is happening. Now, excuse me. I'll go back to work."

He rose and picked up his helmet.

Sady and Orsan went back down into the station hall, where it was noisy, hot and smelly. Most of the people were still seated, but there were some pockets of disagreement, people yelling at the guards who kept them on the platform.

"How are you coping?" Sady asked a guard, and his voice sounded muffled in the helmet.

"Only just, sir. Ideally, we'd need a lot more people. And someone to talk to them."

"We're working on that. Meanwhile, keep them occupied and show that we're doing something. There should be some young men to work as interpreters soon. Start by organising these people into groups so they can be transported to the camp we'll set up. I want you to select any that are severely ill or injured . . ." He hesitated. ". . . or very young or pregnant."

He looked over the crowd, but couldn't see the pregnant woman.

CHAPTER 26

IN THE MORNING, Isandor still sat huddled under his cloak at the tent entrance. His legs were stiff from sitting in this position all night, and his arm ached from clutching the dagger.

He didn't think Jevaithi, in the tent, had slept much. He had heard her cry and he'd ached to comfort her, but he didn't dare leave his post. She'd been right; they weren't safe. He still shuddered at that moment of panic, when the shadow had loomed over him, the horror of feeling the shorthair cloak under his hands. By the skylights, these were *Knights*. Not only that, they were hunters.

But when the light grew from blue to white to pink, he was happy to see that the rogues with their van had indeed gone. He'd heard an engine after the attack, but it had been too dark to be certain. Additional vans might have appeared in the night.

Time for breakfast.

He stretched limbs stiff with sitting in the same position, huddled up under his cloak, and finally slid his dagger into his belt.

He checked in the tent, and found Jevaithi still asleep, her hair fanned out over the pillow. His heart ached to touch her, but he didn't want to wake her.

Next, the goats. They already stood in the corner of the pen closest to him and when he collected the bucket from the back of the truck, a few let out plaintive bleats. Their udders were swollen with milk, and they jostled each other to be first in line.

Isandor got the stool and bucket and sat down with the first animal, its warm smell all around him.

Milking had become an easy, relaxing task.

Milleus said that they were on their way to Tiverius. Apparently, he had a brother there, but Isandor wished they didn't have to rely on Milleus. He couldn't muster the courage to tell Milleus that they were going their own way. He didn't even know if he wanted to go his own way. Alone, he and Jevaithi would be so much more vulnerable.

But by the skylights, Tiverius.

There were a lot of people in the city and people meant danger. He couldn't imagine that Tandor would be the only southerner ever to travel to Tiverius. There had to be other southerners who regularly crossed the borders. They would recognise Jevaithi.

Isandor wanted to find somewhere safe for them to live, not to keep running, but for now it seemed everyone in Chevakia was running. Maybe people in Tiverius were running, too. Milleus had explained why they were running, but Isandor still didn't quite understand how an increase in icefire had everyone in such a panic. Yes, he knew that icefire was lethal to Chevakians, but somehow deep inside he didn't really *understand*. Chevakians were people just like southerners. They even had Imperfects. Yesterday he had spotted an old man on the road, pushed in a chair with wheels by a younger woman.

How could Chevakians be killed by icefire? They looked just like him.

By the time he finished milking, the sun had gone and grey clouds were rolling in. A gusty wind tore at the trees around the clearing, making them whistle and sigh.

The young mother from the family they had met yesterday came to buy some milk. Isandor poured the rest into a container and sat down with a cup of the frothy, tangy liquid.

Isandor stoked the fire and fed it some wood. Meanwhile, he put out the plates and then judged it safe to go to the creek to get water.

When he came back with the pot, a man he hadn't seen before stood at the fire watching him. He was middle-aged, dressed in a rough woollen jacket, loose trousers, wearing a scarf on his head against the sun. A typical Chevakian peasant.

"You can share some of our water for tea." Isandor nodded at the man and went on with his business, pouring a bit of water in the teapot and scrubbing it out, and then adding tealeaves.

When he looked up, the peasant had come right up to the fire, squinting at Isandor.

"You are from the south?"

Isandor straightened. "Yes, I am."

The next moment, the man took a swing at him. Isandor saw it coming and ducked.

"Hey, what are you—"

Another punch missed his head.

Isandor managed to get hold of the man's arm to stop him punching again, but he had the strong arms of someone who worked in the fields.

"What have I done?"

"It's because of you that we have all this trouble," the man said, spitting between his teeth. "You're filthy, raping savages, that's what. You're ruining our country."

"Hey, calm down, let him go." This was a new voice. Milleus pulled the peasant's arm, and he let go of Isandor, but continued to glare with hatred in his eyes.

"These young people are refugees just like all of us," Milleus continued.

The man spat on the ground. "They're southerners. They are raping savages, the lot of them. Why do you defend them, mister? Even as we're all running for our lives because of them. They burned my farm. They killed my animals."

Milleus snorted. "What—these youngsters?"

The man squinted at Isandor. "I don't care which of them did it. They came on their damn birds and set fire to the house. They killed my father-in-law in front of my eyes. Ran a sword right through him, like that." He made a slashing motion. "And you . . ." He pointed a trembling finger at Milleus. "You dare come here with a pair of them. Protecting them. Letting them touch our food."

"One southerner isn't the same as another."

"They're all the same to me. Evil *magicians*. Much as the idiots in Tiverius tell us that there is no *magic*."

"There isn't. The Scriptorium has explanations for everything."

"Oh, there is no magic, huh? Then tell me mister, how come we're all running from this non-magic we can't see but that kills us nevertheless? Are you going to tell me the south doesn't control it either? Are you going to tell me that those vile southerners are doing this to us by accident? Are you telling me that the southerners are not doing this so that they can send rampaging hordes into our land to take our farms? And that while this goes on, we should smile kindly at any southerner we meet?"

A deep anger welled up in Isandor's chest. "The City of Glass wants none of your land. They wouldn't even know what to do with it—"

"Raping savages, the lot of you!"

"I've done nothing. We have fled ourselves—"

"Isandor." That was Milleus, a steady presence behind him. "Ignore him."

"But this man is saying untrue things about us."

"Leave it. He's angry and hurt. Arguing will not change his mind about southerners."

"Too right, Mister. I will *never* change my mind about southerners."

"But they're lies," Isandor called out. "No one in the City of Glass wants your farms. They don't even know what a farm is."

"Then tell me: why did they come to our farmhouse and burn it? Why are we all running from this menace? Why did the barrier break?"

Isandor shrugged. He thought he knew why the hunters—those who had tried to kill him last night—burnt the farms: to mark the ones they'd searched. And the reason they were searching was Jevaithi. But he couldn't tell anyone that. As for the barrier, he had truly no idea. He hadn't even known Chevakia *had* barriers.

"Oh, give the boy a break," Milleus said. At least twenty curious onlookers had gathered. "I found the two of them in my barn before any of this happened. They are young lovers having eloped from their families, fleeing an arranged marriage. They know nothing. They are innocent and can answer our questions just as much as you or I can. If you want answers, you should look at your local authorities."

Several people laughed at this.

A man said, "Destran's probably too busy covering his own backside to look out for any of ours."

Another said, "What have the authorities done to keep us safe? None of them warned us of this magic."

"They did talk about it a bit, but no one ever said it was urgent."

A strange expression came over Milleus' face. He straightened his old back. "Did they ever send suits?"

Several people laughed at this.

A woman shouted. "They promised they'd send some ages ago. They finally sent twenty, for a town of thousands. And they were all a huge size."

Another chimed in. "Yeah, like all their promises. Has Destran put in the road he promised? The school? The hospital? All the things that made the district vote for him? Of course not."

"So why didn't you vote out your representative?"

"He's all right. A local man. In the job for years. We couldn't vote against him. There is no one else, really."

"No? But your mistaken loyalty has consequences. Because you vote for him, the local representative gets away with doing nothing, because he knows that he doesn't have to work for your votes."

Milleus looked like he had grown, and shed ten years in age. Like this, he was formidable, nothing like the old man on the farm. An echo of something he used to be, Isandor thought. Something he no longer wanted to be, but couldn't help breaking through at times.

A flutter of movement stirred the air at Isandor's back. Jevaithi had come out of the tent, her hair mussed, her skin still warm from the blankets. She took his hand behind his back and rested her head on his shoulder.

"Let me guess," Milleus went on. "The council says that in order to get these things approved, they need to be signed by the doga, and in the doga, with all the regional factions bickering against each other, your road, your school, your hospital becomes unimportant, because they are debating other problems in districts more important to them than yours. Because you re-elected your representative, who is a longtime supporter of Destran. I tell you something else . . ." Milleus now discarded the farm jacket he'd been wearing for the past few days. They had gathered quite an audience. Women, men and little children had come out of the vans and watched. "The money that goes into paying your council, and paying their trips to Tiverius, and paying their meals and their work clothes and the buildings they sit in—that money—where do you think that comes from? Tell me where? Out of Tiverius?" He pointed at the peasant, who took a step back and mumbled something.

Milleus continued. "No, it comes from your pockets, and you should determine what is done with it."

Jevaithi looped her arms around Isandor's waist while standing behind him. In a way, he was glad that Milleus had diverted attention away from him and the issue of southerners. On the other hand, something strange was happening.

One woman on the other side of the fire elbowed her neighbour and whispered in her ear. The other gaped, and then elbowed the next one.

"They know him," Jevaithi whispered.

Yes, she was right. And Isandor thought of the library and all the books on warfare he had seen in Milleus' sitting room. "Do you have any idea who he is?"

She shook her head. "It's been a long time since we had any visitors from Chevakia at the palace. When they still came, they'd have to come to the palace all suited-up. Mother wouldn't let me be there when she received them, anyway. I was too little."

"Could he be a retired army general or something?"

"Could be, but I truly don't know any of their names."

And Chevakia, Isandor remembered reading, was governed by a large council of representatives chosen by the people.

But there was the fear and the stories. Things he had been told in his brief time as Apprentice Knight. Chevakia had resoundingly defeated Arania in the year he was born. A few years later, Chevakian weapons made mincemeat of Knights who had been caught in the border villages. Apparently, Chevakians didn't like the idea of Chevakian girls being offered the chance to be well-respected breeders in the City of Glass. The girls had *volunteered*, never mind the whole thing had been a mistake with results none of them could have foreseen. The Knights had reduced icefire to a point it hardly existed, and still it killed Chevakians.

Milleus finished talking and a good number of bystanders cheered, before moving back to packing their tents.

Milleus, Jevaithi and Isandor went to do the same. Milleus put his jacket back on and changed back into a farmer.

Isandor rolled up the tent. Milleus rounded up the goats, chased them up the ramp onto the trailer. Jevaithi packed away the dishes.

When Isandor carried the tent to the van, he found Milleus leaning on the trailer's railing, scratching goats between their ears. He looked deep in thought.

"I thought, Milleus, when you were talking to those people. I thought you said that really well."

Milleus sighed. "Yes," he said, patting a goat's furry back. "I think they liked it. That's the trouble."

He stood silently for a while. No, he wasn't going to say anything; Isandor would have to ask.

"Milleus?"

"Yes."

"Were you ever an important person, when you were younger?"

"Don't know that you'd call it important."

Guess that meant yes.

"What happened?"

"It doesn't matter. What happened was that for all the work I did and the lives I saved, I wasn't wanted. I was discarded. That's when I went to the farm, and I wanted to ignore people. I guess . . ." He shrugged, and fiddled with something in his pocket that sounded like paper. He blew out a heavy breath. "That time can never come back. I made mistakes, bad ones. I can never take those back, either." He lifted his head and met Isandor's eyes with his clouded brown ones. "I want you to remember, if you have a passion, and you believe you can make life better for everyone, don't wait until someone comes to ask you to fix it. Because by that time, it's too late."

By the skylights, fleeing the City of Glass had been the biggest mistake he made in his life. Taking Jevaithi, handing the power to the Knights, who only abused it, who seemed to have used it to unleash the biggest disaster the City of Glass had ever seen. They'd been looking for a reason to kill the Queen, and he'd just given it to them. And they were now doing something that could be felt even in Chevakia.

"I know," Isandor said, the truth on the tip of his tongue. *Nila is*

Jevaithi, the Queen of the City of Glass. He felt like he wanted to say it, because he was sick of hiding.

"You can't know. You are what you are, Isandor. What have you been, other than a teenager who ran off with his girlfriend?"

Actually . . .

Isandor hesitated, but the moment for confession slipped.

CHAPTER 27

SOMEWHERE, IN a place between life and death, a voice said, "Tandor."

It was a female voice, and one he knew well.

He turned around on the chair; his head was the only part of him he could move.

She was coming into the room behind him, a mere ghost of a form, barely visible. Everything about her was white, from her dress—which he recognised and definitely wasn't white in real life—to her hair to her hands.

"Tandor, some Chevakian soldiers just came to the door. They wanted me to come and speak to a large group of refugees that are at the station. Apparently, these people have fled a large explosion and destruction in the City of Glass. I thought your stupidity had harmed only you, but now it seems you have taken down the entire country with you. Why did that happen?"

"I don't know, mother." He'd done all the calculations, and should have been able to control the Heart with all his children there. Why had it possessed them? Why had icefire taken their corporeal beings and turned them into evil beings of light? Why had Ruko stopped listening to him?

He added, "Because the Knights meddled with things they did not understand."

"You should have seen what they were doing. Compensated for it."

"I couldn't!" Without his children, he hadn't even been able to get into the palace until it was already too late.

"I am not happy," she said. "You are stupid and incompetent."

Ruko laughed somewhere in the room. "I've always said that."

Lady Armaine gave him an irritated glance. "You have destroyed everything we have worked for all these years. Now I have Chevakians accusing me, and if I were to show my face amongst those refugees, they would surely rip me to pieces. Tandor, these people were meant to see the *splendour* of what can be done with icefire, not its deathly force."

Tandor wanted to say, *Maybe you cannot have one without the other,* but he kept it to himself.

"If you'd only used your brain, we could have won already. We would have been on our way to show the people the glories of the past, show them how the Knights repressed all that was wonderful in our land. Because of you, people will now be saying that the Knights were right in trying to stifle icefire, that it *has* to be used for evil. And as we all know, it does not."

"I couldn't—"

"You have caused this to happen, son."

"But it wasn't possible . . ." He thought of that moment when he'd stood there watching the enchanted children walk from their prison towards the Heart. He'd yelled at them to listen, but they couldn't. He'd known what the Knights had done, and he had been unable to do the only thing that could have averted the explosion: kill them. He couldn't kill the children. He cared too much for them. Because it was too dangerous to show affection for his own two children, he cared for the ones he had saved.

"You're the biggest failure of my life. I don't understand how the Thilleian royal family could have birthed such a weakling. All the conditions were right for us to take over. People loved Jevaithi; people hated the Knights. We had support from the Brotherhood. Think of it, Tandor, the biggest and richest independent organisation in the entire world. Not just in the City of Glass—I've worked hard for their support right here in Tiverius. And what can they do now? What can we tell them? They cannot continue to defend the good of icefire when people start to die. The Knights have arrived in Tiverius. The doga will trust them, because we cannot give them anything positive.

It's all your fault, Tandor. We spent years planning this. There will not be another chance."

Tandor had nothing to say to that. She was wrong. It was not his fault, and he was sick of her continuous taunts. But unless he was released from this in-between world, there was nothing he could do about it.

"I think we'll take over from here. We are lucky that at least the hybrid child is safe. We must have the child, Tandor. If you cannot control its mother, we will be forced to send someone who can."

"She is Pirosian. You can use all the icefire in the world on her, and it won't have any effect." He felt victorious saying that.

Dear Loriane, good, down-to-earth, Pirosian Loriane, the Pirosian princess his mother's minions had exchanged for the baby Maraithe. He saw her smiling face, the crinkling skin around her eyes and his incorporeal body flooded with warmth. He'd loved Maraithe, of sorts, out of duty to his family. He'd been young and at that age, any beautiful woman would have captivated him. Loriane was different. She was neither pretty nor impressionable, but for that, she owned his heart.

"There are ways to control Pirosians that don't involve icefire."

"Don't you dare touch her, mother!"

She laughed. "You are giving me orders?"

"She is innocent. She doesn't know anything."

"Ah, I think we've found your soft spot. Keep an eye on this lady, Ruko."

"As you wish, mistress."

"No, Ruko, listen to me. You're my servitor. Keep your hands off Loriane!"

But Ruko approached him from behind, and the cold of his touch froze his movements. He returned to the crowded platform amongst the press of people. He was on the ground and Ruko was holding his head in his lap, stroking the ravaged skin on his forehead. What a mock gesture. The very person who kept him imprisoned. Tandor wanted to scream but the icefire that flowed from Ruko's fingers made his muscles stiff.

CHAPTER 28

LORIANE SAT dazed, crammed on the platform amongst the press of stinking bodies. The Chevakian leader had come and gone. He had spoken with some of the soldiers, gesturing as if telling them what to do. He had gone upstairs, where she could still see him through a window. He took off the helmet that made him look like a bug. Underneath, his hair was curly, short and greying at the temples. Loriane liked his face; he looked like someone who would care.

But now he was gone, and one of the Chevakian soldiers yelled, and some semblance of quiet fell in the crowded hall. It looked like something was about to happen.

A suited Chevakian came up the stairs in the company of two young men without suits. One was tall and lanky, with long black hair hanging down both sides of a narrow face, the other was broader and shorter, and wore his hair short.

Someone seated close to Loriane muttered, "Who are they? Were they on the train?"

"No way," someone else said. "They're too clean."

"They're Knights," someone else said, and someone else made a shushing noise.

"How do they dare to show their faces? The Knights caused this trouble. They should hide in shame," Dara said, a bit too loud for Loriane's liking.

Ontane said, "Shut your trap, woman, if you want to survive."

For once, Loriane agreed with him. Because surely, the Knights had fled the City of Glass on their eagles, and they only had to wait at the end of the train line for all the city's surviving citizens to show up, and they would look very carefully for supporters of the old king. Who knew how many of the Knights had survived?

"I don't care who they are. I just hope this means we can get out of here," Myra said, patting little Beido on his backside.

Beyond her, Ruko cradled Tandor in his lap, his hand stroking the ravaged skin. There was something eerily mechanical about the gesture. Loriane didn't think Ruko had ever done something like that before. His eyes were distant, focused on the two southerners, and the expression in them chilling.

"Ruko?" Loriane said.

He turned towards her, and she thought she saw a glint of fire in those black eyes, something that said, *don't interrupt*. He went back to staring at the two men, one of whom was now clambering on a chair which a Chevakian guard had brought.

"Citizens!" he called out. "Citizens, listen to me."

There was more grumbling in the audience. Citizens was a word most often used by Knights when speaking to the public.

"I have a message from the Chevakians."

"When will they let us out of here?" someone at the front yelled.

Someone else added, "We don't want speeches. We want food!"

People close to Loriane stirred. Someone muttered, "We were hoping to get *away* from the Knights, not to be bullied by them again."

A number of people agreed with this, so Loriane couldn't hear what the man at the front said.

". . . The Chevakian army is setting up a camp for everyone here. They have food. They have medicines. They will take care of you. Shortly, they will send some vehicles and will need us to divide into groups of about thirty people each so they can be transferred in orderly fashion. Please give consideration to the ill and feeble first, to wounded, elderly, pregnant and the very young. Any of you who have places to go to in this city, relatives or friends they can stay with, let us know. The Chevakian authorities have informed us that resources are stretched and that they will do their best to help us, but the fewer of us need help, the better."

"Who do you think you are?" a voice sounded from the back of the audience. Everyone turned around.

One of the men who identified himself clearly as Brothers of the Light had risen.

Someone closer to him yelled support.

"We've come here all the way to be free of the tyranny wrought upon us by the rulers of the City of Glass. We don't need the Knights to tell us what to do. Think for yourselves, people, and accept what you think is fair. The Chevakians are providing tents for us, but they don't know who we are and who our leaders are. This is the chance, do you realise, to get freedom from the dictators who have ruled us for so many years. They . . ." He pointed at the two young Knights, who were making their way towards him. "They want us to obey. They want everything to continue as before. They want us to meekly submit to their regime of secrecy and misinformation. Do you want that? Don't you, like most of us, think that it is time the Knights came clear about what actually happened back there in the City of Glass? Don't you think it is time for the people to have a say in how the City of Glass is governed?"

Most of the grumbling had died down. The people were staring at him. Someone at the front yelled, "I don't care where it comes from, as long as we get food."

A woman close to Loriane said, "You mean, he thinks there is a chance we'll be able to go back home?" She was a noblewoman, in her middle age, who had somehow ended up caring for a group of six adolescents who couldn't possibly all be her children.

Loriane had wondered if Tandor had been the only Thilleian descendant to have collected children with abilities to see and bend icefire. He might have collected the most, but he was not the only one. Were they organised through this Brotherhood? She had thought that all they did was collect books and educate orphans.

On her other side, Ontane muttered, "They better be quiet, or there be trouble, I tell you. If they go against the Knights—"

The noblewoman turned to him. "Maybe then it's time to go against the Knights and tell them we won't stand for this anymore." Her expression was fierce.

"I agree," Dara said. Her voice was determined.

"But . . ." Ontane turned to his wife, an astonished expression on his face. "Dear, don't you think . . ."

"Don't ye 'dear' me, husband. Ye've been calling me 'woman' all these years, and I've had to come with you all the way to Chevakia to see what a selfish coward ye really be. Back home, when they came to our door, I wasn't allowed to give any of our food to these people. We had to hide. We had to get out so they wouldn't follow us. And you know what? Here we be, surrounded by them anyway. These people be our family. The Knights have ruined the lives of all of us, and I'll no longer stand for it."

"Dara!"

Myra stared at her mother, her mouth open.

"The man be right. We should do something, or the Knights will just treat us like they've treated us before. They will not speak to the Chevakians on our behalf."

"And you want to make an example of your family?"

A man in front turned around and said, "Look, I really don't care about politics right now. I'd rather hear what the fellow is saying so we can get food."

Many others agreed with him.

The two Knights were making their way through the audience, but people were deliberately getting in their way.

The man in black still stood there, defiant. He yelled, "Remember, you do not need to do what the Knights tell you to do. This is not the City of Glass. Demand to see the Queen."

"Yes," someone yelled. "Where is the Queen?"

"Show us the Queen," a woman yelled at the Knights. "If she is safe, we'll believe you."

"The Queen, we want the Queen."

Other voices took up the chant. "Jevaithi, Jevaithi."

The Knights gave each other a nervous glance.

"Jevaithi, Jevaithi!"

One of them reached for his crossbow. The other put a hand on his arm to stop him.

"Jevaithi, Jevaithi, Jevaithi."

A couple of refugee men rose, much closer to the Knights. The crowd was chanting so loudly now that Loriane could no longer hear what they said, but the Knights backed away, first slowly, and then faster as the men followed. Under loud jeers and chants, the two disappeared down the stairs.

People cheered, including Dara, who rose and jumped around with the noblewoman and her six foster children.

It took a while for the crowd to calm down, but eventually, some Chevakians in suits came up the stairs and moved onto the platform. They pointed and waved, stepped over legs and luggage, and picked people out of the crowd and helped them towards the front. A couple of people with injuries, a few elderly nobles, all dirty and dishevelled, the young woman Loriane had seen on the train who was also pregnant. Many people needed to be carried.

"Get out of the way," someone yelled. "They're taking out the people most in need."

People shuffled aside so that the Chevakians could walk between them.

"You go sit at the front with the sorcerer, Mistress Loriane," Ontane said, while pushing Loriane in the back.

Soon enough, a soldier approached the area where Loriane and Ontane and the family sat.

He took one look at Tandor and flinched.

He said something, which sounded funny inside the suit, and beckoned forward.

Ruko rose, and picked up Tandor.

Ontane rose as well.

Dara hissed at him, "It be just the injured they want. Can't see anything wrong with you."

Ontane pointed. "The others be bringing their families."

That was true.

"We're not family," Myra said.

"He be my brother," Ontane said.

Loriane felt like shouting, *You selfish liar!* but she liked Myra and didn't want to embarrass her in front of the crowd, or lose sight of her. In a way, they *had* become family. Besides, little Beido needed fluids and Myra's milk was drying up.

"Come on, women, let's go." Ruko and Tandor were already walking down the cleared path.

Myra's eyes met Loriane's, apologetic. Loriane shrugged. Not that Myra could help having such a selfish man for a father.

Dara held out a hand to assist Loriane up. There was thunder on her face.

"No matter what ye be thinking about us now, in your city ways, mistress, I did *not* choose to marry him."

"It's all right, Dara, really." Loriane cringed with embarrassment.

Dara grumbled, "No, it bain't."

Ontane whirled. "I heard that, woman. Can ye for once do what they say and stop making me feel stupid?"

"Yeah?" Dara turned to her husband. Her cheeks were red and her eye the most alive Loriane had seen. "Ye *be* stupid. Ye be an embarrassment to me. Ye be a coward, a selfish prick and a petty whinger. If this be time for a change, let's have a change: I will no longer be bullied by ye, and I will no longer call ye my husband."

Ontane looked like someone had slapped him in the face. "Dara, please stop being ridi—"

"I mean it."

"Stop it, you two!" Myra yelled. All around them, people were staring.

"No." Dara folder her arms across her chest. "I've had enough."

"Shut up. You're making me feel ridiculous." Myra's voice cracked.

Ontane said in a low voice, "Your mother be just angry. She'll forget this when she calms down."

"I'm serious."

"Dara, dear, please stop—"

"I'm serious."

"Can we just keep walking?" Myra said. "We're holding everyone up."

Ontane gave a glowering look and stomped off. A few women gave Dara victory signs.

Dara balled her fist. And Loriane felt a pang of jealousy for this woman, who had the courage to do what she herself should have done long ago: tell her lover to fuck off. In a way, she felt the explosion was her fault, because she had provided Tandor with a safe place to stay in the City of Glass.

They made their way to the front of the crowd, where a broad set of steps led out of the station. A flimsy barrier had been erected, and on the other side Chevakian guards paraded in neat brown uniforms.

The square outside the building was completely empty. Loriane gaped at the amazing buildings made of stone. There were carved columns and sloping roofs, wide stairs, ornate railings and paved courtyards. Trees grew in little square bits of ground that had been left uncovered, in neat rows.

They waited.

Then, from the other side of the platform came a vehicle Chevakians called a *truck*. It was a big thing, much bigger than any of the farm vehicles they had seen so far, but smaller than the train. The cabin, with window, sat in front of a large barrel, from which rose a chimney belching smoke, and behind the barrel was a covered trailer. Both its metal surface and the cloth cover were dark as the night.

The vehicle came up to where the refugees were waiting, and stopped. A suited soldier got out and spoke to the soldiers who had been waiting with the refugees. One went and opened the back of the canopy. He beckoned.

The line of soldiers opened up and the first injured refugees shuffled towards the truck.

Two more suited figures in the truck helped the refugees climb onto the loading tray.

When it was the family's turn, Ontane went up first and helped Myra; he tried to help Dara, but she refused his hand and climbed up herself, and then held out a hand for Loriane.

As Loriane stepped onto the narrow ladder, a stab went through her belly worse than she had yet felt. She cried out and stumbled back.

Gloved hands stopped her falling.

She stood there, clutching her belly, swaying and panting. *Oh, by the skylights.*

"What is it? The babe coming?" Myra asked, looking down from the truck.

Loriane couldn't reply for the pain. She clamped her teeth to stop yelling out. Was it possible to forget how much this hurt? Two Chevakians in suits picked her up and wrestled her up the ladder. By the time she was in the truck, the pain had abated.

There were mattresses inside the trailer for the worst injured. Ruko had put Tandor on one of them, and he sat at the edge, again stroking Tandor's forehead.

Someone in a suit, a woman by the sound of her voice, guided

Loriane to a bench that surrounded the perimeter of the trailer and indicated that she should sit down. Two men shuffled aside, looking at Loriane as if she had the plague.

There was no room for Ontane, Dara or Myra to sit.

Soon all the mattresses were taken by wounded.

A Chevakian pushed up a panel that closed the bottom half of the opening at the back of the trailer.

The vehicle growled and jumped into motion, which set off another stab to her belly. Loriane grabbed onto the edge of the bench waiting for it to pass. Sweat rolled down her face into her neck.

By the skylights, she wished that this truck would hurry up.

CHAPTER 29

WHEN SADY CAME back to his office, a long line of people was already waiting there. Not just citizens, but senators and city administrators, and—mercy—the doga's treasurer.

Sady gestured at the man, and he stepped out of the line to follow Sady into the office.

As soon as Sady shut the door behind him, the man started, "Proctor, I implore you, before you make any plans, you really need to consult with me about the mo—"

"No. You need to bring me the missing books. Now."

"I'm working on that. We think we know where they are."

"Here. In my office. Now."

"But I can't—"

"Now." Sady was getting enough of this weaselly man. "Or tell me what has happened to them. If you really know. Which, frankly, I'm beginning to doubt."

The man swallowed visibly. "I had hoped you were going to be reasonable about this."

"Tell me what is reasonable about this crisis and suddenly having thousands of extra people to feed and no money to do it."

"Well," he said and didn't meet Sady's eyes. "It was like this: Destran wanted to check a few things, so we lent him—"

"You let the financial records leave the building?" That was completely against regulations.

"Um—yeah. It was only for a little while."

"Before or after his defeat?"

"Um . . ."

"Answer the question, or I'll assume the worst."

He said nothing, because it seemed there was nothing he could say to improve the situation: that somehow Destran had managed to get damaging records out of the building after his defeat.

Sady spoke slowly to control his emotions. "Do you have any idea what corruption and blackmail looks like? Destran wants to cover the mismanagement that he's presided over for the last ten years, so that he cannot be punished for corruption, so that the senators—and I bet they were northern senators—whom he paid in exchange for their support cannot be found out and persecuted. If you care one bit about your country, and care about any of the thousands of sick and injured people out there, bring me back those books, so I can personally find and throttle the people who took money that wasn't theirs."

The man said nothing, just moved his mouth.

"Don't sit there like that, go!"

"Yes, yes, Proctor."

He rose and went to the door.

"And make sure that with the books, you hand in your letter of resignation."

The man nodded, nervously and scuttled from the room. He left the door open, and to Sady's surprise no one came in.

Well, what the . . .

He pushed his chair back from the desk and went to the door, where he was met by circle of stunned faces.

"Anyone else?"

Several of the administrators shook their heads. Others were suddenly very busy talking to their neighbours. Fancy that. He had scared complainers away.

"It's the han Chevonian blood," Orsan said, weaving his way through the people in the foyer. Sweat glistened on his face from being inside the helmet. "I think they were in doubt that you had it."

That hurt Sady more than he wanted to admit. He didn't want the job. He was just warming the seat for when Milleus returned.

"Anything to report?"

Orsan sighed. "Do you want the bad news or the worse news?"

"Start with the least bad."

"The refugees didn't like the two men who offered to interpret. They were lucky they didn't get lynched before they made it out of the station. So now we are again interpreterless and clueless about what made these people come here."

"Who were these men?"

Orsan spread his hands. "I don't think that anyone checked."

"Right, we're not doing that again. Future applicants will have to identify themselves. Any report on Lady Armaine?"

"The men went to see her, but were told she wasn't home."

"Oh, that's rubbish. She likes playing hard-to-get." He would have to chase the cranky old toad up himself. "What's the worse news?"

"The hospital administrator wasn't keen to send people. He said what if Chevakians need the hospital? I don't know how many he had to spare. I don't suspect he has nurses walking around doing nothing in the first place. I guess we have to make do with what he's willing to share."

"Yes. I know."

"He did eventually agree to send a few people, but it's nowhere near enough to help them substantially."

And that would only add to the anger of the refugees.

"And—"

"There is worse news still?"

"I'm afraid so. Finnisius reports that a large batch of the suits in army storage have deteriorated and no longer offer protection. He wants to know if we have any other stores, or his ability to help will be limited."

"Other stores?" It came out as a shout. "He knows what we have, and he already has it."

"He knows that. I think he was trying to put it politely."

Sady blew out a breath of frustration. "Seriously, Orsan, is this entire country falling to bits?"

Orsan's face didn't betray any emotion. He let a silence lapse, and when it became clear that Sady expected some kind of reply, he said, "That's up to the politicians to decide, sir. Not my place to comment."

"Well, maybe not, but promise me, if you see any sign of anything untoward happening, like people having access to things they shouldn't have, removing things that aren't theirs, or being paid for votes, please tell me."

"It's part of the doga guard's pledge to protect senators current and past. I'm afraid I am not authorised to comment."

"But if there is criminal conduct . . ."

"That is for the doga and the courts to decide. It is my job to make sure no one gets murdered in the process." He was very closed about this. Sady wondered what prompted this behaviour. Orsan had only come into his service when he became chief meteorologist. Before that, he had worked for the proctor's office . . . at the time Milleus was deposed, as a young guard maybe? And had, in his enthusiasm, stepped across the line?

Sady blew out a breath and leaned his head in his hands. A waft of sweat-laced air surrounded him. Mercy, he stank.

Then, in that defeated and frustrated silence, he heard a sound he'd thought he'd never hear: the clear stroke of a bell. Once, then, after a couple of heartbeats, again, and again. It seemed like all the sounds in the building and in the square below fell quiet but for that eerie clear sound. *Ting.* Two breaths' silence. *Ting.* Two breath's silence. *Ting.*

Sady met Orsan's eyes. The expression on Orsan's face was haunted. "Sady, the whole country is looking at you to help us through this."

Sady stared at the clouds scudding across the patch of sky he could see through the window. Right then, he could not have felt any more desperate and alone.

Sady hurried through the corridors of the Scriptorium. Across the mosaic-tiled floor of the tower, up the stairs to the mezzanine gallery, where soft carpet muffled his footsteps and handcrafted bookcases lined the curved outer wall. A student scurried past carrying a pile of books. A few others sat reading on leather-covered chairs.

While the ringing of the bell had put a stop to normal activity in the streets, it seemed life within these solid stone walls went on as if nothing had happened. Coming in from outside, Sady was still in the suit that the proctor's guard insisted he wear—although he argued it was overkill—his helmet under his arm. It was warm in here and the suit felt restrictive and hot. He felt like a creature from a different world. Hot, smelly and bone tired.

"Alius!" Sady knocked on the familiar door that brought back memories of his time as student here. Sadly, he never had the time to pay more than a fleeting visit to this venerable institution these days.

He heard voices inside. People stopped talking. There were footsteps, and a moment later, the door was opened and Alius appeared in the doorway. He looked tired and harassed. "Proctor." He looked surprised. "How did I earn this honour?" He kept the door close to his body, and Sady couldn't see who his visitor was.

"I presume you've heard about the trains," Sady said.

"I have indeed."

"We have thousands of refugees from the City of Glass who are contaminated. Finnisius tells me that many of the army's suits have deteriorated to the point where they no longer offer protection, and the army will be hampered in dealing with this emergency as a result. The southerners are desperate and angry. We need people to keep them under control. We need your medicine. Urgently. When can you have it ready?"

Alius glanced over his shoulder as if looking into the room, except the door was behind him.

"Look, is it all right if I come to your office a bit later? I can explain to you where we are at and how long it will take. I'm in a meeting right now, and—"

"No need to spend much time on explaining. The only explanation I'll need is when the medicine will be ready."

"Yes. Yes, sure. I understand. I will come to your office as soon as possible, and I'll show you the work we've done. I know it's important and would like to prepare a bit and get all the data out. It's going well, but . . ." He laughed. "We're *extremely* busy and we're not in any state to receive important visitors or make coherent presentations."

Sady's courage sank. "You're not ready at all, then."

"No, no, proctor, don't misunderstand my words. We're very close, but very disorganised at the moment."

"I understand. I will expect you later today, then."

Alius retreated back to the visitor Sady still hadn't seen and Sady turned to walk back to the stairs. The door of Alius' office shut with an audible click.

Very close, huh? Who was that visitor Alius had been so keen for him not to see?

Orsan, bearing arms and thus not allowed into the Scriptorium's tower, waited in the room provided for that purpose. He was chatting to a guard Sady didn't recognise and probably belonged to a private family, but he couldn't see which one. A guard would only wear family colours when stationed at the gate to the family's estate.

Orsan rejoined Sady and they left the tower through the ornate columned entrance.

"Whose guard was that?" Sady asked when they were well out of the building.

"Young fellow used to work at the doga, but he's gone private. I don't know who he works for. I didn't ask." Because that was again part of the code of honour, but Sady was beginning to feel that it was this code of honour that was stifling Chevakian politics. Don't ask, don't tell. Protect the back of the person next to you, because next time the lions might be after you.

Mercy, that was the way things had operated in Chevakian politics for a long time, but it seemed to have become much worse under Destran's rule. He was well aware of unwritten rules not to stab any other family of power in the back, but since when, he wondered, had that come to mean cover up for each other's crimes?

Even this late in the afternoon, the foyer of the proctor's office was in chaos, with more people than ever lining up to speak to Sady. He bypassed all of them, to increased shouting of *See me first,* and *I've waited here all day*.

He turned to Orsan, "We must really do something about organising this circus. If this is the only way the common people can make themselves heard, it's dire indeed."

Past Orsan's uniformed body, he spotted a boy much too young to have any kind of political interest. He carried a lute. A skinny lad he was, and he was the only one not shouting.

Sady half-stepped into his office and said to Orsan. "Get me that boy over there."

He went inside, sat at his desk and the boy came in, wide-eyed.

"Sit down," Sady said.

"Thank you so much for seeing me, proctor." He bowed awkwardly.

"What is your name and how old are you?"

"I'm Perin, sir, and I'm twelve. My father has broken his leg in a building site and cannot work, sir. The builder says it's my father's fault and will not pay. I am really good at playing the lute, so I was wondering if any of the senators, or you . . ." His face turned red. ". . . have any parties. I can play for you—"

"You play on the street sometimes?"

"I do, sir, but not today. I've been waiting here."

"All day? To play the lute?"

The boy nodded, his expression eager. "Thanks so much for seeing me, sir."

"I'll give you a job, and it's an important one." Sady had to stop speaking to stifle upwelling emotion. This boy, and children like him, looked to the proctor to save the country. Many of the people outside his door expected the same. Much as he felt without a clue of what to do, he could not fail these people. He could not wait for Milleus, who might never come. The people of Tiverius looked to him, Sadorius han Chevonian, to guide them.

He cleared his throat. "Listen. In the guard room of the tower of the Scriptorium is a guard waiting for his master. I want you to wait outside the building, in a place where this guard won't take any notice of notice you, and tell me who leaves the building with him. You think you can do that?"

The lad's eyes widened. "Yeah, I can." He half-rose. His eyes shone. "Does that make me a spy?"

Ouch. The boy was probably too young to be handed this responsibility. "No. And I want you to be extremely careful. Just go and play somewhere like you would normally do. Watch. Don't talk to anyone."

"I won't. Thank you so much. I will do my very, very best." The boy clutched his lute.

"And, Perin, did you hear the ringing of the bell?"

"Yeah, I did, but nothing's happened, has it?"

"You can't see sonorics. If you're outside, you might want to wear a suit."

"We have no money for a suit, sir."

"Being inside a building will give you some protection. Find a covered courtyard or a hall to keep watch."

The lad's eyes went wide. "I know just the place, sir. The music sounds great in there, too."

"Good. Then go, before the man has left."

The boy grabbed his instrument and scurried out the door.

Sady groaned. Mercy. He couldn't expect Tiverians to have suits. There was no money to give everyone suits, and besides, producing them for the entire population would take too long.

And, meanwhile, the bell rang every hour, and the people of the city had questions, and the southerners had questions but no one could understand them.

He hoped by all that was dear to him that Alius would turn up with the medicine soon.

CHAPTER 30

THE TRUCK WAS moving much too slowly, and Loriane's pains were fast getting worse.

She let Myra pull her into a sitting position, leaning against the outside of the truck. The bench was hard and too narrow, so that she hung on with the hard edge of the metal biting into backside, because her stomach got into the way of her sitting, and there was not enough room for her to spread her legs and lean forward. Loriane's neighbours were both men casting her nervous looks. Loriane swore they would feel the sheen of sweat over her skin each time they bumped into her, which was a lot. There was just no room. Myra stood wedged between the mats on the truck bed floor and those well enough to sit on the benches. She hung onto the metal frame over Loriane's head and tried not to step on Tandor, who lay on the mattress at Loriane's feet.

Loriane dug into her thighs when the pains came. It hurt so much that she didn't know what was happening down there. She couldn't move and couldn't see through the forest of legs and knees. For all she knew, she'd already peed all over the floor.

Three agonising pains later, the truck stopped. In her state, her vision blurred by sweat that was running into her eyes, Loriane couldn't see much beyond the standing passengers other than a barren field. There were some trees and a fence.

"What are we doing here?" she asked, her voice hoarse. She wanted out of this damn truck.

"I don't know," Myra said. She was patting little Beido on the backside, but he was squirming and muttering in the sling. "He's hungry." And of course she couldn't feed him like this, standing up in a moving truck. That was if she could feed him at all. More often, Loriane had taken him, but she couldn't possibly do that now—

The pain returned. She clutched onto the edge of the bench and stared at her knees, trying to control her breathing, and trying not to make any sound. Sweat rolled between her breasts.

When it passed, the truck still hadn't moved, and two Chevakians in their weird suits stood at the back.

"It seems we've arrived wherever we were going," said someone near the back of the truck.

"Can you see anything?" asked another man.

"There's tents," the first man said. "And there's Chevakians in suits."

"Hey you," someone else shouted at the Chevakians. "We want to get out."

A Chevakian said something that sounded like a muffled order.

The next moment, the engine let out a huge hiss and the truck jolted into motion again. Loriane could see glimpses of white tents before another pain overwhelmed her. The child wormed around inside her, a sharp bump tracking across her stomach. It felt like a knife cut her there. By the skylights, what was this thing?

They stopped again, and now a Chevakian came and let down the back panel of the truck. He spoke and pointed, and the first people climbed down. More suited Chevakians waited there, and they led the passengers away. Soon they ran out of people who could climb unassisted, or who would leave their loved ones. The Chevakians came into the truck and handed people down to a couple of others, who carried them away.

Ruko would not let them touch Tandor, and one icy look from those hollow eyes was enough to make the Chevakians back off. He put Tandor down near the edge of the trailer bed, jumped off and heaved Tandor onto his shoulder. The Chevakians stepped back when he passed.

What if . . . Loriane got a strange idea. What if Ruko wasn't trying to protect Tandor, but was keeping him in his dream-like state?

She called out, "Myra!"

But Myra was at that moment being led away by the Chevakians.

"I'm not leaving you."

"Myra, we need to get Ruko away from Tandor. Maybe he'll wake up then."

"What?"

Two Chevakians lifted Loriane up. The movement set off another pain. She dug her fingers into the strange texture of their suits, feeling the arms of the people within. Every bump lanced through her belly and back like a knife. She fought not to scream.

They handed her down to two other people.

Outside the truck was a grassy field with tents in neat rows. There was a broad zone without tents and then a fence. Behind the fence, a forest. The field sloped down towards the city where she could see the roof of the buildings poked through the haze.

All the truck's passengers were being taken into a large tent.

There were benches and mats lined up inside, where other suited people walked around and attended the sick. At the far end was a partition screened off with a curtain.

The Chevakians put Loriane down on one of the benches, in between Myra and Dara. Ontane sat on the other side of Myra, trying to make the point that he was not looking at his wife, but glancing from the corner of his eyes anyway.

A Chevakian was going through the room, examining the wounded one by one. Loriane caught a glimpse through the helmet's visor, and thought that this person was a woman. She held a slate with a piece of paper, and wrote something on the slate every now and then. When she had finished with someone, this person was led or carried to the screened area out the back.

People only spoke in soft voices. Sounds of trucks and hissing steam came in from outside the tent.

When the suited woman approached Tandor, Ruko rose and placed himself in front of his master. He was pale—Loriane did not recall seeing him eat anything—but he towered over her. She stepped back, clutching the slate to her chest. She called out something to another Chevakian in the tent.

"See?" Loriane said to Myra next to her. "There is no reason that Tandor should be mute like this. I think it's because Ruko is keeping him that way and he needs to be close to do it."

"Maybe, but who can scare Ruko?"

Loriane didn't reply, because another pain was building. She grabbed the edge of the bench and squeezed it as hard as she could, aware that a lot of people were watching her. She wanted to move around and see if she could find somewhere comfortable where Myra could assist her with the birth. She also really needed to pee.

She wished this woman with the slate would hurry up, but she was still a couple of patients away from her.

There was a commotion at the tent's entrance and a couple of Chevakians came in. They spoke to one already in the tent, who pointed at Tandor. The newcomers marched between the mats. Loriane noticed belts and weapons when they passed her. They stopped at Tandor's mat. Ruko faced them, his arms crossed over his chest. One of the Chevakians spoke; Ruko didn't react at all. The Chevakians waited, but after nothing happened, two of them went to either side of Tandor's mat. One grabbed the bottom corners, the other the top two corners, and they lifted the mat.

At that moment, Ruko whirled. With a roar that sounded like it came from a wild animal, he swung at the Chevakians, hitting one in the head with his elbow. The man dropped the mattress. Tandor fell. The Chevakian tumbled on top of him, while the other Chevakian had pulled a weapon. There was a huge bang. People screamed, and whoever could move, scrambled away.

"Quick, get Tandor," Loriane called to Myra. She tried to get to her feet, but her legs wouldn't cooperate.

Ontane yelled, "Don't be stupid, Myra." But Myra was already pulling Tandor away.

Dara got up to help her.

Ruko had fallen, and all Chevakians were now struggling to hold him down and tie him up.

"He been shot," Ontane said, his eyes wide. "And he just keeps on living."

"You can't kill a servitor unless you kill the master," a rasping voice said.

"Tandor!"

He looked terrible, shiny new skin stretched taut over his face and half his head, but his eyes were alive.

"Loriane . . ." He panted. "Loriane, have I ever told you how much I love you?"

"I sure as hell don't love you." All her anger rose to the surface. If only she could get off the chair, she'd go and wring his neck. All the problems in her life were because of Tandor.

"Loriane, please . . ."

"No, Tandor, the game is over. What did you do to me? Where is Isandor?"

"It's all wrong," he said. "Ruko, my mother . . . watch them. They'll want the child."

"And what am I supposed to do? Protect this hideous creature? Have you ever thought what it would do to me, carrying a child like that? You betrayed me, Tandor. I hate you, and I'll always hate you. When this child is born . . ." Another pain was building. "When it's born, I'll kill it."

"No, listen . . ."

"I hate you." She panted.

"Loriane, you are my princess, the only one I've ever loved."

"I don't love you. I fucking hate you!" The wave of pain built and built. She screamed at him. "I hate you. I hate you. I hate you!"

"Shut up." He grabbed her wrist in a surprisingly strong grip. "Don't draw attention to us."

She struggled. "I hate you!"

"Behave yourself." He slapped her in the face.

She spat at him. Tangled her hand into his remaining hair and pulled. "I hate you!"

He slapped her again, harder this time.

Loriane spat, and screamed, and howled with the pain that felt like she was being torn apart.

Two of the Chevakians came and lifted him under his arms. Tandor struggled, and yelled at them in Chevakian, but they picked him up and carried him out the back. His screams became progressively weaker. Ruko still stood, bound and gagged, in the corner. His eyes shone. As if in slow motion, he ripped apart his bonds, tore off the gag. Two remaining Chevakians rushed to tie him back up, but he mowed them aside, and ran for the exit. The Chevakians ran after him, and their shouts faded, too.

The pain ebbed away. Loriane slumped onto the bench and sat in dazed silence.

Myra said, "Well, that worked. Tandor is talking again. I'm not sure if abusing him was so smart. I thought you needed him to get a place to stay in Tiverius."

Loriane felt like saying. *You don't know what pain like that is like*, except Myra did know, very well. Whatever this child was, it was just another birth, and nine previous births really did not make it any easier. You could have all the experience in the world, but whenever the next time came, it was just as painful, as scary, as tiring, and just as much sheer physical, sweaty hard work as the previous one. She didn't know why she had ever allowed herself to forget that.

The Chevakians came for her next.

They carried her out the back entrance into a second tent, this one not as busy, with a series of cloth-walled rooms on one side. Going past the entrance of one, she got a glimpse of a child being washed by a Chevakian in a suit. The cubicle where the Chevakians brought her had an examination table and a chair. There was also a Chevakian woman in a suit. She indicated for Loriane to undress and get onto the examination table. But Loriane couldn't walk, so she had to call for someone to help Loriane up and assist her. Cold suited fingers undid the buttons on her dress.

"Sorry, is there anywhere I can piss?" Loriane asked

The nurse shrugged and pulled Loriane's dress over her head, eyes widening at the dreadful red marks that criss-crossed her belly. Even her thighs were bruised now.

She made Loriane lie down on the table and proceeded to prod her belly. Loriane clamped her jaws. *Hurry up, hurry up.* By the skylights, if this lasted any longer . . . Then the nurse pushed Loriane's legs apart and slid a cold gloved hand inside her. A stab of pain made her gasp. Warm fluid dribbled onto the table.

The nurse called out.

I told you so, sea cow.

Another woman in protective clothing rushed into the cubicle. The two of them dragged Loriane into a sitting position on the table. One tried to shove a metal bowl under her, but it was much too late. A pain built and Loriane lost all sensation. It was a bad one, and she closed her eyes and breathed in and out slowly. The cloth under her grew sopping wet. Drops plinked onto the floor.

When she opened her eyes, both Chevakians were gaping at the table.

Loriane looked. Her piss was nearly black.

What was this about? What was going on inside her body?

She yelled, "Tandor!"

She stumbled off the table, out of the cubicle, naked as she was, the Chevakian nurses yelling behind her.

But then a pain started building, stronger than before. She couldn't walk, couldn't move. Purple spots danced in her vision.

A number of white-suited Chevakians caught up with her, dragged her back into the cubicle and one of them directed a stream of hot water at her, while another held her from behind. One rubbed a sharp-smelling substance all over her that made her skin burn. Then they hosed it off. Pains lanced through her like hot knives.

Loriane struggled. "Let me go! Let me go! I'll kill this thing as soon as it's born!" She could feel the pressure building. It hurt like nothing had ever hurt before.

"Tandor, I hate you. I FUCKING HATE YOU!" And then the building pain exploded into agony.

Somewhere in the middle of all that, the nurses finished hosing her down and lifted her. Like some sort of out-of-body experience, she was aware of people running into the tent, looking at her. She was aware of being carried. She was aware of the tent flap opening and a couple of important-looking people coming in.

The Chevakians were rubbing her dry. The pain subsided, but the pressure grew worse. And the Chevakians were trying to put some sort of nightgown on her. She hit at them.

"Let me go." She was going to give birth right here.

More Chevakians were still coming in, and held her arms behind her back so that she couldn't move and this stupid woman was trying to put this stupid garment on her. She trembled. Drops of fluid trickled down her legs. The nightgown went over her head.

The Chevakian nurses—now without suits—were talking to each other in calm voices. They lifted her onto the examination table.

Two nurses held her motionless while a third stuck a needle in her arm. There was a thin hose attached to it and attached to that, a fluid-filled balloon.

"What are you doing to me? Leave me alone!"

One nurse spoke in harsh Chevakian. She tapped a few times against the balloon and turned away.

"Hey, where are you going?" They were still holding her. Another pain was building and she really wanted to get off this table.

But the nurse paid her no attention. The pain built and built. It wasn't just pain anymore. She could almost feel the child's head inside her. If this kept up, she was going to embarrass herself and give birth on this stupid table. Very soon.

Help me!

The Chevakian woman put a blanket over her.

Help me!

A wave of dizziness came over her.

The roof of the tent twirled and circled. Oh, by the skylights! She closed her eyes. And then she knew no more.

CHAPTER 31

WHEN THE FIELDS became smaller, and the houses closer together, Milleus found it harder to concentrate. His mood swung wildly between melancholy and fear. He hadn't been here for so long, and all these people who might recognise his face made him nervous. What if they booed him and chased him out of the city? The peasants might listen to his arguments, but the folk in the city would be more cynical. They were, after all, the ones who had cheered when Destran had deposed him, and at times, especially at night when he lay in bed staring at the ceiling in the van, he could still hear that cheering.

He fell into a brooding silence, but the youngsters didn't seem to notice. They found so much to look at or express their wonder about.

Then they crested the last hill of the plateau and came to the lookout. From here, undulating country sloped down to the city. Tiverius lay stretched out before them.

Row after row of blocky buildings made from pink stone crowded rolling hills. Trees lined the roads, which were straight and lined out in geometrical patterns.

In a strange way, he felt relieved. Tiverius was still here. It looked like it always had. Life here went on as normal.

Seated in the back of the van, Nila leaned over his shoulder to look. She pointed ahead at the golden dome. "That is where the Chevakian Doga sits."

"Yes, very good. Do you know the building next to it?" All that was visible of the building in question was a squat round tower four storeys high. There were arched windows all around, which you couldn't see from here.

She frowned.

"It's the Scriptorium."

"That is the place where . . ." Her frown deepened. "You keep books."

"Yes and no. The books go in the library. The Scriptorium is where people work to further their knowledge."

He remembered spending much time in a room on the top floor of that tower. His friend Alius' office.

From the crest of the hill, the column of vehicles snaked down the slope that led into the outskirts of the city. Forest on both sides was used for firewood. Here and there farms dotted the landscape. There were many fields with sunflowers, all pointed in the same direction where the sun, at that moment, wasn't.

Isandor whispered, "Wow. It's beautiful."

"Pretty," Milleus said. "A woman is beautiful." It would be a lot prettier if it were sunny. But the sky was grey with low scudding clouds.

"Isn't a city like a woman? You have to care for her, otherwise she ceases to be beautiful to you?"

That comment hit him in the gut. Like Suri.

Milleus swore that sometimes that young man said things that would be more appropriate to come out of the mouth of someone three times his age.

Like Suri indeed. While he was here, he should go to her grave and bring her flowers, and hope his sons didn't come chasing after him.

What are you running from?

Mercy, the voice of his conscience was starting to sound like Isandor's. He had no time for family business. Most likely, his sons wouldn't have the time either. He wondered if Markian was still with that silly woman—oh, mercy, what was her name again?—and wondered if Parto and Lyvia had their much-wanted girl yet.

"Where are the goats going to graze tonight?" Isandor asked, shaking Milleus from his thoughts.

"We'll bring them to a commercial stable at the edge of the city. You'll see."

The van rolled down the hill, following the column of refugees which slowly made its way down. It grew very crowded here, and progress slowed further and further, and came to a complete stop.

Ahead, the motionless column stretched around a bend.

People were hanging out the windows trying to see what was going on. Others had left their vehicles and stood on the side, or sat in the grass. Some people piled up wood for fires.

Isandor gave him a worried glance. "What is going on here?"

"It looks like the road is blocked further on," Milleus muttered. That was something he hadn't considered, that the doga would simply block the city to keep any refugees out. They wouldn't be that stupid, would they?

He opened the door and slid stiffly from behind the wheel.

The van rocked with the movements of the goats in the trailer. They were bleating and pushing each other. Panicked by all the noise and the barking of dogs and smells of too many people.

He walked down to the trailer and banged his hand on the side. "Oy. Quiet, you."

The familiar voice did seem to calm them some.

When he turned around, a man stood behind him. "Do you sell meat or milk?"

"Yes, I have milk."

The man rummaged in his pocket and produced a fat purse. "How much?"

Milleus frowned. "Not now. At milking time."

"Please," the man said. "The wife has twins to feed and we've travelled for three days without food."

"There will be milk later." Some other people had turned to him. "But I'll need feed, for the goats."

A woman said, "That's no problem. We'll get hay. You give us milk."

A queue had already started forming, and two boys were running towards the forest, presumably to get grass.

"Hey," he said. "I said this afternoon. There is no milk right now. Goats are not machines you can turn on and off at will."

But no one was listening.

Mercy, milk for this many people? He'd never have enough. There were hundreds of people here. Hungry, thirsty, annoyed that they had to wait so close to their destination.

Isandor stood on the truck's doorstep, looking over the chaos from his point of vantage.

Milleus said to him, "I'm going to see if I can find out what the hold-up is." Would it be worth waiting for? "You better keep an eye on the animals."

Isandor nodded.

From the other side of the truck, Nila said, "Can I come?"

"Sure," Milleus said, and then he looked back at Isandor. "Is that all right with you?"

Isandor glanced over the crowd. "I'll be fine."

Milleus saw through his veneer of carelessness. Isandor didn't like this seething mass of people any more than he did.

"You know where the gun is . . . if you need it."

Isandor nodded.

Milleus and Nila went on their way through the chaos of vehicles, campfires, tents, yelling people, screaming children. At the bend in the road, where there was a small glade, several people were trying to turn their vehicles around, but once they were turned, there was nowhere for them to go, because of all the people still arriving from behind. Men were shouting at each other to get out of the way.

Knots of young men had gathered on the roadside, glowering at everyone who passed.

There was a fence across the road ahead, blocking it off completely.

A couple of uneasy city guards stood sentry on the other side of it, in the field where normally circus troupes or travelling merchants would camp if they didn't want to stay in the city. Now there were rows and rows of army tents. Milleus could see some people walking between them, but they were too far away to see who they were.

"Hey!" Milleus called out to the guards.

They didn't react.

"Hey, you! I want to talk!" he yelled again.

"It's no good. They won't talk to us," said a man next to him, a middle-aged fellow who had the clean hands and finely-cut clothes of a small-town administrator.

"What's going on?" Milleus asked.

Nila pressed her nose against the fence and stared in the distance.

"I've been told they are setting up a camp for refugees."

"Why are you all waiting here? The road is blocked."

"We're waiting to be let in."

"Let in?"

"Yeah, they're setting it up for us, surely. We got nowhere else to go."

A lot of things started to make sense now. "How long have you been waiting?"

"Most of yesterday and today. I hope they hurry up. People are getting very impatient back there."

"Have they said anything about how long it's going to take?" Would there be a way to get out of this queue and contact Sady? "I have a brother in Tiverius. I don't need to get into any camp."

The man shrugged. "I can't help you there."

Nila was still staring at the tents down the hill. He touched her shoulder. "Come, we're going back." He was surprised by how angry he felt, a sensation he remembered well. He needed to get really fired up about something to act, but once he did, there was no stopping him. Yes, he would march into the doga with his signatures and face Destran, if only it could mean that his countrymen could be properly helped.

Nila came without speaking a word. He noticed how tired she looked. He'd promised them they'd sleep in a real bed, safe from the world, safe from their countrymen.

Around the corner, the attempts to turn some vehicles around had escalated in full-scale shouting matches between families.

A woman was shouting, "Oh, I didn't? And then what about you, fat cow. I saw you take two loaves of bread yesterday . . ."

More young men had gathered to watch. They stood with hands in pockets or arms crossed over their chests. They watched Milleus and Nila walk past with suspicious looks.

Nila said, "We shouldn't get involved." As if she felt that he was on the verge of doing just that.

"I don't like this," Milleus said. "People are angry. I don't understand why those soldiers don't let anyone into the camp. There's going to be grief if they don't."

"Soldiers in a position of power don't care about anything except maintaining that power."

He glanced at her sideways. Mercy, where did she learn things like that at her age?

Back at the truck, a huge queue had formed. Many people were sitting in the grass, prepared for a long wait. Many were holding buckets. Isandor sat on the railing of the trailer, holding Milleus' gun.

He said nothing, but Milleus saw in his eyes that he was glad to see them return.

"We can't get through," Milleus said. "The army is setting up a camp in a stupid place, and there is an idiotic fence across the road. No one knows when they're going to let people in. Ridiculous."

Isandor flicked his eyebrows. "Can we turn back?"

"That's not so easy." Milleus looked up the hill, where the long line of refugees completely blocked the road.

Whoever's stupid idea it was to block the road. Did they *want* the people to start fights out here? Was this the way Destran thought to control who came into the city?

Mercy, the doga had no idea, absolutely no idea at all. Who ever could have approved of such a *stupid* idea—

Isandor was still watching him, eyebrows raised as if he wanted to say, *What's the matter with you?*

Oh, mercy. The kid couldn't understand. He stomped away from the truck. "Right, people, listen to me."

A few people gave him strange looks, but many gathered around, probably for the lack of anything else to listen to.

"It's pretty clear that no one's getting through this way. And some of us have families in Tiverius and don't need this camp, so let's organise for everyone who wants to turn around and get into the city by some other road. I want this path . . ." He waved at the right side of the paved road. ". . . cleared of all vehicles so those who want to leave can do so." He waved at a truck which blocked the road. "Move aside, please, sir, so people can get past. Move aside, move aside!"

The truck's owners, and extended family, started pushing the vehicle aside. Others also moved to make room for them.

"Move aside, move aside, so people can get out!"

More trucks moved.

Milleus progressed further up the road, but there, people had made a huge fire right in the middle of his intended path.

Someone had caught an animal that looked suspiciously like a goat —mercy—and which was now roasting over the fire. On both sides of the road were trees and fenced paddocks. People had set up tents. There was no way any trucks could get through.

Milleus let his shoulders slump.

"Pity. Good try. We'll try to keep going tomorrow," one of the drivers said. He had a young family and didn't look entirely unhappy to have found a place where people had food.

Well, important things first, huh?

Milleus went back alone, still burning with anger inside, and fearful for Isandor and Nila, and his goats.

Isandor was making preparations to start milking. Most of the goats were inside the pen, watched by Nila. He had put grass on the feed trough, placed his stool on the trailer bed. The animals were pushing each other to be the first to be milked. Their udders were fat and swollen, some already leaking milk.

A male voice behind him said, "Are these animals yours?"

Milleus turned around. Behind him stood a soldier in uniform. "Yes, I took them all the way from my farm." What did he mean *are these goats yours?* Didn't he have anything better to do than harass people?

The man's eyes narrowed. "There have been reports of theft from farms."

"That's what happens when you let people wait for too long. They run out of food. They start getting it wherever they find any."

"We've told people that there is no point in waiting here. Everyone should clear this area as soon as possible."

"Let me tell you, I'd love to get out of this mess, but we're stuck here because no one can turn around, and there are still people coming. Why do you even let them come here?"

"We're dealing with that right now. We'll start at the back of the column tomorrow, so we can have everyone on their way to the processing posts tomorrow."

Processing posts. What a load of rubbish. Why block a major access route unless the intention was to keep people out of the capital?

"I don't need processing. I have family in Tiverius."

"You'll have to verify that at the processing post."

Milleus clamped his jaws. Oh, for mercy's sake.

They turned back to his van, where Nila was handing out the first cup of milk to a young boy. The queue had grown, but for now, was orderly.

Milleus went into the truck to find something for their own dinner.

Apart from hay, Isandor had collected donations of blankets, some jewellery, a coat, boots, a set of cups and a small heap of coins. Whereas earlier in their trip, there had been eggs and ham and fruit, it seemed people had no food left.

There was some bread and cheese and a few eggs left in the store, but that wouldn't last them more than a day.

A glance out the back window showed Isandor and Nila still handing out milk, and the queue growing longer. There was no way there would be enough milk for all those people.

Milleus cut up the ham, balancing the cutting board on his lap. He would normally take it outside, but he was afraid that he'd be mobbed.

There were clangs of metal from Isandor shutting the goats back in the trailer. He climbed up on the railing and sat there, the gun in his lap.

Nila opened the door and climbed into the cabin, her face harrowed. "Those people are crazy."

"They're hungry."

He passed her the bread and she ate, quietly.

Milleus cut bread for Isandor and then left the cabin.

It was starting to get dark, earlier than normal because of the heavy cloud cover. A cold wind made the trees whistle.

The line of people wanting to get milk had dispersed, but several people had put up tents in the space Milleus had planned to use as corridor to get out tomorrow morning.

Mercy, he was powerless against chaos like this. Where were those soldiers? Why weren't they organising the crowd?

"You go inside and eat," he said to Isandor in a low voice. "I'll watch here."

Isandor stiffly climbed off the railing and handed Milleus the gun.

Milleus took position on the trailer, and sat staring into the darkening sky. Campfires burned everywhere. On the other side of the road, people were chopping up fence posts for firewood, the animals inside the paddocks already stolen or eaten. Mercy, what a mess. Wasn't this typical of Destran? How could he contact Sady?

He wanted to do something, but needed help. The more he thought about it, the more he concluded that if turning people around wasn't practical, there was only one way get out of this mess: by using the road that was intended for that very purpose. Even if that meant destroying the stupid fence. The camp didn't look particularly well-patrolled, and as a farmer, he never went anywhere without a pair of wire-cutters.

CHAPTER 32

THE GUARD at the gate waved his hand, and the truck entered the camp. From behind the glass, in the sheltered environment of the truck, Sady studied the neat rows of tents, most still unoccupied, since the first of the refugees had only just been decontaminated and were being shown their tents.

Mercy, he was tired and annoyed. It was starting to get dark, and normally, he should have been home long ago.

But problems multiplied. For once, Orsan's scout had not been lied to. The Lady Armaine was *really* out, as were her daughters, and of course the guards wouldn't say where she had gone and how long she would be.

On top of that, the station guards had reported fighting on the second of the trains. Not angry citizens trying to smash their way out of the carriage, but people fighting *each other*. It looked like the refugees were from two different factions, and he might have to separate them to keep the group under control. Except he didn't know who was who, and needed the interpreter worse than ever. And Lady Armaine wasn't helpful by disappearing at this crucial time.

Meanwhile, the young musician he had sent to spy had come back from his task and caused him worry by reporting that Alius' secret visitor was none other than Destran. Yes, he understood why Alius wasn't happy about the timing of Sady's visit, but what did he have to discuss with Destran, who continued to serve as senator?

There was still no sign of the missing account books. And, as predicted, Tiverians lined up in front of his office grumbling about money being spent on housing the southerners. He didn't know which of those things worried him most, but he resolved to tackle the easy problems first. Part one: since he could find no Chevakians who spoke the southern language, he had to find southerners who spoke Chevakian. Southerners who were respected by those in the camp. He'd already made the mistake of not checking people who offered themselves once, he was not going to make it again. So that was why he was here, at the camp.

The truck stopped at a tent where a number of soldiers waited.

Sady climbed out of the cabin to salutes and nods.

"We have five people for you," a soldier said.

"Five? Is that all?"

"Sorry, sir. We asked everywhere, but only five responded. Either people are too scared to come forward or there are only a few people in the south who speak Chevakian."

Wonderful. Just what he needed: people too scared to speak out. Scared of what or whom? "Let's go and look at these ones, then."

Sady and Orsan went into the tent, which was an administration post. A Chevakian officer scurried from behind his desk. "Ah, proctor. We have the people here, as you requested. . . ."

The five sat on a bench, three men and two women, all clad in southern fur cloaks, not talking to each other. Only two met Sady's eyes. One of them attempted a clumsy greeting.

"Thank you. I'll talk to them now. I'm very busy."

"I understand, proctor. Please, use my desk."

Sady sat down.

The first person to join him at the table was an elderly man. He was dressed in a black shirt that had smears of slime or some other goopy substance over the front. His hair was thin, greying, and tied together at the nape of his neck. He had a straggly beard that hadn't seen a barber's knife for a long time, with the long pointed end hanging down from his chin yellow with dirt.

He bowed deeply.

"I understand that you speak Chevakian?"

"I have learned a bit your language," the man said.

"Where did you learn it?"

"I learn as young man. When travel to your country."

"As merchant?"

A blank look.

"Were you selling things in Chevakia?"

"No. I was in army."

Mercy, that would go down well with the doga. One of the men who had raided the border regions. Probably had done his fair share in raping and pillaging.

The next person was a young woman with wide eyes, who gave confused answers to Sady's questions. She had her well-endowed bosom half hanging out of the shirt and fixed his gaze with wide eyes. Whatever she wanted, being an interpreter it was not.

The next person was a young man with intense eyes. Although he seemed to understand Sady well enough, he answered with mono-syllables.

The fourth person was an older woman, a favourite auntie type, rotund and smiling. At least she didn't appear to have an ulterior motive, but her Chevakian was worse than that of the others.

The last person was a middle-aged merchant who, when Sady asked questions, came up with a huge jumbling theory about market advantages of *something* that Sady didn't understand.

Sady cut short the torrent of incoherent babble and turned to the administrator, who stood by the door.

The man gave him an apologetic look. "These were the only ones who applied."

Sady sighed, and put a hand on the man's shoulder as appreciation. They were doing their best, all of them. "It's not your fault. I think they're spooked, afraid that if they speak up, they'll be singled out. Understandable, although not helpful. Do you think it would be safe enough for me to walk through the camp and ask for volunteers informally?"

"In that part where people have been given beds and food, yes. Don't go near the processing area, because some of them get pretty violent."

Sady nodded. He could understand that being asked to remove their clothes, being scrubbed with soap and hot water while they didn't understand why, could make people angry, especially if they were tired and hungry.

"Tell these people I may need them later. I'm going for a walk."

Orsan raised his eyebrows, but followed.

"Honestly, I cannot use any of them," Sady said to Orsan when they were well out of the tent. "It seems like the only people who volunteered are at least mildly disturbed."

Orsan said, "The guard mentioned that he thought the people might be scared. I think he's right. Everyone comments on how subdued these people are."

"Well, we'll see if any come forward if I talk to them directly."

They went into a few tents where refugees lay on mats, and where no one replied to Sady's greetings, and Sady was cursing himself for having been part of the government that allowed this country to become so isolated that no one spoke each other's language.

Then, as they were about to enter the next tent, there was some sort of commotion behind them. A woman was screaming and people yelled out in Chevakian, "Stay here!"

Another called for assistance.

Orsan glanced at Sady, who nodded, "Let's go."

Orsan and one of the guards went first, then Sady and another guard.

In the tent, the found the woman he'd seen at the station, stark naked, her belly like a balloon, screaming and fighting two nurses, who held her. Her belly was vividly coloured with bruises and red lines. Mercy, he had never seen anything like that.

Orsan didn't have time to help before she collapsed, and the nurses heaved her onto a bed.

Sady felt a little queasy. He was a politician, not a physic.

Mercy, he'd never had a wife, let alone witnessed a woman grow with child—except Suri, hidden under her clothes. Were those marks and bruises normal? No wonder women hated it so.

The woman now lay on the bed. Sady walked to the table, trying to focus on something other than her hideously swollen belly.

The woman was not what you'd call beautiful, but her face had strong angles that made her look like she would put up a good fight. Her black curly hair was tied in a loose ponytail. Curly wisps had escaped the tie and danced around her head. She was older than he would have guessed, with faint wrinkles around her eyes and greying hair at her temples.

"Can someone please cover her up?"

"Sure, Proctor." A nurse rushed over with a sheet.

"What are you going to do with her?" he asked the physic at the table.

"We're waiting for a midwife to come. We hadn't envisaged dealing with these sorts of problems."

"How long will it take before she's here?"

The physic shrugged. "Hard to tell. There is so much work to be done, we need all our people."

Sady glanced at the mound under the sheet. "Is she having twins?" He could not remember Suri having looked anywhere near as big as that. If anything, he remembered her looking rounded and cute, but that brought the uncomfortable thought that he wished the child would be his and not his brother's.

"No, a single child."

Mercy. "I didn't know that women could get like . . . this." He felt like squirming.

"It won't be easy," the physic said. "She's going to need a lot of help."

Sady felt goosebumps crawl over his skin. Even he had heard some stories that made his hair stand on end.

There were voices behind him in the tent. A man said, "Proctor, excuse me. We've located someone who claims to speak for the refugees." The sheets of the temporary barrier rustled.

"Yes, I'm coming," Sady said, started to turn, glanced at the woman again, and asked, "What kind of help, exactly?" Not really wanting to hear the reply. The subject made his skin crawl.

"Well . . ." The physic hesitated.

"Not pretty." Sady filled in the blanks.

"No. The child is too big to be born the normal way."

Sady shuddered at the thought of what had to be done. He'd heard stories about that, too. Many women died horrible deaths.

"Proctor, please—" the man at his back insisted.

"Wait. I'm talking to someone!" It came out more sharply than he intended. Yes, he knew that following the disaster with the previous two interpreters, it was important that they find someone else.

The physic raised her eyebrows. "No help needed, proctor. We have everything under control here."

Sady said, "About this woman, I've heard that there is this thing, where you can cut out the child without killing either it or the mother . . ."

"Yes. We do that for our women, but I honestly think we're going to be far too stretched to extend the procedure to refugees. It's very expensive—"

"I'll pay."

The physic's eyes widened. "But—"

"From my own personal funds. That's allowed, isn't it?" He couldn't quite say what possessed him. Maybe the chance to save one person from a horrific death, the chance to make a difference. He had never seen injury and suffering on this scale. This looked like a problem he could fix, with a happy outcome.

"Um—yes."

"Well, then, what are you waiting for? Take her to the hospital. Bring the physics you need here. Whatever. Get it done."

"She can't go to the hospital, sir. We have an exclusion zone in place around the camp. Until we've decontaminated everyone, taking anyone outside would place the citizens of the city at risk."

Mercy. He'd been so caught up he'd forgotten about the exclusion. Mercy. He wiped his face with his hand. The skin of his palm scratched over his chin. Since when had he last shaved? He was so tired.

"Proctor?" the man behind him insisted.

"Yes, I'm coming." Sady sighed. "Is there anything else we can do? Anywhere else she can be treated?"

The woman lay there, her face peaceful, unaware that her fate was being decided. Sady knew he could not let her die. He could also not leave her child to be killed by the hands of butchers.

"If we took her into the city, she would need to be in an isolated place, possibly underground, or with thick walls, away from any other people."

A place where other people were a long way away. The solution was crystal-clear. "My house."

"What?"

"It's huge, and mostly empty." *Ever since I failed to marry.* "We can put enough stone walls between me and her, and her family. I'm hardly ever there at the moment. Take her and her family to my house and let the physic come there."

The woman raised her eyebrows, but started to make arrangements.

As Sady left the tent, he looked over his shoulder. The woman lay peacefully, as if she was asleep, her dark hair draped over the side of the bed. She looked tough. Someone who wouldn't have time for nonsense. He hoped she and her child would both survive.

He and Orsan left the tent . . .

. . . and walked into a menacing circle of people, all facing the tent entrance.

Sady found himself shoved aside by his guards. Orsan, a head taller than him, stepped in front, protecting him with his sheer size.

"What's this?" Orsan said, in his most intimidating voice.

Between the guards' bodies, Sady could see the faces of men. More than the occasional few had beards. A lot of them were dressed in black, like the man who had applied to become an interpreter.

Sady's guards drew guns.

"Who are these people, and what do they want?" Sady asked.

The woman he had seen earlier, the one with the suggestive clothing, came out of the group. "I see what people want."

"Who are they?"

"From the Outer City."

Sady remembered having seen the community referred to as the Outer City on his trips. No one went there, his hosts had assured. The workers lived there. It was full of criminals.

And those would have been the people most likely to survive a disaster. If anything, they were used to surviving. Living in the southern land was about surviving.

"Tell them that if they threaten me, it is unlikely to impress the Chevakian doga."

She spoke. Sady had no idea if what she said was anywhere near accurate, but there were protesting grumbles.

"They say they want bodies of their dead. They want . . . ceremony." Someone in the crowd commented. "Funeral," she corrected.

Sady wasn't even sure where the army had taken the bodies of those who had died on the train. It was a horrible thought, to have lost a loved one, and then not to know what happened to the body.

He raised his voice, hoping that at least someone would understand. "Select a couple of representatives, make a list of which bodies you need, age, gender, clothing, and we'll speak tomorrow."

"Today," a man said, in heavy accent. He also had a beard. This was not someone who had come forward as interpreter.

"Tomorrow. It is late. We need interpreters. Why didn't you come forward when we asked?"

"When we do that, everyone can see us."

Another man yelled something in a loud voice.

Several of the black-clad men yelled back at him.

The guards raised their guns.

"Stop," Sady called. "I will meet with you. Both groups. I'll meet with anyone who feels they should have a voice in his camp. Tomorrow. You're safe, fed and you have beds. There is nothing that can't wait until later."

Several of the black-clad men still protested, but others calmed them. Who were these people in black? Mercy, he needed a crash course in southern politics and culture.

With that, Sady's guards cleared a path and Sady walked through the group who formed a strange kind of honour guard all the way to the truck. There were a lot of these black-clad people. With a disturbing feeling, he noticed their age, too. Many young men. Angry young men with beards.

Into the truck. The door shut, and while the driver fired up the engine, Sady felt safe enough to remove the hot suit. His clothes underneath were sweaty and dusty. Outside the window, the groups of refugees lined the road. There were so many, and the Chevakians so few.

"What's with the black and the beards?" Sady asked.

"Apparently, they call themselves the Brotherhood of the Light. Those guys are trouble," Orsan said.

"Yes, and I have no idea who they are and what they stand for," another guard added. "There seem to be a lot of them in the camp, but I don't know that they would speak for many of the refugees. I don't even know that anyone speaks for any of the refugees."

"We have to ask Lady Armaine." Orsan again.

"No," Sady said.

Orsan frowned.

"Lady Armaine offered to help us. She was much too keen to give me the money for my trip. I think she might be part of the problem. The south is not at war with us. It's a civil war, and we have the two groups here, or whatever is left of them. Something done by one of the groups caused the explosion. As outsiders, we don't know who the groups are and what they stand for. We don't know who did what. And we don't know who, if anyone, we should support."

They had arrived at the gate, manned by two Chevakian guards. Far too few, Sady realised, to contain a conflict within the camp. But the army was already stretched. Finnisius had sent units to Twin Bridges, and to help ready the balloons, and to manage the camps, and to patrol the curfew imposed by the bell.

The doga wasn't just running out of money; it was running out of people.

CHAPTER 33

CARRO SAT at the desk, and leafed through the book, his hands trembling. The columns of numbers danced before his eyes. He was back in the warehouse. He felt the biting cold. He heard his stepfather's footsteps.

So that was what his father thought of him?

Death by accountancy.

The Knights in the room were all busy at work, reading through Chevakian documents, or writing notes on tiny pieces of paper to be carried by gulls. The squawks of those birds drifted in from the courtyard.

No one took any notice of Carro. He could make a scene about how much he hated this work, but no one would care. So he opened the book.

The account book was Chevakian. He claimed a bit of knowledge of the language, but a lot of lines had long words that were unfamiliar to him.

Someone thunked another book onto the desk.

Carro slid it towards him and read the Chevakian text on the front sheet. *Planned and actual expenditure of farm operations.*

By the skylights.

He turned around, glaring at the back of the Knight who had brought it. "Hey, what the fuck am I supposed to do with this?"

"Check it. The Supreme Rider says you know about this stuff."

Carro turned the first page. Crops, fences, many words he didn't recognise. He let his shoulders sag. "What is this? A farm budget?"

"You got it. Didn't think this place ran on thin air, did you?"

"So . . . it belongs to us?"

"Smart boy."

A few men laughed.

"Anyone got a dictionary?"

"You're smart, you make it up."

Carro cursed silently. "Why do you need me to do this?"

A few quick footsteps, and the man leaned over him, menacing. He wore a Senior badge. "Look, pup, I don't care who you are, but in this room, we shut up and work."

The figures at the end of the page do not add up. Carro sits and stares at them, through eyes gone teary with cold. His hands hurt and his feet hurt and his father is waiting outside the room. But he knows his numbers, and these ones do not add up.

His father yells, "Hurry up, the tax collectors are nearly here."

"But something is wrong," he says. In fact, it's more than that. The numbers are very wrong, and to check them, he needs a lot more time than his father is willing to give him. There are so many stupid mistakes.

"Then make the numbers right."

Carro squeaks, "I can't." The tax collectors will notice. He knows these men and they can add up better than he can. They will notice that there is a huge sum missing from the books.

But his father grabs his collar and shakes him. "Make it right."

So Carro does the only thing he can think of: he rubs out a few lines and a few numbers. He makes expenditure higher, and income lower. Quickly, he adds the amounts until the columns balance, and hopes the tax collector will not ask to check the money in the safe.

Carro worked, his pencil scratching over the paper. Sweat rolled over his back. He didn't want any of these Knights to notice that he drifted off; he didn't want these visions. He wanted nothing to do with this book.

The draft that went through the room was cold, reminiscent of the warehouse. There was no fire, also like in the warehouse. The Senior Knight was pacing like his father used to do. With every step he heard his father coming closer.

Add up numbers.

No, that was wrong. He rubbed out his calculations.

Add up again.

The result was wrong. The two columns didn't match, like in the warehouse. Any moment now and his father would come and scold him. He was no fighter, not much of a spy, no hunter, and he'd also fail at accounting.

"Why are you all blue around your neck?" Isandor asks.

Seated on the lid of a rubbish container in a narrow alley, Carro sips his soup and tells Isandor of the columns of non-matching figures. He tells Isandor of how he rubbed out and changed the numbers, with his father watching over his shoulder. He tells how his father grabbed him around the neck as if he was going to choke him to death, but then shoved him in the cold cupboard and left him there while the tax collector went over his father's books, saying things like, "Your business hasn't done very well this year."

And all the while his father was explaining about how he was robbed and how his wife's family was asking for return of a loan they had given only a few years earlier.

"It was all nonsense," Carro says and looks into Isandor's blue eyes. There's despair inside him, bursting to come out.

"Maybe your father doesn't want to pay his taxes," Isandor says.

"But he should. He makes a lot of money."

Lies are the worst thing in the world.

Yes, Carro remembered that. He'd been ten or so, just a little boy.

And now all these figures danced before his eyes. They didn't add up either, far from it. Someone had made a big mess of this book.

The touch of a hand on his shoulder made him gasp. He whirled around and looked into the face of Rider Cornatan, smiling.

"I'm glad to see you made it, son."

Carro didn't know what to say. What had his father heard from the hunters? That they hadn't killed the Queen? That he'd let her escape?

Finally, he said, "I'm glad that you're safe, too."

His father laughed. For all that he was a refugee, he was extraordinarily well groomed. His uniform was as crisp and clean as it had been in the City of Glass. Not like Carro's which had stains that didn't come out no matter how much he scrubbed it.

"We managed to get away just in time."

"But . . . what happened in the City of Glass?"

His father's face went serious. "There was a huge explosion. Some saboteur blew up our experimental installation, and it set off a chain reaction."

"The Heart?"

"No longer there, I'm afraid."

Carro thought of the cellar where his father had taken him, where he'd seen the merchant treated with that machine. He remembered the table with metal implements. The eerie feeling as he hesitated to touch anything. The metal of the staff going cold in his hands. It seemed such a long time ago. Back when his life had been innocent.

"Much of the City of Glass has been destroyed. There is too much icefire even for us. It will take a long time before it is safe for anyone to go there again."

"What about . . . all the people?" His father—no, not his father— the merchant, his snarky wife, his sister, Isandor's mother. By the skylights, would he ever find ichina to cure his infliction now?

"Many of the Knights got away," Rider Cornatan said.

"And the other people?"

Rider Cornatan's eyebrows went up, as if surprised Carro should even ask. "The Outer City was destroyed in a fire. I don't know how many got out."

Carro stared at him. *What, are you saying that they're all dead?* His eyes pricked, and that made him angry. He'd always said he didn't care about the merchant and the rest of the family. But . . . all gone?

His neighbours, and Isandor's mother, and the girls he'd eyed in the marketplace, and . . . all gone?

Rider Cornatan's voice came from far off. "I understand that you didn't find the Queen."

"No."

Carro sat stiff, with his hands clasped in his lap and waited for his father to speak, for punishment.

But Rider Cornatan said nothing.

Hatred burned in his father's eyes, but Carro didn't know who was the object of the hatred. So he sat and waited to be punished.

Then his father said, "Come."

Carro stands in his father's study. By the light of the fire, his father sits at his desk. His face looks old.

"Why are you so late?"

"I was out with friends."

"You don't have any friends. Only that cripple boy and if I see you with him again I will come and chop off his other leg. He gives you ideas."

"What ideas? I only want to play." Isandor comes from a poor family, but he still has more toys. He has a box of colourful blocks made from real wood. He has no father, but Isandor's mother cares a lot about him.

Rider Cornatan went out the room, a little way along the dark corridor, and in through another doorway. The room on the other side was huge, with dustsheet-covered furniture towards the far end. The windows were dirty, with lots of cobwebs in the corners.

Carro's footsteps echoed back from the ceiling.

"Nice mansion, isn't it?" Rider Cornatan chuckled. "This is the country house of the old southern ambassador. While the people starved in the City of Glass, the King's cronies lived in luxury."

In the far corner of the room, near the window, the sheets had been pulled off two couches and a low table between them. On a cabinet against the far wall stood a selection of bottles.

Rider Cornatan gestured that he should sit, so Carro sat, the muscles in his legs stiff with tension.

"And, what have you found out so far?" said Rider Cornatan while settling on the other couch.

"What do you mean?"

"You've been checking the accounts, as far as I know."

"Yes, but why—"

"With what's happened in the south, we're going to be here for a while. The icefire bubble is still expanding. This place has been allowed to become run-down, and I'm aghast at how poorly the care-taker has looked after it. I had hoped there would be a nice little bit of farm income for us to buy essentials, such as food. But the care-taker fled as soon as we turned up here, and the books are not up-to-date. At this rate, we can't support the troops still coming from Arania. We need money, and we need to obtain it in such a way that is not going to anger the Chevakians. Your work is extremely important. You need to find us that money."

Carro nodded, but his inner voice squealed, *But what if there is none?*

Rider Cornatan continued, "Of course, it could well be that it could take us a while to retrieve that money. In that case, we'll need to look for opportunities to get some."

"Why don't we hunt our own food?" The Knights always did that.

"There are too many of us here. The Chevakians would be upset. There are not enough large animals in this country anyway."

"Why don't you offer to help the Chevakians? Then they might give us food or money?"

Rider Cornatan smiled. "That's exactly the idea. Except that damn upstart of a new proctor is too suspicious. I sent two men to act as interpreters for the camp of refugees, but the refugees didn't like them and now the Chevakians are suspicious. We need to work harder at gaining their trust. Us, over the Brothers. But the people in the camp can't be allowed to see who we are. I must remain hidden. I want you to be the face of the Eagle Knights."

❄

Carro's father says, "Don't be afraid. They only ask stupid questions."

But Carro feels very small and scared. His father leaves the room and goes to open the door.

Carro sits at the desk in the chair where his father never allows him to sit. He can hear the footsteps in the warehouse. The voice of a man. Laughter.

"Go and see my son, sir. He does the accounts."

Carro glances at the books, and counts the steps. One, two, three.

Any moment now and the tax collector will knock on the door.

Carro turned to the window, feeling chilled and sweaty at the same time. He was no prince, and he was no leader, and he had no intention of becoming the person to blame if things went wrong. Forcing the common people of the Outer City into accepting Knight rule was wrong. Knights did not rule, they protected. The queen ruled.

"Pour us a drink, son, and I'll tell you our plan."

Carro crossed the room to the cabinet against the wall, where dusty glasses stood amongst an assortment of jars, carafes and bottles. He wondered why the ambassador had left all those years ago, and why he had such a wild range of chemicals in his drinks cabinet. A jar of salt, all gone hard and stuck together. Lumps of an unidentified white crystal in a bottle of oil. Carro opened the lid. A sharp scent made him cough. Phooey. What was that awful stuff?

A tiny glass vessel with an ornate glass lid contained something he did recognise: light blue cyan crystals. Weren't they used as a crude method of assassinating your political opponents?

What sort of man had this ambassador been? Maybe his departure had less to do with the south's involvement in the border raids than with his own behaviour.

"What are you doing over there, son? The carafe of bloodwine is on the shelf," Rider Cornatan said.

Carro hesitated, the jar of cyan crystals in his hand. Drop a crystal or two in someone's drink and they would die a painful death. He imagined the merchant writhing on the floor, but got no satisfaction from the image. Everyone in the City of Glass had died.

This was not about him and his petty problems; it was about the people of the City of Glass. It was about the City of Glass not existing anymore, and all its citizens being forced to live here.

Rider Cornatan had known what was happening and had not warned the people. Rider Cornatan wanted to destroy the royal family, and anything that was outside his control. Rider Cornatan didn't care about the Chevakians, the ordinary people who had done nothing wrong.

"What's keeping you, son?"

"Um—nothing." Carro set the jar of crystals down, hidden behind two larger bottles. "It seems you expected something like this to happen."

He picked up the carafe, poured two drinks, and handed one to his father. Rider Cornatan drank deeply, then breathed out satisfaction.

"Always be prepared for everything, son. Now let me tell you what we're going to do. I'm going to send you to talk to the Chevakians."

A Word of Thanks

THANK YOU very much for reading *Dust & Rain*.

As author of this book, I would appreciate it very much if you could return to the place where you purchased this book and leave a review. Reviews are important to me, because they help readers decide if the book is for them.

In book 3 of the Icefire Trilogy, *Blood & Tears*, the saga concludes, as the Chevakians scramble to defend their homeland against an ever-expanding cloud of icefire, and the refugees fight against the power of the Eagle Knights.

Also be sure to put your name on my mailing list, which I use to notify subscribers of news and new fiction. For everything else, please visit my website at *pattyjansen.com*.

BLOOD & TEARS

BOOK 3 OF THE ICEFIRE TRILOGY

CHAPTER 1

IT WAS WELL past midnight when the truck stopped at the gate of Sady's house. Orsan got out of the seat next to the driver, walked around the side and opened the door for Sady, who let himself down, pulling the sides of his cloak together against the biting wind.

"Thank you," he said to the driver.

"My pleasure, Proctor. Get some rest. I'll be back here tomorrow morning, as usual."

Sady nodded. Thank the heavens for faithful staff.

He walked through the gate, where Orsan exchanged a few words with the young guard Farius, then across the path flanked by meticulously clipped bushes, up the steps to the front door.

The night was darker and quieter than normal. Low scudding clouds kept any moonlight from reaching the ground, and ever since the bell had rung the people of the city kept indoors. For the first time in Sady's memory, the famous streetlights of Tiverius remained unlit.

The only light in the hall was the lamp that Lana lit every day after dark and that normally burned all night. By its flickering light, Sady turned to Orsan.

"Any word from my house guests?"

Orsan shook his head and fixed him with an intense stare. "Sady, they can wait until morning. Get Lana to make you some soup and go to bed. I'll be out at the gate if you need me." He gave a customary bow and left.

Sady couldn't argue with Orsan's reasoning. Soup sounded great. Bed even better, although he suspected that once he lay down, sleep would be the last thing that came to him.

After the skirmishes in the refugee camp, he had gone back to his office to deal with the polite unhappiness of the senators, and with the much more rude complaints of the citizens, who told him bluntly that they did not want *this southern menace* in their city. Mercy, could these people just explain to him what they would have done with all those refugees? Turn the trains around and send the poor wretches back to their ravaged country?

He took his cloak off in the hall, and with it, the stoic façade of strength. He let his shoulders sag and dragged his hands across his stubbled face. He didn't think he'd ever been so tired in his life.

But even here, in the comfort of his house, he still saw the people on the platform. He saw the stack of bodies. A tangle of arms and legs, coated in indescribable filth. He saw the wretched survivors with weeping sonorics wounds. He smelled the incredible stench. He saw the angry faces of the refugees in the camp. They only asked to have the bodies of their dead relatives returned to them to observe the proper rituals. They'd been robbed of all dignity, and clung onto what little they had left. But all those bodies would have to be burned to stop contamination. He didn't look forward to dealing with the aftermath of this necessity. From what he understood, burning your dead amounted to sacrilege in the south; burying them was even worse. It made sense how the southerners left their dead for animals to eat, so that the people could eat the animals in turn. But you just couldn't *do* a thing like that in Chevakia's climate. Not to mention the uproar it would cause to the citizens of Tiverius.

How could he possibly solve this?

Bed, Sady, go to bed.

But first, something to eat.

He walked into the kitchen where a single light burned against the back wall. The benches were empty and clean. A bowl of fruit stood in the middle of the table.

"Hello? Lana?" He expected to hear a voice from the pantry: *I'm in here! Wait a moment. Do you want roccas or some soup?*

Now that he came to think of it, he was more than hungry. It could be the reason why he felt so ill. He couldn't even remember his last meal.

"Lana?"

The pantry door was closed. The back door into the laundry was closed. The corridor to the servant quarter was dark.

That was strange. Lana was always here. He couldn't imagine that she had gone to bed; she never did before he was home. But then again, it *was* very late, and he *had* told her repeatedly to go to bed if he was late. He was just . . . disappointed that she seemed to have taken his advice on this night, when he needed to talk to someone calm and sane.

He left the kitchen and knocked on the door to her private room. "Lana, I'm back." She would want to know; she would worry if he stayed out too long.

There was no reply.

Neither was there a sign of life from anywhere else. The noise he made should have brought out Serran, because he was responsible for the grounds, or the young Merni, because she was a gossip, and would make sure that she didn't miss anything.

Where was everyone?

Sady walked into the dark living room, feeling stupid. Here he was, the great leader of the country, and he was unnerved by being alone. Unnerved by feeling so *strange* in his own house.

The living room window looked out onto the courtyard, where he could only see a stone bench lit by a lantern on the patio, a little island of light in the dark. There was a statue in the middle of the yard, of Eseldus han Chevonian, one of his great forefathers. Today, Eseldus was only a dark silhouette.

The windows in the guest wing to the right hand side of the courtyard were dark. The surgeons must have already gone home. He was relieved about that; Sady had no desire to become more intimately acquainted with women's business than absolutely necessary.

He could still see the woman's bruised and red-blotched abdomen. The thought made him shiver. He hoped she survived. He hoped the child survived. That would be one point of light in this misery. He'd never thought this would be the way his house would see a baby.

He went back to the kitchen and scouted for some food, cringing at every noise he made. The clank of a plate on the stone bench, the rummaging in the cutlery, the rumble of pouring coal into the stove, the hiss of the flame under the kettle, it all sounded incredibly loud. He found some bread and a bit of goat's cheese, which crumbled all over the bench when he cut it up into clumsy, too-thick slices.

He sat down and ate, listening to the silence of the house.

And the sounds of the day. The ringing of the bell. The yelling of the men in the camp. He didn't understand their language, but he could feel the despair and anger in their words. It brought back many bad memories of his youth. Hundreds of people crammed into a cellar for days without food. The stink of too many bodies in a confined space. There had been that boy, a bit older than himself at the time, who projectile-vomited on those around him.

Sady could still smell it. He could still see the mother's embarrassment, her despair. Her son was seriously ill with sonorics, and yet her immediate concern was the irritation of the people around her.

Sady could still hear her, and the boy's muffled cries. And the ringing of the bell. He would never forget that. Today, the bell had rung again, after more than ten years of silence.

Somewhere in his mind, he registered that the water was boiling and probably had been for a while. Now, where did Lana put the teapot?

As he pushed up from the seat, there was an enormous crash at the back of the house, and the breaking of glass.

He froze, heart thudding. What in all of mercy's name was that?

"Lana?" he called at the door. Surely, that crash would have woken the whole house up.

But again, there was no reply.

He ran into the living room, unlocked the cabinet in the corner and took out the powder gun, a solid and heavy thing given to him by Milleus back in the days when they used to go hunting. He hadn't taken the weapon from its cabinet for a long time, but now the metal barrel lay cold against his arm. Comforting. Familiar. He pulled out a box of bullets, inserted two into the gun and slipped a handful into his pocket.

Still, none of the staff had come to investigate.

He made his way through the corridor to the back of the house. His footsteps echoed loudly in the silence. His mind churned, trying to come up with innocent reasons for the breaking of glass. Maybe the family had been scared by a door they couldn't figure how to open. He'd travelled in the southern land, and everything was so much more primitive there.

He opened the door to the guest wing. All dark. No signs of movement. The lamp in the hall was out.

"Hello?"

His heart was pounding.

The only reply was the soft keening of a whistling ground squirrel out in the garden, an unpleasant, creepy noise that made his skin crawl. The damn things were a menace, destroying plants and digging holes everywhere, dislodging tiles and cracking walls. He'd remind Farius to put out some baits.

A fresh breeze stroked his skin, making the hairs on his arms stand on end. There should *not* be a breeze here.

As quietly as he could, Sady walked into the living room, clutching the gun.

In the washed-out light from the lamp in the courtyard, broken shards of glass glittered in the window frame. More glass lay on the ground. A chair lay upside-down on the carpet. Then . . . there was a human-looking shape on the floor, a few paces into the room. Booted feet of a man, face down on the carpet, surrounded by a dark stain.

Sady ran across the room, and crouched next to the prone form. The man was dressed in thin trousers and a jacket that could be white or some other light colour. He was wearing thin gloves. Sady grabbed him by the shoulder. The weight was heavy, with no sign of movement. He didn't recognise the face. As Sady turned him over, a metal instrument fell out of a breast pocket. This had to be one of the surgeons, with a huge gash across his stomach where his bowels spilled out. The man's open, staring eyes spoke for themselves. Nothing he could do for this man.

Just inside the window was another body. Another man, on his side.

Sady recognised the jacket in han Chevonian maroon with gold piping before he could make out the man's face: Serran, the off-duty groundsman who should have been asleep in his room. He would not be going anywhere ever again. Rivulets of blood had run from deep gashes across his lower back and soaked his jacket and the carpet.

Sady pushed him on his back to see that his chest had been cut to the bone. His eyes were glassy and open.

Next to him, another unknown man in white shirt, arm ripped to shreds, the side of his tunic slashed open to reveal a dark mess of blood and intestines.

Sady rose, feeling dizzy with the cloying scent of blood and death.

Was anyone left alive in this room?

Where were the southern woman and her family?

One of the beds had been taken from the bedroom into the middle of this room, and stripped of blankets. It was covered only in a bottom sheet, neatly tucked-in as only nurses and soldiers could. Next to the bed stood a surgeon's kit of instruments. Unused, as far as Sady could tell. There were towels and sheets. Clean.

But someone had used the bed. There was a dark patch of something wet that wasn't dark enough to be blood. And a wet patch on the floor with in the middle a glistening heap of . . . something that looked like a disorganised bunch of dark entrails.

Sady's stomach churned.

On the floor, on the far side of the bed, was another body, this one a woman.

Sady's insides went cold as he recognised the bun on her head, the dress, and the apron, the sturdy shoes and the chubby arms and dimpled hands that had so often brought him tea.

Mercy, Lana.

"No," he whispered. For a moment, his vision went black.

No, Lana!

He dropped to his knees, put the gun down and reached for her as if in a nightmare.

Her shoulder felt limp and lifeless.

Her face was a bloodied mess. He couldn't even see her eyes for the blood. Half her cheek had been ripped off.

"No, Lana." His voice came as a rough whisper.

Sady took her arm. It was barely still warm. There was no pulse. The room blurred before his eyes.

Lana, and her cheerful jokes. Lana, who would not go to bed before he came home. And he'd been eating in the kitchen, maybe even while she was bleeding to death and he could still have saved her.

The silence of the room, the smell of blood and the staring eyes of four bodies made him dizzy.

He breathed slowly through his mouth, trying to think. He needed to get guards out here, to comb the grounds to find out who had done this.

Where were the southerners, the pregnant woman and her family? There was no sign of them, although a fur cloak lay draped over the back of the couch.

He said, as loud as he dared, "Hello? Where are you?"

There was a sound in the garden.

Sady froze. The killer might still be out there. For all he knew, the killer might *be* one of the southerners.

He pushed himself up, picked up the gun and went to the broken window, walking over the carpet so that his footsteps didn't make any noise.

The bushes in the garden looked like big angry trolls against the dim sky. Old Eseldus was like the king in their midst.

The sound came again, a snort, from somewhere in the yard.

He cocked the gun, once, twice to fill both barrels.

Click-click. Loud in that heavy silence.

"If you're out there, give yourself up. I have a gun." His voice echoed in the courtyard.

There was no reply.

He slowly stepped through the broken window, avoiding shards of glass, into the garden. His boots crunched more glass. A couple of bushes had been ripped out of the ground, their stems broken. A trail of dark spots led down the paved path, but stopped before they reached poor Eseldus.

There was that snort again. He raised the gun, holding his breath, his finger on the trigger and stood like that, as quiet as he could, until the need to breathe overwhelmed him. Nothing moved.

On the other side of the garden was a pavilion which the architect had probably intended as a garden room, but which, in the absence of the large family that would normally live in a house like this, the staff used as storage.

The door stood open.

The door was not normally open.

He crossed the yard and looked inside, but it was far too dark for him to make out anything.

"Hello? Anyone in here?"

Something moaned softly in the darkness. It wasn't an angry or a dangerous sound, but the sound of an animal in pain.

Clutching the gun, he stepped into the pavilion. Years of accumulated dust crunched under his feet. It was so dark in here. There were stacks of unused furniture in here somewhere but he hardly ever came in this room, and couldn't remember where exactly they stood. And if only he was looking into the light, he might have been able to see some silhouettes. Still holding the gun poised, he waved his left hand about and shuffled forward, feeling where he went.

"I'm here. I have a gun. Don't try any funny business." He hoped it sounded confident, because he didn't feel confident. Somewhere in the back of his mind, it occurred to him that it was probably an exceedingly stupid idea to pursue this alone, and that he should go and find Farius or Orsan.

The sound came again. This time, it was clearly a human voice. A woman. He couldn't make out the words, but she sounded distressed.

He found the owner of the voice in the far corner behind some garden furniture. He remembered the garden table, the big one from Milleus' house that had a candle well in the middle. He could see the table in his mind the last time he'd come in here, and remembered that there was wax in the well which no one had bothered to clean out. He ran his hands over the table, found the well and lit the wick. The paltry smoking and sputtering flame revealed that his quarry was the southern woman, legs pulled up against her chest, hugging herself.

She blinked against the light, her eyes intense blue. Her cheeks were wet with tears. She said something in her language.

"Hang on, I don't understand a word you're saying. Do you speak any Chevakian?"

She only responded to that by crying.

"Come, let's get you some place safe."

He clicked the safety back on the gun, looped the strap around his shoulder and bent down to help her up.

Her hair felt wet and the naked skin on her shoulders cold and clammy. The muscles in her arm shivered when he pulled her up. Her belly was blotched and bruised, but floppy. Her thighs were smeared with blood and she left a puddle of it on the floor. She almost fell and he put a steadying arm around her waist. She was completely naked, and her arms had multiple scratches as if she'd crashed through the bushes.

"Where is your baby?" Because clearly, the child had been born. He made a cradle of his arms and pretended to rock an infant, but he'd never had children, and maybe they didn't rock their infants in the south; in any case, she didn't understand him, and his first priority should be to get her out of here.

"Can you walk?"

He pulled her towards the garden. She stumbled and said some more words in her language, crying. Rivulets of blood ran down her legs. It was clear that she couldn't walk. Not well, anyway. Also, she wore no shoes and there was glass in the courtyard.

"Come." Sady looped his arm under her shoulders, put his other arm around the back of her legs and lifted her up.

Carefully, he walked through the garden to the guest pavilion. She was heavy, and her legs were wet and slippery with blood, but she clung onto him like she was a little girl. Curly hair tickled in his face.

He made his way back into the guest pavilion, past the bodies still on the ground.

When he entered the corridor, Orsan came the other way in big strides, carrying a torch.

"Proctor, what has—" He stopped. Looked at the woman and the broken furniture in the living room. "What happened here?"

Sady explained quickly, to Orsan's increasingly horrified expression. "Did you hear the window break?"

"No, but I thought I heard the side gate open. What has happened to her?"

"No idea. Have you seen her baby?" Sady asked. "Have you seen the rest of the family?" There should be two other women, and a man.

"No. I was at the front gate."

The woman moaned. Her face was wet with tears.

Orsan said, "Give her to me. I'll take her to the domestic wing."

"No. Take her to the second bedroom." The one next to his. "She needs a physic. She's bleeding."

Orsan took the woman from Sady and his arms thanked him. He was no athlete.

"Sady!" Fast footsteps in the corridor announced Merni. She came into the room, skirt flapping. Her hair was messy from bed. "What happened? I can't find Lana—" She stopped. Her gaze found the booted feet of the surgeon. Her eyes widened. She clapped her hands over her mouth to stifle a scream. She stumbled about, her eyes popping wide and dropped onto a bench, where she sat, panting. "They're dead, they're dead, they're *dead*."

Sady sank down next to her and put a hand on her shoulder.

She jerked towards him, her eyes still wide enough for the whites to show on all sides, and let out a scream.

"Shhh, calm down. It's all right."

"No, it's not all right There's *dead* people in there. How can you call that all right?" She screamed again, and clawed at her face. Her eyes were so wide, he wasn't sure if she even saw him.

"Shhh—screaming is not going to help them, or the guards looking for the killer."

"You mean there's a killer still out there?" Her voice spilled over, hysterical. "You mean he's going to come back and kill all of us, too?" She screamed again, shrill. Her nails left red marks on her cheeks. Sady felt like clamping his hands over his ears.

"Quiet!" he shouted, perhaps a bit louder than he'd intended, but the screaming jangled his nerves. He grabbed her hands, so she couldn't scratch herself again. The muscles in her arms were tense and fought him. "They're dead. They're dead!"

He tightened his grip. "Merni, stop it!"

She looked at him, breathing fast. Tears tracked over her cheeks. He mouth quivered. "But . . . but they're dead."

"I know, but screaming is not going to help anyone."

Her chest moved in rapid expansions, as if she'd burst out screaming any moment. But she kept her mouth shut.

"Calm down, breathe slowly, that's it."

She was young, much younger than Lana, and had started working at his household last year at Lana's recommendation, but Sady had found her excessively formal and nervous.

Her breathing slowed somewhat. "That's it," he said, trying to sound as soothing as possible, even though he didn't feel that way at all. "Now, follow Orsan and look after the poor woman."

"Yes," Merni said, and she nodded, clamping her lips to stop them trembling. "Yes, certainly."

She rose and ran off, leaving Sady with the bodies. He slumped on the bench. What now?

Where was he going to get a physic and an interpreter at this time of the day during a level one sonorics warning? The physics held emergency clinics, he'd heard, but he had never been to one. At the hospital, he assumed. He had to—

There was a sound behind him. He whirled around to see that the door to the guest wing's bedroom had opened and three people were coming out. There was a man, a hairy, unshaven fellow in a woollen robe, a middle-aged short and squat woman and a teenage girl, presumably their daughter, cradling an infant in a sling. Ah, that solved the issue of the missing baby.

The girl advanced into the room, her grey eyes wide. The baby started crying, and she patted it on the back.

"You . . . live here?" she said in heavily accented Chevakian.

"I am the owner of this house." He couldn't believe it. He'd spent all day looking for someone who spoke Chevakian, and all the while such a person had been in his house? "I sent you here. What happened here? Is that the baby?"

She backed away when he pointed at the child in the sling, putting a protective arm over it.

"I only wanted to know if the lady's child was safe."

"Is my child." She stuck her chin into the air.

At her age? No way.

"Mine," she said again. Her grey eyes blazed with protectiveness.

"Then where is the lady's child?"

He had to repeat the question before she understood.

"You not see it?"

"No. I found the lady, but not the child. Where is it?"

She shrugged. "We go in." She pointed at the bedroom door. Her mother said something and the girl replied in a sharp tone.

"You didn't see any of what happened?" he tried again.

"We hear . . . Whaaa . . . Whaaa." She waved her arms presumably to mimic screaming and panic. Her mother again commented. She returned another sharp reply.

"Didn't you go and help?"

She spread her hands. "I . . . not . . ." She rolled her eyes at the ceiling.

Sady struggled on for a bit longer, but clearly her Chevakian was inadequate to tell him the full story. He did get that her name was Myra and that Dara and Ontane were her parents. The pregnant woman's name was Loriane, and he didn't think she was related to the family.

Orsan returned, carrying a plank and a hammer. He leaned the plank against the couch and put the hammer down on the seat.

"For the window," he said when Sady raised his eyebrows. "I just spoke to Farius at the gate. He says he heard the side door, too. I'm going to take a light into the yard and see if we can find out where the killer went."

"You may need to find a newborn baby."

Orsan nodded, his face grim. "I thought it was the child the girl carries, but it's too old. Merni showed me."

"What would someone want with a newborn baby?"

Orsan shrugged. "We'll have a look if we can find the bastard."

Sady made a decision. "I'm coming."

"Do you think that's wise? It could be dangerous—"

"I'm coming. I'm not letting you go out there by yourself." His voice was definite. Better in danger than sitting inside grieving over Lana's death. There would be time to get the family's story tomorrow, or whenever he located a translator. "It could be a while before the guards are here. The trail will be long cold by then."

CHAPTER 2

A ROUGH MAN'S voice woke Isandor from his sleep. It was a shout —garbled words that his brain couldn't process in its sleepy state, somewhere close outside the tent. He looked around, to find that he wasn't, in fact, in the tent, but had been sleeping on the passenger bench of the truck. Well, that explained why he felt hot and stuffy.

It was still dark outside, and the orange glow of firelight flickered through the cabin, lighting the seat backs and the wheel and dashboard.

He now remembered Milleus suggesting that two of them sleep in the truck, for safety, while the third person guarded the goats against refugees desperate for milk or, heaven forbid, meat.

He sat up, feeling sweaty and shivery. The seat had been none too comfortable, its leather sweaty. His neck was sore, his back was sore and he had lost feeling in his left hand.

Jevaithi sat in the front passenger seat, her cloak drawn around her. By the way she held her head up, she was awake.

Outside the front window dark shadows moved in groups, all going down the hill. The firelight was not from the campfire—which had gone out—but from people carrying burning torches. There was purpose and aggression in the way they moved.

He had a memory of a mob of young men, most older than himself, running through a snowy street, setting fire to limpets.

Shouts, and fights. The night sky lit up. That had been the night that the Outer City burned, the night they had fled.

"What's going on?" he asked. His voice was croaky. By the skylights, his neck really hurt.

Jevaithi's face looked pale in the flickering firelight. "I don't know. A lot of people are going down there. None are coming back."

"Where is Milleus?" Isandor had seen him earlier that night, when he'd come to relieve Isandor from his guard duty in protecting the goats. Isandor had been stiff and cold, sitting on the trailer's railing, with the goats asleep behind him, all piled half on top of each other, because there wasn't enough room in the trailer for all of them to lie down. Isandor had sat there, with the metal railing biting in his backside, clutching the gun, jumping at every sound. And Milleus had come out of the truck for a change of guard.

"I haven't seen him. He should be outside," Jevaithi said, just as Isandor had reached that same conclusion.

Isandor pressed his nose against the glass. There were so many people going down that road. Their shouts sounded muffled through the glass, and he couldn't make out the words, but the voices were rough with anger. He thought of all the young men he'd seen yesterday, standing around bored and angry, attracted to wherever there was an argument. The goats were bleating and jumping around, and their movement rocked the truck. Surely Milleus was out there somewhere.

"I'll go and have a look," he said.

"No." Her eyes were wide, with little bright spots where the torchlight reflected in them. "Don't go outside."

"How else can I find out what's going on?"

"Please. I'm scared. This is just like the night . . ." She didn't need to finish the sentence. He knew. The night he'd rescued her from the Knights, and they had escaped the blue giant of a servitor. The night that the Outer City erupted in fights.

"If there is trouble, I need to help Milleus."

Jevaithi's eyes met his. She didn't argue with that. "Please, be careful. If something happened to you . . ."

"You'll be fine." She'd be completely lost without either of them. "Just stay here, all right? Don't talk to anyone. Don't let anyone into the truck."

She nodded, her eyes wide. "What if those hunters come back?"

"Lock the door after I've gone. You'll be fine." He repeated it to convince himself. By the skylights, he really didn't like the look of what was happening outside.

He rummaged around in the back of the truck and found a length of wood that Milleus sometimes used as a walking stick. "Here."

She took it from him. The determined expression on her face made him cringe. She would be nothing against trained Knights even if she had a gun. They had only one gun, and Milleus had it, or so he hoped.

He retrieved his cloak, dragged it over his shoulders and opened the door. A gust of smoke-scented wind blew grit and ash into his face. People were talking in nearby tents. Agitated voices. Somewhere in the darkness, someone started a truck engine with a hiss. He looked past the side of the truck.

"Milleus?"

No reply.

He let himself onto the ground, shut the door and walked past the truck. The goats stirred.

"Milleus?"

Milleus wasn't sitting on the trailer bar, where he had been when Isandor went to sleep. The truck's toolbox stood on the ground, open, but the truck's panels were all closed, and there was no sign of Milleus fiddling with the engine. The canopy had been pulled over the trailer as if they were on the road. Two goats stuck their hairy noses out between the bars of the railing, one of them curling its tongue to get hold of a piece of rope.

"Milleus!" Isandor's heart thudded. Jevaithi's heart, in his chest. Through it, she would feel everything.

"I'm here!" came a voice from behind him. Isandor whirled. A group of people stood between tents. The light was too feeble to distinguish faces, but he thought he could pick out Milleus' old vest.

Isandor made his way between packs and vehicles, dogs and guy ropes. It wasn't easy with his wooden leg. He almost tripped over a pack and had to steady himself against a tent pole, and a man inside shouted at him. Dogs started barking.

Milleus stood in a group with three men and a woman. The woman was saying, ". . . and I heard from my brother that the Mekta

Road is very busy but still moving, but he's not been able to get a word from Tiverius."

One of the men said, "The lines are down."

The other said, "All this newfangled telegraph technology. Pigeons would have gotten through ten times."

And the woman, "You did well to get through at all."

They stopped talking when Isandor joined the group. The woman raised an eyebrow at him. She was a middle-aged woman with the soft, pale-skinned features of an administrator. "This is the young man you were talking about, Milleus?"

"Yes," Milleus said.

She eyed him up and down, but said nothing. Isandor thought her face was disapproving.

"What's going on?" Isandor asked.

"He speaks Chevakian well," the woman said, looking at Milleus as if Isandor wasn't there.

"He's a fast learner."

"You did well, teaching him. Theirs is such a strange language."

"Excuse me, what's going on?" Isandor asked again. Why did these people think that because he was young and not Chevakian, they could talk over his head?

"We'll be moving soon," Milleus said.

"But it's still dark." And where were they moving to, anyway?

"Some young fellows have cut a hole in the fence and we're moving through. They say that a lot of the tents in the camps are empty, and are wondering what the hold-up is. We'll be travelling through the camp now, before someone can come and stop us. We'll be at my brother's house in the morning."

Isandor looked from the truck—and the open toolbox—to Milleus. "You gave them the wire cutters, didn't you?"

"It was a ridiculous place to put a fence. Come on, let's go."

Isandor guessed that meant yes. Strange. Milleus had struck him as being someone who liked rules.

The woman and two men left and Milleus and Isandor went back to the truck, where Jevaithi was watching, a pale face behind the window. All around, people were busy dousing fires and packing up tents. Isandor grabbed the hay people had brought yesterday and stuffed it into bags Milleus had for that purpose. The goats could smell it and thought they were getting fed. They jostled each other to be in the position closest to Isandor. He scratched the animals behind the ears.

At the bend down the hill, the first trucks already started moving.

Isandor helped Milleus fire the furnace. All around, people were talking in eager voices. *Hurry up; let's get going.* After being stuck here for what felt like a long time, they were moving again; they were doing something. Just like in the Outer City and in the Knights' Eyrie, people got up to all sorts of trouble when they were bored or frustrated.

Soon, the convoy was rolling again, very slowly at first, and there was a long wait before the way ahead was clear enough for the truck to join the downhill convoy. While they waited, Milleus leaned his elbows on the truck's wheel, and talked about his brother, who worked gathering information about the weather. Isandor hadn't known that Chevakians made such detailed observations of weather patterns. He didn't know that icefire rose and waned in cycles. He had known that Chevakians could measure it, but didn't know that it determined so much of their weather.

Whichever way Isandor looked at it, there could be no peace between the two countries unless icefire was controlled. If the Knights, as he had seen, were experimenting with it, that could upset the entire climate in Chevakia and it would become as cold as the City of Glass. That would be a disaster.

In the City of Glass, people could hunt and eat meat—this habit of eating bread was very strange to him anyway—but Chevakia had no ocean where Legless Lions could live, and without them, the people would starve. They had camels and goats, but those ate grass and there would be none of that, either.

Their houses were also too flimsy for the cold. If the climate changed, many people would freeze before new houses could be built. And that was even without any of the deadly effects icefire itself had on Chevakians.

The truck before them jolted into action, and Milleus followed, still at walking pace, but soon going faster.

When they rounded the bend, an amazing scene unrolled before them. The column of trucks moved through a large opening cut in the fence, with the wire mesh rolled away in both directions. The camp down the hill was dark, with just a few lamps burning between the tents. Further down the slope, the camp merged into the streets of Tiverius: lights in neat rows and the dark outlines of square buildings.

Tiverius, the legendary Chevakian capital. Isandor had often wished, but never truly believed, that he'd ever come here. As butcher's assistant in the Outer City, he'd been too poor. As Apprentice Knight, he would have been unwelcome.

Milleus steered the truck through the fence, held open by a couple of youths waving to the passing trucks.

The convoy chugged onto the grassy plain of the camp, towards the tents.

Jevaithi leaned on his backrest; Isandor could feel her breath in his hair. She'd been quiet. For her, all these refugees would mean getting back to her old life, because someone would recognise her. She could run from her heritage, but she would never be free from it.

The truck in front slowed down and then stopped.

"What now?" Milleus muttered.

Someone ran past the truck from the direction of the camp, shouting something Isandor didn't catch. Two more people followed.

Someone else came running after them. "Stop, stop! Go back or I'll fire!"

That man was joined by a second person, carrying a torch. Both wore uniforms Isandor had seen a few times on their drive from Milleus' farm. Soldiers of the Chevakian army.

Milleus opened the door on his side and slid out of the truck. "Stay here."

He walked past the front of the truck and said something to the soldiers.

"Get back into your vehicles, and turn around where you came from immediately," the Chevakian soldier shouted back. "You are not allowed here."

"We are refugees from Ensar and are on our way to Tiverius." Milleus planted his hands at his sides, as he did when arguing. "We've been waiting on the other side of that fence for more than a day, and we're fed up. We demand to use the road, which is a public road for all Chevakians. We will not go back there and wait. We can't turn the convoy around. Too many vehicles are still coming from behind. Food is running out. Some people here have nowhere to stay in the city. They need to stay in the camp. They're fed up with waiting."

The man replied, but Isandor didn't hear it because a number of people ran past at such speed that one crashed into the soldier with the torch, and stumbled before regaining his balance. The soldier yelled at him and the skinny youth ran for the truck. From the sounds and rocking, he had climbed onto the trailer. The goats scrambled and bumped into the side rail.

"Hey, you!" Milleus shouted. "Get off! You're scaring the goats."

Isandor opened the door on his side. "I've got to go and help him. Stay here." He jumped onto the grass.

A couple of other youths had arrived, and while the soldiers fought his mates, the youth on the trailer inserted his hand in between the cover and the mesh sides. The goats were bleating and jumping around trying to get away.

Isandor grabbed the youth by the back of his coat. He yanked. The youth lost his grip on the trailer and fell back.

Isandor jumped onto the railing to shield the goats with his own body. "Get away from my goats."

The youth scrambled up, looked as if he was going to fight, but then his mouth fell open. "The . . . the Queen's champion?" He spoke the southern language and those words took Isandor back to a time he'd almost forgotten. Flying on the back of an eagle, a time when his only worry was Carro's unusual behaviour.

Yes, he had won the medal, and that had been the beginning of all this misery.

"I'm Isandor," he said, and his voice sounded strange even to his own ears, having spoken Chevakian to all others except Jevaithi for so long. "How did you get here?"

"Like everyone else, on the train." He used the old southern word for train, one that had been in use at the time of the old king.

"What train?" Isandor used the Chevakian word.

"The one that brought us here. You didn't come on the train?"

"No, we came with a Chevakian farmer. These are his goats." He grabbed the bars of the railing. The press of the warm and hairy bodies against his hands was comforting. They had become *his* goats as well.

"We came on the train, and the Chevakians put us here."

"How many of you?"

"All of us. The whole camp."

Isandor let his eyes roam the hillside dotted with tents. There were thousands of people here.

More even. Now he understood. Milleus had assumed the camp was for refugees from the Chevakian border regions. But it was for southern refugees.

"Why did you flee?"

"There was a massive explosion. They say the Knights messed with the Heart of the City, and the Heart took revenge. Some say there was a war. Some say the Knights did it on purpose. —Hey, guys!" the youth called out to his mates, some of whom still jostled with the Chevakians. "Hey, come here, guys. The Queen's champion is here!"

Some people came running out of the darkness—a boy of about ten, a girl and a young woman. They looked dirty, pale and emaciated. Their furs were filthy and matted.

"We all thought the Knights had killed you," the girl said. She was about Isandor's age, but her face was scabbed and oozing fluid. Her eyes were wide with pure adoration.

Isandor felt sick. While he had been eating well and frolicking with the Queen, the people of the City of Glass had suffered a terrible disaster. The next moment, panic clawed at his insides. *Mother.* Where was she?

More people came running towards the Chevakian convoy. "The Queen's Champion is here!" The shout was repeated by people across the grassy field. "The Queen's champion! The Queen's champion!"

"Go back to your tents immediately!" a Chevakian soldier shouted. There were only two soldiers, and at least thirty southern people. Isandor recognised the emotions in their faces from that night in the Outer City. They were hungry, desperate, frightened, bored, all recipes for a riot.

Isandor didn't want to start a riot. He wanted to know where his mother was.

One of the Chevakians from the truck convoy joined the soldiers, and yelled at the southerners, "If anyone touches any of us, I'll shoot."

Isandor shouted at the southern youths. "Go, before there is trouble."

The group made a half-hearted effort at retreating, but didn't go very far.

Chevakian men gathered next to Milleus' truck. Isandor remained in the shadow, feeling their angry gazes on him.

One man said, "So Destran gives all this to southern scum while we have to wait outside and get nothing?" Isandor recognised the driver of the truck in front of Milleus'.

"And why close off the road?" another said. "That is the most stupid thing I could think of doing."

The first man said, "Why isn't there a camp here for us? We have nowhere to stay."

"And no money to pay for their expensive inns," another added.

"Now you people here, listen." The grumblings grew quiet at the sound of the clear male voice of a Chevakian soldier. He looked to be of senior rank, with glittering buttons on his uniform.

"I'm going to have to ask you to turn back. I don't know how you got in, but—"

"We made a hole in the fence, that's what," Milleus said.

The soldier looked at him, briefly raised his eyebrows, and went on, "You have to leave for your own safety. There was a disaster with sonorics in the City of Glass, and these people have fled—"

"We have fled, too," a woman said, and some people cheered.

"These people are contaminated and a risk to your health."

"Any more of a risk than starving to death?" someone yelled.

Several others agreed.

"You have to go back the way you came," the soldier shouted over their voices. "Turn your trucks around immediately and go back the way you came. Follow the Mekta road into the city."

"Where we will find what? Have you got something set up for us, too or is this just another way to keep us out of your hair? This camp looks good enough for us."

"We can't allow you to go through here. Return where you came from. That is an order. Disobey and you risk being fired at." The soldier's voice rose.

"Come on, mate, you wouldn't really shoot at a fellow Chevakian." This soothing voice was Milleus', and he pushed his way through the group. "That is against the army's mandate."

The officer turned his head to him, swallowed visibly, clutching his gun. "Who are you?"

His nostrils were wide, and his chest moved fast.

Isandor knew the type; he'd seen them in the lower ranks of the Knight officers. They had some responsibility but didn't have the experience or aptitude for higher command. They were used to having their orders obeyed and panicked when they were not. He wished he could tell Milleus to watch out. Such men could do strange things at no notice and this one looked at the end of his rope.

Milleus put his hand on the man's shoulder and said some quiet words that Isandor couldn't hear.

The officer's eyes widened. He sprang into a military salute. "Honoured to meet you, sir."

Milleus said something else.

The officer listened, and then said, "The command won't like that, sir."

"No," Milleus said. "They probably won't, but they'll like the alternative even less."

The man nodded and they spoke more. Milleus gestured at Isandor to get into the truck. By the skylights, it looked like Milleus was actually going to convince them to let the convoy through.

Isandor made his way towards the truck when there were fast footsteps and more Chevakian soldiers arrived. They spoke to their comrade and Milleus.

Milleus protested.

One of them said, "It's our orders to keep the camp sealed and remove these people."

"Let's be realistic. There is nowhere for them to move to," Milleus said, his voice calm. "The road is blocked with too many people still arriving. People out there are angry and hungry. Let us pass through to clear up the jam. Seal the fence afterwards."

And so it went on. Milleus argued in favour of common sense. Someone in the Chevakian army had given the order to remove the Chevakians from the camp, and some soldiers thought it was all right to interpret that as letting these people out on the other side of the camp, and others said it was not.

Over their heads, Isandor noticed that southern people were gathering further down the hill. Some were pointing at him.

Another group of Chevakian guards arrived and tried to shoo the southerners back to the tents. Isandor heard shards of shouting, some mentioning his name. Milleus was still talking to the other Chevakians.

A scuffle broke out further down the hill.

"Be calm! Don't fight!" he shouted in his own language over the heads of Milleus and the soldiers. His voice sounded thin on the wind.

Voices shouted back. "Champion, champion."

"Don't fight. They will kill you!"

"Champion, champion, champion!"

Now several of the Chevakians civilians of the truck convoy turned to Isandor.

"That's one of them," Isandor heard a woman say.

"What is he doing here?"

"I saw him with the old man."

"He's the one who gave us milk." This was a child's voice. "I like him."

Down the hill, the scene descended into chaos. Isandor spotted a man in a Chevakian uniform beating a refugee on the ground. Some southerners threw rocks at that soldier. Other Chevakians went after the rock-throwers. Most of them ran up the hill to the shelter of the Chevakian trucks, where Isandor spotted one man clambering in the back of a trailer, and one crawling underneath the vehicle. Another climbed on top of the wood stack. The truck's owner, who had been tending the boiler, yelped when he found a stranger behind him.

Chevakian soldiers walked past the column inspecting each truck. They caught the southern youth hiding in the trailer, dragged him down and kicked him.

In all that chaos, Milleus came back to the truck in great angry strides.

"Get in," he said to Isandor.

"But they're beating up my—"

"Get in. Now."

There was no arguing with that voice. Isandor climbed into the back, where Jevaithi put the gun aside and clamped her arms around him. Her skin was clammy and cold.

"The people in the camp are all southerners," he whispered. "They're refugees from the City of Glass."

"Oh!" Her eyes were wide, but she said nothing else. She stared into the distance and he could only imagine what she felt.

"Don't be afraid," he whispered.

"There will be Knights."

"If there are, they'll have me and Milleus to deal with, but I haven't seen any."

"You don't understand what they can do if they don't get things their way."

"We'll be fine. Milleus is with us." But he understood very well. *He* knew what the Knights could do. The pain of having his very essence sucked into an icefire sink was not something he'd forget easily. Now that the Chevakian barriers had failed, they were no longer immune from icefire.

He kissed Jevaithi on the lips.

From his position, he could see four or five Chevakian soldiers, walking past the trucks. One yelled and swung his baton, clanging it against each truck. "Move, move, move! Turn back!"

The truck in front jerked forward in a cloud of steam, stopped with squeaking brakes to avoid running over a youth who was being chased by a couple of Chevakian guards, and then completed the half-circle and went off back up the hill. A couple of southern youths chased after it and jumped onto the back.

Chevakian soldiers ran after them and tried to pull them off. One of the youths fell and was besieged by Chevakians. A fight broke out.

Milleus had started the engine.

More and more trucks from the front of the column were now driving back towards the hole in the fence, many with people hanging off the back. Chevakians tried to pull the hitchhikers off. They didn't get all of them. The Chevakian soldiers were too few in number to stop the fights that broke out. Isandor could do nothing but watch, clutching the edge of his seat, while Milleus waited for boiler pressure to build.

"Are we going back?" he asked.

"No way. We'll be sleeping at Sady's house tonight."

Now that the truck in front had gone, Isandor had an uninter-rupted view of the camp, where more and more people were streaming out, up the hill, many carrying burning torches.

A soldier came to the window. "Move please, sir." He flapped his hand in a general uphill direction and said a few words Isandor didn't catch.

Milleus grumbled, "Old man? I'll show you who's an old man." With a sharp clink, he dropped the truck into gear. "Hold on, youngsters."

The engine roared, blowing a cloud of steam by way of a threat. The soldier didn't move.

"Get out of the way!" Milleus shouted out the window.

"Sorry, sir, you can't pass. Proctor's orders."

"And do you know what you can do with that dishrag of a proctor?"

He cranked the truck into reverse, shot back as far as they could without hitting either of the two trucks that were still following, and made a sharp turn to the right, over the edge of the road, ploughing through the grass and past the soldiers. The goats in the trailer protested with the jerky movements.

"Hey, hey! Stop!" The soldier ran beside the truck, but he couldn't keep up. There was a loud bang.

Milleus gunned the truck as fast as it would go. "Did you hear that? They fired at us! They shot at honest Chevakian citizens. Hang on, this will be a rough trip."

Isandor grabbed the handholds on the side of the door. Jevaithi clung into him. Milleus steered the truck around bumps and gullies. He seemed to enjoy himself. They rolled down the hill faster and faster and soon Isandor couldn't see the running soldier anymore. He glanced over his shoulder.

Jevaithi's eyes were wide.

Isandor held her. He was scared, too.

The truck bumped and creaked and clanged. They kept going downhill, getting closer to the first line of tents. There were no longer other trucks in front. The sky showed faint blue at the horizon, and the glow lit Milleus' determined face. He muttered obscenities to himself.

The truck clunked back onto the paved road with a sound that Isandor hadn't heard before. The engine roared, but they were not going as fast as Isandor would have expected.

Milleus swore. "They shot the tyres."

A few loud bangs echoed over the field, these ones further away, presumably aimed at the trucks trying to follow. The truck laboured down the road. They were now coming up to the first of the tents. Refugees thronged at tent entrances to watch the spectacle. People of all ages, all southerners in fur cloaks. Skinny, filthy refugees. Many of them were wounded. There were hundreds, thousands.

While they progressed slowly, some of the refugees cheered. Children ran with the truck, barefooted.

"I wish all these people would get out of the way," Milleus muttered. He glanced over his shoulder, where a group of Chevakian soldiers fast caught up. "The old lady can't pull much with a couple of flat tyres. We'll probably have to stop soon, when they catch up with us. You're ready?"

"Ready for what?" Isandor couldn't run with his wooden leg.

"We're likely to get arrested by the soldiers, and they'll take us into the city. You'll have to come up with a story that will convince them that you're not southern spies."

Isandor met Jevaithi's wide eyes.

"Whatever your reason for being in my shed, it can't be political or have anything to do with the government of the City of Glass."

By the skylights, were the Chevakians that scared of the south?

Jevaithi's breath was coming fast. Her face glistened with sweat. Isandor held her tightly, and could feel his heart racing in her chest.

If there were any Knights in the camp, this wouldn't end well. If they were caught by Chevakians, this wouldn't end well.

A Chevakian soldier caught up with the truck, jumped on the outer step, yanked the driver's door open and half-pulled Milleus from his seat. The truck stopped abruptly when Milleus' foot left the accelerator.

Jevaithi let out a squeak and buried in Isandor's arms.

Milleus struggled to free himself of the soldier's grip, cursing, but the soldier was stronger and dragged Milleus from the cabin.

Champion, champion, champion, the southern people were chanting.

Some of them climbed onto the front of the truck. Soon, they would come inside, and then . . .

"What do we do now?" Jevaithi cried. "It's over. We're lost."

"No, it's not," Isandor said.

Something clicked in Isandor's mind. The people he'd talked to briefly were Outer City people, because people from the City of

Glass proper would never have recognised him. It made sense that if something had caused an explosion of icefire, most of the refugees would be from the Outer City. Knights would have eagles, and he'd seen none. Maybe there *were* no Knights here. He had to take the risk.

The Outer City people he knew well, and those people loved the Queen. Jevaithi had another protection: her name.

"Wait." He released Jevaithi and turned to the door.

"What are you doing?" Her voice sounded like a squeak.

"Wait. Come out when I ask you."

"No, Isandor."

"Yes. I have an idea."

He pushed the door open. The scene outside was utter chaos. People were fighting the Chevakian guards, or each other. Three people were on the trailer, trying to get it open. The goats were bleating and jumping about. Milleus had vanished in the seething mass of people.

Still in the door opening, Isandor pulled himself up onto the truck's roof, his trembling hands slipping in the layer of soot and dust that covered it.

He put his fingers in his mouth and whistled as hard as he could.

"Stop. Fighting!"

Not that it made much of a difference. The wind carried his voice and the words were lost in the chaos.

But then a man yelled, "There is the Champion! See? I told you so."

A woman replied, "Our Champion!"

"That can't be. The Knights killed him."

Isandor yelled, as loudly as he could, "I'm not dead, as you can see."

Fights stopped. A few people laughed.

Cheers went up all around, and all the southerners in the vicinity of the truck gathered to watch. Isandor spotted Milleus with the Chevakians at the back, also watching.

He asked. "Are you all from the Outer City?"

A woman replied, "Most of us, yeah."

"Are there any Knights here?"

"If there are, they're keeping their cowardly heads down." The man who had spoken was dressed in black, and when he spoke, voices quietened.

By the skylights, since when had the Brothers of the Light been so visible? There must be truly no Knights here. "Are you the leader of these people?"

"I'm Simo," the man said. He was perhaps in his thirties. He had a thin beard and a balding patch at the top of his head. "Leader is probably not the right word, but we are leaders, of some kind, for the freedom of the people of the City of Glass. I'm glad to hear that you survived. The last we saw of you was when you were being taken away by Knights."

That time seemed like years ago. The man must have been in the audience at the arena for the ritual killing, like most of these people here.

Isandor bent down and stuck his hand into the window. "Come out."

Jevaithi stared at him, looking into the window upside-down.

"Come. These are good people, from the Outer City. They won't harm you. They'll protect you."

He could see the whole world go through that frightened expression in her eyes. Did she want to go back to being their queen? She had said she didn't, but she'd been very quiet the last few days whenever the subject came up. She was scared, and lost, and too groomed for the position to do anything else.

She came out of the truck, took his hand and let him haul her on top of the roof, where the grey pre-dawn light silvered her face and her no-longer-white bear skin cloak.

There were gasps, and a stunned silence.

Then someone cried out, "It's the Queen!"

Several voices repeated the cry. "It's the Queen, it's the Queen. The Queen lives."

Isandor met Milleus' eyes over the heads of the crowd; his mouth was open. Isandor mouthed, *I'm sorry*.

Men climbed up on the truck and lifted both Isandor and Jevaithi onto their shoulders.

From his position, Isandor glimpsed a whole convoy of Chevakian trucks still coming into the camp through the broken fence, and soldiers trying to turn them around. Fights were again breaking out on the edge of the camp, and the Chevakian soldiers, too few in number, retreated. The southerners were throwing up barricades. Fires burned in some places, sending clouds of smoke through the camp.

But there was nothing Isandor could do about any of that. The people carried him and Jevaithi into a large tent, where many people sat on the ground. Mothers and children, older people, all huddled under cloaks. In here, it smelled of bodies and damp earth.

The young Brother Simo yelled, "Listen to me, people. There is good news! We have the Queen. The Queen is back!"

CHAPTER 3

SADY GUIDED the southern family in the direction of the main part of the house. He could hear Merni's voice in the kitchen, much calmer now. She would tell them what to do. Hopefully the bedroom in the guest wing was unaffected, and they could still use that. If they could sleep at all.

He went to get his dark winter coat and returned to the yard. By that time, Orsan had returned from taking the southern woman Loriane into the bedroom. He had also stocked up on weapons: he carried not just his guard's gun, but had retrieved his pistol. Sady and Orsan started combing the courtyard by walking in a grid pattern so as not to miss any clues. Farius joined them a bit later, carrying a torch in one hand and a pistol in the other. He was only a young fellow, an apprentice under Serran, twenty at most and with a face that retained some of the angles and bony corners of an adolescent. He would have had little practice with the weapon.

"Look here," Orsan said from the darkness.

Sady and Farius went to where Orsan kneeled on the pavement of the path that led to poor old Eseldus' statue. Sady had seen the dark trail of spots when he went out here, before he found the woman Loriane in the pavilion. Sady kneeled and reached out, but Orsan said, "Don't touch it."

"What is it? Looks like blood to me."

"Could be. Could be poison. We don't know until we investigate. Best to be safe."

Farius followed the trail, which went halfway to the pavilion and stopped there.

Orsan crouched and examined the grass and the path and the small hedge and rockery adjacent to the path.

"See anything?" Farius asked.

Orsan shook his head. "It looks like he just vanished at this spot."

"Didn't you hear the side gate?" Sady said. The gate was on the other side of the courtyard, with no clear sign of how the killer had crossed that distance.

Farius went over to the door and tried the handle. "It's locked." He hit the wood; it sounded solid. The door was fairly new; Sady remembered it being replaced about five years ago.

"That's strange. I swear I heard the door." Orsan's bushy eyebrows knitted together. "Any other way out?"

Farius raised the torch. The wall on the side was too high and there were no trees or features that would allow someone to climb it easily, or at least not without leaving tracks.

Farius searched the pavilion where Sady had found the southern woman and found nothing except the puddle of blood she had left. The pavilion had only doors into the garden and no access to the street.

"The only way someone could have escaped without having to go through the house is over that wall," Orsan said.

"Look, we're losing time," Sady said. "Let's just assume he got out over the wall without worrying about how he did it. Let's have a look on the other side."

Sady pulled out a key and turned the lock on the side gate. It creaked; the door was only opened when a lot of material needed to be carried into the garden and that hadn't happened since the end of winter.

The alley on the other side led past the walls and gates of neighbouring houses. In the past, these alleys were used by servants who were not allowed to enter their family's house through the main door. These days, people used the side entrance only to cart rubbish away.

A wind gust tore between the buildings and blew all his hair to one side. Mercy, this biting wind didn't feel like summer at all.

Orsan and Farius came out as well. By the light of Farius' torch, they examined the paving and walls, but could see nothing that wasn't supposed to be there.

They were wasting time here. The killer had long since fled. "Let's assume that he fled into this alley, which way would he have gone?"

"That way." Orsan gestured to the east, where low hills rose over the surrounding houses. "Any criminal would probably flee out of the city, rather than into it." He came out of the side gate, and shut the door behind him. Sady registered the noise, and tried to remember if he'd heard it earlier that night, when he'd been sitting in the kitchen. He didn't think so.

They walked through the alley, Farius with the light, Orsan clutching his pistol and Sady between them, his hand on the grip of his hunting rifle.

It was dark. The wind howled around corners and blew sand and leaves through the street. Farius' torch made long eerie shadows on walls. There was no sign of life anywhere on this night. Even the ground squirrels hid in their infernal burrows. The wind carried distorted sounds of the bell tower's hour chime. Then a single strike of the bell, the continued warning for Tiverians to stay indoors.

Sady remembered that before he left his office, he had been keen to look at the sonorics measurements for tomorrow morning. All things going well, the contamination should be going down now that the southerners and the trains had been cleaned.

Somehow, the world of the office and the doga seemed incredibly far away.

They continued through the deserted streets, seeing nothing and no one. A feeling of darkness grew inside Sady's heart. Walking around here was useless; they would not find him tonight. He felt guilty about not being at home when he could probably be more useful there than here. He was about to suggest that they turn back when footsteps sounded in a nearby yard, and a bolt was shoved back.

Orsan held up his hand.

Farius slammed the dimmer over his torch and ducked into a shaded alcove. Sady followed, pressing himself against cold stone. Orsan hid in a corresponding alcove on the other side of the alley. Sady heard the click-click of the cocking of Orsan's gun.

A bit further down the alley, a door opened. Two men came out, talking in relaxed voices just outside Sady's hearing. They wore the long cloaks commonly worn by men from Tiverius' well-off families. Sady could only catch the occasional snatch of conversation. *Have to have a meeting* . . . and . . . *says it should be ready for review soon* . . . One man pulled the door shut behind them and they walked off, away from Sady, Orsan and Farius, all the while in oblivious conversation.

When they had gone, Orsan gave the sign to keep moving again.

"Who were they?" whispered Farius.

Orsan said, "People are allowed to use these alleys."

"But there is a level one sonorics alarm active. People should avoid going outside."

"*We* are outside."

Point made. And Farius was right, too. It was strange.

They walked past the gate where the men had come out. Lights blazed in the yard and lit those parts of the house visible over the wall. The wind also carried the sound of many voices talking and laughing. Who would have a party on a night like this?

"Wait—isn't this the Lady Armaine's house?" Sady asked.

"Yes, it is."

Hadn't Orsan been turned back at the Lady Armaine's house because *she was away*? He stopped, studying the wall. The gate where the two men had come out was a double door, wide enough for a cart, but made from solid wood. "Any way we can look into the yard?"

"You'd have to climb the wall and we can't do that without a warrant," Orsan said.

"And who signs warrants?"

Orsan's eyes met his. Everything about his stance with his hands at his sides, the muscle moving in his jutting jaw and his heavy brow screamed defensiveness. "Aren't we here to find a killer?"

"Do you think we'll find anyone? Wherever he is, he's long gone."

"The city guards won't like if you go over their heads."

The city guards were the ones who normally applied for warrants, and the proctor approved them, not the other way around

"You are a member of the guard. You have a warrant as of now. If you want an official one, I'll write and sign it in the morning. Get me up on that wall. Over there, near the tree."

It was Farius who helped Sady climb up. Orsan stood back and watched. It was too dark for Sady to see his expression, but his silence probably meant that he didn't like it.

Dear Orsan was way too fond of the rules. These people had become so reliant on their inflexible bureaucracy.

Once he could see over the wall, Sady recognised the house with the large garden room where he'd met the Lady seated at her huge desk.

The room was brightly lit and the doors wide open, as they had been during Sady's visit. All the furniture had been moved to the sides to make place for rows and rows of chairs. There were a lot of people on these chairs, talking to each other, all of them wearing warm clothing as if prepared for the cold. They obviously knew of the Lady's propensity to have all doors and windows open. Sady recognised many people, merchants, the doga's chief accountant and some of his staff, Destran, Alius, and a couple of young people who were probably students. Many were in their work clothes, but some dressed in dark clothing—so as to sneak in and out of the house through the back entrance without attracting attention?

Something happened at the back of the room that made people cheer and clap. A thin figure in a powder blue robe walked along the aisle between the seats, her hair piled in an enormous bun on top of her head. While she walked, Lady Armaine spread her hands, and many people reached out to touch them. She smiled and talked to them.

She reached the front of the room, faced the seated people and bowed. A man Sady didn't recognise wheeled a small table towards her. He was a young fellow, dressed in a black robe. He wore his hair tied back at the nape of his neck. His thin beard hung halfway down his chest. Sady couldn't see what was on the table he had brought, because two people at the side of the crowd blocked his view. They stood watching the proceedings, hands clasped behind their backs. The lady's guards, he guessed. They also had beards.

The lady lifted a gold-coloured cloth off the table. The object underneath radiated such a bright glow that it washed colour from the surrounding furniture and people. What was that thing?

People cheered and clapped.

The guards shifted, and Sady saw that the table held a brightly glowing sphere on a stand about waist high.

He had seen this type of light in the houses of the rich in the City of Glass.

They were, his guides had explained to him, remnants of old technology that had been common under the reign of king Caldor. His guide had said these words with much disapproval on her face.

One by one, the people in the room came forward to touch the globe, bow, kiss their hand and return to their seat.

What was this strange group? Why would all these people care? They were Chevakians. Half the important senators were here.

Sady watched, but the queue was long and it didn't look like anything else would happen soon. He was getting cold, Orsan and Farius were waiting, and they had a killer to find, so he let himself down, his head reeling.

It seemed the Lady Armaine had her fingers everywhere in Tiverian politics.

"Anything interesting?" Farius asked.

"Puzzling," Sady said.

"Not the murderer," Orsan said.

Sady met Orsan's eyes, emotionless. Orsan had tried to dissuade him from looking in the yard. He had a discomforting thought: did Orsan know this party was going on? Did Orsan know why these people met here?

Sady's heart pounded. Doga guards worked for the doga, and not for individual senators. They swore to secrecy to protect the privacy of the senator they served. If that senator was preparing to challenge, his guard could not go to the rival senators and talk about any of the senator's recent meetings. Guards knew a lot, and never said anything, unless presented with a summons to a formal interview. And Sady was going to have to order such an interview. It troubled him especially that Destran was there, because that would make any investigation political in nature.

An uncomfortable silence lingered.

Farius said, oblivious to the tension, "I don't think we're going to find a trace of the killer tonight. It's much too dark, and he's been gone a long time. Maybe even went into the other direction."

"I agree," Orsan said.

"Yes, let's go." Sady's heart pounded. Interrogations were not his favourite. Orsan had been with him for a long time. He *should* be trustworthy.

"Home?" Farius asked.

"Yes. Lead the way," Sady said.

Farius uncovered the light and he and Orsan started walking.

At that moment, there was a muffled shout that came not from Lady Armaine's yard, but from the other side of the alley.

Sady stopped and whispered, "Orsan!" as loudly as he dared, and gestured for them to come back.

But Orsan and Farius had walked down the alley and didn't hear him.

They'd just passed a gate into the yard, this one a lacework of metal. Sady remembered glancing in, but had noticed nothing out of the ordinary, just the standard courtyard with central statue and clipped hedges.

Sady ran back, and was followed a moment later by Orsan. "In there," he whispered, and tried the gate. It was open.

"No, I go first," Orsan whispered and he gestured to Farius, who came with the torch.

Both men went into the yard, and Sady followed. There were no sounds other than the burbling of a fountain.

Then another snort, a cough and a sniff.

"Who's there?" Orsan lifted his gun.

Farius held the torch higher.

Long shadows trailed over the yard's walls. Clipped bushes made eerie shapes on the stuccoed walls.

"There," Orsan said, pointing to the far corner.

Behind the backs of both men, Sady saw little, but he could feel the tension in Orsan's voice. Farius raised his gun. Someone tried to run away, judging by the sound of shoes slipping on stone.

"Don't move," Orsan said.

Farius ran forward, and held his torch higher. "Here he is!"

In the corner of the yard stood a man who resembled a walking skeleton. Half his hair was missing, his skull a mess of weeping scabs. His only remaining hair, a patch around his right ear, hung in dirty dreadlocks down the side of his head. His face, deathly pale, had deep scratches from which blood flowed freely. His shirt may once have been white, but now it was grey where not soaked in blood. In his hand he clutched a knife. In place of his other hand, he had a golden claw.

He stared into the light with wide eyes, his chest moving quickly in shallow breaths.

When Orsan came closer, he turned around with a panicked whimper, and tried to clamber up the wall. It was far too high and smooth for a healthy person to climb, let alone one as crazy and injured as this.

Orsan and Farius closed in. The man lunged at Orsan with the knife, but the attack was jerky and clumsy. Orsan avoided and deflected the slashing knife with ease. One strike with the butt of Orsan's gun and the knife clattered onto the paving. Sady bent to pick it up, but the hilt was slick with blood, so he pushed it with his foot, well out of the man's reach.

After a short struggle, the two guards had him tied up with the sleeves of his own shirt, pinning his arms to his sides. The prisoner made no effort to fight or talk. His eyes were expressionless, the pupils tiny, and whites showing on all sides.

His ghostlike face made Sady shiver.

"I think we have our killer," Orsan said, pushing the man in front of him. He was barely panting. "Who are you?"

The man said nothing, and continued to stare out of those blue eyes. Southern. His felt trousers were definitely southern.

Orsan checked the man, rifling through pockets and patting the front and back of his pants. The prisoner didn't object to any of Orsan's searching. Orsan found nothing.

"Come on, who are you?"

The prisoner responded with silence.

Orsan snorted and picked up the knife and swung it in front of the man's face. "It this what you used to kill all those people?"

Nothing.

"Come on, come on." Orsan pushed him in the chest with a flat hand—and Orsan's hands were enormous. "Answer me when I ask a question."

The man stumbled back, but made no sound. His face showed, not fear, but the distant, haughty arrogance of a madman. Not someone who regretted his deeds.

Orsan pushed him further back. "Who the fuck are you, and what were you doing sneaking around like this?"

Nothing.

Orsan hit him in the face. "Talk to me when I ask you a question. Why were you sneaking around with a knife, looking like you just killed someone?" He grabbed him by the collar of his filthy shirt—

"Wait," Sady said.

Orsan turned to him, and relaxed his grip on the prisoner's collar. Orsan's face glistened with sweat, and his eyes were wild with anger. It was not a good time to be reminded of the fact that Orsan was half Sady's age, two heads taller and twice the width. Nor of the fact that prisoners often died "accidentally" in interrogations. Nor of the fact that Orsan, and other members of the guard, would certainly have had their fair share of involvement in those "accidental" deaths. And that these deaths were, if not entirely condoned, certainly not questioned by the doga.

Sady breathed out tension. "This man is southern. It's likely that he doesn't understand Chevakian. We should take him to the courthouse and let the guards interrogate him in the presence of an interpreter."

"What is there to interrogate? He has a knife and is covered in blood."

"I'd like to know: how did he get out of the camp, and why did he target my house in which southerners happen to be staying?"

Orsan gave an impatient snort, and shrugged.

"We don't know, and he can't tell us what he knows when he's dead. I want him in the courthouse prison, and I want him interrogated."

Orsan sighed. Some of the wild anger went out of his face. He wiped his upper lip with the back of his hand, and nodded. "Yes. Let's take him there." And a bit later, "I cared a lot for Serran, that's all."

Sady nodded, and the sadness of his loss again settled over him.

"Come," Sady said to Farius, whose young face showed a wide-eyed expression. He was probably afraid that he had been about to witness his first killing. "Let's take him to the jail."

He met the prisoner's eyes and noticed that he didn't look so arrogant anymore. He was sure: despite his southern appearance and attire, this man understood every word he said.

*

Sady, Orsan and Farius went home after having made sure that the prisoner was securely locked up in a solitary cell.

The jail, that place of death, made Sady's skin crawl. One single corridor of cells for an entire city of criminals. Average stay, five days —he had seen the figures. Next stop, the court, and then the gallows room. High numbers of death sentences made sense in times of food shortages, but railways and farm machines had made life better for over thirty years. Nobody had thought to adjust the law.

All lights blazed at the house and two city guards stood at the porch before the closed door.

When Orsan pushed the gate open, both turned around. "Oh, there he is."

The guards turned to Sady with polite nods. "Proctor."

"You just arrived?" He was sure the guard had been called before he left the house. Had they taken this long to show up?

"Yes, sorry, Proctor, but we've been very busy tonight."

Sady remembered windblown and empty streets and was tempted to ask if that busy-ness involved games of dice, but he bit his tongue. He'd spent enough time feeling annoyed at the misguided "independence" of guards. "How long have you been waiting here?"

"Not too long."

The other guard nodded, but Sady had the impression it was longer than both wanted to admit. Where was Merni?

"Well," he said, trying not to let his worry show through. "We've had four people killed by what appears to have been a southern madman. We've done the work for you, because we found him. He's already in the courthouse prison."

He almost enjoyed the shocked look on their faces. Served them right, playing games while on duty.

"Now all we need to do is find a newborn baby. I'm sure you can manage that."

"Sure." The guard completely missed Sady's sarcasm. "Could we see the scene of the disappearance of this baby?"

Sady led the men through the house to the guest quarters, where someone had lit a couple of lamps, although there was no one in the room. The harshness of full lighting made the horrors worse. There were smears of blood on the carpets, furniture and walls. The glistening blob of unidentified tissue on the floor looked like bloodied entrails. One of the guards told him that it was, in fact, an afterbirth. It seemed that the child had been born normally and that the madman had come afterwards.

Then a chilling thought: what if the madman had been part of the family? The large window had shattered outward because most of the glass was in the yard. Sady had asked for Loriane and the members of her family to be taken to the house. He'd thought it was the right thing to do, rather than splitting them up. He thought there had been the woman, the man, and the girl and the infant. But he could not be entirely sure. He'd been too busy to take note.

The thought made him sick and made him realise that he did not understand these people and their strange habits.

And because he'd thought to be *charitable*, four good Chevakians were dead.

He sat on the couch, clenching his hands in his pockets, staring at the form covered in a sheet that was Lana's body, while the guards combed the room.

Mercy, if they were dead through his fault.

He stared at the carpet, his eyes sore with fatigue or tears or both. Somewhere in the distance, a man and a woman argued.

The guards studied everything, and wrote down notes. They asked Sady what he had seen, which wasn't much. They approved for the bodies of the surgeons to be taken away.

Farius came in not much later. "The people from the hospital are here."

Sady rose, feeling dizzy. Farius had held up remarkably well, seeing his young age and inexperience, but now his face looked pale and haggard.

"Go to bed as soon as you can," he said.

"Do you think I could sleep?"

Sady let the question hang between them and sighed.

"Try for the sake of the household," Sady said. "We'll need you more than ever."

"Yeah," Farius said and his eyes glittered briefly. "Merni's not so good."

Pieces clicked into place. "That was her shouting a little while back?"

Farius nodded. "She refused to make the southern family tea. It was their fault that Lana was dead, she said. I tried to calm her, but she's hysterical about it."

Sady closed his eyes. "That's not . . . particularly helpful."

"No. I said that, too. Didn't make her listen, though."

"Where is she?"

"She went into her room and slammed the door. Hasn't come out, not even to open the front door when the guards came."

Great. One more thing to deal with. "I'll deal with the hospital people first."

Farius left and two men and a woman came into the room, the woman and one of the men in hospital uniforms. The other man carried a rolled-up stretcher.

The woman bowed and greeted him. Her face was anxious, her eyes brimming with tears.

"I'm sorry for the loss of your colleagues," Sady said. He felt helpless. Tomorrow, he'd have to face Lana and Serran's families with the same news.

She nodded, pressing her lips together. Her chin trembled.

Sady put a hand on her shoulder, not feeling so steady himself. "If there is anything I can do . . ."

"Is it true you caught the killer?"

"We think so."

"Why would anyone do something like this?"

Sady shook his head, thinking of the mad youth and his unfathomable black eyes.

"It's just . . . incredible. We don't have many people like them," she said. "We can't miss their experience, especially with all those refugees in the camps. Why would someone kill people who are doing so much good work?"

Sady spread his hands. He didn't know. He didn't understand either. Yet the look in the woman's eyes was accusing, as if it was his fault that her colleagues were dead. And to an extent, it was. *He* had brought the southerners here; *he* had insisted that the surgeons treat the woman. To add insult to injury, his intervention appeared to have been unnecessary because the child had been born normally.

He felt fragile, crumbling under pressure and fatigue. *I was only trying to help*. Why? Because he'd met the woman Loriane's eyes across a seething, disgusting mass of people on a crowded train platform, and had *felt sorry for her*.

The three busied themselves putting the closest body on the stretcher.

Having nothing more to do, Sady slouched down the corridor to his bedroom. Tears rolled over his cheeks.

CHAPTER 4

CARRO STARED out the window in a little bay off the wide corridor of the farmhouse that was the Eagle Knight's base. Large rooms to the left and right were dormitories, each with eight or ten beds. His fellow Knights slept there, in stuffy rooms designed to sleep only two or three people, but he had been tossing and turning on his mat until he grew too annoyed to pretend he was asleep.

The courtyard outside was dark and quiet. Eagles slept in their shed, a low open-walled building on the other side of the courtyard. Carro couldn't see them from here under the dark overhang of the roof.

He'd made this little alcove his workspace, with a flat piece of wood for a desk that looked like it had started life as a door, and two narrow shelves for the books. It looked homely and tidy, and reminded him of his sleeping shelf at home in the Outer City. Except that little homely space no longer existed, and the books stashed under his bed were gone, those books he and Isandor had risked much to acquire. The books his sister scoffed at, and his father—no, the merchant—had threatened to burn.

Just what had happened in the City of Glass?

A candle flapped with the draught that came in through the cracks where the window didn't close properly.

He'd been sitting here since midnight, going over the documents that Rider Cornatan had given him in preparation for future negotiations with the Chevakians. The books about Chevakia were interest-ing, although he could not hope to remember everything about the Chevakian council—doga they called it.

He had more trouble with the hand-written notes from Rider Cornatan.

They said things like, *The Eagle Knights have been destroyed by this disaster, and there are but a few left.*

"That's a lie," he had said to Rider Cornatan while walking in the courtyard that evening.

Rider Cornatan had stopped and faced him, so that the light from the lamps around the farmhouse's courtyard lit his eyes. "The Chevakians don't know that."

His father smiled, and his expression held pity. He stood in his typical proud position, with his thumbs tucked in the metal loops at the chest strap of the riding harness. Another discon-certing fact Carro had found out since coming to Chevakia: his father did still ride. He had a magnificent bird that parted the air like the sharpest sword and had never been housed with the other eagles and therefore Carro had never seen it before. He flew it steady as if he'd been born on the back of the bird, with just the stirrups and reins. The saddle weighed the bird down too much, he said.

And it made Carro feel inadequate and clumsy. He needed the saddle.

He pushed the books aside, heaving a sigh.

Was he meant to accept these lies without comment? Was there any truth in anything Rider Cornatan said, even to his own son?

Go to the Chevakians, pup. Pretend that you're the most senior Knight left. Tell them lies as if they're idiots.

Carro leant his head in his hands.

Lies, lies.

He didn't want to be a leader, not even a fake one. He hated to be told to do things he didn't understand, or things he didn't want to do. Or things he understood how to do, but didn't understand why he had to do them. Or things he could do but disagreed with why he had to do them. Not just disagreed, but thought they were fundamentally wrong.

There, up on the wall opposite the window bay was the Eagle

Knight's crest with the motto. *Obedience, honour, honesty, humility and silence.* Those five words haunted him no end.

What was the honour in killing people who couldn't defend themselves, like Isandor and Jevaithi? Where was the honesty in hiding yourself behind a fake leader who had no real power, but whose only function was to give an impression of weakness? And where was the humility in assuming you were worth more than others, like the people from the Outer City, who were in the Chevakian camps? That you were worth so much more, that you could disregard their lives as if they were rats. Silence, there was plenty of that. Codes of silence amongst the Knights were everywhere. You did not tell on your mates. Not even if they did terrible things.

Obedience was the one that worried him most. All his life he'd obeyed. He'd obeyed the merchant by changing the books for the sake of the tax collector. He'd obeyed his father in going with the hunters, and helping them set fire to the houses of innocent farmers. In his sleep, he heard those people's screams. Obeying had given him nothing but trouble. Obeying had made him betray the only person who had ever cared about him, because he hoped that his father would be genuinely happy with him.

Yet, did he have a choice? That was always the question.

"Hey, there's not much privacy in those dorms, huh?"

Carro gasped and turned around.

It was Nolan, sneaking up from behind. The bluish light from outside silvered his curls and made his eyes glitter. He pressed himself against Carro's back and gently folded his arms around Carro's shoulders. "We see so little of you these days. I miss you whenever we fly out. It gets boring watching Farey and Jeito fool around."

"Yeah—um—I've been really busy. What have you been up to?" He wished he could fob Nolan off with some sort of excuse. He wished he'd never, ever said yes to his advances.

"Not much. Keeping an eye on this crowd of Chevakians where the Queen is. Can't do anything until they're on the move again. Maybe not even then. She'll be in the city. Too many people there. But we'll keep an eye on her. Me, I've been patrolling. On foot, by the skylights. Talk about boring."

The camps. Someone in the Chevakian army had thought it was a good idea to build a camp for the refugees who had come on the trains from the City of Glass. Trouble was, they'd built it in the middle of the road that led to one of the southern provinces. And those silly Chevakian vehicles were too heavy to travel on sand or anything that was not a paved road. A mass of Chevakian refugees had built up on the other side of the fence. They all knew that Isandor and Jevaithi were in that crowd, protected by a mass of Chevakian people and out of the Knights' reach.

"Come. Enough talking," Nolan whispered and pulled Carro up.

Carro cringed; his skin tensed with dread for what would happen next, anticipating the touch of Nolan's sweaty fingers under his shirt.

Obedience. He could not say no without consequences worse than what he wanted to avoid, but oh, how did he want to avoid it.

Nolan led him to the linen cupboard where it was dark and musty and where it smelled of soap and freshly-washed sheets. He lifted Carro's shirt over his head and let it whisper to the floor. "I really want you."

His breathing sounded loud in that silence. He pulled Carro into his embrace. His mouth closed over Carro's. He tasted like cheap bloodwine and smelled of sweat. There was nothing tender about his kiss. Nolan's wet lips slobbered over what felt like half his face. Carro fought to repress his desire to shove Nolan away, a feeling that became stronger every time Nolan touched him.

"You seem so quiet when we meet these days," Nolan whispered.

Carro glanced out the door of the laundry cupboard into the corridor. He hoped someone would come. "I guess I'm nervous. We're not alone in this place. What if someone comes? Are you sure it's the right thing to do?"

"Why do you always bring that up? I've told you so many times: no one cares. This is how we look after each other. Like wolves."

Once, Carro had found that term interesting. Now, the word made him sick. He had enough of being pestered by Nolan every night. Were you allowed to say that you found sex disgusting and smelly, and that it felt too much like rape to be nice or comfortable, that it flat out didn't interest you?

"Come on, relax." Nolan's hand found its way between Carro's waistband and his skin. His hands went over his naked buttocks. He pushed Carro's pants down and pressed himself against Carro's back. Carro felt the slimy hardness of his cock. A wave of despair washed over him. How could he stop this without appearing soft, without making an enemy of Nolan? He'd asked himself that question so many times, and had not yet found an answer. He liked Nolan, but not like this. He hated how his body betrayed him and feigned emotions he did not feel. Regardless of how much he hated the invasiveness of Nolan's touch, there was always a point where what he wanted no longer mattered as long as Nolan made him come, and Nolan was good at that. But afterwards, when the high ebbed and Nolan whispered soft words of love and believed that he enjoyed it, the shame set in. He didn't know how to break that cycle.

There were fast footsteps in the hallway. Someone called out, "Carro?"

"Shit," Nolan whispered and ducked into the back of the laundry. Carro hoisted up his pants, slipped out of the cupboard and sat down at his makeshift desk, his heart thudding. He recognised the voice: his father. He had never been able to work out whether the Knights condoned or punished sexual relationships between each other. His gut feeling told him that it didn't fall under *honour*, and that, if a superior didn't like you, it could be used as a reason for punishment. But that it usually wasn't. Only that rape was used *as* punishment, and that some superiors enjoyed it.

"Working hard?" Rider Cornatan joined Carro in the alcove. If he noticed the door to the storeroom moving, he didn't show it.

"Um—yeah." His heart was still going like crazy.

Rider Cornatan leaned over the makeshift desk and leafed through the book on Chevakian government. "Interesting, isn't it?"

"Um—yeah." Carro struggled to remember what he'd been doing.

Rider Cornatan turned around and fixed Carro with a penetrating stare. Carro felt like his father looked straight through him, saw his weird relationship with Nolan, and disapproved. All sorts of excuses were on his tongue: *I don't want it either,* and *He came to me, and I didn't ask him.* But they felt like that: excuses, making him look like a spineless dud, which, by all accounts, he was.

"We may be moving in sooner than we thought."

Moving in? Moving where? Rider Cornatan made it sound like a military operation. They had no hope of gaining control of anything with the few Knights at the farmhouse. There might be a few hundred of them, but that was not an army. "I thought you wanted me to go and talk to the Chevakians."

"Yes, but the time is not right for that now. There is no reason why the Chevakians would want to talk to us. We need to give them a reason first before you'll get the talk you're so looking forward to. I have another job for you and your hunters to do first."

By the skylights, another job with the hunters? He'd barely seen Jeito and Farey since they had arrived here. He'd presumed that part of his task was over. Jeito would kill him if he came too close to her.

"We have reliable reports that the Queen is indeed in the refugee camp and has made herself known to the people. Unfortunately, a large percentage of the camp population is made up of rogues."

"Um—rogues?"

"The Brotherhood of the Light. The trains that came from Fairlight are full of them."

That made sense. Most of the survivors from the explosion were from the Outer City. "But I thought you said that the Chevakians had isolated the camp and we didn't need to worry about those people?"

"The Chevakians did, but there has been a development overnight which is unexpected and we might call interesting. A number of Chevakian civilians broke into the camp from the south. The official line is that they thought the camp was for them and grew tired of waiting to be let in. But since we have good evidence that the Brotherhood has its fingers through much of the Chevakian doga, I wouldn't be surprised if the so-called southern Chevakian refugees included a good number of Brotherhood supporters."

Carro nodded. His close examination of the farm's accounts had shown that. By all evidence, the manager had sided with the Brotherhood and that was why he had left the place in chaos as soon as the Knights had arrived, taking the important financial records with him. "But I still don't understand why Chevakians would support them. Icefire kills them."

"You tell me, son. I have no idea either, but clearly, over the years that the ex-royals have lived here, they've built up quite a following and have convinced a good number of important Chevakians of the amazing things that can be done with icefire. It would sound stupid that Chevakians would believe that, except that there are now claims that they have found some sort of medicine that allows Chevakians to withstand icefire." His voice was grave.

"Isn't that a good thing? I mean—if it doesn't kill Chevakians anymore then we don't need to worry so much about it?"

"Have you learned nothing from all I've told you?" Rider Cornatan's voice was fiercer than it had ever been, even when Carro had deserved a scolding.

Carro retreated outside the immediate pool of light cast by the lamp. He could imagine Nolan trying to stifle laughter in the cupboard.

"Think of it, son," he said, his voice low. "Us Pirosians are at a disadvantage because we can neither see nor use icefire, so the Thilleians can use it against us without our notice until it is too late. Chevakians, with or without medicine, also cannot see it. Now their barriers have broken. If the Chevakians allow the Brotherhood to start using icefire, they won't care, because it no longer harms them, and they don't believe that icefire is more than the energy in air particles which they can measure. Everyone might live peacefully for a while, but ultimately, someone starts using icefire for the purpose of gaining power again. For making servitors who do their master's bidding. Icefire is an excellent device for changing someone's mind. I hope your reading about Chevakia has at the very least impressed upon you that their society relies on people speaking their minds." Oh, he was angry now. He took in a deep breath through flaring nostrils and continued, "From all reports, it looks like we will be unable to return to the City of Glass for some time, so this affects us, too. The Chevakians simply won't know what hit them, and we will be too few to fight this evil for them. The important Chevakians will be under the influence of those who can use icefire and will side with the Brotherhood. Son, those barriers that were broken after the explosion need to go up again as soon as possible or this entire country, as well as our own, will be our enemy."

"But if they have this medicine, the Chevakians won't need the barriers anymore."

"Exactly, and that's why we can't wait any longer. We must act against the Brotherhood now. Before that medicine is a reality."

Act? Like how? A chill went over Carro's back, as he imagined

Rider Cornatan's plans, most of them involving innocent refugees' lives, and none of them nice.

"And this is where your task comes in." Rider Cornatan licked his lips. "We've had a problem with communication."

Oh?

Again, Rider Cornatan waited for what seemed a long time before continuing. "A messenger was supposed to have come in by now." He looked into the corridor, which was just as empty as it had been before, and his gaze lingered on the half-closed door of the linen cupboard, as if he realised that it was usually wide open. "We are not the only surviving Knights. There are a lot more of us. I ordered other units to hide at our field bases, because to bring this many of us into Tiverius would arouse the suspicion of the Chevakians. But now, with the new developments in the camp, we'll need all of us here."

"How many have survived?" Carro thought of Jono and Caman and the other bullies he had left behind in the City of Glass and had assumed dead. There had been thousands of Knights at the Eyrie.

"Most of us were able to get out, thanks, in part, to the fact that a good number of us were on duty at the Newlight festival."

And that was not a coincidence, wasn't it? Carro had spent a lot of time thinking about the machinery he had seen in the dungeons below the city, and what Rider Cornatan had been doing there. And the fact that no one seemed keen to explain what had caused the explosion.

A chill went through him. Ever since the fall of the king, the Knights had tried to destroy the Heart of the City, first by taking apart the machine—which they couldn't—and then by dragging it underground and encasing it in sheets of metal. But it was a self-containing energy source, even when disconnected from the wires that fed it. Having failed to dismantle the machine, Rider Cornatan had decided to experiment with the power. Had it exploded during some sort of experiment?

"The other units of our army are spread over a couple of locations, the most important one of which is directly south of here. However, I haven't heard from them, and we should have, by now."

He unrolled a piece of paper on the desk. It was a map with marked on it, Chevakia's southern border, the mountainous region with the cliff-surrounded town they called Solmeni, and a couple of black connecting stripes that were train lines. Rider Cornatan pointed. "They should be here. I sent some scouts to check up on them a while ago, but haven't heard from them either. I want you to go there." His finger rested on a town called Twin Bridges. "And then track south from there. Look for a small abandoned woodcutters' village surrounded by forest. Last we heard was that there were storms and fires in that region. They may have kept the eagles inside to stop them panicking."

But Carro could hear in his voice that he didn't believe that. A well-trained eagle didn't skitter that easily. Somehow, the messengers had not come through. They might have fallen into the hands of the Chevakians. Or something else . . .

How far away was this, and where was the location where he had seen the giants made of fire before falling from his bird?

He couldn't possibly tell his father about them. Pirosians were not meant to see things like that. But that had to have been much further south and surely, icefire wouldn't reach this far into Chevakia.

"I want you to go there and return with the army." Rider Cornatan met his eyes with a penetrating look.

Carro tried to read the meaning in those grey eyes, but all he could see was the hardness of his expression and the cold calculating look.

CHAPTER 5

WITHIN MOMENTS of Isandor and Jevaithi having entered the tent, Simo started ordering people about. Some men dragged a mat into the middle. Two other men placed a crate on top, which they covered with furs.

Simo bowed. "Here you are, Your Highness. We don't have much, but we give you the best we have."

The crate made a cosy little bench. Jevaithi sat down, and Isandor followed, with the weight of many stares on him, as if the people questioned his right to sit next to her. He took her hand, cold and clammy. His heart beat like crazy in her chest.

Her gaze darted over the seated audience, as if she expected Rider Cornatan to emerge from the crowd any moment.

Several people dressed in black stood out in the audience, the men with beards. They were, like Simo, Brotherhood of the Light.

It felt absurd, sitting here while he could hear fights going on in the rest of the camp.

She went on in Chevakian. "Who are these people in black?"

"The Brotherhood of the Light. They run schools and orphanages in the Outer City. They are known to support the old royal family. They often sell and collect old things from the palace."

She frowned. "Is Tandor one of them?" Still in Chevakian.

Isandor shrugged, feeling uncomfortable. He didn't know for certain either, and disliked to be reminded of Tandor. What *did* the

Brotherhood do, other than teach poor orphans things that the Knights didn't think they should learn? He'd considered them to be a quaint relic of the old royal family in a quiet, unassuming sort of way.

Meanwhile, people streamed into the tent. Simo yelled at them to sit down around the makeshift throne. Jevaithi sat with her back straight. Isandor wondered where Milleus was. People raised their eyebrows at him, whispered to each other while looking at him. Simo gave him annoyed glances.

Soon, the questions came.

How had Jevaithi escaped, since the palace itself had been completely destroyed?

Did she know the whereabouts of Rider Cornatan and the senior command of the Knights?

Were there any other southern refugees with the Chevakian convoy?

"Quiet!" Simo yelled over the cacophony. "Her Highness will answer questions one by one."

Isandor wondered what gave Simo the right to boss everyone around. It seemed like everyone in the camp accepted him as leader. Was it because he was loud, and no one else had volunteered, or for some other reason?

"I would like to ask you some questions first," Jevaithi said, and although she hadn't spoken loudly, talk stopped immediately, and all those people fell into an expectant silence. Many faces displayed bright expressions of hope.

Simo bowed. "By all means, Your Highness."

But Simo's voice betrayed a measure of annoyance. Maybe Simo hadn't expected Jevaithi to return at all, and he was irritated at her for taking his leadership position.

Jevaithi asked, "Are there any Knights in the camp?"

"We don't think so, Your Highness," a woman said. "The guards are all Chevakians."

"There was a Knight at the station," a man said. "We chased him off."

Some people laughed.

When it was quiet again, Jevaithi said, "Some Knights have survived. I've seen them; they've been following us. A group of hunters tried to kill me."

Several people in the audience gasped.

Isandor wanted to say, *But not all Knights are like that. I was a Knight, and most of them are honourable.* Instead he jammed his hands between his knees and said nothing as the ex-citizens of the City of Glass recounted wrongs done by the Knights. He thought of Carro, who would probably be dead by now, and was sure Carro was honourable, or had been honourable, under his veneer of despair to be liked by others.

The perimeter of the tent had filled up with people, and extra onlookers were trying to cram into the tent entrance, but there was no room for anyone to move and still more people were trying to get in. People lifted children onto their shoulders, held lovers on their laps, and leaned on others while standing on tiptoe at the back. Everyone looked at Jevaithi. By the frowns on their faces, everyone wondered who Isandor was, and why a *cripple* ex-Knight should be with *their* queen. Isandor wanted to run. All this *Your Highness* business was starting to get on his nerves.

It was time for Jevaithi to tell her story. In that clear-voiced way of hers, she told the people how the Knights had been worried about something afoot in the palace on the morning of the explosion, of secret dialogue between Rider Cornatan and his senior-ranked offi-cers. She told them how she was sure that the Knights were doing something unusual. That was because she could feel icefire, but she didn't tell anyone that. She told them how none of the Knights would tell her what was going on, and that Rider Cornatan hadn't wanted her to go to the Newlight festival.

That was because the Knights had *wanted* Jevaithi to be killed, someone in the audience yelled. Because they knew the explosion would happen and they expected Jevaithi to be one of the victims. There was much cheering after this, and Isandor grew angrier. That was just *not* true. The Knights adored Jevaithi.

Next she talked about her life. How she lived practically in a prison, of turning sixteen and of how she'd been wanting to escape from the palace to dance with normal boys during the Newlight Festi-val. She showed them her missing hand. That earned some gasps, but many others said that they had always known. Those people were mostly Brothers in black.

Simo said, "We have saved many children. There is not one family in the Outer City that isn't secretly mourning an Imperfect-born child." After some cheers, he concluded, "This idiocy has to stop."

Several people shushed him and urged Jevaithi to keep talking.

She told them of Rider Cornatan's refusal to hand over power and to let her sit on the Knights' Council. Of his insistence that she wear stupid, gauze-thin clothes that made the Junior Knights drool over her body. Of his constant threats to rape her.

Everyone went very quiet when she said all these things.

A woman at the front cried and said they'd never known. She would have done something had she known.

"No one could do anything," Jevaithi said. "I was surrounded by Knights all day."

Then she told them how she'd wrangled the trip to the Newlight Festival out of Rider Cornatan, of attending the races and of that confusing night in the Outer City, when, after choosing the champion and the escape of the Legless Lion Isandor was meant to kill, she couldn't go back to the palace because the bears and the driver of her sled had been murdered. She told them how an unseen form, a blue-skinned servitor, had tried to kill her, and how she had escaped, with the young apprentice Knight whom she had chosen as champion and his servitor Legless Lion. At this point everyone looked at Isandor and their expressions showed that they had added up the facts.

There was no icefire here to hide the fact that he was Imperfect. They stared at his leg, and increased the size of the circle around him. He was sleeping with *their* queen. They didn't want him. It was acceptable for the Queen to be Imperfect, but a random boy—no. But to his surprise, someone said, "Hurray for Isandor."

A number of people cheered, and some clapped, and a man behind him put a meaty hand on Isandor's shoulder. Isandor turned and saw that the man was a Brother, dressed in black. His eyes twinkled with mirth. "Anyone but that shrivelled prune will do as father for the next queen. I hope you gave it your best."

He laughed, but Isandor felt angry. So that was it, now? That was his function? As Outer City boy, they probably thought he was not smart enough for anything else. He wanted to tell them that he knew how to read and speak Chevakian, but that would make him look stupid.

While Jevaithi told the listeners how they had come here with

Milleus and what had happened on the way, he drew his knees up to his chest and looped his arms around them, feeling the wood of his missing leg bite into his buttocks.

The people, mostly citizens of the Outer City or Bordertown, told their stories, of a massive explosion in the City of Glass, of a ring of icefire expanding outwards, of the shattering of the Chevakian barrier, of the forest fires, and the harrowing trip in the train.

People held conflicting opinions about what had caused the explosion.

"It was the Knights," one said.

"No, it was a servitor," someone said, and others argued and suggested that cycles of icefire happened by themselves.

"There were many servitors," a woman said. "Big shapes made from icefire, destroying everything in their path."

"Those were not servitors," a man said, and people argued about what exactly servitors were, which no one seemed to know, apart from the fact that they had no hearts and obeyed their masters blindly.

"The city is a mess," one man said. "Most of the buildings were destroyed that I could see. No one will be going back there in a hurry."

"But why were you not safe even in Bordertown?" Jevaithi asked.

"After the explosion, these . . . people, servitors, things, whatever you want to call them, made of icefire came out of the ground. They formed a bubble of icefire that expanded outwards."

A woman said, "Yes, and those things were still following us off the plateau. Setting fire to the forest."

Jevaithi looked at Isandor, her eyes wide. "I don't even understand what they're talking about. Shapes of icefire?"

Isandor shrugged. His knowledge from books failed him. He'd never read about anything like that.

Simo took up a stance with his hands behind his back and his legs slightly apart, as if he was teaching. He said, "We're fighting icefire itself. Through the Knights' trying to stifle it, it has become so strong that it has burst from the ground and has taken possession of people's bodies. Somebody did something to those people and they're angry with us."

The woman said, "And these monsters have taken possession of our city? Are they ever going to leave?"

"We may have to fight," Brother Simo said, spreading his hands in a grandiose gesture, as if fighting was something glorious.

A man said, "How would you fight beings of icefire anyway? You can't."

Isandor was tempted to jump up and tell them that all knowledge on icefire held in the City of Glass was based on myth and that there was no proof for any of the things in Simo's conclusions, but he had no proof to the contrary either, and he was sure most of these people here would support Simo. Who'd listen to a boy whose only task was to fuck the queen and get her pregnant?

The debate carried on around him.

Simo said, "Someone unleashed this power, so there must be a way it can be defeated. Icefire can be collected. Sinks do that. We need sinks. Lots of them."

Then there was debate about what sinks were. It was all so futile. They didn't have sinks, and if icefire was strong enough to blow up buildings, no number of sinks of the type the Eagle Knights had was going to have any influence.

Isandor glowered over his drawn-up knees at Simo's back and the people seated around the makeshift throne. Faint sounds of shouting and crashes came from outside. He wondered where Milleus was.

Jevaithi's eyes met his briefly. Her expression looked resigned, and that made him even angrier.

"What he says is all rubbish," he said to her in a low voice, in Chevakian. "Milleus' brother knows more about how icefire works than these people."

"These Brothers have a lot of support," Jevaithi said, her eyes wide.

"Yes, these people believe anything. Just because a Brother says so doesn't mean it's true. We should say something."

"Please, let's make sure we are safe first—"

"We can't be safe until this type of idiocy ends. We have to speak out or they will be just as bad as the king was, or the Knights—" All of a sudden, his voice was the only one in the tent.

Brother Simo had turned around and everyone watched Isandor. Their looks were suspicious. A worthless Outer City boy was one thing, but a worthless Outer City boy who spoke Chevakian to their Queen? Outrageous.

Yes, he got the message.

He unlooped his arms from his knees and rose, awkward because he placed his wooden leg on someone's boot and he nearly tripped.

In the silence, he said, "We should not make up our minds while no one knows what is going on and what caused the explosion. I think there is someone who may know more about it. The master of the blue servitor that killed the bears and the driver is a middle-aged man named Tandor. He does not live in the City of Glass, but he poses as a travelling merchant." Tandor, his mother's lover. He saw a sudden flash of his mother coming out of the door to the inner room of the limpet. The expression on her face was one of worry. Emotion threatened to overwhelm him. He finished with a lame, "Has anyone seen him in the camp?"

An older Brother near the entrance said, "I think I know the one you mean. Wasn't he the fellow collecting old stuff in the Outer City?"

"That would be him," Isandor said. "Have you seen him since leaving the Outer City?"

"No, sorry."

"I think he was on the train," a woman said.

Another said, "No, I know the one you mean, but I didn't see him."

"Yes, he was here," the original woman said. "But he was badly burned. He was with a family, and they got taken away to some medical place, I heard."

"That can't be him. Tandor doesn't have a family," Isandor said.

Simo sniffed. "How can one man make such a difference?"

"He asked me to be his apprentice." People gave him odd glances. Some expressions were clearly annoyed. Feeling the situation slip from his control, Isandor continued, "Before all this happened, he came into the Outer City with a servitor, and tried to recruit me for his plans."

"Why you?" Simo asked, in a who-do-you-think-you-are kind of way.

"Because he saved the lives of many Imperfect children put out on the ice floes. I'm one of those he saved."

Simo held his gaze briefly, and those eyes were full of pity, before turning away to talk to Jevaithi about people in the camp, and how her wish was his command.

Jevaithi answered him politely. Why didn't she see that Simo had no intention of giving up his position?

What did she know, having been locked up in the palace all that time? Knights or Brothers were all the same: they only wanted power. Failing power, they'd suck up to someone who had status, just so that they could grovel their way up.

He pushed himself off the bench. Why ever had he introduced Jevaithi to these people? Why had he even agreed to come with Milleus? There was no need for them to flee advancing icefire. They should have let Milleus go alone. Offered to look after his farm, so that they could learn to be farmers.

"Where are you going?" Jevaithi asked.

"Out," Isandor said, and he knew he sounded angry and Chevakian was an excellent language for being angry.

"What's going on? I thought you agreed with these people?"

"These people are idealists, and they won't stop poking the Knights until they hit back."

"I thought you'd been betrayed by the Knights."

"I was betrayed by *one* Knight."

"I can't believe you're saying this, after Knights tried to kill us. The Brotherhood is for the people."

"And who is to say they won't form another group that will end up just as evil as the others? I want to know what they stand for. What do they believe in? What do they want?"

"Who cares? All of those ideals are useless if we can't go back to the City of Glass. The Brotherhood wants to help us."

"They don't. They want power. They're annoyed that we've turned up."

"That's nonsense. They're helpful and courteous."

"You're too trusting. The Knights aren't the only ones with dicks to rape you."

Her eyes widened and Isandor cringed. That was a tactless remark, but her naivety was so infuriating.

"You are so suspicious."

"That comes with living on the streets. You should try it once."

Her nostrils flared. "Are you saying that I am dumb?" Her eyes flashed with true anger that made him feel chilled inside.

"No, I'm not. I'm just—" Although in a way, that was the translation of what he'd implied. She was so innocent as to be a danger to herself. Knights had always protected her.

"Yes you are. Don't you think that living with the threat of being raped every day does nothing to you? Do you think that I have been living an easy life?"

"I never said that." But she'd known no hunger, no worry of disease.

"Yes, you did. What do you want us to do then? We can't be farmers. We can't hide. These people need our help. They are *our* people."

"I never said they weren't and that we shouldn't help."

"Then what? What is your problem?" She spread her hands in a frustrated gesture.

People watched. There was sure to be someone who understood some Chevakian.

Isandor started to say *I don't like being treated as a nobody* or, *I'm not just a dick with a pair of eyes* but that sounded stupid and selfish, and it wasn't really that. It was that he didn't like all the men in black, and didn't like their mysterious organisation. They had the crowd just as much under control as the Knights had, only the people seemed to subject themselves willingly; and he was angry about that, because he'd thought people would be smarter after so many years of repression by the king or the Knights.

Jevaithi repeated, louder now, "Come on, tell me, what is your problem?"

"Shhh, calm down," he said.

She whirled to him. "No. I've had enough of being treated like I'm a toddler."

"All right, all right, I'm going." He gave a mock bow. "Your Highness." He left the tent, but his legs were trembling and his heart—her heart—was beating like crazy. Why couldn't she understand him?

CHAPTER 6

WHEN THE LARGE mob of southerners carried the youngsters off amongst the tents, relative quiet returned to the hillside on the south side of the camp. With no illumination, and a heavy cloud cover blanketing the sky, it was pitch dark.

The remaining Chevakians gathered by the light from their trucks. Squally wind brought cheers of many voices, presumably from the southern tents. News came that the soldiers had repaired the fence, although the soldiers appeared to have vanished. Milleus could make out a faint glow of light uphill, at the spot where they had entered the camp. He also thought he could hear the sounds of wood being chopped. So someone had finally used their brains and was cutting a road through the forest, or more likely, widening an existing track, so that the people behind the fence could move. He was unsure how many Chevakians had made it into the camp with him, but the vast majority had turned around. The sight of soldiers had frightened them off, or maybe it had been the thought of contamination, or the fear of "magic" folklore ascribed to southern people. It disappointed him that so many people lacked the courage to push on.

For the remaining foolhardy Chevakians, too few to force their way out of their situation, there seemed nothing else to do but to stay put for what remained of the night. They arranged the trucks in a circle and pitched tents inside this circle. Some people had dogs, which they tied up on the outer periphery. As for himself, he had to fix the truck's tyres before he could do anything, but that didn't take long.

And then there was nothing more to do except pay homage to that old Chevakian saying, *If all else fails, make tea.*

"We're not going to sit here and do nothing," Milleus said.

They had gathered around the pot bubbling on the fire. Orange light danced on attentive faces. There were about thirty of them, twelve trucks besides Milleus', men and women, old and young, all of whom had been on the road for days. It was a mixed crew: there was a family of five with a child that needed medical attention, a young couple who had no money and knew no one in Tiverius, and were afraid of the cost of staying there, an elderly couple whose truck had a trailer that contained at least a hundred chickens, and two sisters who were looking for a brother who had travelled ahead of them on the Ensar road, but whom they had been unable to find in the crowd.

"Then what can we do?" said the man who had introduced himself as Artan, the owner of the chickens. The days on the road had left him with grey-flecked beard.

"We're going into Tiverius. Or at least any of you who want to come."

"But aren't you afraid that the soldiers—"

"The soldiers can go polish their guns and shine their boots. They cannot stop us travelling in our own country."

"Maybe not, but they have the guns."

"They will not fight Chevakians. It's in the charter of the army."

"How do you know that for sure? I'm not keen to be a test case."

"Because they will listen to me." And when everyone's eyes were on him, Milleus added, "Because I used to command them."

Milleus took the pot off the stove, added tea leaves and stirred, aware that everyone around the fire looked at him.

A man whispered, "Milleus han Chevonian?"

"The very one."

The man smiled, and some of the people started laughing.

"Milleus han Chevonian? In a southern refugee camp? With goats?" There was more happy laughter, and cheers.

"How did you end up here?" a woman asked.

"I run a farm now, and I'm rather attached to my goats. You won't find better milking goats anywhere in the country."

"Hey, let's drink to that!" A man called.

Someone brought glasses, and a bottle was passed around.

When it came to him, Milleus shook his head, the previous time that he'd drunk still vivid in his mind. At that time, he'd almost lost the youngsters. "I don't drink, thanks. But I do have some tea."

Glasses and cups were shared and a man carried an elderly grandmother to the fire. The old lady turned out to have been a great supporter of Milleus back when he was in power. "Best ever, best ever," she said, moving her lips with great flexibility in her toothless mouth.

Milleus smiled awkwardly, because he hadn't been the best ever, and by being stupid when Sady came for him, he'd missed an opportunity to make a difference.

"So," said Artan. "How are we going to get out of this camp?"

"It was my plan to simply go up to the lower camp gate and tell the guards who I am. I guess they are likely to let me through. It may not be easy, and we may need to create a fuss, but they won't want to keep us in here, because the news that we're here will get out as soon as the others reach Tiverius and there will be a lot of questions about the mismanagement of this situation in the doga. So they will let us out, if they want to or not. And then when we're free, I'm going straight to the doga. I'm fed up with their incompetence. They are too disorganised to make sure emergency supplies of suits and salt pills were available in the regional towns, but no, keeping those supplies up-to-date would have been too easy. And now this debacle." Mercy, he was angry, about everything. Why were there no soldiers here to keep order? Why had they closed the road? Why had no one built a camp for the Chevakian refugees?

A woman asked, "Do you think anyone in the doga will listen? They're too busy with their regional squabbles, especially those from the north."

"They will listen, or I will make them. Before all this happened, my brother came to ask me to return to the doga. He said he had the necessary votes. I said no, let the past be the past. I should never have let him leave; I should have gone, and we might not be in this mess we're now."

"You changed your mind?" The man sounded hopeful. He was older, and would remember Milleus' time in office.

"I had no idea of the severity of the situation."

A man said, "Destran is an idiot, letting all this happen. If the army can't control a couple of unarmed refugees, then what have we come to?"

"It's not quite as simple as sending in the army. It is not an invasion of a foreign army. These are refugees. Everyone still alive from the City of Glass is here. Something happened there that destroyed the city."

"Their filthy magic," whispered a woman.

An uncomfortable silence followed. Many people glanced at Milleus, knowing that during his term, the doga had tried to stamp out the use of the word magic. Magic was fear. Magic was unknown, something no one understood. The Scriptorium had progressed to a different stage with sonorics. They understood it now. They could measure it. Sonorics was *not* magic.

But he had no energy for that debate.

"Magic or no, it doesn't matter what name you attach to it." Was this him talking? They must think he'd gone soft. "I don't know what else is going on, but I'm planning to push on into Tiverius, maybe tomorrow when we can see where we're going, and go into the doga. This camp, and the guards, is a shambles. Either the army keeps the refugees under control, or they don't. They'll need someone who makes the decisions."

One of the men clapped. "And get the southern knights out of our country. There have been too many sightings for them to be untrue."

"Shoot them down. Let the whole lot go back to their own country."

"We'll come with you."

"Tomorrow," Milleus said. "When it is light."

This satisfied the Chevakians, and people retreated to their trucks and tents to sleep.

But dawn was not that far off and Milleus felt too restless to sleep.

In the distance, he could see the city lights, turning the heavy cloud cover a sickly orange. He leaned on the railing of the pen and sighed. The hurt that started with the revelation that the delicate Nila was really the Queen of the City of Glass refused to go away. She was not just an innocent highborn girl. Both of the youngsters had played him, and he had been too dumb to see it, and worse, now he'd lost them and they never even found out who he was.

Both he and she could have put their contact to better use. What a waste of opportunity.

And damn it, he *still* liked the two of them.

To his right, a bit further down the hill, the sound of many voices came from the big tent. Well, they had what they wanted, although it was unclear to him exactly why they had fled. It didn't matter anymore. They were safe, and with this many people around, whoever had tried to kill the youngsters would not get a second chance.

It was just that . . .

To be honest, he wanted to return to the farm.

He didn't look forward to going back to Tiverius. There was too much unfinished business for him to attend to. Andrean and Kalius would have a few things to say to him, none of them nice. How he'd walked out on them, how he'd driven their mother to kill herself and then failed to even put up a plaque at her alcove where the jar with her ashes stood. Trouble was, he couldn't think of anything suitable that was also appropriate. He'd wanted to say, *I never loved you as much as you deserved, and I should have set you free*. But at the time, he couldn't stand the thought of Sady, young, smart and cocky Sady, getting his hands on her. While he was away, his brother was screwing his wife. So Suri was dead and Sady had never married. Had Sady ever touched a woman since?

He did *not* want to deal with this.

He stood there, leaning on the fence. The goats were all settling down for the night. The lights in the other Chevakian trucks and tents winked out one by one.

If he wanted to be gone tomorrow, he should go to bed. The time that he could work through the night unaffected had gone with his youth and his strength. Bluff aside, there was no guarantee that he'd be able to talk his way out of the camp, and there may still be long days of dangerous negotiations and riots ahead. Heck, the soldiers might even decide to take them to jail for disobeying their orders.

He *should* go to bed.

He straightened and turned to the truck. As he put his hand on the door handle, a cold gust of wind tore over the hillside and blew his hair to one side. The air was humid and cold as winter. This weather got stranger every day.

Then a screech that echoed over the hillside made him shiver deep in his bones. Whatever that was, it sounded close. He peered in the direction of the forest. A huge shape flew low overhead, lazily flapping huge wings. It came straight over. For a moment, Milleus saw a dark form, a leathery belly lit from below by the glow of the few remaining lights.

It was as if the wind stopped, the sounds from the city stopped and the whole world turned to silence. Then a gust of warm air followed in the creature's wake.

What in mercy's name was that thing?

Milleus stood quiet, watching the sky. None of the other Chevakians appeared to have seen the creature; no one seemed to be still awake.

And why was it so hot all of a sudden?

CHAPTER 7

TANDOR ACHED like he'd never ached in his life. Not when he became engulfed in icefire, not when Loriane peeled burnt skin away from his face, not when his hands thawed out after the long ride through the snow, had he felt like this. It was as if a piece of his soul had been ripped out of him. As if Ruko's mind had grown roots inside him that had been torn out when Myra and Loriane cut the bonds. Yet he had still managed to maintain the merest wisp of a connection with Ruko. He could still feel Ruko's presence, and see shards of what he was doing.

After his escape from the tent, Ruko had simply vaulted the fence and the Chevakians hadn't even noticed. Now, he was running with the same superhuman strength through the Chevakian country, on his way to join his friends. Whenever he needed to eat, he'd steal a pigeon or duck from a farm and eat it raw, annoyed at the weaknesses of his body that needed food.

He ran, and ran, and ran. All he wanted was to find the other children. Once he reached them, he would discard his mortal form and become one of them once more. With him as their leader, he would push them into revenge. They'd seek out the Knights, and find Tandor, and punish all of them for hurting his girl.

The hatred was so strong that it burned in Tandor's mind.

But Tandor could do nothing to stop the visions coming. And he could also do nothing to stop Ruko reaching his goal.

Tandor himself had been lucky to escape the refugee camp once he confused the camp guards by swearing at them in Chevakian. Claims about his membership of a good Tiverian family were not lies, and when the soldiers left him to confer with their superiors, he'd simply walked out without being questioned; the Chevakian army was that short on personnel.

He'd even been lucky to have overheard where Loriane had been taken. He'd managed to climb into the yard of the senator's house and waited outside the window of the house's guest room, hiding behind a hedge under the cover of gathering darkness. The room had flimsy doors with large panes of glass. He studied them so as to break in quickly, after everyone had gone and the lights were off. After the child was born. He could taste victory. He'd grab the child and take it to his mother's house. If the books were right, it wouldn't take long before the child's first turning. Then he could start to repair the damage, defeat Ruko, sweep up the expanding field of icefire and bring the plan back on track.

For now, he waited and listened to the Chevakians talking. There were two men, in medical gowns. By the skylights, why would this senator go to the expense of getting in surgeons?

What did a Chevakian care about Loriane? She was Tandor's princess. When all this was done and fixed, and the Thilleian family once more held the throne, she would be his queen.

He remembered a hazy flash of memory from yesterday. Loriane shouting at him, "I hate you." She did that often, when he visited her, but she never meant it.

Then there was a ruckus inside the room. Loriane cursing. And then her voice again, a beastly cry that made Tandor shiver deep inside. He tried to imagine Loriane's face, but could not. He could only see Maraithe, grabbing her swollen belly. In his mind, he heard Maraithe's cries. And the voice of the royal nurse, "By the skylights, this one is Imperfect."

And panic. He had to save her children, both of them.

So when Maraithe slept, and the Senior Knight came in to take the boy to be left on the ice floes, Tandor jumped out of the wardrobe and overpowered the man, put on the man's uniform and took the baby to a safe place. And of course, he had been caught when he returned to the palace. By now, the Senior Command knew that

Maraithe's baby girl was Imperfect and understood that the young Chevakian merchant whom they'd deemed safe company for the Queen was not what he claimed to be.

If the Chevakians thought their courthouse prison was bad, they hadn't seen the prison under the palace in the City of Glass.

Tandor remembered lying naked on a table, the feel of rough wood against his naked back. He remembered the Supreme Rider grabbing a handful of his manly bits. He remembered the glint of a knife—

—and he tried to push away those memories as he sat there hiding behind the hedge, and tried to listen for signs or sounds that Loriane's child had been born, and that the surgeons had left. But there were no clear sounds—Loriane said screaming was for first-time mothers; she had told him often enough—so he risked looking over the hedge.

The light was still on in the room. Loriane sat propped up against pillow in bed. A serving woman brought tea to the surgeons. There was also a guard in the room. Tandor could see a basket next to Loriane's bed, but he couldn't see inside it.

By the skylights, what if, for all his calculations and study, the child was *normal?* His mother would kill him.

He was flooded with memories from even further back, when he sat on the little stool in his mother's big garden room, surrounded by luxurious furniture he wasn't allowed to touch—because little boys only made things dirty. She would tell him of all the riches in the City of Glass. He would ask why the City of Glass was no longer rich, and she'd say that the Knights were stupid. She said that he was a prince and that all those riches were his.

And he believed all of it.

Except when he mentioned at school that he was a prince, the Chevakian kids just laughed. Then he would try to make sparks with icefire as his mother had taught him, but he couldn't do it while they watched. Icefire was too weak in Tiverius anyway, even before the barriers went up.

And then the kids would laugh even more, and he got called into the teacher's room and this big fat Chevakian man would rant at him about how there was no magic. Tandor tried to throw sparks at the teacher, too, but it didn't do anything except earn him a cuff on the ear.

There was a shout and the light went out in the senator's guest room, casting the courtyard in deep darkness.

A low, sibilant sound came from the room. Someone shouted and another said, "It must have been the wind."

Where before, there had been no wind at all, there was an icy breeze which found its way through the gaps in Tandor's clothing. The air tingled with icefire.

He rose and grabbed his dagger, and headed for the darkened room, but before he reached the door, and before he could force his way in, a terrible hiss came from inside, and then a muffled scream, cut off suddenly. Another growl and hiss. Tandor couldn't see anything inside that dark room, where there were now crashes and growls, and the sound of breaking crockery, and the splintering of wood.

The window exploded outwards and a huge shape emerged, shaking broken glass off its back as a bear might shake water from its pelt. It moved in a stealthy way like a sabre wolf, with powerful strides like a huge predator. Its neck was long and its head was an extension of the neck, without ears. It had no hair. It walked on powerful claws, but soundless like a lion.

It unfurled its leathery wings. Tandor leapt forward, onto its back. The skin was rough and scaled like a snake's, and was incredibly *warm* under his hands. The creature bucked to try to throw him off. Tandor held onto the place where the wings joined the body. He threw all icefire he could muster at the animal, but it wasn't much, and it sank into the skin without trace. Tandor cursed.

The dacon turned its head and regarded Tandor with an angry blue eye. Then it snorted and jumped into the air. The power of those wings!

While it flew over the courtyard wall, it shook its shoulder blades and rolled. Tandor did his best to hang on, but his clawed hand couldn't get a grip on the creature's back, and he slid off. Fortunately, he landed in bushes, where the Chevakians had found him.

After discovering him in the yard, the three Chevakians, a doga guard, a family-employed guard and a higher-placed man, had taken him to the Tiverian courthouse jail, where the guards had locked him into the dungeon. He was accused of killing four people. He saw no point in arguing; they wouldn't believe him anyway, not until they saw that locking him up wouldn't be the end of the killing. They tied him to a crate with bonds so tight that he couldn't sit down without the rope cutting off circulation in his arms.

Meanwhile, the dacon was loose in Tiverius, and it was only a matter of time before it killed again. It needed lots of food.

He needed to find the hybrid, and fast, because crossbreeds lived one day for a normal person's year. Even when healthy, the crossbreed would not last to see the end of summer.

Once Ruko rejoined his fellows, he would send the children on a rampage of revenge. Maybe Ruko would seek out the crossbreed in order to kill it, which meant Loriane was in danger, too. But Tandor was trapped in this stupid prison by unbelieving Chevakians, and weak from the trip without much food, and still aching from where Loriane and Myra had cut the bonds with Ruko.

"In prison, tied to a fucking crate," he mumbled to himself, and laughed so that he wouldn't cry, and his laugh developed into a wet, hacking cough. He spat out phlegm, wishing for a drink.

Tandor fought a tickle in his throat that wanted to become a cough. His breath rattled with stringy phlegm. He tried swallowing it, but couldn't so he spat. And then coughed up more phlegm.

He peered into the darkness. There was only one small oil lamp at the far end of the corridor, and it cast the feeblest of light by which he could just make out the bars to the opposite cell.

It grew cold in the cell. Tandor was mortally tired but couldn't lie down. He dozed a bit only to find that his arms became painful where the metal bands clamped around them. The scabs on his face itched, but he couldn't scratch. He also needed to pee, and he hoped someone would come and untie him before he embarrassed himself.

But no one came.

He could feel a whisper of a cool breeze stroke past his skin. There was a vent somewhere, and where there was air, he had access to icefire . . . if it was strong enough . . . if the guards untied him and he could get near the vent.

Then he was back at the palace in the City of Glass, and relived that moment where his Imperfect children walked out of their prison into the corridor. With stone sinks embedded in their bodies, they would not listen to his commands. Those sinks also stopped him making them his servitors. They were walking towards the Heart of the City, and he should have killed them, knowing that they would absorb the icefire and that something disastrous would happen.

But those children had been the only people he had really cared about. Not his mother, with her scheming plans and her shady money and her large band of supporters who would all abandon her as soon as they realised what she wanted. Not his merchant stepfather who had been as clueless as he had been rich. Not his haughty half-sisters, who took after his mother and only cared for money.

Having lived the life of a scrawny bullied kid with the fake hand, he wanted those kids he saved to have good lives.

He enjoyed bringing them presents and organising parties for them. He loved the smiles on their faces, even though he knew they thought he was a bit creepy and he didn't know how to be nice to them. He enjoyed seeing them fall in love with each other. Like a dirty old man, he had spied into lofts and rooms watching them fumble making love.

He wanted them to live, and have lots of Imperfect children. Apart from Myra, two other girls had fallen pregnant. He couldn't possibly kill them.

But he should have, because now their bodies had been filled with icefire, and they had slipped from his control. And now the only thing that could control them—the hybrid child—was about to slip from his control as well.

I cared too much, Mother. He'd hoped to give the children the childhood he'd never had.

How to get out of this cell to salvage whatever he could of his plan? He had to change his tactics, and talk to the guards, convince them that they had the wrong person, if they could still be made to change their minds.

Icefire was still very weak in Tiverius. All the way down here under the ground, it was far too weak for him to get rid of the metal manacles, but there was one thing that didn't require so much power. He closed his eyes, and blinked, and blinked again. Ideally, he needed a mirror to do this, and he hoped that just thinking of brown eyes would be enough.

By the skylights, that exhausted him.

He must have dozed, because suddenly there was the jingle of keys and the creak of the cell door, and two guards came in, one of them carrying a torch.

"What do we do with this one?" one of the men said. He carried a slate. "Wanted for quadruple murder, needs a translator."

"I'd say he needs the rope," the other man said. He held the torch close to Tandor's face.

Tandor's eyes watered from the brightness of it, and he could not make out more than the men's outlines and brown Chevakian uniforms.

"Urgh, he looks like a troll. What has he done to himself?" The glow from the torch moved across Tandor's face.

Tandor took a deep breath and plunged in, hoping his disguise, feeble as it was, had worked. "Please, untie my arms." His voice wouldn't cooperate and it came out as a rasp.

The guard cursed. "He speaks Chevakian. Did anyone know he speaks Chevakian?"

"Who cares? It makes the matter simpler. We have a trial today and hang him tomorrow."

"Please. I'm a Chevakian citizen," Tandor said. "I have the right to a fair trial." Not tomorrow. He needed more time before icefire was strong enough for him to escape.

The guard laughed. "You murder four people and dare talk about rights?"

"I did not murder anyone. It was all a misunderstanding."

"A misunderstanding that involved a knife and a lot of blood, huh?"

"The blood was mine." And it was. Scratches from when he'd fallen into the bushes. "Please. I think it was an Eagle Knight. I was trying to stop him by jumping onto the bird. I couldn't hang on and I fell off."

The guards glanced at each other with an expression that said *Eagle Knights?*

"Hmm," one said. "I wonder why you didn't say anything before."

"Because I fell off. I was dazed."

They continued their non-believing glares.

"Please," Tandor repeated. "Untie me. I'm an honest Chevakian citizen. I won't try anything funny. Only for a short while." Only to untie his pants and piss. His bladder was so full that it hurt.

"I don't know about that. You don't look Chevakian. Why do you speak Chevakian so well?"

"Because he's a spy," the other said, and understanding dawned on the first man's face. By the skylights, not only were they obnoxious, they were stupid as well.

"Please," Tandor said.

The man looked at him, his face sneering. "Why should we trust you? We should tell the doga about you."

No, not the doga. His mother had ties all through the doga. They would report him to her. And he didn't want to face his mother before he had the hybrid, or Ruko, or preferably both.

"I'll do whatever you say. Please."

"I don't think so," the guard with the torch said. "Come, let's go." He went to the cell's entrance.

The other man followed, then stopped, turned and hit Tandor in the stomach.

Doubled over, Tandor heard his voice come from far off. "That is what we do with traitors."

When the pain subsided, Tandor felt the cold of piss having soaked his pants.

From elsewhere in the prison came a voice, rough and gravelly. "Hey, new guy, what you be in for?"

"Nothing. I don't belong here." Even to his own ears, his voice sounded too cultured.

A couple of men laughed.

Another voice said. "That's what they all say, the first day."

"Ha, ha, until they are taken into the gallows room." Another voice joined. "And then they'll say whatever the guards want to hear, and the guards don't care, because they love hanging prisoners. We can hear them scream from here."

Tandor shivered. Without the dacon, he couldn't prove his innocence, and the court would have no trouble finding him guilty and the hangman would come quickly. No use in wasting resources on people who killed.

"I stole Lady han Silvanian's jewels," said the first man again. He seemed proud of it, too. Thievery carried the sentence of deportation to one of the labour farms outside the city. Some destitutes stole simply to get a roof over their heads.

The other laughed. "She has too many jewels anyway."

"Yeah, fat cow."

"Will you shut up!" came a voice from further away.

A brief silence, and then the thief said again, "Don't listen to him. He's the one who raped the Vinalissi girl and then killed her when she screamed too much."

"Yeah, he'll be hanged real soon."

Tandor felt sick. In here, status mattered nothing. If he didn't get out, he would be remembered as worse than them. Much worse.

"So, new guy, what did you do?"

"Nothing," Tandor said again.

"Whoa, a cranky one," the talkative prisoner said. "Yeah, all right. Suit yourself. Just trying to be friendly that's all. Good night to you sir."

There was some rustling and grunting and creaking of benches and it grew quiet.

CHAPTER 8

ISANDOR PUSHED his way out of the tent, past the crowds cramming in to see the queen, past the self-styled guards, into the darkness.

"Hey, where are you going?" someone asked.

"I can go wherever I want," Isandor said. By the skylights, he was angry. As if the Brotherhood had suddenly taken over ordering people about when the Knights had gone. And Jevaithi believed them, by the skylights.

The stupid civilian guards had no authority to boss him about, and no one was going to stop him seeing Milleus. But when the guard held the lamp up and Isandor could see his face, he realised that the youth was younger than him.

"By the skylights, it's the champion," the other guard said, this one a woman.

"Really?" the boy said.

"Hey, you," someone else called from further down. "Didn't Simo say that we had to guard the tent?"

"That's what we're doing," the woman called back. She gave a derisive snort.

"So, Simo is pretty much the boss here?" Isandor asked. He tried to make his question sound as casual as possible.

"Pretty much," she said, shrugged, and then let an awkward silence fall.

They were afraid to say more, Isandor guessed. Afraid to be on the wrong side of whatever the Brothers wanted. He asked, "What's your name?"

"Kenna. This is my brother Zito." The boy looked about thirteen, and he had a dirty bandage around much of his left arm.

"Are your parents here?"

Kenna shrugged. "My father sells fish. He was away to get supplies." There was no need to say more. The fish markets were closer to the City of Glass proper than to the Outer City.

"Are all people here supporters of the Brotherhood of the Light?"

"I think so." Kenna looked over her shoulder, but the third youth had vanished. "Not that I've talked to any and know much about them. You know what they were like, quietly going about their business. You're from the Outer City, too, aren't you?"

Isandor nodded. He knew. The Brotherhood school was for orphans. No one cared much about what went on there, except the young people who left the school were usually very smart and did well for themselves in a quiet, unassuming sort of way. None of those people, the merchants, the administrators, the teachers, ever mentioned that the Brotherhood stood for anything, except education. It seemed people were glad the Brotherhood was looking after orphans, so that no one else needed to worry about them.

"When did they start coming out so openly?"

"When we were on the train. There were more and more people in black. Not just men with beards, but women, too. They were saying things like this was our chance for freedom, and we could defeat the Knights."

"A lot of people liked that," the boy said.

"Did they say how they planned to defeat the Knights? Did they have any real plans, or were they just saying things because they sounded good? They do know that just because there are no Knights here, it doesn't mean that they're all dead?"

She shrugged. "I thought they meant to recruit people to fight. They set up an army, and gave people tasks to do. You could join the guards or the cooks or work in the supply tent. Everyone joined these groups. I mean—there is nothing else to do here, and it sounded like a good idea because no one else was organising anything." She cast him a nervous look. "I mean—you *did* get banned from the Knighthood, didn't you?"

Isandor let the uncertainty hang between them. "Have you spotted anyone using icefire?"

"But we're in Chevakia. There is no—"

"Not anymore. The barriers broke and now it's everywhere." Isandor held up his hand and let a spark dance over it. Young Zito's eyes widened.

"No, I haven't seen anyone use it," Kenna said.

"What about Simo?"

They both shook their heads.

"He yells a lot at people," Zito said. "People are scared of him."

"He knows Chevakians," Kenna said.

"Chevakians?" Isandor frowned at her.

"Yes, I saw him with some of the ones who came into the camp. They seemed to know each other well."

Isandor glanced uphill where the remaining Chevakian vans were clustered around a fire. He recognised Milleus' truck. "Any of those Chevakians?" It didn't look like they knew anyone in the camp. Milleus had told him he hadn't met any southerners for many years.

Kenna peered. "I don't think so. A lot of Chevakians left."

The fence had been repaired and he could see fires and tents on the other side. The group still on this side sat around the fire, where people were talking. Milleus was one of those people. Isandor didn't see him, but he saw the familiar truck, and the trailer and goat pen. He ached to go there, but the Chevakians would probably think the was an intruder, and he didn't want to lead Brotherhood thugs to Milleus, so he sat with his knees pulled up to his chest and watched from a distance until the meeting with Jevaithi in the large tent broke up and people streamed out talking to each other, oblivious to him sitting in the darkness. He caught a snatch of conversation about how pale Jevaithi looked.

An older man in black strolled past, semi-casually, but Isandor didn't miss glances at him and at Kenna and Zito who stood on both sides of the tent entrance, not moving and not saying anything. When everyone had left the tent, two new sentries came, both dressed in black, and Isandor finally got up.

Both glared at him as he walked past into the tent, but didn't challenge him.

The people had turned the throne room into a makeshift bedroom by draping Chevakian blankets over upright planks, which partitioned off half of the tent. An oil lamp sputtered, about to go out, on a table in the other half of the tent. A couple of crates and boxes formed chairs and a table.

As he stood there, a cold chill went through him, tugging at his senses. Something above the tent, in the air. He froze, looking uselessly at the tent's ceiling. For a moment, it seemed the world had died. But the feeling passed, leaving the air warmer and without the edge of icefire.

By the skylights, the Knights were flying over the camp with their sinks. No Knights here? Who believed that? They were hiding, waiting to attack.

On the other side of the partition, Isandor found a bed covered in furs. Jevaithi lay there, already asleep.

Isandor undressed and lay down next to her, pulling the fur covers over him. The skins smelled grimy and retained a lingering scent of animals. Cocooned in the smell, he lay staring into the darkness. He liked Milleus and his rational way of dealing with people. He liked the way Milleus looked at something, and tried to understand it. Milleus did not judge based on beliefs or birth. He did not discount facts because they were provided by his enemies.

Isandor realised he had become a lot more Chevakian since being with Milleus, and he liked it. No one in Chevakia had questioned his wooden leg. They'd just assumed it was from an accident, and, unlike the people from the City of Glass, didn't judge him any less for it.

Jevaithi loved her adoring masses, but he felt more comfortable with getting knowledge. He'd always been like that, wanting to question what people told him. He wanted proof, not beliefs or rumour. It was, he thought sadly, something that his mother had taught him.

He could still hear her voice. *I've seen so much stupid belief about birthing babies, and a lot of girls would be dead if I didn't speak out against it.*

By the skylights, where was his mother now?

He nodded off and woke with a shock to the screeches of an eagle in the distance. He jumped out of bed, still in the dark, but when he checked outside, he could only see the side panel of a trailer moving in the wind, and the flapping of a tent awning. It was pitch dark. There was no one to be seen. Even Milleus had gone to sleep.

He went back inside, shivering with the cold, too worried to sleep. Too many things went on in his head. Daytime would come soon.

He relit the oil lamp and sat at the table, wondering if he should go outside and find a fire and make tea. Was it safe to do so? The camp had gone quiet, but there might still be troublemakers about— Southerners or Chevakians, he didn't know. Who could he trust, anyway?

He wondered how many people they had displaced in this large tent and what the poor people of the City of Glass had given up just so that the Queen could have her own tent and big bed with furs. Jevaithi accepted it without question. She was used to being given things without asking for them.

The table was clearly a Chevakian thing, being made of wood, but the crate that formed the seat was something different. In fact, it looked like someone's travel luggage, very old and very Chevakian. He wondered what it was doing here. When he lifted it by one handle, the contents slid against the far end of the chest. By the skylights, it was heavy.

Curious, and because there was nothing else to, he tested the lid and found that the lock was damaged, and open. The lid creaked. The golden light from the oil lamp lit a jumble of clothes and books all thrown in at random, as if someone had searched the chest.

There was a large stopper of the type of jar his mother would use in her practice, but the jar was missing. Whatever had been in it must have been stored in some kind of spirits and must have broken during travel, because the smell still lingered in the chest.

The clothing was mainly men's felt underwear, southern style, but there were some long-sleeved felt shirts and a leather vest.

They were southern clothes, too. Well enough made to belong to a rich person. The chest also contained a variety of pots and stones and metal instruments like rulers and a quadrant, and some instruments he didn't recognise and . . . very old books, with dusty and worn spines.

He took one of the books out and opened the silky pages of vellum. It seemed a diary of some sort, in a very old style of handwriting: Southern, and dating from before the Knights. This was something he would once have paid a lot of money for, when he collected this sort of stuff with Carro.

The writing was hard to read and loopy. The entries were dates, and the text detailed such things as meetings and things that needed to be done, many unfamiliar to him. What, by the skylights, did "temper the feeder lead" mean?

He leafed through and was about to put the book aside when he came to the last entry, scrawled sideways across the page in a hasty hand.

They are at the door. My son and his wife have hopefully fled the palace. Look after them. My life will be short.

By the skylights, he noticed the date, fifty years ago. And the seal depicting the leather-winged creature, some mythical all-powerful figure called a dacon, which was the symbol of the Thilleian house. This was a diary of the old king himself. This travel chest must have belonged to Tandor.

There were two more books, one equally old and incomprehensible, and one full of notes and calculations. There was a diagram with maps and numbers, using a Chevakian word: motes? What did that mean?

He turned a few pages and read of a chamber outside the City of Glass, where one could control the thing called the Heart of the City. Someone had made elaborate notes on settings and levels of all kinds of elaborate levers, similar to the ones Milleus had on his truck. The type of work the Brothers did, with very detailed instructions. By the skylights, it looked as if Tandor had been messing with the Heart.

At the end of the book, he found a diagram in tiny writing spread over two pages. It held names and birth dates. None of them older than himself. His name was on the scheme as well.

Tandor x Maraithe—Jevaithi and Isandor.

He read the line several times. Underneath his and Jevaithi's names was a date of birth. Jevaithi's. He'd always been told his birthday was a day earlier.

He stared at the text, while the diagram blurred before his eyes.

Tandor had betrayed them all. He *was* Isandor's father, the mysterious man who had fathered Maraithe's children while the Knights were bickering, the merchant in disguise. Jevaithi was his twin sister. They were both the old king's great-grandchildren.

CHAPTER 9

MILLEUS ROSE at first light, much earlier than he would have liked, and still feeling tired after a few measly hours of sleep. Mercy, he was way too old for these nighttime escapades. Outside, the light was still dawn blue, filtered through a grey-blue haze. The air smelled of fire, although from his position any evidence of the fights from the night before was well hidden. The tent entrances were shut, and the alleys between tents were empty except for a few black-clad sentries by the large tent, hands in their pockets. The Chevakian tents, too, were still closed.

Heaving a sigh, he opened the door and let himself down from the truck. As soon as he set foot on the ground, the goats started jostling each other to the corner of the pen, clanking their hooves in the food trough.

He ran his hand over the hairy heads, while they pushed their noses into his palm, bleating and shoving each other out of the way.

"Shh, Ladies, people are sleeping."

He found the milking stool and started the daily process of milking with hands that had become unused to the task. At home, he had the milking machine, and since leaving the farm, this had been Isandor's job, with his stronger hands and suppler back; and there was a kind of sadness in the fact that he now needed to do this. But there was no point in complaining. He'd been on his own for ten years, after all. Still, his fingers felt sore and stiff and the joints ached from the weather. More than anything, he was so *tired*.

He was well into the job when a voice said, "Can I help with the goats?"

Isandor. In the faint morning light, he looked exactly like Milleus felt: tired and weary. Had the boy slept at all? He'd noticed activity in that big tent until he had fallen asleep.

The boy clambered over the railing. Blue eyes met his with an expression of concern. "Are you all right, Milleus?"

"I'm just a grumpy old man. A very tired and grumpy old man with weather in his bones."

"I don't like the weather either. It looks like bad weather coming. In the City of Glass, the sky goes like this when there is a snowstorm on its way."

He was right. The ill-defined, low-hanging clouds were typical for snow. At least, they were in the southern highlands. It didn't snow in Tiverius.

Isandor picked up the bucket.

Milleus heaved himself off the too-low milking stool and let Isandor take his usual spot. They fell into the familiar routines, milking, feeding, changing drinking water and brushing the goats, including passing milk to waiting people. All those were Chevakians who had been around the fire last night. There were not many, so they had milk left over, which Isandor poured into two cups, took one himself and handed the other to Milleus. They drank, leaning on the railing of the goat pen.

Artan and his wife had come out of their tent and were now cooking breakfast, and a few others were starting to pack their tents. It wouldn't be long before the Chevakians would leave. And Milleus, damn it, had promised to lead them. Yet seeing Isandor's young face made him wonder whether the youngsters were up to meeting all the trouble they might face here. He had so little time left to tell them all he wanted to say. He didn't even know where to begin.

"The Queen, huh?" Milleus said.

Isandor shrugged. "I'm sorry. I didn't want to lie to you, but we were running away from the Knights and she wanted it like that."

"Why did you run?"

"Jevaithi is scared, for a good reason. She had nowhere to go."

Then he went on to describe a life locked up in the tallest tower in the City of Glass, kept away from the people who adored her. A life of constant put-downs and threats. A life where the young princess had seen her mother slowly wither away, both in mental and physical strength, locked up in the tower for her protection by the people who controlled every aspect of her life. And he told of the mystery surrounding Jevaithi's father, and how the Supreme Rider Cornatan, the regent, kept telling her that he would rape her so that he could have his own blood on the throne.

While Isandor was talking, he met Milleus' eyes through a curtain of ratty and greasy black hair. "Tell me, knowing all this, wouldn't you have fled?"

"I guess so." Milleus couldn't imagine a life of hardship like that. "But if she lived so protected, how did you become involved?"

Isandor spoke of how he'd been an Eagle Knight, how he flew in a race, won and how Jevaithi had crowned him her champion. The first time they met each other's eyes, they had felt a connection. "We're both Imperfect." He glanced at his wooden leg. "But soon after I won, my friend betrayed me. Imperfects can't be Knights."

"Just because you have a part of your leg missing, you're considered inferior, and not allowed to sign up?"

Isandor nodded.

"Mercy. In Chevakia you'd be branded a hero, an invalid having beaten more able men."

"Not invalid. Imperfect," Isandor said.

"Well, that's pretty much the same, isn't it?"

Isandor shook his head. "Imperfect means not just that we are missing parts of our arms or legs, but also that we can feel icefire."

"Sonorics."

"Icefire. Sonorics is what Chevakians call it. Chevakians don't understand it."

"It's the same thing."

"No. When Chevakians say sonorics, they only mean the parts they can measure. The things they can't explain are called magic. And magic is something that's not real, no? And something people don't believe in."

The intense look in his eyes gave Milleus a chill. For years, the doga had waged a public campaign to weed out the use of the word magic, because it made people fearful where they didn't need to be. Sonorics was *not* magic. You could measure it, and make it harmless. Sonorics was under control, and did not need to be feared. But understand it . . . he suspected not even the Most Learned Alius fully understood it.

Isandor continued, "Imperfects are Imperfect, because we can feel icefire in the air."

Milleus knew about the southern resistance to the effects of icefire, but now apparently their bodies had built-in sensors? He thought of the sonorics meters he had seen Sady carrying around, big clunky boxes that contained magnetised strips of metal that attracted the motes, which were then fed into a gel-filled tube, which then needed to be processed in the dark by rolling it over a sheet of silver paper. It was a cumbersome process that made the bellows air-pressure meters look like child's toys. Was he saying that these Imperfect people could do that within their bodies? "What exactly do you mean by *feel*?"

"Like . . ." Isandor raised his hands and let them fall again. "Feel. It's in the air."

"Here and now?"

"Yes. Not much, but there is some. We can . . ." He held out his hand, palm up. A tiny spark lit up, like a miniature bolt of lightning. "It's very weak."

Milleus stared at Isandor's palm, now very normal and pale-skinned. "You did that?"

"Yes. I told you."

"And everyone can do that?"

"Only Imperfects. Ones with arms or legs missing."

That meant both the youngsters. "And what can you do with it?"

"Not much, unless you know a lot about it, but lessons are forbidden. Normally, if an Imperfect baby is born, the Knights leave it on the ice floes for the wild animals to eat."

Milleus stared at Isandor's leg, hidden under his trousers. "Yet the Knights allowed you to become one of them?"

"Yes, I . . ." Isandor looked down. "When I think hard about the leg I don't have, it seems that people don't notice that it isn't there."

Magic. Illusions, ghosts that were said to roam the southern slopes as far down as the barrier. Insubstantial beings that ripped apart livestock that strayed onto the southern slopes. He remembered his own struggle keeping goats safe from what he had always thought were sabre-wolves, but he had never actually seen a sabre-wolf. Magic beings, magic people. He shivered. "Surely you did something to cover up your wooden leg." It wouldn't be that hard, since he had his knee. A good prosthetic on a boy who was young enough to learn to run with it might be barely noticeable.

"I have a shoe that fits the end of the wood."

"There you go." But what a brave kid he was to have enlisted regardless of the threat that he'd be punished severely if found out. Milleus tried to remember his own sons at that age. Andrean insecure and shy, Kalius thinking he knew it all, and popular with the girls. Compared to this young man, they'd lived such luxurious, protected lives.

"You don't believe me." Isandor lifted his trouser leg. "I'll show you."

The skin on Isandor's leg was unbelievably pale, with sparse black hair. The wooden stump was tied to his leg below the bony knee, but an insubstantial white veil marked the place where Isandor's calf would be, had his leg been complete.

Milleus stared and blinked, as if that would make the illusion go away.

"Feel it."

Milleus did. His hand went straight through the illusion, but the wispy form made his fingers ice-cold.

"Mercy."

"It's not very good. It was a lot stronger yesterday."

Not very good? This was scary. Some form of optical projection of light. The white veil slowly faded.

Was there another word for this other than *magic*? "I still don't get it." He cleared his throat, because his mouth seemed to have gone dry. "If they were intent on killing you, why did you sign up for the Knighthood?"

Isandor shrugged. "They seemed . . . honourable, and noble. I thought, because no one said anything about my leg . . . that it didn't matter anymore. All those persecutions of Imperfects were a long time ago. I thought people no longer cared." He let a small pause lapse. "Also, I like animals."

Milleus nodded; he'd noticed that, too. "But once you were in the Knighthood you found out it wasn't as you thought?"

"A lot of bad things happen there. The Knights are so afraid of the supporters of the old royal family that they punish anyone with items that used to belong to the royal family. But a lot of people have those things. After the king was killed, people went into the palace and stole everything the royal family owned. And among the Knights themselves, at the Eyrie, superiors use beatings and rape to keep new recruits under control. Everyone is afraid of everyone else. I had a friend . . ." His eyes looked distant. "His name is Carro."

"The one who betrayed you?"

He nodded. "The Tutors singled him out for punishment. I don't know why, but he's kind of awkward. He always says the wrong things to people, and seems to think everyone conspires against him. And then he does things like telling the superior what the Apprentices got up to last night just so that the superior will be pleased with him."

"Some friend."

"I don't think he can help it." Isandor blew out a breath. "He's probably dead now."

Milleus felt sick. "What a barbaric world." He had known this, of course, but it had always been a distant thing. "How did you two even get to this age?"

"The Knights couldn't kill the princess, because the people love the Queen and would have rebelled. About me, I never knew why I'd been saved."

"Surely someone there must think that this is barbaric. Isn't there anyone who does anything for these poor invalid children?"

"Yes, there is a group called the Brothers of the Light, who run orphanages. They save Imperfect children, sometimes. Not me." His expression was intense.

"So what about you, then?"

Isandor's face went tense. "I wanted to show you. I found this last night." He slowly drew a couple of books from inside his cloak. "I found these in a travel chest that's in the tent. I'm not sure whose they were." Isandor put the top book into Milleus' outstretched hand.

Milleus turned it over, studied the very southern leather cover, and opened the book with its soft vellum pages. He ran his fingertips over the page full of curly southern letters. He didn't know the language well enough to easily read it, but he recognised that certain lines were dates, which, in the south, went back to some past war. "A diary?"

Isandor nodded.

Milleus turned another page. The vellum was of extraordinarily fine quality. He didn't even know they made things like this in the south. Spread over two pages was an intricate drawing of a strange creature. Its body was vaguely wolf-like in shape, but it had no hair and its skin was grey and wrinkled. From its shoulder blades sprang two huge leathery wings, with claws on the end. The drawing showed it slashing sharp nails at a white bear. The white fur was bathed in blood. A small diagram in the corner showed the creature in flight. He froze.

It was the thing he'd seen last night. Or was it?

"What is this thing?"

"It's a . . . dacon. This is the symbol of the royal family." He pointed to a stylised representation of the creature, arranged within the border of a circle that looked like a family seal. "If the Knights find this symbol on anything, they take it off you. Any old cups and plates, and books, and things that came from the old king's household."

"Could I . . . could it be possible that I saw one of those creatures?"

Isandor turned sharply to Milleus. "It would have been an eagle."

"I felt . . ." Milleus put his hands together. "First, the air was cold. Then I heard this beastly cry. I saw a creature fly over. It wasn't an eagle. I've heard those. I've seen those, too. This creature was dark, and had no feathers. When it passed, the air became warm."

Isandor nodded. "I felt that, too. But, this creature . . . people in the City of Glass say it's just a story. It doesn't exist."

"You're absolutely certain of that?"

Isandor met his eyes, but said nothing. He let a silence lapse before continuing. "Anyway, I wanted to show you something else. It's on this page." He flipped through the pages, until he reached the two-page diagram with lines of what looked like names.

Milleus looked at it, silently.

"They're all names—"

"I can read those," Milleus said, running his finger down the list. "Just not very well or fast." And he was clearly meant to find Isandor's name. Indeed, there it was. *Maraithe x Tandor: Jevaithi and Isandor.* Milleus looked into Isandor's eyes and said nothing for a long time. A tear tracked over Isandor's young face. He sniffed.

"This changes everything," Milleus said, slowly.

Isandor nodded, and wiped his cheek. "This is bad—"

"Bad?" Milleus raised his eyebrows.

"Bad for me. They only want the queen, and they only want her to shut her mouth and do as they tell her. I have too many opinions. The Knights will kill me. The Brothers won't know what to do about me. They already think I'm trouble. They'll try to kill me, too, if they can. They just want Jevaithi to be their puppet queen. They don't want anyone to interfere." His eyes were wide.

Milleus nodded, slowly. "Possibly, but have you considered—"

"And Jevaithi will be angry with me."

Yes, he could understand that. "She couldn't have known?"

Isandor shook his head. "Tandor was always telling everyone how he'd lost his . . . manly bits and couldn't be my father—"

Milleus winced.

"He lied to everyone." He let a silence lapse. A tear rolled over his cheek. "I slept with my sister."

"But you didn't know she was your sister." And then he had to suppress a shudder because of the implications. In Chevakia, it would have been a punishable crime. He hoped the City of Glass didn't have such laws. After all, if no one knew who their parents were, then it was bound to happen more often. He continued in a low voice, "You can only do one thing."

"I have to tell her, and then she'll be upset and then everyone will know. And then they'll kill me because they can imprison a Queen, but they're afraid of another king."

"Yes, you have to tell her. But you also have to find a way to use it. You will be stronger together than she can be alone."

"But no one listens to me. I'm only an Outer City boy. No one listens to a boy. No one listens to the queen, even. They don't even want us here. I bet they were disappointed when we came into the camp."

"No one listens to an old man either, but you can make them."

There was a clang of tent post and the squeal of children as one of the Chevakian tents came down.

"You're leaving, aren't you?"

Milleus sighed. "We are. I'm sorry. I am hoping that the guards will let us through just to be rid of us. Then we'll go to the doga and demand that they deal with the situation, that they let all the Ensar people through, or clear the road, and take them to a different camp. I'll be back with help, I promise."

Isandor's mouth twitched. "I would have loved to go to Tiverius."

"You can come with me."

Isandor pressed his lips together but then sighed and shook his head. "I have to stay here, and Jevaithi couldn't come, even if she wanted. I have to stay with her. I think she trusts these people here far too much. Because they're not Knights, it doesn't mean that they won't try to use her in the same way the Knights did."

Milleus nodded. He didn't look forward to leaving the youngsters behind. "It would have been a lot easier had you told me who she was. I could have prevented most of this from happening. For one, I would never have taken the main road, so we would now be safely at my brother's house." He would have been able to take her into the doga, and it would have helped his standing, too. Never before had there been much of a relationship between the Proctor, or indeed anyone in the doga, and the southern royal family.

"If I'd told you, you would have handed us over to the local army post."

Milleus thought back to a time that felt like it was years ago, when he did everything to avoid being a public figure and taking responsibility for the district in which he lived. "Maybe." A bit later, he added, "Probably, yes."

Not much later, the Chevakians had finished packing, and the convoy was ready to go. Milleus climbed into the truck, alone, and found it horribly quiet and empty in the cabin.

Mercy, if only the youngsters had told them who they were earlier, he would never have gone into the camp—but no one had known that the inhabitants were southerners. He would never . . .

He sighed. He must do his best to make sure that they were safe and to make sure that no fanatics got control over the camp, and that, for once, Chevakia and the people of the City of Glass spoke openly and worked together.

The column of trucks started moving downhill.

Milleus closed the escape valve and his truck jumped into motion. Isandor and Jevaithi waved.

"I'll be back as soon as I can," Milleus called out the window. He tried to sound optimistic, but oh, how he wished to take the youngsters with him. They were only children, and this camp seemed a hotbed of conflict, even within the southern population.

The large tent, the gathered onlookers and Isandor and Jevaithi slid from view.

The convoy rolled down the hill, past tents that had been taken down, past the burnt-out remains of the feeble barricade that would never have been adequate to hold back the Chevakian army. Milleus was sure: the Chevakians had been ordered to retreat. Possibly because they had no interest in the conflict, or because they had established a more effective perimeter to isolate the riots. And what had the fights been about, anyway? Just southern refugees being frustrated and angry, and Chevakians being frustrated and angry.

There was no one in the lower third of the camp. Whatever tents had not been pulled down had been divested of their contents. Beds, blankets and whatever sparse furniture had been dragged to the top of the camp, leaving the ground dusty and muddy with occasional black spots. There would be trouble in Tiverius over this. The people would say that the southerners didn't deserve their support if they started burning things provided by the Chevakians. They should be more grateful and have respect. He could almost hear the voices in the doga. That self-righteous prick Janus, if he was still alive.

Ahead were the camp gates. The two metal-barred panels. Closed. Milleus slowed down, and then stopped. The trucks behind him did the same. He had expected to have to argue to be let through, or to be arrested. He'd expected a fight. Whatever he had expected, it was not this.

He honked the horn, but no one came, so he opened the escape valve, parked the truck in neutral and let himself out of the cabin.

There was no one in the gatehouse.

Mercy, what stupidity was this? Milleus rattled the gate. Through the strips between the bars he only saw the Ensar road snaking down the hill.

He banged his fist on the metal. "Hey, is anyone here?"

Artan came up behind him.

"What's going on?" he said.

"I have no idea," Milleus said. In his day, the army didn't just abandon a job. He banged on the gate again. "Hey! Can anyone open this?"

No one came. Artan peered through the gate and the restricted view it offered of the world outside the camp. "I guess we could use your wire-cutters again."

The other Chevakians had also come out of their vehicles and inspected the gate and fence. Several men rattled the gate. Others discussed how they could possibly open or break it, or cut through the fence.

Others suggested they go back to the south side of the camp.

"The gap we made has been closed," someone said.

"But we can easily make another one."

They discussed this for a while. Other people had also noted the activity of trucks in the forest and concluded that someone had made a route through the forest for the traffic on the Ensar road to escape.

"Hey, someone's coming!" Artan said.

Everyone crowded at the gate, or prised aside the tightly-strung cloth that covered the fence on either side.

A small panel opened in the gate, and a man said, "What's going on here?"

Milleus was dismayed at the young and innocent voice. This was only a junior officer. He was wearing a sonorics suit over his uniform, complete with hood and visor.

"Let us through," Artan said, and his call was repeated by some of the others. He gestured for Milleus said, "We're Chevakians and we got stuck in here last night. We ask to be let out."

"I'm afraid I can't allow that, sir." His voice sounded muffled under the mask. "The camp is to be sealed off. General's orders."

"Finnisius?" Milleus said.

"Yes. General's orders. Chevakian or southern, everyone in the camp is contaminated. You'd endanger the population."

"Rubbish," Artan muttered. He held out a bare arm. "I don't feel anything."

Milleus said, "Surely what little sonorics these people contribute is not going to make a difference to overall levels within Tiverius."

"The Chief meteorologist says differently. The General has ordered the camp sealed off, sir. I cannot speak against my orders."

What? Sady had given the orders? Sady would not do such a thing as isolating people unless it was warranted. Just how badly contaminated were the southerners? What again were the early symptoms of sonorics illness? Surely sore joints were a symptom of old age! Or were they?

"I am here on the invitation of the doga." He groped in his pocket, but the letter with the signatures was in the truck. "We need to get through, for the safety of the Chevakian refugees."

"They are being dealt with."

"For mercy's sake, use some sense. Let us out."

But it was a waste of breath. The man was too junior to argue with, and would never make a decision on his own. Milleus knew that too well.

"Can I speak to your superior officer?"

"I'm afraid he's not available, sir. You understand that we are very busy."

"Then go and get him. Tell him Milleus han Chevonian is in the camp and wants to have a word with him. He's an old mate of mine." Not quite. Finnisius had been a junior officer, a bit of a self-righteous prick if Milleus remembered correctly, one of those people with slavish attention to rules.

The man flicked his eyebrows in a kind of *is that so?* way. But he didn't respond, and Milleus had an awful feeling the soldier didn't believe what he said.

"Look, just get him here, and let me do the talking."

"Sorry, sir, he's busy. We're all busy."

The man turned and walked away.

Several of the men banged on the metal panels of the gate. "Hey. Let us out."

The soldier came back. "I'd advise you against cutting through this fence. We have a perimeter set up, in that line of bushes over there.

Anyone coming out will be seen as a threat to Tiverius, and hostile to us."

They were actually going to shoot at Chevakian citizens? "You have to be kidding."

The man met Milleus' eyes for a moment, turned on his heel and went back to his truck.

What now?

Artan was looking at Milleus, and he wasn't the only one. They all expected him to know what to do.

Milleus shrugged. "Guess the only thing we can do is go back and wait until a senior officer comes into the camp."

CHAPTER 10

"SADY." A voice spoke in his dreams, a voice that wanted him to come into a dark mire. He couldn't see the speaker from where he stood, hesitating, on a tall wall, surrounded by mist, with no idea how he'd managed to get up there. Everyone he loved—his parents, long dead; Milleus, missing; Suri, dead at her own hand—was down there and wanted him to jump. But the water—that dark substance underneath the mist must surely be water—was cold and there were weeds that would drag him down.

Another voice called from behind him, "Sady!"

This voice he recognised as Lana's, except the woman who had spoken wasn't her. He didn't know where she came from, but this was a dream and things happen like that in dreams. She looked like an old shrivelled prune of a woman, probably twice his age. She was wearing a wedding gown and carrying a wilted bunch of flowers. He had promised he'd marry her, but he couldn't possibly, not like this—

"Sady, wake up."

Sady woke with a shock. Opened his eyes in bleary morning light. Recognised that there had been someone calling him for real.

Sady said, "What?" Only it came out like a croak, and his mouth felt like sewage.

The remnants of the surreal dream fled his mind.

The voice belonged to Orsan, who stood in the doorway, poking his head into the room. Bright daylight peeped between the curtains. What was the time?

Orsan continued, "Sorry, Sady. I'd like to let you sleep, but there have already been two messengers from the doga for people demanding to see you."

"What for?" But the moment he said that, reality rushed back to him. Lana dead. The trashed guest quarters, the four bodies, the deranged killer. They'd be the victims' families, or other people attacked by this deranged youth, or people from the hospital protesting the loss of two surgeons, or—

"Give me a moment. I'll be there soon—and Orsan, wait."

Orsan came back into the room.

"Any clue about where the baby is?"

"No. Not yet."

Orsan left, and Sady rose from the bed. He'd slept in his clothes, too, and they smelled of sweat and dust, and bloodstains marked the front of his shirt.

No time for a bath.

He retrieved clean clothes from the wardrobe, raked a comb through his hair and shaved as quickly as he could. It made him feel slightly better, but did not dispel the dirty feeling.

In the kitchen, he found the southern family eating breakfast at one end of the table, and Farius staring into a cup at the other. Merni stood at the stove, stirring the pot that Lana used for making roccas.

The southerners looked tired. Sady presumed the city guards had interviewed them last night, at least if they had been able to find someone who could translate.

No one said anything when Sady came in, but the southern girl rose from the table, the baby still in the sling, and gave an awkward bow. "Thank you, thank you."

Sady wasn't quite sure what he was to be thanked for, but he returned a polite nod and sat at the table, feeling empty and bleak. Lana's absence was like a big hole inside him.

Merni gave Sady his breakfast. Her eyes were red. Yes, Lana would do this normally. Serran would be at breakfast, too.

Sady smiled at her, but her expression was hollow, and she turned back to the stove without saying anything.

"It's not fair," Farius said, in a low voice. "He was like a father to me. What do I tell his family?"

"I'll deal with it," Sady said, not looking forward to that task. When families provided sons and daughters for service to doga households, they expected them to be safe.

"What sort of person would do this?" Merni said, whirling around. She cast a furious look at the southerners, none of whom met her eyes.

"Merni, please."

"It's because of them."

Sady sighed. He rubbed his hand over his face. Mercy, he was tired. "Let's be rational. I don't know what happened and why." But the man they caught *was* a southerner, and he could fully understand her anger. "All I know is that we can't turn it back. We have to ride the cart we bought."

She gave him a hard look. Yes, that's right. She didn't like old sayings.

"Besides, we caught the killer. He is likely an escapee from the camp. He will be questioned and dealt with." Last night, Farius had confirmed that the man had not been with the family when they arrived at the house. "Meanwhile, please treat these people as you would like to be treated yourself. The woman has lost her baby. I doubt that was her choice. Give me some bread and I'll take it to her room."

"I'll do that," Merni said, meeting his eyes squarely. She sounded offended.

"Then do it soon," Sady said. "Please, look after her as you would if she were my sister. They are our guests."

Merni grumbled and went to get a tray.

Sady drank his tea. His eyes pricked.

He turned his attention to his bowl, filled with a gluggy substance with bits of grain.

Cooking roccas was Lana's specialty. Merni had left the grains in the water for too long. The skins had burst and the grains were no longer separate and juicy, but had gone like jelly, were hard to scoop up, and stuck to the inside of his mouth. Trying to swallow made him gag, and he had a distant memory of being forced to eat a plate like this as a young boy at his grandmother's house; she had been a particularly careless cook.

Merni watched him, and said nothing. The southern family at the other end of the table sat like statues, pretending not to be there. All three of them had eaten Merni's attempt at roccas, no doubt out of politeness.

But he wasn't so afflicted. He shoved the bowl aside. "I'm going to work."

From the fire into the war zone.

The truck was waiting outside the gate by the time he left the house, and, by the looks of things, had been there for some time.

Sady got into the van, with an apology to the driver and guards. Orsan sat in the front passenger seat. He was one of those people who could survive on hardly any sleep, and right now, Sady would give everything to be like that.

The vehicle drove through the near-deserted streets under a cover of low clouds. Wind whipped fallen leaves, still green, and dust and rubbish through the streets. Doors and windows were closed and obscured by boards or curtains, as the guidelines for a level one sonorics warning dictated.

He tried to force his thoughts to the problems at hand. As he had become accustomed, someone in the office had left a folder with important items on his seat. They were documents on the financial crisis, which was a bad enough problem by itself. Several senators were pushing for a criminal case to be brought against the doga's chief accountant, who had allowed the missing books to leave the building. Destran said, of course, that he'd never taken the records out of the building and had returned them. But they were nowhere to be found.

Today, those problems seemed minor. While the truck drove through the streets, he kept reading the same passage of the document over and over, and could not stop the memories playing through his head.

Lana in the kitchen, smiling as he came in. "I heard you won!" Her eyes shone. "Congratulations, Proctor."

Lana, with her open smile, with her hearty laugh. She wasn't pretty or seductive, and had accepted her role as housekeeper, while she should have been his wife. Never mind that she wasn't from the right family. She lived for him. She never looked at another man. She had, once, even covertly suggested that he sleep with her.

It was a few days after Suri's funeral, when Sady had come home from staying with Milleus and Milleus looked unlikely to follow her in killing himself, and all the fuss had died down. They were in the kitchen. Just he and she, and they'd been talking about Suri and how desperate she must have been to take her life, and if only he'd known he could have told Milleus. He had trouble keeping his emotions down. Lana was making tea, and she lifted the kettle with boiling water off the stove. Through the steam, her eyes met his. She said, "If it would help you feel better, Sady, I can stay with you tonight."

He remembered saying, "But you already stay with me every night," when he realised what she meant. It shocked him so much that his reaction had been immediate. "I would never ask you to do such a thing."

She had turned back to her task without saying anything, but all night he'd lain awake wondering about the strange remark, and about her silence following his too-sharp, shocked reply. She had never mentioned it again, and he'd often wondered what would happen if he'd said yes, or, after one of their late nights talking politics in the kitchen, instead of waving and disappearing out the other door, he'd come up to her, and put his arm on her shoulders. Would she shrug it off, or would she turn up her face so that he could kiss her if that was what he wanted? Which he probably would.

Now it was too late.

Two women he loved gone without ever having felt his touch. That was what was wrong with him: he never made a move when he should, always trying to think up excuses as to why a relationship was inappropriate. With his brother's wife, or with his housekeeper.

People might say he just chose the *wrong* women, but both of them had led deeply unhappy lives because of him, because he kept them on an emotional leash, giving them hope, but keeping what they wanted just beyond their reach.

And now it was too late.

Too late.

The truck jerked to a stop, and Sady, deep in thought, lost grip on his documents. They slid onto the floor. He scrambled under the bench to retrieve them.

The driver opened the door. "You're all right, Proctor?"

Sady rose, the dishevelled papers in his hand. "I just dropped these." He climbed down from the cabin, feeling the driver's questioning gaze on him.

Mercy, he was in no state to run his household, let alone the country.

He clamped the papers under his arm and, accompanied by Orsan, entered the gates to the doga building. The guards at the gate to the forecourt greeted him with salutes. Honest, open faces. They expected him to have all the answers. He crossed the courtyard and climbed the steps. In the hall, he gave his cloak to the wardrobe boy and turned towards the stairs, where the sound of many voices echoed in the high hall.

What was the ruckus up there? The crowd was halfway down the stairs.

Someone yelled, "It's the proctor!"

The shout was repeated up the stairs all the way to the foyer in front of the office.

Sady said, in a low voice, "I thought we had set up a process for people to submit their complaints or issues in the morning." He'd hated how the citizens used to crowd in front of the proctor's office shouting like they were at a camel auction.

"I warned you that a lot of people had come to see you," Orsan said.

So it seemed. Guards shooed the people to the side so that Sady could pass.

Sady met the eyes of a man on the side of the stairs, and the next moment, the man had shoved a dead bird under his nose.

"Look what they did," the man said, shaking the carcass so it almost touched Sady's robe. It had duck feet, but no head. The feathers on the belly were bloodied. "This isn't the only bird. We lost six, all with their heads chopped off."

"Same here," a woman said.

And another man added, "We lost a goat. I took the others inside, but you can imagine the wife isn't too happy with animals in the house."

"And the infuriating thing is that whoever did this just left the bodies there, and didn't even bother to eat them."

"It's vandalism, that's what it is."

"Wait." Sady held up his hands and the people fell quiet.

"We caught someone last night," Sady said.

The audience erupted in cheers and applause.

"Good for you, Proctor."

Sady held up his hand again, and silence returned. "This person attacked my house, and killed four people there." His eyes pricked all of a sudden.

Several people gasped.

"It's an attack on our government," a man said in a low voice.

"I very much doubt this person knew who he was attacking," Sady said, fighting his emotions. "We went and chased after him, and found him not far from my house. The credit for capturing him should go to Orsan and my personal guard Farius. The killer is in the courthouse prison."

"Who is this criminal?"

"We can't be sure. He said nothing. It looks like he's an escapee from the camp, but he doesn't seem to be right in the head."

"None of them are right in the head," a woman said.

A rotund man growled, "A filthy southerner? The prison's too good a place for him."

Several people agreed.

Sady thought of the man's strange hollow eyes, and his horrific scars, and the blood on his hands. "Has anyone seen the latest sonorics figures? Last I'm aware, the bell rang once on the hour. Unless something has changed that I'm unaware of, you should go inside your houses and stay safe. The madman will not kill again."

The news of the killer's capture travelled faster up the stairs that Sady could walk, and by the time he had arrived in the foyer, most people were making their way back down the stairs towards the entrance, many of them smiling at Sady and giving him victory signs.

Some hollow victory. If the man was mad, then how could he gain any satisfaction out of condemning him to death?

Sady went into his office, and heard from his secretary that Viki was waiting for him with the weather reports Sady had asked for.

At least someone was organised.

His former student sat in the visitor's chair, having spread maps and graphs all over Sady's desk, all over his papers and neat piles of documents. Whatever remained of the student too shy to say boo?

"Um, Viki?"

"Oh." Viki jumped up and took a number of rolls of paper from Sady's chair. Two of them tumbled out of his arms.

Sady picked them up, put them on the desk and sat down with a sigh. "Viki, do you always need to carry your entire office around with you?"

"I need to be prepared for every question." Viki sat down again. To Sady's shock, he had not shaved himself since Sady had last seen him and his chin sported a rough cover growth of hair.

"How long have you been here?"

"Um—I thought I'd come early . . ."

"I mean—have you been living in the office?"

"It's been very busy and there's a lot of work to do."

"All right. How does it look?" *Sonorics stabilising, still locally high, in the vicinity of the camp, but tapering off . . .*

Viki hesitated. "I don't understand what's happening."

"Show me." But it did not sound like the result he'd hoped for. Sady didn't like that little catch in his reply at all.

Viki rolled out the latest pressure map on the table. Normally, in this time of the year, an area of high pressure sat over the south, pushing a band of clouds into southern Chevakia, which manifested in a continuous progression of low-pressure cells. Instead, there was only one pressure cell, and it sat over the southern platform. Since Sady had last looked at a map, it had deepened and appeared to be moving—no, expanding—north. Sady stared at the crowded isobar lines.

"I've never seen anything like this before. Have you checked the records?"

"Yes, but I can't find any precedent."

"How many data points did you use for these maps?"

"Not as many as I would have liked. All of these measurements are from recovered balloons. A lot of the ground stations are out, or their reporting is unreliable."

"What measurements are we still getting? Twin Bridges?" He thought of the group of scouts he'd sent there.

"Yes, Twin Bridges, but most of the southern stations have stopped responding."

"Mekta? Solmeni?"

Viki shook his head. "None of those. Ensar, too." He pointed at the map. "Look, the storm front has moved into the southern regions and likely lines are down. People are reporting wildfires."

"In this weather?" Mercy, why hadn't he dragged Milleus home with him?

"There is a lot of wind, and some of those forests are very dry before the spring rains."

"What about sonorics? Have you mapped those?" They knew the barrier at Fairlight had shattered, but it might still be intact elsewhere, never mind that there didn't seem to be a way of finding out.

"I have. And that's even stranger." Viki rummaged between his rolls of paper, pulled one out and unrolled it on the desk. Lines of sonorics were superimposed over a map of the city and surrounding areas.

There was a bright hotspot of fifteen motes per cube with many lines around it.

"That is the location of the camp," Viki said, unnecessarily.

"I thought we'd decontaminated them."

Not well enough, obviously. And another thing: if this relatively low level of sonorics showed up as a bright spot, what had happened to the base level? Sady checked: nothing. Sonorics levels were barely measurable, lower even than normal for the time of the year.

He pulled the map onto his lap and studied it. After a long silence, he said, "This is strange."

"I said so."

"Really, really strange."

"Anyway, that's last night's readings. Look at the difference this morning." He passed Sady another map with—mercy—levels as high as a hundred and ten motes per cube at the army balloon base to the south of the city.

Sady put one map on the desk and the other on his lap and looked from one to the other.

"What caused such a sharp change?"

"Do you want the honest answer?"

"Is there another kind?"

Viki met his eyes, and his expression said, *One we don't tell the citizens*. Sady nodded.

Viki averted his eyes. "I don't have a single *fucking* clue."

Coming from his mouth, the expletive was doubly shocking. Shy, even-tempered Viki, who wouldn't even know how to harm anyone. Yet the strain was visible on that young face, as were the bags under his eyes.

Sady reached out and touched his student's arm. "Viki . . ."

"I don't have a clue, all right? Sack me if you want. I don't know! Everyone expects me to know. I don't!"

"Calm down, Viki."

Viki took slow, deep breaths.

"Have you asked Alius for advice?"

"Do you think I have suicidal tendencies?"

Yes, that was right; though Sady didn't understand the issue, Viki was terrified of his tutor. "Mercy, Viki, one hundred and ten, just outside the city. That's getting into danger territory. Have you sent out any warnings?"

"Warnings?"

"Sending out warnings is part of the Chief meteorologist's job. Those levels are high enough to justify two rings of the bell."

Viki's eyes were wide. "I . . . um . . ."

"Go, order it." That was part of the job, though Viki had nowhere near the training required to do it. While he had the confidence to do the technical part of the job, he had none of the skill with people.

Viki rose and scrambled to collect all his rolls of paper. He scurried for the door.

"And Viki?"

The young man froze. "Yes, Proctor?"

"What's with the facial hair?"

"This?" Viki rubbed his hand over his unshaven chin, dropping a roll of paper. "Something different. I thought it looked good." He bent to pick up the paper. "Beards are very popular right now. I thought—"

"You look like you have a hairy caterpillar plastered on your face. Look, tell me this: what's with the group of men who wear beards?"

"Group of men. . . ?" Viki frowned.

"Yes, they hang around with Alius and other people from the

Scriptorium. Some senators, too. Please tell me who they are and what they're about."

"I . . . I have no idea what you're talking about."

"Then will you please shave yourself before someone assumes you to be something you are not?"

"Um—yes, Proctor. Surely." Viki went red in the face and scurried from the room.

Sady slumped in his seat and sighed, feeling an ache for his old job and the anonymity that came with it.

Instead, he led a country that faced a sonorics crisis of uncertain nature, with financial irregularities that would sink a few political careers in normal times, with a huge population of refugees with whom no one could communicate, while a large group of prominent citizens appeared to be conspiring against the doga.

At least they had caught the killer.

CHAPTER 11

LORIANE AWOKE from her first good sleep in days to the sound of a door opening. For a moment, she thought she was at home in her limpet, but then she saw windows and curtains and she realised that she wasn't—not only that, but she was no longer pregnant, and she was in Chevakia.

Dara was crossing the room to her bed, carrying a tray. "How be ye today, Mistress Loriane?"

Her voice sounded hesitant and uncomfortable, and Loriane remembered snatches of an argument last night, of Dara shouting, "I can't stay here like this!" somewhere in a corridor, while a young woman helped Loriane wash herself in the bath.

"The Chevakians gave me this to bring ye for breakfast," Dara said.

She set the tray down on the bed and backed off a few steps. Ontane and Myra had followed Dara into the room. Ontane left the door open as if he was prepared to flee at short notice.

Breakfast consisted of a bowl with a jelly-like substance which contained many little brown balls, like fish eggs, except it didn't smell like fish, and a cup of tea, which at least smelled like tea.

Loriane slid the tray onto her lap. The scent of food made her stomach churn. She had hardly eaten anything yesterday.

She poked at the sticky substance in the bowl. The little balls resisted being scooped up by remaining firmly stuck in the jelly. The Chevakians called this food? "What is this?"

"I don't half know," Dara said. And after a silence added, "These Chevakians be ignorant of how to cook."

"I didn't mind it," Ontane said.

"Ye'd eat anything."

Loriane managed to hack some of the substance off and put it in her mouth. It was so gluey that it stuck to the roof of her mouth, which made it hard to swallow.

She swallowed the mouthful, with difficulty, and poked about in her bowl for a bit that wasn't so gluey. By the skylights, she couldn't eat this.

"The Chevakian didn't eat it either," Myra said. She patted Beido on the back. Loriane hoped he was hungry, because her breasts felt like rocks.

Ontane said, "Yeah, but he be the head of the household, and not some murdering refugee from a hated country."

Dara glared at her husband with something like a look of warning. He shrugged and crossed his arms over his chest and glared back at her with a look that said *What?*

Dara muttered something under her breath that sounded like, "We agreed not to mention it."

Not mention what? If they had anything to say to her, they should say it. No doubt it had something to do with being the mother of a monster that had killed four people. As if she could help it. Damn Tandor and his machinations.

Loriane poked the spoon at the bowl's contents, ignoring the tense silence. She tried a couple of the round grains, but the jelly-like substance that coated them made her feel sick, and her anger made it worse. She jammed the spoon in the bowl and shoved it aside.

"The tea be good, mistress," Dara said, her voice timid.

Loriane blew out a breath and met Dara's eyes. "Look, just what is going on?"

"Nothing. Ye need to recover, mistress."

"Nothing? And you're all behaving like I have some sort of disease?"

"We . . . we be sorry about the babe." Dara averted her eyes.

Myra clutched Beido to her chest, her eyes wide.

"We have to do more than just be sorry. We have to find it."

Dara said, "Ye'll need time to recover, mistress. Let's not worry about it now."

"We must worry about it. That monster killed four people. It's out there somewhere."

Her only response was blank faces.

Then it clicked in her mind. "You don't believe me, do you?"

Ontane said, "Now, mistress, that be a big thing to say. Ye may be confused, that be all."

"By the skylights, you don't think that I killed those people?"

More silence. It was clear they did. Loriane's heart thudded in her throat.

She remembered, somewhere in her haze of pain after having arrived at the house, Ontane declaring his dislike of "women's business". That he was going to wait in the other room. Myra had wanted to stay, but the Chevakians wouldn't let her.

"I didn't say that, Mistress Loriane."

"But you believe it."

"I didn't say that neither."

But Dara believed it, judging by the look on her face.

"You have to believe me. This is the truth: I didn't kill anyone. I *tried* to kill the child before it could do any damage, but I didn't. It's out there somewhere, threatening all who come across its path." She met their gazes one by one, feeling increasingly cold. They had travelled with her, they knew Tandor. If they didn't believe her, then what chance did she have with the Chevakians?

The uncomfortable silence lingered.

Eventually, she asked, "Whose house is this?"

Ontane said, "Someone Chevakian. He be rich."

Dara shot him an angry look.

"What? It be true. All the other people be his servants."

"Where is Tandor?" Loriane asked.

"Tandor's still in the camp," Myra said, softly. Little Beido was making happy baby-gurgling noises. "You were right. Tandor was being controlled by Ruko, and we broke the bond by separating the two, but Tandor made such a fuss that the Chevakian guards took him out of the tent. We haven't heard from either of them since."

"You left him in the camp?"

"It wasn't our choice. The Chevakians took him away. I have no idea where to."

"And no one thought to make sure he came with us?" By the skylights, Tandor was the only one who knew what was going on. He was the one who had wanted her child. If he was free, he could go and complete whatever evil plan he had cooked up. Use icefire to kill the Chevakians, seize the throne, kill the Knights. Whatever. And the child had a place in his machinations. If he could find it, which he probably could. Maybe he already had.

She threw the blankets aside. "I need to know where Tandor is." She rose.

Dara said, "Ye should stay in bed. Ye still be recovering."

"By the skylights, I won't. I'm going to find that monster." But a spell of dizziness took her and she had to sit on the edge of the bed.

"See? Ye need more time to recover."

Loriane looked around. "Where are my clothes?"

"The woman left some bandages in the bathroom."

"I'm not talking about bandages. I want my clothes. Where are they?" Not on the chair next to the bed. Not on the two chairs near the hearth. Maybe in the cupboard?

"Ye shouldn't get up yet."

"Why not? I've never stayed in bed. I've had ten children."

Dara's eyes met hers.

Loriane thought she saw disapproval. "Look, I'm not staying in bed, and I'm not crazy. I need to find Tandor. Please give me my clothes."

"Um, I be thinking they went to the laundry."

"Then get me something else."

Dara sighed. "I'll ask."

The family left, and Loriane sank back onto the bed with a deep sigh. Dara was right in one, no, two things: one, the tea was really good; and two, she didn't feel up to walking around much. Her backside hurt. It had not been a normal pregnancy and neither had it been a normal birth. Just trying to get up exhausted her.

By the skylights, what could she do? She would have expected at least some support from the family.

Her memories from yesterday were so distorted, she had trouble to tell what was real. It had to have something to do with the stuff the Chevakians had used to knock her out.

She knew that she'd suddenly awoken to a sharp pain, that she had jumped off the stretcher, because she could not possibly push out a child while on her back, and that the Chevakians—what were they doing here anyway?—had tried to stop her. That it was much too late for all of that, because she could feel the child drop into position between her legs.

She thought to run from their grasping hands before they could put her back on that table. But she was in a strange room with no memory of how she'd ended up there. She'd opened a door—which turned out to be a cupboard—got in, shut the door and crouched in the corner. She remembered that overwhelming feeling of pressure. Unable to do anything else except push that damn child out. And push, until she was short of breath.

She remembered reaching down there and her hand meeting something slime-covered that wasn't any body part she recognised. And panic, and that overwhelming urge to push. This thing was happening to her and she had no way to control it.

She clearly remembered that the Chevakians yanked the door open and she was standing there, leaning against the back wall of the cupboard. They tried to pull her out. She screamed at them. What was it with these people trying to interfere with a woman giving birth? They backed off. She felt the burning pain of the head crowning, knelt down in that pitch dark cupboard, and reached for the child down there where she couldn't see. In the palace, other women would do this for the mother, like she had done for Myra. Usually, there would be a group of women sitting around the birthing mother, chatting and offering drinks and words of courage, ready to pass along the items the midwife asked for. These Chevakians were men and had no idea what to do, they didn't offer any help. They just watched.

She remembered, as the child came out and she tried to get hold of it, reaching awkwardly around her belly, grabbing something that felt like the child's shoulder. The skin was rough, and the bones were too sharp and poked at the skin. The little arm came free and felt not-so-little anymore. It *flapped*. A gust of air wafted past her thighs wet with birth fluids.

She'd been scared and shivery with panic, but could do nothing except what her body told her to do.

But by the time the child was out and she'd sunk down on the floor, and the Chevakians shone a light into the cupboard, the thing in her arms was just a baby.

A girl.

The Chevakians brought blankets, and helped her out of the cupboard, dripping blood everywhere. They chatted and seemed happy. A woman brought a cold drink. Loriane sat on the bed when the babe squirmed in her arms and opened her eyes. They were nothing like she had seen before. They were blue and the child *looked* at her. Normal newborns didn't look. Their eyes were hazy, black and barely open. They were certainly not bright blue. And as she watched, the babe's nails became like little kitten's claws, digging into Loriane's skin. Her chubby little shoulders became less chubby, the limbs grew and extended into large leathery wings—

A demon creature.

She shouted and grabbed the child by the throat, pushing it into the mattress.

The Chevakians rushed to stop her. Everyone in that room was shouting.

She remembered the feel of the child's skin under her hands, and that the soft neck grew in size and roughness even as she was trying to throttle it, that the arms grew into huge wings, that she lost her grip, and that the demon-like thing grew and hissed and pushed her onto the floor. And that the two Chevakians, and some other people, had tried to restrain it. She remembered the vicious slashing of claws, spraying blood, screams. Hiding under the bed, on her knees, while blood dripped onto the floor. The demon-like creature prowled around the room, ripping up everything in its path. It hissed and slashed and growled. And then it charged straight at the window, smashed it and disappeared into the yard.

After seeing the bodies on the floor, she'd run out through the broken window, to hide in some other part of the house and waited ... and waited, shivering and bleeding, her back against a cold wall.

That was where the kind Chevakian had found her. And he was the only one who had been nice to her all day, even though she couldn't understand him and he couldn't understand her.

Loriane finished her tea and had another go at getting out of bed, slowly. First, her legs over the side. Then off the bed, onto her knees. The pad against the bleeding felt thick and wet between her legs. She would have to change that. Then, one foot under her, her hands on the side of the bed. She pushed herself up. By the skylights, her muscles hurt.

But she didn't feel dizzy this time.

Very carefully, she padded to the window, which looked out onto a courtyard surrounded by a stone wall. On the other side, she could see into a neighbour's yard with neatly clipped hedges and statues and a bench where a child had left some toys. Wind whipped the bushes and blew leaves around the paving. Nothing moved; the curtains of the house were closed.

She ran her hands along the window frame, but didn't understand how it opened, if it opened at all.

She opened a few cupboard doors. There were blankets and pillows inside, but no clothes. Did this man really live here by himself?

One of the doors had a mirror on the inside. She lifted her night-gown and wished she hadn't. Her belly was floppy, with a skin flap hanging down from below her navel, and wrinkled and crisscrossed with bruises and angry red marks. At least she didn't have a husband who had to pretend that she was pretty.

She'd had ten children, and where were they now? Where was Isandor? She couldn't imagine anyone having survived in the City of Glass.

On a top shelf in the cupboard, she found a box that contained books with coloured pictures. Children's books, with simple pictures of everyday objects, and words written next to them. She supposed that those letters said *house*, and those ones *mother*. She spent some time leafing through the book and made a decision: if Dara and Ontane weren't going to help her, she'd learn to say what she needed in Chevakian herself.

By the time Loriane had finished inspecting every item in the room, no one had come and she had heard nothing outside, so she decided to go for a walk. The nightgown was gossamer thin, but in the bathroom she found a towel or some sort of cloth to wrap around her lower body so that anyone she met wouldn't see her bandages and floppy belly through the fabric.

The corridor on the other side was familiar to her—she had been taken this way last night. If she remembered well, the main area of the house was to the right, down a flight of stairs.

The door to the room next to hers stood open. Inside stood a large bed with fine silky sheets rumpled and hanging off the side. A man's shirt lay on the floor and a couple of mismatched shoes stood half under the bed.

She hesitated near the door, both embarrassed to see this and eager to tidy the room up. One of the people killed had been a woman who had been kind to her yesterday, someone who was probably a housekeeper here. Maybe the younger, unfriendly woman was a daughter who hated having to do this work as well as trying to cope with her loss.

She continued down the corridor and came to the staircase, where her footsteps echoed in the cavernous hall. A huge metal structure with lots of oil lamps hung from the ceiling. She counted twenty-one lights. The stairs themselves were made from a white polished stone with carved railings. A mosaic in different types of stone, depicting a man riding an animal of some kind, took up most of the floor in the hall.

By the skylights, she had thought that the large hall in the palace in the City of Glass was a display of splendour. Just how rich were these Chevakians?

The sound of voices drifted from downstairs, so Loriane descended the steps and remembered the way to the kitchen.

Inside, she found Myra washing dishes. Sounds of hammering came from elsewhere in the house.

Loriane sat down at the table, thankful that Myra's parents weren't there.

Myra gave her a scrutinising look. "You're feeling all right?"

"Yes." This insistence on asking about her wellbeing was getting annoying. She'd given birth to ten children. Why should she *not* be all right?

Except with this one, there hadn't been a happy father taking the child away, and she'd received no money. The child had just . . .

vanished and was out there to threaten everyone, wild and dangerous. Except no one would believe her.

"Where are your parents?"

"Ma is cleaning the room we were in yesterday, and Da is in the garden."

"The Chevakians let you do work?"

"They're busy fixing up the mess from yesterday. It's the least we can do."

Loriane nodded.

"Do your parents speak any Chevakian?"

"Not much. Just a few words."

That was still better than Loriane. It annoyed her to be dependent on someone else to make herself understood. "You speak some Chevakian."

"Only a very little bit."

"Better than your parents."

She shrugged. "I guess . . ."

"Could you teach me?"

"I don't know that much either. Most of the things people say I don't understand. They speak so fast."

"That's more than I understand."

"True."

There was an uneasy silence. Loriane looked at her hands.

"Myra, your parents don't believe me, right?"

She turned away from the washtub, and shrugged. "I guess not. It's hard for them to believe that something like that could exist."

"Do you believe it?"

Myra's eyes met hers, direct. "I believe you're a good woman, Mistress Loriane." Which was not an answer, but close enough.

She sighed and went back to her washing up. "My parents, and everyone in Bordertown, was scared of Tandor. He paid us, but no one understood why."

Loriane nodded. That was pretty much the deal with Tandor.

"We, the Imperfect kids, thought he was the best thing ever. He brought us presents and sweets. He let us have parties, and boys. He also showed us all these old books. We also thought he was weird." She paused to tip the water out of the tub. "Anyway, some of those books showed winged creatures. We asked about them, and he said they were real. He said they were powerful, and he also said that they were on our side."

"What is that supposed to mean?"

"I don't know, mistress Loriane. I really don't know. I thought his talk was boring. I wished I'd paid better attention. He was clearly trying to tell us something, but I have no idea what it was. If he meant that winged creatures were going to take over, I somehow prefer the Eagle Knights."

Loriane nodded.

There were voices in the hall outside the kitchen, and the sound of footsteps.

A woman's voice, unfamiliar.

Then the door to the kitchen opened and the cranky housekeeper Merni came in, together with a woman Loriane hadn't seen before. She had white hair and a face lined with age, but walked straight in the manner only someone of high birth can. Like the nobles in the City of Glass. In fact, she was very much like the nobles of the City of Glass, down to the richly embroidered robe that was surely too warm for the Chevakian climate.

She advanced into the kitchen and turned to Loriane. Her eyes were dark blue.

"You're the Pirosian?" she asked.

It clicked in Loriane's mind. This was Tandor's mother.

Loriane returned the woman's stare. What business did she have asking questions like that? *You're the Pirosian?* As if that was all that mattered about her.

She returned a mock bow. "I am very well, thank you."

"You *are* the Pirosian." The woman's gaze went to her belly, and her eyebrows rose. "Where is the child?"

"I'm sorry. I didn't catch your name."

In a few steps, the woman stood in front of Loriane and grabbed her chin. "Where is the child?"

"Why do you want to know?" Loriane swiped her hand away. She was *not* a naughty child. "Please don't touch me. The child is contracted to a man called Yanko in the City of Glass."

"The child is my son's."

"Can't. He's got no dick and no balls."

"Rude language doesn't suit a simpleton like you. Where is the child?" Her hand returned, the grip tighter this time, and she also held the front of Loriane's nightgown. For her age the woman was surprisingly strong. Loriane struggled to pull away, but didn't want to yank too much, for fear she'd rip the nightgown that belonged to the kind Chevakian man. They had already wrecked so much in his house.

"I don't have to tell you or give you anything. I don't recall Tandor ever speaking of you."

"You're a Pirosian whore, that's why. What my son has to say is of no concern of yours."

"Stop insulting me, and leave. The child is mine and I don't see why I should tell you where it is."

The woman said something in Chevakian, and a hulk of a man whom Loriane hadn't noticed entering the kitchen came forward. He grabbed her shoulders and pinned her to the wall with one hand while holding a dagger under her chin with the other.

Loriane yelped.

The grumpy housekeeper stood in the door that the man had left open, yelling at someone in the hall. Myra just stared.

Tandor's mother pulled a medallion from under her clothes. On it was depicted a creature the size of an eagle, but with wings of skin. Loriane had seen this creature before, on the cover of one of the books Isandor was fond of reading. It was the crest of the Thilleian house, the dacon. She'd always tucked those books away quietly, without commenting on them.

"Does this look familiar to you at all?"

"Um . . ." Loriane said. The tip of the dagger pricked in her skin. "I'm not going to tell you, and you can't kill me, because then no one can tell you."

"You insolent—"

People ran into the kitchen.

"Keep your head down, Mistress Loriane!" someone yelled near the door. Dara.

A blur in a brown shirt—Ontane—shot through the kitchen, knocking the guard half off his feet. He stumbled back. The dagger clattered onto the floor. Ontane scrambled to pick it up.

"You idiots. You don't know what you're playing with!" Tandor's mother held up the medallion.

Clearly, it gave off light or power of some kind, which Loriane couldn't see. Dara shouted.

Myra clapped her hands over her eyes.

In the corridor, the housekeeper screamed.

Loriane glared at the woman. "That thing can't harm me. I can't see icefire, and it has no effect on me."

"Me neither," Ontane said, brandishing the dagger. "I be fed up with this darned sorcery. Ye be going to leave Mistress Loriane alone. Or ye will have me to deal with."

The guard clambered to his feet, clutching his shoulder with one hand. He didn't meet anyone's eyes. He took the woman's arm and together they left the kitchen. When they had gone, Ontane shut the door and stuck the dagger in his belt.

Dara and Myra stared at him with wide eyes.

Loriane whispered, "Thank you."

"I protect my women, even though they don't always deserve it and don't appreciate it." He glared at Dara, who glared back at him. "There be no use in freedom, woman, unless we get rid of all self-righteous idiots, not just the ones we disagree with."

CHAPTER 12

CARRO DIDN'T DARE mention the visions to his father, or the figures he had seen made from fire at the time when he and the hunters had been trying to get back to the City of Glass, before they knew about the explosion. Heck, he didn't know himself what was real and what was a vision, and his father wouldn't like it if he heard that his son saw things. Carro was still waiting for the punishment he would inevitably receive for failing to meet his father's expectations.

So he trudged off and went to find Farey and Jeito in the dorms. Nolan, already aware of the task ahead, followed silently.

Then, under the jealous eyes of a few fellow Knights, who stood guard in the courtyard and who had been cooped up in the farmhouse for days, they went to the stable. The eagles started protesting as soon as he entered wearing riding gear—they had probably heard the tinkle of the metal rings the moment he'd left the farmhouse.

They, too, had been inside for days—to keep Chevakians in balloons from seeing them—and didn't like this situation. They stood in semidarkness in the musty farmhouse. They were all snapping at each other, and hissed at Carro as he walked past. His own eagle bent its head low down, spread its wings and fanned out its tail feathers, a strange mating behaviour that the females displayed if they were begging their riders for food or attention.

Carro scratched the animal on the head and untied the leather straps of the headgear. The bird jumped up and flapped huge wings.

The giant wing feathers brushed Carro's hair. A couple of other birds squawked. Carro's eagle hissed.

A stable boy scurried out, but Carro whistled hard and the birds calmed. In a very pleasing way, it surprised him. It seemed he *had* learned, even though the hunters still thought him a clumsy fool.

Jeito and Farey's eagles stood at the far end, eyeing Carro's bird. Compared to all these fresh, skittery birds, they looked sleek, but well used, and careworn, and rather blasé about their surroundings. Jeito and Farey needed only snap their fingers and they came strutting through the stable. Jeito hissed back at a bird that tried to peck at her eagle's feathers. Her hiss could almost pass for an eagle's.

"Trouble is, those birds don't get out enough," Nolan said.

"Tell us something we don't know," Farey said.

They led the birds outside in complete silence. Carro's eagle took large steps and lifted its feet high, and tilted its head this way and that to look at the surroundings. Carro held tight onto the reins even as it tilted its head all the way back to inspect the sky. Rider Cornatan stood watching, his arms crossed over his chest.

Carro met his father's eyes and a chill went over his back. This wasn't just a simple mission to find this army, or Rider Cornatan would have sent someone else. As for every one of Carro's tasks, there was a message in it. If only Carro understood what those messages were.

Carro mounted his bird and for the first time in days, rose into the air. The breeze through his hair reminded him painfully of his races with Isandor. The hunters were close behind.

"Better make some headway before daytime," Farey said.

At first daylight they had progressed deep inside Chevakia's central district, an area of farms and little villages interspersed with bits of land too rugged or steep to farm.

In an embarrassing way, Carro was glad to stop flying. Because they didn't want to be seen, they had to fly very high, where it was cold and squally winds tried to unseat them from their birds. It was hard to make out where they were going because a blue-grey haze hung over the landscape, turning the landscape into a grey soup. At times, Carro thought he could smell fire, but he was sure that was only his imagination playing tricks with him. He sat hidden deep within his cloak and spent a lot of time fighting visions.

When the night had become a grey and listless dawn, they made camp in a cave, in a rock wall overlooking a river. They went through the usual routines. Nolan made the fire while Farey plucked the bird that Carro had shot. He was proud of the kill—using a dart in mid-air —although he half-suspected that it had been an escaped domestic bird.

His next job was to haul water from the river.

He half-slid down the steep incline, holding himself by whatever trees and bushes were available. The water in the river was murky brown and churned in little eddies. The current carried sticks and leaves.

Carro dipped the bladder into the water and held it under until it was full. When he was putting the stopper back in, a tree trunk drifted past, its surface black and charred from fire. He noticed other blackened branches, too, washed up on the banks. And his mind went back to those apparitions of fire. These burnt tree trunks proved that there *was* a fire out there, up on the southern slopes.

He did not mention the burnt wood when he returned to the others. They had seen the same things he had, and would have the same worries, save that they didn't have memories of people made of fire. And even those worries wouldn't change the task they'd been given.

Nolan had the fire going and Farey had plucked the bird. Jeito sat a little apart from the others. She held a map, but wasn't looking at it. She sat staring into the hazy morning air. Carro poured water into the pot and put it on the fire to the side of the duck, which was already dripping fat and starting to smell good. Farey added the bird's wings and feet to the water. All this without anyone saying a word.

Carro sat down with his back against the rock wall of the cave. When he'd bent to get water, the Pirosian medallion around his neck had dangled free from his clothes, and now Farey glanced at it. Carro put it back under his clothes. Increasingly, Farey and Jeito's silence and looks made him nervous. Nolan tried to make small talk, joking about certain commanders at the farmhouse, but even he fell quiet until all that could be heard was the whistling of the wind around the cliff face and the occasional distant rolling of thunder.

Carro felt alternately hot or cold depending on the direction of the wind. Dark visions clouded at the back of his mind. The Outer City. Limpets on fire, the staff with the sink in his hand, the feeling of frost biting into his hands as the stone absorbed icefire. He tried to push those images away, and he must have drifted while staring into the fire because suddenly Nolan exclaimed, "I don't get it! What are you two on about?"

"Shut. Up," Jeito said.

"But you're behaving like idiots. We know we can trust him."

"He was the one who fucked up when we almost had them."

Carro was fully alert now. He met Jeito's eyes, which burned like furious coals. No, he didn't belong with this group, and had never truly been part of it.

"It was an honest accident," Nolan said.

"Oh, shut up, pup."

"What? Now I'm the pup?"

"You behave like one, so you get called pup. You have no idea what I'm talking about."

"Then enlighten me."

Nolan crossed his arms over his chest, his nostrils flaring. He was probably half a head taller than Jeito and twice the width.

Jeito snorted. "Anyway, I don't care if it was an accident or not, I don't want him with us if he's likely to fuck up again."

Farey said nothing, but he likely agreed. Nolan spread his hands, his eyes pleading, most likely for Carro to say something like, "But it was really an accident!"

But it hadn't been an accident, and Farey and Jeito would always know that.

Carro rose. He felt like he was trembling all over.

"I could leave, if you don't really don't want me along," he said.

"Leave?" Nolan said, his eyes wide.

"Yeah, go somewhere else. I've thought about leaving a lot."

"Deserting?" Nolan squeaked. "Your old man would go mad."

Carro nodded. "Sure he would." Rider Cornatan probably wouldn't rest until he was found, and punish the hunters for letting him go.

Both Jeito and Farey were looking at him with wide eyes. He had them. They listened to him.

"Why by the skylights would you do that?" Farey asked, now no longer angry. "You got your career mapped out. You will go straight into the upper command."

"Only because of my father."

Their silence surely meant agreement.

"Do you know the motto of the Knights?"

They frowned at the change of subject.

"Course we do," Farey said.

"Say it for me."

"Obedience, honour, honesty, humility and silence." Farey's voice had an impatient tone.

"The Knighthood is a proud institution," Carro continued. "We uphold the law in the City of Glass, we guard the Queen, we protect the citizens. We are what young boys dream of becoming, what young men sign up to join."

He let a silence lapse. Jeito and Farey's faces looked grim as if they knew what was coming. Nolan just looked puzzled.

"You don't have to answer this question, but what is honourable about killing the Queen and one of the citizens we are sworn to protect, when all she has done is to refuse to let herself be fucked by senior Knights? She is not sworn to obey any of us. She isn't in the Knighthood and doesn't even sit on the council."

If possible, the silence grew more intense. Even Nolan seemed to understand now.

"I grew up adoring the Queen. At home, we cried when Maraithe died." Even his merchant father had, he remembered now. "We lined up for half a day to catch a glimpse of her bier being carried to the shore. Our hearts broke for Jevaithi, the little girl in the procession, with her hand held by some stiff-faced maid. The tears on her cheeks were real. I was only eight, but I wanted to go to her and bring her my toys so she would be happy again."

Jeito nodded, her hands in her lap.

"When I joined the Knighthood, everyone spoke of serving the Queen. To us, she was the most beautiful woman in the world, if not the only woman in the world. To be a Knight was to dedicate your life to the Queen. We watched her tower room, we watched the corridors of the palace for glimpses of her. Which Knight has not dreamed of landing a job to escort her?"

No one replied to that question; they all knew the answer. Carro sat down pretending to be calm, but he trembled all over. By the skylights, what had gotten into him? The hunters were likely to kill him for saying all these things. But they were things that had bothered him for a long time. Certainly he could not be the only one thinking them?

In continued silence, Farey removed the cooked duck from the fire and cut it up. When he handed Carro a piece, his eerie grey eyes met Carro's with a burning intensity.

"You know that men have been killed for saying lesser things?"

"Yes," Carro said, although he did not. He was such a naïve fool and these hunters would probably be doubly keen to get rid of him now.

He'd hoped . . . he didn't know what he'd hoped, but all he'd received was silence. And he still didn't know what the hunters thought.

They ate, and tried to get some sleep. Farey and Nolan had no trouble, but Carro found it hard to sleep when it was light. He lay tossing on his mat, feeling the bumps and rough edges of the rock through the thin surface.

He must have fallen asleep, because suddenly, it was much later, and a shadow crouched over him. In one fluid movement, he rose, grabbed his knife and slammed the person into the ground, with the "oof" of breath being forced from lungs. It was Jeito, pinned under him. He was heavier than her and in this position, she could do nothing.

"My, I think the pup learned something," she said, her voice low.

"What the fuck were you doing, sneaking up on me like that?"

In a flash movement, she pulled him down by his shirt, and rolled over so that she sat on top. Her face was so close that he could feel the heat of her breath on his skin.

"Do you want to fuck me?"

"No."

She seemed taken aback by that reply, then one corner of her mouth went up. "You prefer boys, huh?"

"No."

"What's wrong with you?"

"Nothing." He looked into her puzzled face and added, "If, however, you think the things I said are true, I do appreciate your support. You are a good fighter, and I'd like to trust you as a friend."

"A friend, huh?" She gave a crooked smile. "I thought I was way too bitter to have any friends. Friends are for children."

"Are they?" Carro couldn't stop a memory of Isandor, and their innocent friendship.

Jeito crawled back to her sleeping mat, giving him strange looks. "You're weird."

Carro nodded. He had come to accept that.

But as Carro lay back down, he still couldn't sleep. In a roundabout sort of way, Jeito's odd behaviour must have meant that she approved of what he'd said, but that she was too afraid to say so aloud.

CHAPTER 13

THAT MORNING in the Proctor's office had the feeling of being at least two days long. Sady was fighting to stay awake, never mind concentrate, while reading through financial reports. The only thing that kept him from putting his head on the books and falling asleep was the sheer magnitude of the mess. Had no one ever given the budgets more than a cursory look? Not only was expenditure vastly bigger than income, columns had been added improperly, or not at all, entries had been left out of the total, and large amounts of money just vanished in between being transferred to different departments.

He didn't understand how Destran could have let all this happen, and he couldn't imagine how Destran had not known about these problems. Or—and the thought brought an increasing chill—was Chevakia in such perilous financial state that Destran had no choice?

Sady leafed through the books and found large chunks of data missing; and with every page he turned, things seemed to get worse.

There was a knock on the door and his secretary came in. "Um, Proctor, General Finnisius is here for you."

Sady frowned. "Did I forget an appointment?"

"No, but, um—" He lowered his voice. "He doesn't look happy."

What now? "Send him in."

The secretary vanished and a moment later, the general strode in with big steps, stopped in front of Sady's desk and gave an exaggerated bow.

He wore his dress jacket, with its many shiny buttons and medals of decoration.

"Good morning, Proctor," he said, in a tone as if measuring his words out precisely.

"Sit down," Sady said.

The general did so, placing each hand precisely on the corresponding knee. Catching the light that fell through the window, his hair looked more silver than grey. The general was closer to Milleus than Sady in age, and had led the army into Arania: a man of intimidating experience.

"About the refugee camps," the general said, and his voice sounded tense.

"Yes, tell me how the situation is there."

"We're withdrawing from the camps."

"You're—what?" The army was needed to distribute food, and to transport other supplies, and . . .

The general fixed him with an angry look. "There has been unrest amongst the refugees. Overnight, the southern fence was breached and a large number of people came into the camp—"

"Into? Who in mercy's name would want to—"

"—Chevakians, from the Ensar Road. They appear to be refugees from the border region, who thought the camp was for them and had been waiting on the other side of the fence. They'd run out of food, and got so angry that they cut through the fence."

"But what were these people doing there? There should have been signs on the Ensar road."

"I don't know. The fact is that those people were there and assumed the camp was for them."

"I told you to put up signs—"

"I'm running an army, not the roads department."

A tense silence followed.

The general breathed out deeply through flaring nostrils and continued, "Anyway, once they came in, we tried to turn the Chevakians around, but some refused to go. The road behind them was so crowded that they couldn't turn their vehicles, and if they could, there was no way for them to get out. More worrying, the camp's youth took the interruption as a sign to riot. There were fights overnight. They lit fires. Chevakians were injured."

What? "So you've lost control of the camp?"

The general gave him a hard look. "We have not *lost control*. We have set up a perimeter around the camp, because we can contain the site from there. There have been no more fights since dawn. We have also made a temporary road to allow the refugees on the Ensar road to leave."

"And there is a problem? It seems to me that you have the situation under control."

"We have the situation under control and are passing the responsibility for the camp to the city guards. My men are not equipped for this. Our duty is to protect the borders."

What was this? "We have criminals escaping from the camp. I want that perimeter completely closed."

The general nodded. "Done. The city guard is looking after it."

"I want all Chevakians out of that camp. Use health warnings to get them out. The southerners may have been decontaminated, but Viki has just shown me evidence that sonorics levels in the camp are still high."

"Proctor, there are two things you have to understand. First: the primary task of the army is to defend the country. We have a balloon base to run and an army to keep on its toes in case the south tries something funny. I'm sure you are aware of the rumours of a rebellion against the Eagle Knights. Last time something like that happened in the south, it spilled over the border. It is our priority to concentrate on that, and I do not want to take any more personnel from that task than absolutely necessary."

"Yes, I understand." Sady was getting irritated, and he felt irritated about being irritated, too. He should not let anyone get under his skin like this, but why did the man have to behave like such a patronising boor?

"Further, as I mentioned, a significant number of Chevakians came into the camp by their own choice. They remain in the camp *by their own choice* despite our directions for them to leave. They're demanding to be housed there, because they have nowhere else to go."

"They can't stay, for their own health. They are going to have to leave and come into the city. We'll process them here and—"

"They will not. They have their own tents and animals. They want a place to camp. Some of those refugees are quite violent. They are already angry with the doga for having forgotten about them. They have joined forces with the southerners. There will be fights."

Sady spread his hands. *You're commanding an army, for mercy's sake!* "Is that a problem?"

The general gave Sady a hard look. "Yes, and that is the second, and more serious issue. My people are soldiers, trained to fight the threat of war from outside our borders. My soldiers do not fight fellow Chevakians."

Sady looked at him in stunned silence, knew that the general was right—incredibly right—in principle, and knew he'd just made a monumental mistake that would cost him whatever respect he had with Finnisius, if there had ever been any respect in the first place.

The general was sure to think of him as a complete idiot now.

He would think a lot clearer if he wasn't so *fucking* tired.

"Then . . ." He paused to order his thoughts and found they were all over the place. Riots in the camp, murderers loose in Tiverius, no money to do anything, and strange sonorics patterns. "Tell me, what would you do?"

The tiny smile around the general's mouth was triumphant. No doubt he'd come here to tell Sady he was an idiot and succeeded, above expectations. "We have already isolated the camp and the wider area around it, so there is no risk to the citizens of Tiverius—"

"No risk? Tell me then why one of those southern refugees, a madman, is in the courthouse prison after having killed four people at my house?"

He had shouted much louder than intended, and Finnisius looked taken aback.

". . . killed?"

"Yes, two surgeons and two domestic staff. Orsan, one of my private guards, and I managed to catch him. He's a southerner, an escapee from the camp."

"Are you sure?"

"I don't know where else he would have come from. He's either escaped last night, or during transfer."

The general looked as if he'd just been robbed of an argument.

After a short silence, Sady continued, "So, what do you suggest we do about this problem? The one that the city guard is so brilliantly coping with?" And where had the general's mandate to pass major jobs like this onto the guard without the doga's approval come from?

General Finnisius' expression was hard. "Increase the number of people. Look, that is a matter for the high command of the guard."

"The city guard is not equipped to deal with large-scale riots." Sady glared back at the general.

"And I told you: we have a country to protect—"

There was a sharp knock on the door and Orsan came in. "I'm sorry to interrupt—"

Finnisius rose. "That's all right. I'm just leaving."

No, he was not. "I haven't finished."

"But I have." Finnisius left the room in complete silence.

Orsan stared after him, his eyebrows raised. His expression said, *What was all that about?*

Sady felt like saying, *Well, Orsan, that was about Finnisius being a prick and having assumed authority he does not have, and challenging me to put him in line.* And he didn't have the people to put Finnisius in line, and likely Finnisius knew that, too. The question was: who runs Chevakia? Between the army, the city guard and the doga, Sady wasn't sure he could answer that.

Orsan closed the door behind him, leaving an uneasy silence.

Sady sighed. "What's the matter?"

"Um, we just got a message from Farius. If you could please come home as soon as possible."

"From Farius?" He'd left the young guard with the southern family this morning. "Did he say what it was about?"

"No, sorry. It was a courier, not Farius himself. The message was short, but it said it was urgent."

What had happened at home now?

"All right." He rose from his desk, while the fear of last night reached cold fingers into his heart. Walking through his house in the dark, finding bodies surrounded by puddles of blood. Intestines spilling out. Lana's face ripped off—

Orsan left the room with him. As soon as he entered the foyer, people wanted to speak with him, including someone from the courthouse prison, presumably to talk about the interrogation of the prisoner, but Sady waved them all aside, left the building and got into the truck.

While the driver scrambled to build pressure in the boiler—usually he had notice of when the truck would be required and could prepare in advance—Sady wracked his mind about anything that might have become an urgent problem: Merni's grumpiness towards the southern family. Their quiet apologetic presence in the kitchen. They'd eaten all of the terrible roccas Merni had made just to be polite. They'd said nothing.

The woman Loriane—he hadn't gone to check up on her. Maybe she had collapsed. Maybe she had done something silly. Maybe there was something wrong with her. But no, what could be wrong with her that required his immediate attendance? Anything of that sort required a medic.

All he knew was that he had no time for domestic crises. He would have to send these people back to the camp as soon as the situation there was stable. Much better for them to stay with their kinsfolk—

The driver cursed fluently and hit the truck's brakes with force. Tyres slid over the pavement with a screech.

Sady had to hold onto his seat to keep himself from being flung onto the floor.

The vehicle skidded sideways and came to a halt. The driver cursed again. Orsan flung the door open and jumped out of the passenger seat.

Sady scrambled up. "What was that?"

"A child crossed the road in front of me!" The driver opened the door and let himself out of his seat. "She's stark naked! She didn't even look."

"Did you hit her?"

"I'm not sure. She was only a tiny thing."

Feeling sick, Sady followed him out of the truck, his head reeling. A child. He seemed to fall from one disaster into another.

A small girl sat on the pavement directly in front of the truck. She couldn't be older than two or three at the most. She had her knees drawn up to her chest and her chin leant on her knees. Sleek black hair fell to her shoulders. There was no sign of blood. That was something, at least.

"Little girl, are you hurt?" he asked.

She didn't reply. She clutched her knees and rocked backwards and forwards in a way that chilled him. "Why is a child like that alone in the street? Where are her parents?" Where were her clothes?

"I have no idea. She just ran onto the street." The driver looked around. His voice sounded shaken.

They were on the main street that ran to the hilly part of the City where Sady lived. The walls of the doga complex were to the right, the Chevakian Archive and the Scriptorium Library to the left. This street did not normally get busy with ordinary citizens; today, it was deserted.

Orsan knelt next to the girl. "It's all right. We won't get angry. We're just glad you're all right. Where are your parents?"

The girl looked up. Her eyes were bright blue.

The look on her face reminded Sady of the knife-wielding madman they had caught last night.

"I think she's too young to understand you," the driver said.

"She's southern," Sady said. Those eyes gave him the chills.

Orsan frowned at him. "From the camp?"

"Where else?" Anger flared inside him. That pompous idiot of a General Finnisius. If even a toddler could get out of the camp, then the army was doing a poor job indeed.

Sady held out a hand. "Come, I'll take you somewhere safe." How had she found her way here all the way from the camp? Did she even understand Chevakian?

She ignored his hand. He rummaged in his pockets, but any sweets he kept in there had long since been eaten.

"Come, I'll take you home."

As he touched her shoulder, she jumped up and retreated until she stood with her back against the truck.

"Whoa, I'm not going to hurt you."

She crouched on hands and feet, like a wild animal, and made a hissing noise that made the skin on the back of Sady's neck crawl. He retreated a few steps. Belatedly, he noticed how hot her skin had felt

"Whoa," Orsan said.

Sady said, "Don't be scared. I know people who can talk to you." Curse him. He'd been to the City of Glass twice, and had not learned one word of their language.

She ducked and ran, between Orsan and the driver's grasping hands, into the street.

"Mercy." Sady straightened, watching her cross the road without looking. Her black hair bounced over her shoulders.

"What was that about?" Orsan said.

"I'd like to know what southerners do to their children to scare them that much," said the driver.

"At least the truck didn't hurt her," Sady said.

Orsan said, "I'd like to know what she's doing here alone and why our men can't even keep a little girl in the camp."

"Good question. Make some inquiries."

When he climbed back into the truck, Sady could still see the wild look in those blue eyes. All through the incident, the girl had uttered not a single sound.

The driver dropped Sady and Orsan at the gate to Sady's house not much later. Sady was relieved to see that the house was still there. There had been no fires, the windows were all still intact and, when he entered, there were no dead bodies in the hall. That was at least something. Strange how expectations changed in a matter of days.

He walked into the hall. "Farius?"

There was no reply, but the sound of a male voice came from the kitchen, so he went in.

Farius sat at the table, opposite Merni, who leaned her head in her hands.

"Oh, there you are." Farius' voice sounded relieved. He got up from the table and came to Sady's side.

Merni didn't move.

"What's the matter?" Sady shrugged off his cloak. "I'm extremely busy at jwork." He found himself getting quite annoyed. He hoped this emergency was at least as bad as dead bodies in the hall, because he seriously had much better things to do.

"What is the matter?" Merni screamed, rising from her seat, pushing the heavy bench so hard that it wobbled. "You better ask what *isn't* the matter." Her eyes were wild.

"Merni, Merni. Calm down."

"No. I'm not putting up with any more of this. First we have a murderer attacking our house, then these people take over my kitchen, then this woman just barges into the house and tries to drag people out—"

"What in all of mercy's name do you mean?"

"That southern freak!" Merni buried her face in her hands and sobbed.

Sady frowned at Farius. "Does she mean Loriane?"

"No, we had a visitor. It was the southern woman who lives on Merchant's Hill."

"Lady Armaine?" The question was futile. There was only one southern woman in the merchant district.

"Yes, she came to the house, demanding to see our refugees. I said no, as you told me, but she had a private guard with her, and with Orsan being away, and Serran . . . I'm sorry, but there was little I could do to stop them. They came in anyway. The southerners were in the kitchen. The lady made straight for the woman Loriane. There was some sort of an argument with the woman, and the next thing the old lady attacked her."

"She attacked Loriane?"

"Yes. I don't know what either of them said. But I think she wanted Loriane to come, and Loriane didn't want to come, and then the old lady used her sorcery—"

Merni jumped up. "In my kitchen! Sorcery in my kitchen! Magic!" Her voice rose to a screech. "You always said there was no magic. But I saw it. In *my* kitchen."

"Shh, Merni, it's all right now. I'm sure there is a logical explanation."

"No, it isn't all right. I don't care for logical explanations. What-ever it was, that was no natural thing that she did. Next time she'll use it on us, like they did to poor Lana and Serran. And you expect me to sit here and wait until she comes?"

"It wasn't Lady Armaine who killed Lana and Serran. We caught the killer."

"How do you know that? As long as there is magic, they'll come and kill us. I don't care who they are. They're all evil. I tell you. Either these southerners are leaving the house right now or I am going—"

"You want to turn them out into the street?"

Her face blazed with anger. "You care more about them than about us, that is clear to me. I've had enough. I'm going back to my mother's house." She untied her house apron and threw it on the table. Then she stormed out of the room.

Sady rose. "Merni!"

But she was already halfway across the hall. She opened the front door, went through and slammed it behind her.

Sady slouched back to the kitchen, slumped at the kitchen table, leaning his head in his hands.

"I could have told you that was going to happen," Farius said. "She was extremely shaken by the events—"

"Farius, we are all shaken. Do you see me screaming at people?"

Farius sighed. "I'm sorry. I guess. I'm not sure she was all that well-suited to the job."

He was right, and although it felt wrong to admit it, he had employed Merni because Lana thought highly of her, and not because he liked her. "Suited or not, I don't think she'll be back."

Farius shook his head.

Sady sighed. "To be honest, I've had enough of people who blame me. If she doesn't want to work here, I don't *want* her back."

"I hope that doesn't include me."

"Include you in what?"

"People who blame you."

"No." Sady sighed. "Sorry, Farius. I'm just . . ." *not coping very well.* Tears pricked behind his eyes. He wiped his face with the back of his hand, but that only made it worse. "I'm sorry."

Farius nodded, silently, and made a show of staring at the table. Sady wiped his face again, the back of his hand wet with the tear that tracked over his cheek. He cleared his throat, attempting to get control over his emotions. "I'll need a new housekeeper."

Silence followed.

He sighed. "Do you know anyone?"

Farius shrugged. "I'll ask." Still looking at the table. "I have a cousin who may be interested."

"Tell her she'll have to deal with disruption, murder, and . . . magic."

"He."

Oh, all right, whatever. Farius' young cheeks had gone red.

There was a small noise in the hall. Loriane stood in the doorway, holding a bowl. She was still wearing the nightgown Merni would have given to her. Through the gauze-like fabric, he could see the outlines of her swollen breasts.

Had she been walking around like that all day?

"Farius, see that she gets something more appropriate to wear." And while Farius nodded, he gestured to her. "Come."

She came, and put the bowl on the table. There were brown crinkly things in it, like thinly-sliced, over-fried meat.

She said something and gestured at the bowl.

"What's this?" he asked.

"I have no idea," Farius said. "But it's not bad. The southerners made it this morning. I guess they didn't think much of breakfast."

"I guess they weren't the only ones."

A small smile played on Farius' lips. "They used the big frying pan and almost set fire to the stove. They also used up a lot of salt, part of why Merni was so upset, but they cleaned it all up when they finished. And whatever they call this stuff, it doesn't taste bad."

Sady eyed the stove, but couldn't see a sign that it had been used. He took a piece from the bowl and bit a tiny corner off.

A tang of salt and sugar exploded in his mouth. He put the rest in his mouth and took another piece.

"It's quite good," he said.

Loriane smiled at him and sat down on the other side of the table. Her blue eyes were intense, with long, dark lashes. The skin around her eyes showed some wrinkles and he guessed that she was in her early forties. Her top lip curved into two distinct peaks, and her bottom lip was full and round. She had let her hair out of the bun and it fell in a cascade of dark curls over her shoulders, except at the temples, where white hair mingled with black.

"Thank you," he said.

She attempted to repeat his words, which sounded foreign in her mouth. So she had been the reason that Lady Armaine came here? Lady Armaine wanted something from her? How did Lady Armaine even know that she was here?

From under her arm, she produced a book that he hadn't noticed her carry into the kitchen. He recognised the worn front cover in an instant. *Toki takes the train.*

He used to read this to his little nephews when they visited, when Milleus was doing the job he now did. Suri would bring the boys, and she would sit where Loriane now sat, watching the boys fidget and bounce while he read. He could still see their bright eyes and hear their voices. *Can we read Toki?* Over and over. They loved that book to death. When they stayed overnight with "Uncle Sady" and slept over in the room that Loriane now occupied, they'd take it to bed.

Loriane opened the first page. Sady didn't need the text.

"Toki got up early one morning. He was very excited. Today, he would take the train with its shiny red locomotive and its three carriages." Mercy, the memories. Two little boys and their lonely mother. Brown eyes and honey-coloured hair. Soft cheeks and a pale-skinned neck that he'd often dreamed of touching. Soft lips he had never mustered the courage to kiss. He fought to keep his composure.

Loriane said something, pointed to the written words and her mouth.

Farius said, "I think she wants you to teach her Chevakian."

"I know," Sady said, but his voice wouldn't cooperate. He cleared his throat, but the tide of grief had broken through the dam. Tears streamed over his cheeks.

From the corner of his vision, he noticed Farius rising. "I'm sorry, um, Sady, but I should be at the gate. I'll ask Orsan to come and take you back—"

Sady held up his hand. "Just leave me . . . for a bit." He took a shuddering breath.

"As you wish."

Farius scurried out, and Sady leant over the table, tears streaming over his face. It was a blessing for young men to be so unacquainted with grief that they felt embarrassed by the sight of an older man incapacitated with it. Suri, Lana, the young boys who used to love him and were now prickly adults. Milleus, who was still missing, who he should go and find instead of being Finnisius' pissing post.

He should never have challenged.

He should have kissed Suri, or Lana.

He should have brought Milleus home with him.

There was a gentle touch on his shoulder. Loriane.

He turned aside, meeting her blue eyes, sincere, with not a skerrick of shame or embarrassment in them. She reached out and wiped a tear from his cheek, and said something, her voice soothing. The corners of her mouth turned up.

"Thank you," he said.

She repeated, "Thank you." It sounded close enough.

Then she rose, and, like Lana would have done, poured him tea.

Sady patted the book. "Tonight, we start."

CHAPTER 14

TANDOR HAD NO IDEA how long he'd been in that cell when he heard footsteps and, more unusual, voices coming down the stairs at the far end of the corridor. A light came closer. Someone was shining a torch into each of the cells. Soft voices, in Chevakian. At least one man and a woman.

"This is the one," a man said. The glow of the torch showed a guard's uniform, but not one of the regular prison guards.

A light was directed into Tandor's face. His eyes saw only white. He tried to scramble into a standing position, but his hands were still tied and his side was too sore from where the guard had kicked him. His pants were soggy and wet and the skin underneath felt raw.

Someone stuck a key in a creaky lock. A bolt slid back with a metallic clang. The door opened. That was new. The prison guards only shoved the food into the cell using a long stick.

"Phoo, he stinks." This was a woman's voice.

A man laughed. "What did you expect?"

They came in, and shut the cell door behind them.

"How are we this morning?" another male voice asked in a mockery of friendliness.

"You're here to interrogate me."

"Good guess."

The guard slid the torch into the wall bracket, and slid a light sock over the flame, making the light spread more evenly.

Now Tandor could see who had entered: a guard, a man in the grey robe of the court and a woman wearing a light blue medical outfit. She had brought a bag which she set on the bench against the wall. She was taking things out and setting them on the wood. Glittery, shiny things with sharp points.

A chill crawled up Tandor's spine. "Whatever you have me here for, I didn't do it."

"You had a knife and blood all over you. The court will decide if that is enough evidence." But evidence never held much sway with the Chevakian courts. Someone was dead, so someone had to pay the price. Now that four people were dead, the price would be so much quicker. Chevakia didn't have large or many prisons for a reason.

The man stopped opposite him. "But we want to question you about something else."

He glanced at the woman and the array of metal instruments in the tray, one of which was a glimmering needle.

Tandor's chill increased. Some of the Chevakian poisons messed with your mind. There was way too much in his mind that could do a lot of damage to him, his mother or her cause.

The woman took a bottle with a clear fluid and filled the syringe from it. She tapped the reservoir to rid it of bubbles.

No, please.

She approached and knelt in the straw next to him. She was young, but with a hard set to her mouth. How many prisoners had she killed?

He flinched when she touched his arm, but it was only to wipe the skin clean.

"What are you doing to me?"

"We need some answers."

"You could just ask me."

She smiled, as if she enjoyed hearing the fear edge his voice. "The only reason you haven't already been tried and sentenced is that we need to know where the missing baby is. What you say now may be important for your sentence. If you speak the truth, the court may give you a more lenient sentence."

Yes, like hack his head off with an axe instead of hanging him? "If you release me, I can go and find this baby for you."

"Wouldn't you like that?" She gave a mock laugh and held the syringe up to the light. A drop of poison glittered at the sharp point of the needle.

Tandor flinched involuntarily.

"Where is the child?"

"I don't know. I didn't touch it. I didn't touch the others. I didn't kill them—argh!"

Quick as lightning, the woman had jammed the needle into his arm, and she held it there with one hand while pushing the plunger down with the other.

A sharp, tingling pain spread from his upper arm.

"What is it? It hurts." Already, he started feeling light-headed. "Argh, what is this for?" Part of some new Chevakian torture method? Sweat ran down his back.

She put a cup-like device over his nose and mouth. It had a soft rim that sat snug on his face and sealed it off from the outside air. The inside smelled stuffy. He tried not breathing, and turning his head away from the thing, but the guard came to stand behind him and held his head still. He kicked with his feet, but that brought the pressure back on the manacles holding his upper arms and they hurt so much that he forgot that he wasn't going the breathe and he screamed inside the mask. The poison made his mouth burn. He yelled and coughed, and coughed some more. Strings of phlegm coated his lips.

"What do you remember of last night?" the woman's voice sounded far off. His vision had gone funny, his tongue tingled.

"I don't know." Tandor closed his eyes to stop the world spinning around him. "I know nothing, do you hear? I didn't do it. I didn't kill anyone. I have never killed anyone. It was the monster." Chevakian didn't have a word for dacon.

"What monster?" the female voice came from far away.

By the skylights, he hadn't meant to say that. Why was he speaking Chevakian anyway? Weren't you meant to return to the language of your birth when layers of consciousness were stripped away?

Tandor struggled against the tide of dizziness, feeling himself being pulled away. He coughed, and the burning in his throat increased. He tried to shake his head away from the mask. "Take that thing away from me." He coughed again, big hacking coughs. He couldn't stop coughing.

The woman said something, and her companion withdrew the mask. Tandor drew deep wheezing breaths.

But the world he saw was not that of the dank prison cell. He was outside, in a field under a threatening sky.

He was Ruko, and he came to a halt at a ridge top that overlooked a patchwork of farm plots, roads, hedges and a scattering of houses. A wall of smoke hung at the horizon, black roiling clouds that hid the presence of the beings within.

He knelt in the dirt and pulled his dagger from his belt. He held the weapon out before him on flat outstretched hands. Strands of icefire danced along the blade. It was so strong here.

He balled his fist at the horizon. "What are you waiting for? Come and avenge what's been done to you."

For a moment, the clouds parted, and revealed a giant figure made of orange flame within. Yes, they were here.

First Ruko pulled his shirt over his head. Then he took off his pants. Last, he unstrapped his artificial leg. He bundled these things together and flung them downhill, towards the fire. "Sisters and brothers, I am here. Time has come for revenge!"

A shrill voice cut through the roar of the wind and popping of fire. "Come to me!" His girl. She was there, amongst the inferno. *She was here.*

The ice-cold wind buffeted his naked skin. It pimpled into goosebumps. The power, the majesty of it. And he was stuck in this stupid half-baked body. The girl had done a piss-poor job of turning him back into a young man. The stupid women then did an incomplete job of freeing him of the sorcerer's hold. The sorcerer was still inside him somewhere. He longed to sever those links forever. Life was better when he didn't have a heart.

He gripped the dagger more tightly, his hands trembling. The touch of icefire aroused him to the point of pain. Strands of blue whipped out from the menacing clouds and stroked his skin like a long-forgotten lover. He longed to jump into that ecstasy.

Could he do it?

He eyed the dagger again. In this form, he could never survive being swallowed by that cloud. In this form, his gratification would be short. Like the male spider, he'd risk his life to have sex once, and be eaten by his mate. That was not how he wanted to die.

After a deep breath in, he plunged the dagger into his own chest. Pain lanced through his body. Blood flowed over his hands, rivulets of it running over his naked chest, into his pubic hair. It hurt, it hurt, and it was so good. He lifted the bloodstained dagger and stabbed again, deeper this time. Blood dripped onto the ground and pooled around his legs. Icefire crackled along the edges of the puddles. He watched in a pain-filled haze, the dagger buried into his chest up to the hilt.

"Come to me!" he screamed, his voice hoarse.

They came, towering figures made of icefire, with hollow eyes burning with anger. Smoky hands reached out of the wall and grabbed him. Drew him within. She was there. Her fiery body engulfed him, dug into his chest to lift out his heart, dripping, and still beating. She flung it away. He would never have a need for it again.

He looked into her fiery face and said, "I'm yours." He grew and became one with the fire, and one with her. They tumbled over the countryside, eating up farms and forests and crops in the wake of their flight of love. And then he found release, and they lay, exhausted next to each other while flames digested their loot. With each breath, she grew fatter and rounder and more glowing and powerful. When the little flames had burnt all they could burn, she clambered to her feet in the middle of the blackened earth. She was enormous, her belly huge and gravid. She spewed a gout of fire that engulfed him with its power, and spewed again, and again, great globs of fire that moved, grew little legs, and coalesced into little fire people. She spewed and spewed, and the little people grew. Hundreds, thousands of them.

Tandor fell, and fell through darkness. Wisps of mist rushed past him, shards of voices, people screaming and calling out for him.

He screamed.

The dank prison cell returned, and immediately before him, the face of the woman in the light blue medical suit.

Reality returned. Ruko had joined his kin. They were on their way to avenge what had been done to them. They were after him, and the Knights.

"Interesting," she said, and she straightened. And then again, "Interesting."

He had no idea what she found interesting.

He looked up at her, his vision dimmed with pain.

"Let me go."

She laughed.

"Let me go, or you will all die."

"I don't think so."

"I'm serious. There is a great wall of evil coming this way."

She ignored him and started packing her things. Then she rose and nodded to the guards. They left the cell, locking the door behind them.

Tandor screamed after them. "Let me go. Let me go."

A rough voice came through the darkness. "Hey, new guy. We all tried the madman trick. Didn't work."

CHAPTER 15

LATE IN THE afternoon, when the light filtered by the cover of clouds was fading, a handful of people gathered on the windy hillside on the eastern fringe of Tiverius. Women, mostly, those Lana had maintained contact with during her life. Her sister, a middle-aged woman with a heavy brow, and a cousin Sady remembered sitting in the kitchen at times. Only six of them to watch the bier, with the cloth-covered body, be swallowed by flames in the fire pit. They stood a bit further away than usual, because the wind was particularly fierce and carried gouts of flame up the fire pit wall each time the wood popped.

The funeral celebrant from the Central Tiverius morgue—Sady made sure she got the best one—was unused to ceremonies with so few attendants. She seemed awkward, glancing from Sady and Orsan on one side to Lana's family on the other.

She spoke the rites. A woman Sady didn't know had tears running down her cheeks. How had she known Lana? The other women were glaring at him.

He stared at his hands, clasped before him. He felt too empty even to cry. He remembered the times—too many to count—that he'd come home late and he and Lana had sat in the kitchen. They'd talked about the doga, about Destran, about the weather.

They had never talked about *her*. He had known so little about her life. The celebrant spoke of a warm woman, with time to help everybody. Who had Lana helped, other than him or people in his household? Sady had no idea.

He had accused Milleus of being distant, but he was just as bad. Worse maybe, since he had never attempted to share his life with anyone, but had expected his household to serve him and him alone. Who was he to judge his brother's marriage? What made him remotely suitable to run the country? He was not. Even Viki, in all his inexperience, was doing better than he was. Sady had failed everyone in his personal life, and only did a marginal job of running the doga.

The wind whipped Sady's hair. In the city down the hill, the clock tower played its regular tune, and then the bell rang, twice. It chilled him.

He remembered the sonorics warnings as they had been drilled in to him when he was young. There was a children's rhyme based on it.

Once rings the bell and we stay inside,
Twice rings the bell and school is out,
Thrice rings the bell and we find the shelter,
But when it rings all the time, we run.
They should be inside on this day.

When the ceremony was finished, Sady and Orsan left with the small group of women. Past the walls that held little alcoves which contained the ashes of many great Tiverians of the past. Somewhere out there was the han Chevonian alcove, with the remains of poor Eseldus, and the remains of his parents who had such great hopes for both of them. They'd seen Milleus' rise as proctor, but had never seen how he was deposed.

The truck waited outside, and before climbing in, Sady turned to Lana's sister.

"Be well. I'm sorry we have met again under such sad circumstances."

He was not prepared for the vicious look in her eyes. "You should be sorry." Her voice was full of venom. "My sister looked after you with everything she had, and what do you do? Invite strangers into your house who kill her."

"It wasn't—"

"Just stop your politician's talk, all right? Barely a month into the job, and you're just as bad as the rest of them. Empty promises, excuses for sitting on your backside. Leave us in peace, and don't pretend that you cared for her, because you didn't."

Sady felt like shouting, *Woman, I've been working for my country and my eyes are about to fall out!* But that would only sound like a complaint. He *had* volunteered for the job, and in case he needed reminding, he had to ride the cart he bought, because there was no money for another one. And time could not be wound back.

The constant demands on his time, the constant crises. And now people were starting to accuse him. His time in the job would be short indeed.

He left quickly for the comfort of his truck.

On the way back, Orsan sat, silent, opposite him. Sady was painfully reminded how not even Orsan was a true ally. Orsan would never reveal all he knew. Working for the doga, he would be privy to other senators' schedules and appointments. All those people meeting at Lady Armaine's house. Why were there so many influential people in a setting that was almost worship? He bet Orsan knew who they were.

His household had been violated, his brother was still missing, despite the fact that the mire of the Ensar Road refugees was almost cleared up and all people housed in the city or camped in a field next to the Balloon base. Milleus' absence was like a hole inside him.

Spending resources on trying to find him would be considered inappropriate. Ensar itself was still not responding. If Milleus had been too stubborn to leave, he would now be dead.

The truck stopped at the house, and Sady could hardly carry himself up the stairs, he was so exhausted. Mentally, emotionally. He hoped that Farius had been able to find another housekeeper, and that no more crises had erupted since he'd left the house.

When he opened the door, it was to voices from the living room, which Sady hardly used these days. There was also a sound suspiciously like the banging of a hammer. Sady went into the room, where he found Farius and the southern man Ontane. Farius balanced precariously on a ladder in front of the window while hanging up what looked like a curtain rod.

"Oh, good afternoon, Sady," Farius said. He held a hammer.

"What in all of mercy's name are you doing here?" asked Sady, spotting on the floor a pile of old carpets which, judging by the musty scent, came from the store room. Some of those were from Milleus' old house, before he moved to the farm.

"There was a level two alert," Farius said, his face red. "Ontane says all the windows make our houses vulnerable to sonorics, so we're putting up stuff to cover them. Look." He climbed down the ladder and picked up a piece of paper. It had diagrams with writing in an unfamiliar scrawl and unreadable script. "He says that once sonorics motes get into a building, they bounce around the walls until they've lost all their energy. But now that energy is in the walls, radiating it back onto the people inside. It's less safe inside than it is outside. So that's why you board up the windows. If the house is closed, that makes a cage that the motes won't penetrate so easily."

That made a lot of sense in a warped sort of way. Through his fatigue, Sady regarded the southern man Ontane, who stood holding a box of nails. A scruffy sort of fellow, who strangely reminded Sady of his father's brother, who had never had much time for pomp and ceremony. It was a painful memory, after that funeral service. He fought to keep those thoughts away; tears were closer than any time during the service. He had never cared enough about his family. "But . . . you're putting a carpet up over the window."

"We ran out of boards. We figured this room was less important than some of the others, since you don't use it very often. We've already done all the important rooms. I thought you'd approve."

"I guess I do." Here they were, two complete strangers, making a home for themselves. "I'm just extremely tired." He shrugged, fighting tears. Lana's presence was everywhere in this house. "Do whatever you see fit, I'm going to bed. Just don't make any loud noises." Although he suspected that he would sleep through those as well. Belatedly, he added, "Thank you."

He turned for the door.

"Make sure you go past the kitchen," Farius said. "The women have been cooking."

The women? Did that mean he'd found someone to replace Merni?

"All right." Then he recalled that he had promised Loriane to start teaching her Chevakian.

Mercy.

Sady left the room. In the hall, he almost bumped into Dara scrubbing the floor.

"Oh, pardon me," he said.

She said something in her language. She looked busy and red-cheeked, so he sidestepped the wet patches as much as he could.

He went into the kitchen, where many oil lamps and candles lit the room. It was quite warm in here, contrary to the rest of the house.

"Uncle!"

One of Milleus' granddaughters in the kitchen. Reili was only eleven, but she was already as tall as an adult, albeit half the width. She was wearing one of Lana's aprons, and gave him a soap-scented hug.

"What are you doing here? Didn't you hear the ringing of the bell? Twice. You should stay inside."

"I am inside." She held herself straight with all her aristocratic righteousness. "I came here to bring roccas because Farius said this morning that Merni can't cook, and found a friend."

Myra stood at the stove and smiled at her.

"What about your mother? She'll be worried."

"She knows I'm here. Really, uncle, do you know how old I am?"

Yes, he knew, and eleven wasn't old enough to make her own decisions.

Sady walked to the stove and lifted the lid on the pot that stood there. It contained a concoction of strips of meat, beans and turnips. "What is this?" Sady asked. It smelled considerably nicer than it looked.

"I don't know. Myra made it."

"Is this what they eat in the south?"

Reili laughed. "No, silly. It's what we could find in the kitchen. You really should do some shopping."

Food supplies would be low. Sady had told Lana not to go out when the bell rang.

"If you would let me, I could—"

"No, Reili."

"We have suits, if that bothers you." Most families would have old suits stashed away somewhere.

"No. You should be home." It disturbed him how lightly the young generation took sonorics threats.

"But I'm bored."

"Your mother . . ." He didn't have a good relationship with Milleus' daughter-in-law. She frequently accused him of giving the girls strange ideas. Besides, he had no energy to argue with anyone right now.

The house was clean, and safe, and there was food on the table. What more did he want? Let his niece and her mother sort out their differences at home.

He sat down at the table next to Loriane. Someone had found her a simple woollen dress. Sady had no idea who it had belonged to—one of the past servants maybe—and the thing was probably horribly out of fashion, but it was an elegant dark red and looked gorgeous on her. She wore her curly hair loose, combed over her shoulders.

Toki Takes the Train lay on the table in front of her.

"Give me the book," he said, holding out his hand.

He dragged it over the table and opened it at a random page, which showed the boy Toki's house. "What's this?" he pointed.

"House," Loriane said. The word sounded strange in her mouth.

"And this?"

"Train."

"I've been teaching her some things. She's smart." Reili elbowed Loriane in the side. "You say it."

"You . . . want . . . tea?" Her blue eyes met his.

"Yes, I would love some."

She rose to get a cup. Her hair hung to halfway down her waist, which was quite narrow despite her recent pregnancy. Her hips were broad, and her backside round and full.

Farius came into the kitchen and sat at the table. "Doing well," he said in answer to Sady's questioning eyes. "My brother will come to help me with the guard duties."

"Thank mercy. No sign of the baby?"

"No."

Loriane stood at the porcelain cupboard, staring at the two of them.

"We'll find the child," Sady said, speaking clearly, so she could understand.

She came back to the table with cups. "I must warn," she said.

"You mean plead?"

"No. Warn."

"For what?"

"I don't know. She's been talking about this all day," Reili said while she emptied the washtub. Then she glanced at Myra. "The others don't like it when she brings it up. It's like they're embarrassed by what she's trying to say."

"Why?"

"I have no idea."

Sady took tea and cradled the cup in his cold hands. "Has Loriane been very upset?"

"Not that much."

Sady knew that southerners had strange family arrangements. Loriane was probably what they called a breeder, who bore children for other people. Judging by her age, it was unlikely to have been her first child

Loriane said, "Warn. Get away."

Get away. From what? "I don't understand," Sady said.

Reili said, "I've been saying that all day. It's something to do with the child."

Loriane's eyes were intense. "Yes. The child. Girl. Danger."

"Yes, we are trying to find the baby for you. We'll do our best."

But when he met her intense expression, he felt terrible. Chances that they'd find the child alive were very small.

He continued to go through the book with Loriane. His niece brought more tea, and then dinner, and they all ate around the table by the light of many candles.

They were a strange assortment of people. Farius seemed to get on quite well with Ontane, and it was comical to see the two discuss building methods—Farius' father was a builder—without a common language between them. Reili was disturbingly interested by Myra's baby, and she rocked the boy on her knee while Myra ate. Seeing Myra struggle, Sady resolved to find out how much it would cost to give her a claw hand.

They talked and laughed through awkward language mashups.

The mood was rudely broken up when Reili's mother came to the door. She not only scolded her daughter for staying out so long, but proceeded to tear a strip off Sady for allowing her daughter to interact with *these people,* so that she had to come and rescue the girl *in her state,* poking out her six-month-pregnant belly. Whatever Sady protested, it mattered not. She dragged her oldest daughter out and left Sady to stand in the hall. There was a soft noise behind him. Loriane stood in the doorway, backlit from the kitchen. Imagine what *she* had gone through, coming here on that disgusting train just moments before giving birth.

Sady suddenly felt very tired.

"Going to sleep," he said and mimicked sleeping.

"Good night."

"Goodnight to you, too."

He slowly climbed the stairs, and reassessed his earlier plans to return the southerners to the camp. Maybe what Lana's memory needed was for this house to be as much of a home as he could make it, in her spirit. And a house needed people. He quite liked these ones.

CHAPTER 16

JEVAITHI WOKE in the comfortable nest of furs and the familiar feeling of soft leather against her naked skin. She wondered why she had awoken, because it was still pitch dark. The breeze made the sides of the tent billow inwards.

There was a small noise close by, without a doubt inside the tent. She reached out to the other side of the bed where Isandor had climbed in some time long after she had gone to bed. The spot was empty, but the furs still warm.

"Isandor?" she whispered, straining to see.

The noise stopped.

"Go back to sleep," he said.

"What are you doing?"

"Please, go back to sleep."

She sat up, drawing the furs over her naked skin. The tent cloth flapped with a gust of wind that made her shiver. Something jingled that sounded like the clasp of a cloak being done up.

"Isandor, please. Let me know what's going on." She rose from the bed and padded across the earthen floor where she sensed Isandor standing. She touched his chest, and her fingertips met the warm fur of his cloak. "You're going outside?" She went to kiss him, but he brushed her off, just like he had earlier that night, after finally coming to bed. It opened up a big hole of uncertainty in her. This was the third day that he hadn't made love to her. Did he not love her anymore? The thought closed on her like a vice. Everything had changed since she'd gone back to being Queen. They should never have come here, but stayed on Milleus' farm.

"Where are you going?"

"There is something I need to do," he said.

"I'm coming."

"No. It could be dangerous."

"I'm still coming." She grabbed her clothes and started to pull them on, humid and dirty as they were. "Do you think nothing we've done so far was dangerous? We were going to stay together. You promised. And any trouble you make I will have to deal with anyway."

"All right." He snorted. "Don't tell me I didn't warn you."

She finished dressing and followed him out of the tent, where two shadows fell in step with them.

Isandor said, "These are Kenna and Zito. We can trust them."

At least whatever he was doing wasn't so secretive as to require the absence of guards. That comforted her, a little.

After the Chevakians had withdrawn, people had rearranged the tents in a more familiar pattern of circles. The open space of the circle that included their tent was deserted. The fire in the open-sided cooking tent had died to a feeble glow. Jevaithi could still smell the scent of the animal that had been roasted for dinner, and could still taste its tangy meat which stuck between the teeth.

They walked into the night. The cold and humid air bit into parts of her skin not covered by the cloak. The only sound was the whistling of the wind through the guy ropes and the occasional flap of canvas.

Isandor led the group into a narrow alley sheltered from the wind. At the end, they came to the large tent where Chevakian trucks had brought supplies that afternoon. Isandor pushed aside the flap and disappeared inside. The guards and Jevaithi followed, into darkness. One of the guards lit a torch, a small pool of orange light. Jevaithi was surprised how young the boy Zito was—no older than fourteen. The other guard, Kenna, was a young woman, probably in her twenties. She bowed when meeting Jevaithi's eyes.

"I'm honoured to serve, Your Majesty."

Isandor bade them to be silent. The boy held the torch aloft, and its long flapping flames lit stacks of boxes around the tent's perimeter.

Isandor walked around and studied them all, before selecting one and using his dagger to pry it open. Jevaithi didn't dare say anything, but wondered what he was doing. The Chevakians had brought these things, why should they contain anything other than food and clothing?

Isandor said, "Come on. If you want to be of any use, give me a hand."

She took the dagger Zito offered her and carefully inserted it in the crack in the wood between the lid and side of the crate. She had no idea how to do this type of thing, and felt awkward, afraid that she was going to make a noise and bring *someone* down. The Brothers most likely, since they had overseen the unloading of the trucks.

They worked quickly, and when Isandor lifted the lid off the crate, the torchlight hit . . . the metal barrels of Chevakian guns.

She looked into Isandor's face, sweaty with the effort. "Did you know this was in here?"

He met her eyes, his expression grim. "I wasn't sure, but I had a suspicion. You know how the Chevakians brought in supplies earlier today? Well, I saw Simo talking with one of them and he seemed to know this person. I thought it was odd, because why would he know Chevakians? Also, this happened when the other Chevakian truck drivers were arguing with Milleus and his group. While that was going on, these few Chevakians were unloading these boxes from the truck. I suspected there was something odd going on."

Jevaithi had seen that, too. With nothing else to do in the camp, and a plethora of guards keeping her from going to see Milleus, how could she have missed the supply trucks coming in? However, she had not thought there was anything unusual going on.

"But why—"

Then there was a noise. Isandor froze. Kenna yelped.

A huge man stood behind her and clamped a hand over her mouth. "Be quiet." His voice was rough, his clothing black and beard big and bushy.

Three other men pushed in through the tent flap and moved into the light. Two of them were equally huge. The third man was Simo.

"Well, well, what do we have here?" he started, in his usual sarcastic voice, but then he noticed the open crate with the guns and glared at Isandor.

For a moment, no one said anything. Jevaithi held her breath, expecting Simo or one of his hulking henchmen to lash out at Isandor. She shuffled closer to him. If they wanted to harm him, they would have to harm her first, and she had a feeling that they might *want* to harm her, but couldn't afford to do so. She felt Isandor's warmth behind her and felt for his hand. Their hearts beat in unison.

"So, we have two children snooping around in places where they are not allowed."

Isandor said, "You trade weapons with the Chevakians behind the Queen's back."

Jevaithi tightened her grip on his hand in the hope he wouldn't try to do something stupid. The other man still held Kenna, and Zito stood, wide-eyed and white-faced, clutching the torch. Fortunately, it hadn't occurred to him to use the dagger at his side, because if he had, it would only have led to disaster.

Simo laughed. "You're surprised that the world doesn't revolve around you?"

If Jevaithi had been uncertain about Simo's loyalty to her, she was certain now. To him, her turning up had been a nuisance. The common people's adoration of her was a hitch in his plans.

She said, "Actually, a lot of the world of the refugees does revolve around us."

Simo took a few steps towards her. Side-lit by the torchlight, she could see the pores on his face. His mouth quivered. Jevaithi braced herself to be hit in face, but he breathed out forcefully, and retreated. He gave a mock bow. "Your Highness, how long would your popularity last if, through your actions, the people went hungry?"

She glared back at him. "Is that a threat?"

"If you choose to see it that way." He flicked his eyebrows in a *see if I care* way. "We have Chevakian supporters who bring us supplies we need, rather than starvation rations."

"Is that so?" Isandor said. "I guess we can also eat guns. I think we might complain to the Chevakians that they delivered some wrong crates."

Simo snorted and spread his hands, rolling his eyes at the ceiling. "Why am I even arguing with a couple of children?"

"Because you need us."

Simo whirled at him. "I don't need you."

To Isandor's credit, he didn't flinch or back away. "You do need us, because most people in the camp are curious about you, happy that you're not Knights, but don't support you outright either. They do, however, support the Queen."

That was the truth, and Jevaithi read it in Simo's face. If the Brotherhood had wanted power, they'd failed at making clear what they stood for.

"Who are these Chevakian supporters of yours?" Isandor continued.

"Private Chevakian citizens."

"Chevakians, helping us? Why would they do that?"

"There are plenty of reasons. Maybe to help an overthrow of a regime they don't like. Maybe some of us, whose families were killed, fled to Chevakia." Simo's voice had a distinct sneering tone.

"The old king's family, you mean." Isandor's voice was cold.

Simo glared.

"Say it aloud, if you dare. It's an ill-kept secret that the family of the old king fled to Tiverius. These are families of people who thought it was fine to murder anyone who didn't agree with them, and reigned with terror through heart-less servitors—people who terrorised the City of Glass. These are the families who want to see that regime reinstated!" Isandor was yelling now, and more people rushed into the tent.

"Isandor!" Jevaithi grabbed his arm, but he paid her no attention. His muscles were tight as a spring.

"No," he said, brushing her off. "This needs to be said. Because you know what? We are the old king's family, too. And we never agreed with what he did, and neither do all the people out there."

Simo's eyes narrowed. His voice was low and threatening. "What are you? A spy for the Knights?"

"I'm a *Knight,* not a spy for them. I'm a Knight committed to the honour of the Knighthood, not to the murder of innocent children, the raping of new recruits and the imprisonment of the Queen. Jevaithi and I are a full-blood Thilleians purer than any of you. We are also sick to death of this clan business, which hasn't done the City of Glass any good for the last fifty years or more."

"You are a traitor."

"Not me. You will be a traitor if you accept help from people who haven't lived in the City of Glass for fifty years, a traitor to your own country. The people of the City of Glass don't *care* about the perpetual arguments between Pirosians and Thillei. They want peace. They want this stupid vendetta to be forgotten. Buried. Never to be resurrected."

"How dare you say that to someone whose family was murdered by Pirosians?"

Isandor grabbed Simo's black cloak and drew him so close that their faces almost touched. "Pirosians almost killed me, but the woman I call my mother is Pirosian. A Thilleian sought to turn me and Jevaithi into servitors, but Jevaithi is pure Thilleian and I love her. Let people be judged by their actions, rather than their blood. I've had enough of this stupid clan stuff. Enough!" He let go of Simo's cloak, and Simo stumbled back to keep his balance. His eyes were wide. Clearly he had not expected such strength in a *child*. "I'm going to let the Chevakians know that these weapons are here, so they can take action against the people from Tiverius who brought them. Having heard about the Chevakian laws, I am sure that inciting rebellion is an offense punishable by death."

Simo eyed Isandor as if sizing up his chances in a fight, but decided against it. "You, boy, what do you think you are?"

"I am Isandor. I am Thilleian. I am an Eagle Knight. I am a butcher's assistant from the Outer City. You can choose which of those reasons you want to use to justify killing me, but I am what I am, and I want the clan fighting to stop."

Simo looked like he was about to explode.

Isandor turned to the man who was still holding Kenna. "Let her go. This achieves nothing."

To Jevaithi's surprise, the man did as Isandor said.

He continued, "We're in a foreign country, and none of us know where the main body of the Knighthood is, whether they're still alive, and if so, whether they'll come to join us, and if they'll come peacefully. One thing I know, if they come to fight, none of us stand a chance."

"What did you think the weapons were for?" Simo said.

Isandor nodded. "Point made. But when they turn up, we're better off to talk to them. A lot of Knights adore Jevaithi."

Simo said nothing. Jevaithi didn't think he liked making bargains with *children*. On the other hand, he didn't disagree either.

"Come," Isandor said to the two young guards.

The left the tent, to find that a huge crowd had gathered outside in the dawn light.

A voice came from somewhere at the back. "Mercy, I leave you for a day, and you already create trouble."

"Milleus!" Jevaithi let go of Isandor's hand and threw herself in Milleus' arms. He smelled of goats and smoke and engine oil.

"Now, now." He patted her hair. "Come, you two, let's get some milk."

Some time later, the three of them sat next to Milleus' truck clutching cups of warm milk. Milleus told them of how the soldiers had refused to let the Chevakians out, and Isandor told him of the weapons.

Milleus' eyebrows rose. "You were sure these were Chevakians? Why would Chevakians send weapons?"

Isandor looked over the rim of his cup. "I can think of only one reason: to fight the Knights."

"But there are no Knights here," Jevaithi said.

"They are somewhere. Maybe the Chevakians know where they are."

"Still, why would Chevakians care?"

"I think," Isandor said and let a silence pass as he sipped. "I think that the survivors of the royal family who fled to Tiverius have somehow managed to get a lot of supporters. I think that the Chevakians preferred dealing with the old royal family. They might have been bad to their own people, but they were more open to the Chevakians. Back then, there were ambassadors, and Chevakians came to the City of Glass wearing strange suits. After the king fled, the Knights had this idea of solving the fertility problems in the City of Glass by bringing in Chevakian girls. We were told they came voluntarily, but the Chevakians know otherwise. The Knights haven't attempted to trade with or even talk to Chevakia. I think it's understandable that Chevakia would support anyone who tries to get rid of the Knights."

"Mercy," Milleus said. His eyes were wide and in the wan dawn light, he looked pale. "Mercy," he said again. "I think you could be right. And I think I know exactly who you're talking about."

"Tandor," Isandor said.

"His mother," Milleus said.

"Are you kidding?" Jevaithi said. "She's not even a real princess. She married into the royal family."

"Those are often the worst," Milleus said.

Isandor met Jevaithi's eyes. "They forget one thing: we are old king's great-grandchildren."

"We?"

She met his eyes, and was shocked to see them overflowing with tears. His heart beat in her chest like crazy. Then he said, "King Caldor's son the crown prince was married to Tandor's mother. She was pregnant with Tandor when she fled to Chevakia. Through Tandor's machinations, the baby daughter of the queen installed by the Knights was swapped for Maraithe, who had a lot of Thilleian blood. Tandor posed as merchant and fathered her twins. You were one of those. I'm your twin brother."

CHAPTER 17

CARRO AND THE HUNTERS packed up their camp at dusk. They rigged their gear to the eagles' saddles and mounted their birds, still without many words spoken. Jeito, who had studied the maps, led the way, over the valley through which the muddy river with the burnt logs wound its way, and over the slowly-rising farmland.

The sun came out right at sunset, a rare occurrence with the recent heavy cloud cover. The sky turned deep red with the haze that seemed to have gotten stronger. Lit from below, the bank of clouds in the south looked menacing, as if edged in blood.

By the skylights, it looked like the worst of the weather was still to come.

Soon, the town of Twin Bridges came into view, a loose scattering of houses at the place where two rivers joined. From here, the road split, with branches going off in two directions, each with its own bridge. The railway line did the same, following the road. The main track went to the west and would join with the Fairlight line, and the other branch kept going into the ranges, where it would go as far as a town called Solmeni.

From Carro's height, the train tracks were easy to spot, straight unnatural lines cutting through the landscape. The metal occasionally glistened between the trees. The roads were harder to see: narrow, and often overshadowed by trees.

They circled over the town a few times while Jeito squinted down,

759

trying to get her bearings. There was supposed to be a narrow forest road leading towards a timber town, long since abandoned.

The town of Twin Bridges itself looked peaceful. Sparse lights lit the street and smoke curled from chimneys. The forest to the south was a black mass of trees.

Jeito whistled. She had found the track and they set off in the direction of the highlands, rugged hills with rocky outcrops.

The forest underneath was now so dark it was almost black. The tiny lights of the town faded on the horizon.

It grew dark and the air became very cold. Occasional gusts of wind brought images to Carro's mind, shadows moving beyond the edge of his awareness. Icefire was in the air; he could feel it. He lashed the reins around his wrists, hoping they'd find the hidden army before he got any full-blown visions.

Those clouds on the southern horizon were very scary, worse than blizzards in the City of Glass, worse than the worst weather he had seen. Occasional flashes of lightning flickered within the cloud tops, and endless series of anvil-shaped protuberances jutted from the top.

Jeito whistled and sent her eagle plummeting towards the dark forest. Carro and the others followed.

Now at a much lower height, he could make out a forest clearing with dark shapes that looked like buildings. The abandoned logging settlement. There were no lights.

They brought the eagles down in the middle of the clearing.

Carro's bird skittered, its wings held wide as if ready to take off again. He had to hold tight to the reins to stop it. It pulled the straps, uttering *kek, kek, kek* sounds, the eagles' alarm call.

Farey lit a torch.

Nolan's bird was also protesting, hissing in a low crouch, with its wings spread. Farey's magnificent male gave it a disdainful look.

The pool of light cast by Farey's torch showed nothing more threatening than a forest clearing with a few dilapidated shacks. The roof had collapsed in one of them. Another had sagged sideways. Thick layers of moss grew on the timber beams. This did not even deserve the name *village*.

The grass underfoot was short with longer clumps, a sign that the field had held animals at some time in the recent past. The air was thick with haze and smelled of fire. The wind whipped the treetops, making branches whistle.

Carro shivered. "Where is everyone? You're sure this is the spot?"

Jeito snorted. "Who got the directions, you or me?"

Carro's eagle gave another alarm call.

"Shut that bird up, will you?" Farey said.

Carro threw the long end of the reins around the eagle's beak and pulled the head closer. It strained against his grip, its eye rolling.

One major thing that alarmed eagles was unfamiliar other eagles, often wild birds, which would sometimes attack intruders into their territory. But they were far outside the Aranian border ranges where wild birds lived.

A gust of wind blew his hair to one side. Voices whispered in the air. Isandor, his mother, the merchant, his sister's whiny voice, Caman and Jono's sneering, the Tutor berating him. All those voices yelling at him, or quietly scolding him. *You had the chance, why didn't you say anything?* or *You're a coward.* Yes, he was a coward, and all those people in his past life could tell.

"Over here," Jeito called from the darkness, jolting Carro from the edge of his torment.

They went into the forest, where huge trees towered above them, their straight majestic trunks rising out of reach of the pool of light from Farey's torch.

The eagle, still with the leather strapped around its beak, was growling and pulling so hard at the reins that it cut off the circulation in Carro's wrist. On top of whatever disturbed it, eagles disliked being in enclosed spaces. They were birds of mountaintops and open plains, not of forests.

Jeito stopped and whistled.

Further up the slope, someone returned the whistle.

It was a single man, in a Knight's shorthair cloak, but wearing a Chevakian-style shirt and trousers. He carried a Chevakian oil lamp, with glass sides that stopped the flame being blown out.

He called, "Who are you?"

Carro wrestled through the shrubbery to pass Jeito, pulling the Pirosian medallion out from under his clothes. On this mission, talking was his task. The man was taller than him, with grey southern eyes, and carried a southern-style crossbow.

"We've come from Tiverius. We assume that you didn't get the Supreme Rider's message?"

The man's gaze rested on the medallion. His face remained strangely blank. For someone having lost contact with the rest of the army, Carro would have expected joy at hearing from other countrymen.

"You'll want to speak to the command," the man said. "Come."

He turned and led the group further up the slope. The shrubbery grew dense here, and the eagles snapped and hissed at passing branches. Carro's eagle uttered sharp calls that eagles used to establish each other's presence. Even though he couldn't see them yet, there were definitely eagles here.

The path became steeper and led up to a rocky outcrop, under an overhanging rock. Underneath, a single light marked the entrance to a cave. The ground was dry, sheltered from the weather, and marked with many eagles' footprints.

The cave was much larger than he had thought. Rough walls suggested that it had been enlarged by people. Carro's eagle skittered and pulled at the reins. It yanked so hard that Carro almost lost grip of it.

"The birds go in here," the man said, indicating a dark entrance to the side. It smelled like birds, too. A young boy came out with a basket containing hunks of meat. All of a sudden, the eagles were all over him, pushing each other to get to the food.

By the skylights, those birds had no principles or manners at all. So much for being scared of confined spaces.

The man led Carro and the hunters further into the mountain, along a hewn passage where occasional lights flickered on the walls.

"Who made all this?" Carro asked, and his voice echoed in the passage.

"This used to be an outpost for the Chevakian army," the man said. "Back in the day when the border regions were still independent."

Carro didn't know that much about Chevakian history.

"The army had to hide here, because the border regions had strong armies, and morale amongst the Tiverian army wasn't always high. They used these caves to hide their supplies and give their troops a comfortable life to keep them from starting a mutiny."

They arrived at another opening where soft light slanted into the passage. Inside a low-ceilinged chamber, a camp office had been set up, with proper furniture and other things that must have been here before the group came.

Farey, Jeito and Nolan remained at the door.

Carro and the Knight headed across the floor, with people stopping their work and looking at them. Many fell silent and followed the group with their gazes. Again, Carro had expected the Knights to be cheered by their arrival. And what were all these people writing anyway? No, they weren't all writing. A group of Junior Knights sat around a lamp, sewing fur pelts together. Another group was using twine to lash mesh made from sticks to the bottom of sturdy poles. Those looked like snow walkers.

They came to a halt at a field desk at the far end, where a Senior Knight sat. Carro recognised his short, grey-flecked hair, his alert face and penetrating eyes: Eminent Rider Barton, a member of the Knights' Council.

The man who had brought him here retreated. Rider Barton rose and greeted Carro, his gaze on the Pirosian medallion—Carro started to wish he'd put the damn thing under his clothes—and they both sat down.

Carro spoke into the uneasy silence. "I am glad that we find you well. It's good we had instructions. You would have been hard to find."

"This is a dangerous area," Rider Barton said. "We were forced to hide. The Chevakian army probably suspects that we're here. There are many balloons during daytime. You took a great risk coming here."

"We didn't see any balloons."

"You were very lucky." Yes, Carro remembered this man from the eyrie. Highly ranked, softly-spoken, but with a reputation for being merciless on his enemies in that same, kind voice.

"You didn't receive prior messages from Tiverius?"

"No, we haven't received anything."

"Rider Cornatan sent a messenger. You've seen no sign of him?"

"We've seen no one. What was the message?"

"Rider Cornatan requests that you come to Tiverius."

There was a small silence and the Rider Barton said, "Certainly. We were already preparing for that mission."

With furs and snow walkers? Right. But Carro let it rest. It was not in his power to question, and it wasn't in Rider Barton's interest to discuss the unit's intentions with a messenger.

They went on to discuss the route Carro and his companions had taken, and if they'd run into any Chevakian army outposts.

"We'll leave tomorrow at dusk," Rider Barton declared. "I'll ask the men to put you up in one of the dormitories. It'll be crowded, but dry, safe and out of the wind."

On the way back through the chamber, many gazes followed Carro. No one smiled. When he was in the passageway, the men continued what they'd been doing, never mind that those activities would be futile.

The hunters waited for him, but because they still had a guide, Carro couldn't ask the hunters for their impression.

First they went back to the eagles to get their packs. Now that Carro's eyes were better attuned to the dark, he guessed there were well over a hundred eagles in the chamber. The poor birds were chained up at very close quarters and some had already been biting at each other's feathers. He was glad his own bird would not need to stay here for more than one night. With no air coming in, it stank of dead meat in here. His eagle was tied up with a couple of local birds which were all jostling and hissing at each other. Carro stroked the feathers on his bird's neck to calm it. Then he noticed that one of the birds in the cluster next to his wore a harness. It was well-made, of the type that hunters often wore. His father would have used hunters as messengers.

He stared at the bird, contemplating the meaning of this. Did it mean that Rider Barton had lied about the messenger not having arrived? If so, then why and where was the man? And why would Rider Barton not want to obey Supreme command orders?

The answer seemed clear from what he had seen in the chamber: because they had been planning to return to the City of Glass.

Here, within hearing distance of the stable boys, he dare say nothing, but while another man led them to the dormitory, he held Farey back.

"We'd do well to make sure one of us stays awake at all times. I wouldn't be surprised if Rider Barton is a traitor. I think the messenger arrived, but was killed."

Farey said nothing, but nodded, his expression grave.

The dormitory was indeed crowded, and there was barely any room for extra sleeping mats. Carro's mat ended up being next to an Apprentice with a face so young that he could not possibly have any violent intentions.

Carro remembered how he had joined the Knights, probably similarly fresh-faced and innocent. It seemed such a long time ago. He asked the young man how long they'd been here.

"Too long. The only time we get to go out is for hunting and the older Knights mostly do that." And he added to it, "Sir."

"I'm Carro."

The young man blushed.

"Before we came, you were planning to return to the City of Glass?"

He shrugged. "That's where the command said they thought we'd go next. Many of the older Knights wanted to go, you know, because there'd be people there who might need our help. We heard of people burnt and all. Can't just leave them to die, can we?"

Carro nodded, and saw his family—the family he had grown up with, bleeding and dying in the street of the Outer City, while he slept safely.

These were good men, and his message put them in a difficult position.

But Rider Barton was a true Knight, and he obeyed.

CHAPTER 18

"**O**VER THERE is my house." The old lady pointed a crooked finger past Sady's nose.

The truck turned the corner into another deserted street and stopped in front of a well-maintained house in the merchant district. Orsan got out and opened the door for Sady, who climbed out and assisted the old lady down to the pavement. He took her arm and helped her through the gate and up the path. A middle-aged man opened the door, watching this high-profile visitor to his house with an expression of great surprise. From his clothing, Sady judged him to be a merchant, already in the long trailing dust robes merchants wore in the warehouses, and he presumed he'd dug out this clothing for sonorics protection, because, failing protective gear, residents had been urged to cover their skin as much as possible if they needed to go outside.

"My son-in-law," the old lady said. She shot the man a triumphant look that hinted at a disagreement about her visit to the Proctor's office.

The man bowed. "Thank you, Proctor, for honouring us with a visit."

"I apologise for the lack of warning and I wish it were in better circumstances," Sady said. "Can you show me the scene?"

"Follow me." The man turned and went down a corridor, his wide robes brushing the walls.

The house smelled of cooking. A couple of young children ran to a doorway, giggling. A woman's voice scolded them to be quiet. They watched, wide-eyed, as Sady and his entourage passed. Sady could only imagine how bored they were. School had been closed since he ordered the bell to be rung twice.

Rooms on either side of the hallway were richly furnished with warm touches from loving family members. How empty and cold his own house was, how devoid of life. Although, without Merni's crazy antics, this morning's breakfast had been an improvement, if a linguistic muddle. Loriane was up to naming the items in the kitchen. That dumpy woman Dara turned out to be a pretty decent cook. He'd sent Farius on a shopping expedition while Ontane guarded the gate. It was a strange combination, but it worked, for now. As a bonus, Ontane didn't need to cover up for sonorics protection.

They went through the laundry, and then the man preceded him into a courtyard and stopped. "This is where I found him."

Amongst a bucket of spilled grain and uprooted hedges lay a blood-covered body, an old man, on his side. His clothes had been slashed to shreds, and the skin underneath torn open as if he were a fruit, showing ribs in the gaping cavity. Chunks of flesh lay on blood-soaked paving, and other chunks had been dragged off, as evidenced by trails of blood.

Feathers were stuck in dark red puddles. There were at least two bloodied carcasses of ducks. The front of the duck house had been smashed in, and the remaining birds, about twenty or so, waddled around in a tight group, backwards and forwards along the courtyard's back wall.

"I'm sorry that you have to see this, Proctor," the man said. His voice wavered for a moment. "I don't understand why anyone would harm him. He was frail enough. Wouldn't hurt anyone."

"I know," Sady said, placing a hand on the man's shoulder. And he did know. He tried to push away memories of that night in the guest room. Finding Lana . . .

The rest of the family remained in the doorway: a younger woman, presumably the merchant's wife, and the old woman who had come to get him, his mother-in-law and the dead man's wife.

Orsan walked around the courtyard, careful not to disturb anything that could be of use to the city guards. Each time he came close, the knot of ducks ran, quacking loudly, to the furthest corner behind their wrecked duck house.

"When did this happen?" Sady asked. It felt like a big hole had opened up inside him. He had been so confident they had caught the murderer.

"Early this morning. I saw pa when he went to feed the ducks, as he always does. We started breakfast and I wondered where he was. I went into the garden to check, and we found him like this."

"Did you see anything unusual?"

The man shook his head. "Nothing unusual. That's why no one worried earlier."

"Nothing at all? No sounds?" Surely, somebody would have screamed. With the ripped bushes and spilled grain, the signs of a struggle were everywhere.

"If there was, none of us heard anything. The dining room is on the other side of the house. Pa always feeds the ducks, and he usually comes in while we're having breakfast." He wiped away a tear. Sady had to fight to keep his own emotions in check. He knew exactly how the man felt.

His wife said, "There was a little girl in the front courtyard this morning when I went to pick up the fruit box from the gate. A scruffy little thing. I tried to talk to her, but she ran off."

"A little girl? A toddler, about two or three years old?"

She shook her head. "Older than that. At least eight or nine."

"What did she look like?"

"Dark hair, dirty. Dressed in a large shirt, probably stolen. No shoes."

"Southern?"

The woman nodded. "Not that it has anything to do with this, but it was strange."

It was. Did that mean there were two little girls running around, or had one of them misguessed her age? Then again, who would mistake a toddler for a child of eight?

He shook his head. "I'm afraid I have no idea what's going on." But he felt cold inside. Mercy, he thought they'd caught the killer.

There was nothing more he could do for the family, but the merchant said that they appreciated his visit and offered him tea. Sady declined, because the City Guards and other relatives arrived and it got busy at the house. Besides, he had something he wanted to do before going back to his office and Viki's maps of continued wildly fluctuating levels of sonorics and his continued inability to raise responses from the southern districts. Or, failing that, his inability to find the missing financial records. Or if that was not enough work, Alius still hadn't replied to Sady's request for the pills, and in fact he hadn't seen Alius at all for a number of days.

The courthouse was one of the places in Tiverius where Sady least liked to come. The pompous splendour of the building, with its large dome-capped hall, intricate mosaic floors and crystal chandeliers, belied the decisions of life and death, but mostly death, that were made inside. Since the sonorics alarm had suspended all court cases, there was little going on this morning, just a few guards milling about, two of them on either side of the courtroom door. Both of them dressed in heavy winter gear.

The doors were open, giving Sady a glimpse of the interior of the courtroom, an equally richly appointed room in which people with a lot of money decided over the lives of many with none.

Although he understood better than anyone about the tightrope that Chevakia walked—of having enough food or not having enough —he felt deeply uncomfortable with the ease with which the city guard condemned to death anyone who had committed a serious crime. And even more so that this was done in the name of giving the country's scarce resources to those who deserved it most. In this way, the killing of prisoners tied back to meteorology—if he predicted more rain, the court would feel less pressured to cull the "undeserving" and criminal poor.

When he was twelve or thirteen, he had attended a court case as minor witness—he'd seen the accused run from the house where he was said to have tried to rape one of the daughters. He remembered the man's cries, his scruffy hair and pleading eyes. The prisoner had admitted to breaking in and stealing—he lived on the street and had no money—but had sworn that he would never lay a hand on a girl. The counter-witness was the girl's mother. She claimed to have seen what he did.

The girl herself had been quiet.

The audience had cheered when the judge pronounced the death sentence.

When the session had finished, Sady had asked his father how the judge could be certain that the girl's mother was right, and his father had said they couldn't. And then Sady had asked what they would do when they discovered the man wasn't guilty after all.

He still remembered his father's uncomfortable look. They had been standing there, next to the pillar outside the courtroom.

Sady couldn't remember what his father said next, only that he had never answered the question. The smell coming out of the darkness of the courtroom brought back those memories. This was a place of death.

A guard met Sady and Orsan on the other side of the hall. He was one of the designated courthouse guards, dressed in blue, with the courthouse symbol of the two crossed swords on his shirt. The man bowed several times, and Sady explained why he had come.

"But Proctor, do you need to go into the prison yourself?"

"I want to speak to this prisoner. I presume he's not going to meet me anywhere else."

"Um—no, but the man is out of his mind. What he says is complete nonsense."

"I still want to hear what he has to say. I will decide if it's nonsense or not."

The guard gave him a blank look, and bowed. "Of course, Proctor."

"Good, then; let's go." Sady led the way into the corridor and off the side down a set of stairs, sliding his hand over the railing. The prison guard trailed behind him.

"But seriously, Proctor, don't take him at his word. The man is an idiot. Sometimes he seems to make sense, and other times he is clearly out of it. You don't know when he speaks the truth even when he seems sane. Maybe he's killed in his insanity but I'm not even sure about that—"

Sady whirled. "Enough. I want to talk to him, and I'll draw my own conclusion. I'll not be accused of ignoring things I should have been told."

"But we have no information from our questioning. The man

keeps telling us how we're all going to die from some invasion of creatures of damnation. If we bothered you every time someone predicted the end of the world, you'd have no time to do anything. He's as mad as a ground squirrel in heat. The man is a waste of space."

"That may well be, but do you want to go and talk to the family of the old grandfather who was murdered this morning? I suggest you go and look at the body. It's not pretty."

The man's eyes went wide. "You mean—there are still people being killed?"

"Yes. That's exactly what I mean." That was right; Sady never liked how these guards made up their minds about guilt and motives before the court decided. They were known to coerce confessions from beggars, only because the Tiverians liked their streets clean of anyone who did not look up to their standard.

When all this was over, he should really do something about the court system and the prisons.

Mercy, now he was angry.

At the bottom of the stairs, he turned right, past the entrance that led to the gallows room, and past the little cells that held criminals awaiting trial. The air here was breathless and stank of damp and sweat. As he passed, there were stirrings and curses in the dark cells behind the barred metal doors. Sady guessed many of the inmates had still been asleep.

The prisoner in question was in a solitary cell at the end of that corridor. Sady grabbed the bars of the door and rattled it. "Open it."

Metal chinked against stone as the prisoner moved his arms.

"But we need—"

"Open it." *But we need to have another guard present.* Right; this man was shackled and wouldn't go anywhere. Moreover, he might be mad, but most likely *wasn't* a murderer.

"Sure, Proctor. Immediately." The man inserted the key in the lock, his hands trembling. The door creaked open, and Sady charged in, bracing himself against the smell of excrement and dank rot.

The prisoner sat bound and shackled against a crate that stood in the middle of the cell, a room normally used to house several prisoners. His skin was grey with filth and shiny with sweat. The only thing on him that looked clean was the golden metal of his claw hand. The beautiful thing was clearly of Chevakian origin. In the light of the oil lamp the jailer carried in, his burned and scarred head looked like a skull. His eyes met Sady's, furious. Brown eyes.

Sady was taken aback. When he saw him last, the man had blue eyes. Had he remembered wrong?

He made a show of sitting down on the bench next to the door to give himself time to think, but nothing came to him that could have explained this strange phenomenon. Brown eyes, blue eyes, there was no way he would have seen wrongly. Blue eyes were south-ern. He remembered very clearly judging that the man was south-ern. He remembered the skull-like appearance of his head, the tightly stretched and scarred skin, the patch of hair around one ear. This was the same man, and his eyes had changed from blue to brown.

The prisoner's gaze followed his every move.

Sady said, "We caught you with a knife and blood on your hands near the place where four people were gruesomely killed. When we caught you, you did not speak to us and led us to believe that you didn't speak Chevakian. If you want to walk free, or indeed if you want to live, we will need an explanation."

"I am a citizen of Tiverius." His words were clear and measured, and without accent. "I was defending the country."

The guard at the door snorted. "I'm touched by that patriotic statement. Excuse me if I don't believe it."

Sady glanced over his shoulder. That guard was most irritating. Did all courthouse guards have such a high opinion of themselves? Had Destran really exercised so little control over the courts, and for that matter, the city guard and the army?

Sady leant forward, his elbows on his knees, and fixed the prison-er's gaze.

"I will need to know who you are, your name, your home, whatever you can tell me to prove that you're telling the truth."

"You don't remember me?"

"No," Sady said, staring, puzzled, at the man's scarred scalp.

"I remember you." He gave a chilling chuckle that turned into a phlegmy cough.

The guard moved to hit the man, but Sady held up a hand to stop him.

"But you do remember me, although I may look a bit unconventional. The unassuming Chief Meteorologist is a promotion from watching the bully beat up a defenceless boy."

Bully? Defenceless boy? When had he ever been involved in beating up—

Mercy, this was Lady Armaine's son. The southern spy. "What was your name again?"

"Tandor."

Yes, Sady remembered. But now he was certain: the boy had, or he was certain he used to have, blue eyes. He remembered the boy standing against a wall in a back alley in the merchant district, crying, unable to move backwards or forwards because older and bigger boys surrounded him on all sides. They pushed and kicked him and called him names. Even though he was older, Sady had been too small and skinny to do anything if he had wanted to—which he hadn't, in case the bullies would turn on him instead. Most of the tormentors were now influential men and had probably long since forgotten the incident. And if he was a good, strong leader, he should forget the incident, too. Except he couldn't.

"You remember," the prisoner said, and succumbed again to a bout of coughing.

"I cannot see what this has to do with the accusations against you."

"But it does. Because I am southern, you assume guilt."

"I think it rather had something to do with a bloodied knife. What were you doing in that yard and whose blood was on your hands?"

"I did not kill anyone. I was trying to stop people being killed. There is a great evil coming this way. You can either let me out now or you will beg me for help when it is too late."

The guard snapped back, "Don't push your luck. If you're as Chevakian as you sound, you know where the gallows are. You've never answered where the baby is."

"I tried to stop it." He spat in the straw, and the guard jumped forward again. Sady again held him back. "Tried to stop what?"

"Your murderer. The baby. The dacon."

"The what?"

"He's been talking about this a lot," the guard said. "It's pure non—"

"Please, let me be alone with him."

The man retreated as far as the door. Sady felt like shouting at him to mind his own business. The city guard was another world of its own. Chevakia had splintered into far too many worlds like this, where leaders were kings of their mini-kingdoms and where everyone else had to abide by their rules, or pay bribes.

Orsan pushed himself off the wall and semi-casually went to stand by the door. He was taller and broader than the guard, and the man seemed to get the message. He retreated. Surely there would be questions about this in the doga later. Sady could already hear the complaints. *Any senator wishing to visit the prisons should file a request with the appropriate authorities.* Well, hang the authorities. Any elected senator of the doga should have that authority by default.

Sady rose and faced the prisoner. The lamplight made the weeping sores on the man's face glisten. His eyes didn't close properly, and wept involuntary tears over his cheek. He said, "You're here because the killing hasn't stopped, aren't you?"

"Can you answer my question, please? What is the thing you need to save us from?"

"Have you seen the girl?"

"Girl? Just answer my question." He lowered his voice and glanced at the door where he had no doubt the prison guard would be laughing.

"There is a little girl with blue eyes who wanders around the city streets."

How did he know about that? "What if there is?"

Tandor laughed, and his laugh descended into a phlegmy cough. "See, you've seen her. She's not a girl; she's a dacon. She is your killer and can be our saviour if you let me out to catch her."

"Just a little girl?" Sady did his best to sound sarcastic, but wasn't entirely successful. She hadn't been *just* a little girl, had she? For one, she was southern, and with the strange look in those unnatural blue eyes, he had to admit that she was far removed from *just a little girl*. There were places—madhouses—in Tiverius where people like that were looked after. The thought of her piercing eyes still chilled him. And then there was the question of her age, and how she would have escaped the camp.

Tandor looked at him with an intense gaze. For a moment, it

seemed like a brown layer over his eyes became transparent and the blue underneath shone through. Sady blinked but the eyes were as brown as ever.

He resettled on the wooden bench next to the door.

Tandor spat again, and Sady suspected it had to do with his injuries and not because he was trying to be rude. Tandor's upper arms were raw from the shackles. He could move his upper arms just enough to reach the crate next to him where the guards would put his food. His clothes were so filthy they were crusted with dirt and who knew what else. This man was ill. Even without the death penalty, he would not live long. He *seemed* crazy, but on the other hand . . .

"Tell me about this girl," Sady said.

"That girl is not a girl. She's a dacon. And she is hungry. She will grow years in age with every day, so she needs lots of food. If you let her roam, she will kill a lot more people. If you let me tame her, I can save Chevakia."

CHAPTER 19

BY THE SKYLIGHTS, this truck made a lot of noise. And it bumped and jerked, and it *stank*. Loriane sat on the velvet-covered seat, her back straight, her hands clasped between her knees. She was hot in the stuffy cabin. The dress that the young man Farius had brought was very thick, unusually tight in the waist, and her belly was still flabby from the pregnancy she thought would never end.

Outside, the streets of Tiverius slid past at disconcerting speed, huge houses with walled yards, like Sady's house.

The two men in the front seat seemed relaxed, the driver and the huge dark-haired and dark-eyed guard in his stiff uniform.

He had come to the house especially for her. She'd seen him before, briefly, in the corridor and shadowing Sady when he went out. And this morning, she'd been sitting in the kitchen with her Chevakian book, and this man had come in and had demanded that she come with him. He mentioned Sady, but not much else of what he said made sense.

She worried about being taken back to the camp, where surely the child could easily find her and kill her. She should have let Myra cut it from the womb, this instrument of Tandor's. It was out there somewhere, and if not killed, it would kill again. The thing was a predator, living off raw flesh.

At a time that now seemed long ago, Loriane had seen the misshapen foetuses in jars in the palace birthing rooms. Demon-like creatures with *wings*. She'd thought such children were born dead, but the awful truth was that sometimes, they lived.

Dara and Ontane didn't believe her.

The Chevakians had no idea, and how she could possibly warn them of this thing was a mystery to her. These people with their machines, with their refined tastes and beautiful houses. The people were so rich and so far removed from her. They knew nothing about icefire, and worse, seemed unwilling to believe that such a thing existed.

The truck stopped in front of a building with tall columns at least two storeys high. In the dark space between the columns, Loriane spotted two guards standing on either side of a door. Another guard, in similar blue uniform, came around the side of the truck, opened the door and helped her out. She caught a glimpse of herself in the reflection of the glass. The Chevakian dress didn't look bad on her. It just felt hot and tight. Her hair was still loose from combing it this morning. It hung in a curly mass halfway down her shoulders.

Sady's guard took her arm and led her up the steps between tall columns into the building. This looked like some sort of official building to her. She wished Sady were here, and would feel a lot better if he was.

They entered a high-ceilinged hall, circular, with columns around the sides and a domed ceiling above. The floor underfoot was smooth, with a mosaic of different-coloured tiles. Patterns of leaves and vines slid by underfoot.

They went through the hall into a corridor on the other side, and from there down a staircase. It grew dark here, with oil lamps casting little pools of orange light over rough stone walls. She didn't like being under the ground. By the skylights, this place reminded her of the dungeons in the City of Glass.

The smell was the same, too, of human misery and suffering. A hand of panic clamped around her chest. Were the Chevakians blaming her for the deaths of their citizens? Was she to be locked up?

She turned to the guard. "Can you tell me what is happening?"

But the guard didn't understand and her Chevakian vocabulary didn't yet include the words "prison" or "I did not kill them." She thought her innocence was clear. She thought Sady understood. After all, he wouldn't have allowed her to sleep in the room next to his if he believed that she had killed four people.

Or would he?

They arrived in a corridor where the stink was worse than on the stairs. Metal-barred doors lined both sides of the corridor.

Dark presences rustled in cells off the side. She thought she heard ragged breathing and the rough whisper of a male voice. Leering.

At the end of the corridor, a light burned in a cell where there were silhouettes of a number of people. The guard led her inside. To her immense relief, one of the people was Sady.

He smiled at her.

She returned his smile, her heart still thudding. By the skylights.

Then she spotted the cell's prisoner. Shackled to a wooden crate, his ankles bound. With pale, scabbed skin and his shoulders wasted to bony protuberances, he resembled a skeleton more than a living being, and a disgustingly filthy one at that. But she recognised his scarred face.

"Tandor!"

He squinted in her direction, but she was unsure if the watering eyes saw anything. Brown eyes. She thought he could only use disguises when there was icefire?

He smiled, and coughed. "Loriane, my love."

"I am not your love." She shuddered with revulsion. Was there ever a time that his mysterious craggy face and lilting voice had seemed exotic to her? She'd been stupid for believing that he would carry her off to a more exciting life. Riches, living like a princess, travelling to foreign places—what a load of rubbish.

She turned to Sady. "Where . . ." And then found that all Chevakian words had fled her mind.

"You talk to him," he said, and mimicked talking. "We go outside." He pointed at the door.

"No."

"All right. I watch from here. Talk to him." He leaned against the metal bars of the door. One of the other Chevakians crouched in the corridor. He had a slate with paper and was making notes.

"He wants to check out what I told him," Tandor said. "And the other guard understands what we're saying. But I'll tell you the same I told him already." His Chevakian accent, always very slight, seemed to have become stronger. He chuckled, and then coughed and spat in the straw. A dribble of brown slime ran down his chin.

By the skylights, he was disgusting. This wasn't Tandor. Not as she knew him. This was the evil that hid underneath the disguise of an alluring, mysterious travelling merchant.

"So what happened then?"

He coughed. "Well, they played with something that was too big for them. And it blew up in their faces, huh?"

"The Knights?"

"Who else? They played with icefire but they couldn't see it. They had no idea what they were doing."

"So, whatever you did, whatever your plan was, when we went into the palace with Myra—that had nothing to do with the explosion? Am I supposed to believe that?"

"Whatever you believe makes no difference." His voice lowered. "It is what we do now that can doom us or save us. The Heart has come alive. When I reached their prison, the children who were captured by the Knights had been tampered with. They wouldn't listen to me. The Knights' tampering had turned them into living sinks and they were attracted by the Heart. They absorbed all the icefire from it and became living evil constructs of icefire. Ruko has gone to join them. He has become more dangerous, having returned to his servitor state. His temper was always a problem, but he was a proper servitor and I had him under control. He's been free since the explosion. I managed to keep some control over him, but it took all my wits to do so. Often, I was controlled by him, not the other way around. By removing him from me, you and Myra set him free and allowed him to return to his peers. He is the most dangerous of all the children. He should never have been allowed to escape."

"So now it's all my fault?"

"Loriane, if you only listened—"

"If I'd listened? If I'd listened to my concerns I would have given you up to the Knights years ago, and if I had, I bet that none of this would have happened. Whenever I asked you about your plans, you never told me anything. It was always later, or, when it's all over. But I see now. First everything that was wrong with the world was all the Knights' fault, and the stupid people from the City of Glass who let the Knights rule. Then it was Isandor's fault, and mine, for letting him sign up. And it was the Chevakians' fault, and your mother's. And the Knights' fault again, and the Brotherhood of the Light. Now, finally, the Chevakians are going to make you pay for your own failures."

"Loriane, please, I need your—"

"You don't need anything that I could give you. Because of you, I've lost all I have. My house, my position, my son . . ." Her voice grew unsteady. She glanced at the man in the corridor, writing down everything they said. "I'll tell the Chevakians that you're evil and should never be released."

His voice cut through hers. "Loriane, listen to me!" He coughed and spat on the floor.

His expression was intense. For a moment, the brown illusion of his eyes wavered, and the blue came through. Royal blue.

From the corner of her eye, she noticed Sady's concerned look.

"I need to get out of here, you have to tell them that. Whether or not you believe in my guilt doesn't matter. I need to find the hybrid child." Tandor cleared his throat and spat again. That began to get on Loriane's nerves. "Where is it?"

"I don't know, and that is the truth."

"It hasn't come back to you?"

"No. Why should it? I'll kill it if it comes back."

"Kill it? The most valuable of all your children?" He laughed.

"This is not the time for stupid jokes!" A wave of anger came over her. She lashed out and her flat palm connected with his cheek with a satisfying slap.

Tandor cursed, and met her eyes, his nostrils flaring. His cheek was going red.

"This child is part of your machinations, isn't it? You are the king's grandson, and you wanted to put yourself back on the throne and return the City of Glass to what it was before the king left. I thought all that stuff about Thilleians and Pirosians was over, not important anymore. You said so. But that's what this is all about, isn't it? Isandor is Thilleian and that was why he was an experiment, to see if I could live with him, and . . ." She saw something now. It was part of the experiment. The misshapen foetuses in the palace had not died because they couldn't live, or because the Knights had killed them; they had died because their mothers had killed them. How often, at the start of the pregnancy, had she felt that she wanted to kill the child? How carefully had she planned for Myra to cut the child from her womb and strangle it? But she had hesitated, because the hybrid's evil blood had already mingled with hers. Seeing the baby girl, having suffered for so long carrying her inside her body, she knew she could never kill it. That was Tandor's experiment: to see if, in the face of evil, a Pirosian would kill her own child.

She continued in a lower voice, "Isandor and I were part of this evil experiment. I know how you did it. He is the hybrid's father."

His eyes widened to show that she had guessed correctly. And some part of her had still hoped that she was wrong. Tears pricked in her eyes, and she couldn't have told if they were from anger or grief. Where was Isandor?

"I'm sorry about all of it, Loriane. Help me out of here, please. You're my only hope. I love you."

"You don't love me. You only wanted to use me. Even now, you're lying and grovelling. Anyway, even if I knew where the child was, you are not getting your hands on her. I'm through with your only hopes. You've said this so many times that I don't believe it anymore. I could have died from giving birth to that thing. All you ever think about is yourself." Tears rolled over her cheeks. She wiped them away, angrily.

"Just let me explain."

"No. No more explaining. I'm through with you." She turned away.

"Come join me, Loriane. Tell him to release me. Help me find the child. Come and be my queen. We will rule the City of Glass."

"There is no more City of Glass, because of you. You didn't love me back then. You don't love me now. You never loved me. I do not want to be with a man who made the entire country suffer. I hate you. I hate you." Her voice would no longer cooperate. She buried her face in her hands and sobbed.

Sady said a few soft words and put an arm around her shoulders. She leant into him.

Tandor snorted. "Look at that. You have yourself some powerful friends." He said something in Chevakian and Sady replied in a sharp tone. Tandor spat in the dirt.

The guard sprang forward and thrust the point of his dagger under his chin.

Tandor spat again, on the man's uniform. "Tell your powerful friend, if he listens to you. Tell him that he'll come and beg me for my help sooner, rather than later. Tell him that he'll need the hybrid to stop the icefire storm coming for me."

Loriane clamped her hands over her ears. "Stop this nonsense. Stop it. I don't want to hear it anymore. I'll tell them to hang you and shoot the child."

A gust of wind tore through the cell. Loriane's chest grew tight as if she could barely breathe. She clutched her throat, her breath wheezing. "Tandor. What are you doing?"

Chevakians were shouting around her, evidently some saw something she did not. Her chest grew tighter. She could barely move. Black spots danced before her eyes.

Sady grabbed her shoulders and pulled her away from Tandor, shouting angry orders at the Chevakian guards. Before he dragged her to the door, she noticed, between the bodies of the guards, two men pouncing on Tandor.

Loriane could only properly breathe when she had left the cell. Sady was looking at her with a concerned expression. "I'm fine," she said in her best Chevakian, but she was still trembling. Sady shook his head, speaking soft words, and holding her.

She stood like that for a while, with his arms around her, feeling his comforting warmth and breathing the clean smell of his clothes. It struck her in a way she had not realised before, how much she hated everything to do with the royal family and the City of Glass. The secrecy, the fear of who was watching whom. All her life, she'd pretended to be unaffected, because she couldn't see icefire, but icefire affected the lives of everyone. None of it had ever done anyone any good.

Sady let go of her and started moving again, leading her down the corridor and back up the stairs.

"I help you," she said. Help him deal with Tandor, help him catch and kill the monster child. Help him guide the refugees from the south to a safe and better life.

He smiled. "Thank you." His eyes were kind and honest. He would not betray her.

While she walked back to the truck with him and his guards, the warmth of his touch lingered on her shoulder. She accepted his hand in climbing in and sat opposite him in the cabin. He was finely built, with close-cropped hair threaded with grey at the temples. His intelligent eyes were light brown, his skin several shades darker than hers with a smattering of freckles over his nose and forehead and a small black mole under his right eye.

Cute, both freckles and mole.

Then he looked up, noticed that she was looking at him, and she feigned interest in Tiverian architecture.

As the city buildings slid past the window, she berated herself. Men were no good, and only wanted to further their own aims. At the very best, they only wanted sex. At the worst, they wanted to destroy her and everything she loved. It had started with the Senior Knight when she was sixteen. She was innocent and naive. He had only been kind enough so that she, starry-eyed with his attentions, came willingly to his bed. She had hoped he would care for her as a lover and companion, but he didn't. She had hoped he would love the child she suffered so much for, but she understood Knights never looked after their own children. She had hoped Tandor would care for her, but he didn't, either.

Men didn't care.

And she hated getting that warm feeling inside whenever she met Sady's light brown eyes. She hated feeling giddy when he smiled.

Damn it, Loriane, you're too old and grumpy to fall in love. She'd seen it all before. Love was for suckers. Not to mention that it was the wrong time and the wrong person and, by the skylights, she couldn't even talk to him.

But he liked her. And he seemed open and honest, everything Tandor was not.

Yeah, all right, she liked him. But that didn't mean anything.

CHAPTER 20

CARRO SQUINTED, fighting an acute attack of yawning. He took up a stance with his legs slightly spread and his hands behind his back. Yes, he understood that it was a privilege to be allowed to listen in on the Knights' Council meeting, but how much longer did he have to wait for this meeting to start? He'd been up since dusk last night and was struggling to stay upright, and the stuffy air in this room didn't help.

The three Senior Knights in attendance sat in easy chairs in the large room that his father used for special occasions and had kept free of beds or stored gear. Ever since Carro had arrived with the extra Knight Division, the farmhouse had been bursting with people. But the large previous formal room had remained solely Rider Cornatan's domain, which he used for meetings.

Carro had been given the task of bringing the men drinks from his father's drink cabinet. The men spoke in low voices. Silhouetted against the light was Rider Barton, who had led the unit into Tiverius. He had cleaned up, brushed his shorthair cloak and polished his buttons. Carro knew the other two Senior Knights only by name. Rider Barton was easily the youngest of the three.

Rider Heston was a wrinkled old man who used to look after maintenance at the eyrie, and whom Carro had never spotted going outside. Rider Ataro led the special service division: spies and hunters and other kinds of specialised groups. He had a sharp face and unsettling blue eyes that felt like they could do all the spying work his men did just by looking through people's skulls.

Rider Cornatan was yet to arrive.

Carro had seen him briefly after returning to the farmhouse with Rider Barton and his unit, but after greeting Rider Barton he had gone to some place from which he had not yet returned. The three members of the council did not seem to mind; they found plenty to talk about. Rider Heston complained about the state in which they had found the farm. Rider Ataro spoke about contacts in Chevakia and then the two of them marvelled over the fact that some of those contacts were still alive. Apparently it was a long time since anyone had used them.

Then they started discussing building styles. Chevakian city buildings and Chevakian rural architecture. By the skylights, it was boring.

Carro tried not to yawn too much.

Finally, there were quick footsteps in the hall, the jingling of a riding harness, and Rider Cornatan came into the room. He carried his cloak over his arm, his face looked red, his hair windblown, and Carro suspected that he had just flown in from that mysterious place he'd been. He winked at Carro, and smiled, and said, "Shut the door, will you?"

Carro did, while Rider Cornatan took his place at the one remaining chair.

"Drink?" Carro asked him.

"Just some water, thanks."

Carro took a glass, but there was no water in the room, only spirits, so he had to go to the fountain in the hallway to get some. When he returned, Rider Cornatan had maps spread out over the table. He took the glass without comment and without meeting Carro's eyes.

Carro returned to his previous position and took up a wide stance, his hands clasped behind his back. At least he felt a little bit more awake now.

". . . We have this side covered," Rider Ataro was saying, gesturing at the map.

"There are likely to be a lot of Chevakian troops on this side," Heston said. "We *are* close to the main base of the Chevakian army, and they do have balloons."

Rider Cornatan nodded. "Rather a lot more than we suspected. We'll have to be quick. And we'll have to take birds."

"The Chevakians won't care. They won't use their army to defend a camp full of foreign citizens," Ataro said, his voice scornful.

"You never know with Chevakians," Heston said, taking his glass in a gnarled hand. "They jump in strange directions."

Rider Cornatan said, "They will defend the camp because if it looks like we're trying to occupy it, they will consider that as an invasion of their territory." He gulped the water down and held the glass up for Carro to give him more.

"What is on your mind, Barton?" Rider Cornatan asked, when Carro had retreated. "You look like you have a better plan."

Rider Barton folded his hands on his knees and sighed. "I'm wondering if a full-scale invasion of the camp is wise."

Both Ataro and Heston stared at him.

"What do you mean—wise?" Ataro asked, his voice reserved.

"For all we know, most of the camp's residents are citizens. Ordinary people. How do you think the men will feel about fighting our own people?"

Rider Cornatan raised his eyebrows.

Rider Barton continued, "Many of my men have lost family, or are uncertain of their fate. They were expecting orders to go back to the City of Glass to see if we can find any further survivors—"

"That would be idiocy. Icefire is far too strong. There are no survivors. Any who survived are likely to be in the camp under the thumb of the Brotherhood."

There was a small silence. "Do we know how many Brotherhood men are in the camp?"

"We can't be certain, but they have support from within Chevakia. We have to break that link. We can fight the Brothers, but we cannot fight the Chevakian army."

Rider Barton let a silence lapse that seemed rather long. He cast the briefest of glances at Carro, and nodded. Carro didn't think he looked happy.

Rider Cornatan moved a glass out of the way so he could spread another map. Carro rushed to take the glass and returned it to the cabinet.

Behind him, Rider Cornatan continued, "Right, so let's get this underway. We have the units at the farmhouse, and the ones to the east of here, a total of two thousand men and well over a thousand birds. When I give the order, we start on this side of the camp with Ataro's unit. We'll have half the unit push into the camp, over land, and the other half stationed out here with birds to ward off any curiosity from the Chevakians."

"The Chevakians will view this as an attack on their country," Rider Barton said.

"We can deal with that." Rider Cornatan rose. "Do you mind if I open the window? I find it rather hot in here."

Carro could see that Rider Ataro probably wanted to object, but Knights lived in much tougher conditions in the City of Glass, and complaining about the cold in Chevakia would not look good for him. So Rider Cornatan opened the window and a blast of cold air blew in.

Rider Ataro dived for the map which was about to blow from the table. "By the skylights, the weather is like the City of Glass."

Carro stands in the cold hall, facing the Knight. He feels small and insignificant.

"So, you want to serve our Queen?" the Knight asks.

Carro nods. He's nervous about this. No boy from the Outer City is accepted into the Knighthood. It's a noble place for noble sons. Men of honour.

Serving the Queen is the highest thing he could do. The Queen is his goddess.

"Son, I could use that drink now."

"Yes, sure." Carro's heart was still thudding. Was there a more awkward time for those visions to return? It was the open window, he realised, the air laced with icefire. Rider Barton met his eyes in a piercing way as if he knew what was going on. Carro's cheeks felt hot.

Carro went to the drinks cabinet and took a fresh glass, his hands trembling. Where was that bottle of imported bloodwine? He rummaged between the empty bottles and found various bottles of spirits that were not his father's. He also found a box of playing dice and a little slate with scores. At the top was written *Queen's Wolves*. Much as he despised the wolves and what they stood for—honestly, were all men obsessed with sex?—those men still considered themselves loyal to the Queen. Did they know that their leaders in the council were discussing her death? Did they know that these men were discussing an attack on their families in the camp?

He shifted another empty bottle aside and came across the stoppered jar with the blue poison crystals tucked at the back of the shelf. By the skylights, what was that still doing out here?

A gust of wind made the curtains flap.

Carro stands at the back of the empty shed. He's just seen the older boys go in there, with a younger boy who they always tease. It's pitch dark inside the shed, but he can hear their voices.

"Come on, do it, or I'll beat you up."

Someone is crying. Carro assumes it's the younger boy.

"Come on, we made a bet. You said you can eat shit. Do it."

A silence, and then a wail.

"I said I'd hit you."

Carro's hands grow cold. He should come forward and tell the boys to get out of his father's warehouse, but he's afraid they will turn on him instead. They already call him names. Tattletale, they call him.

The bloodwine almost went over the rim of the glass. Carro stopped pouring just in time, but now he had a too-full glass and it wasn't acceptable to fill the glasses up that much. He tried to pour some wine from the glass, but it ran down the side, making a mess on the top of the cabinet.

Not knowing what else to do, he sipped from the glass until the level of fluid was more acceptable and wiped the glass clean with the end of his sleeve. While he was doing this, he noticed the bottle with the poison crystals again. How careless to leave it here. He could so easily open that bottle and drop a few crystals in his father's glass. How long would the poison take to kill him?

He returned to the table with the glass, feeling light-headed and sweaty.

"Come and sit here, son," Rider Cornatan patted the armrest of his chair.

Carro sat, under the gazes of the three Senior Knights.

"I wanted to discuss how we will take control over the camp and weed out the Brotherhood element. It is very fortunate that we have all the refugees in one spot. There has been unrest in the camp, and if we move quickly, the Chevakians will thank us for getting them under control. Meanwhile, we take the opportunity to get rid of the dangerous elements."

"How do we know who is dangerous?" Carro asked. Isandor and Jevaithi were in the camp; he knew that for sure.

"Some Brothers identify themselves clearly. Any others, we don't know. Any Chevakians in the camp will be suspicious."

Rider Barton said, "Any Chevakians in the camp should be removed and allowed to leave to avoid nasty situations with the army."

The two met each other's hard gazes across the table. Rider Ataro still tried to find something heavy to weigh down the map.

Another gust of wind came into the room.

Carro hears Isandor's voice, sees Isandor's blue eyes. "Then fight back. Tell him what you think."

Rider Cornatan said, "You will take this unit, son, and come in from the east."

Carro licked his lips. "Me?"

"Yes, you heard me. We have a shortage of commanders I can trust. I'll give you the command of a hundred men and birds and you will lead the air attack."

And Carro says to his merchant father, "I'm not going to stand here all night. Tell me why you wanted to see me or I'll go back to my study."

"We need to make sure the Chevakian army doesn't have any balloons ready," Rider Ataro said. "I'll send some of my spies."

Rider Cornatan nodded at Carro. "Those hunters of yours will be good."

"I'll tell them," Carro said. He was nominally still in charge of the hunters. Whether they would listen to him . . . probably, if they wanted to live. The lives of so many, in his hands. Knights who had signed up for a job knowing that it might kill them, many more citizens, whose only crime it was to have survived the disaster.

And then Isandor asks again, "What do you think, Carro?"

Carro thought nothing, ever. Carro obeyed orders. His stepfather's, his father's, his Tutor's. Isandor's even.

What did he think?

He thought nothing of Nolan's affections at night.

He thought nothing of his father's mindless praise that came regardless of whether he did well or badly.

He thought nothing of his father's plan to force themselves into the camp and fight miserable, unarmed refugees. He thought nothing of being given a division to lead. Rider Cornatan made Carro nothing but a front for himself, someone to blame if things went bad. He put Carro in charge because he *knew* that things would go bad.

His father didn't really *care* about him.

He thought nothing of the Knights' insistence on discipline on the one hand and continuous breaking their own rules on the other. The Knight's mantra was worth nothing.

It was all hypocrisy, and fake. No one really cared.

What did the Knights want? A world in which everyone would continuously be afraid of everyone else?

But he was powerless against the machine of war.

He had nowhere to turn. He had nowhere to flee. Not like this. Not alone. And he had no idea where to turn for help.

The penalty for treason was death. And he wasn't even sure that what he felt amounted to treason. Mutiny, yes, the word was mutiny. The penalty for mutiny was death, too.

Rider Barton watched him, his eyes blinking. As if he could read the warring emotions in his mind.

CHAPTER 21

SADY DROPPED Loriane back home. She sat in the cabin opposite him, still pale after Tandor's attack on her. She said she was fine, but a few diamond drops of sweat collected on her upper lip. He deeply regretted having called her into the prison. Deep inside, he'd known that Tandor was crazy and the incident with Loriane only proved it, and he felt terrible about having inflicted this on her; he had not learnt anything new from the exchange.

He made sure he escorted her into the kitchen, where Myra was feeding her baby.

Loriane told her that she'd seen Tandor, and some discussion ensued. Myra seemed cautious, and Loriane frustrated, but the long process of trying to get her to explain what she knew would have to wait until he came home. As it was, one of the prison guards had a rudimentary understanding of the southern language, and had made notes. The report was already on his desk when he returned to the office, but he had no time to look at it. He was already running late for a special doga session, and he ran in to the hall, poorly prepared, where all the senators had been waiting.

General Finnisius would be there, and he hated waiting.

Viki presented the latest sonorics situation. While the levels in the city continued to fluctuate wildly, the shattering of the barriers had allowed a large area of the southern provinces to become contaminated to a level dangerous to Chevakians. How far this area reached was uncertain. Viki's instruments relied on telegraph lines, and many were out. The fate of the people in those areas also remained uncertain. There might well be pockets still safe or people still holding out with suits and shelters. If they had suits.

There were questions about Alius' pills. Not even the army had enough suits for all its troops, and those pills would come in very handy if the army would have to conduct rescue operations.

But no one appeared to have seen Alius for days, and he ordered another senator to inquire.

Why couldn't they send southerners into those dangerous districts, someone else asked, and many thought that was a good idea, but others thought that the southerners were too much of a risk, because they might steal from the abandoned houses or take over Chevakian farmland.

And so the debate went. But in all this one thing worried Sady most: no one had any accurate maps of the sonorics cloud and how it was likely to disperse. It could be that the main farming areas were going to be out of bounds for most of summer, which would mean no crops, and the country would face a winter of shortages.

Even if they could send southerners to farm the land, and if the crops would grow, they could well be too contaminated for the Chevakians to eat.

No, definitely the pills sounded better all the time.

They discussed the camps and what to do if the refugees needed to stay for a longer period. The authorities needed a register of all people inside, of their allegiances, and the people who did not riot and had behaved well could be released to farming districts.

To which a senator from the Fairlight district said that the south had no vegetation and southerners didn't know how to farm. That was definitely a problem.

And so it went on.

When Sady eventually returned to his office, his head was spinning. He had a quick look at the report that the prison guard had delivered. It did not contain anything he hadn't heard before, and that concerned him, too. A flying creature with mysterious power, evil creatures embodied a sonorics storm. He'd better not let the magic-believers see any of this. Either the prisoner was not as mad as everyone thought he was, or he was consistently mad. He ordered some tea and set about making a list of things that needed to be done. Urgent, less urgent and long-term things.

Urgent:

Find out sonorics situation (requires weather balloons)

Make list of camp inhabitants and their names and skills (requires reliable translator)

Catch murderer (requires . . .

Whatever it required. More guards, which he didn't have at his disposal. But . . . a winged monster? Surely that was some sort of southern superstition. Though, frankly, Loriane looked far too smart for superstition. Or at least, he hoped she was, which was not at all the same thing. It worried him. That, and the business with the girl and however she had gotten out of the camp

Sady, keep your mind on your work.

Urgent: take stock of current food warehouses.

Assess how much cropping the north could stand.

His urgent list was growing rapidly while his long-term list was still empty.

There was a knock on the door and the secretary stuck his head in. "Excuse me, Proctor. There is someone to see you urgently."

Every demand on his time was urgent lately. "Send him in."

The secretary retreated and a moment later, a man stumbled into the office in a slow and awkward gait. He met Sady's eyes, and bowed. The movement destabilised him, and he had to hold onto the back of the chair so as not to fall. Sady would have thought that he was a drunk beggar, save for the fact that the skin on his face was covered in weeping blisters. He wore a Chevakian army uniform caked in so much dirt that Sady hadn't recognised it at first.

Mercy.

Sady gestured for him to sit down, and he did so, gingerly as if his backside hurt him.

"Reporting back, sir." His voice was husky.

"Back, from where?"

"Twin Bridges. You sent us with the woman from Solmeni to investigate."

Sady had, and had almost forgotten about it with everything else that had happened. "Where is the rest of the patrol?"

"I *am* the patrol, sir. They're all gone. I'm pretty sure they are. Solmeni is gone. Twin Bridges is gone."

"How?" His heart thudded against his ribs. Twin Bridges was closer to Tiverius than comfortable.

"We went with the woman on the train. When we arrived at Twin Bridges, it was already very smoky, and the air smelled of forest fires. We reported to the local unit that we wanted to go to Solmeni with the woman, but the area officer told us that the line was cut because of fire, so we decided to stay in Twin Bridges and wait. The local meteorology officer said that there was a very bad storm coming and warned people to stay indoors. But they must have changed their minds because later the town guards came around warning people to evacuate the town. We reported to the area commander to offer help and were ordered to go to the station."

A chill went over Sady's back at the memory of stories of another station, another time. This was starting to sound awfully familiar.

"When we got there, many people were already waiting for us on the platform. There were some folk from further up the plateau, and they had burns all over their skin. The stationmaster ordered all trains out of their sheds, even the really old ones. Two of them left, but even while we were loading the third train, the storm front came into town. The sky went so dark that it was like night. The clouds were black like smoke, and when they parted, there was fire inside. You wouldn't believe it if you hadn't seen it. The black clouds rolled over the town and started eating up the houses one by one. It was the scariest thing to see, houses exploding in big balls of fire."

The soldier wasn't looking in Sady's eyes anymore. His gaze had dropped to the area of Sady's mouth or chin, but he wasn't looking there, either. Sady was quite sure he didn't see what was in front of him. Instead, he was seeing the scene he was describing.

"There were some people who didn't want to evacuate and wanted to stay behind to ride out the storm, stubborn as they were. When we'd gone to their doors, they'd told us they were scared that looters would come in and steal their possessions when no one was in the town. Those people now came running from their burnt houses, covered in sores and peeling skin. Many fell while trying to get to the platform. Everyone was cramming to get onto that third train. The driver panicked and the train started moving while we were halfway through loading. People jumped on if they could. So many could not . . . or they fell off. But the train left, and just as we were about to pull out, the front reached the station. It was the scariest thing I have ever seen, this huge wall of black smoke, flames leaping into the air, trees and houses exploding. And the noise, you wouldn't believe it unless you've heard it. Roaring wind, snapping wood. But the strange thing, Proctor: the wind was cold. The fire was not hot, it was cold." He shuddered.

"The train gained speed. We were all screaming for it to go faster. People were blocking the windows with anything they could find. The train was going faster and faster, but it was getting colder and colder, and we weren't going to make it—and then the engine exploded. It sent such a shockwave through the train that it leapt right off the tracks. The carriage I was in was thrown on its side. The wall splintered and people were crawling out over each other. I think some of the younger ones had already died, but I wasn't going to stop and check. We were crawling over bodies. I managed to get out after pushing another fellow through a crack. His shirt had ripped, and he was bleeding. He took a few steps and fell on his face on the rails and didn't move again."

The soldier raised a hand to rub his face but obviously thought better of it even before touching the blisters and, slowly, lowered the hand to his lap. "I was starting to wonder why I was still alive. I started running, and running, but I still heard the roaring behind me. I reached a house in a meadow. I was so tired that I couldn't run anymore. I thought I might try to hide in the house, so I ran up to the door and I made the mistake of looking around."

The soldier's gaze, like his voice, had been dropping steadily, but now he looked up, into Sady's eyes. "You wouldn't believe if you hadn't seen it, but there was a wall of fire following me, reaching to the sky. I could see nothing but smoke and fire. And then, in that fire, something moved. It was a huge thing, shaped out of fire, the figure of a person. I don't know, but I think it saw me. I knew that was the end for me. And then all of a sudden there was a cry of a beast from the other side and I was yanked right off my feet. The next thing I knew, this huge bird landed next to me. There was an Eagle Knight on its back. I would not be here if not for the bird." He frowned. "Did you know that the Eagle Knights have women in their ranks?"

Sady hadn't known. Then again, many balloon pilots were women, too.

"She dropped me off just outside town, probably didn't want to be seen."

That, too, made sense. There had been few Eagle Knights sighted, but some were sure to have fled. They would not be keen to be spotted.

"Did you check if anyone else survived?"

"They couldn't have, Proctor, honest."

Sady met his eyes, watering and cloudy with pain.

"Can I be excused now, proctor? I am not well."

"Go," Sady said. "My staff will take care of you."

The man rose, leaving a wet patch on the edge of the chair.

Sady went after him. "Orsan, take him to the hospital."

Orsan nodded, but his face was grim. This man would probably not live long.

CHAPTER 22

FROM ISANDOR'S point of view, the situation in the camp did not improve, but did not deteriorate either. Simo treated Isandor and Jevaithi with suspicion, Milleus came to see them freely, which he said drew odd looks from the Chevakians, who had re-established their small Chevakian enclave in the camp, and many of the southern refugees were oblivious to the tension between the Brothers, their Queen and the Chevakians, and went to get milk from the goats and eggs from the chicken farmer to supplement the bland army rations brought in once a day by the Chevakian army.

On the morning of the third day, Isandor and Jevaithi sat with Milleus in the big tent, when a man came running in. He skidded to a halt and dropped to his knees in front of Jevaithi.

"There's a lot of soldiers arriving," he said, still panting.

Isandor's heart jumped. Yes, things had been too easy. He translated for Milleus, who said, "Doesn't surprise me. Chevakians don't like messy situations. They weren't just going to leave things like this. They will have brought more specialised troops."

"What will they do?"

"Split the camp, probably. Allocate the healthy people to farms to work."

That made sense, except . . . Isandor met Jevaithi's eyes; she looked worried, too.

"Where are these soldiers?" she asked.

"At the camp entrance," the man said.

"Are you sure they're soldiers?" Isandor asked. Chevakians about to sort people into smaller camps wouldn't send soldiers; they'd send administrators.

The man bowed first to Isandor and then Jevaithi. "They're wearing uniforms. There are a lot of them, Your Highness."

"Let's have a look." Jevaithi grabbed her cloak and rose from her seat.

Isandor and Milleus followed Jevaithi outside.

The windy hillside was covered in a grey-blue haze that whipped over the city from the west. The air smelled of burning firebricks and reminded Isandor of the days in the Outer City when butchers did all their smoking. With all the southern voices around him, he was suddenly reminded of home and all they had lost. His home, his mother. He wished he knew where she was.

At the edge of the tent city, a group of people stood at the remains of burnt-out barricades, watching the camp entrance, which was wide open, and where a number of trucks were coming into the camp. The sound of the engines carried on the wind. The man had been right to warn them. This convoy was a lot bigger than the usual few trucks that came to bring the daily supplies.

The trucks stopped, a door opened and a man in Chevakian uniform came out. He walked around the back, opened the doors, and men jumped from the back, one after the other and arranged themselves into a neat pattern of straight lines. Like Isandor would have to line up as Apprentice Knight. He shivered.

"There's so many of them," Jevaithi whispered.

She was right. At least twenty lines, of at least twenty soldiers each.

"I don't understand," Milleus said, squinting over the field. "Why do they need so many people? It looks like they're getting ready to fight a ground war."

A Chevakian soldier came out of the tent which had become the sole Chevakian army post in the camp, and went towards the trucks. Judging by his gestures, he ordered the trucks to go back.

A couple of the soldiers detached from their neat lines and approached him. He held up his hands and retreated. Two men grabbed him and twisted his arms behind his back until he cried out.

A number of the refugees gasped, and Isandor could feel the chill going through them. He could draw only one conclusion. "They're not Chevakians. They're Eagle Knights disguised as Chevakians."

Jevaithi made a scared noise and clamped her hand over her mouth. Other people cursed.

Two of the Chevakian soldier's mates came out of the tent, only to suffer the same fate as their colleague. The three of them were bundled into the back of a truck. The door shut.

A woman somewhere behind Isandor said, "How could that be? There weren't any Knights on the train. Where did they come from?"

Isandor said, "The Knights know how to save themselves. They've got eagles."

A man said, "With Newlight, the Knights should all have been at the eyrie. They would have died with the nobles." Or so everyone had hoped, clearly. Although even some nobles had survived, those who had been partying in the Outer City.

And of course, a lot of Knights hadn't been at the eyrie either.

"This proves they knew about this disaster beforehand," Simo said, his voice angry.

"They've organised the explosion to get rid of us," another man, also a Brother, added.

Isandor said, "The Knights have outposts and missions away from the city. There were riots in the Outer City and there were Knights to attend them. Those men would have survived and would have gathered at one of their safe houses."

They all looked at him. He saw meaning in their eyes and stared back defiantly. He used to be a Knight, and was proud of it, too. There *were* Knights who were honest and trustworthy, although he agreed with Simo that he suspected that those honest Knights were not the ones now pouring from the trucks.

"I'm not going back to being constantly afraid of them," someone said, and a lot of bystanders agreed.

"Yes, we're going to fight," Simo said.

"We have to call up all able people to fight them." This was one of the young Brothers. "We have to protect the Queen."

"We have no weapons," someone said.

"It doesn't matter," another said. "We make weapons. We erect barricades."

"We have weapons," one of the Brothers said. "Anyone who volunteers will be given them."

Some cheers went up.

Isandor thought of the Chevakian guns in the crates in the store tent. He held his arms around Jevaithi. She was very quiet, white-faced, and shivering.

Simo said, "Come, Your Highness. We must take you to safety. We'll build our barricades around your tent."

"I will fight, too," Jevaithi said.

Milleus was shaking his head and muttering in Chevakian. "This is ridiculous. How can Destran allow this? Being attacked by a foreign force in my own country . . ."

They went back up the hill, where youths were already stacking anything they could find into new barricades. A Brother had come out of the large supply tent with one of the crates, and was handing out guns and ammunition to eager southern men.

Milleus grumbled. "For mercy's sake, do they know how to use them?" And he stomped off to deliver an impromptu lesson on powder guns.

Isandor and Jevaithi had already received that lesson, and Isandor had actually used the gun a few times, so they watched.

"What else can we do?" Jevaithi asked, her eyes wide.

Isandor didn't know. These events were bigger than him, bigger than Jevaithi, bigger than their family. Milleus might have been able to help, but he was stuck here, too.

It didn't take long for the Knights to mount the first attack on the tent city. They came in with flaming torches which they lobbed into the barricade in a hail of fire. Crates, tent fabric and whatever the Brothers had been able to gather made eager food for hungry flames. The wind fanned the inferno, sending clouds of sparks over the surrounding tents. Some of them caught fire, too.

Fortunately, the Brothers had everyone leave the immediate vicinity of the barricade, but many people would now have nowhere to sleep, all crammed in a few large tents in the middle of the camp.

Isandor stood in the second line of defence, amongst men in

Brotherhood black, ordinary peasants, men and women, old and young, holding whatever weapons were available. Isandor had a gun. Milleus stood next to him. He had retrieved his gun from the truck and stared at the scenes of mayhem at the lower barricade with a look of determination that made Isandor feel scared.

Milleus had seen battle. Isandor has assumed that the first action he'd see would be from the back of an eagle. Instead, they would probably face eagles soon. He knew what those birds could do.

And all he could do was watch. Powerless and angry.

Tents burned, sending palls of smoke over the hillside, punctuated by the sounds of battle. People screaming orders. The discharge of guns. It was impossible to see what was going on and who was winning. Too much smoke and chaos. Groups of people running past, all still camp inhabitants.

The low clouds finally delivered on their promised rain. It came down in freezing sheets, whipped by the wind.

"Hey, relax," Milleus said next to him.

Isandor made a forced attempt to diffuse tension. "Is it always like this, when you're in a war?"

"Fighting is mostly waiting for things to happen. And when things do happen, either it's confusing or scary, or it's over so fast that you wonder what happened. You have no idea if you've won or lost. No idea where to go. You may have lost your unit, or they may be dead. That's what it's like for the soldiers on the battlefield."

Isandor nodded. He didn't like this feeling at all. And he thought that, given who he was, he should have more of a say in the situation. But respect needed to be earned. Milleus had said that many times.

They waited.

The Knights posted guards downhill from the barricades and went to sit in their trucks.

A squall of wind brought sheeting cold rain that made the camp inhabitants run for cover. Isandor grabbed Jevaithi's hand and ran for one of the large tents, pulling his cloak over his head.

Inside the tent, everyone sat down, and people shuffled out of the way to make room for Jevaithi.

"Where is Milleus?" Jevaithi asked.

"He was just . . ." Isandor looked over his shoulder. Milleus was not behind him anymore. "By the skylights. He must have gone back to the truck."

"I hope so," she said, and there was fear in her eyes.

"Sit here, Your Highness." Someone had spread a cloak on the ground.

They sat. People watched Isandor and their gazes made him feel uneasy. He thought they should listen, and they probably thought he should do something. But what?

A Brother walked around, doling out dry chunks of bread.

Simo prowled at the far end of the tent, shaking his fist and shouting slogans like "We're winning this battle." It seemed to cheer people up, but Isandor knew enough about the Knights to see that this wasn't a victory at all. The Knights were likely happy to have established a presence in the camp and ousted the Chevakians, and would send in the birds tonight. Then the real battle would begin.

Isandor sat amongst smelly bodies, chewing his dry bread, and wondering where their next meal would come from and what the night would bring.

CHAPTER 23

SO WHAT WAS going on with the sonorics levels?

Sady went to the meteorologist's office—his old office, but he no longer thought of it that way—and he and Viki studied all the available maps. Even though human-collected data from the south of the country was lacking, some of the automated devices were still working. They showed the low-pressure cell in the south still deepening.

Sady stared at the map, and its white area where they had no data.

"It's as if something is still feeding this system," Viki said.

Sady nodded. "But how reliable is this likely to be?"

"Can't be sure, but the barygraph in Twin Bridges was still operating normally yesterday."

Sady had a vision of a machine busily taking measurements in a town where all the people lay dead in the street.

"Based on how long the sonorics spike took to get from Fairlight to Twin Bridges, how long before we'll see it here?"

"A day and a half, two days maybe, if the wind eases off."

Not much chance of that happening, Sady knew. Not at this time of the year, not with a low-pressure cell this strong.

"So what do we do?" Viki asked. He had shaved his beard, but his cheeks looked hollow.

"Go home. Find a place in a shelter."

"But—"

"Go home. No one can do anything without measurements. We don't have measurements, and—"

"We have to do something!"

"Yes. Look after your elderly relatives. Get them to safety. Get them comfortable. Eat something yourself while you're feeding them."

Viki's eyes met his. Sady didn't like the expression. It spoke of worry and deeper problems. Resistance against sonorics varied wildly, even amongst Chevakians. Children, elderly people and some adults were already feeling the effects of sonorics. What if Viki was one of them? Mercy, he should have thought of this possibility before getting angry with him.

He lowered his voice. "I understand your devotion to your work, but—"

"It's nothing to do with devotion." Viki's voice spilled over. "We're all going to die if we do nothing."

A deep and uncomfortable silence followed. It was a truth that had remained unspoken.

Sady sighed. "Possibly, but you've not been doing nothing. You're a wreck and you're not functioning properly. Your family needs you. Go home. I'm going to sit here until you do."

Viki sighed and rose from the desk. He moved slowly, supporting himself on the desk like an old man, and when he put his jacket on, his hand trembled.

"Shall I ask my driver to take you home?" Sady asked.

"I'll manage." Viki shuffled to the door and opened it.

As he turned and met Sady's eyes, Sady had an overwhelming and irrational fear that this would be the last time he'd see Viki. This disaster was bigger than all of them, and there was nothing he, or anyone, could do about it.

Even without a doga session planned for the afternoon, the news of the demise of Twin Bridges had spread quickly, more quickly than it should, had everyone heeded warnings to stay inside. When Sady came back to his office, there were large crowds outside the foyer, and he had to take the painful step of restricting public access to the doga building. There were people wanting to know what had happened to their loved ones, people demanding that the army go over to check, and strangely enough, a lot of boys wanting to sign up as soldiers.

Sady despaired for the younger people, who had never experienced a sonorics crisis. All these people should be at home boarding their windows. They had no concept of the threat, although some of them were probably already feeling the effects.

He was chilled to think that the prisoner Tandor had foreseen this. And he, who had been at pains to take everything into consideration, had ignored it. Because the prisoner spoke of magical beasts. Because Chevakia didn't just ban the use of the word magic, it actively erased the word from common speech. There was no magic; Sady had heard that repeated from the moment he was old enough to speak. Magic was a superstition held by poorly educated people from backward regions.

Southerners believed in it, but southerners were crazy anyway.

But Tandor's prediction had been true. And the soldier, who could not have known what Tandor said, had seen these fire creatures.

Sady wondered how much of what Tandor said was true. A magical beast flew over the city, and as it did so, it absorbed sonorics. And, outlandish as it sounded, it was the only explanation Sady had heard for the wildly fluctuating sonorics levels. Yet he could not, with all the will in the world, bring himself to take it seriously. There had to be a rational explanation

In his days of working as a meteorologist, he would have launched an investigation into air currents, tornadoes and their links to the myths and habits of the southern people. Even old Chevakian mythology was rife with weather phenomena personified into spirits. He would have asked at the Scriptorium; he would have tried to find books on southern mythology. But there was no time for any of that.

All they could do was hide.

So he wrote notes that ordered halls and cellars to be turned into shelters. By some cruel twist of fate, the courthouse jail would be one of the safest places in the city. He ordered the city's thick-walled, marble buildings to be opened up to those who had no shelter. The library, the Scriptorium hall, even the doga's assembly hall. He went to deliver those directives to the guard station downstairs personally, and when he came back to his office, it was to find that someone had delivered a stack of large boxes to the foyer.

Sady prised open a corner. Inside were countless vials stacked one on top of the other, all containing little white pills.

Alius' pills. Not a moment too soon.

"There are a lot more of them in the store," the secretary said.

Sady could have cried with relief. They might actually survive this crisis.

"Distribute these immediately to all troops and all people who have a need to work outside. Then give one vial to each family."

"Yes, Proctor." The man went into the next room and called for help.

While the staff carried boxes away, Sady slipped one vial into his pocket, for his family and Farius.

In the large kitchen, Sady regarded the people gathered around the table. It was late afternoon, still light outside, but the boards over the windows made it dark inside. Persistent wind crept through gaps and cracks and the draught made the flames on the candles flap. Long shadows danced over the table.

Andrean looked out of place in the kitchen in his finery. His business was doing well; he'd gotten quite rotund in recent years. His wife, he said, felt too tired to come. Likely, Sady thought, she refused to come to his house with *all those foreigners*. Reili had come with her father, and she had the presence of mind to make tea for everyone. She was so much more mature than her eleven years. She smiled at Myra and stroked little Beido on the head.

Her father watched, and she met his eyes. She had Milleus' stubborn set of her mouth, and all of Suri's exuberant beauty.

Kalius sat alone and brooding at the other end of the table. With every year that passed, he resembled his father more, down to the hawkish suspicious nature of him. Of course the fact that his wife had walked out on him recently didn't help.

As oldest, he was old enough to remember his mother before he was bundled off to boarding school. He proclaimed to hate his father, but they were so much alike it was scary. His gaze went to Ontane, who had shaved, washed and cut his hair and wore a work shirt, all of which had taken ten years off his age. He looked very respectable, down to the pouch with tools which he had put on the table.

Myra sat next to her father. She had introduced herself politely to the visitors, and while Andrean had been polite in return, Kalius just glared. She had removed their sonorics suits and hung them up in the hall.

Loriane had been friendly to Andrean, who had fumbled through a resemblance of a southern greeting, but hadn't bothered with Kalius. She sat at the far end of the table, her arms crossed over her chest, glaring back at Kalius whenever he deigned to look in her direction. That woman took no nonsense.

"I'm sorry to call you all together like this," Sady began. "But I don't have the time to visit each of you individually. As you probably know, a sonorics-related fire front has reached Twin Bridges, and is expected to come this way. The Most Learned Alius and his colleagues at the Scriptorium have produced a medicine that helps your body deal with the effects of sonorics. I want you all to take some of these." Sady took the bottle of pills out of his pocket and put it on the table with a soft clunk.

Kalius picked it up and frowned at it, before giving it to his brother, who gave it to Myra.

Loriane took it from her, opened the lid, shook a pill out onto her hand, looked at it, sniffed it and said something to Myra.

"And what else are we supposed to do?" Kalius asked, still glaring at Loriane.

"Do not go outside. Board up the windows. Hide in the safest place in the house. Hope that this will be over within a few days. Take the pills, one a day."

"Have you heard anything from Father?" Andrean asked.

Sady had to shake his head. He wasn't game to say that Ensar was out of communication. He hoped Milleus had been able to save himself. He had hoped Milleus was somewhere in the traffic jam on the Ensar road, but it had been cleared from behind and there was still no sign of him. Milleus was resourceful and able to look after himself, but Sady was beginning to fear for his brother's safety.

Reili divided the content of the bottle into three piles: a small one for Kalius, a large one for her own family, and a medium-sized pile for Sady and his household. She put each pile into a small container.

Kalius gave a sniff, pocketed his portion and rose. "Anything else?" His voice was distant and businesslike.

"No." *Except . . .*

Sady's thoughts went to the children's book on the shelf. They surely would have thought he'd lost it if he asked them, *Can we read Toki one more time?*

Kalius was out the door almost immediately. Andrean worried about his wife. Could she take the medicine without it harming her unborn child?

Sady didn't know. He wanted to say, "Does that matter if we're all going to die?" But, instead, he said, "If there was a problem with unborn children, Alius would have said so."

Did Andrean even comprehend the seriousness of sonorics contamination? It did permanent damage to your body. The more exposure, the more damage. Some of it took many years to show up.

Andrean left, dragging Reili, who wanted to stay. "But, Dad—"

"No. You've spent enough time here. You have to help your mother."

"But all she does is ask me to fetch cups of tea." The sound of her protesting voice faded in the corridor.

Sady sighed, meeting Farius' eyes. The young man sipped from his tea, trying to look as if he weren't there. Mercy, they were so terrible at doing family things.

Myra, Dara and Loriane were studying the bottle, talking in low voices.

Myra said, "Loriane wants to know what you do with this?"

"It's a medicine to stop the effects of sonorics."

Myra translated, and Loriane's frown deepened. She exchanged some words with Myra, who shook her head. Dara put a pill on her hand, sniffed it, then broke a piece off and put it in her mouth. She said something to Loriane, who nodded. Dara laughed.

"What?" Sady asked, his heart thudding in his chest.

Loriane said, "This is simple medicine. We use for stomach cramps. This will not help you at all."

"You're kidding, right?"

Myra said, "Loriane knows about these things. She helps many people with medicine. This you can take, but it will not stop the icefire. It is not medicine. You cannot take medicine for icefire if icefire makes you sick."

The bottle now went to Loriane, who also rolled a pill out onto her hand. She sniffed it, put it between her front teeth and bit half off. Chewed. Frowned. Shook her head. She handed the bottle back to him. Her light blue eyes met his. Sad.

"But . . ." He turned his own bottle around in his hands so that the pills rolled against the glass. This medicine came with Alius' guarantee. He'd just distributed thousands of these across the city. The army's support relied on these pills. Alius had an entire team working on this.

If this medicine was useless, why had Alius given it to him? Why had he distributed it throughout the army? If the men took it and believed they were protected, it would kill thousands of them.

Finnisius was going to kill him.

They were all going to die.

Why, Alius, why?

CHAPTER 24

RAIN PELTED down on the tent roof, whipped up by the wind.

Inside the tent, people sat huddled together in too small a space. Milleus ached all over. The ground was cold and his old limbs were unsuited to sitting in such cramped conditions. If he leaned forward, his hips ached, and if he leaned back, someone behind him kept poking an elbow into his side.

Earlier on, he had wanted to go to the truck, but men dressed in black stopped him at the tent entrance. They talked, but he didn't understand them. None of them spoke Chevakian. No one left the tent.

He had given up the idea that he could control any part of what was happening. He should have listened to the soldiers and left the camp when he still could.

Artan and his wife sat next to him, huddled under a blanket. She was crying, and talked about some relative or friend whom they should try to contact.

"Please, just be quiet," Artan said. "What do you think we can do from here?"

"But if we asked—"

"We cannot ask anyone. They don't speak Chevakian."

"Surely they would have someone—"

"Maybe there are people who speak Chevakian, but I don't see anyone. I'm just trying not to get killed. I can't see what any of us can do."

She fell quiet, but Milleus could hear her crying. He could not begin to imagine what it was like for them, never having experienced war. In the Aranian war, his soldiers had been scared enough, and they had volunteered and were trained.

So he sat, said nothing and shivered.

He worried about Isandor and Jevaithi. It was too dark in the tent for him to see who was there, but they would have heard his voice earlier, and would have come to him, if they were here. Maybe the Knights had already found them and killed them, and maybe all his efforts at hiding them had been for nothing.

Why hadn't they told him earlier who she was? Yes, he knew why. Still, he worried about them.

Then he worried about the goats out there in the weather. They had been panicked enough with all the fighting and shooting. They'd need milking and feeding soon. Maybe the Eagle Knights would kill them for meat. And that thought sent shivers down his spine.

From outside, there were shouts and bangs of guns discharging. Someone splashed past the side of the tent and stopped there.

The people in the tent fell quiet. The flapping torch in the middle of the tent showed anxious faces.

It was so quiet that Milleus could hear the breathing of the man outside the tent. He shouted something that sounded like an order. A second man replied, further away. The Brothers at the entrance stiffened and gripped their guns. One picked up the torch from the stand. Ready to fight. A child started to cry and, despite its mother's attempts to keep it silent, only cried louder. The Brother at the entrance mouthed insults at her.

"Keep your head down," Milleus said to Artan.

The tent flap was thrown back, and in the light cast by the Brother's torch stood . . . an Eagle Knight in uniform, the characteristic grey shorthair cloak, made from the skin of the South's curious-looking Legless Lions, and underneath, the thick maroon shirt, without visible markings of rank. He was only a young man, with a characteristic narrow southern face and his sleek black hair tied at the nape of his neck.

Behind him stood another Knight. Two more were coming up, and behind them Milleus could see outlines of birds, and more Knights with crossbows.

The young Knight spoke a few sharp words that sounded like an order. The Brother with the torch replied, his tone angry. He moved the torch in an arc as if to indicate all the people in the tent.

The Knight repeated the same order, but the Brother just glared at him. A second Brother at the back of the tent rose from between the seated people, and then a third one.

"This is not going to end well," Milleus said to Artan, in a low voice.

The two Knights came into the tent, stepping over legs towards the Brothers at the back. The Brother with the torch shouted at them, waving the torch about. Its light glinted on a metal object in the hands of a man close to Milleus.

He had a gun. And so did another man, a bit further. Milleus had his own gun, but it was tucked inside his belt.

First lesson in survival in an armed conflict: when you were in a minority was not a time to start wielding guns, not unless you were in a position from which you could inflict serious damage.

This was going to be a blood bath. He had to do something. The only thing Milleus could think of was *create a fuss*. Surely the Knights would not like any Chevakian witnesses, especially on Chevakian soil.

He pushed himself up. "Hey, you!"

Artan hissed at him. "What are you doing?"

Milleus yanked his trouser leg out of Artan's grip.

The nearest Knight turned; his eyes fixed on Milleus. Like most southerners, he had cold, light-coloured eyes. His eyebrows flicked up.

Milleus continued. "We are Chevakians and we don't belong here. You must let the Chevakians leave, or the doga will consider this an act of war against our citizens." He felt ridiculous. The Knight gave no indication that he understood any of his words.

The Knight spoke in his language, and another, older, Knight gave a sharp reply. A few of their mates came into the tent, several of them with southern crossbows strapped into position. All of them looked at Milleus.

"Sit down, if you want to live," Artan hissed. "See those crossbows? They're bad news."

"I know." He remembered years ago, back when he was still in the army, trying a southern crossbow just for fun, and having difficulty, even as trained soldier, pulling the spring back. When he missed the target, the bolt hit a tree at a distance that matched the range of a gun.

"My name is Milleus han Chevonian, and I used to lead the doga," Milleus continued, and a kind of reckless feeling took hold of him. There was nothing else he could do, and if the Knights decided to shoot him, well, there was nothing he could do about that either. But he suspected they wouldn't do that, given the disturbed looks they shot one another. Oh no, they hadn't expected any Chevakians in the camp, that much was clear to him.

So he went on, recklessly, "I know many people in the doga, and if any of us, or anyone else is harmed, I will let the proctor know. They will consider it an act of war against the Chevakian state. So, please leave the camp before anything happens that would cause me to let my friends know."

It was rubbish, and utter bluff, but it confused the Knights, and while they conferred with one another, someone at the back of the tent ripped a hole in the fabric with a loud tearing sound.

One of the Knights shouted.

Someone at the back made a remark that sounded like an insult.

Two Knights charged across the tent, stepping over legs. People scrambled out of the way.

A shot exploded. Milleus could not see from where. The Brother dropped his torch. It went out and the interior of the tent was plunged into ink darkness. All around Milleus, people were getting up and pushing towards the entrance or the hole at the back of the tent. Milleus could do nothing but go with the flow. He grabbed what he thought was Artan's arm.

"Hold each other," he said somewhere near where he thought Artan's shoulder was.

"I've got Kara. I don't know where the other Chevakians are."

"Over here," someone shouted in Chevakian, but with all the other people shouting and pushing to get out, Milleus had no idea where the voice came from.

He could see nothing, and had no idea where the Knights were. People trod on his toes, and poked elbows in his side.

He shuffled with the stream towards the entrance, through the tent flap, out in the rain, on the muddy field that had been some sort of central point in the camp. The dark silhouette of one of the large communal tents loomed ahead. Milleus didn't know which. He was unsure where his truck was. Uphill, that was all he knew.

There were fires everywhere, even in the rain, screams, rioting groups of people, fortunately still further away. Over all the noise came the occasional loud bang of a gun being fired. The orange glow from fires showed the white-feathered bellies of flying eagles streaking low over the camp: more Knights arriving. Hundreds of them. How had all those men been able to come into the middle of Chevakia unnoticed?

"This way." He led Artan to the dark cover of a large tent, which could be the cooking tent, or one of the dorms, but wasn't the tent where Isandor and Jevaithi had slept. That one was further up the hill . . . and on fire.

A vice of panic clamped his chest. Where were the youngsters?

He couldn't see his truck, which might be a good sign—at least it meant it wasn't on fire. But how to get there? People were running past at high speed, both camp residents and Knights. People were throwing rocks and other projectiles.

He gasped when a couple of dark forms ran around the corner and almost crashed into him.

"Shh, Milleus," a voice in Chevakian said. Isandor, with someone else, a thin figure, smaller than him. Mercy, it was the youngsters, both of them, safe.

"Milleus." Jevaithi gave him a shivering hug. She felt cold, wet and thin.

"I'm so glad you're alive." He was embarrassed how his voice faltered. He wanted to hug them and carry them off to a safe place.

She huddled in his arms. "Please help. They're looking for us."

"If we can reach the truck, they won't find you there."

"They'll search the entire camp. They know that we're here."

"They will not touch the truck when I'm in it. They know that the Chevakian doga will see action against Chevakians as an act of war."

"I hope you're right." But she didn't sound convinced. "But we must get help from outside. I don't know who else can still help us other than the Chevakians."

"Let's go to the truck first."

While they sneaked through the shadowed alleys between the tents, Milleus considered their options. Hide in the truck and then what? Jevaithi was right. The Knights would find her. His threats to warn the doga were empty. The doga would never find out that there had been Chevakians in the camp if none of them got out of the camp.

Which meant they had better get out, and also that the Knights would have no hesitation in killing them.

He could ram the fence with the truck—the fence wasn't that sturdy anyway—but then all of the Eagle Knights would be after them. Eagles flew much faster than the truck could go and he could never reach Tiverius in time.

The Knights had a group of citizens rounded up sitting on the ground in the rain.

As they passed, a woman rose and ran. Two Knights went after her, caught her, pushed her on the ground. She screamed at them and one Knight kicked her.

Mercy, was that how they treated their women? No wonder the south had fertility problems. No wonder the youngsters had fled.

Further up the hill, the black-clad young men of the Brotherhood were throwing firebombs at the Knights. Milleus spotted a man, with a cloth covering all parts of his face except for his eyes, on top of a stack of crates, shooting at random. Smoke billowed between the tents. A line of Knights stood there holding shields against flying rocks and burning sticks that flew towards them.

They reached the truck, an island of safety in this crazy world. Fortunately, there was no sign of activity uphill.

"What can we do now?" Jevaithi asked.

"Be ready to move," Milleus said, opening the cabin door.

Isandor offered to get the steam going.

Milleus went to check on the goats. They were bleating and jumping around. They were probably hungry, but there was no time to look after them.

A couple of loud bangs echoed over the hillside. Isandor froze, and met Milleus' eyes. No words were necessary. The fighting was coming up the hill.

Isandor flung wood into the furnace. The water level was quite low, so Milleus grabbed the goats' water trough and emptied it in the reservoir. The water would be dirty and might clog the steam nozzles, but he'd sort that out later. Damage to the truck was a worthy price to pay if they could escape.

Isandor was trying to light the fire, but the wood was wet and his hands cold and clumsy. The small pilot flame would not ignite the kindling. His hands trembled.

"Here." Milleus opened the lid to the first aid box, which contained a flask of spirits. Isandor tried to screw the top off, but couldn't get it, then he slammed the bottle against the metal barrel so that the top broke off, and splashed the fluid over the wood. With a *whoosh* from the pilot flame, the fluid turned into an inferno.

Then they clambered in the cabin and the wait began. Milleus closed all valves, hoping that none would burst, and settled in to wait.

A couple of men marched up the hill, weapons drawn. Milleus ran his hand over the barrel of the gun that leaned against his leg.

"Hide behind the seat!" he told Isandor and Jevaithi but they already huddled there. He threw the bag that contained the tent over them. Watching the pressure needle move.

Come on, come on. He wasn't sure what he'd do. Ideally, he would have wanted to ram the fence on the lower side of the camp. Going to the higher side meant that he would have to backtrack along the Ensar road, and it would take quite long before they'd get to Tiverius. That was if no one punctured the tyres. After the last mishap, he had no spare. The lower fence, however . . .

This warming up was too slow. The shouts were coming closer. And closer. He was irritated that he couldn't see anything for the smoke, the darkness and the steam.

A number of figured resolved from the mist, running towards the truck.

Finally. With a hiss of steam, he dropped the truck into gear. The vehicle shot forward, but still didn't have much speed. They were going uphill and the truck was heavy. He should have disconnected the trailer, but he cared too much about his goats. They were not going to make it. Or maybe they were. People ran next to the truck, and the truck was slowly inching ahead.

A huge shape descended from the sky.

"Eagles!" Isandor called from the back seat.

More shapes swooped down, so close that the truck rocked with their passing. Milleus peered into the sky, but couldn't make out where the eagles had gone.

The heavens opened in all earnest. Milleus could hardly see anything for the water that ran down the window. There were screeches outside. The eagles were following. Damn it, they were not going to make it—

A series of shapes loomed up out of the rain. Trucks. Milleus slammed on the brakes, but the weight of the truck sent it skidding in the mud. Milleus yanked on the wheel.

The truck slid sideways, missing the other vehicles by as little as a hand's width, and came to a stop. Milleus gunned the engine, but the tyres slipped in the mud and didn't find traction.

The engine hissed steam. Rain pelted down on the roof.

Milleus wiped his face.

"What happened?" Isandor asked from the back seat.

"We're stuck!"

A couple of figures came walking through the rain, men with cloaks. "Shh, don't say a word." His heart was still thudding.

One of the men outside shouted something, and gestured for Milleus to come outside.

There was nothing for it. Milleus half-opened the door. Cold and humid air gusted in, mingled with raindrops. He debated taking the gun, but decided against it. It was only a hunting rifle, and would bring more anger from the Knights than protection against them. The best thing he could do was try to create another diversion. And stay within reach of the gun.

As he clambered from the vehicle, slowly, to win time, a group of people caught up with the truck and positioned themselves around it.

They were ordinary people, not Brothers, not fighters, but young people and old people and children, their mothers, fathers and grandparents, about fifty of them.

A young boy he guessed to be about ten carried a gun. Water dripped from his hair into his eyes and his clothes were soaking wet, but his face showed determination.

These people knew where Jevaithi was and were ready to protect her.

Eagle Knights were coming from all directions, some of them

leading their birds, until the refugees were surrounded and huddled around Milleus' truck.

Lightning flashed.

Milleus could do nothing but watch. In all the wars he'd fought, he'd never felt so helpless. He had no army to command, no idea what was going on, and why there were no Chevakian soldiers here. *They* would have listened to him. Now all he could do was wait while the Knights inspected everyone, and hope the doga would do something, but with Destran in charge, he didn't hold out much hope.

They would find the youngsters, and then what would he do?

CHAPTER 25

IN THE EVENING, under the cover of growing darkness, the main tower of the Scriptorium was like a ghost town. Since Sady had ordered the bell to be rung, there had been no more lessons, no more students talking quietly in alcoves, no more bows and whispers as an academic passed. Just a solitary door attendant on the ground floor who assured Sady that yes, the Most Learned Alius was in the building.

Sady made his way from the ground floor entrance hall up the spiral walkway that circled the inside of the tower. A soft red carpet absorbed his footfalls, and the rich handcrafted bookcases along the walls spoke of history and knowledge contained in this place.

Orsan walked behind him like a shadow. Under normal circumstances, anyone bearing arms was not allowed in the Scriptorium, but the gatehouse guard had waved Orsan through, because "It's not as if anyone's here to notice."

Sady knocked on the door of the familiar office. The sound carried in the eerie silence. He pictured Alius sitting behind his desk that always overflowed with books and papers, slowly getting up and walking to the door. And he found himself in that mental space he had occupied during most of his own studies. Even back then, most of the students saw Alius as a god, quoting his words at every opportunity. Back then, Alius was working on the barrier, and he was Chevakia's hero.

Why did he take so long to open the door?

He knocked again. "Alius, it's Sady."

Sady held his breath

But nothing happened. He looked around, but the mezzanine gallery and the hall below were empty except for Orsan, who leaned against the banister, his face without much expression.

What to do? He really needed to talk to Alius about these pills, and he didn't have the time to chase Alius all over town. Where did he even live? Sady had no idea.

Maybe there was some clue in the room where he would have gone. A note about a meeting or something. The thought *Lady Armaine's house* came unbidden. Her house had been like an impenetrable fort protected by a wall of excuses uttered by the guards at the gate.

Come on, Alius!

Sady tried the handle, and the door opened with a creak. It was dark in the room, and an odd kind of musty smell wafted out, as if the room had been closed for a long time. Slowly, Sady walked in.

A lamp against the far wall was sputtering the last of its flames, gilding piles of boxes just inside the door, identical to the ones that had been delivered to Sady's office earlier. The room smelled musty and damp, with a cloying sweet scent that he couldn't identify.

Sady nearly tripped over a book that had been carelessly flung onto the floor, its pages open.

What was going on here?

He grabbed for the lamp and turned the wick up so that it gave more light, and held it up.

All through the room, books were spread over the floor, yanked off shelves and left open, pages ripped. Alius' desk stood by the window against the back wall. The high back of the chair faced the door. Alius often complained about the room's layout, necessitating the placement of the desk facing the window. Today, the chair was empty . . . no, it wasn't . . . Someone with grey hair lay slumped over the desk, his head on the books.

Mercy.

"Alius!"

Sady rushed across the room, tripping over more books. He set the lamp down with trembling hands.

Alius' head lay sideways facing away from the door, on the open pages of a book. The eye that stared into nothingness was open, glassy. A trail of blood had dribbled from his mouth onto the book, but it was already dry and black. Some little insects were crawling into his open eyes and nostrils.

His hand, gnarled and aged, clutched a pen. The other lay on his lap.

When Sady touched the Most Learned's shoulder, the flesh was rigid and unyielding under his hand.

Above his head lay a wooden box, the lid open, with inside a tiny glass vial, empty. The matching glass stopper lay on the desk.

Sady had to stand back. The body gave off a cloying scent that suddenly became too much. He ran to the gallery, feeling dizzy and struggling to keep control of his stomach.

"Orsan! Orsan, quickly!"

Orsan had wandered a little away from Alius' room and came rushing back.

"Proctor?" His face was concerned.

"Look!" Sady gestured into the room.

Orsan looked, and swore. He walked around the desk without touching Alius. Sady followed, covering his nose with the sleeve of his robe. That cloying smell was the beginning of decay.

Orsan looked up. "He's been dead for a while." He picked up the wooden box. "What's this?"

"Careful of that box, whatever is in it."

Orsan put it down carefully. "Poison?"

"Looks like it."

Orsan's brown eyes went from the box to Alius' unmoving body. "Why would he do a thing like this?"

"I gave the pills he made to our southern guests. Both Dara and Loriane said the medicine had been made from a common herb, and would offer absolutely no protection against sonorics."

Orsan frowned. "And you believe them over Alius' word as academic?"

"Neither of the women knew what the pills were meant to do. Both are familiar with herb lore, and offered their opinion without knowing any of the story behind these pills. I cannot see why they should lie."

"But why would Alius send us medicine if it doesn't work?"

That, of course, was a very good question.

But Sady got a cold feeling. There was no medicine. That was why Alius had been late delivering it, why he hadn't wanted to promise its delivery nor talk about it, why he had looked nervous or evasive, and had been unhappy that Lady Armaine had mentioned it. He never had a working sonorics medicine.

Why Alius?

Sady glanced at the shelves to the side of the desk. The books were all ones he'd expect to see in an academic's room. Medical volumes, fat books with titles with long, academic words, the meaning of which Sady had long forgotten. There were so many books, so much information in this room.

"Have you seen this?" Orsan asked.

Sady turned. Orsan was pulling a sheet of paper from under the book under Alius' head.

"What is it?" Sady took the paper from Orsan. It was, in fine script that Sady recognised as Alius' handwriting, a letter, addressed to him.

It said,

To the honourable Proctor of Chevakia.

By the time you read this, I will be dead. I have deceived my country and the country will be better off without me. There is no excuse for what I have done. I'm afraid that I've let myself be distracted by politics at a time when I should have been working harder for Chevakia.

It was well over ten years ago, when I was unhappy with the way your brother was unseated, that I made some political comments that led Destran to cutting money for the Scriptorium. It was a necessary thing from his point of view. The wars had drained a good deal of our money, destroyed a lot of factories and converted others into making weapons. A lot of people came back from the wars needing care and housing. These were important issues for the doga to address. The Scriptorium was less important and lost a lot of its funding. Nevertheless, I believed, perhaps foolishly, that the doga should invest in knowledge for the future. The doga did not share my views.

In a public speech, I made no secret of my anger, and afterwards, a woman came to see me at my office. I didn't know her, but she said she heard my plea and offered to pay for some of the work I would no longer have the money to do. I asked her motives, and she said she had come into money and wanted to spend it on a worthy cause. She acted innocent and although she clearly had southern blood, I thought she was well-intentioned but naïve. My work was to find better ways to protect humans against sonorics rays. How could I refuse? That decision has haunted me ever since.

Sady felt cold. Just by pure chance, and a less desperate situation, he had avoided making the same decision. He wondered what would have happened had he not insisted that Lady Armaine's contribution to his travel expenses had been registered as non-political. It had been more dumb luck than anything, that he'd had the presence of mind to ask that. He continued reading.

Over the years that followed, she continued to fund a larger and larger proportion of my work. She encouraged me to work on using sonorics as an energy source. Since our forests are suffering from our need for wood fuel, I thought that was an excellent idea, providing we could find a way to protect ourselves from sonorics.

She said there were ways in which sonorics could be made harmless, and brought me into contact with this group called the Brotherhood of the Light. She told me that when the City of Glass was plunged into the dark ages by the Knights, the Brotherhood kept knowledge about sonorics alive. I soon learned that the Brotherhood wasn't made up of just refugees from the City of Glass. Many of its members are rich Chevakian merchants, disgruntled with the doga, and lured by the prospect of cheap energy and new technology. Many of those merchants had been in close contact with the City of Glass under the royal family, and had lost much trade when the Eagle Knights took over.

They saw an opportunity to regain what they had lost. They knew that the Brotherhood and its supporters planned to bring down the barriers and they supported that plan, providing a way could be found to protect Chevakians from sonorics rays. This is where I came in. There were some hopeful results from a new ingredient, they said.

I was given a huge stack of material. I don't think they expected me to go through it as closely as I did. I might have been gullible, but I will not be accused of substandard work. In the pile, I found results from experiments done on Chevakians who we know to have been forcibly moved to the City of Glass, all of whom had died horribly. The research, while macabre in nature, was interesting, but the main ingredient of the pills I was to make, from a plant that grows in the borderlands, had not been used in any of those trials.

How was this meant to help me find a medicine, I asked, and I was told that there should have been data about another experiment, which they would provide. You have to understand that none of these people were academics and their knowledge of the subject matter in question was rudimentary at best. They would not have realised that these were the wrong trial results they had given me. I asked for the correct results. They promised to send them. Except they didn't, and every time I asked, they gave me some excuse that seemed plausible, if annoying.

Just make the pills, they told me, and we did, because if we were going to test it, we would need them anyway.

Next thing I knew, Lady Armaine had told you about this medicine.

I should have walked out at that point in time, but the problem was that I had no other way of paying all the students I had taken on and I couldn't leave the project without major loss of face, both to myself, my staff and students and indeed all of the Scriptorium.

And there was another, deeper, problem, namely that of deeply rooted corruption. If I walked out, a lot of my colleagues and friends and others in the higher echelons of power would lose their positions. In the beginning, when she first came to me, Lady Armaine had used her own money to fund my work. However, she fled the City of Glass with only the clothes she wore, and married Darius han Lavani, who was always much better at gambling than at merchanting. He was well-off but never as rich as his father and grandfather had been. Then of course he died in suspicious circumstances, and there was no more money coming in.

So she used her ground army of Brotherhood supporters to keep politicians in office, and demanded payment from them in return. Then she recycled those bribes by paying us. We were paid with money that had mysteriously vanished from doga accounts.

If I had walked out, all that would have been exposed, to great upheaval in the doga. Lady Armaine repeatedly let it shimmer through that if I walked, she would harm my family, and they are innocent and know nothing of this.

So they forced me to bring out the medicine regardless of my objections. I can no longer live with the guilt.

Please, Proctor, the medicine does not work. Do not believe anyone who says otherwise. Please evacuate everyone from the path of this storm.

Once the storm has passed and Chevakia is safe, please take the book underneath this message to the doga. It contains everything they need to know. I believe in Chevakia. I believe you are by far the best leader the country has ever had. I will not have any more Chevakian deaths on my conscience.

With trembling hands, Sady opened the book.

There were columns of financial data. Sady recognised references to the books that had gone missing. Those books Destran appeared to have deliberately hidden. Alius had received *how much* money from Lady Armaine? She had received how much from Destran? And the money had gone where? To an account in the City of Glass, for *what*?

Lady Armaine's riches were paid from money scammed from the doga. Mercy. He met Orsan's eyes.

"Did you know about any of this?"

But Orsan, proper as he was, didn't answer the question. If they came through all of this, he must remind himself to pass a ruling that doga guards could be questioned about this matter.

Who was involved? Worse—who wasn't involved? He stared at Alius' lifeless body, his heart thudding. The entire doga was short of money. Every senator had been a target for Lady Armaine's group. Any of them might betray him. Any of them might still believe that the pills worked.

He'd run out of ways to protect the country. He'd given the orders for people to find shelter. Now he could only go home and prepare his own house for the inevitable. He wished there was something else he could do. And in the back of his mind, he still heard the rough, pain-laced voice, *You will beg me to help you by the time it's too late.*

In the cosy darkness of the kitchen, Sady ordered everyone in this house to sit down for dinner. He'd deliberately left Orsan at the gate, so that Farius and Ontane could be inside. Young Farius sat next to Myra. They talked in low voices and judging by their coy looks, he had a suspicion there was something going on between those two.

Dara had finally stopped fussing with pots and pans and sat down at the head of the table. Reili had shoved her study books out of the way of the plates, and it was as if everyone understood that the spot next to Sady was reserved for Loriane. She had come into the kitchen quietly. Myra said that following the family meeting, she had gone with Andrean to look at his pregnant wife, because Andrean had complained that with the sonorics warnings, no one would come to see a patient unless they were about to die. Sady suspected that Andrean was bluffing, and that his wife was perfectly fine, but Loriane had gone and come back looking impressively professional.

Myra had confirmed that apart from a breeder, Loriane was a midwife.

The soft light from the plethora of lamps and candles around the kitchen gilded her hair and made two bright spots of reflection in her eyes. Her broad-lipped mouth curved into a smile, and Sady noticed that she had little dimples in her cheeks.

"How was my niece?" he asked her.

Loriane waggled her hand. "Not time yet."

Thank the heavens for that. Sady might not like his nephew's choice of wife, but he could hardly think of worse times to have a baby than in the middle of a sonorics emergency.

"Mother is just bored," Reili added.

It struck Sady how normal life continued in the face of danger, and he hated to shatter that small bubble of normality.

He said, "I don't know how much of this you will understand, but I'm going to need your help."

They all looked at him.

"Reili, Farius, please help me explain if anything is not clear. The medicine doesn't work. It seems it was part of a conspiracy to assure Alius' cooperation with a group called the Brotherhood of the Light." He used the southern term.

Myra repeated it in the way it was supposed to be pronounced, and said something else. Dara nodded.

"You know these people?"

Loriane spoke. "They have . . ." She stopped, and said something to Myra.

Myra said, "Schools? Is that word for place for children?"

"Where children learn?"

"No, they live. With no family."

"You mean orphanage." As far as he knew, the City of Glass didn't have schools.

"Yes." Her eyes lingered on his. "Brotherhood of the light have orphanage. In City of Glass."

"What do people in the City of Glass know about the Brotherhood?"

Myra quickly translated the question.

Ontane said something, spreading his hands and rolling his eyes at the ceiling.

"Father says they crazy."

Dara nodded.

Loriane looked more pensive. She spoke to Myra.

"Loriane says that in City of Glass Brotherhood teaches about icefire. The have old books from king."

"Caldor," Sady said.

She flinched.

Sady understood the situation with a clarity that should have been obvious long ago. Fifty years ago, the City of Glass had been prosperous. He had only been a very young boy, but vaguely remembered the envious talk of his parents and grandparents. At the time, there had been a regular trade between Tiverius and the City of Glass. But, while the Tiverians were both enchanted and fearful of the south and its technology, within the country, a revolution was rising of people who had been abused for the sake of that technology. This was the part that Chevakians in border regions called magic, and that academics in Tiverius had always denied existed.

The resistance against the abuse of magic—let's call it side effects of sonorics—led to the rise of the Eagle Knights, who blamed the icefire technology for their ills and banned it. At the same time, Chevakia was developing steam technology, and found out how to build the barrier to stop sonorics. But all of the southern sonorics technology, their "magic" and Alius' barrier were part of the same academic discipline, and in both countries, those who saw good in the power of sonorics were driven underground. They had formed one large cross-border alliance, which, in Chevakia with its eternal limitations on cropping and land use, had drawn strong support from influential people.

And now, the sonorics supporters had done something to the source of the power and it had gone badly wrong.

"So, here is the situation: a large storm is coming this way, clouds heavy with sonorics—icefire. The Chevakian who knew most about sonorics is dead. Without shelter, many of us will die. Since we had the barrier, no new shelters have been built, and they are not big enough to hold the entire population. There is no time to build more shelters. Many people will die. Except, the prisoner Tandor claims that this . . . dacon . . . thing is the only way to reduce sonorics. My question is: do you think there is any merit in what he says?"

Acknowledging the potential existence of the magical being felt like making a hard confession. He would have preferred to ignore the issue if another option had been available. Which there wasn't.

Myra said, "I don't know what the creature is."

Loriane shook her head. "Is real. I seen it."

Dara said something in a harsh tone. Loriane replied, equally harsh. Myra loosened the sling and took Beido out. Ontane glared at Loriane from the corner of his eyes.

Loriane glared back at him.

"Is real," she repeated. "Is kill people. Baby."

Dara made another sharp comment.

"She says Loriane is not good in the head."

"It's true!" Loriane said, her eyes blazing with anger, and then she added something to Myra.

Dara snapped back at Loriane, and Ontane said some soothing words.

Myra rose. "Have to do work now. Make the house safe. Tandor is crazy. Bad."

When Sady came in, they had been working on the bathroom, which Farius had determined to be the safest part of the house, and supplies and beds were being moved in.

Everyone left, except for Loriane. Sady now understood the argument he'd sensed the morning after the killings. Mercy, if even the southerners were unsure of Tandor's words, then how much hope did he have? A small part of him had wanted Tandor's story to be true, because he wanted to be able to do something.

And Tandor said that this *creature*, if it existed, could be used to reduce sonorics, but he had no control over it, and neither did anyone else, and Sady could not see what else he could do to stop the sonorics cloud reaching Tiverius, with or without people made of fire—that detail hardly mattered anymore. Thousands of innocent citizens would die, and he could do nothing to stop it.

He let his shoulders slump. They'd go into the bathroom when the storm came. He'd put on his suit, and accept any family whose house did not have a safe place, and hoped they would survive, and if they survived, hope that they'd still be able to grow food, and that the farm animals had survived. *If* they survived, and that was a big question.

He blew out a heavy breath.

A hand moved into the field of his vision, and closed over his.

He met Loriane's eyes, their strange colour mesmerising. She didn't look away and didn't smile, but continued to meet his eyes with a steady expression. "Sorry," she said.

"You can't help it," he said. He shrugged. He hated being powerless. He had done all the right things, prepared the people as best as the situation allowed, reopened the shelters; he had settled the refugees and given them food. He had settled the Ensar people, and ordered the army to be ready for an attack. Except this wasn't the kind of attack that could be fought.

"What do you want me to do? Just sit here and wait until we can die?"

He was unsure Loriane understood.

"Chances are that when this storm has passed, you will be the only ones alive in Tiverius."

Maybe that was what this Brotherhood had wanted all along, and gullible Chevakian businessmen had bought into the dream of free energy while being told lies about the side effects.

"You will live," Loriane said in the oddly disjointed way of a foreign speaker. "You are a good man."

"This is not about good or bad."

"You are good."

Her hand slid up his arm. That must be a southern thing, because Chevakians didn't touch there, unless . . .

Her steady gaze did not waver from his.

Sady's heart was thudding. When had the atmosphere changed from one of comfort to something overwhelmingly suggestive?

He lifted his hand to cover hers, feeling her skin, soft, but with bumps and calluses on the fingers, under his hand.

How long had it been since he had last touched a woman like this?

"Loriane, I . . . don't want you to think that you have to do anything to stay in my house. I require no payment of this kind."

She didn't react, but continued to meet his eyes, and smiled. Her lips curved and her lips drew back to make little hollows at the corners of her mouth. Her cheeks dimpled.

Woman, don't do that or I'll . . .

Do what?

It hardly mattered if they were all going to die.

Would he go to his death regretting not having shown his affection to three amazing, brave and beautiful women in his life?

He reached out and touched the soft skin of her neck, threading his fingers through her hair. It was lush and bushy and smelled of flowers.

"I won't do this if you don't want me to."

Who was he kidding? Who was the most scared here? Twenty years, thirty years, since he had last kissed a woman.

He was scared to death that she would get up and walk out. That she would slap him in the face. He was waiting for it.

But nothing happened.

And then slowly, he closed the remaining hand's width distance between them and kissed her, fleetingly, on the lips. Giving her the opportunity to back out.

She didn't. Still meeting his eyes in that intense look, she slid her hand up his arm, to his shoulder, and pulled him closer.

He kissed her properly, and she kissed him back, unleashing a flood of feelings deep inside him. Relief, regret, desire. She was an amazing woman, strong in the face of incredible hardship, and if he had only night left to live, he was going to spend it with her.

For a blissful time, he forgot about the problems. He wanted to hold her and never let her go. He wanted to take her by the hand and shout *Look, I found the best woman in the world and she's mine.*

He had never, ever, been in love. Oh, he'd liked Suri, and had dreams about her. He'd liked Lana, as companion, but there was a reason why he'd never taken any intimate steps with either of them: because he hadn't wanted to.

The kitchen door opened, and someone said, "Sady—oh!"

Sady let go of Loriane, his heart still thudding.

It was Orsan at the door, dressed in a cloak dripping rain, his eyes wide.

"Um—I'm sorry for interrupting your—um . . ." His cheeks had gone red.

"You have interrupted. Tell me." Sady was surprised at how unapologetic he felt.

Orsan pushed down the hood of his cloak, still watching Loriane. Oh, yes, he disapproved.

"There is fighting in the refugee camp. The camp commander confirms that his men were overwhelmed by Eagle Knights."

Sady's first thought was *Fuck the camp and fuck the Eagle Knights*, but managed not to say that. He took a deep breath, still tasting and smelling Loriane and wanting, oh so badly, to take her upstairs. His second thought was *and Finnisius said they had everything under control*, but he didn't say that, either. His third thought was very different. "Orsan, tell me what the *fuck* are Eagle Knights doing in Chevakia?"

"Um—General Finnisius sent me to report. I don't know the details."

"What is General Finnisius doing?"

"He asks for advice."

Sady pushed himself up from his seat and grabbed his suit. "Well, I'll give him some advice. He's been giving me nonsense about these camps for days. Withdrawing from his job. *We don't fight civilians*. I bet my life that there is someone, or several someones, inside that camp who attracts this kind of weird behaviour." Likely the Brotherhood had infiltrated the army. "Come." He grabbed Loriane's hand. "Get a cloak. It's raining."

And as he followed Orsan out of the kitchen, another thought came to him: supposing this mythical creature existed, and supposing it roamed wild in the Tiverian skies, turning from a little girl into a flying monster at will, the only place they could find someone to tame it was amongst the southern refugees, and maybe that someone was a person with experience in dealing with large flying creatures and they had none such people in Tiverius.

CARRO DID NOT want to go out. By the skylights, the weather was awful. Rain lashed the metal sheets of the shed, which creaked and rattled with gusts of wind. Carro stood at the central bar, fussing with his eagle's reins. The bird snorted and shook its head, scattering bits of down, and gave Carro the evil eye. It had been asleep, beak tucked in its feathers, when the order to fly out came.

It looked like it wanted to do this just as much as Carro did. No piece of clothing would keep him dry in weather like this. The eagles hated it, and hated it even more because it was dark.

All around him, Knights were saddling up their birds to go out, part of the second wave of attacks, as Rider Cornatan had ordered. They had word that the trucks were in the camp, now it was the Eagle Knights' turn to fly in under the cover of darkness and flush out Brotherhood leaders and find the Queen. She was to be brought back to farmhouse. Alive. Rider Cornatan had vacated and prepared a room for her, a storeroom, without a window, with a heavy lock on the door, and a large luxurious bed with satin sheets.

Anyone defending her was to be killed, and the Queen brought back to this prison, where she would again be paraded out to the people as mascot, and where the Junior Knights would again talk about her puppies. Except this time, Rider Cornatan would waste no time in getting her pregnant.

And when the Brotherhood was defeated and its members killed, and the Queen safely imprisoned, the Knights could go on being just as dishonourable, disrespectful and disobedient as they wanted. Nothing would change unless *someone* changed it.

As Carro stood there, surrounded by eagles, unnecessarily fiddling with the harness, he was struggling to hold visions at bay. Icefire was strong tonight, and it made him alternately shiver or feel hot.

Jeito glanced at him. She had been doing this ever since they had started preparing, as if looking for an opportunity to do something unexpected, like stick a knife in his back. Since their conversation at Rider Barton's hideout, she had not spoken to him.

Farey had told him that Jeito's mother and sister were likely to be in the camp.

Carro thought, *My family could be there, too* until he remembered that the merchant was no longer family, and that the scornful dumpy girl wasn't really his sister, and never cared about him . . . except he remembered walking through the streets holding her hand. And he remembered her walking up the stairs to his sleeping shelf carrying broth. He'd been sick for days, and the soup was the best thing he'd ever tasted, even though he would never tell her. He remembered her wanting to dress him up in some garishly-coloured thing she had made with offcuts from her father's fabrics. He remembered screaming at her, and his mother telling him to be nice to her. He remembered yelling, *I hate her!* And his mother boxing him around the ears for being horrible to his sister, after which he had screamed that he hated his mother as well. He enjoyed looking at the hurt expression on her face.

At one point, his family had cared about him.

In later years, they had given up caring, because he had never given them a reason to care for him. He liked it when people hated him, because he could stay angry.

The world had hated him, because he had expected the world to hate him. By hating himself, he had made himself be hated. Except for Isandor who had, in some way, seen through the hate.

Whatever had possessed him to tell on his friend? Why had he cared about Rider Cornatan's approval?

Rider Cornatan didn't care for him. Perhaps his real father cared for him less than the merchant had. Rider Cornatan didn't care for the any of the people of the City of Glass. Rider Cornatan didn't care for the Eagle Knights' mantra, or their task: to keep the order and protect the Queen.

And he *did not* want to go into the camp and fight other people from the Outer City. But everyone around him was getting ready with grim determination.

Knights were already taking their eagles out into the rain. The birds made protesting noises.

Farey jerked his head in a *let's go* kind of way.

Carro nodded. Several pale-faced Knights under his command looked scared. They didn't want to fight either.

He turned around to needlessly adjust the saddle on his eagle's back—and met Rider Barton's eyes, intense.

Why were they all staring at him? But he knew why. If there was ever someone who could stop this, he was that person. Rider Cornatan would not listen to anyone else.

With trembling hands, he retied the eagle's reins and crossed the stable. At the open doors, groups of birds were taking off into the stormy night.

Rider Barton met his eyes in silence. His face was exceedingly blank, as if he was afraid to show any of his thoughts.

Carro said, "I noticed at the meeting that you were reluctant about sending the men into the camp."

"My excuses. I didn't mean to question the Supreme Rider. I was merely voicing the feelings of my men."

"Loyalty and Honesty." Carro forced a smile.

Rider Barton nodded and returned an equally forced smile.

"You backed off because you didn't want to push the Supreme Rider for what you feel is right."

Rider Barton flicked his eyebrows. "I don't know what that is supposed to mean."

Carro met his eyes, and felt like screaming, *Come on, give me some help, I know that you don't like this either*, but he said nothing, and Rider Barton said nothing, and Carro couldn't be completely sure that Rider Barton's remark about his men expecting to go back to the City of Glass in order to rescue people meant that he disagreed with Rider Cornatan's order. He was trembling so much that he couldn't think of anything safe to say.

Rider Barton nodded. "I'm sorry. I have a unit to lead." He clipped the loops of his riding harness together.

"Yes, sure. Let's go."

Trembling, Carro went back to his eagle. Now what did that mean? That Rider Barton distrusted him? That he didn't agree? That he was scared of being found out as dissenter?

He led his bird out of the stable, feeling that an opportunity had just passed him. By the skylights, if he wanted to reinstate the Knights' honour, if he wanted to lead a movement, a rebellion, a *mutiny* against the upper command, he would have to be bolder than this. Yet he needed numbers. Jeito and Farey might support him, and some of their friends, but he needed Rider Barton. Rider Barton's men might support him . . . but he couldn't see who they were in the dark and chaos of the shed where half the men had already left for battle. He had no way of reaching them.

So he grabbed the eagle's reins and followed Rider Barton outside. Rain pelted down, freezing and biting his skin. Not even his thick cloak was going to be enough to keep him warm in weather like this. He was already shivering.

They took off over the forest. Driving rain cut into the skin of Carro's face and hands and he could barely see.

First was the darkness of the forest that separated the farmhouse from Tiverius, and then some fields and dotted lights of farms.

He was nervous, shivering. Worried that Jeito or Rider Barton had been told to act as they did in order to test his loyalty and that either of them would run a dagger through his heart as soon as they landed.

Worried that they might think that he was a spy for Rider Cornatan.

He could already see the glow of fire on the horizon, and palls of smoke rising into the night air. He didn't have long to think about what to do.

Carro stands in the emerald room where he first met his father. The door rumbles open and three men come in. They stop a few paces inside the door and stare at him. They're Knights, of a fashion, but their standard of uniform would never be approved inside the eyrie.

One wears a faded shirt, the other non-standard trousers. They wear shorthair cloaks, and are just recognisable as Knights, but clearly not ordinary Knights. One of the men he recognises: the tall and skinny Farey whom he met in his father's bathroom, the one with the Aranian face. A second man is quite young, with a head of honey-coloured curls. His eyes are light brown. The other is slight of build, with sleek black hair and piercing eyes.

"Um—I'm Carro," he says, and the small man glares at him in a way that says, "See if I care."

The men must obey you, his father has said. If they do not, punish them until they do.

Punish these men? Rider Cornatan has to be kidding.

The camp was closer now, and Carro could make out burning piles of wood and people running. Shouts and screams. The first Knights had gone into the camp in trucks, to despatch the Chevakian soldiers. There were the trucks of the Chevakians which people had said were in the camp. There were the trucks that had held the first wave of Knights. He peered into the stinging wind. Where were all the camp's inhabitants? Where were Isandor and Jevaithi? What if they had already been captured?

The eagles landed on a field uphill from the tents. Knights jumped off and formed groups according to orders, while the stable boys looked after the birds. Everyone with their unit. Carro found Jeito, Nolan and Farey in the dark. He was cold, wet and his muscles were stiff, so his steps were awkward. Men shouted orders. Someone lit a torch, which almost flapped out in a strong gust of wind. Carro pulled the sides of his cloak closer against the rain and shouted to his command to follow him.

The Senior Knight walked back and forth in front of the lined-up men. "At the moment, most of the fighting is on the other side of the camp. We are going to come in from this side. We will get everyone out of the tents and line them up. We search the tents to make sure no one hides. First pick of beds tonight for the unit that finds the Queen. Go, go, go."

"Kick him," the boy says.

Carro looks up from the boy who crouches, sobbing in the snow to the bully standing next to him. The bully is older than him, a head taller and almost twice his width.

"Come on, kick him," he says.

Carro wants to ask, "Where?" Or, "How?"

He doesn't need to ask why; he knows. Because if he doesn't, the older boys will hit him. Not that he really wants to kick the boy, but it's easy because he's younger and smaller than Carro, and he's too scared to fight back.

Carro glances at the door to Isandor's house. Isandor would tell the big boys to go away, but Carro hasn't seen his friend all day.

He swings his leg backwards and kicks the boy. Not as hard as he can, nor softly enough for the older boys to notice that fact. He hates the soft feeling as his boot connects with the young boy's back.

By the skylights, this was not a time for visions.

The first Knights were already marching into the camp. Carro followed. He was wet and freezing. He couldn't see anything through the mist and smoke. He no longer knew where Nolan, Farey and Jeito and the rest of his command were, because the torch had been doused and everyone around him reduced to dark silhouettes.

Ahead, Knights arrived at the first of the tents. A man threw a tent flap open and shouted for the people to come outside.

They did, slowly, into a pool of light of a torch held up by a Knight. There were old men, women, children, some making pleas to the Knights. Many of them sported bandages. A man spat at the Knights at the entrance, and retreated when one of the Knights lashed out at him. A woman screamed.

They weren't Brotherhood people, men dressed in black with beards, but ordinary citizens, most of them from the Outer City. Carro tried to find familiar faces, but most people pulled their cloaks over their heads and hid in the darkness underneath.

Rain came down in sheets.

The Knights made all the people sit in the rain, and went to the next tent. Carro looked over the group. Some people attempted to sit on their knees so they wouldn't get wet from the ground. Mothers took children on their laps.

He couldn't see Jevaithi or Isandor, but it was only a matter of time before they were found. And what would he do then?

He stood there, avoiding the people's gazes, and shivered, and wished something would happen that would make all this go away. He wished he knew where Rider Barton had gone, or even that Rider Barton had given him a less ambiguous reply about who he supported.

He wished he'd never betrayed Isandor, and he wished he'd had the courage to tell Rider Cornatan that he wanted nothing more to do with him.

The Pirosian medallion burned against his skin. He longed to take it off and fling it as far as he could.

But that would solve nothing, because everyone would continue doing all these stupid things without him. Pirosians versus Thilleians: was that what it all came down to? It was stupid, stupid that people would die for this vendetta. Stupid.

NOT MUCH LATER, Sady and Loriane arose from the truck at General Finnisius' field office while rain pelted on the roof. The canvas sides of the tent billowed in with gusts of wind; and the flapping of the fabric, and the rain, almost drowned out the sound of the truck idling. Sady had ordered Orsan and the driver to wait. From further away came the blasts from burners which kept a unit of balloons in perpetual readiness.

Sady had shed his hood, but had kept the rest of his suit on, dripping water all over Finnisius' chair. Loriane wore only a cloak over her dress. If he understood correctly, she was of the type of people on whom sonorics had no effect whatsoever and could not see it. She didn't seem to be cold either.

Finnisius came to the table with a map, raising his eyebrows at Loriane. "These talks are confidential," he said, meeting Sady's eyes.

"If there is an answer to the problems we're facing, it will be with the inhabitants of the camp. We'll need to talk to them and we'll need southerners for that."

"But she doesn't need to be here now."

"She will not leave this tent. You, Lady Loriane, and a handful of others are the only people we can trust, and I wish you'd stop being such a precious prick about my judgement." It was Finnisius' poor judgement that had left the camp underprotected, and he wanted to rub that in, but he could not afford an argument right now. He glared at Finnisius, and Finnisius glared back. Sady had no idea what sort of relationship Destran used to have with the general, but he guessed that, like the city guard and the courthouse guards, Finnisius could do pretty much as he pleased.

Sady continued in a milder voice, "Now, tell me what is the situation?"

General Finnisius blew out a breath through his nose. He spread the map out, on which someone had outlined the field of the refugee camp and the perimeter around it.

"A number of trucks arrived here," Finnisius said, stabbing at the place on the map where the lower camp entrance was. "My men thought they were supply trucks, but there weren't any supplies scheduled. When they went to speak to the drivers to find out what was going on, a great number of Eagle Knights came out of the back and overwhelmed my men."

"You're sure they were Eagle Knights?"

"Oh, yes, no doubt about it. They were in uniform."

"Where did they come from?"

"A farmer saw the trucks turning onto the road a bit north of the camp. They came out of the forest. Other than that, we have no information. We need to get airborne to find where their base is but we can't see anything until daytime."

By which time there were probably more important matters to take care of, such as seeking shelter against sonorics.

Sady glanced at the map. The perimeter checkpoint was closest to Tiverius. It was probably the last place anyone would expect an attack.

General Finnisius hit the table with his flat hand. "Eagle Knights, performing military operations inside our borders. That's an act of war."

"That, it is."

Finnisius' eyebrows rose. Maybe he had expected an argument. "If the Eagle Knights take over the camp prior to the storm, they can move under cover of the weather, and who knows if we won't find ourselves occupied by the time we can come out of hiding."

"I agree completely."

"We will not tolerate any southern occupation of any part of our country."

"And we will not tolerate any political foreign influences to dictate our decisions."

"We seem to be in unusual agreement. Tomorrow, I'll apply for permission of the doga to retaliate."

"You have permission now." That was it. Declare war. Sady had never envisaged it to be as easy as this.

"Now?" Finnisius frowned.

"Immediately. The sooner, the better."

"But the doga has to vote—" Normally, the doga would have to approve any military action by vote in the emergency council.

"The doga will be disbanded at the next sitting."

In a few sentences, Sady told him of the medicine and the content of Alius' letter. Finnisius listened without speaking a word, an increasingly stunned expression on his face. "So the pills don't work at all?"

"No. We have less than a day to stop the Eagle Knights, or anyone else, invading the city. That's even with suits. By tomorrow morning, I want everyone in the shelters."

"The entire doga could be affected with this corruption."

"The entire doga *is* affected."

"Is there anyone we can still trust?"

"No. Just you and I, and Viki and Shara Diadoro. And Lady Loriane. I declare emergency rule until this crisis is over. We tell no one of this decision and carry on as normal, but meanwhile, all decisions are taken by us. And we're going to go into the camp."

A small smile played around Finnisius' lips. It seemed this was what he had wanted to hear. "You'll have access to any of my soldiers who have sonorics suits."

"Thank you." The question remained if the suits would be up to the task of protecting the soldiers, but no one could answer that. "Prepare to go into the camp as soon as you can. I want the Eagle Knights evicted from the camp or taken into custody. I want to make it clear to them that I consider this invasion an act of war. The refugees are here by our invitation and are on Chevakian soil."

The general gave Sady a calculating look, as if he was already working out the logistics in his head. His expression showed reluctant respect. Sady thought of the words in Alius' letter. If the Most Learned had really thought he did such a good job, why hadn't he said so earlier? He wouldn't have made so many mistakes.

He said, "It is also important to remember that not all southerners in the camps support Lady Armaine or the Brotherhood."

"There is no time to find out what's going on and who everyone supports. My men will fight anyone who creates trouble."

"I want you to do more than that. I want you to dismantle the camp and take everyone out to supervised shelters. Consider as hostile anyone who resists. Take the ordinary citizens and guard them elsewhere in the city. Gather the people who identify themselves as belonging to the Brotherhood and lock them up separately. Take everyone's names. Employ southerners to help, but don't tell them what it's for. Do not accept money—bribes—for anything. The Knights themselves . . . when you have defeated them, I'll talk to their leaders."

"Certainly, sir." Finnisius strained his legs as if to get up.

"Wait, I haven't finished."

Finnisius sat back down, all his attention on Sady.

"Do you have a courier here?"

"Yes." The general's voice made it sound like a question.

Sady dug in his pocket and took out the symbolic key to his office. "Tell your courier to take this to Senator Shara Diadoro."

Finnisius stared at him, horror written on his face. "You're resigning?"

"No. I'm giving this to her in case."

"In case of what?"

"I'm going to go into the camp with you. In case I don't come back."

"No way," Finnisius said.

"Yes, and my decision is final. We'll travel in one of the rear balloons, out of the way of the likely site of battle. I won't sit on my hands while you are fighting."

"It's my job to fight, not yours."

"Nevertheless, I'm coming. There is nothing more for me to do except hide and hope that some of us will survive. Except that there may just be someone in the camp who can help us. The lady here will come with me."

CHAPTER 28

ISANDOR RAISED his head enough to see over the back of the front seat.

Outside the truck, Milleus faced the Knights across at least ten paces of muddy ground. Only a few drops of rain were still falling down. The wind chased wisps of mist and smoke past him.

The Knights stood quiet, holding crossbows. They had all the time in the world. They had the refugees surrounded and wouldn't do anything that would risk their advantage.

Jevaithi looked at him with wide eyes, her face a pale oval in the sparse light.

The other refugees were still under or behind the truck, forming a living wall between the Knights and their queen. Isandor could hear their voices. Even so, Isandor didn't think their presence would be enough to stop the Knights if they set their mind to reaching the truck—which they would if they knew who was aboard.

Lightning flashed, showing the fence line where, a few days ago, the Chevakians had cut through into the camp, desperate for *something* to happen. Milleus was right; Isandor should have told him who Jevaithi was before entering the camp.

Now that fence, and freedom, might as well be miles away. They could never reach it.

Thunder rumbled in the distance, and a bell rang, a thin and high sound carried by the wind. Milleus had explained about the bell and what it meant to Chevakians. Milleus should be inside. If he stayed out here, he would be exposed to icefire levels high enough to do both short-term and long-term damage.

But Milleus didn't move. He stood straight-backed, with his hands in his pockets just like he did when looking at the goats. In fact, the truck rocked with the jumping of the goats. They had been inside for most of the day and Milleus' smell probably made them think that he was about to let them graze.

The Knights didn't move either.

Milleus said, projecting his voice so the Knights would hear, "We ask to be let out of the camp. I am Chevakian. These people are ordinary citizens who do not support your conflict. Let them go so they don't get hurt."

The Knights said nothing and showed no sign of having heard Milleus' words.

"They don't know Chevakian," Jevaithi whispered. "He's wasting his breath."

"Some will understand." Knights came usually from the upper class families. They had tutors. More than a few would have a basic knowledge of the language.

Milleus was still talking. ". . . If you use any violence towards us or anyone else in the camp, the Chevakian doga will see this as an invasion of their territory. If Chevakians are killed, they will declare war. So, if you let me go, I will take this matter to the Chevakian doga and we will negotiate—"

A voice shouted a harsh order.

One of the Knights marched up to Milleus. The man was almost a head taller, but Milleus faced him defiantly.

"He's so brave," Jevaithi whispered.

She was right. Through all of their trip, and before that, Milleus had faced any risk. He might be old, but Isandor felt a twinge of jealousy. Why couldn't he stand out there and tell the Knights to go away?

Because they wouldn't listen to him. Respect had to be earned. He was an exiled junior apprentice who had run off with the queen.

A Knight gave an order and a number of men marched forward. Milleus took up position between them and the truck, but there were too many of them and they simply walked around him.

"Why doesn't he shoot?" Jevaithi asked.

But Isandor knew that would make matters worse. If Milleus did, the Knights would kill him instantly.

The refugees tried to bar the way, but they had no weapons. The Knights pulled people out from underneath the truck or trailer.

"They're coming for us," Jevaithi whispered. "They know we're here."

"We're not giving up that easily." He grabbed Milleus' walking stick and pressed it into her hand. "Here. Mind the door on that side."

She took the stick from him, and then pulled him close. Her breath came fast and her skin felt sweaty. It was so good to feel her against him, to feel their hearts beat in unison. It felt like coming home. Then he thought of his mother stirring concoctions on the stove in the limpet that was his home, her warm hug. He could smell the faint scent of herb extracts that always hung around her. Those feelings made him so angry. Yes, he would fight for Jevaithi and his mother.

Jevaithi stroked his hair. "I love you."

"I love you, too."

"I don't care that you're my brother." She pressed her lips on his for a fleeting kiss. The smell of her was intoxicating.

"Don't give up," he said. "Whatever happens, we never give up."

She nodded, her face pale. "My mother always said that. Our mother."

That hit him harder than expected. He'd never thought of Queen Maraithe as his mother before, but she was, and she had withered away in the luxurious prison the Knights had created for her.

"We owe it to our mother to fight. To our mothers."

Jevaithi settled in next to the door holding the walking stick aloft, ready to strike at anyone who came in.

Isandor took Milleus' shovel and waited by the other door.

Voices yelled outside. Something hard struck the side door with a thunk. A squall of rain lashed the window.

Then the door opened on Isandor's side. A blast of icy wind came in. Isandor swung the shovel at the dark silhouette. It hit a hard object with a clang. The handle jarred in his hands and he almost dropped the shovel. The Knight went down without a sound. Immediately, a lot of people ran to the truck, shouting. It was too dark to see who they were and who was fighting who. He could only guess that refugees pulled the unconscious Knight away. More Knights ran onto the scene and fistfights fights broke out everywhere. Refugees crammed around the truck.

Two Knights dragged a woman away. They dumped her on the ground, and then one Knight stabbed her. She did not move again. The Knights now had hold of a smaller person. Several other people were screaming.

By the skylights, the Knights were going to kill everyone just to get him. Where was Milleus?

Isandor shouted for him.

His voice was lost in the tumult. Behind him, people were trying to open the door to Jevaithi's side of the cabin. She hung onto the door handle with all her might.

"Wait." Isandor slammed and locked the door on his side and scrambled over to help her. "Lock it."

"I have." Her voice spilled over with fear. "They'll break the door." The truck rocked with the efforts of the Knights yanking at the door handle. Hard objects hit the window. There was already a big crack in the glass.

Then the door burst open and a Knight climbed into the cabin

Jevaithi screamed and flung herself in Isandor's arms, but the man pulled the back of her shirt.

"No, no, Isandor, help me!" She grabbed his arms.

Isandor put his arms around her and wedged his feet at the back of the driver's seat. The Knight half-climbed into the cabin and pulled on her legs.

She screamed, "Keep your hands off me!"

The door on Isandor's side sprang open. A cold breeze went through the cabin. Large hands grabbed Isandor's shoulders and yanked. He tumbled backwards out of the truck. Jevaithi slipped from his grip. The Knight dragged her out the other side of the cabin.

He could hear her scream, "Isandor! Isandor!"

People jostled him. He managed to get upright, and yanked his cloak out of the Knight's hands. People were attacking the man from all sides.

Milleus' gruff voice came from somewhere Isandor couldn't see.

"Mercy, let go of them. It's a disgrace. How do you dare act against a couple of children?"

Isandor shouted, "Milleus! Milleus, where are you?" It was so dark, and there were so many people fighting, and the rain was running into his eyes.

"Over here!"

Isandor spotted Milleus standing on the beam that connected the trailer to the truck. He wrestled through the crowd. Milleus stuck out a hand and hauled Isandor up.

"You hurt?" Milleus asked.

"Jevaithi. They took Jevaithi." Panic clawed at his insides. All around, people were fighting hand to hand. He stuck his head out to look at the other side of the truck, but it was too dark to see who was who. Too dark to see any trace of Jevaithi.

Isandor screamed, as loud as he could, "Jevaithi!"

A couple of people took up the chant. "Jevaithi, Jevaithi."

"Shut up, everyone. She's missing! The Knights took her."

More voices now chanted, *Jevaithi, Jevaithi. Peria, Peria!*

Isandor climbed on top of the trailer. "Shut up everyone."

Several people made shushing noises.

"Hey, who are you?" a man asked.

There was nothing left to say except the truth. "I'm Isandor, Jevaithi's twin brother. The Knights just took her. They'll kill her if they get the chance. They've been trying to kill us ever since we escaped from the palace."

There were gasps.

A man shouted, "Revenge! Revenge!"

"Glory to the queen and king!" someone else yelled. Other people repeated those words. Isandor cringed. He was no king, and the south definitely didn't need another king. He only wanted Jevaithi to be safe. He had failed her.

When he saw the Knight behind him, it was too late to run.

CHAPTER 29

THE WORD CAME from somewhere uphill, and went through the Knight army. "We've got the Queen!"

While many around him cheered, Carro went cold inside. He'd known this would come, but had hoped that it wouldn't; that Isandor and Jevaithi had found a way out of the refugee column and were safe in Tiverius. He wanted to ask if the report was true, and if anyone knew anything about Isandor.

His eyes met Jeito's by the faint light of the impending dawn. Jeito's face was grim, and Carro thought of Farey's words. Jeito had family in the camp.

He followed the others up to the commotion on the hillside.

A ring of Knights had cornered a group of at least a hundred citizens and a truck with a trailer. Carro's heart skipped a beat. It was the truck of the old man who had given Isandor and Jevaithi shelter, and a couple of Knights marched downhill with a struggling prisoner he recognised a moment later as Jevaithi.

She was cursing and her hair was tangled. As they passed, her eyes met Carro's for a fleeting moment. There was mud on her face and on her simple Chevakian peasant dress. The hot anger in her expression shook him.

Next came a couple of Knights carrying a blanket with a blood-covered body. A deep cold went through Carro. Isandor was dead? Was this the end of it? Jevaithi back under the influence of the

Knights and her lover murdered? The only person who had ever cared about Carro without any motive other than friendship?

His head reeled.

Knights bustled around him, but he hardly noticed. Up on the hill, voices took up a chant. *Peria, Peria, Peria!*

That was the name of the southern land under the reign of the old king. Carro had never heard anyone say the name aloud and didn't realise that anyone still used it. This was the Brotherhood's doing. But why? Why revive a regime of a tyrant who tortured his people?

What were the Brotherhood fighting for? The right to torture again?

The conflicting emotions became too much for Carro. He clamped his hands over his ears, wanting to shout, *Enough!*

Most of the refugees were not Brotherhood people; they were ordinary citizens who cared nothing about the feud between the clans. Most of the Knights were not Pirosians. Many could see icefire and knew how dangerous it could be.

The Pirosian medallion burned against his skin. He and his father were spurring on this war by their very existence. The people were fighting just because they disliked the Knights' hold on power, not because they wanted the Brotherhood to rule.

Enough, enough, enough. This war had to stop.

Carro's heart jumped when someone put a hand on his shoulder. "Can you do something for me, son?"

His first, stupid, reaction was to salute.

The hand, of course, belonged to Rider Cornatan, and he laughed at Carro's hasty salute, but his eyes showed concern. "Are you all right, son?"

"Um—yeah." Carro's heart beat furiously against his ribs. That had been a stupid thing to do. "Um—tell me what you want me to do." By the skylights, what would his father do when he found out about all those thoughts Carro just had?

"I need someone reliable to stand guard. Come." He led Carro downhill where two Junior Knights stood guard on either side of the entrance to a large tent. While going in, Carro met one of their gazes, wide-eyed. Was he going crazy or did he see fear of his father in everyone?

Inside the tent stood a table with a woman tied to it.

Filthy and blood-smeared, Jevaithi was still the most beautiful woman he had ever seen. They had tied a gag around her mouth, but she growled insults that needed no explaining. Her grey eyes were vicious.

"I want you to make sure no one comes in here," Rider Cornatan said in a low voice.

Carro nodded, his gaze on the Queen, and the way the torchlight gilded her skin.

"No one, right?" Rider Cornatan held up a finger. "Not even any other Knights, especially from the Council."

"Yes," Carro said, trying as hard as possible to appear calm and careless. He glanced around, but couldn't see the blanket with the blood-covered body.

"There are subversive elements amongst us," Rider Cornatan continued.

Carro's heart skipped a beat. "There are?" His mouth felt dry.

"You heard Rider Barton at the meeting. Don't trust him. Don't let him into the tent."

"Um—sure."

Rider Cornatan gave him a penetrating look, then held the tent flap open. Carro went outside, where it had started raining again, and took up his position with the two Juniors.

He could only think one thing. Rider Cornatan knew that he had reservations. He had no idea how his father knew, or whether it was only a hunch, but he knew nevertheless. This was a test of his loyalty. He'd be watched. There would be spies somewhere.

But no matter how much he looked—and he didn't dare crane his head too much—he could only see the two terrified Junior Knights, scrunching their faces against the biting rain.

Rider Cornatan had gone back inside the tent and left the flap open. Carro could see the queen's legs through the gap, and the filthy cloth that held her ankles to the table.

His father said something that Carro didn't catch, and next followed a scream and barrage of swear words from Jevaithi.

Rider Cornatan laughed. "That is uncouth language for a young lady, let alone our Queen."

She spat. "If you think I'll go back to living in your prison, you're mistaken." Carro shivered with the anger in her voice. "I will rather die than help you."

The Junior Knight next to him shifted, and his boots made squelching sounds in the mud. Carro glanced aside, but the young man was staring intently at the next tent.

Rider Cornatan said, "Then be prepared to die, Your Highness."

The young Knight took in a sharp breath, noticed that Carro was looking at him, and turned his head so that Carro could no longer see his face. When he turned around, the young man on his other side did the same.

"I hate you," Jevaithi said.

"You make one mistake, Your Highness." Rider Cornatan's voice was mocking. "You seem convinced that we need you alive."

"I don't care if you kill me."

"I had something else in mind."

There was a sound of fabric ripping, a snarl and then a hard slap of a hand on naked skin. Carro cringed. That *had* to hurt.

An angry growl, also from Jevaithi. And Rider Cornatan's chuckle.

Carro shivered.

"Rape me, if you cannot get what you want elsewhere, you disgusting old man. I will never, ever give you the pleasure of seeing your daughter on the throne."

Rider Cornatan laughed in his dangerous, amused voice. "We'll see about that."

A bit later, the tent flap rustled and Rider Cornatan came out. He stopped and smiled at Carro. "Good work, son. Another job for you. Take her to the farm."

"Er—how . . . er . . ."

"Don't be so shy. Grab these young men, and one of the drivers. Someone will look after your bird." He turned to leave, but turned back. "And feel free to teach her a lesson in humility."

"Er . . . sorry?"

"My dear son. Do with her whatever you want. You do remember how to fuck a woman, don't you?" He laughed, and then he was off.

Carro remained in front of the tent while the Knights were still fighting rebels in other parts of the camp. He could hear the cries and shouts, the pop of fire and the firing of Chevakian powder guns.

He turned aside to see that the young Knight was staring at him.

He went into the tent, where a lone oil lamp flapped a sooty flame.

Jevaithi lay on the table. The ripping cloth he had heard had been her skirt. She was now completely naked. Carro stared at the rising mound of her pubic bone and the mussed-up black hair that covered it.

By the skylights.

The remains of the dress had fallen onto the ground and had been trampled into the mud. He picked the cloth up, but it was wet and disgusting.

One of the Junior Knights was peering into the tent. He met Carro's eyes, flinched.

"You have a cloak or something I can borrow?" Carro asked.

The young man took off his cloak and handed it to Carro, who approached the Queen.

She turned her head, the only thing she could still move.

"I'm not afraid of you." The anger in her eyes made him shiver.

Carro wanted to say, "There is no need to be afraid of me," but he figured the less said, the better. He draped the cloak over her. A small frown crossed her face.

Carro's hands trembled. The breeze that came in through the tent flap carried alternately warm and cold air. Dark figures moved at the edge of his vision, but he forced himself to think of other things. He had no time for hallucinations. If he was going to act, he had to do so before Rider Cornatan came back. It scared him witless, but there was no option. *Mutiny*.

He gestured at the Junior Knight. "Come inside, please."

The Junior Knight did, his eyes wide, no doubt wondering what he had done wrong.

"What is your name?"

"Minno, sir."

"Minno, do you want the Queen to be killed?"

The young man's widened even further. "I . . . I don't know, sir." His gaze flicked to the table behind Carro, and acquired a telltale glitter.

Carro answered the question for him. "You don't want the Queen to be killed. Do you want the Queen to be raped?"

"Um . . ." The glitter became more prominent.

"No, Minno, you don't want the Queen to be raped. No matter

that she's Thilleian."

The man looked at the ground and shook his head. "No, sir. I don't want the Queen to be raped."

"Serving the Queen is one of the honours of the Knighthood."

"Yes, sir, it is."

"Minno, were you happy with what you were ordered to do here?"

"It's not up to me to say, sir. I follow orders."

"But if I asked you, as a man, not as a Knight?"

The man's eyes widened. Carro thought he understood. Again, the less said, the better. "Minno. This is important. I want you to go to Rider Barton and tell him to come back here to me. Tell him that he knows what it's about—"

"But what about my orders to guard the tent?"

"Fuck your orders. We're going to do what I should have done a long time ago. Run. Quick."

Minno's whole attitude changed. He smiled. "Certainly, sir." He ran out.

Carro turned to the table, freeing his dagger from its sheath.

Jevaithi's eyes were wide. She said nothing—probably too scared—but surprise did not need words to show itself.

No time to explain. He bowed. "I'm sorry, Your Highness, but I'm going to have to touch you." He lifted the cloak, inserted the dagger between the wood and the fabric that tied her ankle to the table leg and sliced through in one movement. Then the other leg, her upper body and her arms—her stump and her wrist on the other arm. She sat up, stiffly, her stump rubbing her opposite shoulder. Her feet were bare, and he would have to carry her.

"Keep the cloak. You'll need it when—" Splashing footsteps sounded outside. "Ah, there is—"

The tent flap rustled and in came . . . Rider Cornatan. He stopped. His gaze went from Carro to Jevaithi seated on the table.

"You told me to move her," Carro said, trying to sound as innocent as he could. His heart was thudding against his ribs.

Rider Cornatan's hand moved so fast that Carro didn't see it until it, and the staff with the sink at the end hit his face. He reeled back. When he wiped his face, the back of his hand came away covered in blood. It ran from his nose down his lip and chin, then dripped onto his shirt.

"Fight, you coward. Straighten up." Rider Cornatan poked the staff in his side.

Carro straightened, his head still reeling. He licked his lip, but new blood trickled down almost immediately.

Rider Cornatan had taken up a fighting stance, with his legs apart and both hands holding the staff. That thing didn't work here in Chevakia, did it?

Carro stumbled a few paces so that Jevaithi was at his back.

"Stand aside so I can take the girl, if you're not going to do it."

"She is the Queen."

"She's just a dumb girl. Stand aside."

"No." Carro was trembling. He clutched the hilt of his dagger so tightly that his fingers hurt.

"What's this nonsense? Instead of incompetent, are you now dumb as well?"

"No," Carro said, louder this time. "I am a Knight and swore service to the Queen—"

"I recall that I just said you could service her—"

"Don't talk of her like that!" Carro lunged, raising his dagger. It was an automatic gesture, learned while hunting Chevakian creatures for roasting on the fire.

Rider Cornatan swung the staff just in time. It hit Carro's hands and dislodged the dagger from his grip. It bounced over the muddy ground before coming to rest under the table where Jevaithi still sat, wide-eyed.

Rider Cornatan came closer. "My dear son, just *what* are you up to?" His voice was cold as a blizzard.

"I am a Knight. I have sworn to the Knight's pledge: Obedience, honour, honesty, humility and silence."

"And you will obey me."

"There is no honour in attacking our own people. There is no honesty in ordering your slaves to kill the Queen. There is no humility in encouraging rape, and there may be silence in not saying anything about any of these despicable things, but I am sure that this is not the type of silence the motto intended." He was angry, oh, he was so angry that he trembled all over.

Rider Cornatan's voice lowered. "Do I hear that right? You dare challenge me? I have done so much for you. Given you a good home. Fished you out of the cesspit of the Apprentice Knights . . .”

Carro wanted to say that the merchant had not provided a good home, that the merchant had mistreated him, but he had not. The merchant had hit him only a few times, when he was little, and when he deserved it.

He fought images of the merchant coming to the table in the central room of the limpet, bringing the box of dice for a game. Carro loved those word games.

Rider Cornatan put a hand on his shoulder. “Come on, son. Let’s just forget about this. Let’s stop this nonsense and take her—”

“I am not your son! Here . . .” With trembling hands, Carro fumbled under his clothes and pulled out the Pirosian medallion. He flung it onto the table, where it came to rest against Jevaithi’s leg. “You can take that back. I don’t want it. I thought the Knights were about honour and courage, but they’re about repression and thuggery, about serving yourself at the cost of others. That is not the Knighthood I joined, or one I want to be part of.”

Rider Cornatan’s face hardened. “All right, if you want to play like that.” He retreated a step, and swung the staff. A hissing trail of steam zipped over the ground.

Carro jumped aside. By the skylights. He’d thought it didn’t work here. If Rider Cornatan attacked him with that thing, he was as good as finished. He tried to back away, but the edge of the table bit into his back.

If only he could reach his dagger . . . He lunged for the table.

“Not so fast, boy.”

A stream of light cut through two of the table legs. As if in slow motion, the table lurched, and Jevaithi started sliding off. She crashed into him and they both fell on the muddy ground. Jevaithi scrambled onto her feet, holding the cloak around her naked body.

Rider Cornatan laughed. “So, you think we served you badly?”

Carro glared up at him while on his hands and knees in the mud. He pushed himself onto his knees, picking up one of the severed table legs.

“So, you think no one noticed all the mistakes you made, clumsy pup? The fact that through your bungling, I lost two very good men. The fact that you had to tread on a stick to let the Queen escape?”

"I am no ace fighter. You had all the right to tell me off and made sure I wouldn't do it again. You could have returned me to where you found me. I didn't want the attention. I am a scholar or an accountant." He never thought he'd say that, but he knew how much he meant it. His stepfather, no, the man he knew as his father, was a cold, hard bastard, but if there were any ethics to be taught, he was far better at it than any Knight had been.

"You're right," Rider Cornatan said, and his voice was cold. "I could have done that. Yet, I did not. Time and time again, I gave you a chance. I sent you with the hunters—"

"To murder my best friend!"

"I gave you a patrol—"

"And told me to rape them!"

"I gave you a job at a desk—"

"So that I could take the blame if something went wrong!"

Carro runs home through the street. The snowy ground is lit by orange light from the blazing warehouse fire behind him. The ground shakes from explosions. Fires in the Outer City are always dangerous, but this, in a tanning warehouse, is worse than usual.

People are running through the street, while burning debris rains down from the sky.

His mother stands at the door of their limpet, holding his sister. His father is looking anxiously into the crowd of people fleeing.

Then his eyes meet Carro's.

He smiles. He opens his arms.

Carro runs, stumbling over his feet as another explosions rocks the ground.

Into his father's arms. The familiar smell of his fur cloak. The smell of his shaving cream. His hands ruffling his hair.

Tears pricked in his eyes. His father cared. He was harsh and at times unreasonable. He never showed his emotions except on rare occasions, but he cared. Why had Carro taken so long to remember that?

In all the memories of bad things, this was what really mattered. There was nothing wrong with his family. It was him. He was a whiny, ungrateful kid who didn't appreciate what he had.

And now the merchant was dead and his real father would kill him soon with a weapon that used icefire.

Rider Cornatan laughed. "And I had great hopes for a son of mine. You're a pathetic weakling, too fragile for the Knights. I should simply kill you when you're off-guard, but I'm going to give you a chance. Come on, stand up straight and fight."

He swung the staff and Carro thrust out the table leg. He had no great sword skills and the move was inelegant. The staff hit the wood with a great clunk. The table leg jarred in his hand and he almost dropped it. He stepped backwards, and almost tripped over the remains of the table. But something was pressed against his back.

"Take this." Jevaithi, with his dagger.

He freed one hand without taking his eyes off his father. "Give it."

Jevaithi put the dagger in his hand, blade first. By the skylights, what use was that? He needed to hold it by the hilt. And he needed two hands to change his grip, and his other hand needed to hold onto the table leg.

He gestured to Jevaithi. "Your Highness, turn it around."

The moment Carro glanced aside, a hissing beam shot through the air. He ducked, without knowing where the beam was. Lightning crackled.

Carro lunged, his dagger poised. Rider Cornatan put up a hand and the blow deflected. The blade of the dagger ran through the sleeve of his tunic.

Carro regained his balance. By the skylights, he was no fighter. He was going to lose this badly, even though Rider Cornatan was now bleeding from the cut in his arm.

He held the staff in front of his face. The metal was rimed with frost.

There were splashing footsteps. The tent flap opened, letting in a blast of icy air. Minno came inside followed by—thank the skylights— Rider Barton.

Rider Cornatan glanced over his shoulder.

Carro pounced. He could only see Rider Cornatan's weak spot: his throat. He'd learned to hunt large animals with a dagger. He knew how to cut a throat. The movement was mechanical. Rider Cornatan toppled backwards onto the tent fabric and Carro fell on top. He drove the dagger down and sliced. Blood spurted everywhere.

Carro scrambled up, unable to tear his gaze from Rider Cornatan's convulsing body. Blood had drenched the front of Carro's pants. It was sticky and hot, though cooling rapidly. The fountain of blood from Rider Cornatan's throat weakened until it was a mere ooze. The body twitched a few times and finally lay still.

Rider Barton bent and retrieved Carro's bloodied dagger and returned it to its owner.

Much calmer than he felt, Carro took it with blood-covered hands, wiped the blade and stuck it back in his belt.

Rider Barton gave a Knights' salute, which was only performed to superiors. "I am glad you read my signals." His voice was soft. "Let's get the south back to being a respectable country."

Then he knelt before Jevaithi, who stood there muddied and covered only in a cloak, shivering.

Carro also sank to his knees. A feeling of relief washed over him. The fight had left him exhausted. He swelled with the enormity of his actions. This was his decision.

Rider Barton said, "I am an Eagle Knight bound by honour to serve the royal family of the City of Glass with fairness and obedience to our laws. I, and my men, are at your service."

Carro picked up the medallion that lay in the mud and put it in Jevaithi's hand.

She studied it, and then met Carro's eyes. "You're Rider Cornatan's son?"

Carro nodded, pressing his lips together. He'd gained a father, he'd lost a father. Maybe he'd never felt like Rider Cornatan was his true father.

"It is time that this feuding was forgotten," Rider Barton said.

Carro put a fist on his chest. "It is time that the Knighthood behaved according to its motto."

"Agreed," Rider Barton said. "Give the order, Your Highness, and I and my men will carry it out."

Jevaithi said, "Stop the fighting between our people."

Rider Barton bowed. "At your service."

He turned on his heel and left the tent. Carro followed him.

CHAPTER 30

THE FORMATION of balloons had left the army base and was making its silent and deadly way over the outskirts of Tiverius, under the cover of menacing clouds and occasional squalls of rain. Seated in the centre of the gondola, in seats normally reserved for ground troops being transported, Sady was uncomfortable in his sonorics suit. He hadn't worn the suit since his trips to the City of Glass, and the smell of those trips lingered inside. The rank scent of meals consisting of nothing but meat, the restrictive atmosphere, the claustrophobic feel of hearing his own breath echo back at him.

Chevakia was in uncharted territory now. No one knew how bad sonorics was going to get, or how long it would last, how far it would reach and whether or not anyone would survive.

Sheets of rain lashed the side of the gondola, rocking it from side to side. Sady pulled his legs as close to the seat as possible, to keep them out of the way of the crew who were running around opening and closing flanges. Every now and then, the pilot would shout an order, or would start up the burners with a roar that echoed over the landscape.

Sady felt cold and hot at the same time. He couldn't see the ground over the edge of the basket. The feeble light from the vessel's bridge only reached to the railing to allow the armsmen to see. The gunner in the corner closest to him scanned the sky with binoculars attached to his weapon. He wore an army-issued khaki sonorics suit so badly scuffed on the knees that Sady wondered if it still worked.

On the empty seat next to him stood a portable sonorics meter and a rack of gel-coated measuring tubes. He'd taken on the task of taking air samples in a sampling balloon, blowing the air through the tube and inserting it into the machine, because he knew nothing about military action and this was something he did know well. But he might as well have given up on the measuring thing. Each time he shoved another tube into the meter, the measurement was wildly up or down. He'd plotted a graph, but it was all over the place. There was no logic to it. In the back of his mind, he wondered if that meant the flying creature was about.

Loriane sat on his other side, wearing a Chevakian army outfit. The trousers were too big for her so she had rolled up the hems. The shirt and jacket fitted better. She had her hair tied at the back of her neck, but did not wear a suit. She stared into the darkness, clutching the safety belts over her shoulders. Occasionally, their eyes met. For someone who had never seen steam engines until a few days ago, she was holding up well.

She also cast regular glances at the balloon's pilot, a sturdy woman of about Loriane's age, who bossed the crew about in a loud voice.

General Finnisius had been adamant that Sady travel in one of the support vessels at the back of the column. There were about twenty balloons ahead, an army of menacing dark bubbles punctuated by tiny lights in each gondola and the occasional flare of a burner. Already, the merest of dawn light silvered the horizon.

"You see that, Proctor?" The pilot pointed.

Sady pushed himself out of his seat, and quickly crossed to the railing to keep out of the way of the crew. The floor rocked with the wind.

They were flying over the farmland immediately to the south of the city, neat rectangular plots interspersed with roads and farm-houses. The southern forest started on the crest of the hill, a dark mass of waving pine trees.

The pilot pointed at the blackness of the clouds threatening to the south, which had grown into a huge roiling wall with the occasional flash of lightning within. It chilled him deep inside. Sady had never seen anything like it. He even doubted that this used to happen in the days before the barrier. This weather cell was deeper and more vicious than anything this country had ever seen.

"How long before that is here?" the pilot asked.

Sady eyed the clouds, trying to remember Viki's maps. "Half a day, I guess."

"We'll need to be out and packed before that hits."

Sady nodded. Having balloons packed away would probably be the least of anyone's worries once that storm front hit.

"Has the wind carried the sonorics away yet?" the pilot asked.

"The sonorics levels are all over the place. On average, it's probably not safe to go without suits."

"I feared as much," she said. "Much as the men hate wearing them. Anyway, we're almost there."

They had come over a ridge and the camp was easily visible, the source of firelight and smoke. Up here, dressed in the muffling suit, Sady couldn't hear anything, but there were people running between tents with flaming sticks.

The balloon's signaller was waving lights to communicate commands. General Finnisius travelled in the next balloon and his gondola was a frenzy of flashing lights. Sady understood a mere fraction of their coded meanings.

A number of dark shapes rose from a spot uphill from the camp.

The pilot cursed. "Eagles incoming."

Both gunners, one on each side of the gondola, already had their weapons aimed.

"Everyone to their stations! Everyone else, out of the way!"

Sady rushed back to his seat and buckled up his safety belt with trembling hands. He met Loriane's eyes which were wide with horror.

He took her hand. "We're safe here."

She nodded, pressing her lips together, but she looked scared more than anything.

"Watch it. Here come the eagles," called the gunner. He swung the gun around, following a huge dark shape swooping past.

Bangs echoed over the hillside from the firing of the gun on the other side of the gondola. Gunners in other balloons were firing as well. Loriane clapped her hands over her ears.

Sady put an arm around her shoulders, shielding her with his body as much as he could.

The birds lost their formation, swooping between the balloons. When they had passed, one fluttered to the ground.

One balloon appeared to be losing air, but the rest held formation. The eagles had disappeared into the darkness. The gunner searched the sky for them through the binoculars.

Sady didn't dare move. His muscles felt rigid as if he'd frozen in place. Loriane trembled under him. He had volunteered to come, had even demanded it, but he regretted his decision now. He was no soldier.

A squall brought stinging rain from the sky, lashed against the side of the balloon's gasbag. Even the suit could not keep out the fingers of cold.

One of the gunners shouted. A flash of lightning blinded Sady.

The birds returned, huge flying shapes plummeting towards them, with menacing claws outstretched, accompanied by the war cries of the riders on top.

The balloon shuddered when a bird hit it. The gunners on both sides were shooting into the air, the pilot screaming orders at the crew. One of the men jumped onto the ladder and scaled the side of the air bag. He vanished out of sight. A moment later, two loud bangs echoed, the balloon jerked and huge wings flapped past so close that Sady could feel the air rushing past, even through the suit. The basket swung from side to side. A crewmember slipped on the wet floor and hung onto the railing until the movement stopped.

Loriane stared, her eyes wide.

"How did we come through? How many of them are there?" Sady asked.

"I've counted at least twenty." The pilot peered into the sky.

"That's not many."

"They won't have their entire force active, with this type of attack."

"Looks like they're in trouble," the gunner said looking ahead.

Sady pushed himself up in the harness high enough so that he could see where the man pointed. An eagle had its claws stuck in the netting that covered a balloon at the front of the formation. Its huge wings flapped as it tried to take off with the balloon struck to its claws swinging violently underneath.

Light signals flashed between the remaining balloons. *Hold fire.*

It would be easy to finish off the eagle, as it was a pretty large target and well within range for the crews close to it, but bringing it down would unbalance the entire balloon and would endanger the men in the gondola underneath.

But it managed to free itself, releasing the balloon with such force that it swung almost vertical. Something fell out—Sady hoped it was not a person—and it swung a few times back and forth before it stabilised. The eagle flew off slowly before it was shot from two different directions. It fell, soundlessly.

Meanwhile, the other birds came back around and unleashed an attack of arrows. This time, Sady's balloon was in the firing line. The shield netting deflected the crossbow bolts, and one fell into the basket next to Sady, a southern thing made from bone and feathers. The two gunners on either side of the gondola were going gang-busters, swivelling their guns on their mounts as they followed the eagles swooping past. A small projectile pierced the balloon skin above Sady's head. Hot air whistled out. The pilot fired the burners with a roar.

Then the eagles were gone for another fly around. Sady made a quick inspection of the balloon's crew and found them all unharmed. Two other balloons had now sunk so low that they weren't going to make the camp. General Finnisius was busy signalling commands to these men, and a bit later a third balloon went to join them, presumably so that they could lead an attack from outside the camp. Sady suspected that this had been a potential strategy.

There was a shout, and the eagles were back, silhouettes against a flash of lightning in the nearly black sky. There were a lot more than twenty this time. A thunderclap shook the ground. Sady could hardly see anything after the flash, but heard the lashing of rain against the side of the balloon.

The guns went off again. There were soft pops of things bouncing off the balloon netting. Another eagle went down, a flutter of feathers and claws that plummeted past. Sady kept as still as he could. Loraine clutched onto his suit.

General Finnisius' signalling light changed to red, indicating that they were going down.

They were now close enough to the camp that Sady could see the people running between the tents, as well as huge bonfires, and fighting. Shouts reached up to the balloons. The three balloons were already down outside the camp, their crew having jumped clear of their deflating gasbags.

The eagles swooped again. New volleys of arrows came from below. Sady sat as still as he could, feeling the thunking of the arrows hitting wood under his feet.

Many people down there were cheering, too, but Sady couldn't see what was going on. Now that they were almost on the ground, the eagles couldn't attack anymore.

The first balloons touched down, and their fighting crew jumped out. The basket rose again once their weight was no longer inside. Each balloon would hover for as long as they could, given the prevailing wind, containing a pilot and gunner to help defend those troops on the ground.

Sady's balloon was one of the last to come down, and by that time, the soldiers had secured that area, holding back a crowd of refugees.

General Finnisius yelled, "Hold your fire for the proctor of Chevakia, by whose grace you are in this country and whose food you're eating."

Sady clambered out of the basket, accepting a hand from one of the men, and then helped Loriane out, into the circle of Chevakian troops.

The people behind the troops were all southern refugees by the look of their clothing, and more of them crammed from behind. Loriane studied their faces.

"Do you know anyone?" Sady asked.

She shook her head.

Jammed in between a wall of soldiers, Sady couldn't see anything. Fights raged on the other side of the closest tents. He couldn't see who was fighting. He couldn't see General Finnisius. Eagles flew over. Shots rang out. Smoke billowed, reducing visibility to a few paces. How had he ever thought of finding something of use here?

He would have been better off hiding in the shelters.

CHAPTER 31

AFTER THE KNIGHTS had gone with both the youngsters, first Jevaithi and then Isandor, Milleus slumped against the side of the truck. He felt sore and tired, and incredibly *old*.

The refugees stood huddled around the truck. A man leaned on another's shoulders. A woman cried. What were the Knights going to do with the youngsters?

He could sit down and cry himself. He might have been half-decent at running a wartime army, but ever since, he had failed everyone he cared about. Suri, Kalius and Andrean, Sady and now the youngsters.

He stuck his hand through the bars of the trailer and scratched a hairy flank. His goats were all he had left.

The Knights had retreated to a position from where they could watch the truck. He could see six of them, watching like silent statues, silhouetted against the threatening sky. The southern horizon was a broiling mass of black clouds. If he had been at home he would have said there was a snowstorm coming.

But first things first. The goats needed milking, or they would dry up or their udders would become infected. He had run out of hay and he would have to set up the pen so that they could graze whatever grass had not yet been trampled into the mud. But it would have to wait until the situation calmed a bit. Milking couldn't wait.

So he climbed in the trailer. The animals bumped and jolted him. There was barely enough room for him to sit. The goats pushed him. They nibbled his clothes. The bucket fell over twice. A couple of animals dunked their heads in the bucket and drank their own milk.

When he finished, he had only half a bucket left. He poured some in a container for himself, and was just distributing the rest to the refugees when the ground shook with a roar. Several of the refugees ran for the cover of the truck. A young girl squealed.

But Milleus would recognise that sound in his sleep: the sound of a burner. And indeed, there were the dark shapes of balloons in the northern sky. The Chevakian army had turned up. There was hope yet. Destran wasn't half-stupid after all.

Milleus put away the bucket and climbed over the trailer railing. The goats bleated and pushed him.

"I'm sorry, ladies, but I don't have anything for you." He would have to do something soon because the poor things were going crazy.

The Knights had gathered in a group, and looked uncertain as to what to do.

Milleus wanted to be ready to move, as soon as he had the opportunity. Join the Chevakian troops; tell them what was going on here. Get them to free the youngsters.

He checked the furnace and threw in a couple of logs. The boiler was still full of steaming water.

The first of the balloons had come down on the downhill side of the camp, to sounds of shouting. Groups of Knights were running down the hill. The refugees around him were getting restless. Milleus closed the escape valves, allowing steam to build up in the boiler.

A Knight came up to him and said something.

"You can say whatever you want, but I'm going to join my countrymen."

The Knight didn't move. He flapped his hands and gestured. Milleus had no idea what he meant.

"Look, I am Chevakian, and it is my right—"

The man gestured again, more angrily now.

One of the goats in the trailer behind Milleus stuck its nose between the bars of the railing and managed to get hold of his shirt. It pulled, hard. "I need grass for the goats. They're hungry."

He was sore, tired and hungry, too. And angry.

The man yelled. A couple of refugees argued back. Over their heads, Milleus could see smoke rise into the air. A number of Knights came running back up the hill, took positions behind tents and aimed crossbows.

"Come on, Mister. I'm Chevakian. I don't understand. I don't want to get out." He pointed uphill.

The Knight repeated the same command and pointed to his right, where there was a dark and empty field. Go there? No, not likely.

Burners roared. Gunshots rang out. Tents went up in flames.

The goats were jumping and pushing in the trailer.

The Knight raised his crossbow . . .

And Milleus pulled the pin out of the trailer's tailgate. It fell down with a clang and an avalanche of goats burst out. The Knight was caught in the middle of the stream of hairy bodies, waving his arms to stay on his feet. They jumped against him, pulled his clothes. He screamed, pushing the animals away.

The refugees cheered.

At the same time, a number of Chevakian soldiers surged onto the hillside and took possession of the terrain like a well-oiled machine. Most of them were wearing sonorics suits. There were a few warning shots, but they outnumbered the Knights on the side of the camp by at least ten to one, and guns were more effective than crossbows. Some Knights whistled—presumably for birds—but none came and the Chevakians rounded them up.

Strangely, the goats had settled to graze peacefully amongst all these goings-on. Well, at least someone was going to get a good meal today.

A group of five suited people came up the hill towards Milleus, four khaki-suited men surrounding one man in a civilian suit. Their khaki suits sported the insignia of the proctorial guard. The man in the middle was too short to be Destran . . . Besides, he couldn't imagine Destran coming into battle.

"Milleus!" The voice sounded muffled inside the suit, but it sounded like . . .

"Sady?" What in mercy's name was he doing here, with the proctorial guard no less?

"Milleus, you're safe!" Sady ran, and took Milleus into a hug.

Milleus hugged him back. "Mercy, Sady. I am glad to see you." And he was.

"I was so scared for you. I should never have left without you."

"And I should have come with you."

"I should have realised that you were one of the people trapped in the camp when we didn't find you with the Ensar road refugees."

"Don't blame yourself. I'm here now, ready for whatever you want me to do. You know I still have that damn letter. We'll show Destran, huh?"

Sady didn't respond to that and an uneasy silence followed.

The four guards had positioned themselves in a rectangle around them. There was something eerily familiar about the way they *watched* Sady.

"Sady, what is going on?"

"Well . . ." Unease crept into Sady's voice. "I wanted you to challenge, but you weren't there and . . ."

All of a sudden, it became plainly obvious. Sady, his little brother, was doing the job he had asked Milleus to do. The job Milleus had come back to do.

Then the second shock. Sady had allowed the traffic to build up on the Ensar road? Sady had understaffed the camp? Sady had made this mess?

"Milleus?"

"I'm . . . happy for you." He couldn't possibly challenge his brother.

He would never have expected Sady to consider himself for the job. His brother always had his nose in maps. Sady, run the country?

"It has nothing to do with happy, Milleus. We're in a major crisis. I need your help. I need help from every person I can still trust. Are you with me?"

"Yes, certainly."

"Well then, listen. The only reason I am here is because there is a huge front of sonorics coming this way, none of us can do anything about it, we don't have enough shelters, Alius was supposed to have given us a medicine against sonorics, but it never worked, and Alius has killed himself, and all there is left for us to do is hide and hope we survive. We have until midday, and I'm not going to spend that time doing nothing. You've lived with the southern people. If there is anything or anyone who can make a difference to our survival, no matter how small—"

"Did you know I was here?"

"No."

"Surely you haven't come here just because of some vague hunch. I know you better than that, Sady."

"Well—um—no." Sady hesitated. "This is going to sound like I've gone crazy, but, it's like this: I'm trying to find a giant winged creature called a dacon."

Milleus' first thought was that his brother had gone crazy. Then he remembered the book Isandor had shown him, and he remembered the screech in the night, and the warm air.

He said, "Larger than a southern eagle?"

"Yes." Sady's gaze was intense. "Please, can we leave the mockery until this is over?"

"I'm not mocking you. I've seen that thing. When it flies over, the air that follows it is warm."

"Where did you see it?"

"Exactly where I'm standing now. It came from the direction of the city and went over there, to the forest."

Then he told Sady of Isandor's book, and the spark on Isandor's hand, and when he finished, Sady swore loudly.

"What?" It chilled Milleus. Sady never used such language.

But Sady turned to one of his guards. "Can you contact the prison urgently, and tell them to release the prisoner."

The man bowed and left.

The battlefield had quietened.

By the weak dawn light, Chevakians marched Eagle Knights off to repossessed trucks, which Sady said the Knights had stolen from farms. Their birds were harder to control, because none of the Chevakians knew how to control them.

A group of soldiers approached. Their suits hid their faces, but they stopped and the first man saluted.

"Proctor, the situation is under control. We defeated the Knights, and more than half of them switched sides."

Milleus recognised that stiff voice: General Finnisius.

Sady said, "Good. Sweep the camp and ask anyone who has ideas about our safety to come forward. Make it clear that they will be rewarded."

Finnisius gave a small bow. "Certainly, sir." And he was off again.

Milleus stared after his retreating back. Finnisius was a self-important, arrogant piece of work. If Sady had him acting like this, his brother must be doing something right.

CHAPTER 32

IN THE DARKNESS of the eternal night in the prison cell, Tandor could tell day from night by the number of meals brought by the guards. During the day, there would be three meals fairly close together, followed by a long time without any meals. Also, during the day, guards came and went, jangling keys, and taking prisoners away, to the courts or the gallows room. Every time someone left, other prisoners took bets as to whether he would be back.

But today, they'd received only two meals, and no one had come to get the prisoners. In fact, no one had come yesterday either. The other inmates went into a frenzy about this. They said the guards never skipped a meal, and sentencing went on every day, even during festivities.

With his knowledge of Ruko and the other children, Tandor feared that this was the beginning of the end. The guards didn't come because either they were too busy trying to organise people into shelter or, and what was worse, they were all dead, and in that case, the prisoners would starve to death in this hole.

What a way to end a life that should have ended in triumph.

When a guard finally did show up, he marched past all the doors, to loud protests of the inmates.

"Bring our bread."

"We're hungry!"

The guard walked past all of them, while the patch of light from his lantern moved down the corridor. He set the lantern down at the door to Tandor's cell, extracted keys and opened the door. He picked up the lantern, and set it on the bench inside. He didn't close the door. By then, Tandor knew.

"I told that idiot of a Proctor that he'd beg for my help," he said, and coughed. "He still wouldn't believe me. So what's happened now?"

"The Eagle Knights have attacked, and there is fighting in the refugee camps. A large sonorics storm approaches. Someone seems to think that you can do something about it."

The guard knelt next to Tandor and unlocked the shackles that held his legs. "Don't get too cocky. Also, don't think that this means that's you're innocent."

"I don't think my innocence or guilt matters."

The man swore under his breath. Next, he unlocked the shackles that held Tandor's arms, then quickly backed off.

Tandor let his arms rest by his side, relishing the feeling of freedom.

"Come on then, go," the guard said. "Before I change my mind. I don't like this order one bit."

"Good for you then you didn't have to give it." Tandor struggled to his feet. He was stiff and sore, and clumsy. In slow, shuffling steps, he walked past the guard into the corridor.

Prisoners stirred in their cells.

"Hey, they let him go."

"What about us?"

"You can ask him," Tandor said, jerking his head at the guard. "But I doubt he'll be in the mood. To be honest, you'll be safer down here."

It cost him much effort to climb the stairs.

The courthouse corridor was deserted and lit only by a few flapping lamps along the walls.

A guard stood just inside the building's entrance, looking bored at a temporary guard station that would normally be outside. Tandor half-expected to be challenged, but it seemed the order to release him had been genuine, and the guard only watched him.

He opened the door and walked onto the porch of the building. Cold air buffeted him in the face, and with the wind came a familiar tingle. He drank in the icefire, and searched the sky for the flying dacon. He didn't see it.

To the south, the sky was pitch black, a dark mass of roiling clouds with the occasional flicker of lightning within. The base of the clouds glowed orange. That was the direction of the camp, where all the action was taking place. But he was too stiff and sore to get there in a hurry.

He moved in a kind of shuffling run. Through the merchant quarter past the houses of families he knew. The sky was dark and ominous punctuated with flashes of lightning.

The wind whipped around corners, sometimes warm, sometimes cold. Sheets of rain lashed his face. When his muscles cramped, he stopped and studied the sky, but never did he see a dark form fly over, not an eagle, not the dacon. Where would it have fled?

Finally, he stumbled up the steps to his house. The windows at the front were dark, at least those he could see over the wall.

The doorman stuck his head out of the gatehouse and called, "Halt, what are you doing here?"

"Don't be stupid, let me into my house."

The man came out, carrying a torch. He shone it into Tandor's face and stared, his mouth open. "Master?"

"Open the gate, you idiot. I don't have all night." In fact, it was almost morning.

"Yes, yes, sure." The man unlocked the gate and pushed one half of the solid metal gate aside.

There was light on in his mother's back room, and he heard voices.

"But it was your guarantee that none of us would be harmed!" said a male voice.

"That depended on your work." That was his mother. "You didn't do the work I required."

"No, that was not what I heard. This medicine was to protect us all from sonorics."

"You lied to us!" Another voice.

"You are responsible for Alius' death."

Tandor opened the door and went in.

His mother sat at her desk, surrounded by her rich Chevakian men, the ones she had convinced to support her. Their clean and cultured faces twisted into masks of horror. Tandor could only imagine what he looked like to them, dirty, with his hair burned off, his face scarred so that he could barely close his eyes and his clothes filthy from the prison.

The rule was that when family turned up, guests left, so the men rose and left the room. One of them was the former proctor Destran.

No one said anything until the door closed.

His mother gave him a cold look.

As he took his time sitting down, he noticed that his sisters were also in the room.

Rosane wrinkled her nose at him. "You stink."

He felt like telling her off, the arrogant cow. Always thought she was better than him, and never did any of the hard work.

But his mother glared his sister into silence. She regarded him from behind her desk, her elbows leaning on the surface and the tips of her fingers touching each other. "You took your time turning up."

"Yes, well I got held up."

He hadn't expected sympathy and got none. She flicked her eyebrows; her gaze lingered on the hairless part of his skull. "Where is the dacon?"

"That's why I'm here."

"I don't see it. You were meant to bring her."

"I *will* bring her, but I need a vehicle. I can't chase anything like this."

His mother's lips twitched. "Very well, but I'm coming. I'm not letting you ruin a perfectly good truck." She rose and retrieved her cloak.

"Thanks for the confidence," Tandor muttered.

His mother crossed the room in a few steps and held a finger under his nose. "Look, without me, you'd be nothing, and if you ask me, you're still nothing. What is so hard about bringing a newborn baby here?"

"If you'd come to my help, you would have found out. But no, you let me deal with the escaped servitor by myself, and now you blame me for all that's gone wrong."

"You never knew where the baby was."

"I did, but she turned before I could get to her, and I tried to climb on her back, but she wouldn't obey me."

His mother stopped. "What? Isn't the dacon meant to listen to Thilleians?"

"She didn't listen to me."

"Where is it now?"

"I don't know. I haven't seen it, because the Chevakians caught me and put me in the courthouse jail. Where were you? Why didn't you check on me?"

"I had other problems. Alius decided to jump sideways on the issue of the pills. He stalled and stalled bringing out the pills until it was too late, and then he killed himself rather than issue the medicine to keep everyone happy. Next thing, all our supporters have questions."

"Why?"

"They say that people have warned them that the pills don't work."

"And—do they work?"

He had trouble transporting himself back to the situation before he left: his mother in discussion with Chevakian business people about opportunities that would open up with increased icefire. The barrier was silly, she said. There were better ways for the Chevakians to protect themselves.

"That hardly matters." But he saw the answer in her eyes. She didn't care about any of the Chevakians who had given her money. "We need to control this beast or the entire country is going to demand the death penalty for us. We need to find it. I'm coming with you. Two of us will be stronger than one."

CHAPTER 33

ISANDOR STRUGGLED, but the Knights bound his arms behind his back and dragged him away from Milleus' truck. He yelled out, "Jevaithi!" But his voice did not rise above the screams of the people, and the hiss of engines.

People chanted, "Jevaithi, Jevaithi!"

A lot of people were screaming, and over the noise, there was a thunderous roar that shook the ground and made the air vibrate. The Knights stopped behind a large tent, with Isandor suspended between them, hanging from their grip on his upper arms.

"There," one of the men, a Knight Leader, said, his gaze directed downhill. At least twenty huge dark objects were floating down into the camp, massive round silhouettes occasionally punctuated by a flame and another roar.

Balloons. The Chevakian army.

A volley of arrows flew from the camp but most fell well short of the baskets, which were bristling with soldiers.

There was a moment of eerie silence before the first bangs echoed over the hillside: Chevakian guns.

Voices on the ground screamed orders.

The balloons landed.

The Knight Leader shouted, "Everyone, come with me. You two, take him away. We don't need him."

Isandor felt a surge of fear. *Don't need him* was a Knights' way of pronouncing a death sentence. He struggled, but with his hands bound, he could do nothing. The two men dragged him across muddy ground. More balloons were still coming down and the sounds of battle changed as the Chevakians joined. There were people cheering. Groups of Knights ran downhill towards the scene of the fights. A flash of lightning turned the whole camp white and a moment later, a clap of thunder shook the ground.

The air tingled. For a heartbeat, he thought he could see icefire strands in the clouds. Blue and pulsing

They arrived at a couple of trucks guarded by one single Junior Knight standing on the steps into the cabin peering over the camp. "What's going on down there?"

"Trouble. Chevakian army has turned up. Go join the unit."

The Junior Knight saluted his superiors and left Isandor with his executioners.

They looped a rope under his arms and tied it so he stood with his back against the truck. Then another rope around his legs. Isandor kicked, but they were too strong. The ropes were really tight and cut circulation in his hands, but he suspected that he would not have use for blood circulation much longer.

Please, let it be quick.

"Now, let's see how brave our boy king is."

"I don't want to be a king." The people had called him that and it embarrassed him. The people of the City of Glass feared kings, and he was no king.

He glanced at the sky. Where were those balloons? Where was Milleus? If he whistled, was there a chance that his eagle would turn up?

The Knights laughed. "You're a worm, nothing but a worm, from the Outer City. You really thought you could defeat us with your pathetic rebellion?"

"We will defeat you." Although he wished no part in the rebellion. By the skylights, he had to keep them talking, until someone, *someone* would see him.

One of the Knights lashed out with a rope.

A sharp pain exploded across his legs, as if someone burned a glowing rod into his skin. Isandor bit his lip to keep in the scream. He braced himself for the next hit, which came soon enough, and the next one, on his stomach. Each felt like it dug deeper into his skin. With the fourth hit, he screamed.

"Change the tone of your cockiness now?"

"We will win!" He turned his face to the sky, and with all the breath he had left, whistled for his eagle.

He had to keep believing, or all was lost. Believing that Jevaithi was alive, believing that Milleus would find him, that the Chevakians would defeat the Knights.

He lost count of how many times the Knight hit him. With each hit, his anger grew. Once he had respected the Knighthood, but these men were rotten, evil.

His shirt felt wet, with blood, he guessed. The icy rain was probably the only thing to keep him from feeling the pain. Because there was no pain, only anger.

With each hit, he screamed. "Fuck you!"

The rope lashed him. "Shut up, you worm."

"Never!"

Again.

"Never! You'll have to kill me first."

Again. His throat was raw from screaming.

"Never."

There was no next hit. The Knight stood before him, his face shining with sweat, his chest heaving.

"Getting tired, huh?" Isandor said. His skin was itching like crazy.

"You are a tough bugger." The Knight grabbed the collar of his shirt and pulled him up, dragging at the bonds that held Isandor to the truck. "You like playing games, huh?"

Isandor spat blood into the man's face. Behind the Knight's head, roiling clouds parted, and something *moved* between them, blazing blue icefire. "By the skylights, what is that?"

"Trying to distract me?"

"No, look!"

But the clouds had covered the crack again. The first Knight stared. He had seen it; Isandor had seen it, but the second Knight had not.

He said, "Looks like the Chevakians are beating the stuffing out of our boys. Come, we got to help them. Just get on with this job."

"I hear ya." The first Knight unsheathed his dagger, but he still looked nervous.

Isandor screamed, "Jevaithi! Milleus! Mother!" But a gust of icy wind tore past him and carried any sound his voice made. It was so cold that it hurt. All around him were flurries of . . . snow?

His mind drifted off into a place where he kept his secrets, a place where he and Carro sat on mounds of snow and read old books, a place where he led Jevaithi by the hand in the warehouse where they had exchanged hearts. And a small hunting shack in the Aranian mountains where he had first made love to her.

The dagger came down.

One moment, it glittered in the light, the next it plunged into his chest. He screamed without making a noise. The clouds burst open and released a lightning bolt of pure icefire. The world stopped moving around him. He felt no pain, and no sense of having a body.

The Knight stumbled back, wide-eyed.

Voices, thunder and battle sounds went quiet. Was he dead? He tried to move, but his arms were still tied to the truck. Not dead, then?

A screech above the camp made all the hairs on Isandor's neck stand up. The Knights shouted at each other and looked up.

A waft of warm and humid air went over the camp. The air wove into blue strands that were sucked up into the sky.

Isandor had only felt something like this once before: in the City of Glass, when he tried to escape through the Outer City with Jevaithi, and when Carro and his patrol had attacked him with an icefire sink.

Isandor sensed a lot of people running up the hill. There were cries and screams.

A huge shape came plummeting out of the air. At first Isandor thought it was his eagle, but it was much bigger than that. The thing —whatever it was—landed on top of the truck, where he couldn't see it. He tried to twist around, but his arms were still tied to the truck. His back hurt, his legs hurt, his chest hurt. His movements dislodged the dagger from his chest. It fell into the mud at his feet. A strand of icefire played over the hilt and the blade, which had withered to a useless stump.

The animal behind him snorted, and no, that didn't sound like an eagle. It didn't sound like a camel, or a bear, or like any animal he knew, but it was a large-animal snort. A very large animal. He felt the warmth of its breath. The icefire strand on the dagger curled itself into a little coil and sprang off, over Isandor's head, to the creature on the roof of the truck.

A woman's voice screamed, "Look! Look at it!"

The truck wobbled at his back. There was a thud of a heavy weight landing on the ground, and then the thing came around the side of the truck. It was . . . a girl.

She was about his age, and stood barefoot in the mud. She was stark naked, thin, her skin grey with engrained dirt. Her cheekbones were strong, but her cheeks rounded. Her hair was curly and deep black, like his mother's hair before it started going grey. Her eyes . . . were deep royal blue, like his own. She was strange and alluring and the most beautiful and most wild girl he had ever seen.

"Who are you?" *What are you?*

She didn't reply, but her eyes remained fixated on his. She came closer and ran her nose over his shoulder, like an animal sniffing its master. Her breath was so hot that it made him shiver.

She reached out a claw-like hand, with long and pointy nails, and ran it over his blood-soaked shirt. The blood dried, turned to powder and blew away on the wind. His skin burned and itched. She ran her hand down both his thighs and the skin there itched, too, *knitting* back together. Then she hooked the long nail under the rope that tied his arms to the truck and ripped it.

Oh, the freedom.

Oh, fuck, the pain.

She ripped the rope that tied his hands together, too.

While he cursed with pins and needles, the girl knelt at his feet and ripped the bonds to his legs as well. Her back was unusually broad for a girl and triangular in shape. Her backside was not full and rounded, like Jevaithi's, but muscular and strangely asymmetrical, and her legs—wait, what was the snake-like thing that curled around her upper leg? She had a tail?

"What are you?" he asked again.

She rose and bent over him, and kissed him on the forehead. He leaned into her warmth. She smelled like home, as if he had known her for years. If there were any good spirits, this had to be one.

At the edge of his consciousness, a truck engine roared. People shouted.

"Give her to me!" a rough voice yelled.

Someone stumbled towards him. The man looked like a living skeleton, dressed in filthy clothing, with a skull-like head devoid of most of its hair. The face had suffered horrific injuries, burns probably, and the skin was stretched tight over his forehead and cheeks. The lidless eyes were permanently open. But the irises were royal blue.

By the skylights. "Tandor."

Was this girl creature a slave of his?

Tandor stopped, panting. "You're in great danger. Stand very still and don't speak, and I'll come to take that creature away. I know how to deal with it." He inched closer, his hand outstretched.

The girl turned her head, and gave a low hiss that made the hair on Isandor's neck stand up.

"Why should I give her to you? She seems to like me a lot better."

"She's a dacon."

A magical shapeshifter, the symbol of the Thilleian house. Isandor wouldn't have believed it if he hadn't seen the girl. "Why should I give her to you? You lied to me about everything else." Isandor was surprised how quickly his anger resurfaced. "You lied to me about who you are, and what you wanted, and about everything. About my sister. You used my mother—"

"Come now, there is no time for talk."

Isandor laughed, an action that made his stomach hurt. "Everyone is watching. These two tried to kill me. And you're just going to walk out of here?" He noticed an elderly woman having come out of the truck. That was the Lady Armaine, daughter-in-law of the old king?

"We're not going to walk. We're going to fly," Tandor said. He had come even closer. His left eye didn't close properly and was weeping. By the skylights, what had happened to him?

Isandor laughed again. "We'll fly because I'm a magical being since someone just stabbed me and I should be dead?"

"You stupid boy. You're a servitor, that's why."

A servitor that couldn't be killed unless the master died. When the master died, the servitors died. Which meant that no one could kill him when Jevaithi was still alive, and that he died when Jevaithi died.

And that no one could kill Jevaithi while he was alive. That thought filled him with hope.

Tandor continued, "We're going to tell that beastie to turn into its dacon form and take us out of here."

"You can't tell her what to do. She doesn't even understand you, or doesn't speak."

"Come, you stupid boy." He grabbed Isandor's arm.

He yanked himself loose. "Let me go, you don't own me."

The girl snorted and shook herself like a bear. She positioned herself between Isandor and Tandor, jamming Isandor up against the side of the truck. Her body was much hotter than a normal person's would be. It . . . grew. The skin became rough, the body became thicker, the shoulders extended. Hands and feet became huge claws. The head elongated like a bear's snout. Ears and hair vanished into the leathery skin. And the snake-like thing against her leg grew into a huge tail.

Lastly, protrusions on her shoulders unfolded into giant leathery wings.

The creature turned its head towards Isandor. It had retained the girl's blue eyes.

"Watch it!" a male voice yelled. One of the rebels, with a gun, pointed at the creature's head. He wore the black of the Brotherhood, and Isandor recognised Simo, wild-eyed. "I'll kill the abomination!"

"No, don't!" Isandor jumped forward, but his muscles were still sore from being hit. A mighty wing swooped over his head. There was a bang.

He vaguely heard Milleus shout. The next moment, a rain of burning embers came down. The creature hissed and spread its wings. Simo fired again, and this time, Isandor saw the bullet hitting some kind of invisible shield in mid-air. It exploded into millions of glowing fragments. The dacon hissed. Simo fumbled with the gun that had to be reloaded.

"It's a construct of the old king!" someone yelled.

"It's a servitor."

"Kill it! Kill it!"

Isandor held his hand on the creature's neck. He could feel muscles relax under the hot skin. The creature understood the insults? It had nothing to do with the old king, and was not a servitor. It was something of icefire itself, some poorly understood part of it, some part that, possibly, the Brotherhood denied for fear of frightening the people. The Brotherhood desperately wanted icefire to be a positive force. And it was not.

The creature bowed its head and breathed out a cloud of warmth. As the air stroked past his skin, he could feel a sense of longing, and a savage hunger.

She finds nourishment in icefire, Isandor realised. And he also realised what he could do to save Tiverius from the same fate as the City of Glass and the southern Chevakian towns.

"You fly, huh?"

She crouched and held out her wings.

By the skylights, they were massive.

He grabbed a handful of leathery skin, put his good foot onto a bony protuberance that might be an elbow, or a shoulder, and heaved himself onto the broad back.

The huge body under him felt warm, and *right*. This was what he did best: working with animals.

He bent over the long neck. "You ready?"

The giant wings flapped and he rose into the air.

CHAPTER 34

"**T**HE IDIOT!" Lady Armaine cursed, and Tandor was unsure if she meant him or Isandor, who had become a black speck of ever-diminishing size in the sky. This was something neither of them had considered: the dacon could only be controlled by its Thilleian parent.

He stood a little apart from his mother and her retinue.

The Chevakians were returning to their balloons, ignoring hundreds of bodies in Eagle Knight uniforms. Chevakian commands rang out over the camp. *Quick, quick, get to the shelters.*

It was futile. Not even the shelters would be enough to weather this storm. The front was already at the next ridge, and whenever the clouds parted, human-like forms made from icefire peeked through.

"So." His mother spat. "The storm comes. We all hide. Tiverius is destroyed, and everyone who manages to survive is convinced that icefire is the worst thing in the world. No one will want to support us anymore. Our family is ruined. Can you think of a worse outcome?"

Tandor held his silence. As a matter of fact, he *could* think of a worse outcome, one in which Ruko destroyed all of Chevakia. Even his mother didn't understand the depth of the boy's anger.

"Come, let's get out of the weather." His mother walked towards her private truck. Tandor followed, for lack of inspiration of what else to do.

Loriane had the Chevakian senator. His children despised him.

His mother had never loved him, and both his countries disowned him.

They joined the long column of Chevakians going into the city. The camp inhabitants watched the vehicles roll past. These people would all die, even though they thought they could survive the icefire cloud. They were people like Loriane, most from the Outer City, most innocent, tired, injured and confused by the succession of battles fought in the camp. Tandor couldn't bear to look at them.

Isandor was flying a zigzag pattern over the city, creating a lace-work of icefire in the sky. It was as pretty as it was futile. A stupidly brave boy. Given some training and a few hard life lessons, he and his sister would make a good king and queen. The Knights were defeated. He'd even heard rumours of a rebellion from within. Rider Cornatan killed by the hand of his own son. The younger generation was taking over.

"Why don't you ever listen to what I'm saying?" his mother said.

She sat opposite him in the lavishly appointed cabin.

Old money. Old values. Corrupt values. After the mistakes he made—and they were his mistakes—the survivors from the City of Glass would never accept him as their ruler. His mother certainly didn't deserve to get that position. The throne belonged to Jevaithi, or Isandor, or Loriane even, people who cared.

And as his mother talked about hollow victories and corrupt plans, and as the doomed city that was his home slid past outside the window, one thing became clear to him: it was never too late to make a stand. Even if it would be his last.

He knocked on the glass that separated the driver compartment from the rest of the cabin. "Stop the truck."

The driver did. His mother stopped halfway through her rant. Tandor rose from his seat and opened the door.

"What are you doing?" His mother spoke as if he was a small child.

Tandor didn't answer. He let himself onto the pavement and slammed the door shut. The truck didn't move, but he walked away from it. His mother opened the door and shouted, "Tandor, come back!"

But Tandor kept walking. There was one reason that Ruko still sought revenge, and he was that reason. He walked into a side street and shouted at the sky, "Ruko! Come and get me if you dare."

CHAPTER 35

WITH A FEW lazy wingbeats, the dacon turned and flew back over the city. Isandor loved flying on her broad and muscled back. Her movements were majestic and powerful. He had never flown a stronger mount.

The wall of smoke loomed before him, a mass of broiling black clouds. Fires consumed farmland and forest, thick smoke spreading from the fire front. Wind whipped the trees on the ground, throwing up eddies of dust. The air tasted of smoke and grit. And icefire. It streamed through the air, forming ever-strengthening cords that danced over the dacon's skin. Isandor felt none of it; she drank it all in, like a camel in desperate need for water. With each wingbeat, muscles became more powerful and confident. With each wingbeat, she came closer to the front.

Soon, tendrils of smoke detached from the clouds and reached for her, long strands of wispy substance, whirling with grace that belied the violence within. Isandor's skin tickled with their power, and these were only offshoots that escaped the dacon's skin. The cold was biting, and he wasn't dressed for it.

The dacon swooped back and forth, feeding from the roiling clouds, *halting* their progress. This was then, how the storm could be beaten, unravelled from the outside like a ball of knitting wool.

Back and forth, back and forth.

But when the outer layer of grey-black peeled off, the inside of the clouds glowed an angry fiery orange. Shapes of blue icefire moved within. By the skylights, something lived inside those clouds, shapes that knitted the outer layer back together. Shapes that picked up entire trees and hurled them at the dacon. She managed to evade their projectiles, but Isandor felt the whooshing of wind of the force with which they were thrown. The burning projectiles fell amongst farms yet unaffected, and started new fires. The fire front roared and billowed outwards. Lightning cracked and thunder shook the ground. The dacon absorbed power, and flew backwards and forwards.

It was not enough.

Not enough to stop the fire, not enough to halt the progression of the front towards Tiverius.

We are going through the clouds, Isandor thought at the creature. If we break apart the storm, it may lose coherence.

He sensed a measure of glee. *Finally. Why did you wait so long?*

She banked sharply and plunged into the roiling mass. Blackness closed all around him. The air was so cold that his hands became stiff. Wind buffeted him. Icefire grew much stronger here. Blue strands of light zapped through the darkness without notice. They struck the dacon's back, its head, its wings. She absorbed all the power without flinching.

Angry orange flames lit up, and a human-shaped figure made of flames rose from the fire. It had dark holes for eyes, and gouts of fire for hands and a mouth that blazed with white icefire.

Attack it! he thought at the dacon.

She dived into the fireball. Air crackled around Isandor, protecting him in a cage of sizzling strands. Flames pulled at the cage, but wherever they broke though, the cage knitted back.

The fire-being hefted a burning tree and swung it around as if the dacon were an annoying fly. Sparks flew off the burning wood. The trunk hit Isandor's protective cage with a juddering crack. Some of the strands broke and reknitted around the burning tree. Isandor was lifted off the dacon's back with his protective cage when the fire-being swung the tree in the other direction. Sparks rained down on him, freezing onto his skin and clothing.

He screamed in his mind, *Help!*

He couldn't see the dacon anymore.

The fire-being roared triumph. Isandor crawled as far into his cage as possible, but the fire-being wasn't roaring at him. The dacon had taken hold of its arm with its mouth. It shook its head like an eagle trying to kill a larger animal by shaking it, and sparks of fire rained from the fire-being's arm.

It dropped the tree. Isandor fell, and fell . . . and was snatched up just before hitting the ground by the dacon, carrying the icefire cage in its mouth.

It flew at crazy speed, dodged and twisted. At least twenty other fire-beings had come to the first fire-being's aid. It was shouting at the sky, sparks spewing from its mouth and still leaking from its injured arm. Icefire streamed from its damaged form into the dacon.

A second fire-being tried to grab the dacon, but it swung its tail, unleashing another shower of sparks from the fire-being's side. Isandor understood. The sparks were blood, and once the skin of the fire-being had been broken, it didn't easily repair.

"Put me down!" he yelled over the roar of fire and wind.

The dacon did, and Isandor climbed onto its back, anchoring the icefire cage to the dacon's shoulders.

As he did so, he noticed how the skin of the dacon had darkened . . . and wrinkled. As if she sensed his thought, she turned her head. Her eyes, once bright and blue, had clouded. Eyelids sagged, wrinkles surrounded her nose.

She looked . . . old.

He understood. "By the skylights. Taking in icefire makes you age quickly."

Her eyes were sad. How long did she have?

The lumbering fire-beings were coming for them, and there were a lot more now. The idea was to injure them. Two were already 'bleeding', one staggering aimlessly, leaking sparks from its side, the other kneeling on the ground, and much smaller than it had been before.

Isandor unsheathed his dagger and held it to a strand of icefire to imbue the blade with it. Then he threw it at the nearest fire-being. Straight into the chest, and out the other side. It left a gaping hole in the fire-being's body. It seemed surprised for a heartbeat or so, and then the sparks gushed out, the being howled at the sky and fell flat on the ground. Isandor cheered. He kneed the dacon around. Hauled up his dagger on its thread of icefire borrowed from the dacon.

Threw it at the next construct, which it hit in the shoulder. Turn around, and again. The fire-beings were not very smart, if determined to fight to the death. Several lay on the ground, their lifeblood oozing out of them in the form of sparks, reabsorbed into the dacon's skin.

Isandor collected the dagger, threw it, retrieved it, threw it. And the fifth one, he missed completely. His arms were getting tired and too cold to aim effectively. By the skylights, how many of these things were there?

Also, he noticed that the fire front had started moving again. There were only two bleeding fire-beings left on the ground. The others had all come back to life.

A thought went through his mind. *You cannot kill a servitor until its master dies.*

These were not regular servitors, but what if they had a master? If so, who was this master? How could he find out in the short time he still had?

He became aware of the sound of a voice. Somewhere outside the cloud, a man was calling his name.

No, when he steered the dacon out of the clouds, he heard that the man was calling, "Ruko, Ruko."

It was Tandor.

He steered the dacon to a glide and landed next to Tandor—his father. He screamed, "Do you command these fire beings? Tell them to stop!"

Tandor shook his head. "Sadly, I do not. But I know who does." And he raised his voice. "Ruko!"

A huge being detached from the clouds, with shimmering flames for arms and legs. The body was transparent, and the head a construct of delicate flames. Isandor could see the eyes, hollow and dark, the shimmering flames that formed the hair. The figure, a young man, had a broad, square face and a jutting chin.

"Ah, there you are. Come and get me if you dare." And then to Isandor, "Stand back."

"But he will kill you!" And somehow, that mattered, because Tandor was his father, and there had to be some good in him.

The fire-being that was Ruko bent down, showing Isandor all the intricate detail of the head. Smooth skin, a flat nose with flaring nostrils, heavy brows. With a chill, Isandor recognised the giant who had locked him and Jevaithi into the butcher's warehouse.

"Yes, he will kill me. Revenge is the only thing he has ever wanted since losing his girl. If not me, he'll go after the Knights, or the Chevakians. He'll find a reason to suit his murders. The only way to stop him is to give him what he wants. I'll tell you something I've learned. Servitors are a bad idea, not because they obey evil people, but because they are evil, and you cannot control them unless you're more evil than they are. I was never evil enough to do what would have been required to keep them under control. I must pay for that. Look after the City of Glass, son. It is yours."

The fire-being's hand touched Tandor, and the world exploded in a flash of white. The wind knitted into strands of power that were sucked into a roaring vortex of icefire. Isandor was flung high into the air. The wind sucked him up as if he was a flurry of snow and dropped him on the ground in a whirlwind of dust and leaves. Thunder rumbled. Huge hailstones pelted down, bouncing all around him. He pressed himself into the mud shielding his head with his arms. Those hailstones *hurt*.

Furious as the storm was, it didn't last long. The hail stopped, the torrential rain eased, and Isandor pushed himself up. Somewhere in the struggle, he had lost his wooden leg, and he fumbled in the mud until he found a tree branch to support himself.

The branch had come from a copse of trees next to a ruined farmhouse. Isandor limped to the building. The roof had been blown off and the exposed beams seared by fire. Piles of blacked coal that had once been items of furniture were still smoking. He found no sign of life. Rain drizzled down, and mist and smoke restricted his vision. Where was he?

A soft whimper attracted his attention. On the other side of the farmhouse, he found a duck pen with all the ducks in the hutch, burnt to cinders. The sound came again. The grassy field next to the duck house was strewn with burnt wood and splinters, and amongst them, he found an old woman. She lay in the dirt, naked, her back horribly twisted. Her eyes were closed and her lips formed inaudible words.

"I'm here," he said. "I'll help you."

She didn't react. A tear ran over her cheek. Her breath came shallow, although he couldn't see any injuries. The skin on her face was pale and thin as paper. White hair was plastered to her head. Curly hair.

Breath caught in his throat. He knelt, clumsily without his wooden leg. "Can you hear me?"

She turned her head towards him and opened her eyes. They were blue.

With trembling hands, Isandor tried to turn her lower body. If only she'd lie straight, she wouldn't have so much trouble breathing.

But her lower body was limp and he feared that she had broken her spine and he'd do best not to touch her. He took the wrinkled right hand into his. The nails were still sharp, but the skin no longer hot.

"Please, live," he whispered. "For me."

She gave his hand a tiny squeeze. Her blue eyes blinked, once, and remained open.

Isandor didn't know how long he sat there before the sound of an approaching truck made him look over his shoulder.

An unfamiliar vehicle had stopped on the farm road. The passenger door opened and someone climbed out.

A female voice called, "Isandor!"

Jevaithi. He struggled to his feet. She rushed to him, jumping over the debris, and came to a halt when she saw the body.

"It's all right," he said.

She didn't look convinced, but ran into his arms, enveloping him with her familiar scent. He was so happy that he pulled her close and kissed her, until he remembered he shouldn't do this anymore, because she was his sister and it was not proper. But there was a time for being proper later. He kissed her again, because he loved her so much. She broke the kiss by pushing herself against his chest.

"Hey, silly. We're not alone, you know." Her chest heaved with deep breaths. Their hearts beat in unison.

"I love you. I don't care what anyone says."

"I love you, too."

"I was so scared for you. How did you escape the Knights?"

"Someone helped me." She turned around and behind her stood . . .

"Carro?"

Indeed. It was Carro, but he looked much older than when Isandor had last seen him. He came forward, glancing at the old woman's body.

He stopped in front of Isandor, and dropped to his knees.

"Your Majesty, could you forgive me? Could you forgive all the Knighthood for the things they have done? Could you accept a new Knighthood of men and women who are honest and obedient for all the right reasons?"

"Get up, you silly," Isandor said. "We're friends."

"*Were* friends," Carro said. "I did great wrongs because I believed that I must do those things to please people in power."

Isandor shrugged, suddenly full of emotion and memories. Him and Carro playing in the snowy alleys of the Outer City, him and Carro leafing through old—and illegal—books. Him and Carro flying in the race for the Queen's Champion. The strange discipline of the eyrie, with its rules and bullying by older Apprentices. Carro had not been given an easy time.

"Can you forgive me? Your Highness?"

"I accept your apology," Isandor said. "But please do not call me that again. I am no king and I have no desire to lead a country."

"But we have to," Carro said. "There are so few good people left. We have Rider Barton, you and the Queen. That's it."

"The Knights of the Council are dead? Rider Cornatan?"

Carro nodded, and looked away. Isandor sensed a story that was too raw yet to be told.

"Come on, silly, you're embarrassing me. Get up." He gave his stick to Jevaithi, grasped her shoulder and held out a hand. Carro took it and Isandor heaved him to his feet while holding himself upright on Jevaithi's shoulder.

"Look at me." Carro laughed. "Helped by a man with one leg. What happened to your peg leg?"

"No idea," Isandor said.

"I'll make you a new one, if you let me."

"I would be honoured." He took the stick back from Jevaithi. And with Jevaithi on one arm and Carro on the other, he clambered into the cabin.

❄

The truck took them to the refugee camp, where a huge cheering crowd had gathered. They weren't just southerners, but also Chevakians, soldiers and civilians, and some Eagle Knights with their birds, which looked none-too-impressed with all the noise.

As soon as Jevaithi helped Isandor from the truck—how annoying was it to be without his damn leg?—a man in the audience called, "Peria!"

Others repeated, "Peria, Peria!" Isandor did not want that name to be used, with all it stood for, but it seemed the name had stuck and he could do nothing about it. The southern land again had a name.

And there was Milleus' truck, Milleus himself, and a younger man who looked like Milleus, and with him was . . .

"Mother!"

Isandor ran, limping, into her arms. She was crying, and that made him cry as well. Milleus hugged Jevaithi, and then the younger man, who must be Milleus' brother, put one hand on both Isandor's and his mother's shoulders. "Let's go home. You're all my guests."

Sady took everyone into his house. Milleus, the young royal couple, the Knight commander Rider Barton and his young second in command, who seemed to be the prince's friend.

And not to forget Milleus' goats. The latter much to Farius' chagrin.

They talked and ate, and Viki came past to say that sonorics levels were falling rapidly, and got invited to the feast as well.

Some time when it was almost morning, when everyone had gone to bed, he walked with Loriane up the stairs. He stopped at the door to his bedroom. Dara and Myra were sharing the next room, that had been hers, so that the two Knights could have the other room.

"This means that eventually, you'll be able to go back to the City of Glass."

"Yes." She smiled, but the smile faded quickly. "Is safe for you?"

"I don't know. And besides, I belong here." There was so much work to be done.

She gave him an intense look. "I . . . can stay."

"If you want to go home, I don't want to stop you." He had trouble saying this, and he had to look away.

"Hey." She reached for his face and put a warm hand on his cheek. "What you want?"

"I had hoped . . ." He licked his lips, breathed deeply and plunged on. "I'd hoped that you would choose to stay here."

"With you?"

"With me." He licked his lips again. Another calming breath. "In my house. As lady in the han Chevonian family." Another deep breath. "I've been crazy about you since I first saw you on the platform. I love you. I haven't loved anyone like this for more than twenty-five years."

She stared at him. Her eyes glittered with tears. Sady held his breath. She was surely going to refuse and tell him to quit behaving like a child.

But then she closed him in her arms, and buried her face in his shirt, and cried. Sady turned her face up and kissed her. She clung onto him, kissing him back, while the tears ran down her cheeks and dripped on his shirt.

He broke the kiss. "Hey, it's going to be fine. I love you, that's all that matters."

She wiped her cheeks with the back of her hand, smiled, and her smile turned into laughter. "Shhh," Sady said, putting a finger on her lips.

He opened the door to his bedroom and for the first time in more years than he cared to recount, led a woman into his private domain.

EPILOGUE

IT RAINED in Tiverius for a further three days, and then the sun came out. The sonorics levels dropped dramatically, and people came out of the shelters. The tide of sonorics was receding, but it would be some time until the border regions were accessible again, not to mention the southern platform.

When the losses could finally be counted, the figure was staggering. Ensar, Solmeni, Fairlight. Entire towns wiped off the map. In addition, much cropping land had become inaccessible and crops lost through the weather or lack of care. Viki had given approval for all districts to farm as much as possible, and fortunately, the bad weather had delivered more rain further north than usual, but still, this would be a hard winter in Tiverius.

One morning, Milleus left his brother's house and walked to the cemetery. He wandered through the rows with familiar plaques and familiar names. So many of his former senators had already died.

He stopped at the wall that contained the han Chevonian cubicle. There was a small statue of Eseldus, a smaller version of the one that stood in the courtyard of the house. Sady's house now. Milleus could have the guest quarter, Sady said, but after today, he wasn't sure he wanted to intrude in Sady's life. Sady had never intruded in his life either.

Kalius had offered him rooms, since he was living alone as well; but he liked Kalius as much as Kalius liked him, and the less said about that, the better. In all honesty, he considered leaving the city for good. He had his goats; he could set up a travelling farm, taking the animals where the milk was needed and where hay was plentiful. Else, he might follow the youngsters up the platform if the issue of sonorics would indeed be gone forever. He figured they could use someone experienced to talk to.

Today, however, was about family. He had brought a cloth and cleaned and polished the plaque that said Suri han Helonian and put a bunch of flowers in the cubicle. He tried to think of her, but after all that had happened recently, he was ashamed that her face would not come as easily as it once would have. It was so long ago. He'd made mistakes, but he could do nothing to change them.

"Father."

He jumped at the voice behind him.

Andrean stood there, already in his formal dress. "Uncle said I could find you here." His son's gaze went over Milleus' comfortable woollen robe.

"No, I'm not going to the ceremony like this," Milleus said, meeting his son's eyes. Mercy he looked just like his mother when she used to nag him.

An uncomfortable silence hung between them.

"I just wanted to ask . . ." Andrean hesitated. "What do you think about this marriage?"

"You ask me about marriage?" Milleus snorted. His son had always been the first to condemn him for Suri's death.

A further uncomfortable silence.

"Well, I think that my brother is old enough to make his own decisions. Your uncle has also acquired the responsibility for a large group of southerners, and if history is anything to go by, many of them will never leave. War, sonorics, other disasters, it's happened before and will happen again. I do not see it as a problem that he takes his wife from amongst those refugees. If I'd have been less lucky in winning the Aranian war, we might have been those refugees, trying to eke out a living in hostile Arania, and we would have been grateful for a friendly hand."

Andrean shrugged, opened his mouth as if he was going to say something, but thought better of it.

Milleus tidied up the cubicle, shut the ornate grille that kept the ground squirrels from eating the offerings, and walked with his son out the cemetery gates.

Neither said anything because that was their way of dealing with each other's differences, but that didn't worry Milleus. The sun was shining, the sky was blue, and all Tiverians had decorated their fences, front gates and doors with flowers, most of them woven from straw for lack of the real thing. Already, people lined the road to watch the parade. Never in living memory had a proctor in office gotten married. And it was a perfect day for a grand wedding.

The next spring:

A soft breeze stirred Isandor's hair as he crested the ridge, a breeze scented with green and flowers. The sky was deep blue above and little streams trickled between the rocks on either side. At the head of the column, he kneed his camel up the last of the slope.

Bordertown.

Blocky houses lay scattered in the landscape, but the southern platform was a far different place from the one they had left. It was *green*. Flowers bloomed in the fields as far as the eye could see. Flowers bloomed even on the roofs of the houses, which had lain abandoned throughout summer and winter, until, finally, it was safe to come onto the platform again.

The line of camels inched into the grass, so green it hurt the eyes. Isandor reached out to his mother. In her white dress, she looked divine. Her hair stirred in the breeze, loose locks falling over her shoulders. It was going grey at the temples. But she looked healthy. Her cheeks glowed. The breeze made her dress flutter about her so it drew taut over her full breasts and slight rounding of her stomach. She had not spoken to him about it, but he knew the signs, even if only in the amusing way her Chevakian man treated her like a goddess. After a life of being a breeder, she would be able to keep the last child she would ever bear.

She had asked to come on the trek, to have one more look at her homeland before turning back to Tiverius and her new husband.

The line of camels cut a track through the grass and flowers so tall that the heads grazed the animal's belly. It was slow going, because

Isandor's camel, in the front, needed to tread carefully to avoid obstacles hidden in the grass.

"Ee-yup!" someone called from behind.

Ontane had steered his camel off to the side to a house with a shed in the front yard. He tapped the beast on the neck to make it sit. After it did so—protesting and stretching and twisting to graze—he slipped off the saddle. The shed door stood half open, broken and splintered, and halfway to the front door of the house lay a hump of dirty fur, from which white spokes protruded.

Isandor made his camel backtrack to where Ontane waited.

"This is your house?" Isandor asked.

"So it be, Sire, in none-too-happy condition. The wife will be devastated."

Isandor nodded, but he thought Dara was far too content in Sady's household to ever be serious about returning to Bordertown. Not to worry about that right now.

Jevaithi had also halted her camel to look at the odd arrangement of fur and white sticks. "What is it?"

"I have no idea." But as he said that, he knew what it was. "It's a bear."

Jevaithi's face twisted into a horrified mask. She lifted a hand over her mouth. "The poor thing."

Isandor felt a chill. The poor animal might have been lost or abandoned, hadn't been fed after everyone left, and when it had managed to escape from the shed, had been too weak to find food. Bears were fish eaters. The only ocean here was green with flowers.

The desiccated carcass and the flowers encapsulated what the destruction of the Heart meant for the south. New life, but also the death of some old life. By the skylights, what would the City of Glass look like?

"Well, this is where we leave you." He tapped his camel on the shoulder and it sank to its knees.

Ontane bowed. "Your Highness. I would like to thank ye for everything. I'm sorry about your loss, Sire."

Isandor glanced over his shoulder. Behind him, the rest of the column had come up the plain. Two camels carried the stretcher between them that held his father's body, dried and preserved in layers of cloth, as it had been found recently in a field by a Chevakian farmer. Some people had wanted to burn Tandor's body like that of a traitor, but although he had been a traitor, he had also given his life to put it right. And it might well be the only right thing he had ever done. He was a Thilleian prince, and deserved to be remembered as one, for good or ill.

"We will bring him home," he said, staring at the horizon. "We will rebuild the city. We will find a way."

Loriane came to him, her arms wide. She whispered, "Son."

Isandor took her in his arms and smelled her perfume. She was warm and soft, and familiar. She would stay here with Ontane who had promised his wife to bring some of their items from their house and return to Tiverius with Loriane.

Other people from Bordertown already fanned out to their houses, while the majority of the column waited. The packing camels carried supplies to survive the coming months, until they could give the sign that the rest of the people from the City of Glass could return home. Whoever wanted to return home. Milleus had said that if it was safe, he wanted to come.

Isandor hugged his mother. Her eyes glittered with tears.

"Be well, my son. I wish you could stay."

"You'll be very happy," he said. "He's a good man." And she wouldn't be alone. Dara would probably stay, and Myra, too, if Farius' family gave their son permission to marry her.

"I know." She returned a weak smile, and moved her hand to her belly as if scratching it. "If it's a boy, he will carry your name, or a girl, Jevaithi's."

Isandor kissed her on the forehead. "I love you. We'll visit soon."

While his mother hugged Jevaithi, Isandor signalled for the column to start moving again.

His eyes met Carro's. His friend sat atop his camel, wearing full uniform. His face was blank, an expression Isandor had come to accept as normal from Carro. Isandor didn't know what went on in that head, but he knew that Carro, and the new Supreme Rider Barton would serve the royal family for the good of the people, and not to strengthen their own power.

"Well, let's go then." He swung his wooden leg over the camel's back and slid in the saddle. Ouch. This mode of transport had much to be desired, but it would be a while before they could fly eagles again. With no snow, sleds had become useless. Balloons, maybe. Yes, Balloons. He must talk to Sady about that.

He dug his heels in the flanks of the camel and it unfolded its awkward legs—back first—with a howl. At Rider Barton's whistle, the column set in motion once more.

They had a task to do.

The trilogy is finished here, but in the *Moonfire Trilogy*, we return to the world of Isandor and Sady twenty years later. Everything they thought they knew about icefire is turned upside down. The people have one chance to save all life on their world.

Sand & Storm is the first book.

ABOUT THE AUTHOR

Patty Jansen lives in Sydney, Australia, where she spends most of her time writing Science Fiction and Fantasy.

Her career started in earnest when her story *This Peaceful State of War* placed first in the second quarter of the Writers of the Future contest and was published in their 27th anthology. She has also sold fiction to genre magazines such as Analog Science Fiction and Fact, Redstone SF and Aurealis, before making the move to independent publishing.

Patty has written over fifty novels in both Science Fiction and Fantasy, including the *Icefire Trilogy* and the *Ambassador* series.

pattyjansen.com

BOOKS BY PATTY JANSEN

MORE INFORMATION:

PATTYJANSEN.COM

For a complete list of books, scan the image below with your phone.